Chris Bunch was part of the first troop commitment into Vietnam. Both ranger and airbourne-qualified, he served as a patrol commander and a combat correspondent for *Stars and Stripes*. Later, he edited outlaw motorcycle magazines and wrote for everything from the underground press to *Look* magazine, *Rolling Stone* and prime-time television. He is now a full-time novelist.

Find out more about Chris Bunch and other Orbit authors by registering for the free monthly newsletter at www.orbitbooks.co.uk

SHADOW WARRIOR

CHRIS BUNCH

www.orbitbooks.co.uk

An *Orbit* Book

First published in Great Britain by Orbit 2004

This omnibus edition © Chris Bunch 2004

The Wind After Time
First published in the US by Ballantine Books
Copyright © 1996 by Christopher Bunch

Hunt the Heavens
First published in the US by Ballantine Books
Copyright © 1996 by Chris Bunch

The Darkness of God
First published in the US by Ballantine Books
Copyright © 1997 by Chris Bunch

The moral right of the author has been asserted.

A CIP catalogue record for this book
is available from the British Library.

ISBN 1 84149 332 5

Typeset in Garamond 3 by M Rules
Printed and bound in Great Britain by
Clays Ltd, St Ives plc

Orbit
An imprint of
Time Warner Book Group UK
Brettenham House
Lancaster Place
London WC2E 7EN

CONTENTS

BOOK ONE

THE WIND AFTER TIME

For
Lance LeGault:
A damn fine
Wolfe

ONE

The seventeen-year-old walked into the circle of smooth-raked sand. Around it sharp boulders, reaching toward alien stars, made the circle an arena. All else was silence and the night.

A corpse-white grasping organ appeared, extending toward him. In the center was a Lumina. It glowed.

'Take the stone.'

'I am not worthy.'

'Take the stone.'

'My years are not sufficient.'

'Take the stone.'

Joshua took the Lumina into his own hand. His fingers brushed the Al'ar's tendrils.

'Have you been instructed?'

'I have.'

'Who lit that torch?'

A second Al'ar spoke. 'I did.' Joshua saw Taen standing to one side of the sand circle.

The Guardian forsook the ritual: 'This may be forbidden.'

'No,' Taen said, voice certain. 'The codex did not see, so it could not enjoin such a turning.'

'So you said before, when you came to us, and told us of this Way Seeker.'

The Guardian stood without speaking, and all Joshua heard was the whisper of the dry Saurian wind. Finally:

'**Perhaps we should allow it, then.**'

Joshua Wolfe came awake. There was no sound but the hum of the ship, no problems indicated by the overhead telltale. He was sweating.

'Record.'

'*Recording as ordered,*' the ship said.

'The dream occurred again. Analyze to match previous occurrences.'

Ship hum.

'*No similarities found. No known stress at present beyond normal when beginning an assignment.*'

Wolfe slid out of the bunk. He was naked. He walked out of the day cabin, glanced across the instrument banks on the bridge without seeing them, then went down the circular staircase to the deck below. He palmed a wall sensor, and the hatch opened into a small chamber with padded floor and mirrored walls and ceiling.

He went to the middle of the room. He crouched slightly, centering his body.

Breathe . . . breathe . . .

Joshua Wolfe, nearly forty, had used his body hard. Ropy muscles and occasional scars roadmapped his rangy high-split frame, and his face appeared to have been left in the weather to age. His hair was bleached as if by the sun. He was just over six feet tall and kept his weight at 180 pounds. His flat, arctic blue eyes looked at the world without affection, without fear, without illusion.

He began slow, studied movements, hands reaching, touching, striking, returning, guarding; feet lifting, stepping, kicking. His face showed no stress, effort, or pleasure.

He returned to his base stance abruptly and froze, eyes changing focus from infinity to the mirrors on the wall, on the ceiling. For an instant his reflections blurred. Then the multiple images of Joshua returned.

He sagged, wind roaring through his lungs as if he'd finished a series of wind sprints. He allowed a flash of disappointment to cross his face, then wiped sweat from his forehead with the back of his hand.

He controlled his breathing and went to the fresher. Perhaps now he would be able to sleep.

'Accumulators at near capacity for final jump.'

'Time to jump?'

'Ten ship seconds . . . Now.'

Blur. Feel of flannel, memory of father laughing as he danced in his arms, bitter — bay, thyme, neither, in the mind. A universe died, and space, time, suns, planets were reborn.

'N-space exited. All navbeacs respond. Plus-minus variation acceptable. Final jump complete. Destination on-screen. Sensors report negative scan, all bands. Estimated arrival, full drive, five ship hours. Correction?'

'None.'

Wolfe's ship, the *Grayle*, darted toward the field on a direct approach.

'Where shall I land?'

A screen lit. The field below was just that — a huge, bare expanse of cracked concrete. There was no tower, no port building, no hangars, no restaurant, no transport center. There were perhaps half a hundred starships, from long-abandoned surplus military craft to nondescript transports to small well-maintained luxury craft parked helter-skelter on the sides of the tarmac. There was no sign of life on the field except, at one end, a grounded maintenance lighter and two men intent on disemboweling the engine spaces of a heavy-lifter.

'Put us down not too far from those ramp rats.'

Seconds later, the braking drive flared and the ship grounded. Joshua touched sensors; screens lit and were manipulated as he carefully examined every starship of a certain description. One drew his attention. He opened a secondary screen on that mil-surplus ship, once a medium long-range patrol craft.

'ID?'

'Ship on-screen matches input data on target fiche. Hull registry does not match either numbers from target fiche or the ship listed as carrying those numbers in Lloyds' Registry. Sensors indicate skin temperature shows ship active within last planetary week. Drive tube temperatures confirm first datum. No sensor suggests ship is occupied.'

'It wouldn't be. He's already about his business. Maintain alert status, instant lift readiness. I'm going trolling.'

'Understood.'

Joshua dressed, then went to an innocent wall and pressed a stud. The wall opened. Inside were enough weapons – guns, grenades, knives, explosives – to outfit a small commando landing. The ship itself hid other surprises: two system-range nuclear missiles, four in-atmosphere air-to-air missiles, and a chaingun.

Joshua chose a large Federation-issue blaster and holstered it in a worn military gun belt with three magazine pouches clipped to it. Around his neck he looped a silver chain with a dark metal emblem on it, stylized calligraphy for the symbol *ku*. It also supported, at the back of his neck, a dartlike obsidian throwing knife.

Joshua considered his appearance. Gray insul pants, short boots, dark blue singlet under an expensive-looking but worn light gray jacket that might have been leather but was not, a jacket that obviously held proofed shockpanels. Pistol well used, all too ready.

Someone looking for a job, any job, so long as it wasn't legal. Just another new arrival on Platte. Just another one of the boys. He would fit right in. He stuck a flesh-toned bonemike com over his left clavicle.

'Testing,' he said, then subvocalized in Al'ar: *'Is this device singing?'*

'My being says this is so.' He *heard* the ship's response through bone induction.

'Open the port.'

Joshua's ears crackled as they adjusted to the new pressure. He walked onto the landing field, and the lock doors hissed shut.

He started whistling loudly when he was still some distance from the mechanics. One of them casually walked to his toolbox, picked up a rag, and began wiping his hands. Joshua noted that the rag was lumpy, about the size of a medium-sized pistol. Platte was that kind of world.

'Help you, friend?'

'Looking for some transport to get around the hike into town.'

'Town's a fairly dickey label when there isn't but one hotel, a dozen or so stores, three alkjoints, our shop, an' a restaurant you'd best not trust your taste buds to.'

'Sounds like the big city compared to where I'm from.'

A smile came and went on the mechanic's lips, and he looked pointedly at the heavy gun hung low on Joshua's hip. 'I'd guess you came from there at speed, eh?'

'You'd lose, friend,' Joshua said. 'When I lifted, there was nobody even vaguely interested in my habits or my comings and goings.'

The mechanic took the hint and started toward his lighter. 'I can call for Lil. See if she wants to pick up a few credits. But it'll cost.'

'Aren't many Samaritans working the Outlaw Worlds these days,' Joshua said. 'I'll pay.'

The mechanic picked up a com and spoke into it. 'She's on her way.' He returned to the engine bay and turned his wrench back on. The second man appeared not to have noticed Joshua.

After a while Joshua saw a worm of dust crawl toward the field.

Lil was about eighteen, working on forty. Her vehicle was a nearly new light utility lifter that looked as if it'd been sandblasted for a repaint and then the idea had been forgotten. 'What're you doin' on Platte?' she asked without preamble after Joshua had introduced himself.

'My travel agent said it was a relaxing place. Good weather.'

Lil glanced through the ripped plas dome at the overcast sky that threatened rain but would never deliver. 'Right. All Platte needs is water and some good people. That's all Hell needs, too.'

The road they traveled above was marked with twelve-foot-high stakes driven into the barren soil. Some time earlier someone had run a scraper down the track, so there were still wheeled or tracked vehicles in use. The vegetation was sparse, gray, and sagging.

'You'll be staying at the hotel?'

'Don't know. Depends.'

'It's the only game in town. Old Diggs sets his rates like he knows it.'

'So?'

'I run a rooming house. Sorta. Anyway, there's a room. Bed. Fresher. For extra, I'll cook two meals a day.'

'Sorta?'

'Biggish place. Started as a gamblin' joint. Damn fool who set it up never figured people got to have somethin' to gamble before they gamble. He walked off into the desert a year or so ago, and nobody bothered looking to see how far he got. We moved in.'

'We?' Joshua asked.

'Mik . . . he's the one that called me. And Phan. He was the quiet one. Probably didn't even look up from bustin' knuckles. They're my husbands.'

'I'll let you know if I need a place.'

Joshua asked Lil to wait and went into the long, low single-story building without a sign. The lobby was scattered with a handful of benches, their canvas upholstery peeling. It smelled stale and temporary. There were planters on either side of the door, but the plants had mummified a long time before. The checkout station was caged in thick steel bars. The old man behind it blanked the holoset he was watching a pornie on and smiled expectantly. Joshua eyed the bars.

'You must have some interesting paydays around here.'

The old man – Diggs, Joshua supposed – let the smile hang for an instant in token appreciation. 'It prevents creativity from some of our more colorful citizens. You want a room?'

'I might.' Joshua reached into his jacket and slid a holopic across. Diggs activated it and studied the man in the projection carefully but said nothing. Joshua took a single gold disk from another pocket, considered, as greed strolled innocently across Diggs's face, added its brother, and dropped the coins on the counter.

'Tell by the sound they ain't snide,' Diggs said. "Damned poor picture. Doesn't look like your friend was very cheerful at having it taken, either.'

'His name is Innokenty Khodyan.'

'That wasn't what he used here.' The coins vanished. 'Another reason I don't have trouble is everybody knows I'm an open book. He checked out two days ago. Took him that long to get a sled and driver sent down from Yoruba. Two other men came with the armored lim. Hell of a rig. Long time since this dump has seen something that plush.'

'Yoruba, eh?'

'Three, maybe four hours, full power away. Across the mountains, then northeast up toward the coast. What isn't in or around Yoruba isn't worth buying. The reason they don't fancy a landing field is they like to see their visitors coming. From a ways off.'

'I didn't think Ben would change his ways.' Joshua nodded thanks. Innokenty Khodyan was running as if he were on rails. 'Three other questions, if you will.'

'You can ask.'

'Is there any other way to get to Yoruba? If a man was in a little more of a hurry.'

'You can wait, see if somebody's headed there in a lighter. Somebody generally is, once a month or so. That's about it. Second question?'

'How did Khodyan pay for his room?'

'*That's* something you won't get answered. Try again.'

'The two men with the lim? What'd be your call on them?'

'Same sort as you, mister. Except their iron wasn't out in the open. But they had the same kind of . . . call it serious intent.'

'Thanks.'

Joshua was at the door.

'Now I have a question,' Diggs said. 'Will somebody be looking for you in a couple of days?'

'Not likely,' Joshua said. 'Not likely at all.'

Lil had her blouse off, eyes closed, her feet splayed on the dash. She'd slid the worthless dome back into its housing. Joshua took a moment to admire her. Her breasts were still eighteen, nipples pointed at the invisible sun. She looked clean, and Joshua didn't mind her perfume, even if it made him think he was trapped in a hothouse.

'You stayin' here?' She didn't open her eyes.

'No.'

'Do I have a roomer . . . or is it back to the field?'

'Lil,' Joshua said, 'what shape is this bomb in? I mean its drive. I can tell it's not up for best custom finish.'

'It hums. Phan makes sure of that. He says he don't want me to break down out in the middle of nowhere. But I think he just loves turbines. He'd rather wrench than screw.'

This time the gold was dropped on the woman's stomach. Five coins, larger than the two he'd given Diggs. Joshua thought about letting his fingers linger but decided not to. Lil lazily opened her eyes.

'Now, that's the sorta thing that *really* makes a girl smile. I *was* gonna rape you for the transport, but not that bad. Or are we talkin' about other possibilities?'

'We are. I need transport to Yoruba. Leaving now. After I get a few things from my ship. That's the retainer.'

'Yoruba, huh? You just want me to drop you off . . . or will you be coming back through here?'

'Maybe a day. Maybe longer. I can't say. Maybe I'll need transport when I get there, maybe not. Depends. But if you're available, that might simplify things.'

'You just hired yourself a pilot. Ten minutes at my place, then we can flit.'

'Just like that?'

'Phan, Mik, me, we don't tie each other down or make rules. They can fiddle their dees while I'm gone, anyway. Build up energy for when I get back.'

Joshua went around to the other side of the lifter and over the low hull into the seat beside Lil. She started the primary and let it warm.

'You planning on getting dressed?' Joshua asked. 'Or did I just hire my first nude chauffeur?'

'I could put it on, I could take the rest of it off. Whatever you want, since you're paying.'

Joshua made no answer. Lil shrugged and pulled the blouse back on. 'At least I got your attention.'

The track through the mountains had been roughly graded so a gross-laden heavy-lifter wouldn't high-side, but it still was more an exceptionally wide path than a roadway. Joshua asked Lil to take the lifter to max altitude, which gave him a vulture's-eye perspective at about 150 feet constant.

The land was savage, dry brown earth running into gray rock. The scraggly trees and brush were perhaps a little taller than they'd been on the flats, but not much. Lil and Joshua overflew a couple of abandoned, stripped lifters and one thoroughly mangled wreck but saw no other sign of travelers.

There were shacks, but he couldn't tell if they were occupied. Once or twice he saw, higher against a mountain face, scantlings, survival domes, and piled detritus where some miner had tried to convince himself there must be some value to be torn from this waste.

Joshua spotted to one side a sprawling, high-fenced estate. Beyond the walls there was Earth green and the blue of a small lake. There were buildings, big ones, a dozen of them, white in new stone.

'Who belongs to that?'

'Nobody knows,' Lil answered. 'Somebody rich. Or powerful. Somebody private. He – or she, or it – gets supplies once every couple months. Curiosity don't seem welcome.'

She pointed. Joshua had already seen the two gravlighters that had lifted away from one building and now flew parallel to the lifter's pattern. He wasn't close enough to see how many gunnies each lighter held. After they'd passed, the lighters returned to the estate.

'You were in the war?' Lil asked.

'That was a long time ago.'

'Figured, by your rig. My dad . . . anyway, the guy Ma said was my father was some kind of soldier, too. Ma kept a holo of him on a dresser, wearing some kind of uniform. Took it with her when she hooked, I guess. I don't remember seeing it . . . afterward.' Then: 'Any damage in my asking about what happens once we get in range of Yoruba? I mean, I can nap-of-the-earth insert you without anyone noticing. Their sensor techs couldn't hear a fart on a field phone.'

'No need,' Joshua said. 'As far as I know, we can parade right in the front door looking beautiful and getting kissed.'

'There's more'n one front door,' Lil went on. 'You ever been there?'

'No. And my travel agent couldn't seem to find a brochure.'

'You better think about cannin' *that* yonk, you get back from your, uh, "vacation." 'Kay. There's a whole patch of front doors. Outside the gates there's cribs. Shantytown. Bars. Cafés. Independent-run. If you're looking for sanctuary on the cheap or if whoever you're lookin' for is down on his credits, that'll be where you want to go. Somebody'll be around to collect the tariff sooner or later. Everybody pays at Yoruba.'

'I was never much of an alley cat. Except when I had to be. What's the next level?'

'The next stage is straight into the main resort. Up there, what you get depends on what you got.'

'That sounds like a good place to start.'

'You called it,' Lil said. 'You want to spend, I'll put you in Ben Greet's lap, if you want. He's the one who owns Yoruba. He says frog, everybody turns green and starts pissin' swamp water.'

'Glad to see my friend's doing so well,' Joshua said. 'Maybe we'll have a chance to talk about the old days.'

'I hope you aren't bein' cute and Greet really *is* your friend,' Lil warned. 'Greet's nothin' but bulletproof.'

Joshua smiled.

Something ahead caught his eye. 'Well, I shall be damned,' he said. 'What an utterly *charming* little place.'

A nicely paved roadway led up from the main track, a freshly painted white fence on either side of it and demarcating the deep green pasture around the sprawling red-brick house. There was a sign on the road below. Lil took binocs from the dash box and handed them across. Joshua focused. The sign read: TRAVELER'S REST.

'Does anyone actually fall for that?'

'They surely do. Pretty regular we hear of some gravlighter that "just happened" to crash around here. Crash and always burn, real bad, since nobody ever finds the pilot or swamper. Or cargo.

'We call that the gingerbread house. Except you don't have to bring Gretel. The owners'll provide her . . . and anything else that's asked for, or so the story goes. Until you stop payin' attention or go to sleep.

'They got themselves a cargo ship back at the field, and every now and then it lifts, but nobody's ever seen a cargo manifest.'

'Most places I've been,' Joshua said, 'after a while people would see to something that wide-open, law or no law.'

'Not on Platte, mister. 'Sides, as far as we know, the only people that get done are fools or off-worlders, and none of us took either to raise.'

They rode in silence, not uncomfortable, as the track crested the mountain and then wound down across a valley a bit more fertile than the wasteland. There were more buildings, some rich, some poor, no order to their location. A mansion would be next to a hovel, and sometimes there would be a clump of buildings, almost a failed village. Sometimes there would be a paved road, and twice he saw automated ways. The roads, like everything else, started and stopped arbitrarily, as if the builder had built until he got bored or had quit when a completely invisible requirement had been met. There were farmhouses, but each sat in desolation. Occasionally there would be the gleam of a few light manufacturing buildings. Farther on, with no road or track to them,.would be a group of buildings that might shift for a marketplace. It was as if an angry child had hurled his elaborate toys across a sandbox.

'I guess,' Joshua mused, 'when you're studying anarchy hard, logic doesn't come knocking much.'

Lil frowned, not understanding, then looked ahead at the track. The frown persisted. She spoke, again without preparation but as if she'd been waiting for him to speak first:

'You know, when I shook my tits at you back there . . . there was a reason.'

'I didn't figure it for a sudden impulse,' Joshua said.

'I said I had rooms. For a price. Board cost extra, I said. That ain't all that's for sale. Not for everybody, though,' she said hastily. 'We ain't that poor. And I'm not that desperate.'

Joshua maintained his silence.

'If you're gonna be staying on in Yoruba, let me be with you. I won't charge nothin'.'

The turbine hiss was loud in the dead air.

'I know, in Yoruba, there's prettier. If you're really a friend of Ben Greet's, most likely they'll be free, too. But I ain't that bad; give me a little time with a mirror. I won't let you get bored. I know some tricks. I was in a house for a while, till I had to offplanet and come here. I ain't just a country dox, not knowin' anything but flat on her back with her legs up.'

When Joshua didn't reply, her shoulders slumped. 'Didn't figure that'd fly,' she said in a monotone. 'But Jerusalem on a pony, you don't know what it's like bein' in that hellforsaken port. You know everybody, everybody knows you. You know what they're gonna say, and pretty soon you know what *you're* gonna say . . . what you're even gonna think, day in, day out.

'And all the time people pass through, and you know you ain't ever gonna be able to go with them. You're gonna dry and wither, just like this damned planet *grew* you like you were a scatterbush.'

'That's not it, Lil,' Joshua said. 'I've got business in Yoruba, and things might become . . . troublesome. Quite loudly troublesome.'

'Trouble don't get no cherry off me,' she said defiantly; her hand flashed to her boot top, and Joshua saw steel flash.

The small gun vanished. 'Hell with it. I don't beg. There's Yoruba, anyway. You want me to sleep in the lifter, or should I find a room somewhere? I'll have to charge for that, you know.'

Joshua didn't reply. He blanked her presence as the lifter lowered to the track, which became a paved and marked road with planted greenery to either side. Ahead rose Yoruba, sprawling over half a dozen hilltops, its domes, spires, and cupolas gleaming dully. His eyes half-closed, he let himself flow outward, ahead of the lifter as it moved past a guard shack where a semimobile blaster's muzzle had been tracking them. Two heavily armed guards saluted casually as their eyes noted, filed, categorized.

'**Ship, do you still hear this voice and know from where it sings?**' Again he spoke in Al'ar.

'**You are still heard and watched.**'

The lifter went up a side road toward a grand series of towers, all glass and multihued stone, surrounded by the exotic plants of half a hundred worlds. They passed through wrought-iron gates and rode over hand-laid flagstones. There were bubbling fountains and, under an archway, two women, smiling as if he were their lover home from his great adventure.

Lil set the lifter down smartly beside the greeters. 'Welcome to Yoruba,' they chimed.

'Thank you.' Joshua got out and knelt, one hand touching the pavement. He *felt* Yoruba, felt the danger tingle, the sparkle of wine and laughter, the shout as markers cascaded, the blank despair of the gambler's loss, the silk of flesh around his loins, the tang of blood and the blankness of death. But not for him. Not yet. He felt no neck prickle. The flurry vanished, and he was touching nothing but a flagstone in a mosaic.

'Is something the matter, sir?' The woman was trying to sound concerned.

Joshua stood. He took a gold coin from his jacket and laid it in the greeter's suddenly present palm. Lil was staring fixedly at the lifter's control panel.

'No. Nothing at all,' Joshua said. 'It's just been a long trip. Sorry we didn't have time to com ahead. We'll need a suite and a porter. Just one. Neither my partner nor myself has much in the way of luggage.'

A slow smile moved across Lil's face, as if her muscles found the change unfamiliar but welcome.

TWO

Joshua lay flat on one of the enormous beds, eyes closed, half hearing Lil's gurgles and squeals at their room with its private garden and pond; the autopub with its myriad bottles, flasks, bulbs; the elaborate refreshers with surround showers, deep tubs, saunas; the call panel offering personalized dreams from hairdresser to masseur to escort; and all the rest of the suite's silk and gold Byzantine appointments.

He was reaching out, delicate as an Al'ar tendril, again *feeling*. Again – no threat, no danger.

There was a soft thump beside him, and he was back in the room. 'This's the biggest bed I've ever seen,' Lil announced. Her smile became sultry. 'You suppose it works?'

Joshua's fingers reached of their own volition and ran down the side of her face. Eyes closed, she inhaled sharply and lay back, waiting, lips open.

'Unfortunately,' Joshua said, 'I was raised pretty strict and never could handle playing during working hours.'

Lil said nothing, but her hand came up, touched his, then moved down across her flat stomach, hand circling upward and lifting her blouse. She ran a fingernail over one nipple, and it hardened.

She touched her waistband, and the memory fastener opened. She lifted her hips and slid her pants down until her golden down shone. Her legs parted slightly, and she slipped fingers between them, gently caressing herself. Her eyes opened, and she looked dreamily, smiling, into Joshua's.

Joshua got up. He took a breath, made his voice level. 'And you're on the payroll, too, lady.'

Lil sat, still smiling. 'What do I do?'

'Spend some money. Think rich. You'll need an outfit for dinner. Plus something for tomorrow, casual but expensive. Something you can run in, if we have to. Hair, derm, manicure, massage if you want. Don't get too crazy – I'm not *that* rich. I want you to look like –'

He was looking at an extended middle finger. 'I know,' Lil said, 'what I should look like. Close, anyway. Mistress, wife, or pickup talent?'

'Like somebody who's made a big score would want to help him spend it. The somebody's not dumb, so you're not taking him to the cleaners, but he's got a bad case of lust.'

'Who's the somebody? Do I need to know? The guy – woman – you're looking for? Or you? Not that it matters. Like I said, anything you want goes.'

'For me,' Joshua said softly. 'I've never set a honey trap yet. You're camouflage, making it look like I'm just holed up and unwinding.'

'Sorry. The men I grew up around wouldn't think that was an insult. Are you ever gonna tell me why we're here, or am I just supposed to wait for the bangs to start?'

Joshua picked up his small carryall and started toward one of the freshers. 'Take two hours. Three if you have to. I'll be in the bar. Working.'

'There you are, sir.' The white-jacketed barman set down a snifter of light amber liquid and a frosted ice-filled water tumbler. The bar was a long reach of hand-polished wood and brass, and the shelves behind it sparkled with the stimulants and depressants of a thousand cultures.

Joshua sipped from the snifter, then nodded acceptance, and the bartender smiled as if he really cared. Joshua wore a black open-necked raw silk shirt and tight black trousers over half boots. He appeared unarmed. He still wore the deceiving silver jewel on its chain around his neck, and the flaring bell sleeves of his shirt concealed a slender tube projector strapped to the inside of his right forearm.

The fat man came into the bar from an office, saw Joshua, and walked toward him. He wore formal wear, tailored oversize. The man had allowed himself to bald and was smiling, the smile of someone welcoming a friend he hadn't seen for a month or so. In the years Wolfe had known him the pleased expression never had gone higher than his pink jowls.

'Welcome to Yoruba, Joshua,' he said, sitting down, one careful stool between him and Wolfe.

'Ben.' Joshua lifted the snifter in a slight toast but did not drink. 'You look well.'

'I always said someone who doesn't respect himself can't have any regard for anyone else.' Both of them smiled, flat hard smiles, appreciating the hypocrisy.

'What do you think of my operation?' the fat man asked.

'It's a little flash for my tastes, if you want the truth.'

Greet shrugged. The barman put Greet's drink down. It was a single shot of a clear liquid in a spike-bottomed liqueur glass embedded in a small silver bowl of ice. Greet shot the drink back and motioned for another. It did not seem to affect him, and Joshua had never heard of anyone who'd seen the fat man affected by any drink or drug. Greet waited until the barman had replaced the entire setup before replying.

'Garish?' he said. 'Perhaps. But my clientele generally doesn't share your conservative tastes. They like seeing what they're paying for up front and gold-plated. Which brings up the question: Who are you hunting?' The smile remained.

Joshua sipped ice water.

'If it's me . . . we might as well start the game now,' Greet went on. 'And I hope the warrant's worth the risk and you've taken care of your people.' His voice tried to force steel. Joshua turned to face the fat man. Something flickered in Greet's eyes.

'No, Ben,' Joshua said. 'Your sins, far as I know, are still unremembered in anybody's orisons.'

Relief jellied Greet's face. 'Any of my boys? If so, there's a couple, maybe three, I'd have to give a warning to, even if it wouldn't do them much good. A man has certain moral duties, you know.'

'Innokenty Khodyan's his real name. You want a holo?'

'No. I know him. Another one from my old days. He's not using that label, but he's here. Guest, not staff. He wanted secure and had credits, so I booked him into the Vega Suite. You're working a warm track – he only checked in a couple of days ago. But there's just a bit of a problem.'

Involuntarily, Greet's head jerked as he saw the ring and little fingers of Joshua's right hand curl back, thumb over, first and middle fingers extended.

'Problem?' Joshua asked gently.

'Nothing . . . nothing that can't be dealt with, I hope,' Greet said hurriedly. 'You know he's got cover with him? They're contract talent, not working for me, so I can't call them off.'

Joshua showed no concern.

'He's fresh from a job,' Greet went on. 'He's got his stash in a safe in his suite.'

'Half a dozen jobs,' Joshua corrected. 'He went on a spree in the Federation. Hit them high, hit them low. Like he usually operates. But this time he scattered a few bodies around, and people decided enough was enough. So he's mine.'

Greet grimaced. 'I remember – gracious, it must be ten years ago – I warned him about getting excited. I told him most beings don't get nearly as concerned about property as they do about blood. But I guess it's in his genes or something.'

'You still haven't told me about your problem.'

'Not with Innokenty. I can't give him to you gift-wrapped; there's some other guests I've got around who think well of him, but I know you don't give a tinker's darn about that. The problem is, he's got a buyer inbound.'

'Who?'

'His name's Sutro. He's a pro. I've dealt with him before. You bag Khodyan, I'll have to give him some kind of explanation.'

'Tell him what you will,' Joshua said indifferently. 'You'll have something. You always do. As for the real "problem," I assume you're taking a flat five percent off the top.'

'Ten,' Greet corrected. 'And his expenses.'

'You'll get fifteen from me. Before I lift.'

'Then we *don't* have any problems, do we?'

'Not a one,' Joshua said.

Greet's jowls creased as he beamed, relaxed, knocked back his second drink, and raised a finger. 'Leong,' he ordered. 'Two more. And Mister –'

'I'm flying true colors.'

'– Mister Wolfe's bill is comped.'

Joshua drained his snifter without chasing it. He waited until the barman had arrived with another round and then departed. 'Thanks, Ben,' he said. 'As a favor, I'll try to keep things down to a dull roar and not upset your other guests. One thing. Don't get cute. I'm not fond of surprises.'

Once more Greet looked worried. 'Joshua, I gave my word. You'll have no problems from me or any of my staff. I'm telling the truth. You believe me, don't you?'

Joshua ringed Greet's wrist lightly with two fingers of his left hand. His eyes half closed, then opened fully. 'I believe,' he said, 'you're telling the truth. For right here and right now. Don't change. Life'll be a lot simpler that way.'

'You have my promise.' Greet stood, remembered his drink, and poured it down. 'I'll be around . . . if you need me for anything.'

'One more thing, Ben,' Joshua said. 'That Armagnac you're pouring's never been within five light-years of Earth. Maybe you want to have a chat with somebody about that.'

An hour later Lil made her entrance. Two drinkers at the bar swung and gaped, and one emaciated old man at a nearby table rudely forgot what he was cooing to a bejeweled woman certainly not his granddaughter and followed her passage with enchantment.

Joshua stood as she came to the table he'd moved to. Now he was drinking only ice water.

'Well?' Lil wore solid black, her classically lined evening gown high-necked, ending just below the knee but slit on either side to midthigh. A single gem at her throat threw colored reflections back at the overhead lights.

Joshua smiled broadly, and the corners of his eyes crinkled. 'I am honored,' he said formally. 'I surely won't have to worry about anyone noticing *me* tonight.' He bowed her into a chair and motioned for the barman.

Lil giggled as she slid a little awkwardly into her seat. 'I don't have a handle yet on how to do this,' she confided. 'I don't have anything on under this, and you're the only one who gets the leg show for free.'

'Yes, sir?' Leong asked. A professional – his eyes mostly stayed on Joshua.

'Champagne for the lady . . .' Joshua lifted an inquiring eye to Lil, who nodded enthusiastically. 'Water for me.'

'You're not drinking?' Lil sounded disappointed.

'Maybe some wine. With dinner.'

'This outfit really didn't cost that much,' Lil said hurriedly. 'It was on sale. The man said it was last year's, but I really, really liked it. And the rock's a synth, so –'

'Lil. Shut up and look beautiful,' Joshua suggested. 'Nobody's asking about the price tag.'

The drinks came. Lil drank. 'Now what?'

'Now we have dinner,' Joshua said.

'You're not going to tell me anything, are you?'

'When you don't know anything, there's nothing to tell,' Joshua said.

'I remember,' Lil said, 'back on – back where I came from, I heard this story. I probably won't tell it right. But it goes something like this: There were these two guys. Apprentice monks or some kind of religious people, anyway. They were bragging on their masters or teachers or preachers or whatever. One said his teacher could walk on water, see in the dark, and all that, a real miracle worker. The other baby monk said the miracle of *his* master was he ate when he was hungry and slept when he was tired.

'It sounds really dumb, telling it, but I never forgot that story. Sometimes I almost think I understand it. Do you?'

'Nope,' Joshua said. 'Too deep for me. But I surely am hungry. Shall we reserve a table?'

The fish course had just been served when Innokenty Khodyan came into the dining room. The great chamber, all white linen, bone china, and silver, was about half-filled, and Lil had just been marveling not that there were this many crooks on Platte but that there were this many with money when the three men were escorted to their table by the maitre d'.

Khodyan was a completely nondescript human male. He wore conservative formal dining garb, as did his two body-guards. One, who had a closely trimmed beard, came in first, eyes sweeping, clearing the room, gun hand near his waistband. Then he let the other two enter. The second gunnie made sure there wasn't anybody in their wake.

'That's him,' Lil whispered, eyes never leaving her dinner.

'I'm getting sloppy,' Joshua said. 'You never should have known it.'

'You're not sloppy. I spent too many years bein' the victim not to have feelers out. You lose often enough, you get sensitive. So that's him. What do I do? You want me to shoot somebody? Throw a scene? Or do I just jump under the table?'

Joshua, in spite of himself, grinned, full attention on Lil. 'Shoot somebody? Where the hell are you hiding a gun? I thought you weren't wearing anything but that gown you had anodized on.'

'Mister, you didn't pay enough to be told *that*,' she said mock-primly. 'A girl never tells all her secrets. You didn't answer my question.'

'You keep eating the tilapia,' Joshua said. 'But don't distract me for a second.'

Khodyan probably was armed. His two men, Joshua thought, letting his *feelings* swirl around the table the three men were being obsequiously seated at, were as good as advertised. They laughed, smiled, joked with the maitre d' and their client, but their attention never focused, always sweeping the room. One of them turned toward him, and Joshua concentrated on whether he thought his k'lmari might be a little overcooked as he cut off another bite. He *felt* the thug reach a verdict — one of us, celebrating, bed partner an import, not one of Greet's doxes, possibly dangerous in the abstract, no sign of interest in us, hence only worth the note — then look elsewhere. Joshua waited a moment, then subvocalized:

'The one we seek is present.'

'I am aware. I am appreciating him. My senses are concentrated, and I am remembering completely. Will you be taking action at this time?'

'Not yet. Continue remembering.'

He motioned for the waiter as he finished the last bite on his plate, then split the last of the Pantheon Riesling between his and Lil's glasses. 'I think we are ready to order our wine for the main course. Could we have the sommelier?'

'You're not going to do anything?' Lil possibly sounded a little disappointed.

'Of course I'm doing something. I'm going to order us some red plonk and then ask about the entrée.'

'And afterward?'

'I'm not sure. Maybe some strawberries and port?'

Lil relaxed and managed a smile. 'So all you do is eat when you're hungry and sleep when you're tired, hmm?'

'That's about it.'

Innokenty Khodyan seemed intent on a long, thorough spell at the trough. When Joshua and Lil had finished dessert and were leaving, the thief was still ordering, two dishes at each course. 'I wish I could eat like that,' Joshua observed, not looking back as the maitre d' ushered them out. He stopped at the desk, asked questions, and passed a coin across when he received the answers and a brochure.

Lil remained silent until they'd stepped off the slideway and the door to their suite had clicked shut. She drew a question mark in air. Joshua's hand brushed the wall. He *felt* no sensors, no watchers other than the passive monitors Ben Greet had installed in all the resort's rooms.

'As you were saying?' Joshua prompted.

'Never mind. I don't need to ask. The wine kinda slowed

me down,' she said. 'I understand you not making your move down there, in front of his goons and all. But you'll go out sometime tonight, right?'

Joshua took her hand and gently drew her to him.

'*Cease remembering.*'

'*Understood.*'

Her lips parted and met his, her eyes closing. His hands held her shoulders, moved down, found the slits in the gown, and cupped her bare buttocks as she pressed against his hardness.

The gown was a pool of black on the floor, and her hands moved over him, touching fasteners, finding clips, until he, too, was naked. He stripped off the chainknife and the holstered tube projector and tossed them away.

His hand went to the light control.

'No,' she said throatily. 'I like to see.'

He lifted her toward the bed.

It was deep in the night.

'Ah, Christ. Jerusalem. Oh, God.'

'Now?'

'No. No.' She rolled over, pulling a pillow under her hips. 'Now!'

He moved over her.

'Yes. Yes. Now,' she said, voice guttural. 'Now!'

'Like . . . this?'

'Yes, oh, please, yes. God, yes. There! There! And . . . and the other way now! Do it, God, do it to me!'

Her nails clawed his supporting hands, and she arched against him.

His tongue led him to her nipple. His teeth nipped gently. Her breathing, lowering toward sleep, caught. 'Jesus! Don't you *ever* get sleepy?'

'When I'm tired.'

Her fingers moved downward.

'You're . . . *not* tired!'

She turned on her side and slid one thigh over his. He rolled onto his back, and she came to her knees above him and guided him into her. She gasped as he lifted, then lowered his thighs.

'What . . . what about *him?*' she managed just before words stopped for them both.

'Tomorrow . . . *is* another day.'

Joshua's mind told him it was dawn. He and Lil were lying on the floor, the pillows from both beds piled around them. Lil was sleeping soundly, one hand under her cheek, the other between her thighs.

Joshua went to the window overlooking the garden. He brought both hands up from his waist and extended them outward, breathing deeply, gaze fixed on the space between them. He took the centering stance, then began the slow movements, lifting, blocking, striking, guarding.

When he was finished, he showered and dressed in a casual lounging outfit in a nondescript, friendly shade of brown that he'd bought the previous day. He scribbled a note on a hotel pad and set it beside Lil. The note read: PACK AND GET READY. He opened the door, went out, and slammed the door loudly enough to wake the woman.

'Begin tracking.' There seemed to be no reason to speak Al'ar now when he communicated with the ship. He felt the acknowledgment against his breastbone.

He went down the corridor, avoiding the slideway, mind setting aside all things, ship, resort, Lil, the night, the future. All that existed was Innokenty Khodyan.

He carried no weapons.

He asked some casual questions about room service as he sipped a cup of tea in the breakfast room. He studied the brochure he'd gotten from the desk clerk the night before, periodically checking the time. He finished his tea, left a lavish tip in cash, and went toward the lift banks. He stopped at a waste receptacle, tore the brochure into fragments, and threw them away.

He entered a lift that was exclusive to one of the resort's three towers, and touched the sensor for the floor the Vega Suite was on and for the floor above it, as well. The lift went up quickly, floor indicators blurring. It stopped once, and a harried-looking maid got on, pushing a laundry cart heavy with soiled towels. Joshua thought: *warmth . . . sunlight . . . a day off . . . a perfect meal . . . a laugh from a child . . .*

The maid looked at the man in brown, saw nothing worrisome, and smiled impersonally when she got off two floors later. The lift went on to the floor Joshua had first selected.

The resort's architect had understood the needs of those with enemies. The tower was cylindrical, and the ten suites on each floor jutted out independently from the central core, not connected to the floor above or below. From above, the tower would look like a ten-pointed star. Separate corridors led from the lift shaft to the entrance to each suite. In the central area, aimed at the lift, was a sniffer that would be programmed to allow only the weapons a guest, his friends, or the hotel staff carried without shrieking alarm or possibly even opening fire.

Joshua moved swiftly along the corridor toward a suite the desk clerk had said was unoccupied. Halfway down was a niche for a maid to park her room cart without blocking the passageway. He melted into it.

He waited: *wind, wind, blowing, wind unseen, not strong, not moving even the grasses, not even whispering . . .*

Twice the lift doors opened and hotel employees got out. Neither of them took the corridor leading to the Vega Suite. One glanced down the corridor Joshua was waiting in, then went on. Joshua *heard* the door to the Vega Suite open, a low voice, a man's laugh, the door closing.

Wind, wind . . .

One of the two bodyguards, the one with the beard, moved silently into view, near the lift.

Wind, wind . . .

He checked each corridor but did not go down any of them. He went to a window, looked up, looked down. He returned to his post near the lift door and waited, not moving, showing no sign of boredom or impatience.

A few minutes passed.

The lift door opened and a roomboy pushed out a cart laden with old-fashioned covered platters. The roomboy grinned and said something to the guard, who replied in a neutral tone. The bodyguard made sure no one else had ridden up in the lift, then followed the roomboy toward the Vega Suite.

Wind blowing, embers, flameflicker, fire, fire . . .

The heavyset man inside the suite appeared to be listening politely to Innokenty Khodyan's tirade. The thief's whine had stood him in good stead as a child, and the habit was now unbreakable.

The holoset blared unnoticed, and the ruins of the night's snacks were scattered around the large living room. Doors led off to freshers, bedrooms, a small pool, a bar, other rooms. A hide-a-bed sat against one wall. At night one bodyguard slept there, the bed moved against the door. There was a safe near one couch.

'I'll be peeling wallpaper, I tell you,' Khodyan said. 'Look. If Sutro don't show today, I'm gonna get a couple of doxes sent up.'

'No whores,' the bodyguard said. 'You told us you'd be wanting them but you weren't allowed. Not until your connection leaves.'

'Listen to reason, would you? I was bein' a worrywart, right? When you come off a job, you're like that, afraid everybody's out to do you. I took it a little too far. Right? You guys'll be here. Hell, you can even watch if you want.'

'No leg.'

'So all I get to do is whack you guys for matches, try to teach you how to bet right, look out the friggin' window at everybody down there relaxing, or else out at that friggin' desert? Shitfire, I can't even open a window and breathe the local air. I guess I oughta be grateful you let me eat.'

'Those were your orders.'

'Magdalene with a dildo, but you bastards are hard. Look. The essence of gettin' along is knowin' when to go along, right? So how about –'

The door chime went off.

'Breakfast,' Khodyan said in relief.

A gun was in the heavyset man's hand. He checked the screen that monitored the outside corridor.

Wind, blow . . .

For an instant the screen fuzzed.

Neither the heavyset man nor his client noticed. The bodyguard opened the door, and the roomboy pushed the cart inside, the other bodyguard behind him.

Fire roar . . .

A man wearing brown cannoned into the bearded man, driving him into the roomboy, who screeched and sprawled, the meal cart skidding ahead of him.

The heavyset man's pistol lifted as Joshua rolled off the floor inside the man's guard. He snap blocked with his left, and the pistol thunked to the rug. The man had a second to howl, reaching for his paralyzed wrist, as Joshua's open-palmed right hand slipped past the bodyguard's neck, index and middle finger brushing skin near the carotid, and the man slumped, boneless. He was dead.

Innokenty Khodyan had his mouth open, but Joshua did not hear what he was shouting.

The bearded man yanked a heavy pistol from a waist holster as he came to his knees. He fired, but Wolfe wasn't there. The blast spiderwebbed a window, and dry desert air rushed in. Before he could fire a second time Joshua was next to him, left hand tweaking the gun barrel back, and then Wolfe held the pistol. He continued his spin, dropped into a crouch, and was five feet away from the bodyguard, the man's own pistol leveled. He glanced at Khodyan, who wasn't doing anything dangerous.

The bearded man half raised his hands.

'Good,' Joshua approved. 'Stay a pro. You blew the contract. Stay alive so you can feel guilty.'

The bodyguard squatted, grabbing for an ankle-holstered backup gun. Joshua touched the trigger and blew a fist-sized hole in his chest. The roomboy had stopped squealing and was going for the door, scrabbling up from his hands and knees. Joshua kicked his legs from under him and knuckle rapped, with that seemingly gentle touch, against the back of his head. The roomboy went on his face and began snoring loudly.

Joshua held the gun steady on Khodyan. He back kicked the suite door closed.

'We don't need company,' he said. Formally: 'I am a duly constituted representative of the Federation. I am serving a properly executed warrant, issued within the Federation and presented to me by a Sector Marshal. According to this warrant –'

Innokenty Khodyan launched himself at Joshua, fingers clawing. Joshua sidestepped, turned, lifted a knee, and sent the smaller man tumbling, almost onto the heavyset bodyguard's corpse. Khodyan saw the man's pistol and had it, fast for a man who'd begun as just a thief.

It was too far, even for a dive, as the blast crashed past

Joshua's ribs. He fired, and there were three corpses in the suite.

Joshua walked over to Khodyan's body and looked down. The thief's final expression was petulant. He glanced at his own image in a mirror. It matched the thief's. As a corpse Khodyan was worth only expenses.

Outside the suite he heard dim shouting through the soundproofing; then someone hammered on the door. Joshua paid no attention. He knelt over the body, thinking. Then he looked at the safe.

Joshua tucked the pistol in his pocket, grabbed Khodyan's corpse by the collar, trying to keep from getting bloody, and dragged it to the safe. He looked at both of Khodyan's palms carefully. Deciding that Khodyan was left-handed, he pressed that index finger to the porepattern sensor on the safe's door. It took two tries before the door slid open.

Inside was another gun, which Joshua ignored; a wad of currency from various worlds; a vial of tablets claiming to be aphrodisiac; and two medium-sized jeweler's traveling cases. He took both to a table and started to open one. An unexpected sensation – like small chimes felt, not heard – made him hesitate. He opened the second case. There were three rows of drawers. His fingers went, as if drawn, to a drawer in the case's center, and surprise shattered his hunter's mask.

There was one single stone in the drawer. It was oval and uncut but appeared to be machine-polished. The stone was unimpressive, gray, although there were a few flecks of color, like quartz flakes in granite.

It was a stone the Al'ar called Lumina.

This was the third time he'd seen one.

The last time the stone had been on a headband worn by a Guardian who stood just behind an Al'ar leader-officer on the bridge of a warship, the last of his fleet. The officer had spit contempt and scorn at Joshua and his plea for surrender. The stone had flamed, echoing the defiance. Wolfe hadn't needed to translate to the Federation admiral standing next to him. He turned away from the com screen, refusing to look as weapons officers sent missiles flashing into the Al'ar ship, and there was nothing but swirling fire and black.

The first time had been in a sandy clearing, when a Guardian had given the boy human named Wolfe his Al'ar name, the Warrior of Silent Shadows, and told him to become worthy of it.

Wolfe picked up the Lumina.

Quite suddenly the stone flared; the kaleidoscoping colors would have shamed a warmed fire opal.

The fires went out, and Joshua was holding an uninteresting rock. His eyes iced as he regained control. He carefully tucked the Lumina into a pocket. Then, whistling tunelessly, he went to the door.

THREE

'I find,' Sector Marshal Jagua Achebe dictated, 'after a complete survey of the evidence, that the deceased, Innokenty Khodyan, met his death while resisting being served with a correctively drawn warrant for . . . for . . . you put whatever the charges were in, David, before you final this document for my signature. I further attest that Innokenty Khodyan's body was inspected by me, on this date, and I certify the corpus is in fact that of the charged being.

'I also certify the warrant hunter, one Joshua Wolfe, is well known to me as a reputable citizen who has previously served warrants, on a freelance basis, for the Federation and at no time has behaved in an unprofessional, careless, or bloodthirsty manner.

'This inquest is duly closed.' She released the microphone, and it disappeared into the ceiling. Achebe looked down once more, and Innokenty Khodyan's frozen eyes stared back. She slammed the drawer shut.

'That's that. No known estate, no known next-of, nobody gives a rat's ear, so we can crispy the critter after a decent spell. Maybe this afternoon, when we get back from lunch.' She went out of the morgue, and Joshua followed her down a long corridor.

'Hell in a whorehouse, Joshua,' she said over her shoulder. 'When you go and kill somebody, you don't mess around. You could float a lifter through that hole in his chest.'

They went into her office. It was big, intended to reflect the dignity of her position, and Achebe had taken advantage of every square inch. It looked like a crime lab had exploded.

The walls were lined with 2D solidos. Achebe looked at one as if she'd never seen it before. There was a line of soldiers in dress uniforms, waiting to be awarded medals by some forgotten dignitary whose back was to the pickup. One soldier was a younger Achebe. Not far from her stood Joshua Wolfe, also at rigid attention. The scar that now etched the corner of his mouth wasn't there.

Achebe tapped the picture. 'We were a lot prettier then. At least, *I* was.'

Wolfe was looking at another picture. 'That one's new.'

It showed Achebe wearing a shipsuit with the three stars of a Federation vice admiral on it. She was on the bridge of a ship, staring at the pickup in astonishment.

'Somebody sent it to me about three months ago,' Achebe said. 'Said she shot it when the word came over the com about the Al'ar. We were off Sauros then, waiting for the landing order.

'She was one of my weapons officers and thought I might like to have the pic to remember the day. As if I'd forget it, sitting there, trying to handle the idea that maybe I wasn't going to die in the next hour or so.

'Guess nobody'll forget that day, now, will they?'

'Guess not,' Joshua said, his voice flat.

'Where were *you* when you heard?'

'About a parsec and a half under you. Waiting to *give* the signal.'

'You were *with* them when it happened? On the ground? You never told me that.'

'I wasn't with anybody,' Joshua said. 'I was hiding in a spider hole, staring at my watch.'

'So what do you figure happened to them?'

Joshua stared at her, his face blank. After a time Achebe realized he wasn't going to answer her. She slid behind her desk, grace denying bulk.

'Too early for sauce?' she asked, changing the subject.

'The sun's up, isn't it?' Joshua set a skull with a large hole in it on the floor, next to the archaic weapon that might have caused that hole, and eased into a cracked leather chair that didn't match any of the others in the room.

Achebe took two bulbs from a floor unit and handed one to Joshua. He pulled the tab off, waited until the bulb iced, then sipped. Outside, there was the dim hiss of anti-grav traffic and every now and then a high, shaking whine as a ship lifted from the nearby field.

'Just to remind you of something you seem to have let slip your mind,' Achebe said. 'Warrant hunters don't get but their expenses when they bring back the bounty in a meat chest. Even when an upstanding official's willing to say said warrant hunter isn't any more homicidal than anybody else in these parts.'

Joshua did not bother answering.

'You losing it, my friend?'

'Looks like,' Joshua said ruefully. 'I had him cold. I should've hit him with a hypo or a nerve block instead of giving him a chance to make a damned fool out of both of us. Maybe I better start looking for a nice quiet job building bombs or something.'

He stared at Achebe as the grin slowly split her face. 'All right. What are you holding back?' he asked.

'When you pulled down on Khodyan,' the Sector Marshal said, 'that put an equally large hole in that 50K Federation warrant you would've gotten, as I've pointed out. However . . .'

She took a microfiche from the desk and flipped it to

Joshua. 'You need not bother asking for a viewer. Private enterprise triumphs. That's an E-transfer for one *hundred* thousand credits to the being who terminates Innokenty Khodyan's nefarious career. Merry Halloween or whatever holiday you Christians celebrate.'

'Who posted it?'

'One Judge Malcolm Penruddock of Mandodari III. Back in civilization. But not that far. It's about —'

'I've seen Mandodari on the charts,' Joshua said. 'What's his interest?'

'According to the full complaint I used to issue the warrant, he's one of the honest joes Khodyan hit when he was out ripping and tearing. He posted this bounty after you'd already grabbed the official alert and gone snuffling off.

'I guess "Judge" isn't a courtesy title, because he had enough clout to com me instead of sending his message through channels. Interesting note, Joshua. I had to remind him the law isn't a private assassination service for rich bastards, since he wanted to offer the reward on the condition Khodyan wasn't to be taken alive. Judges do go and presume they're the only dispensers of justice, don't they?'

'Has he been told yet?'

'As soon as we got the com that you were inbound with a meat crate, I shot one straight off. He authorized immediate payment. So you aren't as poor as you thought.'

Joshua scratched his nose, thinking. 'Innokenty Khodyan killed some people this time around. Was that what set this Penruddock off?'

'Big negative there. According to his com, he lost a chunk of his gem collection to Khodyan, but there weren't any bodies involved. He was very interested in anything that was recovered. I had him ship me his original theft report.'

'Mind if I take a look?'

'You think it's a little strange somebody gets that antsy about a bunch of rocks, too, eh?'

Joshua studied the printout she passed to him, matching it with his mental inventory of the two jewel cases that now sat in Achebe's safe. Penruddock certainly was a man who knew what to buy. Some of the finest stones were on his list, along with their valuation. The two trays of star sapphires Wolfe had paid Ben Greet with weren't there. But the five four-carat marquise-cut diamonds he'd given Lil were. And one other: *small stone, of unknown composition, semipolished, egg-shaped, approximately three inches by two inches in diameter. SENTIMENTAL VALUE ONLY.*

The Lumina.

Joshua handed the list back. 'I don't know if it's that strange,' he said. 'I knew a man who collected string. He shot himself after he lost it all in a fire.'

Achebe studied him closely, then put the list away and took out two more bulbs. 'That's got to be it Joshua. Just another nut case with money. Surely there's nothing more to it.'

Her voice dripped disbelief.

FOUR

The slender brown-skinned man blocked the saber slash with his own blade and cut quickly with the long straight dagger in his left hand. Blood lined the upper arm of his heavyset opponent, who stumbled back, mouth gaping in seeming astonishment and fear. Blood oozed from half a dozen other light cuts on the man's bare torso.

Joshua Wolfe grunted, stood, picked up his cloak, and edged his way past the big man's knees.

"Samatter, friend? A little blood get to you?'

'I get bored at boat races,' Joshua said.

'You think it's rigged? Somebody better check your pupils, bud. I got a dozen large ones saying Yamamoto's just playing with him.'

'Yeah,' Joshua said. 'Yamamoto's at six to five, Lopez eight to one, and who's doing all the bleeding? Plus nobody'll take a bet on anything beyond the sixth, at any odds. Tell me that's not an invitation to dance.'

'You just picked the wrong boy,' the big man said.

'Maybe so,' Joshua said indifferently, and forced his way into the aisle. 'I make a lot of mistakes like that.'

The big man looked after him, worried.

Joshua was at the coliseum's exit when the roar began. Yamamoto's saber and dagger clanged onto the mat, and his arms crossed overhead in surrender. The crowd didn't sound as if it liked what had happened.

Wolfe pulled on his cloak and went out. The streets were wet with the drizzle that had fallen all day. He walked down a block, checking his back now and then in shop windows. He was clean.

He thought about walking back to the hotel but decided not to. He started to subvocalize, then caught himself. His ship was half-gutted in one of Carlton VI's yards for a long-overdue refit and update, so there was no one to talk to. He took a com from his pocket, keyed a number, and spoke softly. Then he leaned against a building, waiting. There was a doorway nearby he could have sheltered in. But he liked the rain.

After a while a red-painted lifter slid down the street and grounded next to him. Joshua clambered in beside the driver. 'Sorry to take so long,' the driver said. 'Everybody's out and about tonight and scared spitless they might melt.'

Joshua smiled and gave an address. The lifter went down the avenue, no sound in its cockpit but turbine hum and the occasional buzz as the demisters cleared the windows.

The lifter stopped at the address Joshua had given. Joshua had coins ready and dropped them into the driver's hand. He got out of the lifter and went across the sidewalk quickly, into the café's brightness.

The house musician had a metronome-bass going and was weaving a polyphonic line across it. His eyes were half-closed, as his fingers plucked notes from the squares holoed irregularly in the air in front of him. Joshua thought the piece might have started life as a medieval lieder.

The musician said hello to Joshua as he went past.

A red-faced man wearing a gold woman's wig waved and shouted at Joshua to join them before they got too drunk to see. Joshua smiled, shook his head no, and went to the bar.

He ordered Armagnac and ice water. He sipped, staring at the antique mirror behind the bar, not seeing it. He was thinking about a gray stone and a judge who'd tried to take out a murder contract for a hundred thousand credits. A woman wearing loose silk harem pants and a bare-midriff blouse slipped up beside him. 'You don't have to drink alone,' she said in a voice that sounded worn-out.

Joshua nodded to the bartender, who busied himself at the mixpanel. 'Jean-Claude's out of town?'

'Out of town or with somebody else,' the woman said as if it didn't matter very much which. She took the tall glass from the bartender, made a slight toast in Joshua's direction, and sniffed deeply at the gas as it rose from the mouth of the container.

'Thanks for the offer, Elspeth,' Joshua said. 'But I'm not fit company tonight.' The woman shrugged, patted his hand, and went away.

Joshua finished the Armagnac. He dropped a coin on the bar and went back out into the rain.

The streets were as deserted as the sidewalks. An occasional lifter hissed by, sending water swirling up as it passed. Joshua thought he could hear surf crash against the cliffs behind his hotel. A coryphodon honked wet unhappiness from the zoo half a mile away.

The hotel's huge lobby was deserted except for two desk clerks trying not to yawn in each other's faces and a middle-aged man with a short haircut frowning his way through the headlines projected on a portable holoset. There weren't any messages. Joshua considered a nightcap, but the taste in his mind was wrong.

He went to one lift and touched the porepattern lock. The door opened, and he entered. As the door closed Joshua turned and saw the man with the crew cut looking at him, then away.

The lift had only one sensor. Joshua touched it, and the

lift soared toward the hotel's roof. When the door opened, he waited a moment before he went into the wood-paneled corridor. There was no welcoming committee. Staying close to the wall, he walked toward the door at the end. It opened as he reached it, and he went into his home.

The penthouse had a huge multileveled living room, two bedrooms and freshers, a library, and a workout room. Glass doors showed the terrace garden that could serve, and had, as an emergency landing platform. In the master bedroom, hidden in a windowsill compartment, was a steel-wired ladder that could drop two floors to the balcony of a small room he'd leased through a cutout.

Joshua checked the security board. The sensors showed one entry by someone using an approved key and giving the current code. Fires crackled in the living room and bedroom fireplaces. Loughran, the nightman, had followed his instructions

Joshua closed his eyes, then opened them, looking around as if seeing everything for the first time. It was very neat and looked as if it had been decorated by a man with a lot of money, time to make up his mind, and quiet tastes. It also appeared as if the occupant was a man who'd owned very little for a very long time and who had to keep that little in perfect condition. The penthouse appeared to be just as he had left it at dusk.

Joshua frowned, corrected the slightly skewed hanging of one of the Hogarths, then crossed to a cabinet. He took a medium-aperture blaster and a fume mask out and went to a couch that faced the entrance. He put the mask on a table and sat down with the gun in his lap, thumb resting on the pistol's safety, index finger touching the trigger guard.

Some time passed. A smile touched Joshua's lips, and he swept his hand through the air. His motion opened the penthouse door.

A man stood there. A look of surprise ran across his face, then vanished. He walked into the suite, hands held up to either side, palms facing Joshua. Joshua gestured, and the door closed.

'You're still hard to sneak up on, Joshua.'

'You'd better give your boy downstairs some peripheral vision training,' Joshua said dryly.

'Hard to find a good op when peace breaks out all over. Harder to keep him in Intelligence after he's trained. Can I sit down?'

'Pour yourself a drink first. Third decanter from the left's got your brand in it.' Joshua put the pistol on the table but left his hand draped over the couch's arm.

The man went to the sideboard, found a glass, and poured a small drink. He did not put ice in the glass. 'You want something?'

'I'll get it myself. In a few minutes.'

'Aren't we being a little untrusting?' Still moving carefully, hands in view, the man sat across from Joshua. There was nothing special about him. One would never remember his face an hour after meeting him. He would fit seamlessly onto any street on any world and never be noticed. He wore casual clothes in quiet colors. The name he'd given Joshua fifteen years before was Cisco.

'I'm a creature of habit,' Joshua said. 'Every time you show up out here in the Outlaw Worlds, life's got a tendency to get interesting.'

Cisco painted on a brief smile, then took it away. 'I've got something special.'

Joshua made no response. Cisco tasted his drink. 'I understand you blew a warrant recently. Or was that on purpose for some reason my leak didn't know about?'

'You heard right. I slipped. What do you have?'

'I said this one was special, and I meant it,' Cisco said. 'First I'll give you the terms. Federation Intelligence guarantees all expenses, no questions asked. One hundred K payment on top, even if you draw a blank. You make the recovery intact, we'll pay one million credits. Delivered here on Carlton or anywhere else you want, in any shape you want. It's an NQA – no questions asked.'

'You *did* say special, didn't you?'

'I did. And you're the only one being offered the contract.'

'I've heard that before, believed you, gone out, and found every amateur headhunter and half of your operatives stumbling around playing grab-ass in a fog they made up themselves.'

'You can't blame me for something like that. You know you can't always give an operative all the data before you put him in the field. You never did, when you were running someone.'

'That was during the war.'

'Maybe mine went on a little longer than yours.'

'Maybe,' Joshua said, tired of the fencing. 'Go ahead, Cisco. Let's hear the proposition.'

Cisco leaned forward. 'There's one Al'ar left alive. He's somewhere in the Outlaw Worlds.

'We want you to take him.'

On the terrace outside rain splashed harder. Cisco's eyes glittered.

FIVE

Wolfe forced control.

'Hardly a new rumor, Cisco. Surprised that you're spreading it.'

'It's not a rumor.'

'Look,' Joshua said, trying to sound ostentatiously patient. 'Since the war, since the Al'ar . . . disappeared, there's been stories floating around that they're still out there. Hiding behind a pink cloud or something, waiting to come back and wreak terrible revenge.'

'I know the stories. This one's different, which I'll prove in a second. But let me ask a question,' the Federation agent said. 'They had to go *somewhere*, right? We were pushing them hard, but it was still their choice, as far as anything I've heard. I've never believed that crap about mass suicide. Doors swing both ways.'

'Not this one,' Wolfe said.

'Okay,' Cisco said in a reasonable tone. 'You lived with them. You were their first prisoner to escape. You were our best source for their psychology. So how do you know they're gone for good?'

Wolfe hesitated, then decided to tell the truth. 'I *feel* it.'

'I'm not laughing. Explain.'

Wolfe wondered why he was telling as much as he was; he thought perhaps he had to talk to someone, sometime, and Cisco, at least currently, was no more an enemy than anyone else in the Outlaw Worlds.

'*Feel* is beyond emotion, but there's no logic to it; or, rather, it includes logic and uses other senses.'

'Al'ar senses?'

'Yes. Or as much of them as I learned.'

'Part of why you're so hard to ambush?'

Wolfe shrugged.

Cisco grunted. 'I was pretty sure you had some . . . hell, "powers" isn't the right word. Abilities, maybe. Something that the rest of us don't. Anyway, you've got this "feeling." But I can't – Intelligence can't operate on something that vague. We've got to be ready for almost anything.

'Hell, we've probably still got contingency plans tucked away somewhere in case Luna attacks Earth-gov.' It was about as close as the agent could come to a joke. Joshua allowed himself to smile to acknowledge it.

'Set that aside,' Cisco went on. 'What put us in motion was the market in Al'ar artifacts. You know there's a ton of people out there collecting anything and everything that's claimed to be Al'ar?'

'Happens after every war,' Wolfe said. 'The winner collects stuff from the loser and the other way around. I'm not surprised.'

Cisco moved a hand toward his pocket but stopped as Wolfe's hand touched his gun. After a moment Wolfe nodded. Cisco, moving glacially, took out a small egg-shaped stone, gray, with flecks in it.

'This is the current hot item. Asking price starts at a mill – and goes up. It's a –'

'I know what it is,' Joshua interrupted.

Cisco handed it to him.

As Joshua touched it, the gem sparkled, sending a dozen colors flickering against the walls. He held it for a moment, then passed it back to Cisco.

'It's a fake.'

Cisco blinked in surprise. 'You're probably the only one – outside of an Al'ar – who could tell that. It is. Our labs have built about twenty of them. We've been using them for stalking-horses.'

'Any luck?'

'None. All we're getting is real collectors, guys who want a Lumina to finish off their collection. If the Al'ar used flags, they'd want one of those, too,' Cisco said.

'Why do you give a damn about anyone who wants to buy stuff like this and what's it a cover for? Or what else is somebody getting into that interests the Federation?'

'I don't know,' Cisco said. 'Those were my orders. Look for anybody after a Lumina.'

'So whoever your boss is really looking for must have the same ability I've got – to spot a phony Lumina. Or else you would have nailed someone besides souvenir hounds.'

Cisco started. 'I hadn't figured that out yet,' he confessed. 'I forgot . . . you were pretty good at systems analysis.'

'So you're drawing blanks on one end and looking for this mythical Al'ar on the other, which is where you want me. How am I going to know where to look – if I take the commission?'

'I'll give you everything FI has.' Again Cisco's hand slowly moved to his pocket, took out a microfiche, and handed it across. 'That's the summary. I'll give you the raw data if you want.'

'I do. What did this give you?'

'We've worked various directions. The only one that seemed to give us anything were these Lumina stones. We've found four so far.

'There's a second commonality. All four show up within a given time frame and in a logical order, as if someone was going from world to world and selling these stones or possibly putting them into a network that's already been set up.'

'That's a thin supposition,' Joshua said. 'But say it's valid. Why me? This kind of detailed work is what your paper shufflers and door knockers do best.'

'Right,' Cisco said, his normally flat voice showing sarcasm. 'What an excellent idea. To have a whole group of people, who'll sooner or later be identified as Federation Intelligence, wandering around out here bellowing, "Anybody seen an Al'ar?" What sort of rumors do you think *that* would start?'

'Point conceded,' Joshua said. 'But still not enough for me to come in.'

'Next I want to show you some film. I can't let you keep it, and I won't even let you put your hands on it for fear I'll walk out with a switch. Where's your projector?'

Joshua rose, went to a wall, and touched a sensor; vid gear emerged. He pressed buttons. 'It's ready.'

'Before I show you what we've got, let me give you another bit of data. Maybe you don't know it, but we've got all of the Al'ar capital worlds under surveillance, including Sauros, your old stomping grounds. If it wouldn't draw attention, we'd have them under fleet interdiction – assuming we've still got enough ships in commission to mount a blockade.'

'I didn't know that.'

'The given reason, even to our own agents, is we're trying to prevent looting until the Federation decides what to do with these planets. The Al'ar had some weaponry we still don't understand, even after ten years.

'But that's not the real reason. We put the coverage on because of that damned rumor about the Al'ar being alive.

'Our surveillance is both passive and active pickups. What you're going to see comes from an active bird. Offplanet sensors picked up an inbound ship and decided it was on a low-profile orbit, not wanting to be seen. That aroused some interest.

'By the time the bird launched, the ship was on the ground. One . . . person came out as our craft was incoming. Here's the pickup.'

Cisco put a disk into the vid slot, and the large screen flashed to life.

The tiny robot Cisco had called a bird flew at low altitude through the streets of an Al'ar city. Wolfe thought he remembered some of the buildings, even though time and weather had already begun to shatter their radiant delicacy. He repressed a shudder.

'Now the bird's coming into the open, into one of the Al'ar parks,' Cisco said.

'They weren't parks,' Joshua said absently. 'Call them . . . reaching-out centers.'

'Whatever. Pay attention – the shot only lasts for a few seconds.'

The screen showed a medium-sized starship sitting on its landing skids. Wolfe didn't recognize the model but guessed from its design that it was civilian, most likely a high-speed yacht. The port hung open. As the robot soared closer, Wolfe saw movement, and the port closed. The bird had almost halved the distance when the starship's secondary drive activated, and the ship lifted under full power. It roared across the open ground, gaining speed as it went. Wolfe saw the shock wave ripple from its nose, wrecking small buildings as it smashed overhead. The ship pulled into a climb, then appeared to vanish as it smashed toward space.

'Just out-atmosphere, it went into N-space before we could even think about putting any E-tracers on it.'

'Somebody has very fast reactions,' Joshua said.

'Or some very developed "feelings,"' Cisco said dryly. 'Now, here's the blowup of the air lock area.'

Even with the resolution, the picture was still very grainy. It showed the ship's lock, and now Wolfe saw someone moving slowly, as if underwater, up the ramp into the ship.

'Too far,' Cisco muttered. 'Let me run it back.'

The figure backed down the steps, then turned and walked out a few feet into the open ground.

Cisco froze the frame. 'Well?'

The being on-screen wore no spacesuit but a plain coverall with a weapons belt. It was very tall and thin, almost to the point of emaciation. Its face looked like a snake's seen from above, eyes vertical slits, nostrils barely visible holes.

Joshua found himself shaking uncontrollably.

Cisco blanked the screen.

'Now,' he said, noting Wolfe's reaction, 'Now will you go out there and take that Al'ar for us?'

The exercise room was mirrored like the one on Wolfe's ship. The mirrors showed nothing at all.

Outside, dawn was close, and the last of the night's rain clouds scudded overhead.

There was a shimmer in the mirrors, and Joshua reappeared. He held the Lumina in front of him in both hands.

He looked at his multiple image closely. No strain showed on his face.

He stared into the Lumina, and once more his image shimmered, just as he lifted a foot to take a step. There was nothing to be seen for an instant, then he returned to full visibility.

He nodded once, then went to his bedroom to pack.

SIX

'Anything to declare?'

Joshua shook his head.

The customs officer put on a smile like a cruising shark, said 'Welcome to Mandodari III,' and kept a close eye on the detector screen as Wolfe passed through.

Wolfe went to the lifter rank and slid into the backseat of the first craft, putting his black nylon case beside him.

'Where to?'

'Acropolis Hotel,' Wolfe said. He'd chosen it from a list the liner's steward had given him. As the lifter rose, he turned, looking back. It was an old habit.

The hotel was as advertised, large, intended for the upper-end business traveler, unlikely to pay much attention to Joshua's comings and goings. It had been built just after the war in anticipation of the peacetime boom that had never come to Mandodari.

Joshua 'freshed, made a vid call, and found he was expected. He went down to the lobby and outside, ignoring the doorman's inquiry. He hailed another lifter, got in, and gave the address of a restaurant he'd chosen from the hotel's courtesy list. At the restaurant he used their com to call a second lifter and gave that driver the address he wanted.

For a change, the man was no more in the mood to talk than Wolfe was. Joshua concentrated on the city.

Mandodari III wasn't dead, but it was hardly healthy. During the war it had been one of the Federation's biggest fleet ports, close to the Al'ar sectors. It had been hit by raids twice, and Wolfe saw at a distance the shattered hills where something big had gone off.

With the war's end and demobilization, Mandodari III had begun to decay. The streets were potholed and unswept, and the buildings on either side were boarded up or just dark, vacant, their owners not even bothering to pull down the last, despairing LIQUIDATION SALE banners that flapped in the dusty breeze blowing across the city. The people he saw wore the styles of the last year or last decade and were intent on their own business but in no particular hurry to accomplish it.

The lifter went into the hills that ringed the city, past mansions, some empty, some occupied. It grounded outside one, and Wolfe paid the man off.

It was a vastly gardened estate, high-walled with spear points atop the wall, studded with security sensors. Far up a winding cobbled drive was the main house, white-painted with a columned porch, big and square enough to be an institution.

Wolfe touched a com panel and announced himself; he heard a hiss, and the gate opened. As he walked up the drive, he saw movement from the corner of his eye and noted two auto-sweep guns tracking him.

The door opened, and a woman invited him in. 'I'm Lady Penruddock,' she said. 'Mister Wolfe?'

Joshua nodded.

The woman was about ten years younger than Joshua, beautiful in a chilly way. She wore an expensive-looking skirt and off-the-shoulder jacket in gray and a dark red blouse that fastened at the throat. Her low voice suggested that she knew quite well what she wanted and most often got it.

'You don't look like one of my husband's usual visitors,' she said.

'Oh? What do they look like?'

'There's an old word. Drummers. It generally meant –'

'I've heard the term.'

'They're men who've gotten something that is more than they are, more than what they should have,' Lady Penruddock went on, 'and want to sell it before they're found out.'

Joshua's lips quirked, looking enough like a smile to show acknowledgment.

'I *was* going out,' the woman said. 'But you might be . . . interesting. I think I'll stay. My name's Ariadne. Wait here. I'll get Malcolm.'

Her footsteps tapped away across the marble. The mansion's foyer was huge. One wall was hung with the heads of game animals. Joshua recognized a few of them: an Earth Kodiak bear, an Altairan phract, a Jameson's beast from Nekkar IX. On the other wall was an alcove occupied by a twenty-foot-tall rearing six-legged monster Wolfe had never seen before. He walked closer and admired the taxidermy. He noticed a small square in midair that fluoresced green, barely visible, like a holograph. He touched it.

The creature shrilled rage and slashed at him. The heavy rifle was coming to his shoulder, and he almost stumbled on the green, slimy stones of the planetoid, stepping back . . . and the beast was still once more and Joshua was in the mansion's alcove.

'Clever,' he said softly, then frowned and put his hand back on the sensor.

Again the monstrosity came for him, but Joshua paid no attention to it or to the rifle the diorama had given him. Instead, he looked about the canyon he appeared to be in. He looked up at one crag. That was where the shooter, and pickup, had actually been. He smiled, real humor on his face, stepped away once more, and returned to Judge Penruddock's mansion.

The judge was just entering the room, his wife behind him. He was a large, bluff man in his late sixties, white hair carefully coifed, body well tuned. He wore dark, formal clothing, as if to remind everyone of his former profession.

'Mister Wolfe,' he said. 'I am truly pleased to meet you.'

'Judge,' Joshua said.

'I see you were "in" my little device,' Penruddock went on. 'I've got half a dozen more like it around the house, but that's my favorite. I came around the path, and the bastard was waiting in ambush for *me*. Almost got me before I touched a round off.'

'Indeed,' Joshua said, and his smile came and went again.

'Ariadne,' the judge said, 'Mister Wolfe is one of the heroes of the Al'ar War, although not the sort the public heard much about. He's also the man who recovered those jewels that bastard stole from us.'

'Ah.' Lady Penruddock's gaze was assessing. 'I sensed he was something . . . special.'

'That's a good way to describe him, and we're honored to have you here, sir. Come to my study. We can talk there.'

The three started down a hall.

'I thought you were going out, my dear.'

'I was. But I thought I might stay on. Whatever Mister Wolfe's business is, it certainly sounds fascinating.'

'I hate to be a spoilsport, but it is fairly private. And I'd rather keep what we're going to discuss sub rosa. Unless you mind?'

Ariadne Penruddock looked at her husband. 'No. I don't mind at all. I'll see you later, then, dear. It was nice meeting you, Mister Wolfe.' Her voice was nearly a monotone.

Penruddock watched her walk away, then produced a booming laugh. 'Women! Aren't they always trying to hang on, even though they ought to know they'll just be bored listening to man talk.'

Joshua said nothing, followed the judge.

The den was as he'd anticipated – all dark wood and leather, with maps, guns, and trophies.

'A drink, sir?'

'No, thanks,' Joshua said. 'Maybe later.'

'One of the virtues of retirement,' the judge said, 'is being able to do what you like whenever you want. I've found a brandy and milk goes very well before the midday meal.' He went to a sideboard, poured a drink from a nearly empty crystal decanter with too many facets, added a bare splash of milk from a refrigerated container, and drank about half before lowering the glass.

'I'm delighted, sir,' he said, 'that you were able to put paid to that vile scoundrel Khodyan. I've learned over the years that there's but one way to deal with men like him, and that's in the manner you did.'

'I suppose,' Joshua said, 'you might feel that way, having been a judge. I've never had that much confidence.'

'That's not confidence, Joshua, and I'd like to call you that, if I may. That's just plain common sense.' Penruddock emptied the glass and made himself another. 'You know, when that Sector Marshal sent me the com of what had happened, I wondered if you were the same Joshua Wolfe friends told me about during the war.

'I did a little checking and found out. Damned pleased to meet you, sir. You did good work, turning all they'd taught you back against those bastard Al'ar. The service you did our Federation was of the greatest, the greatest indeed.' Penruddock's voice had gotten louder, as if he were giving an after-dinner oration. 'Why didn't you stay on in the service, if I may be so bold?'

'The war was over,' Joshua said.

'But the Federation can always use men like you, even

in peacetime. A great loss, sir. A great loss. Heaven knows I tried to serve, tried to join up, but you know, my heart . . . well, it just wasn't one of those things that was to be.

'But I can tell you, I did my part as best I could. Even though my training was in the civil field, I set up Loyalty Courts and made sure there wasn't the slightest bit of dissent on Mandodari. Men like you, men out there fighting on the frontiers, didn't need to have people backstabbing them with either deeds or words.'

Penruddock looked at Joshua for some gratitude and was disappointed when he didn't get it. Joshua walked to one bookshelf.

'Behind this is your jewel collection?'

Penruddock was startled. 'Well . . . yes. But . . . how could you tell?'

'Would you open it, please.'

Joshua watched carefully as Penruddock fingered a sensor and the false books lifted into the ceiling, revealing a vault. Penruddock touched several spots on the vault's face that appeared unremarkable and then turned the handle, and the colunterbalanced door swung open. Inside were rows of shelves. Joshua pulled one shelf out, and gemstones shot up multicolored starlight.

'How many other people know where this is? The police report on the robbery said the thief or thieves –'

'Thieves, sir,' Penruddock said. 'There had to be more than just one man. They took away half a dozen trays, and I've never known a burglar so bold as to make more than one trip.

'But to answer your question. Myself. My wife. One . . . perhaps two of my servants. Long-time employees, still with me today.

'But all that doesn't matter, does it? You've recovered what you were able to recover, for which I am grateful, and

Innokenty Khodyan is dead, which makes things still better.' Penruddock looked anxiously at the open door and sighed in relief when Joshua nodded. He closed and relocked the vault.

'Now I must ask the question that's been puzzling me, Joshua,' the judge said. 'I was told you are a warrant hunter now. Your business with me is over, isn't it?'

'No,' Joshua said. 'Sometimes I hunt other things than men. I'm interested in the things that weren't on Khodyan when I killed him.'

'You mean the diamonds?'

'And one other thing.'

Judge Penruddock started and tried to cover it. 'Oh . . . you mean that little stone? That was just something of sentimental value. Something I bought when I was a boy, and, well, I guess it was the cornerstone, without intending the pun, of my collection.' He had deliberately kept his eyes on Joshua, trying to force belief.

Wolfe stared back until Penruddock looked away. The silence climbed about them.

'Very well,' Penruddock said. 'I don't know why I'm so secretive about it. It's not illegal to own, after all. It was an Al'ar Lumina stone. How did you guess?'

'I didn't know exactly what it was,' Joshua lied. 'But that "sentimental value only" jumped at me. Since no one died in the robbery, there had to be something important for you to post the reward you did.'

'You came to the correct end, sir, but you took a wrong turn. I would have wanted the thief hunted down regardless. Have you ever been robbed? It's like . . . like being raped. They came into my house and defiled it. So of course I wanted revenge. Consider this, Joshua. If my wife and I had been here on that night, wouldn't we have most likely been hurt or worse? The police told me this Khodyan had no hesitation about using violence.'

'Let's get back to the stone, Your Honor.'

'Since you were among the Al'ar, you know what it was used for.'

Joshua hesitated, then told the truth. 'No. I don't. Not completely. The Lumina gave them focus, like I've heard crystal does a meditator. But it also was an amplifier and allowed greater use of their powers.

'Was that why you had it?'

Penruddock turned around and looked out a window at a huge Japanese rock garden, its effect ruined by size.

'No, or not exactly. I'd heard stories about the Lumina. But I'm not into such metaphysical –' Penruddock hesitated before going on, '– stuff. I wanted it as a trophy. Most of my gems have a history, and I know their value, not just in money. Some have been the ruin of a family or a dynasty, some have been part of a reluctant bride's price, and so forth. This Lumina was the price of empire for us.'

Joshua knew Penruddock was lying.

'What do you think happened to it?' the judge went on.

'I don't know. Innokenty Khodyan hadn't linked up with his fence when I took him, and supposedly nobody else on Platte had gotten any jewels from him.'

'Then he must have sold it before he reached whatever godforsaken world you killed him on. Certainly there's no market for it on Mandodari III.'

'Possibly,' Joshua said. 'Or else he had already made the delivery to his customer.'

'What do you mean?'

'Innokenty Khodyan was a professional. Some of the dozen thefts he pulled before I took him were general – he'd found out about someone's stash and gone after it.

'But this would appear to be something different. I'd suspect the theft was commissioned.'

'For the Lumina?' Penruddock looked shaken.

'There are other collectors of Al'ar gear,' Joshua pressed.

'Do you know any of them? Better, have any of them come here and seen the Lumina?'

'No to both of your questions,' Penruddock said flatly. 'I've heard about those wretches, with their bits of uniforms and parts of shot-down ships . . . thank you, I am hardly of their ilk.'

'Where did you get the Lumina?'

'I can't tell you.'

'Was it here on Mandodari?' Joshua caught and held Penruddock's gaze.

'I said I can't –'

'You just did. Who sold it to you?'

'A man contacted me directly,' Penruddock said grudgingly.

'How did he know you were interested?'

'I'd mentioned what I wanted to some friends.'

'Other gem collectors?'

'Yes. One had told me he'd heard of a Lumina – actually that there were two, for sale, but they were far beyond his price.'

'Where is he now?'

'He's dead. He died . . . natural causes . . . about two months after I bought the stone.'

'The man you bought it from here. Was he a native of Mandodari?'

'No. I met him at the spaceport. He said he was between ships.'

'Do you know where he came from? Where he was going?'

'No. I only cared about what he wanted to sell.'

'How'd you pay?'

'Cash.'

'How much?'

Penruddock looked stubborn.

'How much?'

'Two million five hundred,' he said.

'That's a great deal of money for something you're just going to leave in a vault and just look at once a week or so. What else did you plan to do with it?'

'I already said – nothing. It was merely to *have* it! You're not a collector, so you wouldn't understand.'

'Maybe I wouldn't,' Wolfe said. 'Have you ever heard of a man named Sutro?'

'Never.'

Joshua searched for his next question.

'I didn't expect this when I allowed you to come here,' Penruddock said. 'To be grilled like I was some kind of criminal.'

'So the Lumina's gone, and you have no idea who might have taken it,' Wolfe went on, paying no mind to the judge's words. 'Do you want it back?'

'Yes . . . no.'

'Make up your mind.'

'I don't want that stone back. I don't think you could recover it,' Penruddock said. 'Especially if what you said is true and another collector sent that son of a bitch Khodyan to steal it from me. But I want another one.'

'That doesn't make sense.'

'I don't have to make sense, Wolfe,' the judge said, trying to regain control of the situation. 'Perhaps I just realized it myself. You said you came here looking for warrant work. Very well. You've got it. I'll cover your expenses and pay you a finder's fee when you secure me a second Lumina. I'll pay the same price as I did for the first.'

Joshua walked across the room and stared down at the mansion's front entrance and driveway. He heard a slight noise, and a small metallic green lifter came into view, hovering down the drive and out the gate. Joshua turned back.

'If I take the warrant,' he said, 'I'll want the rest of what you're not telling me.'

'What are you saying?'

'I'll need to know who the man was you bought it from, how he got in contact with you, where he came from, and why you trusted him enough to go to a spaceport with that much cold cash. Just for a beginning.'

'I told you everything!'

Joshua Wolfe took one of the hotel's cards from a pocket and laid it on a table.

'You can reach me here.'

The gate closed behind Joshua, and he started back toward the city. He heard a turbine whine, turned, and saw the metallic green lifter. Ariadne Penruddock was at the controls. She stopped the craft, and the window hissed down.

'It's a long walk, even if it's downhill. Need a ride?'

'I never walk unless I have to.'

Joshua went around the back of the vehicle and opened the door. He looked back up the drive at the house. In an upper-story window he saw a white blur that might have been a face.

He got in and slid the door closed.

'I'm at the Acropolis,' he said.

'Mister Wolfe, would you mind if we had a talk?'

'Not at all. What about?'

'My husband. Lumina stones.'

'I *felt* someone else's presence while we were talking,' Joshua said. 'Were you eavesdropping . . . or are you more sophisticated?'

Without taking her eyes from the road, Lady Penruddock opened her purse and showed him a small com. 'Sometimes a woman needs to know what's being said about her even if she's away from the house. I had the pickup put in his study just after we were married.'

'Maybe,' Wolfe suggested, 'you'd better pick a place for our talk where you're not known.'

'The Acropolis is fine. Nobody in our circle goes there.'

The bar was automated, which meant one less witness. It was empty except for two salesmen nursing beers and glowering at their notebook screens as if they were the supervisors who'd given them this awful territory. Ariadne studied the menu set into the tabletop.

'Deneb sherry,' she decided, and touched the correct sensor.

There were no Armagnacs, but there was a local pomace brandy. The delivery slot opened, and Lady Penruddock's drink and Wolfe's water and brandy appeared. He fingered the tab sensor, touched the snifter to his lips and drank ice water.

'Let me tell you about my husband and myself,' Ariadne said without preamble. 'We married for our own separate reasons, and for me at least, nothing has altered my intent.

'Malcolm and I largely lead our own lives. What he does is his business. If he wishes me to accompany him, I am delighted. If not . . .' She shrugged. 'I have my own friends, my own pursuits. Malcolm cares little what I do so long as I do not embarrass him or force him to take notice.

'If I found you attractive, which I do, and we happened to spend some time together, that would only concern the two of us.

'I am not sure, though, that that would be wise. For me. But I am still thinking about it.' Her fingers touched the fastener of her blouse for an instant, then went away.

'What Malcolm perhaps does not yet realize is that I require the same from him. He must not embarrass me or force me to have to apologize for his sometimes unusual predilections.'

'Such as the Lumina?'

'Exactly. Did you know he was lying when he said he only wished to own the Lumina for itself?'

'I did.'

'My husband is a devotee of power,' Ariadne said carefully. 'He chose to become a civil judge for that reason, instead of criminal law. That was well before the war, when our world was thriving.

'Malcolm made his decisions wisely over the years, not so much for justice as for how they might benefit him. He was quite successful.

'Then the war ruined him, as it ruined this world. When it was over and the Federation left, all the wonderful wheelings and dealings with land, and estates, and investments, on- and offworld, were mostly gone.

'Malcolm had planned to use his Loyalty Courts to propel him into politics, possibly to the highest offices. But with peace came the new government, which holds office by the size of the welfare checks it gives out.'

She shrugged. 'I care nothing about that or about what the working man does or thinks.

'Malcolm retired from the bench at the advice of several lawyers who said there might otherwise be an investigation of his decisions before and during the war.

'So he looked about for other fields to conquer.

'One of them was me. My family had been very indiscreet in war investments, so our standing with the hoi polloi was shaky. Also, I'd been a bit . . . indiscreet once when I was very, very young. Mandodari doesn't care what goes on in its bedrooms so long as the windows are blanked. I wasn't that cautious. The woman and her husband were able to leave, but I was trapped here, and Malcolm was a most convenient salvation.

'You look surprised, Mister Wolfe. Isn't a woman permitted to be honest about herself and her chances?'

'I'm just surprised you're telling all this to a stranger.'

'Why not? Better to a stranger, one that'll be offworld in a few days, than to the whale-mouthed gossips I normally associate with. As I was saying, marriage benefited us both. Malcolm received certain material advantages, perhaps what was known as a dowry in the old days, and I became a quote honest end quote woman.

'After we were married, Malcolm started hearing about the Lumina stone. He already had his collection of jewels, which I truthfully believe is the only thing he completely loves, and so it didn't seem that odd for him to want an Al'ar stone.'

'The Lumina is not a jewel.'

'And how many people know that? Let me continue. He felt that possession of a Lumina stone could bring him some feeling for power that might guide him to his next step.

'At least that was what he thought when he began his quest. Then he heard about the *ur*-Lumina.'

'The *what*?'

'Now it's my turn for surprise. I thought you would have known of that, since I heard Malcolm say you were among the Al'ar, although I'm not sure I completely understand.

'Malcolm heard stories of a great Lumina, although I don't know if anyone ever said anything about its physical size. I've heard him call it a "king Lumina" or a "mother Lumina." He didn't tell me what it was used for, what it was meant to do. But if a small Lumina had the purpose you told Malcolm, the great one would surely be worth possessing.

'He was going to use the Lumina he had to track down the big one. I don't know how. Maybe he thought it would lead him directly; maybe he thought whoever he bought the stone from could help him. He was never that specific. Now he wants to hire you for the search.'

Joshua rolled brandy round his mouth, concentrating

on the burn, letting the words find their own meaning. He took a second swallow.

'Very well,' he said. 'You were honest with me, and I'll return the trade. I've never heard of this ultimate Lumina, not even when I was a boy and was among them. I don't see how such a thing could even exist. If it did, it would have been at least hinted at in their ceremonies.'

'You could be right?' Ariadne said indifferently. She touched the menu for another sherry. 'It doesn't really matter to me.'

'All right,' Joshua said. 'So what do you want me to do about your husband?'

'You can take the commission if you wish,' Lady Penruddock said. 'All I ask is you keep Malcolm from making an utter fool of himself – or getting hurt.

'I can guess you have your own agenda with this Lumina stone and don't know what it is or care.

'All I'm concerned about is Malcolm. Do what I want, and I'll be a friend. A very good friend. Otherwise . . . well, my family may be in disgrace, but we still have enough power to make life exceedingly miserable for you even if you are some kind of war hero, even out into the Outlaw Worlds.'

She drank most of her drink. 'As for that other thing I spoke of, whatever might happen between you and me . . . that can wait until another time.'

She dipped a finger into the dregs of the sherry, touched it to Joshua's lips, got up, and walked out of the bar, not looking back.

Joshua sat very still for a time. He picked up his snifter, was about to drink, then put the glass down, signed the tab with a fingerprint, and went out of the hotel into the dusk.

SEVEN

'Twenny-five credits for straight, thirty-five for a suckoff, fifty for roun' th' worl', an' for a hunnerd you can have me *an'* Irina,' the woman said, trying to sound as if it mattered which was chosen. Her partner smiled in Wolfe's general vicinity, then turned as a lifter approached and saluted it with her chest. She looked disappointed when the driver didn't slow down.

'Suppose I'm interested in something else,' Joshua said.

'Like what? I don't do pain or shit . . . but I can send you to somebody who does.' The woman leaned back against the wall of the bar. 'Shoulda known you weren't th' kind who wants somethin' normal. Guys who look like you never do.'

'Not that, either,' Wolfe said. 'I think you might be needing a new fancy man.'

'Not a chance. Keos takes real good care a me an' Irina an' the other girls.'

'I didn't say I was asking.'

'Get on your scooter, bud. Or you're gonna get hurt.' Joshua didn't move. The woman's hand dove in her purse and came out with a silent alarm. 'You're lookin' for trouble, you're 'bout to get on kissin' terms with it.'

The other woman came closer, her eyes wide. She licked her lips in anticipation.

A man came out of the bar, hand inside his vest. He was

big and walked with a limp, and the surgeon who'd rebuilt the side of his face hadn't done a very good job.

'What is it, Marla?'

'Him,' the first woman said. 'He wants t' be our new mack.'

'Shit!' the man spit, and came in on Joshua, hand coming out of the vest with a sap. Joshua stepped into him, and two fingers rapped sharply on the man's forehead as Wolfe struck the pimp's forearm with the side of his blocking hand.

The blackjack hit the filthy pavement before the man did.

The two whores looked scared. Joshua kept one eye on them while he knelt and rifled through the man's pockets. He found a knife, a wad of cash, a vial containing a brownish powder, and a flat blaster in an ankle holster. He threw the vial and knife into the street and tossed the credits to Marla.

'Thanks,' he said, slipping the blaster into his pocket, and started away.

Marla stared after him, completely bewildered. 'Hey! I thought you was –'

But Wolfe was around the corner and gone with what he'd gone into the port district for.

The message light on his com was blinking when he got back to the hotel.

'Mister Wolfe?' It was Penruddock's voice. 'I've been considering what you said earlier. Perhaps it would be convenient for you to come back out here, and we can continue our discussion. We'll be in all evening.'

Joshua carefully checked the gun he'd acquired before returning the call.

'This'll be fine,' he told the lifter driver, and gave him credits. He got out and started for the eight-sided, five-story blue monstrosity the band's efforts blared from.

The lifter took off, and Joshua turned in his tracks and went down three streets and over two until he was on the street where the Penruddocks lived.

He buzzed the gate panel and was admitted.

Panels sensed his approach and lit, and the driveway was a long, cobbled finger of soft light through the night.

The Penruddocks met him at the door. Malcolm wore a soft red dressing gown over black dress pants and an open-necked shirt. Ariadne Penruddock wore a green silk robe that would have been modest except for the long slit that ran up the left side to her hip. She caught Wolfe's glance and moved her leg slightly, and Joshua saw tanned smoothness ending in close-cropped darkness. Both Wolfe and Penruddock pretended not to notice what she'd done.

'I'm glad we're going to have a chance –' Penruddock broke off at the scream of the engines.

Two gravlighters came in above the tree line. Wolfe saw the gunmen on the open deck and dove into Penruddock.

Ariadne's mouth gaped with surprise. Wolfe kicked the door closed, grabbed her leg, and pulled her down as the guns opened up.

They were solid projectile weapons, and rounds smashed through the walls, glass and masonry shattering, bullets whining up from the stonework.

Wolfe lay flat, trying to hold Ariadne. 'The lights,' he shouted. 'Where's the cutoff switch for the lights?'

Ariadne didn't answer, struggling in blind panic, kicking, clawing, trying to get away. She kneed him, he gasped in pain, and she scrambled up, trying to run anywhere, nowhere.

The guns crashed once more. There were three fist-sized holes in Ariadne Penruddock's back, green turning black as the woman skidded to her knees, then collapsed facedown. Joshua was reflexively half-up; the gunmen sent more rounds chattering through the house, and he went down again.

Joshua rolled on his back, pulling the now-futile blaster as the lifters made two more passes, bullets tearing the night apart.

The door above him tore away, and there was a glow from the still-burning path lights.

Now it's over, he thought. Now they come in with grenades and finish it.

But the lighters put on full power and were gone. Joshua barely heard the sound of their receding engines through the ringing in his ears.

He got shakily to his feet.

Dust hazed the foyer, and he had the iron taste of blood in his mouth. He saw movement, and belatedly, his gun was in his hand. Judge Penruddock staggered toward him. His hand was clasped over one arm, trying to stop the pulsing blood. His lips moved soundlessly.

Joshua heard a cracking, and Penruddock's trophy, legs splintered from the bullets, crashed down onto the judge. Joshua dove away, rolling, down the hall, as the beast smashed into pieces.

Then there was silence.

He went back to the foyer.

Malcolm Penruddock's body was crushed under the shattered monster, except for one hand and forearm. It twitched and was still.

Wolfe went to Ariadne Penruddock's body. He didn't turn it over. He didn't want to see her face.

He reached down, touched her hand, then went quickly out of the house and around the side, away from the road, the light, and the building scream of sirens.

EIGHT

'You were there when they slotted them?' Cisco asked.

Wolfe nodded.

'How'd you get out? They have their best cops, such as they are, on it. Penruddock was a big name, and so was his wife.'

Wolfe just looked at Cisco.

The FI man shrugged. 'All right. I didn't think you'd tell me. Did you leave any trail at all?'

'Not much of one,' Wolfe said. 'I was moving under my real name, but the only link would be two com calls, one to Penruddock's house, one back to me.'

'The cops aren't even looking for a Mister Inside. But I'll make sure you stay clean.'

'What's the best theory?'

'Their murder squad is going on the assumption that one of Penruddock's old partners in corruption was holding a grudge and waited until now to settle it.'

'Ten years after the war, after he retires? That's thin.'

'That's all they've got.'

'What about the triggermen?'

'Import talent. There was a freighter that landed two days earlier, had an open exit clearance, and lifted twelve minutes after the first reports of gunfire came in. No guns, no gunnies, no aircraft found so far, so everything must've gotten back aboard that ship.'

'What registry?'

'Micked. The ship came in with recognition numbers from a Halliday Line freighter that we have a positive location for on the other side of the galaxy. As for its papers,' Cisco went on, 'Mandodari isn't too particular about who lands there these days.'

'A pretty goddamned pro touch on somebody who's been retired as long as the judge has. If he was telling me the truth,' Wolfe said.

'Okay. There's another theory. Khodyan had friends who are doing paybacks.'

Wolfe snorted and didn't bother answering.

'It didn't fly for me, either,' Cisco agreed. 'Try another one. His wife. Any angles there? Word is she led a pretty spectacular life.'

'No,' Wolfe said. 'It has to be the Lumina.' He leaned forward. 'Cisco. *Who else is in the field? I've got to know!*'

Cisco shook his head. 'I don't know. I swear, Joshua, I'm not lying to you.'

His gaze was bland, sincere.

'Are we screened?' The on-screen Ben Greet glanced around as if he could somehow see any taps.

'Now, Ben, that's your problem, not mine. I can guarantee the com link is sealed on this end. I'm using the Sector Marshal's own set.'

Wolfe was lying. He was linked to Platte on one of Cisco's secure coms.

'What do you need, Joshua? You didn't leave any loose ends here when you left, did you? I don't have the . . . the things you gave me anymore.'

'Not interested in those. What I want to know is everything you have on Sutro. The fence that was going to meet Innokenty Khodyan.'

The pickup was good enough for Wolfe to see sweat bead the resort owner's forehead.

'Joshua, I swear, I don't know anything at all. And even if I did, you know I couldn't tell you anything. I've got to stay known as a man who can keep it buttoned.'

'Ben, talk to me. I don't want to have to come all the way to Platte and have this conversation again.'

Wolfe let the silence linger and held Greet's eyes. The man winced as if he'd been struck.

'All right. I've met him four times. Big man. Might have been a fighter once. Let himself get sloppy. He told me once he was going to get back in shape as soon as he had the energy. Black hair, don't remember the color of his eyes; he had a beard this last time, black, going gray. I'd guess he's in his early fifties.

'He speaks like he has a bit of education but sometimes slips into street talk. Generally travels with half a dozen guards. He has his own ship. I don't know where it's registered.'

'Is Sutro his real name?'

'It's the only one I've ever heard him use. He or any of his . . . clients.'

'Where's he out of?'

Greet's expression slipped for an instant, and the complacency showed. 'Now, that I don't know, and I haven't inquired. Joshua, I know what the most idle curiosity can cost, remember?'

'What happened when he arrived this last time?'

'Now, that is interesting,' Greet said, a note of animation coming into his voice. 'He ported where you did, about a day later, had his own lifter, and came straight on in without notification.

'He found out about you — don't look at me that way. I said I didn't know who you were, just some kind of FI warrant hunter. Anyway, he heard the news and flitted like a stripe-assed ape within the hour. He seemed really unhappy, too.'

'Go back to the other times you met him. Does he illicit buy anything, or is it just jewelry?'

'He'll deal in anything that's high-dollar and easily transportable. I've known him to handle art, minerals, company certificates. He's clean, slick, pays twenty-five percent of the legal price, which is better than most. I've heard he gets away with it by preselling what he buys – or else being the go-between for commissioned "work."'

Wolfe found that interesting, but his face showed nothing. 'What about his pleasures? Whores? Drugs? Liquor?'

'He'll tumble a dox as long as he can pretend he's not paying for it directly. He drinks a bit. No drugs. His main vice is gambling. That's one reason he likes Yoruba, because my games are straight.'

'How does he pay his bills? Or do you comp him like you did me?'

'Of course not. He pays his way like any other member of the profession. Hold on. I'll call his account up.'

Greet stepped off-screen, was gone for some minutes, then came back. 'Uses a standard debit card on a draw account.'

'What bank?'

'Numbered only.'

'Give it to me.'

'Joshua . . .'

'Come on, Greet.'

Greet heaved a reluctant sigh. 'You're recording this, I know. Here it comes.'

His off-screen hand tapped a keyboard, and numbers scrolled across Joshua's screen.

'I'll save you some work, Joshua But please don't ask me about Sutro, not ever again. And I don't think you'd better come back to Yoruba'

Joshua didn't respond.

'The card was issued on some planet called Rialto. I don't know anything about it at all. That's all I've got.'

'Thanks, Ben. I'll leave you in peace. For now. But one thing. Don't even think about tipping Sutro. He's a maybe, but I'm certain.'

Joshua touched the sensor. The connection must have blanked on Greet's end first, because before the image broke up, Joshua saw the fat man's face pucker in a frenzy of rage as he spit into the pickup.

The great house teetered in its abandon like an archaic top hat that had been set upon by mice and small boys. It was back from the road, closed off by a sagging and rusted razor-wire fence. There was a large, new stainless-steel cylinder sticking up out of the ground that was the input side of a pneumatic delivery system.

The gate sagged on its hinges. Wolfe eased through and went up the cracked and overgrown walk. Grass grew thick around the main building, and the trees were long unpruned, broken branches caressing the ground. It had gotten worse since the last time Joshua had been there.

The house looked tired, gray, as if its date with demolition contractors had been broken and never remade, and now it just waited, knowing time could do no more, and the final collapse would be welcome.

Wolfe touched a com sensor. It was ten minutes before the box crackled.

'Go away.' The voice sounded as cracked and old as the house it came from.

'Mister Davout? This is Joshua Wolfe. I need some help.'

Another long silence.

'Wolfe? Commander Wolfe?'

Joshua took a deep breath. 'That's right.'

'I'm sorry. Very sorry. There's been some young vandals. I didn't mean to be rude. Come right in.'

There was a *clack* as the door auto-unlocked and swung open.

Wolfe smelled damp, decay, rot and entered. The house's central hallway was stacked with neatly bundled and tied newscoms reaching high over Wolfe's head. The door to a front room stood open. It was almost full of boxes. Wolfe looked into one. It held unopened music-fiche shipping containers.

'I'm upstairs, Commander. Be careful. I've added some new precautions.'

Wolfe went down the hall toward the stairs. Another room he passed was stacked high with the gadgets of the moment from the last ten years in their original packaging.

His stomach churned as he caught the reek from the kitchen. It had been a long time since it had seen a scrub unit or, for that matter, cooked a meal. He saw a sink stacked high with dishes, green and black mold spilling over the stainless basins toward the floor. To one side were row after row of freezer units and, beside them, the interior outlet of the pneumo-tube.

The stairs were a tunnel of baled papers arching close overhead, and Wolfe had to turn sideways to go up them. He moved very slowly, hearing the creak of the uncertain bales and seeing every now and then bright steel wire carefully laid where the careless would be certain to step and bring tons of paper tumbling down.

He didn't look in any of the rooms on the second floor but went up to the top floor.

That had once been a single room, probably a conservatory, since there were double-panel glass squares overhead that had been sloppily painted black. The room had been divided and divided again by more baled papers, except those papers came from the huge, if elderly, superspeed printer.

Waiting was a small man who, like his house, smelled of decay. He wore a tattered set of coveralls and slippers.

'You're not in uniform,' Davout said in relief.

Wolfe frowned in puzzlement.

'If you had any bad news about my brother,' the little man explained, 'you would have come in uniform. And there would have been a doctor or priest. That's the way they always do it.'

Davout's brother had been a civilian com tech on a world that had been one of the first seized by the Al'ar when the war had started. Like Joshua's parents, he'd been interned. But unlike them, there'd been no confirmation as to his fate. It had merely been missing . . . missing . . . missing, presumed dead . . . and then, when all the prison worlds had been fine-combed, the flat report: DECEASED.

Davout had never believed any of the reports, and so he'd kept everything from the day he'd heard of his brother's capture, sure that one day, one hour, the man would stride up the walk and want to know what had happened while he was away.

'So how is the war going? Never mind. You don't have to tell me. Well, well enough, or else I wouldn't be able to reach out to as many worlds as I can. Sit down, Commander, sit down. I'll make tea.'

Davout picked up a stack of microfiches from a rickety chair, looked about helplessly for a place to put them, and finally set them on the floor. Joshua sat awkwardly. Davout left the cubicle they were in and went into another, where Joshua could see a tiny heating plate and micro oven. Another cubicle beside it held a chemical toilet that from the smell Davout had forgotten to recycle for a while.

All that was in the paper-walled cubicle was the chair Wolfe sat in, a second torn office chair, a stained canvas cot, and the console that had brought him there. It was an amazing assemblage of electronics, none appearing less than five years old, most still anodized in various mil-spec shades of dullness.

'You know, Commander,' Davout's voice came. 'When this war ends, I think we should consider war crimes trials for the Al'ar. I mean, it's just not right for them to treat people the way they do.

'Don't you agree?'

Joshua made a noncommittal noise, almost felt like crying. Once, three years before, he'd tried to tell Davout, tried to show him. The little man had stared as if Wolfe had begun speaking in a completely unknown tongue. He'd waited until Wolfe had stammered into silence, then had continued their conversation where Wolfe had so rudely interrupted it.

Davout came out, cautiously balancing two mismatched dirty cups holding a dark substance.

'If you want milk or sugar, I'll have to go below-stairs,' he said. 'I don't partake, as you know, so I keep forgetting my manners and keep some on hand.'

'That's fine, Mister Davout.'

'So what brings you this time? You know, I don't ever think I've really thanked you for what you're doing for me. I mean, I know who you work for . . .' Davout looked cagily at Wolfe through thick, tangled eyebrows. 'You don't need to tell me. I've read about you intelligence operatives. I'm glad you trust me enough to help with your projects. It keeps me from . . . thinking too much. About things.

'I just hope I'm doing my share to win the war.'

Wolfe coughed, clearing his throat. 'This time it should be easy, Mister Davout.'

'Go ahead.' Davout picked up a v-helmet and held it ready. 'Oh, I've forgotten to tell you something. I've made a new acquisition.' He pointed to a second helmet half-hidden behind a pile of paper. 'If you want to ride along, you're welcome.'

Wolfe set the cup down, walked over, and got the helmet. It was even older than the one Davout held and, like the little man's, had been extensively modified, the jerry-rigged modifications e-taped or glued in place.

Wolfe pulled out the rubber bands that retracted the headphones, put the helmet on, and slid the black visor over his face. He started as something crawled across his throat, then realized it was the helmet's microphone.

'There we are,' Davout's voice came. 'Now, what do we need?'

'A planet named Rialto. I don't know where it is, what it is. But I need to find out something about its banks.'

'Ah.'

The universe spun around Wolfe, a whirl of figures, starcharts, stardrive blur that could only be a latent personal memory, more figures. Wolfe's stomach came up, and he pulled the helmet off.

Davout must have sensed something, because he turned from his place at the console and lifted his own visor. 'Is something the matter?'

'It's been too long since I did this,' Joshua said truthfully. 'A little vertigo.'

'Oh.' Davout was disappointed. 'It's always better to have someone along. It's sort of like – like having a friend. But never mind. Let me see what there is to see.'

'Now, here we are. Rialto, more or less Earth type – ah hah, I can see why you mentioned banks. I read: 'Rialto's biggest source of income is its banks. They are privately chartered, but with the full encouragement of the government behind them, and all transactions are completely secret, as are depositors and all other financial data. All attempts by Federation law enforcement have failed to secure any degree of cooperation, and all known attempts to penetrate the so-called golden veil of Rialto have failed; hence, the planet is a well-known monetary sanctuary for criminals, tax evaders, and others who prefer that their financial business remain secret.' Mercy. How can they do something like that? Don't they know there's a war on?'

'So we're screwed?'

'Hmmph. Make yourself some more tea, Commander.'

'Oh, my. That's cute. That's very cute. They have a wonderful little booby trap set up so that anybody who tries to crawl his way in using an ANON password gets back blasted.

'Very sexy,' Davout said admiringly. 'So let's try another way.'

'Damn! Pardon, Commander. But a man living by himself gets careless about his language.'

'What's going on?' Wolfe was getting a little bleary. He'd been sitting in the chair, and occasionally on the cot, for six straight hours with no breaks other than what Davout considered tea and a visit to the redolent toilet.

'I tried another way in and got my paws slapped,' Davout said. 'Hmm. This may take a little thought.'

'Ah hah, ha hah, ha hah,' Davout crooned. 'You didn't even see me dip past the gate, now, did you?'

'You're in.'

'I'm in. Isn't it a good thing that we're honest people? We could be very rich if we weren't.

'Now, what, or who, did you want to know about? Rialto is an open ledger, as their bankers might say.'

'That's the second problem. All I have is a single name. Sutro. Spelled like it sounds. It's a person, male. I'm not sure if he uses or even has a second name. It would be an active account, very active, with lots of credits going in and out. The only action I know of for sure would be a bill paid to an account called YORUBA or possibly BEN GREET.'

'Very good, very good. That's what I like about you, Commander. You never come to me with the easy stuff.'

'Sutro, Sutro, there you are.'

As Davout spoke, the printer beside him clicked, and sheets of paper spat out.

Wolfe started up from his drowse. It was after midnight, and Davout hadn't said anything at all for the last hour and a half.

'We now have everything there is to know about your Mister Sutro. My, but he's rich. Spends it, too.'

'What's his home world? Do you have that?'

'I have everything he had to file with the bankers to set up his call account.' Davout lifted the helmet off. 'Rialto, it appears, is very sensitive about exposing themselves to any risk, so I have quite an extensive dossier on Mister Sutro, which you'll be holding in about five minutes. But to end the suspense, his home world is a place called Trinité. If you want –'

'I'm familiar with it – at least where it is. Mister Davout, you're a hell of a guy. I can't say how grateful I am.'

The little man smiled shyly. 'Thank you, Commander. Thank you.' He was silent for a time. Wolfe waited, knowing he was trying to find the courage to ask something. Finally:

'You said I've helped you. Would it be out of place for me to ask for a favor?'

'Anything I can do.'

'I know there's a thousand, maybe a million like me, who've got family held by the Al'ar. But would you mind, would it be possible, for you to see if you can learn something? I mean, I don't know what kind of connections you Intelligence people have behind the Al'ar lines, but is there anything you could find out?'

The little man's eyes were pleading, desperate.

'Joshua, this stinks on ice.' Sector Marshal Achebe held the microfiche as if it belonged in a fume cabinet.

'It's a perfectly legitimate complaint,' Wolfe said, trying to suppress a grin.

'Legitimate, maybe. But don't you think there's something somewhat irregular when a complaint gets filed about some resident of the planet of Trinité, by name of Sutro, on a charge of conspiracy to violate Federation statutes up to and including murder and further alleges that this Sutro also conspired to conceal his part in said crimes and further is likely to commit even more heinous crimes if not brought to the bar immediately?'

'What's wrong with that?'

'It reeketh when the person filing said complaint happens to be a warrant hunter named Joshua Wolfe,' Achebe complained. 'Now what are you going to do? Go out and serve your own warrant?'

'Of course.'

'Samedi with a new derby,' Achebe swore. 'Are you also going to post a reward?'

'Nope. Thought that might be a little much.'

'Joshua, Joshua. Why?'

Wolfe's smile vanished. 'Because I might run into some trouble with whatever passes for law on Trinité. I'd like to have some cover.'

'You know this Sutro doesn't have any record with the Federation? At least nothing I could find.'

'I know. That's another reason for the complaint.'

'Trinité's quite a planet.'

'Never been there.'

'Let's say it's got a *lot* of gold. I'm glad it's not in my sector. The people there seem to think they can do pretty much what they want and buy off any complaints afterward.'

'Are they right?'

'Damned close,' Achebe admitted. 'Which brings up my last question. If the shit hits the fan, what do you think I'll be able to do to help?'

'Send flowers, maybe.'

Achebe sighed in relief. 'Okay. I'll approve and E-post it. I assume you don't want any real circulation but just want it there for the record.

'I was afraid you'd slipped a notch and thought the law in the Outlaw Worlds maybe was going to actually be able to do something.'

'I know better than that, Jagua.'

'You have time for a drink? Might be your last, you know.'

'With a cheery invite like that, how could I refuse?'

'So you're alive.'

'*Alive? I do not know if that is the proper concept. All systems are locked into green. All circuitry is performing better than before I was refitted, and my sensors advise that all parts of me are as good as or better than when I was first launched. Thank you.*'

Joshua was astonished.

'Thank you?'

'*My programmer said you would be startled,*' the ship went on. '*She said a bit of a personality was needed. I have no computation on the value of her belief.*'

Joshua chuckled. 'All right. It's nice to have you back, if your circuits can now interpret that. I could have used your services a couple of times in the last month. Is everything go?'

'*Affirmative. Destination tape running. Tower clearance granted. At your command.*'

'Let's do it.'

The *Grayle* shuddered, came off the shipyard ways, hovered down a solid-painted line to a lift point, then rose still higher, canted to near vertical, and screamed up off Carlton VI.

The unobtrusive man wearing dark, sober clothing put his binocs back in their case and started unhurriedly toward the com booth at the back of the observation deck.

NINE

The first Al'ar struck the boy from behind, sending him sprawling. Joshua, as taught, tucked and rolled, coming up as the second Al'ar youth flashed a hand across the boy's stomach, a seeming touch that made Joshua scream in agony and stumble back.

The third was maneuvering to get behind him, and Joshua spun kicked, his boot crashing into the Al'ar's thigh. The alien fell but made no sound, although his hood flared wide in pain and both hands grasped his leg.

The first came in once more, thin white arm darting out like a pointer, touching Joshua's wrist and sending pain burning up his arm.

Joshua had the alley wall at his back, and he waited, trying to keep tears from welling and blinding him.

The Al'ar attacked again, and Joshua ducked his head to the side and sent a hammer strike into the Al'ar's chest. The alien squealed and fell, and one of his friends dragged him back. The other two hesitated, then grabbed the third by the shoulders and were gone into the evening mist.

Joshua fought pain, fought collapse.

Another Al'ar moved out of the darkness.

'You fought well,' he said. 'For a groundworm.'

That was one of the Al'ar terms for terrestrials.

'To the mud with you,' Joshua managed. 'If you wish to share what your friends found, you have but to ask.'

'I desire no self-proving this evening,' the Al'ar said. Joshua only half understood his words. His family had been stationed on Sauros for only three E-months, and he was still being tutored.

'Then remove your worthless self from my way.' Joshua limped forward.

'I will help you,' the Al'ar said, seemingly undisturbed by the insults. He stepped forward, and Joshua managed a guard stance.

'You need not fear me. I have spoken my intent.'

Joshua hesitated, then, for an unknown reason, let the Al'ar lift his arm around his neck. All the Al'ar appeared emaciated but were able to lift far more than most terrestrials – another mystery unanswered.

'I live –'

'I know your burrow,' the Al'ar said. 'You are the hatchling of the One Who Speaks for All Groundlings.' Astonishingly, the Al'ar continued in strangely accented Terran: 'Your word is "Ambassador"?'

Joshua stopped in his tracks. 'You speak my language! No one has ever done that.'

'There are a few of us who are . . . weird? No, aberrant. It is not thought good to . . . reduce yourself and speak like a Lesser One.'

'Thank you for very little. I will not embarrass you any more,' Joshua said. 'I must learn your words better, anyway.'

The Al'ar made no response, and they limped on.

'I was interested seeing the way you fought,' the Al'ar said. 'I have never seen a groundworm do that.'

'It has the name of –' Joshua was forced back into Terran. '– tae kwan do.' Then he returned to Al'ar. 'It is a discipline you must work at. My father is a master, and when I learned all he had, he found one who was his master to teach me more.'

'Perhaps you should learn our ways of fighting. They are very deadly. Those hatchlings were but toying with you. If they had learned their skills well or intended real harm, you would not be on this plane. So I would say our ways are better than your tae kwan do.'

'Who would teach me?'

'Perhaps,' the Al'ar said, 'I might. If I wished.'

Joshua stared at the alien but decided not to question him.

'Why,' Joshua asked, 'did they attack me?'

'Because they were curious.'

'Three of them against one? And hitting me from behind?'

The Al'ar turned his snakelike head toward the boy. 'But of course,' he said, and Joshua thought he distinguished surprise. 'Would you have us fight one at a time from the front? That way dictates loss. Pain.'

'That is what we call –' Joshua hunted for the word, couldn't find it in Al'ar, and switched to Terran '– a coward.'

'That is a word I have seen but do not understand.'

'We do not respect those who lack courage to fight –' Again there was no Al'ar word, so he returned to Terran '– fairly.'

'I think my mind can hear that last word and know it. We have our customs, you have yours.'

'So why are you helping me?'

There was a silence.

'I do not know,' the Al'ar said finally. 'Sometimes I think I am mad.'

'You are the first Al'ar who has been anything other than a . . . a worm turd to me.'

'As I said, there are those who think me mad. But you do not have my name. You may call me Taen. Perhaps that explains my behavior, for it would be, in your language, the One Who Stands Aside and Wonders.'

Joshua's eyes opened, and the ship noticed and brought the lights up slightly. He lay without moving for a while.

'Now why,' he mused, 'didn't that dream bother me?'

After a while his eyes closed, his breathing became regular, and the ship, after the programmed time, dimmed the lights.

The *Grayle* came in on a lazy braking orbit, the ship circling Trinité three times before closing on the main island of Morne-des-Esses, giving Wolfe a chance to turn computer images into reality.

Trinité was mostly water and islands, with two desert landmasses near the equator that cut the tidal action of the triple moons and made the equatorial islands habitable and the shallow seas around them navigable. North and south of the continents the waves rolled ceaselessly, hammering at the few rocky skerries that still jutted from the boiling seas.

Morne-des-Esses curled like a protective snake around half a hundred tiny islets. The world's capital and only real city, Diamant, sat on Morne-des-Esses's largest bay, its streets twisting up the steep hills that ran almost to the water's edge.

'*I have Trinité Control on-line. Need input.*'

'Patch 'em through,' a speaker went on. 'Trinité Control, what's your problem?'

'*Negative problem,*' the voice said, and Wolfe wondered why it was obligatory for all pilots and navigation points, human or roboticized, to drawl as if there were all the time in the world. *'We have two landing options, as your ship was advised. One is Wule, conventional spaceport, all facilities, on land. The other is Diamant Port, just offshore from the city. Your charts should indicate details. Ships berth like watercraft at buoys, com links available at buoy head, water taxis available on call or signal.*

'Wule Port is ten credits a day, Diamant fifty. Have you reached a decision?'

'That's affirm, Trinité Control. We'll take Diamant.'

'Understood. Turning you over to Diamant Subcontrol.'

'Take it on in,' Wolfe said. 'Try to land like a rich bitch's yacht. Blow spray in somebody's face or something.'

'Assumption: That is not an order,' the ship said. *'You are making a joke.'*

'Thank you for informing me.'

The ship lowered into the water like a suspicious matron into a bathtub, and Wolfe heard hissing through the outside mikes as the atmosphere-seared hull sent steam boiling. On secondary drive the ship cruised into the harbor and down a row of buoys, some with yachts, others with starcraft moored to them. It found the assigned buoy, and mag-grapples shot out.

'Diamant Subcontrol advised there are anchors available for an additional fee, which they recommend in the event of a storm. Should I signal for them? I have no familiarity with such gear.'

'Disregard. They're getting enough of our credits as is. Instructions: If I am not in the ship and a storm does blow up, take whatever measures are necessary to keep yourself safe, including lifting off.'

'Understood We are now landed.'

Artificial gravity went off, and Wolfe's inner ear complained slightly. The ship moved gently to wave-rhythm.

'Open up and let's see what we've got,' Wolfe said.

The ship opened the lock and slid the retractable loading

platform below it. Joshua walked out onto it. He was about two feet above the ocean.

The water was blue, calm, peaceful, and the sun glared white on the rooftops of Diamant. A breeze ruffled the water like a mother's fingers, then passed on. It was a day, and a world, that said that nothing much mattered beyond the moment.

'Hey, Cap'n!' The voice came from a gaily painted boat that to Joshua's surprise looked as if it were built of wood. Its owner had close-cropped hair and freckles and looked about fourteen. She was slim-built and wore shorts and a baggy exercise shirt with LIBANOS WATER TAXIS on it.

'You need to go ashore?'

'In a bit.'

The young woman expertly gunned her boat toward the *Grayle*'s platform, reversed the drive, and let it drift up until a fender touched the ship.

'What's a bit? If you're coming now, fine. Otherwise I'll come back on my next run.'

Joshua didn't answer; he walked back into the ship, touched a blank wall, and took coins from the drawer that slotted out. He went back out.

'What's your hourly?'

'Two credits.' The girl grinned. 'More if I think you're good for it.'

Joshua sent the coins spinning through the air, reflections bouncing off the water. The girl caught them one-handed and made them disappear.

'I'm yours for . . . two hours. What do you want? The grand tour?'

'As soon as customs comes out to clear me.'

The girl laughed raucously. 'Captain, there isn't any customs on Trinité. They've already checked your credit balance before they let you land, especially here in the harbor. If you're solvent, you're welcome. I hope you're not carrying anything real contagious. My shots aren't up to date.'

'Healthy as two horses. You are . . . ?'

'You can call me Thetis.'

Joshua grinned. 'You pick that yourself, or did somebody with a crystal ball come up with it?'

'My grandfather gave it to me. Said he never liked what I'd been birth-named with.' She shrugged. 'I don't even remember my other name now.'

'My name's Joshua Wolfe. Hang on while I grab a couple of things.'

The *Grayle*'s lock hissed shut behind Joshua, and the platform retracted as soon as he'd stepped into Thetis's boat. He wore white trousers, deck shoes, a light green shirt, and a coarsely woven silk windbreaker. He did not appear armed.

'Where to?'

'Like you said, the grand tour. I'd like to get an idea of what the island's like. Never been here before.'

Thetis put the boat into drive and sent it hissing away, its wake purling white. The boat looked very old-fashioned, about eighteen feet long with a covered foredeck, a glass windshield, and three rows of seats. The hull was lacquered, and the detail was gleaming white.

'Is this real wood?'

'It is,' the girl said. 'Hand-laid by Granddad, but now I'm the one who's got to keep it afloat. Keeps me busy, but I don't mind. Wood feels different than resin or even metal. I wouldn't trade *Dolphin* for anything.' Without a noticeable pause she asked, 'You on vacation?'

'Why else would anybody come here?'

'Lots of reasons,' Thetis said.

'Such as?'

The girl looked at him, then away at the harbor. 'My grandfather said, when he turned the boat over to me, never to ask the customers more than they want to say and tell 'em even less.'

'Your grandfather sounds like he's been around.'

'And then some. He mostly raised me. He said I didn't need to go to Diamant's schools as long as I passed his teachings. I guess I did all right.'

'Who was Thetis's father?'

'Ask me a hard one. Nereus. His folks were Pontus and Gaea.'

'Where are your forty-nine sisters?'

The grin vanished from the girl's lips.

'They didn't live through the war,' she said tonelessly. 'Any more'n my mother and father did. My grandfather tracked me down in a crèche.'

'Sorry,' Joshua said, apologizing. 'I lost my own folks when the war started.'

The girl nodded but didn't respond. After a moment: 'Diamant,' she began, 'has about fifty thousand legal residents, maybe sixty now. There's about double that who're visitors, or who have job permits, or who're just here without bothering anybody. The island's industries are tourism, fishing –'

'I read the Baedeker coming in,' Joshua interrupted. 'How many casinos does Diamant have now?'

The girl turned. 'Now I've got your ID. You didn't look like a banker on the run or somebody here to toast his toes. You a pro or just somebody who likes the action?'

'Only a man who's interested in the sporting life.'

'You just gave me the rest of it,' she said with satisfaction. 'Granddad says that anybody who's careful of what he says about gaming generally is somebody who'll make you a bet he can make the jack of diamonds jump out of the deck and piddle in your ear, and you'd best not play with him unless you want a real wet ear.

'We've got five big casinos, plus there's who knows how

many quiet games or even full-scale joints. There's enough action to keep anybody happy. You see all those islands?' She pointed out away from the harbor. 'Those are all private. Could be anything on any of them. The Diamant Council doesn't care much once somebody buys or leases them. If there's complaints or troubles, they'll send somebody out to see what's going on and levy a fine if it's real bad.'

'Do gamblers have to register?'

'They're supposed to. But nobody bothers. What kind of gaming you looking for?'

'Thetis, anybody ever tell you don't act like – what, fourteen?'

'Fifteen next month. Thanks, mister. Nobody with a sure fix on anything wants to be a kid any longer than she has to, right?'

Joshua inclined his head in agreement. 'You ever hear of anybody named Sutro? He's supposedly a resident.'

'Nope. But I don't ask much, either.'

Joshua took a bill from his pocket, folded it, and tucked it in the girl's shirt. She looked down into the pocket and looked surprised.

'That's just for asking?'

'It is. But ask quietly.'

'Mister Wolfe, I don't do *anything* noisily. It doesn't pay to attract attention unless you want to. I'll find out and get back to you.

'You still want the tour?'

'I paid for it, I'm going to get it,' Joshua said, and lounged back on the brightly colored canvas seat.

The girl looked at him speculatively, then went on with her description of the scenic wonders of Morne-des-Esses.

'Here,' Thetis said as Joshua stepped out of the boat onto the dock, and handed him what appeared to be a thick calling card. 'Press on the little boat symbol if you need transportation, and that'll buzz me. Twenty-four-hour call.' Without waiting for a response, she tapped the drive into gear and shot away.

Joshua turned to the gangplank and stretched like a great cat in the sun, then went up the cleated ramp.

A man who, with his baggy multistriped pants and cotton shirt that reaffirmed that he really was on TRINITÉ, SO BEAUTIFUL GOD SHOULD HAVE QUIT HERE, could only be a tourist was staring into the back end of an elaborate camera. The camera sat on a tripod of absurdly thin and shiny metal that should never have supported its weight.

The camera was focused on a woman at the edge of the dock. She was some years younger than the man and perhaps half again his weight.

Joshua looked over the man's shoulder curiously. The camera's rear showed an exact duplicate of the harbor in front of them. The man held a small pointer and, one by one, eliminated all the anchored ships. To one side of the frame a large sailing yacht was entering the harbor. The man touched the pointer to it and moved the image closer to the center of the screen. He saw Joshua's shadow and turned.

'Morning, friend. Isn't this the way it's supposed to be?'

'Damned if I know,' Joshua said. 'I didn't know there was any right or wrong way for scenery.'

'Sure there is. The man who teaches the class I take said that the object of attention – that's my wife, Dorena – should be at the lower third of the picture. Then the eye should move upward, to the right, which is why I moved that boat where I did. Then the eye goes left again, to that big building up on the hill that looks like a toadstool, whatever it is –'

'That's one of the casinos.'

'– and that's what makes good composition. Right?'

'Guess so. What do you do next?'

'Seal the image, then print it.'

'One thing you might want to do,' Joshua suggested, 'is move that lamp standard that's growing out of your wife's head.'

'Well, I'll be . . .' The man laughed at himself, obliterated the pole, then touched buttons, and a print obediently slid out the base of the camera. 'C'mere, hon. Meet the man who just kept me from doing it dumb again. Mister . . .'

'Wolfe. Joshua.'

'I'm Arabo Hofei. We just came down yesterday on the *Darod*. We'll be here for two weeks and enjoying every minute of it. I saw you come in from that starship anchored out there. Is it yours?'

'It is.'

The man shook his head. 'Wish I could figure out a way to make those kind of credits. But then, some of us are meant to have it and some of us meant not, right, Dorena?'

'We do all right,' the woman said. 'Besides, what would we do with a big hulk like that? Keep it on our balcony? I imagine docking fees must be astronomical.'

Joshua laughed, and after a moment the woman decided she'd just been clever and joined in. She suddenly broke off, looking behind her.

Two unobtrusive men wearing dark sober clothing walked past. Their faces were calm, and their low conversation was of serious matters most likely beyond this world's concern.

'Now, don't those two look like they're having a swell time,' she said a bit loudly – loudly enough for one of the men to look at her calmly, then turn his attention away. Dorena blushed.

'I didn't *mean* to be overheard,' she almost whispered. 'Wonder who they are.'

'Chi something, I think,' her husband said.

'Chitet,' Joshua added.

'What are they? Some kind of priests?'

'Sort of,' Arabo said. 'I read something about them once. They're like a cult, aren't they? Don't believe in emotions or things like that, right?'

'Pretty much,' Joshua said. 'They're an old group. Men, women, children. They pretty much keep to themselves. They have half a dozen, maybe more worlds of their own.

'There's a story that three or four hundred years ago they planned a coup against the Federation. They thought they were entitled to run things because they never let emotion get in the way. They thought they could take a few key posts, or so the story goes, and the Federation would shrug, realize the Chitet were the best possible governors, and let what'd happened go on.

'The coup never came off. The story says that at the last minute their leaders ran probability studies and decided they had only a fifty-fifty chance and called it off.

'Supposedly the authorities arrested their leadership but couldn't get anyone to talk. Since there hadn't been any bodies in the street or government houses blown up, the Chitet weren't proscribed.

'But that was a long time ago. Since they're like you said, priding themselves on always using pure logic, they're considered pretty respectable, and a lot of businesses, even governments, use them for comptrollers, auditors, and things like that.'

'Pretty good, Joshua,' Arabo said admiringly. 'You rattled that off like you were reading it from a screen. What are you, some kind of professor?'

'When you're between stars,' Joshua said, 'there isn't much else to do but read. Sorry. I guess I did sound a little pompous.'

'Nothing wrong with that,' Dorena said. 'Lord knows we could all do with more learning than what we have.' She leaned close to Arabo, whispered something, then giggled. Arabo chuckled.

Joshua lifted an eyebrow.

'My wife wondered if these Chitet, uh, make love.'

'I guess they do,' Wolfe said. 'There's supposed to be a lot of them.'

'I knew *nobody* could stay sobersided all the time,' Dorena said. 'We're going out on the glass-bottom boat, Mister Wolfe. You want to go with us?'

'No, thanks,' Joshua said. 'I just grounded and want to look around.'

The Hofeis gathered their photographic gear, and Joshua moved on toward the road that led to the big mushroom-shaped building on the hill.

In the daytime, the Casino d'Or was cheap-looking, smelling of broken promises and stale perfume, like all whores in sunlight. There were only a handful of people on the tables trying to spend fast enough to catch up with their fleeing dreams.

Joshua leaned against a wall, picking out the various games. A beefy man wearing a tunic tailored to hide a gun drifted up and pretended interest in a gaming machine a few feet away.

Joshua walked over to him.

'You work here.' It was a statement, not a question.

After a moment the man moved his head a trifle verti-cally.

'I'm looking for a friend of mine by the name of Sutro. Since he likes to gamble, I thought you might be familiar with him.'

The man's dead eyes gazed at Joshua.

Wolfe took out a bill, folded it, and held it out. The man didn't take the note, nor did he respond. Joshua put the bill away.

'My apologies, friend. I thought you were sentient,' he said, and started for the exit.

TEN

Joshua jerked back from the display as an Al'ar glared at him.
Around the holograph, words formed:

**THE
SECRETS
OF THE
AL'AR**

**Their Secret Weapons!
Their Covert Society!
Their Hidden Ways!
Their Murderous Skills!
Their Perverted Culture!**

. . . which was coming very soon, less than two E-
months away, to Morne-des-Esses, fresh from triumphs on
Worlds A, B, C, and so on, and Joshua would be well
advised to buy his tickets in advance, for the demand for
this Educational Opportunity would be Most Great . . .

'Never underestimate the absolute goddamned stupidity,' Joshua began in some disgust, about to punch out of
New and Notable on Trinité but he was interrupted.

'*We have visitors,*' the ship announced. '*It is the girl Thetis
and an old man. Shall I extend the loading platform?*'

'Go ahead.' Joshua got up, started for the lock, then turned aside, opened the arms cabinet, and tucked a small blaster in his waistband at the small of his back.

'Give me a visual.'

He saw Thetis and a fierce-looking old man with archaic sideburns that ran up into a walrus mustache that bristled rage. He shrugged.

'Open the port.'

It slid open just as the man and girl were getting out of the wooden speedboat.

'Good evening,' Wolfe said civilly.

Without preamble: 'I'm Jacob Libanos. You gave Thetis quite a bit of money today. I want to talk to you about it.'

'I'm listening.'

'Trinité can make you think everything's for sale. There's some things that ain't. Thetis is one of them.'

The girl looked embarrassed.

'I never thought she was,' Joshua said dryly.

The old man studied him for long moments, then nodded. 'I'll work on the assumption you're telling the truth. But that isn't the only thing I wanted to talk about. You asked her to look around for somebody named Sutro. You puttin' her to risk?'

'No,' Joshua said. 'Sutro's a legitimate resident of Diamant, or my sources say he is. I just want to know more about him.'

'I'd say you was law, but I checked your ship's registry. Damned odd sort of Federation man'd come out of Carlton VI.'

A half smile came and went on Joshua's face. 'You've been there.'

'I have. It tries just as hard to be decadent as Trinité, but it ain't got the credits to pull it off.'

'That's a pretty good description,' Joshua agreed. 'Come aboard if you want the grand tour.'

Libanos nodded and followed Joshua inside.

'Damned big ship,' he observed, 'for just one man. Or is there crew out of sight?'

'Just me. Ship's automated.'

'Heard they'd finally got that down. Haven't been aboard one yet.' They went up to the control room. Libanos studied the main station carefully. 'Looks pretty easy to run,' he observed. 'All those damned gauges and readouts that did nothing but beep at you – glad to see them gone. All they did was clutter the mind, anyway. By the time they told you were in trouble, generally you were 'most dead.'

'You have your papers?'

'Commercial master, passenger master, the mate buttons to go with 'em. But it's been a long time.'

Joshua waited for the man to volunteer his current occupation, but nothing came.

'Let me ask you something, Mister Wolfe.'

'Joshua.'

'We'll keep it mister for a while, if you don't mind. Thetis . . . or maybe me . . . finds out about your Sutro, what happens then?'

Joshua didn't reply.

'I didn't figure you'd answer that one.' Libanos thought for a while, trying to stroke his mustache back into some sort of order.

'All right. We'll do what we can.'

Without saying more, he turned toward the port.

Joshua put one hand over the two cards, waited while the bettors made their decisions, then pushed counters across the line.

'*Carte,*' he said, and a card slid across the green baize. He looked at it calmly. '*Non.*'

The banker turned his cards over. He had seven. He took another card. A queen stared haughtily up.

Joshua turned his cards, showing six, and let the croupier's paddle take away more of his counters.

The banker touched the shoe, and Joshua *felt* what would happen.

'*Banco*,' he said.

The banker looked pointedly at the small pile of credits beside Joshua. Wolfe reached into an inner pocket of his formal jacket, took out a small plastic card, spun it across. The banker looked at it, buried surprise, and handed it back.

Two cards whispered out of the shoe to Joshua, to the other man playing, and to the banker.

Joshua, without looking at his hand, flipped his cards over. He held a natural.

The banker lifted the corner of his cards and grimaced. The croupier carefully pushed the large stack of credits across, then ceremoniously moved the shoe to Joshua.

The man who'd been banker stood, bowed, and left the table. Another player slid into his seat.

'Gentlemen,' Joshua said, and waited for the bets.

Joshua cashed in his winnings, turned away from the cage, and noticed the beefy man. Joshua nodded politely, stepping around him.

He hesitated, then started for the dinner theater. 'If you're going to be one, be a big red one,' he said to himself wryly.

The line stretched out the door of the theater almost into one of the main gambling rooms. Joshua saw his photographer friend and wife. They beckoned, and he went over.

'Is the show that good?'

'Supposed to be. Sold out an hour ago.'

'Oh, well,' Joshua said, putting mock sorrow into his voice. 'Guess I'll settle for plain food, then.'

'Hang on a second, Mister Wolfe. We've got a whole table reserved,' Dorena said. 'Whyn't you join us?'

Joshua smiled thanks and joined them in line.

'More wine?' Arabo Hofei said.

Joshua shook his head. 'I'll have a drink with the show.'

'So what did you think of the meal?'

'All right,' Joshua said. 'But it seems that places trying to feed your eyes don't pay that much attention to the rest of you.'

Arabo laughed loudly. He was a little drunk. A couple at the next table looked over and smiled, pleased to hear someone enjoying himself. 'Now isn't *that* the truth,' he said.

'It wasn't that bad,' Dorena said, 'but there sure wasn't very much of it.' She patted her stomach with a bit of pride. 'I'd be a shadow if I had to eat here every night.'

'So what are your plans when the show's over, Joshua?' Hofei had assumed first-name terms before the salad.

'Have a drink at the bar. Maybe go back on the tables. Maybe go for a walk.'

'You do a lot of gambling?'

'A bit.'

'Would you show me – show us – how that doggoned red-dog game works? I've always wanted to play it, but it goes so fast, I'm afraid,' Dorena said.

'That's the way the dealers want it,' Joshua said. 'Keep the action going, never let people think, and you end up with a bigger piece. But you don't want to play red-dog.'

'Why not?' Arabo asked.

'Because the odds will eat you alive. They're about fourteen to one, plus the house generally takes five percent or so off the top.'

'I never understood numbers,' Dorena complained. 'It just looked like fun.'

'Winning is fun. Losing isn't,' Joshua said flatly. 'If you want, I'll show you –'

He was interrupted by an orchestra fanfare. The dance floor opened like a gigantic clamshell, and dancers spun frenetically as the stage hydraulicked up.

There were acrobats; comedians blue, straight, and robotic; tigers; aquabats; jugglers; horses; giant sloths; singers; musicians; and women. Mostly there were women in every stage from nearly naked to spacesuited, dancing, posing, singing, and talking. Joshua guessed it was a very good show for those who liked that sort of thing.

His eyes kept roving the crowd, trying without luck to pick out a man who might match the description he had of Sutro. Once he saw the two Chitet, now joined by a friend, sitting near the stage, watching as intently as they might observe a spreadsheet run.

One dancer caught everyone's attention. She was small, Afro-Oriental, Joshua thought, with long black hair and a pert figure. For a moment he thought she was nude, then realized she was wearing a bodysuit. Her partner was equally striking: tall, strong-muscled, white, platinum blond. The two of them performed alone with no music other than a metronomelike drum and a swirling synth-tone that might have originated on the Japanese long bamboo flute.

The woman floated, hung, turned, seemingly only to touch the earth or her partner's waiting arms for a moment's rejuvenation before taking off once more.

'How does she *do* that?' Dorena sighed. 'I used to dance before I met Arabo and he told me it was all right to eat. But even at my best I never dreamed I could . . .' Her voice trailed away, and she looked momentarily disconsolate. Hofei patted her hand.

The tune ended, and the two dancers took their bows and left the stage.

The next act, a hatchet-throwing comic, complete with blond and brunette barely missed 'targets,' seemed flat to Joshua and his companions. Joshua slipped a debit card into the table's slot before Arabo could get his out in spite of the man's protests.

They were in the lobby when they heard the woman scream, the scream choked off.

The tall white-blond dancer cowered beside the casino's entrance. His partner, the small Afro-Oriental woman, lay sprawled on the concrete nearby.

There were three men in front of them. Two of them were heavy, hard-faced, half grinning, enjoying their work. The third was thin, average build, expensively dressed. He reached down, jerked the dancer to her feet, snarled something, and drew his hand back.

Joshua was across the lobby and through the door. 'I'm sorry, sir. But artists aren't permitted to mingle with the guests.'

'Funny man,' the small man snapped. 'Now butt out or get hurt.'

'Sorry,' Joshua said, and strolled toward them.

'Take him, Bej.'

'Right, Elois,' one of the goons said, and started toward Wolfe. His hand went into his pocket and came out with a whip club; he slashed as it sprang open. Wolfe ducked, let the lash go overhead, and rapped the man's elbow with the heel of his hand. The man yelped, dropped the club, and grabbed his crazy bone. Wolfe raked a kick down the front of his leg, crashing onto the arch of his foot, and the man screamed loudly, the scream broken into silence as Wolfe's hammerblow struck the front of his skull.

The second thug came in, hands in a shifted cat stance. Wolfe took the same stance for a moment, ignored the other's feint, blocked the following midsection punch, then snapped his blocking hand up, smashing the goon's face with the back of his wrist, ripping his nose away from the cavity. The man gurgled agony, lost interest, and stumbled away.

The small man Wolfe had heard called Elois was backing away. His hand slid into his jacket and came out with a small nickel-plated gun, lifted as Wolfe's hand blurred to the back of his neck, then darted forward.

A shiny dart of black obsidian protruded from the man's wrist. He let go of the gun, stared at the bubbling blood, said 'Oh' in a surprised tone, and sat down on the concrete.

Wolfe stepped over, pulled the knife free, wiped it on the man's jacket, and resheathed it. He paid the short man no further mind but turned to the woman. 'You need an escort somewhere?'

The woman smiled shakily and touched a finger to the corner of her mouth, where the bruise was beginning to blossom. 'I don't know,' she said. 'You appear more dangerous than he is.'

'No, ma'am,' Wolfe said. 'I've spent my spleen for at least another week. From now on out I'm a pink pussycat.'

The woman hesitated, then said, 'All right. If you'd walk me to my lifter.'

'My privilege.'

The woman gazed at her partner. 'Thanks,' she said. 'Thanks *so* much.' The tall blond man shrank back as if she'd struck him.

Joshua looked about, saw the Hofeis standing wide-eyed, waved a farewell, took the woman's arm, and led her away, leaving a crowd gathering around the two sprawled men. It had taken just a few seconds. There was still no sign of security or police.

Joshua concentrated on his breathing: in through the nose, out through the diaphragm. After forty breaths his heartbeat was normal.

'You follow the Way,' the woman said.

'You have sharp ears,' Joshua said. 'One of them . . . and another discipline.'

'I once became curious about things like that and studied enough so I could write a dance that would be realistic. Perhaps I should have paid more attention to the effects rather than merely the motions.'

'And perhaps,' Joshua said dryly, 'I should have paid more attention to the end product of the motions myself.'

'You mean you should not have intervened.'

'I won't say that. But someone taking a quiet vacation doesn't need the sort of attention I most likely just set myself up for.'

'Yes,' the woman said. 'A "vacationer" mustn't ever get in the spotlight.' She put obvious quotation marks around 'vacationer.' 'When you are not on "vacation," might I ask how you spend your time?'

'Traveling. Meeting people.'

'That covers quite a range of professions,' the woman said.

'It does, doesn't it?' Joshua agreed. 'By the way, we haven't formally met.' He introduced himself.

'I am Candia Hsui,' the woman said. 'One-half of the Null-G Duo. I'm afraid, the way I feel at present, I may be all of the troupe. Damn Megaris, anyway!'

'Your partner?'

'At the moment. What a shit! You have no idea, Joshua, what it is like to look for a dance partner. I don't care that they're always boy-crazy or that they have the courage of bush babies.

'What I just said is a lie, but I try to be content with what Allah wills. None of them seems to think they have to be strong. I've spent more time in clinics getting patched up because some wavy boy dropped me than anything else.' Joshua realized she was babbling, a little shocky from the blow and the blood.

'Shows what happens,' he said, trying a mild joke, 'when

you take your job home with you. You should've left him at
the office.'

Candia giggled suddenly. 'You have humor in you,' she
said. 'That is good. That is better than Elois or most of the
men I generally choose.'

'Elois is – was, rather – your companion by law?'

'Choice only. I would never contract with anyone. Love
does not live as long as lawyers.'

'You have humor, too,' Joshua said.

'I think you must,' Candia said, 'especially when you
are as long from home as I am. Here. This is my lifter.'

It was a sleek black-silver sporter. She touched the lock,
and the bubble opened.

'Let me ask you something,' Joshua said. 'Where are you
going?'

'Why –' Candia broke off. 'I was going to say back to my
apartments. Which I share – shared with Elois. I do not
think I am thinking clearly.

'Hell! What a pain that will be. I'll have to get my cases
tomorrow and no doubt have to put up with another session
from the bastard. Although he never struck me but once
before.'

'If you want to pick them up now, I'll ride along,' Joshua
said, wondering why his tongue was behaving so foolishly.
'I'll help you get a room at whatever hotel you choose. If
you're short on a payday . . .' He let the suggestion trail into
silence.

'No. Money is not something I am short of, but rather
common sense. Get in. Let us go, get my things, and be
gone before Elois finishes getting his arm sewn up or
plassed or whatever they'll do to him.'

Joshua went to the other side of the lifter and clambered
in. Candia touched buttons, and the bubble closed, the
drive started and the vehicle lifted off the ground.

The lifter went through the resort streets swiftly, past

the still-raucous bars and restaurants, then into the hills, past the dark, blank-faced palaces of Trinité's elite. She drove the winding roads fast, skillfully.

'What was it you did to Elois? I thought I saw a knife, but it was black.'

'It was a knife. Of sorts. I'm sorry I had to use it. Usually there's an easier way.'

'Pah! I hope the pigfutterer bleeds to death!'

Elois's 'apartments' were a rather luxurious town house atop one of Morne-des-Esses's peaks.

Wolfe looked at it. 'Quite a place. What does Elois do to pay for it?'

'Some of this, some of that. Mostly smuggle. Nothing seamy, he swore. Just papers that are worth money on other worlds that people wish to have in other places without handling them themselves. I should have known what he was, seeing his bullies always about him.' She shrugged. 'At least he was fun for a while.'

Candia touched the lock, swore when nothing happened. 'He already took my porepattern from the lock! Now I will have to come back and listen to his bullshit!'

'Maybe not.'

Joshua touched the tips of his fingers to the sides of the lock and *listened*. The lock clicked, and the door swung open. Candia looked at him in astonishment.

'How did you do that? Elois said this lock was unbreakable! In his trade having a safe place is very important.'

'Perhaps he should complain to the manufacturer,' Joshua suggested.

Candia's possessions were indeed no more than three cases. Joshua lifted the last of them into the baggage area of the lifter, slammed the lid closed, and got in the vehicle.

Candia climbed into the driver's seat. 'Now, what hotel would you recommend, my fearless paladin?'

'One with two big doormen,' Joshua suggested. 'Elois looks the type who doesn't take no for an easy answer.'

'Probably not,' the woman sighed. 'In which event I shall have the law take him by the balls and pull hard. Let me think. Perhaps the Diamant Novotel?' She looked at him in a curious manner.

'You know Diamant better than I do,' Wolfe said. 'I've only been onplanet a day.'

'We'll go there,' Candia said, giving him the strange look once more.

There were two doormen at the Novotel even at that late hour, and both of them were very large. They hurried out as the lifter slipped up the drive.

'There is an advantage to an expensive toy like this,' Candia said. 'People scrape and bow when they see you come. I could be an ax murderer and no one would notice.' She sighed. 'What a bother it will be giving it back to Elois.'

The bubble opened, and the two men bowed Candia and Joshua out, then picked up her luggage.

'I'll wait until you sign in,' he said, 'then let you sort things out in peace.'

'You know,' she murmured, 'I am starting to believe you might truly be *sans peur et sans reproche*.'

'Don't put big money on that,' Joshua said. 'Unless you change *reproche* to *raison*. But thanks for the compliment. Why?'

The doormen withdrew discreetly out of hearing.

'You never suggested that a good place to stay might be your hotel and the safest place of all would be your room and your bed. I've not known many men who wouldn't try to take such advantage.'

'But I'm not staying in a hotel.'

'Your villa, then.'

'Nor there.'

Candia glared at him. 'I do not know whether to stamp my foot, hit you, or laugh. Very well, then, Joshua Wolfe. Where are you staying?

'My ship's moored in the harbor. The *Grayle*.'

'Thank you, Joshua. Perhaps your chivalry will be rewarded. We shall see.' She came close, stood on tiptoe, kissed Wolfe on the lips, and went into the hotel without looking back.

Joshua stood, bemused, still feeling that butterfly touch. He realized one of the doormen was grinning at him.

Wolfe licked his lips, tasted something like jasmine, and went down the hill to the harbor.

ELEVEN

There were two scribed messages on the com when Joshua awoke:

> I would appreciate a few moments of your time at ten in the morning, in my office, if it would be convenient, so that we can both avoid possible problems.
>
> Falster Samothrake
General Manager
Casino d'Or

and:

> Perhaps my hero would wish a bit of a reward this afternoon. If so, please have an appetite and be waiting at one in the afternoon.
>
> Candia

Joshua looked at them and grimaced. 'So the tiger gets his innings first.' He yawned and went to the workout room.

Falster Samothrake was the bullet-headed man Joshua had taken for a security thug.

'Mister Wolfe,' he said in a flat voice, expressionless. 'Please sit down.'

Joshua obeyed. 'I suppose I owe you an apology,' he said.

'No. I've never minded being thought stupid. You should know what an excellent tool that becomes.'

'I've been told that.'

'You made quite a stir in my casino last night,' Samothrake said.

'I didn't figure that you'd want one of your performers messed up.'

'We have security for problems like that.'

'I didn't see any around. So I did what I thought was necessary.'

'Wouldn't you say you might have been a little excessive? There are three men in the hospital this morning. One will need extensive plastic surgery before he'll be happy looking at his face in the morning, the second has a shattered humerus, and the third will probably lose about thirty percent of the use of his hand.'

'They brought the guns to the party,' Joshua said. 'What do you propose to do about what happened?'

'I wasn't sure, which was why I asked you to come here. I decided if you failed to show up, then my course of action would be clear. But you did.

'Mister Wolfe, I now plan to do exactly nothing. Let me explain, so you may choose to regulate your actions here on Trinité accordingly.

'First is I watched your baccarat dealings yesterday. Very professional, sir. I like having a freelance such as yourself at my tables. It encourages others to play against you, since all wish to tear down the master, and every time the fools bet, the house takes its percentage.

'Second is that I'm familiar with Mister Elois. He is, to put it bluntly, an arrogant pain in the ass. He's been a problem here before. Perhaps, when and if his hand heals, he will moderate his behavior, although I doubt it.

'Third is I intensely disliked his involvement with Miss Hsui. I would never dream of intervening in one of our performers' personal lives, but I am most content when *they* are and I knew that to be unlikely with anyone who chooses to company Mister Elois.

'The fourth reason is the most significant, however. You have important friends.'

Joshua raised an eyebrow.

'I refer to the Hofeis. They were happy to tell me just what happened outside the casino last night and wished to make certain I didn't get any incorrect ideas. Since they are the principal owners of Thule Investments, which owns twelve points in this casino, I was, of course, most interested in what they had to say.'

'The Hofeis?' Joshua was incredulous.

'Indeed. They prefer to travel without fanfare, and their tastes tend toward the commonplace. Perhaps that is why Thule Investments is so successful. I truly believe the Hofeis could almost buy this world if they wished.

'You still appear astonished at who your friends turned out to be, which is another clue I chose the right course to take, since I loathe a gold digger.'

'Thanks,' Joshua said. 'But what about the Diamant police?'

'They see and know what certain people in this city, of which I am one, wish them to. No more, no less.

'One other, minor point. You asked me about someone named Edet Sutro. Might I inquire as to your interest? I must add that if you're planning anything with him such as occurred last night, you will be in serious jeopardy. Mister Sutro is one of the most honored citizens of Diamant and a valued patron of this establishment.'

'Not at all,' Wolfe reassured him. 'Before I decided to

visit Trinité, I discussed matters with some of my colleagues, particularly as to men they knew on this world who might be fond of some exclusive action. He was but one of the names given me.'

'Exclusive action.' Samothrake mused. 'That would mean, to a man in your evident profession, someone who likes a high-stakes game and isn't that quick at calculating the odds.'

Wolfe inclined his head, said nothing.

'I'll give you this, Mister Wolfe. Your friends advised you poorly. Mister Sutro is quite a capable sportsman. I can attest to that by personal experience.'

'Thank you for the information. While not questioning your word, I'm well aware each shepherd prefers to have his own flock to shear.'

The two men exchanged wintery smiles.

'Feel free to test the truth of what I said when Mister Sutro returns to Trinité.' Samothrake rose. 'Now, I'm afraid I have problems more complicated than yours. Thank you for coming to see me, Mister Wolfe. Please feel free to continue using our facilities, although I will caution you that the next set of unusual events may be seen in a less forgiving light.'

The *Dolphin* cut its drive, and Thetis tossed a line around a mooring cleat on the *Grayle*'s loading platform. Her only passenger was Candia, who wore a translucent wrap of swirling colors, sandals, and a beach hat. It was exactly one.

'Good afternoon, my brave knight,' she said. 'You look rested.'

'Candia. Thetis.'

The girl's greeting was a bit clipped, and she turned away, busying herself with a rag on the instrument panel's brasswork.

'Shall we be on our way?' Candia asked. 'I have all that

could be desired by the hungriest dragon slayer.' She indicated a large cooler behind her seat.

'I didn't know what you'd planned,' Joshua said. 'Am I dressed appropriately?'

Candia eyed his sleeveless cotton vest, shorts, and ankle-strapped sandals.

'You are perfect. Now get in.'

The *Dolphin* nosed into the beach and grounded with a slight scrape. Joshua leapt over the side. The water was cool, perfectly clear. Candia struggled with the heavy cooler, and Joshua took it from her, waded to the islet's beach, and came back to help her out of the boat. Candia had a small mesh bag in her hand.

'I'll be back when you told me to, Miss Hsui,' Thetis said. 'I hope you two have fun.'

Without waiting for a response, she moved controls, and water frothed as the *Dolphin* backed off the beach, turned, and headed back toward Morne-des-Esses.

'That one does not like me,' Candia said.

'Why not?'

'Because she sees me as a rival.'

Joshua blinked. 'But she's just a kid.'

'I know some men who would think that an attraction,' Candia said. 'And what if she is? When you were young, didn't you ever wildly love someone who did not know you even breathed?'

Joshua's face softened. 'Yes,' he remembered. 'She was nineteen. I was sixteen. She was the daughter of the Federation secretary of state.'

'What happened?'

'Nothing. I was trying to get courage enough to ask her to my academy's formal ball. Of course she would have laughed. She was a very cool one with an eye for the main chance, and my parents were vastly outranked by those of the boys who usually came calling. But I was lucky, and my father was transferred to a new post, off Earth, so my heart was only chipped a little bit around the edges.'

'So you have been on Earth?' Candia's eyes were wide.

'Born there. Grew up all over the galaxy. My parents were career diplomats.'

'How interesting. I shall be interested in hearing your stories and seeing if perhaps we have visited the same worlds.

'Now, come.' She took a small clock from her bag and put it on the top of the cooler. 'There is much to be done before the young one returns to make sure I have not stolen your virginity.

'First a swim. That is good for the appetite.'

Candia stripped off the robe. She wore a black fishnet one-piece suit that had a silver-looking fastener strip down the front. She ran to the edge of the water. 'But I hate the feel of clothes when I am swimming,' she called back. Her fingers opened the fastener, and she pulled the suit down to her thighs, side kicked it off, caught it with one hand, and tossed it back at Joshua.

'You have my permission to be equally immodest,' she shouted. She ran three steps into the water, flat dove, and vanished.

Joshua shook his head, smiling, then took off his clothes and went after her.

The world was calm, blue, at peace. A small fish looked skeptically at Joshua; its tail wriggled, and then it was gone. Joshua kicked toward a brightly striped mass of sea-weed growing from the sea bottom. It was shallow off this nameless island, no more than fifteen feet deep.

He'd looked for Candia but hadn't found her, above or below the surface, and so swam happily about, with Trinité, Al'ar, violence all of another world and time.

Something tickled his toes, and he jackknifed and was face to face with Candia. She stuck her tongue out and swam for the surface.

Joshua broke water a second after she did.

'You are careless,' she chided. 'What if I were a man-eating fish?'

'Then I would have been doomed, and you would have had to eat the whole lunch yourself.'

'What a tragedy,' she said, and swam close to him, floating effortlessly. She put her arms around him.

'It could be I *am* a man-eater. Be warned.' She giggled. 'I was watching you swim. You are very graceful.'

'Thank you.'

Her eyes closed, and her lips opened. Joshua kissed her.

'Perhaps the reason you swim so well,' she said, 'is the excellence of your rudder.'

She brought her legs up around his thighs and pulled him close against her. Joshua felt his stiffness against her warmth. He thrust gently, experimentally.

'Ah ah,' Candia said. 'If I let you do that, you will not be able to steer yourself and will never navigate back to our lunch.' She broke out of the embrace, eeled backward, and swam hard for the beach.

'I would say we did very well,' Candia said, surveying the ruins. 'The artichoke hearts and olives are gone, as is the caviar. The cheeses have been destroyed. There's a bit of the pâté left if you have not made a sufficient pig of yourself.'

'I'm so full, I'll never move,' Joshua said.

'Ah? Not even for some more champagne?'

'For that I can move.' Joshua lazily extended his glass.

Candia picked up the bottle and leaned back on the picnic cloth. She wore only the rainbow robe.

'Perhaps m'sieu would wish a new glass,' she murmured.

She opened her robe and let a bit of champagne trickle into her navel.

'M'sieu wishes,' Joshua said, a bit hoarse, and slid over to her. His lips caressed her stomach, moved up, his hands slipping the robe aside, and his teeth teased the nipples of her tiny breasts. Then he moved downward, and Candia opened the robe for him and spread her legs.

His tongue fondled, entered her, and she gasped and lifted her legs around his shoulders.

'Next,' she managed, 'it will be my turn for dessert.'

'I feel,' Joshua said, watching the *Dolphin* approach the beach, 'like I'm coming home from an evening out and my mother's about to decide if I was a good boy or not.'

'Don't worry about her.' Candia laughed. 'Of course she knows.'

'How could she?'

'She is a woman, is she not?'

Thetis looked at them both, her lips pursed angrily, and had even less to say on the ride back to the *Grayle*.

'It doesn't feel like a woman has ever lived here,' Candia announced after Wolfe had shown her around the ship.

'No. Not for long. But how did you know?'

'It is comfortable but stiff. A man's place. But that is good. Are you coming to see me dance tonight?'

'I hope so. Are you now a solo act?'

'No. I gave Megaris another chance. I am always doing that, I fear.'

'Afterward, do you want to come back here?'

'Of course.'

'You know, if you wish, you could bring your luggage with you.'

Candia looked surprised. 'I know I am quite good in bed, but this is quite sudden.' A cunning look crossed her face. 'Ah, but perhaps I think too much of myself. Tell me the truth, Joshua Wolfe. I know you are not on vacation here, nor do I believe you are a gambler.

'The men I have known who were could never absent themselves from the tables for long, nor did they have the ability to relax and enjoy a simple picnic and swim.

'Could I be right in thinking that my presence here, with you, might help you do whatever you are on Trinité for?'

Joshua hesitated, then remembered what he'd told Lil back on Platte. 'You're right, Candia. And yes, you could help.'

'Will it be dangerous?' Without waiting for a reply: 'I hope so. I have been living such a dull life of late. That was another complaint I had about Elois. He kept me well clear of his business. All I was good for was as a bed partner, that for not very long, then someone to get angry with and finally strike.

'So excite me, Joshua. I shall try to do my share in return.'

Joshua had just finished dressing to go out when the ship told him the *Dolphin* was pulling up at the platform. He'd eaten on the ship after Candia had left, not wishing to test his digestion against the casino's efforts again.

Thetis was the only one aboard. She had a large plastic envelope under her arm. Wolfe hesitated, then invited her inside.

'I'm a butt,' she said.

'Nice opening. Why?'

'Oh . . . I was rude this afternoon. I wasn't professional. I'm sorry. I thought – anyway, I didn't have any right.'

Wolfe started to say something, remembered sleepless nights and the Federation official's daughter, and changed his mind. 'Forget it. Everybody's entitled to a mood every now and then.'

Thetis brightened. 'That's good. Thanks. I won't do it again. The main reason I had to come out was I've found your Mister Sutro! And I know an awful lot about him!'

She beamed, and Joshua grinned.

'Sit down,' she ordered, and touched the fastener on the envelope and took out papers. 'Now the Sibyl of Cumae will hold forth. Knows all, sees all, and will talk your ear off about it.

'Sutro. First name, Edet. Naturalized citizen of Trinité for about ten years, since right after the war. No police record. Nobody knows where he came from before that. Grampa got that,' she explained, 'from a fishcop he used to be friends with who doesn't know things are different now.

'I'll get a picture of Sutro tomorrow. He's big, people said, and has a beard.

'He calls himself an expediter, which Grampa said can mean almost anything. He owns an island he's named Thrinacia. I had to look that up –'

'I know what it was. He has a nasty choice of names.'

'I think he's probably nasty in other ways,' Thetis said. 'Anyway, Thrinacia is one of the Outer Islands, about forty miles off Morne-des-Esses. I've been out to the islands three or four times. We could get to Thrinacia with the *Dolphin* on a calm day, or you could rent a lifter. I looked it up on the chart, and it's about a mile long by two miles wide. It's got its own robot instrument-approach spaceport, two or three separate mansions, and a sheltered docking area. The island's surrounded on three sides with cliffs. They're not very high, no more than fifty feet, and I think you could climb them if you wanted. The other side, the one with the dock, has some beaches.'

'Let's go back to this cliff climbing for a minute,' Joshua said. 'What do you think I am?'

Thetis looked at him wisely, then back to her papers. 'He

has twelve men working for him. I found that out. Do you know how? I'm real proud of myself.'

'Tell me.'

'There's only about three groceries that cater to the people who live off Morne-des-Esses. Naturally, since I do a lot of the deliveries, I know all of them pretty well.

'Mister Sutro does his shopping at Sentry Markets, and I found out from the manager there's an open charge account with thirteen authorized signatures. I double-checked, and there's twelve different kinds of liquor they keep on hand, so I figured that was a pretty good confirmation.'

She grinned excitedly at Wolfe. 'Wouldn't I make a great spy?'

'No,' Wolfe said. 'You're too pretty and not loony enough.'

'That's what Granddad said. About not being crazy enough. Thank you.

'Mister Sutro has a big fishing boat, a speedster, and two lifters registered. One of them is a heavy gravlighter; the other's a sporter. All of them are on the island.

'He's gone – offworld – about six months out of the year, maybe more. He's gone right now, by the way.'

Joshua grimaced, said nothing.

'I thought you might be interested in when he leaves the island,' Thetis went on, 'so I talked to the harbormaster and checked the log.

'He generally comes ashore once a week or so when he's on Trinité. He always comes to Diamant within a day or two after he's come back from offplanet. Grandpa checked the logs against Diamant Subcontrol's history of landings. They clear all approaches for the islands as well as here. He never lands at Wule that I could find out.

'His men do the shopping and so forth, and they generally use the cargo lighter.

'When he comes in, he does the same thing. He brings a bunch of his guys with him. I found out they're pretty mean-looking people, like some of the rich folks here use for bodyguards.'

'That's exactly what they'd be,' Joshua put in.

'I asked some more questions, but people started giving me strange looks and I had to stop. But I found out that he likes to gamble, like you told me. Generally he gambles up at the Mushroom Tabernacle.'

'The what?'

'That's what we call the main casino,' she explained. 'Sometimes he goes to the Palace – that's the second of the big gambling places – but not very often. I couldn't find out what kind of games he likes to play.

'I even went to one of the girl places,' she said. 'I asked about Mister Sutro, and the madam told me I was quote way the hell too young to be caring what Sutro does with his diddlestick and get the hell out of her front room, so I struck out there.'

'Thetis, you *are* too young to be doing things like that,' Joshua complained.

The girl stared at him. 'Maybe you'd be surprised, Mister Wolfe.' Then she turned pink and started stuffing the papers back into the envelope. 'Anyway. That's all I've got.'

Wolfe got up, went to his cache, and took out bills. Then he remembered something, went up from the living area into his trip cabin, and fumbled through drawers. He found a long case that held something he'd meant to give a woman who'd turned out not to be what he'd thought and went back to the main room.

'Here.'

He gave her the sheaf of credits.

'Hell!' she gasped 'That's too much money!'

'No, it's not. You earned it, plus it comes out of expenses. Your grandfather gets half. I'll be needing him for some night work if he's available.' He gave the case to

Thetis. She looked at it, then at him suspiciously, and opened it.

Inside, on a red plush nest, was a torque bracelet made of precious metals twined together until the ornament gleamed with a dozen different colors, though each appeared to blend seamlessly with the others.

'My. My, oh, my,' she managed in a whisper.

'That's your tip.'

She picked up the bracelet, slipped her hand through it, and examined it. Then she lifted her eyes.

'Thank you, Joshua. Thank you.'

He put on his formal jacket, tucked a small gun into its hidden holster, went to the casino, played half a dozen abstracted hands, and deservedly lost all of them.

He saw the Hofeis as they came in for dinner and thanked them enormously.

'Forget it,' Arabo said briefly. 'Nobody should ever put hands on a woman.'

'And it was so *exciting*,' Dorena added. 'Although I never dreamed a real fight was that bloody.

'If you want to pay us back, you can make good on your promise to teach us a little about gambling.'

Wolfe grinned. 'I have a question. Why would two people who don't know anything about gambling buy part of a casino?'

Arabo looked puzzled. 'I don't see what that has to do with it. I know people like to make love, so if I wanted to buy a whorehouse, would I have to be a customer?'

'You'd better not,' Dorena warned. 'Or you'd be wearing your knockers for a necklace.'

'I know people like to gamble,' Arabo went on, ignoring his wife, 'especially rich people. There aren't a lot of places in this sector of the Outlaw Worlds where it's safe, and the Casino d'Or had the best balance sheet, a good reputation with the Diamant police, and their employees seem to stay on, which is always the sign of a good company.

'What else did I need to know?'

Joshua decided he would never be able to fathom the mind of a businessperson and left them.

He sat through the show, including Candia's dancing, without much registering. He was thinking about a large bearded man, twelve bodyguards, and an island.

TWELVE

Candia moaned, leaned back, hands on Joshua's knees, then leaned forward again and again as Joshua's hand caressed her. Her body jolted, her head went back in a silent scream, then she sagged forward onto his chest, gasping for air. Her breathing slowed after a time.

'You are still ready,' she said in some surprise.

'Next time I'll finish, too.'

'Does your Way teach that kind of control?'

'Yes.'

'Why is it not more popular?'

Joshua was silent for a space, then decided to tell her the truth. 'Because, for one thing, it helps to have been a prisoner of the Al'ar for three years.'

Candia was jolted. 'Oh. I did not know. Joshua, I am sorry. Now you are soft. Please. Forget I spoke. Think of something else. Think of loving me as you did a moment ago. As you will again. As I want you.'

Joshua breathed, measured, bringing control. *Water, flow . . . water, move . . . water, change*, and his body responded.

'Now,' she whispered. 'Now we shall do it my way.'

Without freeing him, she pushed herself up and lifted a leg across his chest.

'Turn sideways,' she said, 'until your feet hang off the

edge of the bed.' Joshua obeyed. She swiveled once more until her legs were on the outside of his.

'Ah, I feel you. Now, sit up. Slowly. Yes. Now I shall do all the moving. You can use your hands as you wish on me.' She moved her hips up, down, a steady motion.

'You know,' she said, voice throaty, 'I think all dancers dream of having . . . another dancer for their lover. Someone who has the muscles they do, someone who can move with them. Why we do not think of a fighter, a lover . . . Oh. Yes. Touch me there more. But . . . it seems men dancers always choose each other. Oh! Like that, Joshua. Oh, yes. But now I know the place to look. Ah now. Now I am coming. Come with me. I want to feel you let go!'

Her body pulsed around him, and he jerked upward, stifling his outcry.

'You said your ship talks to you.'

'Yes.'

'It sees what's going on outside?'

'It does.'

'Inside, too?'

'Yes.'

'So it knows what we are doing?'

'I don't know if it can interpret what it sees. Perhaps it can. Does it matter?'

'I don't know. But I have never been watched by a machine before. I don't know if I find it exciting . . . or creepy.'

Joshua threw another bucket of cold water on the stones, and steam swirled through the small room.

'That is all,' Candia gasped. 'I have suffered enough for my sins! Let me out. I'm boiled!'

She pulled the sauna door open and staggered out, and

Joshua heard her splash into the pool before the door swung to.

Two bucketfuls later he, too, stumbled out into the chilled air of the bathroom. Candia lay in the small pool, her splayed legs on its rim, head pillowed on an inflatable cushion. Water bubbled around her.

'I tried to talk to your ship,' she said, 'but it ignores me.'

'It *can't* acknowledge you. That's in its basic programming.'

'It's probably jealous.' She sighed. 'But that's all right. You have a very sexy ship, you know.'

'No, I didn't know.'

'Look. As soon as I got in here, pumps started up. I could just lie here like this, letting myself be loved by the water, and sooner or later forget about men.'

'Candia, you are oversexed.'

'I would certainly hope so,' the woman murmured. 'I want to be able to keep up with you.'

'Enough fooling about,' Joshua said. 'We've got to be out and about.'

Reluctantly the dancer came out of the pool. 'So what are we going to do?'

'We're renting a nice, comfortable house on our own island. I've decided I need more privacy. A house and a lifter, and I'd like to put them in your name.'

Joshua stayed in the background while the sleek, dapper little man danced attendance on his client. Candia looked at Wolfe when a question came that she couldn't answer, and he'd nod – slightly.

It took only four islands before they had what he needed. The island had a single house, a sprawling, fully roboticized villa, so there wouldn't be any nosy staff. There was a boathouse and a dock. The nearest occupied island was three miles away.

It was about ten miles off Morne-des-Esses, far enough to be able to lose any pursuit.

The realtor beamed when Candia gave her approval. He went to fetch the lease papers from his lifter.

'Tell me,' she whispered, 'why you chose this one. Was it the mirrors on the bedroom ceiling? Or the size of that big bed?'

'Neither,' Joshua said. 'It was the goat I saw out back.'

'Pervert!'

The ship hovered up to the dock, and the lock slid open. Joshua set two travel cases on the dock, then stepped out.

The lock closed. Joshua touched his bonemike, spoke inaudibly, and the ship turned, went out about fifty meters, and disappeared beneath the water.

'That is eerie,' Candia decided. 'What happens if she decides not to come up again when you call her?'

'Then I've got a very expensive salvage problem.'

'The water is very clear. Someone might be able to look down and see her, you know.'

'If anybody's looking straight down for a spaceship, my cover's blown, anyway. All we can do is hope and think clean thoughts.'

Candia picked up one case with the dancer's strength that Joshua was still surprised at, and they started toward the house.

'Now what do we do? Besides make love, I mean.'

'Mostly, we wait.'

'So what'll you want with me? I'll guess it ain't real legal or you'd have Thetis do it.'

'Nothing illegal about it, Mister Libanos. Let's just say it's a bit chancy.'

'Whyn't you use that fancy lifter you've got?'

'Lifters send up spray. I want something quiet.'

'Why not?' the old man grunted. 'Nothing much happening this time of year, anyway.'

'Can I ask you something, Joshua?'

'You can *ask* anything.'

'But you might not answer. It is a personal question. Very personal. You were a prisoner of the Al'ar, you said the first night we made love.'

'I was.' Joshua's voice was suddenly dead.

'I wish the light was on. I would like to see your face, to know when I should shut up.'

'Don't worry about it. What's your question?'

'Were you a soldier?'

'Not then,' Joshua said reluctantly. 'When the war started . . . when the Al'ar attacked the Federation, I was on Sauros. That's one of the Al'ar Ruling Worlds, as they called them. They didn't have to centralize their capital, since they had ways of communicating between stars almost instantly. We still don't know how they did that.

'My family had been sent there two, almost three years before, when the first incidents occurred and things started heating up. They were supposed to try to defuse the situation with words.

'But after a while the Al'ar decided they didn't want to listen. I guess there weren't many on our side who wanted to, either, by then.

'When they blindsided our fleets without bothering to declare war, they rounded up every Federation being on any of their worlds. They didn't bother with the difference between soldiers and civilians. Not then, not later. I ended up in a camp.'

'What about your parents?'

'They died, like most of the people around me. Disease. Malnutrition. Neglect. The Al'ar weren't deliberate bastards, but it worked out the same.'

'But you escaped.'

'I escaped.'

'And after that?'

'I was the first human who'd been that close to them for that long, and so the Federation was very glad to see me and use what I knew. Later on there were a few more like me. But not very many. The Al'ar didn't take many prisoners, since they never surrendered themselves.'

'Then the Federation made you a soldier?'

'Of sorts.'

'I have known soldiers,' Candia said softly, 'and I have learned that none of them, none of the real ones, ever want to talk about fighting. So I shall not ask about what you did or where.

'But I have another question. How could you stand to be around those creatures? I never was; I only saw them on the vid or on holos. But they made me shudder. Like . . . like seeing a slug on your walk. Or a spider on your wall.'

'That's the way most humans feel . . . felt. The Al'ar felt the same way about us. That's the real reason the war happened.'

'But you didn't?'

'No.'

'Why not?'

Wolfe was silent for a long time.

'I don't really know,' he said slowly. 'Maybe it's because spiders never bothered me. Or maybe because I got moved around so much growing up that I was always on the outside. Every place we went was new, and the people were strange. Most generally they didn't like me, because I was different.'

'But they killed your parents. So you hated them and must hate them now.'

'No,' Joshua said. 'No, I didn't. Not then, not now.'

*

After two weeks no one much noticed Joshua around the casino. He was just another sleek gambler who happened to be Candia's latest lover.

He would take her to work and back to the island most nights, generally spending the time in between at the table, where he usually won. Always courteous, always reticent, he kept himself to himself and became invisible in that world of flashy transients.

One night he pulled the lifter close to the employee entrance and escorted Candia inside. He'd timed his appearance close to showtime, so the ramp to the backstage entrance was deserted.

He went back to the lifter, took out a black satchel, and reentered the casino. The corridor was still empty. He went down it to an unmarked door and opened it. He'd picked the lock earlier in the day.

He closed the door behind him and used a jamb lock to secure it. The stairwell was gray and smelled of moisture, concrete, neglect.

He opened his satchel, took out coveralls that were marked CASINO STAFF with a name tag of KYRIA, and pulled them on. The only other thing the satchel contained was a gray metal box. It was stenciled: RELAY BOARD. DO NOT OPEN WITHOUT PROPER PRECAUTIONS. He touched the paint, made certain it was dry.

He went up two flights of stairs, opened the landing door, and came out in another corridor. He went past five interior doors, paused at the sixth. His hands blurred around the lock, and he heard a click.

He opened the door and looked out on the catwalks that spidered above the main theater. There were the lights, pulleys, lifts, flats, and ropes remotely operated by the production crew backstage, a level below. He found the open section of wall he'd chosen, turned four studs on the back of the metal box, and held it against the wall.

It held firm when he released it. He went out, relocked the door, and went on down to the main level. He stripped off the coveralls, then opened the door a crack. The corridor was vacant.

He left the building, drove to the main entrance, and entered, this time politely greeting three or four people he knew, pausing long enough to ask one of them the time, frowning, and pretending to reset his watch.

'Wake up! Joshua, wake up!'

'What is it?'

'You were dreaming. Not a good dream,' Candia said. 'I heard you grunt. You're sweating. And you were speaking a language I do not know. It gave me the shudders.'

'Something like this?' He spoke a few words in Al'ar.

'Yes. That is it.' She turned on the light, got up, went into the bathroom, came back with a towel, then began drying him gently.

'Do you want to tell me what the dream was?'

'I was dreaming about Sauros,' Wolfe said slowly.

'What were you doing?'

'I was with my Al'ar friend, Taen. I guess he was my friend. I never asked him, and he never told me.'

'What were you doing?'

'He was showing me places on the body where, if you just touch them, the person must die.'

Candia shuddered. 'No wonder you were grunting. What a terrible thing to dream!'

'No,' Joshua said. 'I was fascinated. Taen was helping me translate those places on an Al'ar body to the same spots on a man.'

'This was a friend?' Candia's voice was incredulous.

'A friend. A teacher.'

'Did he teach you anything other than ways to kill people?'

Joshua started to answer, stopped. His words had gone on too long. 'Yes. But nothing worth talking about.'

'I do not believe you,' Candia said after a pause. 'But each of us must have secrets. There. Now you are dry. Think happy thoughts.' She kissed him, turned off the light, rolled away from him, and pretended to go to sleep.

Joshua lay awake for a time. Thinking. Remembering:

'Very well,' Taen said. 'I have decided I am mad. I shall teach you how to fight. But it will be necessary for you to learn more of our ways. A virai cannot fly unless it studies the winds.'

The boy bowed.

'You will not like me as I teach,' the Al'ar warned. 'I did not – perhaps do not – like the one who taught me. But this is as it should be.'

Without warning, his grasping organ came out at stomach level, struck the boy, and sent him stumbling down. Joshua hit hard, rolled sideways, tucked his feet under himself, and was back up.

The Al'ar moved closer. Joshua snapped a kick; Taen's grasping organ touched it, and Wolfe lost his balance and fell heavily.

Once more, without outcry, he got up.

'Good,' the Al'ar said approvingly. 'Showing pain like a hatchling means your shell, your body, is not learning. But this is the last I shall praise you.'

Another time:

'I know the ways of being invisible,' the boy complained. 'They're of another Way, but I've studied them.'

'Tell me, wormling, of thy brilliance.'

Joshua took a breath.

'You're not really invisible. You just move beyond someone's perception. To the side, above, below. Or else you use misdirection. Touch them on one shoulder, duck under when they turn, and they'll think they've observed the area.

'Another way is to use light, darkness. Move toward the greater light, the greater darkness, and you'll remain unseen.'

'I shit on such mummeries,' Taen said. 'This is the Al'ar way.' He moved to one side, then back, and Joshua's eyes hurt. He looked away, then back. Behind Taen was a table, and on it was a vase.

Now he could see the vase clearly.

The air shimmered, and the Al'ar returned.

'That is what I mean. It is harder when someone is looking directly at you, easier when their focus is set elsewhere and then they turn to you. But this is another thing you shall learn.'

Joshua smiled in the darkness.

The Al'ar shuffled toward him, moving in a semicircle. Joshua turned, kept his face toward Taen, moved sideways. The Al'ar's grasping organ swept out, and Joshua ducked under it, tapped the organ with three knuckles, and *felt* Taen's pain. The Al'ar's leg lashed, and Joshua kicked it away.

Taen tottered, and Joshua snapped a frontal kick into his midsection, sending the lean alien sprawling. Taen curled his legs under himself for the rebound, saw Joshua standing above him, fist ready for the killing knuckle stroke, and let himself down.

'You have learned all I have. Now it is time for us to go out and seek a name for you. You must then study, but with other teachers. I must consult our Elders and study our codex for permission, but I feel it is time. When – if they agree, we shall go beyond Sauros, out into the dry lands, at night.

'Someone shall be waiting for us. I shall teach you the words you must use to him. You must study them so you make no mistakes and cause me to look like a blind one.'

A final memory came to Joshua.

He was twenty. He was alone by the green haze that

marked the limits of the prison camp. Cross into the haze and you died.

He paid the haze no mind. After almost three years it had become a part of him, as much a part as the long shabby huts, the constant hunger, the torn clothes, and the cold.

And the searing loneliness.

He did not allow himself to think of that.

Instead, he began his movements, as he did every day at dawn and dusk. Slowly, letting his mind be taken away.

'Hey! You!'

The peace left him. He turned.

There were four of them. One was the son of a man who'd been one of the embassy's lifter drivers before the war, before internment, and was his age. The second was one of the Marine guards who preferred being with younger men instead of the few survivors of his detachment. The other two he did not know other than that they were always seen with the driver's son.

All of them were heavier than Wolfe and had found ways to acquire more food than the allocated rations.

Wolfe did not respond.

They formed a semicircle around him, keeping about eight feet from him.

'We wanted to set you straight,' the driver's son said. 'Teach you we all gotta hang together an' remember we're men, not friggin' slugs. We ain't gonna be here forever, an' we'll need t' be ready when th' time comes to fight back.

'It ain't right, you doin' all this Al'ar shit. Tryin' to be like one a them. We been watchin', seein' you study them. Prob'ly wishin' —'

Joshua was suddenly next to him, less than a foot away. Two fingers touched the young man's skull just at the angle of his jaw. He screamed in mortal agony and stumbled back.

The Marine was coming into some sort of a fighting stance, but before his hands came level with the ground,

Joshua struck him with a backhand and he fell, trying to breathe, eyes popping.

The third and fourth were backing away, hands lifted.

'Pick up these other two,' Wolfe said. 'And do not ever come to me again. Do not speak to me, do not think of me.

'Am I understood?'

He did not wait for a response but turned his back. Once more he began the slow movements, facing the green haze, letting his mind study it, reach toward it, through it, beyond it.

He barely noted the scraping sound as they dragged the two men away.

The memories faded. Wolfe put his head down and slept.

'They're pretty alert, aren't they, even when the boss ain't around?' Libanos said, lowering the night glasses. 'I count three. Two walking in the open, number three hangin' back waiting to see what happens.'

'Four,' Wolfe corrected. 'There's another one about twenty yards in front, keeping just off the walkway. He's still . . . now he's moving again.'

'Mister, you ain't even used the binocs. How'd you know that?'

'Good eyes. I lead a clean life.'

The old man snorted and continued examining Edet Sutro's island. The *Dolphin* sat, drive idling silently, about two hundred meters offshore, tossing in the surf.

'All right. I've got their cargo lighter. Pretty standard. I make it as a Solar 500. Been on 'em. Run 'em. They're power pigs but fast. Maneuverable enough to get by. One man can run 'em; takes two if you're on instruments. Hell if I know what the inside'd be like. Anything from bare cargo space to yacht city.' He handed the binocs to Wolfe, who examined the lifter.

'What about visibility?'

'Normal electronics, night amplification with helmets, maybe screens. Normal vision'd be the windscreen, the four ports on either side, and there's a screen in the overhead rigged to a pickup in the stem.'

'Entrances?'

'Two hatches on either side of the driving compartment, one roof hatch, a big hatch for cargo on port and sta'board.

'Oh, yeah, there's two emergency exits. One right in the stern, high up, the other in the bottom of the hull, in case the thing flips.'

'Very good.' Wolfe mused. 'I like something with a lot of doors.' He fixed the craft in his mind, then handed the glasses back. 'Shall we go, Mister Libanos? It's getting past my bedtime.'

Candia shuddered and gasped as Wolfe drove inside her, then lifted her leg up, curling it around him, heel at the back of his neck, bringing her hips up against him.

A moment later she did the same with her other leg, linking her ankles, pulling hard as Wolfe convulsed and spasmed. Moments later she followed him, and her legs sagged down.

They returned together, hands moving on each other's sweat-slick bodies.

After a time she murmured, 'You know, Joshua, sometimes I almost think I'm . . .' Her voice trailed off.

'Yes?'

Candia sighed. 'Never mind. I almost said something that would have embarrassed us both.'

'So that's what should happen,' Wolfe finished. 'When I'm finished, I'll be gone. What kind of back door will you three be needing?'

'Depends,' Libanos said. 'How many bodies'll be lyin' around for the heat to notice?'

'None, I hope.'

'It don't matter, really,' Libanos said. 'Me an' Thetis, we'll have half Morne-des-Esses swearin' we were singin' hymns with them. People don't realize there's a whole lot more folks on Trinité than th' rich an' putrid.

'We'll have no problems, Mister Wolfe.'

'I didn't really think you would. Candia, what do you want to do? Since we've been seen being together, you'll most likely have to answer quite a few questions.'

The dancer shrugged. 'I, too, am not unfamiliar with fooling the law. But is that my only choice?'

'What would you rather do?'

Candia looked pointedly at Thetis and her grandfather. Libanos took the girl's arm, ignored her angry glare, and walked out onto the beach house's verandah.

'I'd rather go with you,' the woman said, then held up a hand. 'Wait. I didn't mean for it to sound like it did. I meant . . . you'll be leaving Trinité after you get whatever you want from this Sutro, am I correct?'

'Yes,' Wolfe said.

'I would like a ride to wherever you're going, if I would not be in the way.'

'What about your contract here?'

'Eh! It had only another month to run, and I am getting very bored of that horrible band's *crash-bang-boom* and being dropped by Megaris. I seek other pastures.

'And as you saw, I travel light.' She looked away from Wolfe, out the window, the sunlight a white glare on her face.

'That would be good,' Wolfe said. 'It'd leave nothing but questions with nobody to answer them.' He paused. 'I'd feel a lot better, as well.'

After a moment Candia turned and smiled at him.

They were on the beach. Candia had her head pillowed on his stomach. He was half-asleep, listening to her tell him about her early days in dance and how hard it had been to choose between ballet and what she did now.

'But eventually I thought perhaps I might like to live without constant pain and have a credit or two as well, and so –'

The com buzzed. Wolfe picked it up.

'Yes.'

'I just heard on my scanner,' Thetis's voice said. 'Edet Sutro's ship has just been cleared to land on Thrinacia.'

The sun and Candia and the dappled water vanished, and the darkness drew Wolfe in.

THIRTEEN

The man who'd named himself Edet Sutro grinned jovially as the lifter settled at the dock. 'All right, boys, who plays and who stays?'

One of his bodyguards, whose expensive suit hung like it was still on a store rack, grimaced. 'Me an' Pare lost th' roll.'

'Look at it this way, Baines. You're saving your money keeping away from the tables.'

'Right, boss. Thanks, boss. Three weeks on th' ship each way, plus sittin' in that damned jungle waitin' for a month, and now I'll get to wait till next time we come to town to spin down. I feel *lots* better. Thanks again.'

The big man boomed laughter. 'All right, boys. Let's go see what kind of mischief we can get into.'

The smooth machine went into motion. Two men went up the companionway, doubled to the far side of the dock, looked over, saw nothing, then ran to each end of the pier, hands hovering inside their jackets. The second two went no farther than the top of the companionway and waited for Sutro to come up the ladder. They and the two behind the fence were as big as the bearded man.

If guns went off, it would be their duty to throw themselves on top of him and take the blast if they couldn't shoot first.

The last two came up onto the planking, ignored the others, and turned, scanning across the harbor.

Sutro strolled up the dock as if unaware that he wasn't alone.

'Man takes care,' Libanos said. 'You think we stand a chance?'

'That's what makes life interesting, isn't it?' Wolfe said. They appeared to be two idle strollers considering the rigging of a yacht that just happened to obscure the line of sight between them and the cargo lighter moored at the casino's dock a few dozen yards away.

'Mister Sutro,' Samothrake said, voice as smooth as his slight bow, 'it has been too long.'

'It surely has, Falster,' Sutro said. 'It surely has.'

'I trust your business offworld went well.'

'My business almost always goes well,' Sutro said. 'I spend a great deal of time and care making sure.'

Samothrake looked to either side and came closer. 'There was a man asking about you.'

'Ah?' Sutro beckoned his chief guard, Rosser, over.

Samothrake described Joshua Wolfe, named him. Sutro looked mildly interested, and Rosser's eyes vacuumed the casino. The other seven men pretended to pay attention to the hotel manager, but their eyes were always moving, always elsewhere, waiting.

'Is he here tonight?'

'No, sir. But I do expect him. He is friends with one of our dancers and generally arrives with her before the dinner show.'

'I see. Perhaps when this Mister Wolfe shows up you'd do us both the honor of introductions.'

'I would be delighted.' Again Samothrake bowed, and Rosser, at Sutro's nod, unobtrusively passed him a bill.

'Now,' Sutro said, his voice booming, several passersby turning to look. 'What first? Drinks, then some action, eh?'

His bodyguards chorused enthusiasm, and the small throng moved toward one of the casino's lounges.

Candia stepped onto the dock.

'You'll be right here?' she asked skeptically.

'I'll be back here as soon as I make the call,' Thetis said. 'I promised Joshua. Nobody'll bother me.'

She opened her windbreaker, and Candia saw she had a pistol stuck in her waistband. 'Granddad gave me this and taught me to use it, to make sure I'm not bothered. There's been folks who thought they were buying more'n a run-about when they gave me money. They didn't think that way for very long.

'You just worry about being seen and establishing your alibi, like you're supposed to do. As soon as the excitement starts, you come running.'

The girl and the woman exchanged looks of mutual dislike, then applied smiles, and the dancer hurried toward the casino.

'*Faites vos jeux, messieurs,*' the *tourneur* said, teeth flashing white under his thin mustache.

'*Passe,*' Sutro said, and tossed credits onto that square. There was a gabble in various languages as other bettors chose their lots.

'I like a live game like this. I surely can't stand playing roulette with one of those goddamned robots,' Sutro observed.

'Might as well play a vid game,' Rosser said. The *tourneur* bobbed his head, indicating agreement as he twirled the wheel's cross-handles. At the same moment he spun the small ivory wheel against the wheel's turning.

The ball bounced, skipped, red, black, then red, slowing.

'*Rien ne va plus,*' the *tourneur* announced unnecessarily — most of the numbers were filled. The ball bounced once more, then came to rest.

'*Sept,*' the tourneur said. One croupier pulled in credits with his rake, and a second paid the winnings. Sutro watched his money depart, expression neutral. He held out a hand, and Rosser put another sheaf of bills in it.

'Mister Sutro?'

Sutro frowned at the interruption, turned. Samothrake stood beside him.

'The gentleman you wished to meet will not be in this evening,' the casino manager said, attempting to sound as if the news were personally tragic. 'I was advised by his friend that he is ill.'

'Perhaps another time,' Sutro said indifferently.

'*Messieurs, faites vos jeux,*' the dapper little man said once more.

Sutro sipped champagne, considered the wheel.

'*Dernière douzaine,*' he decided.

Thetis slipped thin gloves on, put a coin in the vid, touched sensors. She fitted a round filter over the vid's mike. As the screen swirled into life, she blanked her own pickup with a square of plas.

Wolfe stepped out of his coveralls and was wearing a skintight black plas suit. Libanos stood beside him, holding a very large, very antique projectile weapon.

'Put it away,' Wolfe advised. 'Nobody needs to see you waving that cannon around.'

Libanos muttered, obeyed.

Wolfe took a dart gun from a small pack, clipped the gun to a catch on the suit, put the pack on, pulled the suit's hood over his head, and went down the ladder into the water.

He entered it without a splash and swam slowly, effort-lessly, across the dark harbor, hands never coming above the water's surface. He swam to the rear of the lifter and then clung to the still-warm drive outlet.

Breathe in . . . deep, deep, diaphragm deep . . . out . . . in again . . .

His heart was a slow, steady metronome.

He reached out, *felt* the man lounging behind the con-trols of the ship, *breathe . . . breathe . . . found* the thin man at the port, eyes watching the dock.

A shadow came out of the water and pulled itself onto the narrow step at the lighter's stern. Wolfe eyed a pickup mounted above him, decided it wasn't turned on, and found the emergency hatch. It was latched shut on the inside. Wolfe pried at it, tore a nail, flinched. He took a thin-bladed knife from its sheath at his waist and gently probed between the hatch and the hull, eyes closed.

The blade met resistance, and Joshua pushed. The latch's *click* was crashingly loud, but only to him.

He looked behind, saw nothing in the harbor that would outline him, and lifted the latch.

Baines grunted. 'Your turn. My eyes are bleedin'.' There was no response.

Baines turned away from the port, frowning, saw Pare's body slumped in the seat, and black blurred at him; a finger speared, touching his forehead, and the thin man folded to the deck.

Wolfe put plas ties on both men's hands and feet, took a red-shielded flash from his pack, and blinked it once, twice toward the wharf where Libanos was waiting.

'Calm down, Dorothy. What is it?'

'A bomb, Mister Samothrake! Somebody planted a bomb here!'

'Don't get excited. No matter what's going to happen,

you won't make it any easier if you get hysterical. How do you know?'

'Someone just called. They wouldn't give me a picture. They said there was a bomb – bombs – and we were all going to die for our wickedness!'

Samothrake's voice remained calm. 'You're new here. We get those kind of things all the time. They're either fruit-bars or kids. What did the voice sound like?'

'I couldn't tell. It sounded synthed. Flat. Maybe a woman.'

'What *exactly* did it say? Try to remember.'

'I can remember.' The woman shuddered. 'I'll never forget it. "Ye . . ." That's what the voice said – ye. ". . . are the spawn of evil, wallowing in your degeneracy. Ye have been called, and there is no escape. I have set bombs to destroy your works unutterably. There shall be one for a warning, then others to destroy everything." That's exactly what was said. I was trained to remember things like that.'

'That's why we hired you on the switchboard,' Samothrake said.

'What do we do?'

Samothrake considered, looking at the thronged gaming floor.

The glowing hand swept across the top of Wolfe's watch, and his thumb touched a sensor.

The 'relay box' exploded, sending metal shattering across the empty attic, the blast tearing lifts, ropes, cascading them down through the false ceiling onto the still-vacant stage below.

Screams knifed from the tourists just beginning to crowd into the theater.

Dorothy squeaked as she heard the detonation, then ran hard for the exit.

Samothrake took a com from his tuxedo's inner pocket and touched a single sensor.

'All stations, all stations. Begin immediate evacuation of the casino. This is not a drill! Security . . . alert the police, advise them bombs have been planted in the casino. I repeat, this is not a drill!'

His voice was still unruffled.

Candia pelted down the dock and jumped down into the *Dolphin*.

Thetis already had the drive on. She cast off the single mooring, reversed away from the dock, and at quarter speed pulled out into the harbor.

Sutro's security element retreated toward the only place they knew to be safe slowly, carefully, skilled combat veterans.

As before, four of the biggest surrounded the fence, while the others leapfrogged each other's movements, guns in their hands, ready.

An old woman saw them, squealed in fear, and limped out of the way.

The men with the guns paid her no mind.

They reached the dock, ran down it. As they did, the lighter's side hatch opened. A man stuck his head out.

'Get the drive started! Some asshole set off a –' Rosser flattened as a metal cylinder tumbled through the air from the lighter. It hit a foot away, bounced, and went off. A thin mist hissed out.

Rosser came to his knees, lifted a gun that was suddenly too heavy, tried to aim at the man in the lighter hatch, and collapsed.

There were other gas grenades rolling around the dock, and men were falling, squirming, then lying motionless.

The two men at the landward end of the dock, rear security, outside the gas's influence, dropped into a kneeling stance. One pulled a wire stock from inside his coat, clipped it to his gun, then went down as a wisp of gas took him.

The other fired, sending a blast of green energy smashing into the empty night, the noise burying the tiny twang of Wolfe's dart gun.

The guard clutched at his throat, tried to find words, half rose, then went down.

Wolfe leapt onto the dock, Libanos behind him, and went to where five men lay. Three were faceup, and he paid them no mind. He rolled the fourth over onto his back and saw the heavy beard. He took out the light and blinked once into the harbor.

He and Libanos dragged the other eight to the lifter, tied them hand and foot, and dumped them into the cargo compartment. Libanos got behind the lighter's controls and keyed switches; the drive surged, and the lifter moved against its moorings.

A few seconds later the *Dolphin* cruised in.

Wolfe picked up Sutro's body, seemingly without effort, carried it to the boat, and slid it down into the stern seat.

He waved to Libanos, who brought the cargo lighter up just clear of the water, spun it, and at half speed headed out of the harbor toward Thrinacia. Wolfe jumped down into the *Dolphin*.

'Any time you're ready,' he said.

Thetis gunned the boat away, and the dock was bare and empty, the last gas mist fading against the glare from the casino as firefighters and police vehicles swanned toward it from ground and air.

FOURTEEN

Edet Sutro's body was strapped to a door that had been removed from its hinges and laid across two stone benches in the mansion's wine cellar. Wolfe touched the tip of a spray to Sutro's neck and pressed a stud.

'He'll be back with us shortly,' Joshua said. 'Candia, would you pack our stuff. We'll be leaving as soon as we finish our chat and Mister Libanos comes back with the lighter.'

'How long do we have?' Candia asked.

'You mean before we have to worry about the law? Probably almost forever. Sutro's boys, being illegals, will take a long time to decide it's okay to go legal and holler for help.

'As for the heat themselves – first somebody with the casino will have to make the connection between me and that bomb, which should take three or four days. About that time they'll start checking everybody who has anything to do with the place, and you'll be the only one who turns up missing. Then they'll play connect-the-dots.

'By then we'll be on our third jump out of here, and the Libanoses will have gone to ground wherever they wish.

'Ah. Mister Sutro has returned,' he said, seeing the bearded man's eyelids flutter. 'Now, if you'll excuse us.'

Thetis had been staring fascinatedly at the bound figure. 'What are you going to do to him?'

Joshua half smiled. 'Very little. Mister Sutro is no fool, and so he'll be more than willing to share a bit of his tawdry past with me.'

The girl hesitated and then, at Candia's frown, followed the older woman out and up the stairs. The door closed with a thud.

Sutro's eyes were open, sentience returning.

'Edet, my name is Joshua Wolfe. I know who you are, what you are,' the warrant hunter said without preamble.

'You're the gambler that was looking for me,' Sutro said.

'I was looking for you. But I'm not a gambler.'

'What, then? Law? FI?'

'Let's say . . . freelance talent.'

'Who are you working for?'

'Since I'm the one who isn't tied up,' Wolfe said, 'I prefer to ask the questions.'

'You won't get any answers.'

'Oh, but I shall.' Joshua pulled up two empty crates and sat on one. He reached in his pocket, took out the Lumina, put it on the other crate between the two. Sutro started and then tried to cover it.

'You remember a thief named Innokenty Khodyan?'

Sutro clamped his lips shut. Joshua put a hand on the Lumina, waited until it flamed high, and fixed his stare on Sutro. The man squirmed.

'I do,' he said. 'He got killed before I could meet him.'

'I killed him.'

'Ben Greet said he'd been taken by a warrant hunter.'

'That's one of my trades.'

'There aren't any warrants on me.'

'I know that. At least not under the name of Sutro. And I don't have much interest in knowing what your parents tagged you with.'

'What do you want to know?'

'Innokenty Khodyan was a pro. He'd hit ten, a dozen

worlds, then go to his fence – I don't know if he always used you or if there were others to dump what he had.

'I'm guessing he mostly worked off tips and the obvious targets.

'He did that on his last run. With one exception. This stone.'

'How do you know that?'

'Sutro, I'm not a fool. You're big, you're good, but I don't think even you would know just where to fence an Al'ar Lumina.'

Sutro didn't answer.

'You know of a man named Malcolm Penruddock? A retired judge on Mandodari III. Crooked, the word had it. He owned this Lumina, and Innokenty Khodyan took it from him.'

'Never heard of him,' Sutro said. 'I bought from Innokenty, bought almost anything he had. He knew what to steal and what it was worth. He never said anything about that Al'ar rock when he messaged me and said he was ready to sell some things.'

'Don't lie, Edet,' Wolfe said, his tone mild. 'You will not be rewarded in the afterlife.

'Who came to you, told you about Penruddock's Lumina, and said they wanted it?'

Sutro shook his head.

'There's two ways I could go,' Wolfe said. 'Three, come to think about it. The messy way, which could get bloody and take a while. The Al'ar way . . .'

He picked up the Lumina and held it in front of Sutro's eyes. The man squirmed, trying to pull away from it.

'Let me remind you of something, Edet,' Wolfe went on. 'I spent six years with the Al'ar. Three as their prisoner . . . and three more before that. Studying their ways.

'Sometimes the Al'ar needed information. Then they'd decide to take a prisoner. You know how often he talked?

All the time, Edet. One hundred percent. Of course, he wasn't worth much afterward. The mind didn't come back like it should've.

'Mostly the Al'ar did the merciful thing and killed them. But a few lived. I guess, somewhere back in the Federation, there's probably still a couple of wards full of those people, rotting, dead except their chests move every now and again. We could do it like that, Edet.

'But I'm not as good as the Al'ar. I might get a little sloppy.'

He paused. 'That's another way. Then there's the sensible way.' He set the Lumina to the side. 'You tell me what I want to know, and I'll give you something that'll maybe keep you alive for a while.'

'Right.' Sutro sneered. 'I go first, of course.'

'No,' Joshua said. 'I'll tell you right now. As I said, this is the sensible way. Penruddock's dead. So's his wife. I was with them when they got killed.'

'Why do I care about a couple of bodies I've never even heard of?'

'Lying again, Sutro. Don't do that.' Wolfe reached out with a finger and ran it caressingly down behind Sutro's ear and along his jaw line. The bearded man bellowed in agony, his eyes going wide in shock like a poleaxed steer.

Wolfe waited until the man's moans subsided.

'They were killed in sort of an unusual way. Two cargo lighters full of gunsels came in at full tilt, strafed their house, then hauled to the spaceport where their ship was waiting. From there, they vanished like they'd never been.

'I thought that was a little exotic a way to do paybacks for a little malfeasance in office.

'Now, the interesting thing, and the reason I think he was killed, was I'd shown up on Mandodari III. I was using my real name, which was a mistake. I'm guessing somebody knew who I was, maybe had an ear on Penruddock's com, and didn't want us to get too friendly.

'It takes money to hire a ship and hitters who don't give a shit if they scatter a few bodies around the landscape.

'I'd be a little concerned if I were you, Sutro, that maybe your client might want to police up the other end of the connection.

'Now you know what I was going to tell you. You return the favor, I unstrap you, and before we lift I'll drop a call to your goons to come get you.

'Then you better think about doing a little running yourself.'

Sutro licked his lips, thinking. Wolfe sat completely still.

'All right,' the fence said after a time. 'I've got no choice, do I? The Lumina was a contract job. You're right. I went to Innokenty, gave him the word, told him what it paid.

'It was a lot, Wolfe. Enough for the stupid bastard to just go in, grab the Lumina and get out.

'But you know crooks. Never steal one thing if they can take a dozen.' Sutro tried to shrug but found the straps confining. 'Not that I gave a rat's ass. I thought it'd maybe put up a smoke screen.'

'So who was the client?'

'You aren't going to believe me. It was the Chitet.'

Wolfe tried to cover his reaction but failed.

'That's right,' Sutro went on. 'Maybe you best take your own advice and think about hatting out of town, eh? Maybe whatever commission you've been offered for whatever you're hunting doesn't look so fat once you realize you're going up against an entire goddamned culture, now, does it?

'Also explains how somebody could afford to hire all those heavies that slotted Penruddock, doesn't it?'

'Thanks for the advice, Edet,' Joshua said dryly. 'Now get back to the point.'

Sutro shrugged. 'One of their sobersides came to me, said they wanted something. They, not he. I asked him if he was speaking for the movement or whatever they call themselves. He said as far as I was concerned, yes. Then he told me the details. I told him I didn't know what he was talking about. I wasn't a man who dealt with crooks, let alone jewel thieves. He must be thinking of some other person named Sutro.

'The man just smiled politely and told me . . . well, let's say he told me enough about myself so I would've been wasting time playing innocent any longer.

'They had a complete file on Penruddock. Who he was, who his wife was screwing, plans of their house, data about their servants . . . everything. The file was like what I'd imagine Federation Intelligence might have.'

'What was their price?'

'Ten million credits on delivery. Plus my expenses.'

Wolfe lifted an eyebrow. 'Penruddock told me he paid only two and a half for it.'

'And he was paying top credit. I've seen – heard, actually – of two or three of those things surfacing, and generally they go out for one and a half, maybe two, outside.

'But who was I to tell the Chitet they were wasting their money?'

'What did they want with it?'

'Come on, Wolfe. I wasn't about to ask that kind of question.'

'Any theories?'

Sutro shook his head.

'How do you know it was the Chitet? Couldn't it have been maybe a dozen of them who'd decided to go into some kind of business of their own?'

'Could have been,' Sutro said. 'But I don't think so. I was given a complete list of com sites to use if there were any problems. There were places on ten, a dozen worlds, plus some blankies I don't know where.'

'So you were briefed, and I assume they gave you a retainer. How big?'

'A mill.'

'That tends to make you take people seriously. What came next?'

'I went to Innokenty and put him in motion.'

'Then what?'

'I waited.'

'Did you have any further contact with the Chitet?'

'That was the only physical contact I had and the only Chitet I ever met. Although he had four security types with him. All dressed like they always do, like they're damned religious caterpillars.'

'While Innokenty Khodyan was off being a villain did they contact you?'

'Two, maybe three times.'

'How impatient were they?'

'I couldn't tell. They were always calm, always quiet. I'd never had anything to do with them before, just read about them. They behaved just like I'd imagined they would.'

'What happened when things went wrong and you found out Innokenty Khodyan was dead and the Lumina was gone?'

'I contacted the main number they'd given me and talked to the voice there. They never turned their vid pickup on. And it always sounded like the same voice.'

'How'd he take it?'

'Weird,' Sutro said. 'I could have been talking about the weather. I had the strange notion that if I'd said I had the Lumina in my hand, I would've gotten the same no-bother comeback, as well.'

'How did they end it?'

'That was strange, too. I was told I could keep the retainer, and possibly I would be dealing with them again in the future. They told me to dump all the information I had, though. They'd come to me.'

'So where's the list of com sites?'

'Wolfe, as you said, I'm no fool. When Ben Greet said Innokenty had been nailed by the law, I jumped out of there and reported. I would have blanked my data even if they hadn't told me to. I've stayed clean because I stay clean.'

Wolfe considered for a moment, then loosened Sutro's straps and pulled one arm free. He picked up the Lumina and held it out.

'Edet, touch the stone.'

Sutro hesitated.

'Go ahead. Nothing'll happen to you.'

Reluctantly the fence obeyed. Once more the stone flamed colors. Wolfe closed his eyes, appeared to listen, then set the Lumina down and refastened Sutro's bonds.

'All right. If you're lying, you're lying to yourself, too.'

'That's all?'

'Not quite. Now, you're going to go through every detail, as it happened, from the time the Chitet came to you, what these men looked like, and everything else until you dumped your files.'

'There he comes,' Thetis said. 'See? From just behind that island five points off north.'

The lighter was a white dot against the blue water and sped toward the island at high speed, not more than two yards above the water, foam frothing up on either side of the hull.

Joshua and Candia's travel cases were stacked on the verandah, and Thetis sat on one of them.

The lighter slowed as it neared the beach. But instead of

berthing at the pier, it cut its drive, skewed sideways, and settled down into the water about thirty yards offshore. The front hatch lifted.

'Get down,' Joshua snapped, pulling Candia sprawling behind one of the cases, then yanking Thetis to the cover of one of the verandah's columns. Bewildered, she crouched. A gun appeared in Joshua's hand.

A man stood in the lighter's hatch. He was not Jacob Libanos. In spite of the heat, he wore sober, dark clothing. He had a neat goatee. A man and a woman appeared beside him. One was Libanos. The woman, dressed in quiet, subdued clothing, held a gun against the old man's side.

A loudspeaker crackled.

'Joshua Wolfe. Please surrender. We do not wish to provoke bloodshed. We know you have the man named Sutro, and we wish to talk to both of you. Do not force us to take physical action.'

'Bastard,' Joshua swore, then regained control. 'Candia, you and Thetis go out the back. Try to find a place to hide. I'll try to stall them. They shouldn't look for you too hard.'

'Joshua Wolfe,' the voice came again. 'Please come into the open with your hands raised. Tell the others in your party to do the same, or else Libanos will be shot. This is not an empty threat.'

'Go on, you two!' Joshua said.

'No.' The voice belonged to Thetis.

Joshua turned his head. She had her small pistol out, aimed at his head.

'No,' she said again. 'We do just what that man wants.'

'Thetis –'

'That's my grandfather! Do what I said!' Her voice was shaking, but it was very determined. Candia started to say something.

'Shut up,' Thetis snapped.

Joshua stared at her, then grunted, spun his pistol out into the open, and stood, lifting his hands.

The two men pushed Joshua into the room. He stumbled, nearly went down, regained his balance. He was naked and blindfolded.

He *felt* four others in the room, but none of them spoke. After a moment a woman laughed deliberately.

For a moment Joshua felt comfortable. That was very much part of the familiar basics of interrogation.

The woman spoke. 'Is it agreed that I speak for the Order?'

Three voices agreed.

'Joshua Wolfe, we desire certain information from you. It is expected that you will not cooperate. Unfortunately, we have but a limited period of time to secure this data, and so we shall be forced to use methods that are normally abhorrent to us, save in the most extreme cases.

'This is such a time.'

Wolfe barely had time to sense the blow before it hammered into his diaphragm. He gasped and staggered, and he was hit twice more, once in the kidneys, then in the side of the head.

He went down, curled, protecting his privates, smelling pine oil from the floor, tasting blood and vomit in the back of his throat.

A kick thudded into his back, another into his ribs. A hand grabbed his neck and twisted it, and three times a fist smashed into his face.

'That is enough. Remove him,' the woman said.

This time Joshua had been permitted to wear a thin pair of pajama pants that might once have been white but now were soiled with bloodstains, filth, and dried excrement, none of it his. His eyes were uncovered.

He was pulled from the room they'd picked for his cell, a large, windowless storage room at the back of the mansion. He had no idea where the others were.

One man held a blaster on him; the other two strapped his hands behind his back with plas restrainers. They frog-marched him down the corridor into what had been the dining room. Wolfe saw his own bloodstains on the polished wooden floor. Now the windows had been covered, and the long table had been moved to the side. There were four chairs behind it. Two of them were occupied, one by a woman, not unattractive, in her thirties, hair worn in a convenient pageboy cut. The man was some years older, with gray close-cut hair and a neat goatee. Both wore quiet clothing that came close to being a uniform. There was a gun on the table in front of the woman.

Two of the guards left. The one who remained was squat and heavy-muscled, with narrow eyes that never left Wolfe.

'Is it agreed that I speak for the Order?' the woman said, no question in her voice.

'It is.'

'Joshua Wolfe, I require you to answer certain questions. You will answer them fully and completely.'

'To whom am I speaking?'

'You may call me Bori. It is not my name but will give you a symbol to use.'

'Where are my friends?'

'They are still alive and are being kept secure. You should be aware that their safety depends on your cooperation, of course.'

'When you have what you need, what do you intend doing?'

'I do not think that pertains to the moment,' Bori said. 'I am the one with the questions.'

Wolfe half smiled.

'You find something funny?'

'I was just remembering something I told Sutro a few hours ago.'

'We know a great deal about you, Joshua Wolfe. About your war record, about your time with the Al'ar, even your activities here in the Outlaw Worlds, although you've done an excellent job of remaining nearly invisible.'

'Since you know everything, then what's the point of our . . . chatting?'

'Tyrma!'

The squat man slashed a knife hand sideways into Wolfe's upper arm. Joshua winced and bit his lip to keep from crying out.

'We have little time or appreciation for humor,' Bori said. 'Now, you will please answer our questions. First, the most immediate matters:

'Are there other bombs set in the casino, as the police believe?'

'No.'

'The reason we asked was because if there was going to be further upset to the order of things, it might be well to immediately go offworld before continuing our interrogation. I suspect you are telling the truth and that first bomb was merely to create a diversion.

'Do you have other associates beyond the ones we secured?'

'No.'

'Where is your ship?'

'Offworld. In a parking orbit.'

'Then you lied. There *are* others in your team.'

Tyrma struck again, this time with a side kick to Wolfe's ankle. Joshua almost fell, recovered.

'How many are there in your crew?'

'Two,' Wolfe said.

'How will you summon them?' Bori held up the bone-mike from Wolfe's gear, and he experienced a faint moment of hope. 'This device appears of too limited a range to reach beyond the planetary surface.'

'I use a conventional com,' he said. 'I place a call through the offworld connection to a certain party on a certain world on a certain link. My ship's computer monitors any com that's broadcast of that nature, and the crew'll land at whatever point I told them to.

'If the pickup point has changed, then I can use any microwave transmitter to tell them where to get me once they're in-atmosphere.'

'Complicated,' Bori said. 'But careful, so I am not surprised. We shall require you at a certain time to summon them.

'But not at the moment.

'Who are you working for?'

Joshua said nothing, stiffening for the blow.

'No, Tyrma. Not now. We shall outline our needs to Joshua Wolfe before we apply further stress.

'Are you working for the Federation? Specifically, are you working for Federation Intelligence? If so, we shall need to know all the details of your mission, including controlling agents and when and how you report.

'Are you working for the Outlaw Worlds' own law enforcement?

'Are you working on a matter of personal concern?'

'I'm following my own trail.'

'Which is?'

'When the Al'ar trained me, they used a Lumina stone,' Wolfe said. 'When I served the warrant on Innokenty Khodyan, I discovered the stone.

'I wanted to know where it came from and where I could find others. That is why I went to Penruddock.'

Bori stared at him, reached under the table, took out

the Lumina, and set it in front of her. 'We shall return to that line of questioning again. I am not sure I accept your story.'

Joshua waited.

'There are stories that not all the Al'ar departed . . . or did whatever they did at the end of the war. Have you heard such tales?'

'I have.'

'Do you believe them?'

'No. I checked on a few of them, found they were gas.'

'We are fairly sure you are wrong,' Bori said. 'Next question: Have you ever heard of the Mother Lumina? Perhaps you would have known it as the Overlord Stone. It would have been some sort of controlling or recording device for all Luminas, perhaps.'

'No.'

Bori considered. 'I am not sure I accept that answer, either. We shall ask it again . . . under different circumstances.

'What do you know of the Secrets of the Al'ar?'

Wolfe lifted an eyebrow. 'Bori, are the Chitet going mad? Secrets of the Al'ar? Like what? Like where they went?'

'Tyrma!'

Again the squat man struck Joshua.

'I was referring to the curiosity show called *The Secrets of the Al'ar*. It is scheduled to perform, or do whatever it does, in a few weeks here on Trinité. It also appeared on Mandodari III not long before we learned, through some of our friends who have not yet joined us openly, of Judge Penruddock's acquisition of the Lumina.

'We are wondering if this is a coincidence or not. We have, as a matter of course, close-sieved *all* matters dealing with the Al'ar.'

'The first I heard of it was seeing something on my com

after I landed,' Joshua said. 'I don't know anything about it other than it sounds like a freak show.'

'Let me ask you something,' he continued. 'If your pet goon won't flatten me for it. What do the Chitet want with Luminas?'

'We do not particularly care about this stone or the others that have surfaced. However, there are matters far bigger and more sensitive behind them that we must deal with. We believe our duty is to all humanity, and we know, and you need not ask how, that the matter of the Al'ar is *not* over and settled.

'I will not explain further, except that the questions I have must and shall be answered and answered truthfully.'

'And then what happens?'

'To you? We shall give you a quick and painless death. It is necessary. At one time, perhaps even after the war, you had ties with Federation Intelligence. They must not learn of the Chitet's activities.

'As for your companions . . . we haven't decided what logic dictates must happen.'

'You sure give me a lot of encouragement.'

'Oh, but we do, Joshua Wolfe. It has been a long time since the war, and perhaps you forget just how wonderful the thought of death ending agony can be.

'Return him to his room. Deal with him as I ordered.'

Tyrma jerked Wolfe toward the door.

In the cell he and one other guard coldly beat Wolfe into unconsciousness while the third man kept his gun ready.

It was hot, hot like a fever dream, when Joshua came back to awareness. The light glared down at him.

He tried to clear his muzzy head, looked about for water.

There was none.

A man's agonized screams sounded, and Joshua thought that might have been what had brought him back to awareness.

He thought the screams came from Sutro.

After a moment, his head lolled and he heard no more.

Again he woke, with no idea of how long he had been senseless.

Again he heard screams.

A woman's voice.

'No. Please. Don't do that to me. Not again. Please. Oh, gods, it hurts too much!'

The words faded into agonized cries for mercy that would not be granted.

The voice was Candia's. Then came a man's guttural laughter.

Wolfe staggered to his feet, stumbled to the door, was about to pull at it, then caught himself.

Breathe . . . breathe . . . the earth reaches out, holds you . . . slowly . . .

His hands moved in patterns through the air for a time. Then he went back to the far wall and sat down. His expression was calm.

'It is not working,' the technician said. 'The sensors in his clothing show complete normalcy, tranquility.'

'Shut it off,' Bori said.

The technician touched a sensor, and the screams ended as the voice synthesizer shut off.

'We shall try another method,' she said. She seemed undisturbed.

Wolfe's body contorted against the straps, his face writhing in pain. There were tiny receivers hooked to his nipples and his lower legs.

'It is a simple matter for the pain to stop,' Bori said, her voice sympathetic, friendly. 'All I need is what you know, and then all of this shall go away, and you will be given water, food, be allowed to sleep.

'Or I can increase the level of pain. Or move the receptors. Men have far more sensitive areas than the ones I am currently having stimulated.'

Breathe . . . breathe . . .

She motioned, and the tech moved a slidepot.

Again Wolfe shuddered, then his body went limp, his expression still.

'Shut it down!' For the first time urgency entered Bori's voice.

The technician obeyed.

'Does he have a suicide block?'

The tech looked at another machine.

'I don't know,' the man said. 'I can't tell. But he's under some sort of control. Look, here on the screen. All synapses were responding as a normal human male should under the applied stimuli, then suddenly it stopped . . . *before* you ordered me to!'

Bori thought for a time.

'Disconnect him. We cannot take the chance of finding out what kind of mind/body power he is using.

'Would drugs be an option?'

'I'm not sure,' the technician said. 'We couldn't just hit him with a hard dose. I'll bet the same thing would happen. Maybe if we started with a small dose, then worked our way up . . . maybe.'

Bori turned to Tyrma, who stood behind her. 'You saw what happened. Physical stress techniques, whether like this or of the sort you are trained to practice, will be of no benefit. I'll devise another approach.'

The squat man looked disappointed.

*

Tyrma and the two guards woke Joshua Wolfe from his stupor and dragged him out of his room and through the ruins of the mansion's living area.

Wolfe wondered what they'd been looking for, decided anything, and concentrated on what would happen next. *Breathe . . .*

Waiting on the dock were Candia, Thetis, her grandfather, Sutro, Bori, the goateed man, and two other Chitet. All the Chitet wore holstered guns.

Wolfe noted that a starship lay in the shallows about fifty yards away and that the hatch was open.

The guards marched Wolfe out onto the pier. He could feel the hot boards under his feet, feel them creak as he walked, and he could smell the sunlight.

'Joshua Wolfe,' Bori began. 'You appear to be impervious to most conventional questioning methods, and we do not have the time for further delays. Nor can we chance taking you offworld with us. Therefore, I am giving you one final option:

'Tell us what you know, now, or else your companions will die one by one.'

'Not my granddaughter,' Libanos bellowed, lowering his head, hands stretching for Bori. A guard had his pistol out and snapped its barrel against the back of his neck. Libanos's knees caved, and he slumped to the dock.

Melting . . .

'Will you talk?' Bori drew her gun.

Wolfe did not answer or move.

'We shall start with the least important, to prove our . . . sincerity, if you will.'

Sutro had time to bring up his hands, shielding his face, before Bori shot him neatly in midchest. The blaster made a half-inch hole in his chest and blew most of his back in a bloody spray across the water. Sutro fell back, splashed into the crystalline ocean, lay motionless. The water around him turned brown, then red.

'Will you talk?'

Again Wolfe made no reply.

The air takes me . . .

The gun swung to Thetis. She flinched, waiting for the blow she'd never feel.

Tyrma shouted a warning in an unknown language.

For an instant Joshua Wolfe was not there but was a shimmer in the soft tropical air.

Bori's fingers touched the trigger stud far too late. The bolt crashed out into the ocean.

Tyrma was the first to die. Wolfe temple struck him, then tapped his chest with the heel of his hand; he *felt* the squat man's heart stop and shoved the falling corpse into Bori, who stumbled back, dropping her gun, almost going into the water.

The guards behind Wolfe fumbled for their pistols. Joshua moved easily, without hurry, a blur, around the first one's side, blocking the second's aim; he drove a knife hand into the first guard's carotid and never heard him gurgle death as Libanos, still lying on the boards, swept the second guard's feet from under him, roaring, grabbing the Chitet in his great old, strangling bear hands.

Bori was scrabbling for her gun, and Thetis kicked her, sending her sprawling onto her back. The woman rolled as she hit, had Thetis's foot, twisted it, and sent the girl spinning, crying out in pain.

The goateed man's gun was lifting as Wolfe came in on him; a fist smash into his biceps paralyzed his arm, sending the pistol clattering to the decking. Wolfe's hand curled oddly, cobra touch, and darted into the base of the goateed man's throat. He tried to scream and sprayed blood through his shattered larynx for an instant before Wolfe's forearm jolted up, snapping his neck.

A blaster went off, blowing a hole into the deck as

Candia kicked out, a dancer's kick, and knocked the gunman into the water.

The last guard's fingers opened nervelessly, his eyes cavernous as the world changed about him, and his mouth opened, perhaps to cry for help, as Libanos shot him in the face.

Bori was the only Chitet left alive on the dock. Wolfe could hear shouts of alarm from the ship's open hatchway but paid them no mind.

The woman rolled to her feet in an attack stance, facing him. Her face was as it always had been, calm, controlled, and then most of her head vanished as Thetis shot her once, then again in the body with her own pistol.

'The house,' Wolfe shouted. He scooped up two of the pistols and shot the guard in the water who was floundering toward the ship, and they went running down the dock as a bolt impacted in the water beside them, steam boiling, curling in the clear air.

Wolfe knelt, aimed, weak hand curled around his gun butt, touched the stud, and blasted a smoking hole inside the Chitet ship's lock. Then he ran after the others.

Libanos was overturning couches, pulling tables up for barricades. Joshua paid no mind, running into the mansion's dining room.

The Lumina was still sitting on the middle of the table. Wolfe went around the table, saw his bonemike on the floor behind the chair, grabbed it.

'Ship!'

'*I hear.*'

'All systems full alert! Lift! Weapons station, full readiness.'

'*Understood.*'

'I will correct. Fire when you clear the water.'

'*Understood.*'

He pocketed the Lumina, ran back to the mansion's

living room, and peered through one of the windows. He saw a pod on the starship opening, speedboat on davits, Chitet with rifles getting into it.

A blaster bolt shattered a column outside, and Wolfe ducked back.

Then the ocean boiled, and his ship lifted off the sea floor and broke the surface, water streaming from it. A concealed bay slid open, and the chaingun emerged.

'Target ... starship. Two-second burst, directly into the air lock.'

'*Understood.*'

The dragon roared, and fire spit from the multiple muzzles of the gun, searing like a cutting torch through the unarmored Chitet ship, then shifting aim, and a thousand more three-quarter-inch-diameter collapsed-uranium rounds ripped through the lock door.

The starship rolled on its side, and flames spurted.

'Pickup!'

'*Understood.*'

The ship moved over the water and across the sand, crushing the gazebo as it hovered closer.

'Open the lock.'

The lock door opened, and a ramp shot out.

Wolfe had Candia by the arm, pulling her toward the ship. Libanos scooped up his granddaughter and, puffing heavily, followed.

They clattered up the ramp, and it slid closed behind them.

'Straight up,' Wolfe snapped. 'Get us out-atmosphere.'

'*Understood.*'

The *Grayle* stood on its tail, and its drive tubes hummed.

Flames mushroomed from the Chitet ship's lock. A moment later the ship exploded. A ball of black and gray, red-streaked, climbed toward the *Grayle*, but not fast enough as it soared toward space.

FIFTEEN

Thetis stared, fascinated, at her index finger. She crooked it.

'I never thought,' she said slowly, 'I'd ever kill anyone. Or how easy it is.' She moved her finger once more.

Wolfe looked at Libanos. The four of them stood on the *Grayle*'s loading platform. Tied up to it was a double-hulled boat older than Joshua, its purpose obvious to anyone half a mile downwind.

Libanos touched his mustache. 'I don't know,' he said. 'I got over it.' He sighed. 'But I think I left something behind.'

'We all did,' Wolfe said quietly.

Thetis looked up. 'I'll be all right, Grandfather. It's just . . . maybe I've led too sheltered a life.'

'Go back to it,' Candia said. 'Sometimes the wild side isn't the best.'

Thetis reached out and took her hand. 'Thanks. I'm sorry about the things . . . the things maybe I thought.' She blushed and jumped down into the fishing boat.

Joshua handed Libanos a thick plas envelope. The old man opened it, saw the credits, and stuffed the envelope inside his shirt.

'What are you going to do next?' Wolfe asked.

'First thing is to have Marf, here, run us back to Morne-des-Esses and find out, real loud, that while we were off helpin' him pull his nets, some cheap pricks stole Thetis's boat.

'After that . . . well, I guess I'll close down the house for a while, maybe go sail around the islands in an old hooker I've got moored outside Diamant, and start lookin' for wood to put up and season for the new boat.

'Read some, think some.

'There's a fishin' village on one of the out islands I may port out of for a while. There was a little boy Thetis was sweet on six, seven years ago. Maybe she'd like to see what he grew up like.

'Then I'll put in for victims' relief and start thinking about rebuilding the *Dolphin*. There's a few things I didn't do quite right the first time around.

'I'll stay out of the line of fire for a while, until this settles.'

'Good,' Joshua said.

'How big a stink is this going to make?'

'Big,' Joshua said flatly. 'Explosion in a casino . . . an island about volcanoed when a starship blew up . . . if they run DNA traces, there'll be a pile of bodies to think about. But I think all they'll be looking for is a gambler named Wolfe and his dancer friend.'

'Wasn't concerned about the proper authorities,' Libanos grunted. 'Day I can't make them dance my tune without knowin' they're jiggin' is the day I'll be ready for the long count.

'I was thinkin' of your friends the Chitet.'

'They didn't make a full report,' Joshua said. 'Not after they arrived here. My ship was monitoring all freqs, and there weren't any out-system coms outside of Wule and Diamant. You should be clean.'

'Let's hope, anyway.' Libanos hesitated. 'Do me a favor, Mister Wolfe. Don't come back anytime soon, hear? Life gets a little exciting with you about.

'A little too exciting.'

As they turned back to the *Grayle*, Wolfe noticed that Candia was looking at him oddly.

'You're sure the dancer didn't have any idea you're on a contract for us?' Cisco asked.

'Positive,' Wolfe said.

'So where'd you leave her?'

'I don't think you need to know that. Somewhere she'll be safe. Somewhere quiet. She said she thought she'd like to try a little quieter life by herself. She said . . . things had changed.' Wolfe tried to smile but didn't quite manage it. 'Cisco, drop her, all right? She's not a player. I want to know how many goddamned Chitet there are, and you keep ducking the question! How far do I have to run, how deep a hole do I have to dig, how many cubic feet of dirt do I have to pull in after me?'

Cisco considered his words. 'We don't know.'

'What do you mean? How many worlds do they have . . . how many ships . . . how many people? Those are pretty simple matters. And what in the hell are they doing icing people for these goddamned Luminas? What do they care about the Al'ar? Or doesn't Federation Intelligence know that, either?'

'We know the size of their culture. But we don't know how many of them have gone outlaw or what they want.'

Wolfe blinked. 'Wait a minute. What do you mean, outlaw? I surely got the idea the woman who called herself Bori was speaking for the entire movement or culture or whatever the hell it's calling itself.'

'We think differently,' Cisco said.

'Why?'

'I can't tell you. To be honest, I don't know myself. All I know is I got the word, from people who're far higher in the directorate than I am, that there's only a few renegades who're calling themselves Chitet, and we're already in the process of rounding them up. We're just giving them a little time and a little rope until we make sure we've got all of them in the net.

'The main Chitet culture is just what it's always been. That's an absolute.'

'So one of your boys called whoever speaks for all the Order, and he said cross his heart, we're all just reputable citizens, eh? About the level of analysis FI usually does.'

Cisco made no response. Wolfe looked hard into his eyes. The intelligence executive met and held his gaze. Wolfe began to ask another question but changed his mind.

'But that doesn't alter the problem I've got,' he said instead. 'It only takes one of them and one gun and I'm history.'

'You're under our cover, Wolfe. Don't worry about them. I've already put the word out, and they'll be dealt with. They won't have time to be messing with you.'

Wolfe looked unconvinced.

'But that wasn't why I wanted a face-to-face,' Cisco said. He got up, walked to one of the *Grayle's* screens, and looked at the huge bulk of the Federation frigate that lay half a mile distant, outlined by far-distant stars. Then he turned back.

'The contract has changed,' he said.

'To what?'

'We've had further developments I'm not able to tell you about. We're doubling the fee, and I'll give you some numbers that you can use to get whatever backup you need, anytime, anywhere.

'When you find the Al'ar, you're to take him out.'

Wolfe was on his feet. 'The hell I will! I'm not one of your goddamned assassins!'

'You've done it before.'

'That was a long time ago!'

Cisco grimaced. 'I'm sorry you feel like that. You know, if I'd had done to me what those bastards did to you, I'd be more than happy to put the last one in his meat crate.'

'You're you,' Wolfe said. 'No deal.'

'You aren't being asked, Joshua.'

'And if I tell you to shove it, I'll be out in the open for the Chitet?'

'That,' Cisco said carefully, 'and very conceivably worse. You don't need FI for an enemy, even out here in the Outlaw Worlds.'

Wolfe stared at him once more, and this time the man looked away.

'Get off my ship,' Wolfe said, his voice calm.

'You'll keep the contract?'

'You heard me.'

Cisco took a microfiche from his pocket and set it down on the panel next to him. 'Here's the contact numbers you might need. You've also got open call on any FI warships in your area if it gets that bad.' He went to the open lock door and started to wriggle into his suit. Wolfe followed him, watched, made no move to help.

Cisco's gauntleted hand was about to snap the faceplate closed, when he paused.

'I'd say I'm sorry, Wolfe. But this whole thing is big and getting bigger. None of us has any choice. Come on, man! This is for the Federation!'

Wolfe made no response. Cisco snapped the plate closed and touched a sensor on the hull. The inner lock door irised shut.

Joshua waited until he heard the outer lock cycle open, then went to a screen and watched Cisco being reeled across space toward the Federation warship's yawning lock.

He thought about what Cisco had just said and wondered again who in the government was so interested in Luminas.

'The question is really, I suppose,' he said, 'how many Chitet are inside Federation Intelligence?'

'I see,' Joshua said thoughtfully. 'So you really don't have any way of knowing when I could book *The Secrets of the Al'ar*.'

He waited while his words and image jumped through several subspace transponder units to the screen on the harried-looking woman's littered desk.

'Not really,' she answered. 'I'm afraid Mister Javits is, shall we say, a bit eccentric. Perhaps that's why he chose to use my agency instead of one of the larger ones.

'All I can do is list your number and Carlton VI, and when Mister Javits contacts me, which he does on a regular basis, I'll inform him of your interest. Then I'll get back to you and we can arrange a contract, security deposits, and so forth.

'Certainly it should be no longer than an E-month, perhaps two. But in the interim,' the woman went on, 'you have the show's past itinerary, and you're more than welcome to check with any of the promoters who've booked *The Secrets*. It's one of my most popular attractions.'

'I'd also like to see the show myself,' Wolfe said. 'I've had friends who caught it, but I've learned to never book anything I'm not really enthusiastic about myself.'

'I'll upload the current tour schedule right now,' the agent said. 'Mister Javits – I've never met him, never even seen him – seems to always be on the road.' She giggled. 'Now, isn't that funny that we still say that?'

'It's better than saying "on the ether,"' Wolfe said, 'or "on the hyperspace" and sound like Space Rangers of the Galaxy.'

'I guess so.' The woman fingered sensors on her keyboard. 'There. It's on its way. Oh, wait. One change that won't appear on what you're getting.

'*The Secrets* was booked onto Trinité,' she said. 'Mister Javits canceled that just two days ago.'

'Oh? Why?'

'He said he has a friend there who told him advance sales and interest weren't promising. He also said there was an outbreak of some rather worrisome virus in the capital, which is, umm, Diamant, which he'd as soon not chance catching.'

'But he does that very, very seldom, so you needn't worry, since I know you'll do an excellent job of four-walling.'

'I hope so. One further question. How many people does Mister Javits use on his tour? I'd like to know that so I can plan lodgings and so forth.'

'To be honest, I don't know that myself. I've only seen holos of the presentation. But you needn't worry about putting people up. The show is entirely self-contained. It's very automated, which is another of the attractions, especially for the younger set.

'All you need provide is an open area, permission from your local authorities for Mister Javits's ship to port there and remain during the duration of the performances, and he'll set up everything else, including a good-sized weatherproofed arena he carries aboard ship. He's a *very* sophisticated showman.

'Thank you for your interest and time, Mister Hunt,' the woman said. 'I'm sure you'll be delighted you decided to book *The Secrets of the Al'ar*.'

'I'm sure I shall.'

The screen blanked, and Wolfe's polite smile vanished.

'So how did I avoid catching this mysterious virus?' he said thoughtfully. 'And isn't Mister Javits just the careful one?'

'Ship, we're going to do some plotting. Stand by.'

'So *The Secrets* did play Mandodari, like Bori said,' Wolfe mused. 'Now overlay the FI projections on where the other four Lumina first surfaced on top of the old schedule.'

'*Done.*'

'Any correlation?'

'*None within your parameters.*'

'Dammit!' Wolfe stood, stretched, walked to one wall, and opened a panel. He looked at the array of bottles inside, picked up a bottle of Laberdolive, read the label twice, replaced it, and closed the panel. He went to a second panel, opened the refrigerator door it concealed, took out a bottle of mineral water, and drank.

'Wait a minute. How long after *The Secrets* show played Mandodari VI did Penruddock report his Lumina stolen?'

'*Nearly a year.*'

'Extend my time parameter to a year between the Luminas' appearance and the tour. Now is there anything?'

'*All four appearances now coincide.*'

'Well, hot damn. I think we're getting somewhere. Now overlay the Al'ar capital worlds and the show's previous appearances. Any conjunction?'

'*Yes, on five.*'

'Including Sauros, where somebody filmed that Al'ar?'

'*Including Sauros.*'

'As a matter of curiosity, is there one of the Al'ar capital worlds within reach of Trinité?'

'*Affirmative. Estimated orbit . . . two jumps. Ship time, four days.*'

'But the Chitet and I messed up that one,' Wolfe said. 'Now, take the current tour and plot Al'ar capital worlds around it.'

'*Done.*'

'How many match?'

'*All of them.*'

'Mister Javits, you aren't *that* careful. What's the nearest one we can reach in time to see the show?'

'*The nearest is Montana Keep. Estimated jumps . . . six. Internal time . . . two ship weeks. Date of appearance . . . three E-weeks. The*

Secrets of the Al'ar *is booked to appear there for two full local weeks.'*

'Make the jumps.'

Joshua remembered a painting. It had gone with his family on all of its assignments and was generally hung just inside the front entrance to their residences. The reproduction was a simple picture showing a clown and a young woman staring at him, an odd expression on her face. The boy had spent hours staring at it, imagining what had happened, who the two were, and what they meant to each other.

The painting crashed to the floor, and the Al'ar soldier's booted heel smashed down on it.

He spoke into a microphone, and a cold synthesized voice came from the small box on his weapons belt: 'Come now or face death! Take only what you are wearing! Nothing else is permitted!'

Joshua's father tried to protest, and one of the soldier's companions backhanded him. His mother screamed then and was seized by two more of the squad.

Joshua took one step forward, and three slender gun muzzles aimed steadily at his chest.

'Young one, move no farther or you will die,' the soldier in charge ordered.

As the Al'ar hurried them down the embassy steps, flames roared from the back of the building.

Two of the Marine guards and their sergeant lay dead in front of the building.

Something else rose in Joshua's memory.

A man's white, pale hand sticking out of the dirt, an ornate, old-fashioned signet ring on one finger. Joshua stooped, slipped the ring off his father's hand, stood. He took a deep breath, picked up the shovel, and finished filling in the grave.

He turned to his mother and gave her the ring.

'Do we say a prayer or something?'

'Who do we pray to?' she asked harshly. 'Can you think of a god worth the words?'

He shook his head and took her arm, and they walked away, past the long lines of mounded earth in the camp's graveyard.

Then he remembered coming back from a work detail and seeing four men outside the hut he and his mother shared.

'Don't go in there, boy. Your mother died about an hour ago. We just buried her.'

It was harsh, but it was the camp way.

Joshua shook his head, disbelieving. 'But she was able to sit up this morning! I fed her some broth.'

None of the men answered.

Joshua managed a breath through frozen lungs. 'What did you do with the ring she had? It was my father's.'

'We didn't find anything like that, son,' one of the men said, trying to sound kind. Joshua knew he was lying.

Wolfe got up suddenly from the control chair and walked down the spiral steps and into the ship's kitchen.

Very deliberately, concentrating only on what his hands were doing, he began making a pot of tea.

The mirrors of the workout room reflected two stools. On one sat the Lumina, flaming brilliantly. On the second was a ripe multistriped melon.

The stone 'burned' higher, and then, for an instant, there was the blink of a hand extending, fingers held together in a knife thrust.

The tips of the fingers barely touched the melon, and it exploded, spraying juice and pulp across the room.

Joshua Wolfe was suddenly visible in the mirrors.

He stared at the shattered fruit, nodded once, and began to clean up the mess.

SIXTEEN

BOMBS ROCK
LUXURY HOTEL

1 Killed as Blasts
Shatter Penthouse

<u>Press for More</u>

Two bombs exploded just after dusk today in two
floors of Carlton VI's most luxurious hotel, the
Hyland Central, killing one hotel employee.

Police are seeking the leaseholder of the hotel's
penthouse to aid in their inquiries.

Dead was Peter Loughran, 45, a long-time
employee of the hotel assigned to the night security
detail.

Police bomb experts said the twin devices were
professionally made and set. The lieutenant in
charge, whose name by government policy cannot
be revealed, said, 'It appears the first bomb went
off in the Hyland's penthouse and was triggered
by Mister Loughran, making a routine check of
the apartments as ordered by the penthouse's
tenant.'

'A few moments later,' the lieutenant continued, 'a second bomb, obviously linked to the first, destroyed a smaller room two stories below.'

Police theorize that the penthouse's leaseholder, Mister Joshua Wolfe, was the target of the attack and the bomb was inadvertently set off by Mister Loughran.

The purpose of the second bomb is unknown at this time, and the room's occupant, a Mister Samuel Baker, who held the room on a long-term lease, is being sought for questioning.

Damage to the hotel was extensive and will require rebuilding of both floors the devices were detonated on.

Little information was available on Mister Wolfe at press time. He was considered a model tenant who kept to himself and never caused trouble. Hotel records as to his profession and employment were non-existent, however, which has aroused police suspicions. He is currently believed to be offworld.

Mister Baker was unknown to any of the hotel employees, and no information whatsoever appears available. The relationship between the two men, if any, is also unknown.

Anyone with information as to the whereabouts of either of these men should contact Carlton VI platentary police at C-8788-6823-6789.

34ERS 45MCS MDU89 QZ3RE . . . IT IS IMPERATIVE YOU COMMUNICATE SOONEST WITH YOUR STATUS, CURRENT DESTINATION, AND ANY FURTHER DATA WHICH MAY BE USEFUL, SO MAXIMUM FEDERATION SUPPORT CAN BE MADE AVAILABLE.

CISCO

'*Standing by for response.*'

'There won't be any.'

Joshua crumpled the page from the one-time pad and pushed it into the trash destructor slot, then turned to the screen with the contract he'd been studying when Cisco's message came in.

'And they say there's no such thing as slavery any more,' he finally murmured. He picked up the lightpen and signed it: Ed Hunt. Then he touched the TRANSMIT sensor.

'Hi-ho. Hi-ho. It's off to work we go.'

SEVENTEEN

Steam clouds hissed up and grew larger as the cargo ship's drive nudged it toward the yellow pillars that marched from the shore deep into the jungle.

'All contract workers, Lock Bravo for immediate disembarking. This is the last call.'

The ship nosed up to the floating dock below the structure, and magnetic grapples clanged. The ship rolled slightly in the sullen surf that washed up on the beach about a hundred yards away.

The ship's lock extended out over the dock, and the portal irised open. The half a hundred men waiting inside tasted the world's air. It was humid, sticky, threatening.

'Lumberpigs first, old lags second, virgins last,' someone shouted. Men picked up their duffels and made their way up the lighter's ramp to the dock and into an elevator.

Joshua slung his carryall over one shoulder, then bent to pick up the square leather-bound case beside him. A dark man who'd been in the same compartment with Wolfe in the short jump from Lectat IV to Montana Keep grabbed the case's handles and lifted.

'Jesu, buddy, what the hell you got in there? Rocks?'

'Books,' Joshua said.

'A reader, eh? Be interestin' to see if you can stay awake long enough offshift t' turn a page. I never can.' The man shouldered his own gear, and the two joined the line snaking off the craft.

A man wearing a protective helmet and an officious expression waited on the dock. He held a notebook and checked names as the men went past.

'Virgins, over here. All new hires, let's go. Come on, virgins,' he said monotonously. Wolfe stepped out of line, nodding good-bye to his acquaintance.

'See you up the Centipede,' the man said, and disappeared into an elevator.

'Name,' the helmeted man said.

'Hunt,' Joshua said. 'Ed Hunt.'

The man keyed sensors. 'Right. You're unassigned, right?'

'Right.'

'Go topside, second companionway to the right, down two levels. Personnel will plug you in.'

Joshua started away.

'Hang on.' The man took a sensor from his back pocket. 'I'm assumin' you followed orders and didn't bring any hooch or high, right?'

'I don't get cooked on the job.'

'Yeh,' the man said, disbelieving. 'Nobody does. That's why we don't gotta shake all you lice down to keep you from gettin' fried and fallin' in the scaler.' He ran the sensor up and down Joshua's body. 'You're clean. Open the bags.'

Joshua opened the carryall. The man probed through it, found nothing. He opened the leather-bound case, then hesitated. He looked up and met Joshua's steady gaze. The man looked puzzled for an instant, then shook his head and closed the case without examining it.

''Kay. You ain't carryin' nothing. Go on or you'll be late for noon meal.'

Joshua went into an elevator, rode it to the top, and stepped out onto the structure's flat deck.

It curled from the shore two miles into the jungle, more

than four hundred feet above the jungle floor, and was made of a series of cylindrically legged segments. The deck under him hummed from hidden machinery. Each segment's top deck had a wide, toothed centerline belt with rough-trimmed logs on it. When the belt reached the structure Joshua stood on, it disappeared into the depths of the building, and Wolfe heard the screaming rasp of high-speed saws and smelled sawdust.

He found the second companionway and clattered down the crosshatched steel stairs.

There were three bored clerks in the office. Joshua recognized a few of the men he'd come out with in lines in front of them. He waited until one was free, then went to him and gave the man his name. The clerk touched sensors on a pad.

'You never contracted with us before,' the clerk said. 'Correct.' It wasn't a question.

'Correct.'

'Have you ever done any logging?'

'No.'

'Any idea where we could plug you in?'

Joshua shrugged.

The clerk looked at a screen. 'I got half a dozen slots. Four of them are in the mill here at base. Two outside. You rather work inside or out?'

'Outside.'

'One's oiler on the treadway. You get bored easy?'

'Yeah.'

'Then that isn't for you. You done construction?'

'Some.'

'Ever drive a crane?'

'Once. Four . . . five years ago. For six months.'

'You kill anybody?'

'Nobody worth mentioning.'

'Pat your head and rub your gut, mister. I'm not joking.'

Joshua blinked, grinned, obeyed.

'Okay,' the clerk said. 'You got separation there. Maybe you'll work out. One of the drivers is going below next rotation, so we need a replacement. They'll show you what you need to know up at the head. If you don't work out, report back here and we'll reassign you. That's assuming you aren't dumped for cause, in which case you go below and become their headache. Here.'

He handed Joshua a blue metal disk and a red bar. He said in a bored litany: 'The red one's your debit card. Buy what you want – we got a thorough company store. It'll come out of your wages before you leave or take any rotation leave below. If you lose it, you'll be responsible for any purchases made by whoever found it until you report it. The blue disk has your bunk and mess hall assignment on it. You'll sleep –' The clerk looked at his screen. '– three legs back from the head. There'll be a set of company regs on the shelf above your headboard.'

'Thanks.' Joshua picked up his bags.

'One other thing, Hunt. You ambitious?'

'In what way?'

'You said you like being outside. You got any interest in being a lumberpig?'

'I don't even know what he is.'

'The cutter. The man down on the ground in the suit. The guy who lasers the trees that you're going to be lifting up to the Centipede.'

Joshua shook his head. 'Not me. Looks like a good way to get dead.'

'It is. That's why we keep looking for new blood.' The clerk smiled. 'Sorry. Bad choice of words.'

There were two smaller beltways on either side of the lumber drag. Joshua stepped on the one churning toward the end of the 'Centipede' and set his bags down.

The smell of cut wood grew stronger and the clang of machinery louder as he rode.

He looked over the railing, down at the treetops. He spotted movement and saw a great leather-winged reptile with a drill-like beak hanging from a branch. Wolfe heard crashing in the jungle and looked away but could see nothing. But the tops of the trees waved frantically. He wondered what beast was passing under the shelter of the canopy.

Sitka GMBH practices the most ecologically sound lumbering possible. The use of the MaCallum-Chambers Logtrain enables you, our most important employee, to work in a relatively safe environment.

The Logtrain, sometimes humorously called the 'Centipede,' is built, segment by segment, from an area accessible to transports, either sea- or air-based, deep into uncut forest. It is therefore possible, from overhead, for your foremen to choose exactly the desired trees and communicate their instructions to the men on the ground, the cutters.

Once the log has been cut, it is secured by cranes at the cutting head of the Logtrain, lifted to the conveyor belt, and passed to the rear for processing.

After an area has been logged of all lumber of the type contracted for, an additional segment will be added to extend the Logtrain by you and your comrades, and once again logging will commence.

We welcome you to this, the most exciting and productive form of logging the fertile Human Mind has yet produced.

It is entirely due to the foresight and genius of Sitka GMBH Founder Harold . . .

Wolfe tossed the pamphlet aside, opened the leatherbound case, and took out a battered volume.

'. . . I thought it was a place
Where life was substantial and simplified –
But the simplification took place in my memory,
I think. It seems I shall get rid of nothing,
Of none of the shadows –'

'Hey! You. Cherry boy!'

Wolfe looked up.

'You want in?' The beefy man held up the game counter.
He had more bills in front of him than did the other three
at the small, stained table.

'No thanks,' Joshua said. 'I'm not lucky.'

The beefy man laughed as if Wolfe had said something
funny. 'You're gonna learn, out here, up near the head, we
all gang together. Ain't no place for solo artists. Except
maybe jackin' off. Best do what's sensible and get on over
here.' Two of the others laughed too loudly.

Joshua grimaced, set the book down, and got up.

'That's better,' the beefy man said. 'Time to learn –'

Joshua booted the chair out from under him. The man
sprawled, rolled to his feet, and charged forward, roaring
like a bull. Joshua knelt, sweep kicked, and the man
crashed to the deck. He scrabbled up and came in again,
fists milling.

Joshua's left shot out in a palm-up fist. The strike hit the
man in his upper chest, the blow masking the darting
motion Joshua's right hand made, two fingers tapping the
beefy man's forehead.

The man's arms flew wide, and he pitched backward as if
he'd run into a wall.

Joshua didn't watch him land but turned to the table.
None of the other three had moved, although one man's
hand was slipping toward his coverall pocket. The man's
hand stopped.

Joshua waited, then went back to his book:

'. . . that I wanted to escape;
And, at the same time, other memories,
Earlier, forgotten, begin to return . . .'

One of the gamblers went to the beefy man and began slapping his face. After a time the man groaned, sat up, then vomited explosively.

Joshua turned the page.

A violet laser blast cut through the green below and sliced sideways into the tree trunk.

'Awright,' the crane driver who'd introduced himself as Lesser Eagle said. 'Now, I've already got my grabs on the upper part of the log. Watch close. The pig'll cut it through on both sides . . . see? It's just hanging on the stub, ready for me. Now, I'm moving in a second set of grabs just above the cut. Got it. Now, there isn't any way that goddamned log is gonna go anywhere, unless I want it to.'

The suited man four hundred feet below moved hastily back as black machinery moved in on the tottering tree, a move echoed in various scales and angles by the screens around the crane cab.

There were three other cranes around the head and the same number of cutting teams down on the ground.

'*I'm clear*,' the radio bleated.

'And I've got it,' Lesser Eagle said into his mike. 'Okay, I'm going to want to fell the tree to the left.'

'Why left?' Joshua asked.

Lesser Eagle looked puzzled. 'I can't tell you that. It's just . . . the right way to do it. Maybe after you've been making lifts for six months or so, you'll get it.

'Maybe not. So when you don't know, always drop it where there's the least amount of crap. Liable to foul your lift or maybe kick up a widowmaker and take out the pig.'

His hands swept across the booth's controls as if he were conducting an orchestra.

Far below the tree trunk broke from the stump to the left. The cable to the upper grab went taut, then the lower one, and the tree came up, swinging to the horizontal as it lifted toward the cutting head. Lesser Eagle swung the boom and neatly set the hundred-foot-long tree into the 'basket,' which in turn brought the log lumber up onto the lumber drag over Joshua's head.

'How about that, my friend? A little different than heaving iron, isn't it?'

'Not much,' Joshua said. 'A little hotter, a little noisier.'

'*Hey, Prairie Flower.*'

Lesser Eagle keyed his throat mike. 'I'm listening, McNelly.'

'*I've been down for two hours. Coming up.*'

'Man, you ain't got no. stamina,' the Amerind said. 'You ought to be good for a double, triple shift, the way you go on about what a great pig you are. Paul the goddamned Bunyan or whoever it was.'

'*Stamina my left nut. You get in this stinkin' suit one time and see how many minutes it takes you to start sweatin' off the pounds. Friggin' Sitka oughta put less money in bullshit and more into air-conditioning.*'

'Not a chance, McNelly. I'm one of the privileged classes. Plus you could stand to lose a few ounces. Make you sexier next time you go below. Who's replacing you?'

'*Hsui-Lee. So get ready for amateur night.*'

Another voice came up on the com:

'*Your ass sucks buttermilk, piglet. I'll spend most of my shift cleaning up your shit. I'll be lucky if I send up more'n a few hundred feet of wood. Might as well have a brush hook as a cutter.*'

Wolfe heard machinery grind, and cables lifted the cutter, awkward in his bulky sealed suit, out of the jungle up toward the head of the Logtrain. Another suit came down into Wolfe's view, close enough so he could almost see through the faceplate. The pinchered arms waved or, more likely, tried to make an obscene gesture, and Hsui-Lee went down for his shift on the ground.

The monster came out of the jungle fast, a gray-green blur that hit the cutter and sent him spinning, life-support and lift cables tangling.

The radio screamed something, then cut off, then:

'Emergency! We've got a man down . . . and some goddamned critter's about to take him! Where's the sonofabitchin' shooter?'

There was a gabble of chatter on the circuit that Wolfe couldn't distinguish. He was the only one in the booth – Lesser Eagle had gone to help another driver reprogram his crane, telling Wolfe to keep his goddamned hands off the controls. 'Let Hsui-Lee take the wood down. We'll get it on the ground. If you want to be doing something, boom over to a clear area and practice tearing saplings out or something.'

Now Wolfe could make out the horror below. It stood about thirty feet tall, on four legs, with a body jutting up from the first two. He thought of some kind of lizardlike centaur, but the beast's upper body was a dark cylinder, its head not much more than an enormous maw of dagger fangs. Four arms scrabbled at the downed cutter.

The man's laser sliced toward the creature, cutting away one arm. Wolfe heard the nightmare roar, then his hands were busy on the controls, and the boom swung slowly, far too slowly, back from where he'd been practicing.

The cutter managed to roll away behind a tree trunk, and Wolfe had his boom over the scene. He slapped the cut-away, and his lower grab dropped, smashing down on the horror, missing the sprawled cutter by two yards.

He heard the howl through the sealed glass of the booth. His hands found another bank of controls, pulled, twisted.

The jaws of the upper grab yawned, lowered, took the monstrosity around the middle, and Wolfe lifted it clear of the ground, the cable reeling it toward him.

The grab bit deeply into the beast's side, and a greenish fluid poured out.

Joshua snapped one control up; the grab's jaws snapped open, and the horror fell, tumbling, down through the tree-tops into the jungle.

Wolfe saw the cables for the downed cutter's suit lift him clear of the jungle. At that moment an explosive round slammed down into the area he'd dropped the beast into, and he heard the dim blast of the gunshot from the deck above.

The booth door slid open, and Lesser Eagle burst in.

'Get the hell out of there and let me –' He stopped, realizing everything was over, and saw the limp body of Hsui-Lee moving past the booth, out of sight to the deck above. Sirens were still shrilling, and the radio was still going on about shooter failure and how in the hell and such.

'Guess you did run a crane before, eh?'

'Once or twice.'

'You figure you pulled the muscle yanking that man out,' the medical orderly said.

'I don't know. All I know is it's giving me grief.'

'Hell. I can't see anything's wrong.' The man hesitated. 'But maybe I better send you back to the mill. Let a real doc make sure. I'm just the local specialist in blisters, burns, and whatever genital rots you lice managed to hide when you took your physical.

'As long as you're back there, you might want to look up Hsui-Lee. I'm pretty sure he wants to give you his firstborn or something.'

*

'Just a sprain, Hunt,' the doctor said. 'You wasted your time coming back here. Get on back up to the head and tell them to put you on light duty for a day or so.'

'Thanks, Doctor.'

'None needed. If I hadn't heard of what you did pulling that man away from that chironosaur, I'd say you were malingering like the rest of those lice outside.'

Wolfe stood, left the small clinic, and went down the corridor toward a companionway. In one hand he carried a large, heavy book. He paused outside an open door and looked in at the sleeping, bandaged man he'd last seen being dragged out of the jungle. He went on toward the deck without waking him.

The two men walked past, the first telling a most elaborate story, the second listening closely. Wolfe slipped out from his hiding place and crept to the high stack of supplies on the structure's deck. He climbed onto its top and lay flat so no one could see him.

The world was dark except for the glare of the search-lights that made a finger of light along the Centipede out into the jungle and the glare of the overhead stars.

He opened the book with the cut-out midsection, took out the small bonemike and transponder, and checked his watch. It was still a few minutes short of the hour.

He turned the set on, checked its controls, and dropped the bonemike's harness over his neck.

'Am I being listened to?' he said in Al'ar.

Nothing came for a long moment, then:

'You are being listened to,' the *Grayle* said.

Joshua sagged in relief. 'It would've been a real pisser,' he muttered, 'if this buildup hadn't paid off.' Then: 'Give location.'

'Just entering atmosphere. I have your location. Instructions?'

'As ordered, you'll land two miles from my location, offshore, homing on this signal. Return underwater until you reach a point no more than a thousand yards distant from me, unless the water is less than a hundred feet deep. In that event, go to the nearest hundred-foot depth and remain on the bottom until summoned.'

'Understood.'

Joshua put away the com link to his ship and slid down from the pile of supplies. He looked out seaward, thought he saw the momentary flare of a ship's drive braking, then saw nothing. He took a tiny bottle from his book.

'Now,' he said. 'Now we CYA.'

'I should've known,' Wolfe's shift boss muttered, 'you were too goddamned good to be true.'

'Sorry, boss. But honest, I wasn't –'

'Hunt, don't lie to me. I can smell the stink of the booze from here. What'd you do, swim in it? Where'd you get it, anyway?'

Joshua looked down at the deck.

'Forget it,' the man said. 'There's never been a logger who wouldn't manage to get himself trashed if he was marooned in space. Go clean up, and in your bunk. I'm not putting you on the cutting head with a hangover. You're docked the day's wages, too.

'Lesser Eagle's covered for you, so you owe him a shift.' The man scowled, then turned his attention back to the data scrolling past on his screen.

Joshua left the compartment and went down to the two-man room he'd been assigned to. His bunkie was out, working. Joshua ran a basinful of water, took off his coveralls, and began rinsing out the extract of bourbon.

'All for the shore who's going ashore,' the coxswain sang out.

There were about twenty men strapped into the seats of the small submarine, and the compartment was about half-full. No one paid any attention to the disgraced shooter who sat at the rear, cased rifle across his knees his travel cases beside him.

The coxswain touched controls, and the port slid shut. The air-conditioning went to high.

'You know,' a man sitting near Joshua said, 'until you suck in good air, you forget how every friggin' breath we take stinks of that goddamned jungle.'

'You been with Sitka too long,' Lesser Eagle said. He sat comfortably next to the three soft cases that held his gear. 'This is ship air, not the real stuff.'

'And what do you think you're going to be breathing down below?' the man said.

'The same stuff,' the former crane operator said. 'But I'm going to be so busy making whoopee, I'll never notice.'

'Bet you ten credits you're broke and back topside in a month.'

'I'll take the bet,' Lesser Eagle said. He grinned at Wolfe. 'The man isn't aware of my resolve.' He leaned toward Joshua. 'You gonna look me up, in my new position of great importance, next time you come below? I'll even buy the first round. Maybe try to decoy you into staying.

'You know, only about half of the contract people fill out their time. The rest get hired away, like me.

'The only reason Sitka knows I'm leaving is the Port Authority was nice enough to buy out my obligation. Otherwise, it'd be *pfft* . . . and no more Injun.

'No reason you can't follow my lead. Slinging cargo nets down there's a damn sight better than breathing wood dust and shit topside. Plus you don't get called lice and worse by the whitehats below.'

'I'll keep it in mind,' Wolfe said. 'Thanks.' He looked out the port. The sub was pulling away from the dock, out of the shadow of the Centipede. Air hissed, controls clanged, and the ocean rose and covered the port. Green changed to black as the ship dove toward the sea bottom.

'Welcome to Tworn Station,' the woman said. One of the lumbermen bayed like a wolf in heat. The station greeter kept her expensive smile firmly in place.

The men swarmed out the lock into the undersea city. Wolfe stayed carefully in their midst.

The sub dock was next to the liner docks, where starships could port after they'd made the underwater approach to Tworn Station, the largest of Montana Keep's five deep-sea settlements. There was a lavish terminal there, plush welcome to the Outlaw Worlds' tourists who came to play.

Outside the terminal Wolfe noted a pair of soberly dressed, mild-looking men whose eyes seemed to meet everyone's and then sweep on.

Wind, blow, soft, not moving the grass . . .

The Chitets' gaze swept across Wolfe and moved on.

EIGHTEEN

There'd never been an Earth sky as blue as the roof of the dome. The 'sun' was that of a spring morning. Wolfe consulted the map of Tworn Station he'd gotten from the Centipede's rec room, oriented himself, and started down one of the winding streets. After a few moments he stopped, frowning. He looked up, checked his watch, then looked up once more.

He remembered one of the slogans of Tworn Station: 'Where the Nighttime Is the Best Time.' Cleverly, while keeping to Zulu time, they'd modified it slightly. 'Day' would be, he estimated, about seven-eighths normal, so the 'sun's' motion was slightly accelerated. The 'moon's' travel at 'night' would be slowed to compensate.

From nowhere a bright ball of flame roared down. Involuntarily, he flinched just as the 'comet' exploded and became flaring letters across the 'sky':

GIRLS
Beautiful
Friendly
Lonely
All Day – All Night
Visit Neptune's Landing

Wolfe shook his head and continued walking.

Tworn Station was built in a series of not quite concentric rings. The streets wound and twisted, creating the illusion of a far larger arca.

Contrary to what the logger in the submarine had said, he wasn't breathing dry, sterile ship air. Instead it sang of cinnamon, musk, cumin, watermelon – spices that tanged his nostrils and appetites.

Music roared, hummed, soared around him, coming from shops, bars, apartment buildings whose doors stood open; in them men, women, and children lounged, sharp eyes calculating, smiles offering:

'Hey, lumberpig . . . how long you been down?'

'Read your fortune, handsome?'

'Get up, get down, get all around, guaranteed pure quill, no habit, no regrets . . .'

'Best lottery odds, right here. Six winners last cycle alone . . .'

'You look lost, my friend. Need a guide?'

Wolfe kept his smile neutral, his gaze unfixed.

A woman passed, smiling a promise that her charms would more than compensate for what she'd do to his credit balance.

The buildings were low, no more than three stories at the highest. Their plas was anodized a thousand cheery colors, but not, Wolfe noted, sea-green.

He paused at the entrance to a small square. Across the way was a bar with an open terrace.

Emptiness . . . void . . . all things . . . nothing . . .

The three Chitet were looking at him. One frowned, searching her memory.

Emptiness . . . nothing . . .

Wolfe felt warmth from the Lumina in its pouch hidden behind his scrotum.

One Chitet turned to the frowning woman. 'Shouldn't we be hurrying? I think we're late.'

The other's frown vanished, and she checked her watch. 'No,' she said. 'We have more than a sufficiency.'

'My apologies. I misestimated. It is this strange "sky" we are under.'

The three went on.

Breathe . . . breathe . . .

'I think,' Wolfe said softly, 'someone besides myself may have outthought Mister Javits.'

He crossed the lane and went through the outside tables and into the bar.

There was one man inside, his head on a corner table, snoring loudly. The three women at the bar spotted Wolfe. The blondest and fattest got up and came toward him, chiseling a smile through her makeup.

'Afternoon, big man. Are you as dry as I am?'

'Drier,' Wolfe said. 'What kind of beer do you have?'

She began a long recital. Wolfe stopped her after a few brands and chose one. She went to the bar, reached over it, touched a sensor. A few seconds later the hatch on the bar opened, and a glass with a precisely correct head on it appeared.

'I'm partial to champagne,' the woman said, trying to sound throaty.

'Who isn't?' Wolfe agreed. 'Buy what you really like. I'll pay champagne prices.'

The woman chuckled. 'I drink beer, too. But it's perdition on my hips. Easy on, hard off.'

Paying no attention to her wisdom, she tapped the sensor and drank thirstily when the beer emerged.

'So you're with Sitka?'

'How'd you guess?'

'There's nothin' out-system due till tomorrow, and gen'rally, this close to the port, we get 'em first thing. How long you been loggin'?'

'Three weeks.'

The woman looked disappointed.

'Something wrong with that?'

'I shouldn't say . . . but the longer you been topside, bein' chased by lizards, the readier you are to do some serious carryin' on.'

'And the more credits you have to do it with,' Wolfe suggested.

'That, too, honey. That, too.'

Wolfe took a drink of beer.

'Who were those three prune faces that came past?' he asked. 'Hard to believe they're in a place with Tworn Station's reputation.'

'Hell if I know. They call themselves Chitet. Some kinda straitlaced bunch from back toward the Federation. Dunno if they're a religion or what. There's a whole cluster of 'em down here. Along with their leader.

'I read somethin' on the vid says they're here investigatin' the possibility of settin' up their own dome. More gold to 'em, but I can't see what they'd spend their time doin' down on sea bottom.'

''Sides poundin' their pud. They surely ain't the sort interested in ballin' the jack, man or woman. I could have more fun with a vibrator.

'Damn dull. How many of you come from topside?'

'No more'n twenty,' Wolfe said.

'Damn.' The woman made it into a two-syllable word. 'That ain't enough for a circle jerk, let alone any kinda party. Hope to hell the liner's got some hard-chargin' folks aboard.

'So what's your pleasure, mister?' She smiled hopefully. Her breath wasn't the freshest.

'Another beer . . . and could I use your vid? I haven't been paying much attention to the world lately.'

The woman looked disappointed. 'Should've guessed something like that.'

She brightened a little when Wolfe handed her a bill. She got him another beer and the slender plas block he'd asked for. He found a corner booth where he could see the door, sat down, and keyed the vid.

The man's expression was calm, assured. He was bald, looked to be in his early fifties, and appeared to be no more than a successful businessman. Wolfe looked more closely at the thumbnail on the vid. There must have been some glare from the camera, he decided, that created the strange glitter in the man's eyes.

He touched the sensor for PRINT instead of SPEECH, then the tellmemore.

Chitet Master Speaker Matteos Athelstan, in an exclusive interview with the *Monitor*, said he was most impressed with the citizens of Tworn Station and was so delighted with the cleanliness and recreational opportunities available under our fair dome, he said he was allowing his entire detachment, from all three of the Chitet ships currently docked at Tworn Station, liberty.

He said he hoped the citizens of Tworn Station would take the opportunity to share their lives with his men and women and expressed hope that some of our people might be interested in the Chitet philosophy, particularly as it pertained to economics.

'Very quietly, we are practicing the way of the future, leading the way out of the ruins of the past,' Master Athelstan said. 'Our way has already been embraced by many billions of people throughout this galaxy, and their changed lives have increased their liberty, clarity of thought, and, most importantly, economic well-being. Since

my election three years ago, we've been able to
increase our membership a thousandfold. In
addition . . .

Wolfe touched a sensor, and the screen cleared. He keyed
CALENDAR:

New Show-All Spectacular at Rodman's . . .
Two-Way Theater Opens in Surround-Dome . . .
Men-Only Revue and Dancing at Scandals . . .
Holo-Poker at Newtons . . . Art Museum Hosts
Second Mayan Empire Display . . . The Secrets of
the Al'ar . . .

He hit PAUSE and reread the last entry carefully He
thought for a time, trying to decide if the trap was for him
or for larger game.

Leaving his beer half-finished, he put the vid down, got
up, and left the bar.

The heavy blonde watched him leave, a sad expression on
her face. The man in the corner was still snoring.

Wolfe counted four Chitet around the main entrance to the
prefab building that had been erected on the tarmac next to
the ship and guessed there'd be more.

Breathe . . . breathe . . .

His soul divided

*Fire . . . burn low . . . burn quiet . . . embers only . . . ready to
flare . . .*

. . .

*Nothingness . . . void . . . less than space . . . all matter is
here . . . there is nothing . . . no particles, no sensation . . . the soul
is vacant . . .*

A knot of tourists came down the wide avenue leading
to the docks, saw the color-flashing holobanner, and

crossed to the entrance booth Wolfe was unobtrusively among them.

He fed coins into the slot and entered.

An Al'ar in combat harness appeared in the darkness. Its mouth gaped and it spoke, but the words were not the real speech but instead a simulated garble. The purported translation hissed into Wolfe's ears:

'You of the Federation . . . you have spent too long in your lazy ways . . . now we of the Al'ar have come to challenge you, to destroy you.'

Wolfe's expression was blank.

'Little is known of the Al'ar ways or their culture. Only a few men and women learned their language, and even fewer were permitted to visit their worlds.

'Of those few, most were diplomats or traders, and unfortunately all too many of them were caught up and went to their deaths in the first days of the war.'

Figures ran across the screen. Wolfe lifted his hand until it was silhouetted. It was trembling slightly. He watched it as if it belonged to someone else.

'After the first surprise attack,' the narrator said calmly, as if the spinning, shredded Federation ships in the middle of the darkness did not exist, 'and the total loss of four Federation battle fleets, humanity was put on notice that there could be but one victor and one loser in this war.

'So man girded his loins for the greatest battle that would ever be fought . . .'

There was a field of bodies.

'The Al'ar did not realize, or did not care, that these men and women were trying to surrender.

'But there was a worse fate than death. Some humans

were captured by the Al'ar. No one knows what tortures they were subjected to, for only a few were rescued or managed to escape.'

The screen showed a slumped woman. Involuntarily, Joshua flinched. Twelve years before he had led the team that had rescued her and three others.

Breathe . . . breathe . . .

The red blotches on the starchart shrank and shrank.

'Little by little,' the narrator went on, 'we drove them back and back, off the worlds they'd conquered, back from their outpost planets, and we attacked what the Al'ar called their capital worlds.

'The Federation came in for the death stroke. Huge fleets, thousands of ships, many millions of fighting men and women closed in for the final assault on the Al'ar sanctuaries.

'And then . . . then the Al'ar disappeared.

'No one knows where they went. The ships offworld exploded as one, as if they'd all had bombs aboard, fused to detonate at the same time.

'The handful of Al'ar we'd managed to capture simply disappeared. No prison camp sensor showed any sign of where they could have gone.

'Similarly, when reconnaissance teams were sent down onto the Al'ar capital worlds, they found nothing.

'There are tales that food was found on tables, that Al'ar machinery was running, that their weather control apparatus was in operation.

'These are all false. In fact, it was as if the Al'ar had decided to leave and, before their departure, had cleaned, shut everything down . . . and then simply vanished.

'Where did they go?

'Why did they go?

'There are no answers.

'The Al'ar are gone . . . and they took their secrets with them.'

The starchart vanished. There was blackness, then the lights came up. There were only a handful of people in the circular theater with Wolfe. One of them was a Chitet who looked at Wolfe but did not see him.

'You are invited to visit our museum behind this chamber,' the synthed voice said. 'Also, on your way out, we welcome you to our gift shop and hope you will recommend our exhibition to your friends.'

'Not bloody likely,' one of the tourists who'd entered in front of Joshua grumbled. 'Secrets of the Al'ar . . . by Mohamet, I thought we'd find out how they screwed or something.

'This is just like friggin' school and history shit!'

His friends laughed, agreed, and went out.

Joshua lingered in the narrow corridors of what the voice had called a museum, paying little attention to the mostly false relics, the battle souvenirs, the holopics, which were as tacky as everything else in the show.

He *felt* something – he didn't know what.

Not fire . . . not water . . . not void . . . not earth . . . not air . . .

His hands were curled, held slightly away from his body. He walked strangely, each foot sweeping in, almost touching the other, then out into a wide-legged stance.

There was something . . .

There was nothing . . .

He came to a passage, looked down it, took a step.

A wall fell away, and the Al'ar came at him, its grasping organ blurred in a death strike.

NINETEEN

But Wolfe wasn't there to accept the strike.

He ducked, stepped in, and stood, launching his own attack. But the Al'ar had stopped in midstrike and spun away.

Time found a stop.

Wolfe was the first to speak.

'Taen!'

The Al'ar's head moved slightly. His hood was fully flared.

'You have "seen" me, Shadow Warrior.' The Al'ar changed to Terran. 'And I recognize you, Joshua Wolfe.'

Neither relaxed.

'Have you come to kill me?'

'I was hired for that task . . . not knowing it was you I would find. But it is not a duty my body shall fulfill.'

The Al'ar slightly lowered his grasping organs. 'I should have known that if you survived the war, you would be the one to find me.'

'How did you live?' Wolfe asked.

'Better to ask why,' Taen said. 'Although that is a question I do not know the answer to. Please speak Terran. For the moment I do not wish to be reminded of what is in the past.'

'Sentiment? From an Al'ar?'

'Perhaps. Perhaps that is why I was . . . left,' Taen said. 'Perhaps I had become tainted by my interest in the life of groundworms. Perhaps I was deemed unworthy to make the Crossing. Or perhaps there is another meaning I have not yet discovered.'

'You know you're in one hell of a trap,' Wolfe said. 'And now I'm in it with you.'

'Those men who dress like **hanthglaw**?'

'Yes. They call themselves Chitet.' Wolfe half smiled, remembering the Al'ar primitive creature who kept the colors of whatever he slid across.

'I first *felt* someone was on my trail some time ago,' Taen said. 'When I *felt* you enter my realm, my exhibition, I thought you were the only hunter. But now I can *feel* the others out there.

'It is truly an excellent trap, well laid to take us both, here beneath the water, inside this dome. I fear we shall have to abandon this craft. Not that it matters. I have Federation monies to build a hundred more like it and know the location of many derelicts.

'But that is for the future, and their plan will not be set in motion for a time, so we may speak of the past and determine what actions must be taken next.

'It will take some cleverness for us to escape this snare of theirs. Unless you wish to reverse your intent and attempt to continue the task you were first set and grant me the death. I will warn you, I do not think you can accomplish it, even though your movements are far better than when last we exchanged blows in learning.'

'I do not intend to kill you. And the Chitet weren't the ones who hired me.'

'The Federation?'

'Yes.'

'So where do these Chitet come into consideration?'

'I don't know exactly. They captured me on a world called Trinité and interrogated me.'

'So it was you who caused all the upset with exploding spaceships and such matters. I saw some of what had happened on the vid and decided that that was no place for one such as myself to appear, even though I thought it had great promise in my search.

'So like a gowk, instead of – what is your phrase? – going to ground and seeing what would come next, I continued my rounds.

'You see how blind a being can become when he is alone and frantic?'

'I never heard you talk like this.'

'I was never unable to *feel* another one like myself, either.'

'You said the Crossing. What does that mean?'

'Those are the . . . realms, but that is not the correct word, and I find none in my Terran speech . . . for where my people have gone. But they have gone on, as they once entered your space.'

Wolfe stared at the Al'ar for a long time. 'You – your people – were not of this spacetime?'

'Of course not. How else were we able to move on so easily? Although this time it was into a far different dimension than what you term spacetime.'

'Are they gone for good?'

'Yes. Or, I think so. Let me give you a comparison that you showed me once in one of your books of Earth. Can a butterfly become a larva? Even though what happened cannot be compared to a growing. It was merely a necessary change.'

'Because we were about to defeat you?'

Taen was silent for a long time. He moved his grasping organs together, rustling, like dry wheat.

'Just so. Just as we were forced out of our previous . . . dimension.'

'This is a great deal to understand,' Joshua said. 'And I think I now know more than any other man.'

'That is not unlikely. So come. I will make you a vessel of that potion you so loathed and forced yourself to drink to learn more about us.'

Joshua managed a smile. 'At least, drinking that **valta** crap, I won't know if you've poisoned me.'

'That thought occurred to me as well.'

'It is as terrible as I remember it,' Wolfe said, sipping. 'Worse, even.'

'I often wish,' Taen said, 'I could have understood what you termed humor. It seemed a comfort in times of great stress to your people, and I thought it might be helpful to me.

'But there is no such possibility.'

The two had left the museum and gone back through the building that extended from and was part of Taen's ship. It was the same one Wolfe had seen in Cisco's projection, a time that now seemed far distant.

The Federation craft had been modified internally until it had duplicated Al'ar ships Wolfe had been aboard, bare except for controls and minimal comforts, walls moving with ever-changing eye-disturbing colors. Taen crouched on the spidery rack the Al'ar used to relax on. Wolfe perched on another unit.

'When the war began,' Taen said without preamble, 'I was considered suspect. Perhaps it was because I attempted to speak to the Elders about you and your family and others. They thought I had become contaminated.

'I had not. I merely knew if we did not treat nonfighters with what you told me was called kindness, the Federation forces would fight more strongly, more cleverly.

'But they paid no mind, and so the situation was as I predicted.'

'You know my parents died in the camp.'

Taen inclined his head but made no response for a moment. 'I did not know that. But I knew that you escaped. That was when they allowed me to become a fighter, after the Elders had seen evidence of your thinking, of what we had taught you. I was put in charge of a unit intended to find and destroy you.'

'I wondered,' Wolfe said, 'about something like that. As the war went on, several of the . . . projects I mounted encountered difficulties. I thought then that possibly you, or some of your other broodmates I met and sparred with, had been tasked to hunt me.'

'But we never came close,' Taen said. 'I think we held you in too much contempt, as we held all Terrans. After a time the unit was broken up, and we were sent to other duties.

'I became a . . . a predictor of events. When your fleets closed on Sauros, I was in a tiny ship, one that even your sensors could not detect, far offworld, waiting to give estimations of vulnerability to our fleet commanders. The link was sealed . . . and then . . . then I lost all contact.'

Once more Taen moved his grasping organs together. Wolfe felt dryness, despair, a dying echo, across the chamber.

'Strange,' he said. 'I was just below you. On the ground. Doing much the same task.'

The Al'ar uncoiled violently from the rack, eye slits wide, hood flaring. 'What did you see? What happened?'

Joshua thought he could *feel*, behind the toneless Al'ar accents, desperation.

'I saw nothing. I was hidden. All I knew was that all your jamming, all the communication bands I was monitoring went blank.

'Then there was nothing.'

Taen returned to his perch. 'Then there was nothing,' he echoed.

Joshua picked up the bowl again and sipped at the sharp bitterness of the **valta**. 'What did you do then?'

'I waited until my screens showed that all Federation ships had left the system. I used my emergency power to land on Sauros and find a ship.

'That ship led me to another, one of the Federation ships we had captured and outfitted as a decoy. This craft.

'I fled deeper into our space to a factory world. I activated the machines, set them to building this . . . mummery, I think is the word. I had the machines build me other machines so all this could be run by one being, and actually I am not required beyond the instant to start the apparatus. All else is automated, roboticized. The idea came to me within a short time after my people had . . . left.'

Wolfe had the queer idea that Taen had wanted to say 'abandoned me.' He said nothing.

'Since I must travel in the ways of the groundworms, I remembered a story you had once told me, about how a smart Terran hid something from someone right out in the open. That is why *The Secrets of the Al'ar* came to be. Who would dream an Al'ar would dare to display himself so openly?

'Perhaps the idea is clever, although I must tell you, if I shared any of the emotions you tried to tell me about, disgust would match my sentiments as to what I am doing.'

'That's the question,' Wolfe said. 'Why are you doing what you're doing? What are you looking for?'

'I do not know if I should tell you that. But I knew the link, the place I would find a clue, would be somewhere between the worlds of the Al'ar and the worlds of man. I will find a matrix someday.

'I must.'

Once more Wolfe felt desperation.

'I didn't tell you,' he said, 'just what the Chitet were interested in.' He stood, turned his back, unfastened his clothes, and took out the Lumina.

'Ah,' Taen said. 'You have one of the stones I sold for my expenses. I would guess you have been using it to increase your powers.'

'How did you sell them?'

'It took me a time to establish a method. I watched those who came to see my show, then utilized the resources any computer can access to find out more about them.

'Eventually I found a man more interested in money than in where the Luminas came from or who provided them. He had no problem doing business with a being he never met, never even saw on a vid screen. He remained honest only because he knew if he cheated me, his source of riches would vanish. No doubt he also assumed that I would hunt him down and slay him.

'Unfortunately, he died in what appeared to be an accident some time ago. I should have been suspicious and investigated more fully.

'No doubt if I had, I would have discovered the presence of these Chitet earlier.'

'Taen, you are trying to avoid what we must talk about. The Chitet asked me about a Mother Lumina, something they also called the Overlord Stone.'

Taen made no response.

'Another man, a man the Chitet murdered, was looking for the same thing. Is that what you want, Taen? Is that what you're looking for?'

'That is what I seek,' the Al'ar said reluctantly.

'For what end?'

'I am not sure yet. But it has a . . . congruence on the Crossing.'

'Will you know what to do with it when you find it?'

Taen turned his face away from Wolfe, hood inflating slightly.

'Goddamit, answer me!'

'No,' the Al'ar answered. 'But there will be those who shall.'

'Other Al'ar?'

'Yes. Not all of us were permitted to cross.'

'Who are these others?'

'I do not know them. I was never told directly of them. But they are the Guardians.

'If they exist, if what I believe is the truth and not a story that keeps me from turning on myself and tearing my own vessels of life apart.'

'Other Al'ar,' Wolfe said, returning to Terran. 'Why did they remain? What are they guarding? Why was this Overlord Stone left behind?'

'I do not know the answers to any of your questions. When – if – I find the Mother Lumina, perhaps I shall hold some.

'But I *feel* we are running short of time. This dome's day ends. These docks will be deserted soon. Then they shall attack.

'We must ready our welcome.'

TWENTY

'We may have one slight advantage,' Joshua said. 'Since we have information they want – or you do, anyway – they'll be trying to take us alive.'

Taen held out grasping organs, moved them from side to side: scorn.

'It has been far too long since you have been subjected to the inexorable logic of war. Perhaps you no longer deserve your Al'ar name.

'I am the one with the knowledge, or so they must believe. Therefore, your presence becomes superfluous.'

'Thanks for the correction,' Wolfe said dryly. 'Not that I planned to be around for further tender mercies in an interrogation chamber.'

'Nor I, although no Terran can know how to torture an Al'ar.'

'And thus we reassure the other.' Wolfe once more checked the loading of the medium blaster he'd smuggled down from topside and then inserted gas plugs in each nostril.

'I have a question, Shadow Warrior. I have a special suit that I wear when I fear being seen by Terrans. It gives me a very human appearance. Should I don it? I would rather not, since it restricts my movements.'

Joshua considered, then grinned. 'Go naked. The shock value might keep both of us alive a few seconds longer.'

'That is a cunning thought,' Taen said.

The Lumina on the table flared.

'Do you have any idea what that might signify?' the Al'ar asked.

'Not sure,' Wolfe said. 'But I'd guess the Chitet have a Lumina of their own. Probably they're sitting around staring at it, thinking into it, hoping it's some kind of weapon. I doubt they've had a lot of one-on-one contact with Al'ar before. For all I know, they think they've got some kind of crystal ball.'

'Which is?'

'Something frauds use to befuddle fools by pretending to predict the future.

'All we need to know is they're getting ready to hit us.'

'Since no one knows the exact power of a Lumina,' Taen said, 'I'd first suggest that we communicate only in Terran, unless circumstances dictate otherwise. Perhaps they might be able to track me by my speech. I do not know. But I think it is time to take some action to disrupt their strategy.

'If the station authorities had not disabled my drive when they permitted me to bring my ship into the station, the solution would be simple. I have more than enough power to punch through this dome.'

Wolfe stared at the Al'ar. 'And what about the ten thousand or so people in the dome who don't share our feud?'

'What matter they? I do not know them. And they are not Al'ar.'

'Sometimes I forget,' Wolfe said, 'just what made your people so lovable.

'But there's an idea there.'

There were three 'moons' overhead: violet, orange, yellow. The programmers of Tworn Station had decided to add exotica to this 'night.'

The ship and its attached, extended structure sat in dimness. There were overhead lights along the lanes on either side of the square, and other lights gleamed from the nearby port terminal.

A few passersby paused, looked at the darkened marquee with disappointment, and looked for other pleasures.

Music came faintly, dissonantly, perhaps from a distant calliope.

Here and there in the shadows there was slight movement. A gun barrel gleamed, moved back into darkness.

A tiny hatch atop the ship's hull opened, was seen.

'Stand by,' a Chitet section leader said into his throat-mike.

Something soared out, throwing sparks, smashed into the top of the dome, and bounced back, and the signal flare exploded. White light flooded the station, brighter than the 'sun's' day.

Night observation devices flared, overloaded, went to black, died. Men and women staggered, blinded, seeing nothing but red.

The ship's hatch slid open, and two beings darted out, bent low. A blaster bolt smashed into the deck beside them.

'Only the Terran,' Wolfe heard someone shout. 'Don't shoot unless you're sure!'

A man came up, pistol in a two-handed grip, and Wolfe cut him down. There was a woman behind him, aiming a gas projector. She fired, and the projectile bounced out, spraying a white fog. Taen's weapon, a long slender tube that fitted over one of his grasping organs, buzzed, and the woman screamed and fell, most of her chest seared off.

They ran down the passage, hearing shouts and the clattering boot heels of pursuit.

'You should have walked your escape route as I did,' Taen said.

'I . . . wasn't planning on getting out this way,' Wolfe panted. He turned, sent four bolts at random to the rear, and ran on.

There were milling men and women coming out of doorways, shouting, screaming as the flare overhead died. Some recognized the corpse-white Al'ar, and their shrieks added a new terror to the swirling throng. Gunfire boomed, the screams grew louder, and Wolfe saw a young man gape in disbelief at the bloody mess that had been his knee.

They came to an open square with a deserted bandstand in its center. They ran toward the bandstand, and six Chitet rose from concealment and rushed forward, encircling them.

Wolfe went airborne, his feet lashed out, and he felt bones shatter. He let himself land on the body, scissor kicked the second attacker's feet out, and pulled the woman down on him as the third's rifle butt crashed down.

The woman grunted, and Joshua rolled from under her and was up. He sidestepped the weapon's butt strike. His hand reached and then touched the rifleman's elbow; he shouted, and the weapon fell from pain-numbed fingers.

Wolfe's right hand came out in a finger strike, and the man bent double, trying to suck in the air denied him as Wolfe's left hand tapped the back of his skull; the corpse fell limply to the decking.

Wolfe recovered and saw the fifth man's body spasm as if electrocuted. Taen's grasping organ flashed out once more, and the sixth Chitet contorted and dropped.

Wolfe and Taen ducked for cover, and a blaster bolt from behind crashed into the plas wall above them.

'We appear to be cut off,' Taen said, and fired a long burst behind himself.

Not far from the blackened crater the bolt had made was a panel, one of hundreds scattered through Tworn

Station. Wolfe had seen them; then their commonality had made them invisible.

On the panel were three sealed boxes, one labeled FIRE, the second DOME LEAK, the third GAS. Under them was a warning:

EMERGENCY ONLY
Any person who knowingly sets
off a false alarm will be prosecuted
to the fullest extent of the
Tworn Station Authority.
The most severe penalties will be sought,
including fines, imprisonment, loss of citizenship,
and banishment for life.

'When in doubt,' Wolfe murmured, and shot all three boxes open.

The night went mad. Sirens howled, screamed, clanged. Doors crashed shut. Partitions arched up from the deck, closing off the dome.

'Come on! For the port!'

Lasers flashed overhead, to the side, and then steel walls rose smoothly, above a man's height, blocking Chitet pursuit, continued to rise higher still until they touched the 'sky,' partitioning the dome and sealing Tworn Station against the anticipated blowout.

Wolfe ran for the dome wall, pushing his way through the crowd that had poured from nowhere.

'To your stations ! Emergency stations!' a man bayed. He saw Wolfe, the gun, then the Al'ar. He screamed something, reached into a pocket, and Wolfe snap kicked him into a wall.

The dome wall was just ahead, and a blister yawned open.

'Inside!'

They dove into the survival pod as a gun blasted behind them. The pod was a thirty-foot-long cylinder with a rounded front and a squared rear. There were four rows of plas seats with safety harness and a small control panel with a single porthole above it. The air lock's gray metal was visible outside. Wolfe slammed the SEAL sensor, and the pod's hatch hissed closed.

'Did you know this was here?' Taen asked.

'I didn't. But there had to be something,' Joshua said. 'Shut up. I'm trying to figure out how this bastard works.'

He scanned the panel, ignoring the flashing lights, touched sensors, swore when nothing happened.

One panel was blinking insistently:

DO NOT LAUNCH WITHOUT AUTHORITY PERMISSION! DO NOT LAUNCH WITHOUT AUTHORITY PERMISSION!

There was a crash as the unknown gunman outside sent another shot into the pod.

'Over there?' Taen suggested.

Under the controls was a square box marked OVERRIDE. Wolfe ripped it open, saw old-fashioned manual knife switches, and snapped them closed.

The world lurched beneath him as the pod rolled out into the lock. Wolfe heard the clunks of another pod being moved into position as the lock cycled them out of the dome. Water frothed outside, rising to cover the porthole, and there was nothing but black.

Again the world roiled, and he stumbled, grabbing one of the plas seats to steady himself.

Taen curled himself into one of the seats.

'Your departure from the station was successful,' a synthed voice intoned. 'Alarm signals on all standard distress frequencies are being automatically broadcast.'

Wolfe swallowed, equalizing pressure as the pod shot toward the surface.

'And what happens next?'

'We surface, and I call for my ship. Then we get the hell out of Dodge.'

'And after that? What are your long-range plans?'

'I would dearly like,' Wolfe said, 'to see tomorrow or maybe the week afterward.' He became serious. 'I don't have many options. Federation Intelligence will be after me for not killing you, and the Chitet won't give up.

'I guess there's only two things possible: Either I start practicing how to become invisible on a full-time basis or else go looking for this goddamned Mother Lumina that's got everyone on a skewed orbit.'

'Are you suggesting,' Taen said, 'that you become my partner in my quest?'

'If you wish me to,' Joshua said carefully. The subject seemed better handled in his second tongue.

'At one time, when we were little more than hatchlings,' Taen said, 'I wondered what a partnership would have produced, when we achieved full growth. But I thought in terms of exploration of the unknown or something of that nature, and when I realized we were doomed to go to war with each other . . .'

Joshua waited, but the Al'ar did not finish the sentence. After a heavy silence, Taen continued:

'But I have allowed the dead past to swallow me.

'I observed the way you fought down below. You are a far greater warrior than when last I saw you. You have learned much with no one to guide you. You give great honor to your teachers, your fellow students who tried to help you learn the ways of fighting.

'To answer your question, yes, of course. I welcome you, Shadow Warrior, and it is my honor to be allowed to fight with you.'

Something touched Wolfe, something he had not felt for time beyond memory.

'We are approaching the ocean's surface,' the artificial

voice said. 'Would all aboard strap themselves down, in the event of bad weather on the surface, to avoid injury. One person designated as pod control officer should approach the controls.'

A board slid out from the control panel.

'This pod has a range of approximately a hundred miles at a fixed speed of three knots. You will observe the controls provided.'

There was a joystick, a dial with a pointer, and a single slidepot.

'The stick functions as a rudder, and the other control is a throttle. Use these to steer your craft.

'Warning – do not expend your fuel foolishly. If there is a storm, do not attempt to sail out of it but wait until it has passed.

'The third instrument indicates the nearest broadcast point. Keep the red arrow centered at the top of the dial and you will go toward it.

'It is not likely that you will reach that point, however, since all stations on Montana Keep have been alerted to the emergency.

'Do not become alarmed. You will be rescued in short order.' The program shut down.

'Wonderful,' Wolfe said. 'As if we need to advertise.'

He looked for anything that might access the pod's transmitter, saw nothing.

'We have worse problems,' Taen said. 'Look at the hatchway.'

Wolfe turned and saw water seeping into the pod.

He hurried to the hatch. Halfway down it the metal was torn, blackened. Along the edge was torn, burned sealant with water beading through.

'Our friend was a better shot than I thought,' he said. Suddenly the metal wrenched farther open, and a stream of water gushed in, sending him staggering back.

'Can we block this?' he shouted over the building hiss of the incoming ocean.

'**I see nothing,**' Taen said.

The pod chamber was rapidly filling, water almost knee-deep now. Wolfe sloshed to the control panel, stared out and up. The blackness was less absolute, and he thought he saw light above. He felt pain in his chest, realized the pod's atmospheric equalizer must've been hit as well, and began exhaling steadily.

'Breathe . . . out . . .' he managed. 'Or . . . rupture whatever . . . kind of lungs . . . you've got . . .'

'**The question would appear to be,**' Taen said, undisturbed, '**whether we gather enough water to keep us from rising before or after we reach the surface.**'

The blackness *was* lighter, and then daylight blinded them. The pod shot clear of the water, then crashed back down. Wolfe was slammed into a wall, and his vision darkened, then came back. He looked out the porthole. The ocean was gray, with a small chop.

'Are we still leaking?'

Taen waded to the hatch. 'How interesting,' he said. 'I can observe the ocean beyond. It would appear that the hole is just above the water level, although waves are bringing in water every now and again. If we had pumps, we could pump it dry and be safe.'

'That's one of the many things we're a bit short of,' Wolfe said. The control panel's directional needle was pointing to the right. He slid the control pot up to full, turned the joystick, and centered the needle.

He heard humming, and slowly, laboriously, the pod began moving, the water level now just below the smashed hatch.

You are in the sea . . . so you have allowed it to embrace you . . . turn away . . . you are letting it wash you, move you . . . you are not in control now . . . you are not part of the tide . . . reach for the earth, remember the earth, find your center . . . find the void . . . return whole . . .

His breathing slowed. He *felt* out, found nothing. He took the Lumina from his pocket, held it, not seeing it flame up.

Taen said something, and Wolfe *felt* surprise in his words but did not allow them to be heard.

Beyond there . . . out there . . . land . . . the jungle . . . the earth . . . feel on . . .

Involuntarily Wolfe swiveled, *felt* where the Centipede lay on the continent that stretched in front of him, *felt* its distance.

'As a good guess,' he said, 'we're only about ten, twelve miles from the lumber station where I came down to Tworn Station.' He touched the plas that concealed the bonemike and winced as his fingers found a deep gouge in its surface that had been cut without his realizing it.

'Ship, do you hear me?'

There was no response.

'Ship, do you understand this sending?'

Again, nothing.

'Ship, can you detect this device singing to you? Respond at once on this frequency.'

'I hear a singing in a tongue none speak,' came the response. *'I am responding only because my logical circuits dictate you must be the one sending. If that was you sending previously, be advised your voice pattern no longer matches the one I am required to obey. Please inform problem. Be advised if input does not give satisfactory explanation, all transmissions from your station will be ignored.'*

'The transponder suffered physical damage. Do not terminate transmission. That is an order. Emergency override,' and Wolfe switched to Terran, 'Frangible, Onyx, Three, Phlebas.'

'*Your message received, understood. Emergency override orders acknowledged. Stress analysis applied. No sign evident that you are drugged or under control of a hostile. As instructed, I will obey your orders.*'

'Shit,' Joshua muttered. 'I think I'm a little too careful. Ship, do you have this station located?'

'*I do.*'

'Lift from the bottom but do not break surface until you're a mile offshore. Then, at full power —'

Static suddenly roared against his bones.

'Ship, do you receive this station?'

He felt nothing but the static.

'What is it?'

'I'm not sure,' Wolfe said. 'I hope it's just some kind of local interference. But I'll bet I'm wrong. We've got troubles, partner. I think somebody picked up our transmission and is jamming it.'

'The Chitet?'

Wolfe shrugged. 'I guess our best chance is to ride this clunker to shore, hope the jamming stops, then call again.'

Taen's hood lifted, subsided.

'Then that is what we shall do.'

Thirty minutes later Wolfe saw the outline of the coast rise out of the gray water ahead. He couldn't make out the Centipede yet but kept the needle centered. Less than five minutes after that the steady hum of the drive faltered, then quit. The pod settled, and water began slopping through the hatch.

'We took a harder hit than I thought,' he said. 'How are you at swimming?'

'I will float under this planet's circumstances,' the Al'ar said. 'However, propelling myself through the water will be a very slow matter.' He held out his slender grasping organs. 'But I shall kick and flail as best I can.'

'The hell you will,' Wolfe said. 'I'll tow you. Let's get this hatch open and out of here.'

He hit the sensor. Motors hummed, and the hatch moved, opening a few inches; then metal grated against metal. He hit the sensor again and heard a relay cut out.

'We may not have to worry about swimming,' he muttered. He braced against one of the plas seats, kicked, kicked again. The inner surface of the hatch caved in a bit but didn't open.

Taen stepped in front of him and slid his impossibly slender grasping organs through the slit. He braced himself against one wall and pulled.

Joshua felt the Lumina in his pocket flame, heat. Metal screeched, and the hatch moved a few inches; then the relay cut back in, and the way was open and the ocean crashed in. The pod rolled, began sinking.

Joshua had an arm around the Al'ar's thin chest. He pushed his way out, against the current, and was out of the survival pod.

He fought his way to the surface, swam a few strokes away from the sinking pod, and released Taen. He rolled on his back, forced his boots off, and let them sink. He unbuckled his gun belt, was about to release it, and stopped. He looped the belt around his neck and buckled it.

'Now we swim?' Taen inquired.

There was still nothing but the jamming roar to be felt through the transponder.

'Now we swim. You lie on your back, keep your head above water, and kick with me. Sooner or later we'll either drown or hit the beach.'

'I shall not drown.'

Wolfe wondered what Taen meant, then put the matter out of mind.

Reach deep . . . the way is long . . . you have much power . . . your muscles are not torn, not aching . . . this is sport . . .

breathe . . . breathe . . . now feel the sea, let it take you, let it wash you . . .

The pod was barely visible above the surface, rolling, about to sink, no more than thirty feet away.

A gray-green snake's head as big as Wolfe's body broke the surface, reaching ten feet into the air on a snake neck. Wolfe saw a flipper break the surface and turn the creature.

It glared down at the pod, hissed a challenge, struck, and screeched its agony as teeth chipped against the alloy steel. It struck once more, then turned, seeing the two beings in the water.

Wolfe's fingers fumbled for the holster catch, lifting the retaining loop. The sea monster's head lashed down; its fanged mouth struck the water just short of Taen. The Al'ar slapped the beast on the top of its jaws, a seeming touch.

Wolfe heard bones crunch, and the creature screamed and rolled over, showing a light green belly and four thrashing flippers. It came back up, shrilling, and pulled its head back like a cobra about to lunge.

Wolfe had his pistol out and touched the stud. A wave washed his arm, and the blast slammed past the monster's neck. He fired once more, and the bolt hit the animal just below its skull. Ichor gouted over the water around them, and the animal thrashed, slamming into the sinking pod again and again.

Wolfe had Taen around the neck and was swimming hard, away from the pooling gore and the sea monster's death throes.

'I don't,' he managed, 'want to see what this world imagines sharks to be like.'

'Do not speak,' Taen said. 'Reserve your strength for the task ahead.'

Wolfe obeyed and let his free arm and legs move, move in muscle memory.

He fancied he could see the tree line ahead of him but knew better, for they were still too far out. He refused to allow himself hope, reminded his mind it was a drunken, careening monkey, swam on.

It might have been five strokes, it might have been five thousand, when the sky darkened.

Wolfe rolled on his back and saw the great ship descending toward them.

'Are we being rescued?'

Wolfe brought his mind back from where he had buried it and studied the starship through salt-burning eyes.

'No,' he said. 'That's an old Federation cruiser. *Ashida* class, I'm pretty sure.'

'Then release me. I shall go down to my death before I go into the hands of the Federation.'

'You don't have to worry about that,' Wolfe said. 'All of them got mothballed or broken up for scrap after the war. But this one didn't.'

'Chitet!'

The static blur against his clavicle was gone, and a voice sounded:

'Stand by for pickup. If you have weapons, discard them. Any attempts at resistance will only produce your deaths. I say again, stand by for pickup.'

Wolfe had the pistol out, held just below the water.

'No,' Taen said. 'Release the weapon. They will only shoot us in the water. Is it not better to let them pick us up and then meet our deaths when we have a better chance of taking some of them along to amuse us on our journey?'

Wolfe opened his fingers, saw the pistol sink down into green darkness.

The huge ship was only fifty feet above them, moving to one side, when the *Grayle* broke water, its hatch sliding open, less than ten feet away.

Wolfe was swimming desperately, once more grasping

Taen as he felt heat from the Chitet cruiser's drive sear him. He found a grab rail, pulled himself aboard, and rolled into the lock.

It cycled close behind him.

'Lift,' he gasped. 'Straight off the water, full evasive pattern.'

'*Understood.*'

Gravity twisted and warped; then the ship's AG took over, and he came to his feet.

'Screens!' He saw the bulk of the ship nearly overhead, to one side, the land, the sea below. The *Grayle* was skimming just above the water, accelerating.

Water spouted high to the right, where the *Grayle* would have been if it hadn't jinked a second earlier. On another screen he saw the cruiser's missile port snap closed and another open.

'Immelman, straight back at them.'

'*Understood.*'

He felt vertigo even through the artificial gravity as the ship climbed and rolled.

He grabbed a railing for support. Taen crouched on the deck nearby.

'Target . . . starship ahead.'

'*Acquired.*'

'Launch one!'

The cruiser was no more than ten miles distant when one of the *Grayle*'s tubes spat fire and the air-to-air missile smashed toward it.

Whoever was controlling the ship was very fast, recovering from amazement at receiving fire from what appeared to be no more than a yacht, and the former Federation warship banked away, climbing.

But Wolfe's missile couldn't miss at that range. It exploded into the Chitet cruiser near the stern, and the ship twisted in the blast.

'Offplanet!'

'*Understood.*'

The *Grayle* climbed at full drive.

In a side and then a rear screen, Joshua watched the Chitet ship flounder like a gaffed fish, smoke pouring from its wound.

The ship grew smaller, smaller still, and then they were in space.

'Three jumps. At random. No destination.'

'*Understood.*'

Joshua looked at Taen as the Al'ar got to his feet. He was suddenly very tired.

He *felt* Taen's strength and a chilly, almost robotic companionship.

'And now it begins,' the Al'ar said.

'Now it begins,' Joshua echoed.

The *Grayle* vanished into the cold fire of the stars.

BOOK TWO

HUNT THE HEAVENS

For

Dr Michio Kaku
Professor of Theoretical Physics

Master Hei Long

Grandmaster Toshitora Yamashiro,
The Nine Shadows of the Koga Ninja

ONE

The dead ships were scattered through the night, sometimes sharply illumed in white light, then darkness reclaimed its own as they moved, drifted, the rocky spray of the nearby unborn world occluding the light from the far-distant sun.

The ships were linked by nearly invisible cables that held them in an approximate orbit around a medium-size planetoid. Some of the ships were worn-out and centuries old, others were the energy-devouring military craft of the great war eleven years in the past. Some wore the colors of failed merchant enterprises, others the standards of ones too successful by far. Some appeared intact, others were being systematically cannibalized by their caretaker on the asteroid 'below.'

Half a light-second distant, space distorted, and there was the slight blink as a ship came out of stardrive. A few moments later, a transmission came:

'Malabar Control, Malabar Control, this is the *Grayle*. Request approach and docking instructions.'

The call was made three times before a reply came in:

'*Grayle*, this is Malabar. Request your purpose. This is not a public port. Landing permission is granted only with proper authority.'

'Malabar, this is *Grayle*. Stand by.' The synthed female voice was replaced by a man's:

'Malabar, this is *Grayle*. Purpose for visit: resupply.'

'*Grayle*, this is Malabar. Permission refused. I say again – this is not a public port.'

'Malabar, this is *Grayle*. Message follows for Cormac. I shackle Wilbur Frederick Milton unshackle. Sender: Ghost.'

There was dead air, then:

'Stand by.'

Nearly an hour passed before:

'*Grayle*, this is Malabar Control. Porting request granted. We have auto-approach capability. Please slave your ship controls to this frequency. After docking do not leave your ship until authorized. Cormac advises will meet Ghost personally and strongly recommends it had best be Ghost Actual. Clear.'

The man lounging against the bulkhead wore an expensive cotton shirt faded from many washings, a sleeveless sweater that could have been his grandfather's, and khaki pants that might have belonged to a uniform once.

He straightened as the inner lock door slid open and eyed Joshua as he came out.

'Joshua,' Cormac said. 'If that's the name you're still using, Ghost Actual.'

'It is. And you're still flying your own colors,' Wolfe said.

'Time must've been good to us then.'

Wolfe made no response. Cormac turned to an alcove. 'He's who he said he was, friends. You can go on about your business.'

Two men carrying stubby blast rifles came out, nodded politely to Joshua, and went past into the inner reaches of the planetoid.

'Interesting how you never forget the shackle code, isn't it?' Cormac commented. 'And you're right. I do owe you. What do you need? A ship? An insert, like the old days? I haven't done much direct moving lately, but I doubt if I've lost any moves. If that's what you need.'

'I need a shipyard.'

'Ah? You don't appear to have taken any damage, from what the screen showed me.'

'I didn't. But the *Grayle*'s maybe a little too noticeable. Do you still remember how to do a Q-ship setup?'

'Do I remember?' Cormac laughed shortly. 'Commander, that's one of my most requested tunes these days. There appear to be a lot of men and women floating about who'd rather not have their ships present the same face to the Federation – or to anybody – more than once or twice.'

'Yes. I can handle that little job for you. How thorough a change you want? Snout, fins, configuration, signature . . . I can still do it all.'

'How long for the full boat?'

'Pun intended?'

Again, Wolfe didn't answer.

Cormac considered. 'Normally three months. But I assume these aren't normal times.'

'You assume right,' Wolfe said.

'Month and a half, then.' Cormac hesitated. 'That's a big call-in, I must say.'

'I'll cover your costs, plus ten percent,' Wolfe said. 'I'm not broke. But I'd appreciate a quick turnaround.'

Cormac swept a grandiose bow. 'So let it be written . . . so let it be done!'

Wolfe grinned. 'Where were we the last time I heard you say that?'

'I had that wonderful hollowed-out moonlet,' Cormac said wistfully. 'Not ten light-minutes from that Al'ar base, and they never twigged to me at all.'

'What happened to it?'

'I don't know,' Cormac said. 'I tried to track it down when the Federation started mothballing everything.' He shrugged. 'I suppose someone beat me to it.

'Now wouldn't that make a *great* smuggler's haven?'

'From what I've heard about this sector,' Wolfe said, 'you don't appear to need one.'

'True, true, too damned true. Come on. I'll show you around and start my crews to work.'

'Not quite yet,' Wolfe said. 'I've got a passenger who nobody gets to see. I mean nobody, Cormac. How do we arrange that?'

'We'll set up quarters next to mine. No bugs, no probes, no nothing. Not even mine. You could put the Queen of Sheba there and no one would ever know.'

'Good. I'll need some kind of vehicle to make the transfer.'

'No problem with that, either. Now come on. Let me buy you a drink. You still drink . . . Armagnac, it was, yes?'

'You remember well.'

The two men started down the long metallic corridor.

'Sometimes,' Cormac said a little wistfully, 'it's about the only excitement I have. I swear I sometimes think I miss the war. You ever feel that way?'

'Not yet.'

'You *are* blessed.'

Cormac's quarters were hand-worked wood, silver, dark-red leather, lavish as a port admiral's. Wolfe lounged back against his couch, tasted his drink.

'It's only Janneau,' Cormac apologized. 'If I'd known you were coming I could have had one of the freetraders come up with better.'

'It's fine.' Wolfe looked about. 'You have done well by yourself.'

'It wasn't hard,' Cormac said. 'When peace broke out all anyone wanted was to either get out or find some nice, comfortable sinecure. Those of us who had, well, an eye for the main chance could pretty much pick and choose. And I wanted to stay out here in the Outlaw Worlds.

'I heard they needed someone to take care of all the ships that were going to be decommissioned. Given my modest talents, and a few coms to some friends who remembered what services I'd been able to render, and I had a new career, or anyway the powerbase for one.'

'Doesn't the Federation ever come looking to see what's happening to those hulks?'

'Hell no. There's fifty-eight boneyards around the galaxy. Some of them don't even have caretakers, and I wonder if the ships're even still there. At least I'm disappearing mine little by little. By the way, I could make you one *hell* of a deal on a battlewagon if you're interested. One thing the Federation still has too much of, Joshua, and that's warships.' Cormac picked up his glass of beer, looked at it, set it back down. 'Them . . . and the people who used to pilot them.'

'You do miss the war,' Wolfe said gently.

'And why not? I was only twenty-two then. How many people my age had their own spaceport and responsibility for getting people into – and sometimes out of – places no sane person could imagine?'

'Why didn't you stay in? Federation Intelligence must've wanted to keep you.'

'I don't have much use for some of the people they did keep,' Cormac said. 'I did a couple of . . . small jobs for them after the war. And was sorry I did.'

'Cisco being one of them?'

'That shit-for-brains!'

'He's still with them.'

'Why am I not surprised?' Cormac said. 'Bastards like him have to have a big daddy to hide behind. I can remember . . . no. Leave it.'

The slender man got up, walked to a bookcase, and picked up a model of a starship.

'I wasn't surprised to hear from you,' he said without turning around. 'Not that surprised, anyway.'

'Oh?' Wolfe's tone remained casual, but one hand moved toward his waistband.

'Ghost Actual,' Cormac said, 'you are in a ton of trouble. Two tons.'

'That's why I need the ship-change.'

'You might need more than that.'

Cormac went to a desk, opened it, and touched a pore-pattern lock. 'This came across about an E-week ago. I pulled a copy, then iced the file. Nobody else on Malabar has seen it.'

He took out a rolled cylinder of paper and handed it to Wolfe, who opened it. There was a pic on it of Wolfe that was four years old, and:

WANTED

Joshua Wolfe
Murder, Conspiracy,
Treason,
and
Other Crimes
Against the Federation

500,000 CREDITS REWARD
Must Be Taken Alive

'Alive, eh?' Wolfe read the rest of the sheet. 'But I'm considered armed, deadly, guaranteed to resist arrest, and so forth. That ought to slow them down for a little.'

'Should I ask?'

'Better not, Cormac. It gets real involved. Although I wonder how the hell they figure I've committed treason since I haven't been inside the Federation much since the war.'

'It doesn't matter a tinker's fart to me,' Cormac said. 'Who was it who said if he had a choice between betraying his country or a friend, he hoped he'd have the balls to sell his country out?'

'Don't remember. But I don't think he said it quite like that.'

'Actually,' Cormac said, 'I thought when I got the call you'd be wanting . . . other changes made. Ones involving a doctor.'

Wolfe smiled, moved his hand away from his waist, picked up his drink, and sipped. 'I don't think I'm that desperate yet.' He set the snifter down. 'Cisco's the one who originated that warrant.'

'Son of a bitch,' Cormac said. 'I should have slotted him way back when. Remember when he tried to tell me how to run a snatch-and-grab and there were about a trillion Al'ar looming down on us?'

'I do. I think that's the only time I've ever seen you raise your voice.'

'I was feeling hostile,' Cormac admitted. 'That man doesn't bring out the best in me. Never mind. And forget about paying for the ship mods.'

He pushed through the beginnings of Wolfe's protests. 'That wasn't a question, goddammit. You might need the geetus later. Hell, if you've got an open warrant, I know you will. Sooner or later that frigging Cisco'll change the terms and it'll be dead or alive, no questions as long as the body bag's full. Just you wait.

'And then you'll really be sailing close to the wind. Cisco may be a stumblebum, but he's dangerous. Especially when he's got the whole goddamned Federation for backup.'

Wolfe felt the walls themselves might be pulsating to the music. The circular bar was filled, and the slide-tempo band in the center ring was sweating hard.

Cormac leaned close. 'Well?' he said, half shouting to be heard.

'Well what?' Wolfe said.

'Well, it's been two weeks. You feel any more relaxed than when you checked in?'

Wolfe shrugged. 'I'll relax when the *Grayle*'s ready to go. Lately I get twitchy when I don't have a back door.'

'I'm pushing the crews as hard as I can right now. Most of the material's in-shipped. Oh, yeah – I stole a nifty piece of signature-masking electronics out of a P-boat that got dumped on me last year. Put that in today myself.'

A voice said hello, and Wolfe turned. The woman was in her early twenties, had red hair in a pixie bob, and wore a designer's idea of a shipsuit, made of black velvet with see-through panels. He returned the greeting. The woman held her smile, lifted a finger, and ran it slowly over her lips, then melted into the crowd.

'You been making conquests while I'm slaving in the guts of your ship?' Cormac asked wryly.

'Hardly. Never seen her before. You know her?'

'No. I think I've seen her once. Don't even know if she's pro or just looking for action.' Cormac shrugged. 'You want dinner?'

Wolfe nodded, and they found a wall booth. Wolfe slid the privacy/sound one-way curtain shut and grimaced in the sudden hush. 'I guess one of the drawbacks of the aging process is that music gets louder than it used to be.'

'While everything else gets dimmer,' Cormac agreed. 'So the trick is to never get old.'

The menu glimmered to life between them. Wolfe studied it, then touched the sensors for a conch salad and curried crayfish brochettes.

'You want wine?' he asked.

'Never developed a taste for it,' Cormac said. 'I'll stick with beer.'

To accompany the meal, Wolfe ordered a half-bottle of a white whose description suggested it might resemble an

Alsatian Riesling, and leaned against the back wall of the booth. Cormac touched his own sensor, and a mug of beer appeared from a trapdoor in the table's center.

'Joshua,' he said carefully, 'something I've wondered.'

'Wonder away.'

'The word was you grew up among the Al'ar. Is that right?'

'Not quite,' Joshua said. 'My folks were diplomats. We were on Sauros for three years. Then the Al'ar jumped the fence, and we got stuck in an internment camp.' He paid deliberate attention to the drink menu and found a claimed Earth brandy. The drink arrived, Wolfe tasted it, made a face.

'Somebody's chemist needs a trip to the home planet for research. Anyway, my folks died there, and I got off, and the Federation thought I was a hot item. And the war dragged on.'

'What do you think happened to the Al'ar?'

'They vanished.'

'No shit! Every damned million or billion or trillion of them, zip-gone? I was out there, too, remember? Where do you think they went?'

'I don't know.'

'Can they come back?'

'I . . . don't think so.'

'So we had ten years and who knows how many bodies so they could pull a vanishing act. Why did they start that goddamned war, anyway?'

Joshua considered his words. 'Because they wanted the same thing we do. All the room in the galaxy plus two yards. I guess space can't support but one hog at a time.'

'So much for patriotism,' Cormac said. 'Sorry. I got the idea you aren't real fond of talking about them.'

'That doesn't bother me,' Wolfe said. 'I don't much like talking about the war, though.'

'So what do you want to talk about?'

Wolfe considered, then smiled. 'What about whether that redhead was real or not?'

The trapdoor opened, and their food lifted into view. Neither man spoke as they ate. After a time Cormac looked out.

'Here she comes again. Why don't you ask her?'

'Maybe. After I finish eating.'

'Looks like she's got a question of her own.'

The woman came over to the booth and tapped. Wolfe found the OPEN sensor, and the music battered them.

The woman smiled and started to say something. Wolfe leaned closer.

'Joshua!' Cormac shouted, and went over the top of the table, knocking Wolfe back as a blaster beam crashed across the room and blew a hole in the booth's back wall.

Wolfe was momentarily trapped between the back of the booth and the table. Cormac rolled away and Wolfe squirmed up. The redhead's hand went into a slit in the shipsuit and flashed out with a tiny handgun.

Wolfe curled forward, smashing the table away, and his fingers snapped out and touched the woman's gunhand. She shrieked; the gun went flying and she stumbled back as the first gunman fired again.

The blast took the woman in the back. Her body spasmed, and she flopped aside as Wolfe came out of the booth, gun in hand.

The gunman was on the other side of the band, running for the stairs that led to the upper deck.

Wolfe knelt, free hand coming up to brace the gun butt, elbow just on the far side of his knee.

Breathe . . . breathe . . . the earth holds firm . . .

His finger touched the trigger stud, and the gun bucked. The bolt took the gunman in the side, and he screamed, clawed at himself, and sagged, body slipping bonelessly down the stairs.

The room was screams and motion. Cormac was beside him, his own pistol out.

Wolfe glanced at the woman, saw dead, surprised eyes, and looked away. He went across the room, paying no attention to the hubbub, and kicked the gunman's body over.

He was young, no older than the woman his bad aim had killed, sallow-faced, with the wisp of a beginning goatee. Paying no mind to the blood pouring from the hole in the gunman's side, Wolfe quickly and expertly patted the body down.

He found no identification, but from an inner pocket took out a piece of paper that had been folded and refolded until its creases were about to wear through. He unfolded it.

WANTED

Joshua Wolfe . . .

He passed the paper to Cormac, who scanned it. 'Somebody missed the part about alive, alive-o,' the ship-yard owner said. 'It appears,' he went on in a near whisper, 'I didn't scrub that file as clean as I thought I had. Or else word's gotten offplanet about you being here.'

The room was deadly silent.

Wolfe *felt* no threat, and his gun vanished. A moment later, a woman laughed shrilly, tightly, and the volume went back up again.

'Let's go,' Cormac said. 'I'll fix the local heat when we're back at my grounds.'

Wolfe nodded, and they moved quickly toward the exit. Wolfe opened the door for his friend, who went out and flattened against the wall. The corridor was empty.

Joshua followed him.

'I guess,' he said, 'maybe we *do* need to talk about some . . . further alterations.'

Joshua Wolfe's face filled all three of the large screens. He sat in a chair in the middle of them, his expression blank.

'Are you feeling anything?'

'No.'

There was a hissing, and the screens clouded as gas sprayed out around Wolfe. His face turned frosty white. After a few moments, it began swelling, turning red, as if he were being systematically hammered by invisible fists.

The other man in the white room moved away from his console and walked to Joshua's chair. He was big, imposing, and might, years earlier, before the muscle softened, have played some kind of a contact sport. He'd said he wished to be known as Brekmaker.

He walked around Joshua, stroking his chin, his eyes intent. Wolfe lay motionless in the chair, as he'd been ordered, but his eyes followed the man.

'Are you experiencing much discomfort?'

Joshua's eyes were no more than slits as the skin puffed up around them. 'Not . . . that much.'

'Good. In a few moments we shall proceed. This,' Brekmaker went on, 'is an interesting challenge. You certainly have a . . . lived-in face, my friend. Yes, I suppose that's how I'd put it.' His tone suggested he wasn't used to anyone contradicting his observations.

'Now, if we had enough time, of course we could build you an entirely new face, from the bones out. Turn you into a chubby, happy-go-lucky sort. Then we could take some bone, maybe an inch or so, out of your lower legs, shorten you.

'Do some chemical alterations of your digestive system, and poof, after a few months and a thousand meals, you'd have the body to match your face. Rolo-polo, the grinning fat boy.

'I've always wanted to do a perfect job such as that,' the man went on. 'But I've never had the time . . . or rather my clients haven't. Nor have they properly understood my intent.

'No, they all say they want to be different, but they seldom mean it. You can talk if you want to.'

Wolfe remained silent.

'So what I intend to do,' Brekmaker went on, without waiting more than a moment, 'is to make you into the impossible man to your friends and enemies. First we'll remove all your facial scars and marks, especially that one near your mouth. Fortunately, it's not a keloid, so removal will be quite simple.

'In the process, I'll take all of the aging lines off your neck. Then I'm going to build up your cheekbones a bit, make them a bit more distinct than they already are. I'm going to rebuild that nose, which looks like it's been broken more than once, am I right?'

'Three, maybe four times,' Wolfe mumbled.

'In short, I'm going to be your Ponce de Leon. In case you don't know – '

'I know who he was,' Wolfe said.

'Oh. Not many of my clients have heard about the Fountain of Youth. Yes, you'll be the young man you once were, plus I'll make some improvements the helix didn't give you when you were born. I'll also take some of the pouching off your eyelids, cut a bit of cartilage from the back of your ears and pin them back a little just because they're a bit too batlike for my tastes.

'You haven't had significant hair loss, so I won't need to do implants, but I will do a perma-dark so you won't be a silver fox anymore.

'Of course, you're wondering right now how all this is going to make you unrecognizable to . . . to whoever you don't wish to know you.

'It's very simple but devilishly clever, if I do say so

myself. Imagine this, Mister, uh, Taylor you said your name was, I believe. Imagine you are walking down the street and you see someone who you recognize from your first time in prison, or in school, or whatever, twenty years ago. He looks *exactly* the same as he did then. You are about to hail him and then you stop yourself, barely in time.

'You're embarrassed, because you realize that all of us change in ten or fifteen or twenty years, and of course anyone who looked exactly like your friend of years ago cannot, simply cannot, be that man.

'And so you hurry past, not really looking at this person again, because you're deeply grateful you didn't say anything and make an utter ass of yourself and also don't think on the matter, for none of us wish to remember our momentary near foolishnesses.

'Simple . . . yet very clever, isn't it?'

Wolfe managed to make a noise that might have been agreement.

'I feel that you're experiencing a bit of pain.' Brekmaker went to his control panel, touched sensors. Gas hissed. 'There. That should take it away. Now we can begin.'

His fingers moved over other parts of the panel, and, from the ceiling, tiny projectors appeared and moved toward Joshua's face.

'Culan in a kennel,' Cormac swore. 'You look like ratshit on rye! What'd you look like yesterday when the quack got through? Couldn't have been worse.'

'Don't be so polite,' Wolfe said muffledly. He glanced in the mirror beside his bed, saw the yellow-serum-crusted mask that looked like an inflated balloon, then pointedly turned the mirror facedown. 'Just think of me as about to begin my butterfly imitation.'

'You need anything? You sure that bastard didn't work you over with a bat or something?'

'It feels like he did.'

'You need more painkiller?'

'No. I'll handle it.'

'What can I get you?'

'Nothing. Just make sure Brekmaker doesn't get off-world before this whole thing's over with. I'm not real comfortable with having to pay him up front.'

'Don't worry about that. I disabled the drive on his ship, and I've got one of my boys watching him pretty close. But I don't think we've got any worries, since we've got his pretty little portable OR set up in here and out of his ship. I'm sure he won't skip without it.

'He wanted to circulate, but I told him he couldn't. Not until you said it was okay.

'So he asked if I could set him up with a woman or two. The bastard likes to brag on himself. Couldn't wait to tell the girls I sent him how great a surgeon he'd been and still was even if he'd been subjected to some terrible misunder-standings, how he'd done work on Earth itself, sometimes on some of the most famous people, and so on and so forth.'

'That doesn't sound like someone we want wandering around with his mouth at full drive,' Wolfe said.

'I suggested just that quite strongly, and he pissed and moaned, and eventually said it'd add another ten thou to his bill.'

'I'll pay it,' Wolfe said.

'I wish I'd been able to get somebody else,' Cormac said. 'But you were in a hurry.'

'What're the odds any other disbarred doc'd be different? At least he doesn't have a jar in his nose or an injector in his arm.'

'So far,' Cormac said glumly. 'Look, I've got to get back to it. If I bust ass, about the time you start looking like a human being, I might have something to show you. You sure you don't need anything?'

'I'm sure.'

Cormac left the apartment. Wolfe heard the outer door close, then lock. There was no sound but the soft murmur of music from the player in the apartment's central room and the hiss of the air recycler.

Then he *felt* the presence.

'May I enter your burrow?'

'You may.'

There was a long silence. Then the other said, still in the same language:

'How unusual. Using the same senses you have, I see there shall be a vast difference. But beyond, you remain as you were. I am curious to see, once you are healed, what your own seeing shall grant you. I must say, you are incredibly ugly at the moment, even more so than normal to me.'

'I'm not trying to fool *you*,' Wolfe said, changing languages. 'Just all these goddamned people who want my ass on toast for wanting to help you.'

The other also changed to Terran. 'I listened to what that Cormac said and assume he meant the ship will be ready.

'I have been wondering something. I sought the Mother Lumina, even though I have, as yet, no concrete proof of its existence. Was I correct in that? Or should I have been searching for the handful of other Al'ar whom I must believe were left behind when my people made the Crossing? I bow to your wisdom in this.'

'The Mother Lumina, or your Guardians?' Wolfe said. 'You seemed most convinced of the Guardians' existence when you first explained your search.'

'I was and am.'

'I don't know,' Wolfe said.

He reached in the table beside his bed, took out the Lumina he'd taken from the cache of a thief he'd killed, touched it.

The gray stone came to life, and a thousand colors pulsed through the room, flickering over Wolfe's ruined face.

Joshua came suddenly awake.

'**You shouted**,' said the one beside him. '**Are you experiencing pain?**'

'No,' Joshua said. 'At least . . . not much. No. I was in a dream. No, not a dream. I was being attacked. By . . . I do not know what. I heard a buzzing, though. Such as insects make.'

'There are no insects on this artificial world,' the other said. 'Or there should not be, at any rate. So of course it must have been a dream.'

'I know.'

'Look at your arm,' his companion said suddenly.

Wolfe's forearm showed red ridges, streaks.

'What could that be?'

'I don't know. Maybe a reaction to the painkiller?'

'But you have taken none since this afternoon.'

'I don't know.' Wolfe stared at the marks. Slowly they began to fade.

Then he heard, in his mind, the sound of angry insects once more.

'Actually, I would like to have some trumpets for a proper fanfare,' Brekmaker said. 'You have been an excellent subject. Now, take a look at yourself.'

Joshua looked at the three screens.

'I look like me,' he said. 'Quite awhile ago. And I'm bright pink.'

'That'll change. I'm going to put you out again, and repigment the skin. One thing, Mister Taylor. I must caution you to work on your facial reflexes. If you frown as you always frowned, if you smile as you always smiled, then the lines will start coming back, and your resemblance to your former self will become far more marked than otherwise.

'Now, lie back. You'll be unconscious for perhaps half an hour or an hour while I finish up this last detail. I'll revive you, then we can begin arrangements to reload my apparatus, and, well, the remainder of my fee, which I discussed with your associate.'

'I'd just as soon stay conscious.'

'No, you wouldn't. Even though repigmentation is simple, it can be quite painful. Trust me on this.'

Wolfe stared at Brekmaker, grudged a nod.

'Now, I'm going to give you the deep tan of a man who's been in space, as you wished. Please put your head back on the rest.'

Wolfe obeyed. The doctor fingered controls; two projectors rose out of the chair, aimed at Joshua, and anesthetic gas hissed.

'Breathe deeply now.'

A few seconds later, Wolfe went limp.

The doctor used other controls, and the projectors disappeared and other, similar devices emerged. Brekmaker moved slide pots, then fingered a sensor. He watched the screens closely as a thin mist came out, his fingers dancing across a keyboard. The sprayers moved obediently, and Joshua's face darkened, changed.

'There,' Brekmaker said to himself. He got out of his chair, smiling oddly.

He reached under his console and took out a small tri-di recorder. He snapped an experimental picture, then went to Joshua.

Aiming carefully, he shot a series of pictures from several angles, whistling through his teeth. He frowned, then lifted the recorder for a final shot.

There was a slight sound behind him.

Brekmaker spun, one hand diving into the pocket of his surgical gown. He saw an open panel that he thought had been bare wall.

Nearly on him was a tall, impossibly slender snake-headed being, its skin color the dead white of a drowned man. Its eyes were slitted above the hood that flared around its neck.

Brekmaker's hand came out with his gun, and his mouth opened, to shout, to scream. But as the gun lifted, the Al'ar's grasping organ flashed out, touched the doctor in midchest.

The man's face purpled. His frozen muscles tried to pull in air, failed. The gun fell limply to the deck.

Brekmaker clawed at his throat and once more the alien struck, a bare touch against the man's forehead.

Brekmaker stumbled forward, crashed across his control console, and rolled to the floor, lying faceup, his final expression one of utter disbelief.

The Al'ar looked once at the corpse, then fitted himself awkwardly into the doctor's chair and began to wait.

TWO

'Blackmail?'

'Sure,' Wolfe said. 'You wait till you're at a good safe distance, then let your patient know you just happen to have taken some before-and-after pics for your professional files, and certainly the poor sod would be happy to kick in a few credits to make sure those pics are kept properly secure. It ain't a new racket.'

'I'm not doing too good on the professional recommendation circuit, am I?' Cormac said. He opened up the tiny recorder, took out its microfiche, and snapped it four times in his fingers, paying close attention to what he was doing. Without looking up, in a deliberately casual voice, he asked, 'Brekmaker was fool enough to take these snaps when you were conscious *and* gave you room enough to take him?'

Wolfe made no reply. Cormac looked at him, then away.

'Civilian life's getting to you,' Joshua said. 'You never used to ask any questions about anything.'

Cormac smiled, a bit ruefully. 'Sorry. Didn't mean to be inquisitive.'

'Forget it.'

The Al'ar evaded the blow, knelt, and his leg snapped out. The kick took Joshua in the upper thigh, and he hissed pain, rolled backward, then to the side as the Al'ar leapt toward him.

The Al'ar struck, Joshua sidestepped, blocked, and his return blow was blocked in return.

The two broke contact.

The Lumina stone on the pedestal against the wall of the bare room flared colors, and the Al'ar shimmered, vanished.

Wolfe glanced at the Lumina, sweat beading his forehead. The stone turned to dull gray, and the Al'ar was visible once more, closing on Wolfe.

Joshua jump-kicked, took the Al'ar in the chest, and knocked him flat. The alien backrolled into a crouch, and two fingers of Joshua's right hand hovered motionless an inch in front of his eyes.

The Al'ar froze and his hood flared. He lifted his grasping organs, crossed them.

'You have the advantage.'

Wolfe bowed, stepped back, and the Al'ar got up.

'That trick with the Lumina. I did not know you could do that,' the alien said.

'I did not, either. This was the first time.'

'Shadow Warrior, perhaps it is good that we are searching together. Perhaps, when . . . if we find the Mother Lumina, you might then be more able to understand its purpose than I.

'I might even wonder if this is what the one we went to intended, so long ago, who listened to the words you spoke and gave you your name. Perhaps he was also one of those who remained behind and we may ask if . . . when . . . we meet him. But that is for the future. As I said, perhaps that Guardian sensed that you might be a more worthy user of our devices than even an Al'ar.'

'You grant high praise, Taen.' Wolfe switched to Terran. 'Shall we go one more turn?'

'I think not. I feel fatigued.'

'You're getting old, my friend.'

'As are we all. In my case, perhaps it is being forced to live on Terran food. My body is not content. Last night, when my body was in disuse, I had thoughts come that were disturbing.'

'You *were* corrupted by being around me. I thought Al'ar never dream.'

'Not in your terms. Let me go on. I *felt* that insectlike buzzing you described. With it came a sense of dread, of menace. Then I returned my body to its proper state of readiness, and the sound was gone. Of course, I showed none of the physical signs you evinced.'

'So what does it mean?'

'I do not know. But I think we must accept that this sending, or whatever it should be called, is not a fiction, but something that exists in or close to our space-time.'

Static hummed, clicked, and SIGNAL INTERRUPT bleeped, then the screen showed CONTACT RESTORED.

'Sorry,' Joshua said. 'Thought I lost you for a second.'

'You're still not giving me a picture,' the distorted voice light-years distant complained.

'No. Nor are you.'

The speaker transmitted a sound that might have been laughter. 'Isn't it nice to find a couple of professionals who really trust each other?'

'Just like always,' Wolfe agreed.

'So what can I do you out of?'

'I just wanted to touch base. See if anything . . . interesting's going on.'

There was dead air for almost a minute. 'How clean is your transmission?'

'Clean. It's bounced, well, let's just say more than twice. And it's as sealed as I could make it.'

'Okay. Only because I like to see things stirred up. Cisco's looking for you. Looking hard.'

'That's no news. He's got a warrant out on me,' Wolfe said.

'That's one thing,' the voice said. 'That's the official policy. He's put word out that he wants a meet with you. Your terms, your ground, you know how to contact him.'

'Yeah. Sure. So he can collect the bounty?'

'Come on, Wolfe. Stop playing games. You know the rules.'

'I'm not sure Cisco does anymore.'

'No skin off my ass either way. I'm just passing the word along. There's one other thing that goes with it – he said you can bring your friend from Tworn Station along.'

Wolfe waited until he could control his voice. Tworn Station was the undersea resort where he'd tracked down Taen.

'I got what you said . . . but don't know what it means.'

The speaker stayed silent.

'Anything else?'

'Nope,' the voice said. 'Unless you want the hot gossip on who's sleeping with whom or who backalleyed her latest best friend. One other thing. Shoa InterGee is looking to hire a hotrod to take over their security section. The pay's good, but I gotta warn you, their system stinks. I've been known to go wading in their stuff every now and then for giggles, and there's folks out there far sneakier'n I am.'

'Hardly think they'd be interested in hiring somebody who's on the run from Fl.'

'As I said, I'm just the pipeline.'

'Thanks. Stay clean and I'll catch you next shout.' Wolfe touched the sensor, and the speaker went dead. He turned to Taen.

'I understood the transmission,' the Al'ar said in Terran. 'So this Cisco knows I exist and that we are teamed. I am hardly surprised – there were more than enough people who saw me when we retreated from my ship for Federation Intelligence to draw the correct assessment.

'But it will undoubtedly make life more interesting. My question is, should we agree to this meeting with the Intelligence man?'

Wolfe considered.

'The problem,' he mused aloud, 'is how to walk into his nest and be able to get back out again. Mmmh. I think I can manage that.'

'I was hoping you would say that. I would appreciate any data we can absorb. We are operating with far too little input in our quest,' Taen said. 'Now, once we derive whatever information we are able, can we kill this Cisco?'

Wolfe grinned. 'Taen, you would have made a perfectly wonderful spy, what with your sense of morality and all.'

'Your words are meaningless. If you have an enemy, you seek him out and slay him. All else is nothing but noise to my brain.'

The door to Cormac's inner office opened, and a soberly dressed man with a neat beard came out. He looked at Joshua, said 'Good morning, son,' then went out the door, letting the door ease shut against his hand.

Wolfe looked thoughtful, shut off the com he'd been scanning, and went into Cormac's office.

'The gentleman who just left called me son. I don't think he actually had five years on me.'

'Better get used to it, young man. I've already put the word out for my bars to start making sure you're of proper drinking age. Ain't surgery wonderful? Drag up a chair.'

Wolfe obeyed. 'Can I be nosy?'

'You cut my fingers off when I tried, but go ahead.'

'That gentleman who just left? Was he a Chitet?'

'He certainly was, although he didn't sound like one for

a couple of moments after I turned him down. He got a little dramatic on me. You have an interest in their little operation?'

'I do. They've tried to kill me half a dozen times now.'

'Mercy Maude,' Cormac said. 'All this from an organization that claims to be nothing more than a logical and systematic philosophy and way of life.

'Then you'll be very amused when you find out what he wanted. He put it most subtly, but he was very interested in acquiring, for a very impressive price, in cash to be handed to me directly, some of the mothballed Federation ships I'm supposed to be keeping all safe and secure. I don't mind selling a part here or there, but his ideas seemed excessive.'

'They're on the move, Cormac,' Wolfe said. 'The last time they tried to slot me was with an *Ashida*-class cruiser.'

'Oh? Not the most subtle way to suggest they don't like the way you cut your hair. And here my fine-feathered friend was telling me how they really needed half a dozen big ships to convert into transports for a large shipping deal they're about to sign. He was real specific about what he wanted: those three *Nelson*-class battleships, two of the heavy cruisers I've got, and by the way, there's a C & C rig out there that'd be almost perfect. Looks to me, if they need Command and Control, they're building a fleet. Got a bit hostile when I told him to pack his ass with salt and piddle up a rope. Most civilly and in my most mellifluous tones, of course.'

'Why'd you turn them down?'

'To be honest?'

Wolfe grinned. 'If that's the best option you can come up with.'

'I couldn't figure out what story I'd have if somebody ever came looking for them and asked me to explain a hole in space. Although now I'm getting a little concerned for some of my confreres who don't have the well-developed sense of survival I do. As I said before, there's a lot of available warships out here in the Outlaw Worlds.

'You know, Joshua, people with a goddamned mission in life who know what I should be doing better than I do make me nervous. Especially when they start buying guns.'

'You and me both,' Wolfe agreed. 'A small suggestion – keep your back against a wall for the next few forevers. These Chitet don't seem to handle rejection well.'

'So I gather. Fortunately, my cowardice genes are well developed.'

Cormac got up from his desk. ' 'Tis a parlous world,' he said 'I guess the only option for honest folk like you and me is to have a drink. C'mon.'

'What were you looking for when the FI robot got pictures of you on Sauros and put me in motion?' Wolfe asked.

'I had landed on several of our homeworlds already, looking for any data that might give me a clue to the Mother Lumina,' Taen said. 'I hoped to consult certain files, I think your word is, from our Farseeing Division, what you call Intelligence.'

'Hasn't FI already seized those?'

'They think they have,' the Al'ar said. 'But there are other copies, available for those who know where to look.'

'What data did you specifically seek?'

'What I sought, I never found. Mention of the Mother Lumina, mention of the Guardians, anything that might have been transmitted before my people made the Crossing.'

'And?'

'Nothing.'

'I cannot believe,' Wolfe said, 'that at one signal, a signal you say you didn't receive, every frigging Al'ar in the galaxy went away like a Boojum. So you weren't looking in the right place, or in the right manner.'

'I dislike your levity, but I must concede, logically, you are correct.'

'Which of the homeworlds, what we call the capital worlds, were the most important?'

'Sauros,' Taen said. 'The world I had my birth-burrow on, the same one you lived on before the war. I also sought access to one of our great machine-thinkers, computers, to help me analyze the problem. But I had no time to search for anything before that spy-probe found me.'

'If I can put us both back on Sauros, will you let me help in the search?'

The Al'ar curled on a ladder that was the closest approximation Wolfe could find to his customary seat. He remained silent for a long time. Twice his hood puffed, deflated.

'There are risks,' he said. 'To us both. There will be precautions still in place, unless they were set off by Federation searchers earlier. And I do not believe the Federation even knew where to look.'

'I've seen Al'ar booby traps,' Joshua said. 'They can be managed.'

'So you have a plan?'

'An idea.'

'Which of my two goals are we seeking?'

'Not the Mother Lumina. We'll start with the Guardians. Maybe that'll lead us to the rock in question.'

Taen's slitted eyes stared at Wolfe. 'One thing you have never told me. Not honestly, by what I can feel of your thoughts. You could have abandoned me on Montana Keep, or simply returned me to one of my own worlds, and then gone to ground.

'I do not doubt you have more than enough abilities to avoid both the Chitet and Federation Intelligence. They will not seek you forever, especially when they learn you have taken no further interest in the fate of the Al'ar.

'Why, Joshua Wolfe? Why, One Who Fights From Shadows?'

There was a long, heavy silence.

Wolfe shook his head slowly from side to side.

'She sings, she dances, she sways, she swoops,' Cormac said proudly. He and Wolfe stood on a crosswalk in an enormous bay. Below them lay Wolfe's ship. It looked just as it had when he ported at Malabar. 'Would you care to request your good ship *Lollipop* to go through her paces?'

He handed a transponder to Joshua.

'Do you hear me?' Joshua asked the ship.

'*I hear you,*' came through the small speaker. '*I recognize your voice. Do you have a command for me?*'

Joshua turned to Cormac. 'So what do I ask for?'

'How about "gimme the external dimensions of a *Hatteras*-type 92 yacht?" In case you forget your *Jane's,* that's about twenty feet longer than the *Grayle* and a whole lot humpier.'

Joshua spoke into the transponder.

'*Understood,*' his ship said.

He heard the hiss of hydraulics, and the *Grayle* grew imperceptibly. As she did, a long oval atop her hull lifted, and a portholed bridge appeared.

'That's all false front, of course,' Cormac said. 'It extends back over the drive tubes, so you don't really pick up twenty feet, and the bridge is a dummy, too. I couldn't figure any way to mickey up hull blisters, either, that wouldn't conflict with your retractable ones, so I left that alone.

'The *Grayle* can physically mimic about twenty other ships more or less of her class, from a *Foss*-class tug, to any number of in-system workships, to one of the new Federation *Sorge*-type spyships. That might be an interesting switch if things get sticky with our friend Cisco.

'But that's the frosting on the iceberg, when somebody

gets too close. The real changes are in the various signatures, infrared, radar, and so forth. Onscreen, your little putt-putt can look like almost anything from a medium cruiser down to a miner's asteroid puddle jumper. That's the real prize. I decided that everybody wants to go small when they're phonying up what their ship looks like, so I'd go mostly the other way around.

'Plus your rig's pretty clean anyway, so I wouldn't be able to get much tinier an echo.

'You lost two storerooms and one of your spare staterooms for all the e-junk I loaded in, and you don't even want to think about drive economy, especially if you're using any of the drive-signature spoofers.

'Your performance envelope is still the same, unless you're using any of the physical phonies in-atmosphere. I went for things that had lots of little bitty stickouts, so there's a lot more drag. Be a little cautious about going full tilt when you're surrounded by air if you've got any of that crap extruded. I don't guarantee my welds that far.'

'You through?'

'I think so.'

'Pretty good spiel,' Wolfe said.

'Pretty good *work*,' Cormac replied. 'Now you owe me.'

'I do that.'

Cormac turned serious. 'And that's a favor I'm going to call in.'

Wolfe was almost asleep, nodding over a last Armagnac and *Murder in the Cathedral* when the buzzing grew in his ears. He came fully awake, but the sound didn't stop; it grew still louder.

He felt menace, danger, and in spite of himself looked around the familiar bridge.

Pain seared his arm, and he pulled his sleeve back and saw the red welts emerge.

Then the buzzing was gone, and there was utter silence.

After a time, the welts subsided.

Wolfe got up, made strong coffee.

'De Montel?' Wolfe whistled. 'This is a *serious* favor.'

Cormac ran a thumbnail through the foil and pulled the cork. 'Now that's what a proper bottle-opening ought to sound like,' he said. 'Never could get used to that crack when the pressure seal breaks.'

There were two snifters on his desk. He poured one about half full, about an inch into the other.

'Thought you didn't touch hard stuff,' Wolfe said.

'I'm trying to be sociable.'

Wolfe sniffed, tasted, nodded. He eased himself down into the armchair in front of the desk. 'Okay. What've you got?'

Cormac reached into his desk drawer, took out a holo, passed it to Joshua. 'Remember her?'

The woman in the holo had dark, curly hair that frothed down about the shoulders of the sea-green gown she wore. She was on a promenade deck of a ship, and behind her a planet's curve arced. She'd evidently been told to look happy for the recorder and was trying her best to comply, without much success.

Wolfe blanked the background and the jewels at her throat, and studied her face. 'I think so. From the war?'

Cormac nodded.

'Little bitty thing? A first looey . . . no. Captain.'

'That's her. She was my log officer. Rita Sidamo.'

'Okay. I've got her. What's her problem?'

'She's married to a shithead who won't let her leave.'

Wolfe lifted an eyebrow. 'No offense. But that's a little thin these days. It's too easy to just walk out . . . or scream for help.'

Cormac didn't respond to that, but went on. 'We were, well, pretty friendly for three or four months before the war ended. Against regs, naturally, but who gave a damn? It was pretty intense, actually.

'Since the war ended so quickly, it kind of left us hanging. We weren't sure whether we wanted to stay together, or what.

'She took her discharge, went back to her homeworld inside the Federation. We sent a few coms back and forth, and then all of a sudden she stopped writing.' Cormac picked up his drink, tasted it, and grimaced. He went to the cooler and came back with a beer.

'I got over it. Or thought I did, anyway. What the hell, we all kid ourselves about things.

'Three months ago, I got that pic and a letter. She said she had to pay someone to get it out for her.'

'Out of where?'

'The reason she stopped writing is that she got married. Real quick, for no good reason, she said. I guess it was because the guy was good-looking and rich.'

'This isn't sounding any thicker, Cormac.'

Cormac's lips tightened. He opened his desk again, took out a microfiche, stuck it into the viewer on the desk, and spun the device until the plate was facing Wolfe

An image was onscreen:.

A man about Joshua's size, dark-haired, harsh features, staring into the recorder lens with a challenging look.

'His name is Jalon Kakara. He's a merchant fleet owner. Has his own shipyard.'

Other images, starting with a tab's screamer:

BEHIND THE MASK:
JALON KAKARA'S PRIVATE SINWORLD

'He's got his own planetoid, which he calls Nepenthe. It's inside the Federation,' Cormac said. 'I don't know about the sin part of it. But it looks pretty spectacular.'

Wolfe nodded absently, watching images flash past: a long spaceyacht; two mansions; a gleaming high office building; a domed, irregularly shaped planetoid; a spaceport with its pads about half full, all of the ships with jagged crimson streaks down their sides; laughing, richly dressed people at some sort of party; then a picture of Kakara and the woman, both wearing swimsuits, sitting on the rail of an antique hovercraft.

'He's a shit,' Cormac said flatly.

'I've never heard of the guy,' Wolfe said. 'But that doesn't mean anything. The pics make him look rich, all right. Sorry I said what I did.'

He drank and Cormac refilled the snifter.

'I've done some research. Had some friends inside the Federation get what they could on him. Kakara does most of his business from Nepenthe,' Cormac said. 'When he goes offworld, he has his own yacht. Actually, it's a full-size *Desdemona*-type freighter he had laid down in his yards and modified to his specs.

'Sometimes he lets Rita go along with him. But mostly, she's stuck on Nepenthe. Especially now.'

'I've known people who'd like to be stuck like that.'

'His biggest thrill is getting in the pants of his friends' women,' Cormac said. 'And he's a hitter.'

Wolfe's face tightened.

'She wanted out, told him so, even managed to file divorce papers. He got to the records and blanked them. Told her she's his, she agreed, and that settled things. Period.

'She said he likes it better now that she's a prisoner.'

'Are you asking me to do something about it?'

'No,' Cormac said. 'I wouldn't do that. But I'd like you to come up with a plan for me.'

'For *you*? Cormac, you're a goddamned driver, not an op. You're the guy who gets people like me in and out, remember?'

Cormac stared at Wolfe. 'Eleven years since I've seen her. And even before I got the letter I kept thinking about her, and feeling like a dickhead because I should've gone after her way back then, done something, but I didn't. So this time I'm going to.

'I'd already made up my mind before you showed up. When you did . . . I figured maybe I actually had a chance.'

Wolfe took a deep breath. 'Are there kids?'

'No. She said that was one reason things went wrong.'

'Do you have a way of contacting her?'

'No.'

'So you want me to come up with a way for you to get your butt down on Nepenthe, get to her, tell her your idea, hope to Hades she wasn't having a momentary fit of pique at the old man, and then haul ass out with your lovely like you're a harpless Orpheus, right?'

Cormac nodded.

'You realize you're going to get killed pulling this stupid piece of knightly virtue, don't you?'

Cormac shrugged.

Wolfe picked up the glass of Armagnac and drained it.

'You are not going to like this,' Wolfe said to Taen. 'I'm not sure I do myself. But circumstances have altered our plans.'

THREE

'This was a decision reached without logical consideration,' the Al'ar said. His neck hood was half flared.

'No question about that,' Wolfe agreed.

'I have more input on our dreams of insects,' Taen said. 'I sense blue, I sense hazard, a danger that reaches beyond me, beyond you. That should be our immediate concern, not this person who may or may not desire to mate with your friend.'

'Your data,' Wolfe said dryly, still in Terran, 'was derived from cold, logical analysis.'

'Certainly,' Taen said. 'My brain has no other capabilities.'

'But what my brain does is . . . never mind.'

Taen's hood slowly subsided. He stared long at Wolfe.

'Do you remember our first meeting?' he said, returning to Al'ar. 'You were being tested by some Al'ar hatchlings until my presence interceded.'

'We'll forget that I had just busted one clown's ribs for being so interested in tests. Go ahead.'

'You called them cowards at the time, which there is no word for in Al'ar, because they had the sense to attack you in a group rather than singly. I did not understand the term then and am not sure I understand it now.

'But let me tell you of another occurrence I witnessed. During the war, after my special unit was dissolved and I'd been ordered to abandon my hunt for you, I was on the command deck of one of our ships, the kind we called a Large Ship Killer. We trapped two Federation probes and disabled one's drive unit with a long-lance striker. The second ship would have been able to escape, most likely, while we delayed to destroy the first.

'Instead, it reset its pattern and came back almost certainly in an attempt to rescue those who were aboard the first, which any rational analysis would have determined was futile, since they were doomed. The result was we destroyed both ships and their crews.'

'Humans do stupid things like that,' Wolfe said.

'Is the thought process, or rather emotional pattern, because there is no way it can be of rational derivation, which occurred to the captain of that second ship similar in any way to why you wish to aid Cormac?'

'Possibly.'

'Could this sort of thinking, which no Al'ar could ever comprehend, have anything to do with the fact you were defeating my people before we chose to avoid destruction and make the Crossing?'

'Probably not,' Wolfe said. 'We were just lucky.' He got up from his chair. 'Come on, little horse. We have miles to go before we sleep.'

'I doubt if I shall ever understand.'

'That makes two of us.'

Wolfe knelt in front of the Lumina, naked, his hands on his knees. The stone flared colors around the padded room. His breathing was slow, deep.

I am in the void . . . I am the void . . . there is nothing beyond, there is nothing before . . .

He lifted his hands, brought palms together, clasped them, forefinger extended.

Fire, burn, fire enter, fill, bring wisdom . . .

His breathing slowed still further.

Quite suddenly, he was 'above' the Lumina, 'looking' down at it. He moved still higher, reached the overhead, passed through it, mind giving a 'picture' of conduits, bare, oiled steel, then he was 'on' the control deck.

His breathing quickened, and he was staring at the Lumina as its colors flamed. He turned his head and unclasped his hands; the stone cooled, turned gray.

'Well, I shall be dipped,' he said in considerable astonishment. 'I didn't know –'

He broke off, centered his mind, brought control over his breathing. Once more, it slowed.

The Lumina came 'alive,' colors seething.

Wolfe saw nothing but the stone, nor did his perception change.

After long moments, he stood, without using his hands. The Lumina's colors subsided.

Joshua shook his head in bewilderment, picked up the Lumina, and went toward the fresher.

'In readiness for last jump before arrival off Garrapata,' the ship said.

'Stand by,' Wolfe said. He scanned the screen once more. 'And now we go into the Federation itself and wiggle our butts.

'Let's see how well it works in the real world. We want a physical transformation here, not just a spoof-job. Assume the characteristics of . . . a converted *YS*-class yard-boat. I bought you after the war, did most of the conversion myself. I renamed you the, umm, *Otranto*. Respond to any calls to that designation as well as *Grayle* until ordered otherwise.'

'*Understood. Stand by.*'

Hydraulics hummed, and indicators on a newly installed control panel moved.

'*Conversion complete,*' the ship said.

'Now how the hell can I take a look at . . . extrude damage-inspection recorder fifty yards, give full angle of yourself.'

'*Understood.*'

After a few moments, a screen opened.

'Damn,' Wolfe said in some amazement. 'I'd hardly recognize you myself. I'd say you were gorgeous, except that from your appearance I'm a pretty hamfisted makeup artist if I did the work myself. I better put a beeper on you when we land so I don't get lost.'

'Your friend Cormac,' Taen said, 'did excellent work. He is to be commended. It appears that your ship will serve us well.'

'He's getting his paybacks. Ship, what do you think? I remember your last programmer decided you needed more of a personality.'

'*Your statements I interpreted as showing pleasure. Therefore, I feel the same, although I know not what the term means.*'

'*Grayle*, meet Taen. You'd make a great pair. We'll resurrect ENIAC to perform the ceremony. Okay, *Otranto*. Jump when you're ready.'

The world shifted, turned, and Joshua tasted strange spices, felt memories come to him. Then all was normal, and the screens showed new constellations.

'*N-space exited,*' the ship reported. '*Garrapata two E-days distant.*'

The office, and the little man sitting in it, smelled of failure that'd hung on so long it'd become his best friend.

'Here,' he said. 'It's quite a package. Well worth the price I named, Mister . . . Taylor.' The man's nose twitched above his sparse mustache. He reminded Wolfe of a rabbit about to enter a carrot patch.

Wolfe took the microfiche, hefted it, *felt* it. 'Who made the stonebucket?'

The little man tried anger, found it unfamiliar, gave it up. 'You don't think I did it?'

'I know you didn't. Not enough time, for openers. But I don't give a damn.'

'Okay,' the man said. 'It was put together by a team from DeGrasse, Hathaway. I have a way in with somebody who contracts for them now and again. I didn't figure there was much cause for doubling the work they did. I've never heard anybody complain about their investigations.' The little man hesitated, then went on. 'Plus Kakara's little planet isn't that far away, and he does a lot of business here on Garrapata. He's got a reputation. It's hard to watch your back when there's only one of you.'

'Who were DeGrasse, Hathaway digging for?'

'Don't know. Wouldn't ask.'

Wolfe put the fiche inside his jacket, took out bills. 'Here's your fee. You said you preferred cash.'

'Who doesn't?'

Wolfe left the tiny office, eased the door shut. Its click was the loudest sound in the dusty corridor.

Joshua stepped out of the shuttle, walked unhurriedly to a nearby dock, slipped around it, waited. No one was following after him.

He crossed back, past the shuttle station to a second dock, got into the smaller, personnel elevator, and touched its sensor. The lift went up to the deck of the oval dock. He touched the pore-sensor on the *Grayle*'s lock, entered.

Taen sat curled in the stand the two had welded together a day earlier in the *Grayle*'s tiny machine shop. A heavy blaster lay beside him, on its shelf. His eyes slid open.

'There is a message,' he said with no further greeting.

Wolfe went up the spiral staircase to the command deck and to the com.

The screen blurred as he played back. He saw Cisco's utterly unmemorable face.

'I received your blurt-signal,' the Intelligence executive said. 'I assume you have our mutual friend. I need to meet you. It'll do you more good than me. The situation has altered since we last spoke as regards him . . . and yourself.

'We'll meet on your terms, your turf. Contact me as to details through any of the usual channels. I guarantee your safety, but I know you don't believe me.'

'You're right,' Joshua said to the fading image. 'I don't.'

Jalon Kakara glowered at Wolfe. Joshua got up and walked around the holo, examining it closely.

'Did you notice,' Taen said in Terran, 'how his eyes never quite looked into the pickup?'

'I'll be damned. No.'

'Not in this image, nor in any of the others.'

'If I believed baddies had consciences, which I don't, I'd suspect Jalon has trouble sleeping nights.' Wolfe went back to the controls, continued scrolling the microfiche.

'I have a thought,' the Al'ar said. 'By the way. I think I should speak in Terran until we return to the Outlaw Worlds. Sound can sometimes travel much farther and arouse greater suspicion than what we see.

'I am sorry. I am interrupting your concentration.'

'No, you're not,' Wolfe said. 'I'm just cycling this and letting my subconscious do the scheming. Go ahead.'

'My idea was that perhaps I was wrong.'

'An Al'ar admitting he was wrong? You *were* corrupted by me, and I understand why your people abandoned you.'

'I define that as a joke and pay it no mind, nor will I allow the insult to require a response. Perhaps, in a way, we shall benefit from this idiotic side-turning away from our proper goals.'

'In what way?'

'Very few Al'ar ever left their own worlds and journeyed into the Federation. Possibly this is yet another reason we lost the war, since ignorance is always a weapon that turns in your hand.

'I shall pay close attention to what transpires, since I know we will not manage to reach our goals without interference from the Federation. I must know my enemy better than any Al'ar ever did.'

'Your enemy . . . and mine,' Wolfe said, suddenly grim.

He touched sensors, and once more Jalon Kakara's eyes filled with casual disdain and enmity.

'No,' he murmured, and touched more buttons.

The alien and the man were suddenly in the middle of a party, Kakara the center of attention. Wolfe glanced again at the woman beside him, recognized her as Rita Sidamo, but only with a part of his mind.

His eyes were held by the inaudible conversation Kakara was having with a waiter. The man's face was nearly as white as his antique boiled shirt. Suddenly Kakara's hand shot out, sent the servant's tray spinning.

Kakara was shouting now, and the smaller man began trembling.

Taen began to ask something, stopped when Wolfe motioned for silence. He ran the scene once more, then again.

'Oh, I like a bully,' he said softly. 'Especially on toast.'

The bar was a quiet hush, its liquor almost as old as the money it served. It even had human bartenders.

Joshua Wolfe eased into a seat not far distant from one bartender, whose dignified face suggested he would be more suited on the other side of the long polished wooden slab.

'Your wish, sir?'

'Armagnac, if you have it.'

'We do. Any special label?'

'I'm impressed,' Wolfe said. 'Rare enough to find any Armagnac. I'll have Hubert Dayton.'

'I am sorry, sir. But I doubt if you could find that anywhere but Earth. Possibly not even outside of Bas-Armagnac itself.'

'It can be found,' Wolfe said. 'I've had it.'

'You are lucky. I've never so much as tasted it. Would a Loubère be an acceptable substitute?'

'More than acceptable. With a glass of icewater back, if you please?'

The man brought Joshua his drink in a small snifter and set a pitcher of icewater and a glass beside it. Joshua held out a bill. The barman didn't take it.

'You're new to the Denbeigh,' the bartender said. 'I'll present a bill when you leave. Also, this early in the afternoon I'll have to get a note that large changed in the lobby.'

'This isn't for the drink,' Joshua said. 'I'd like to repay you for a few moments of your time, Mister Fitzpatrick.'

'Ah?' The white-haired man did not take the bill. 'You have the advantage on me, sir.'

'My name's Taylor. John Taylor. I was told you're considered the . . . mentor, I suppose might be the word, for barmen here on Garrapata.'

'A compliment carries its own gold. Your money remains your own, Mister Taylor.'

'A Mister Jalon Kakara drinks here when he comes down from Nepenthe.'

'Common knowledge,' Fitzpatrick said. 'He's not a secretive man. Not in that respect, at any rate. That information is hardly worth the sum you're offering.'

'I have heard it said that he is, let's say, not the most congenial company when he's displeased.'

'He would hardly be the first man of means who might be so described,' Fitzpatrick said.

'Let me make a couple of assumptions. Since he drinks when he's traveling, I would assume that he drinks when he is on his home planetoid. Since he is rich, I would assume that he doesn't mix his own drinks.'

'Again, your money remains your own.'

'I'd like to know whether you, perhaps, know of a fellow barman who might have been employed by him on Nepenthe. I'm sure such a man would have fascinating tales.'

'He might,' Fitzpatrick agreed. 'But those tales might not reflect well on his former employer.'

'Particularly,' Wolfe said flatly, 'if Kakara knocked him on his ass when he fired him, or maybe just screamed and generally treated him like a scut.'

'Are you writing a book, Mister Taylor?'

'I could be. But I am not.'

'You know,' Fitzpatrick said thoughtfully, 'if you spoke to such a man, if I knew of such a man, you might end up with very damaging information. Someone who didn't wish Mister Kakara well, someone who himself might have felt his wrath as an innocent, might relish such an event coming to pass.'

'I'd say so.'

Fitzpatrick picked up a pen and notepad from under the bar, wrote swiftly, tore the piece of paper off, and handed it to Wolfe. 'Here's an address where you'll find someone who'll be helpful. Give him this note. He'll tell you whatever you might be interested in.'

His hand picked up the bill, caressed it.

'Yes,' Fitzpatrick said gently. 'Mister Kakara being a bit taken aback is something to relish, indeed. Your drink, by the way, Mister Taylor, is on the house.'

*

'So Jerry sent you along, eh?' The man yawned once again, then got up from the rumpled sheets that turned the narrow couch into a bed. 'I need some coffee if we're going to talk about a turd like Kakara. C'mon in the kitchenette.'

Wolfe followed the man through a doorway. There was just room for the two of them. The man filled a small coffeemaker and touched its START stud. Water hissed, and the tiny pot filled with brown liquid.

A starship lifted from the nearby field, and the tiny apartment's walls shuddered slightly. The man turned his head.

'Two weeks, and I'll be off on one of those,' he said. 'The hell with the Federation. Things're bound to be better out in the Outlaw Worlds. Can't get worse, anyway.'

There was a bottle on the sideboard. The man lifted, shook it. 'Hell. Isn't even enough for an eye-opener.'

'Here. Try some of mine, Mister Hollister.' Joshua took a hammered-silver flask from an inside pocket and passed it to the man.

'That's civilized,' Hollister said. He found a cup, hesitated, then rinsed it out at the sink, knocking over a couple of the unwashed dishes when he did. 'Now, if there's another cup around . . .'

'Just some water,' Wolfe said. 'It's a little late for coffee for me.'

'All right.' Hollister cleaned a glass that had A MEMORY OF SHELDON SPRINGS etched into it and gave it to Joshua. He unscrewed the cap of the flask, sniffed, looked surprised. 'Lordamercy,' he said. 'It's almost a shame to pour this on top of the crap I've been drinking lately.'

He looked swiftly at Joshua, as if afraid Wolfe was going to agree with him, then poured until his cup was about half full. He added coffee to the mixture, gave the flask back to Wolfe.

Joshua poured two fingers into the glass, then added water from the tap.

They went back into the main room. Hollister pushed the sheets off the end of the couch, sat, and indicated a chair. Wolfe sat, putting his glass carefully on a rickety table.

'I owe Jerry large,' Hollister said. 'And maybe I'd like to come back this way again if things don't work out, out there, so I'll give you whatever you want as a favor. What do you need?'

'Nobody's asking for a free ride,' Joshua said. He took out a bill, folded it in half, and set it on the table.

'For that,' Hollister said, 'you can brainscan me about Kakara and damn near anything else. What do you need?'

'You were on Nepenthe?'

'There, and two or three times he told me to go with him on that tub of his, the *Laurel*. Mister, I hope you're planning to do some serious damage to Kakara. I'd call him a prick, but that's the best part of a man, and he doesn't qualify in my eyes. The only person he treats worse'n the help is that poor goddamned wife of his.'

'What're you going to do to him?'

Wolfe shook his head. 'I'm just interested in hearing some stories. No more, no less.'

Hollister looked disappointed; he drank about half of what was in the cup.

'The first thing I'd like to know is how you got the job,' Wolfe said.

'First question you ought to ask,' Hollister said, 'is *why* I got so friggin' dumb as to want it in the first place. But I'll start where you told me.'

'All right,' the woman snapped. 'You. Taylor. Get in here.'

Joshua obediently stood, moved out of the row he sat in, past the knees of the other waiting men and women, and followed the woman into her office.

She slammed the door hard.

'What in the hell makes you think a good man like Mister Jalon Kakara would ever be interested in hiring you?'

'Perhaps,' Joshua said calmly, 'because I'm one of the best bartenders in the Federation.'

'You say that. But I looked at your fiche. God's blazes, you've got a better record as a vagrant than a barman. Looks like you've worked on a dozen worlds or more. Haven't you ever heard of job stability? That's what employers really want.'

'I haven't found any problem getting work,' Wolfe said, his tone still unruffled. 'Perhaps my trade has different standards than what you're accustomed to.'

'Like hell,' the woman said. 'I've been running an employment agency for twenty years, so don't tell me what I'm accustomed to and what I'm not. Taylor, I wouldn't even bother calling Mister Kakara's personnel director about someone like you. Pity's sakes, I'm surprised I'm not thinking about calling Customs and asking why the hell you were allowed on Garrapata, anyway.'

'I'm sorry to have taken your time,' Joshua said, and stood.

His hand was on the sensor when the woman spoke again. 'Mister Taylor, would you wait for a moment?'

Wolfe turned around. The woman's entire manner had changed.

'Would you please accept my apology for my atrocious behavior?'

Wolfe put surprise on his face. 'Of course.'

'Would you sit down, please, sir? And could I get you something to drink?'

'No. No, thank you.' Wolfe returned to his chair. 'But could I ask what's going on? This entire interview has been very irregular.'

'You certainly may. And I'd appreciate it if what I say not go out of here. When you came in, saying you understood my agency hires experienced service personnel, and that you further understood Jalon Kakara was one of my clients, and you were interested in entering his employ, I, quite frankly, wanted to just ignore you.

'But Mister Kakara pays me well. And often,' the woman added, a note of bitterness in her voice, 'as he damned well should, considering the number of people he goes through.

'The reason I behaved like an utter bitch, Mister Taylor, is that Kakara is one of the most unpleasant beings I've ever had the misfortune to have as a client. I like to form a long-term relationship with my employees, since as you well know there aren't very many good ones in the service sector. Least of all' – and she tapped Wolfe's carefully forged resume – 'ones with your credentials and capabilities, which, of course, I'm actually most impressed by.

'So I determined to test you, to see if I thought you might be able to survive working for him. If you'd shouted back at me, or told me you thought I was an evil-behaved slut, I would have apologized, explained, and then found you another place to work where you'd be far happier. But you appear to have the skin of a rhinoceros and the patience of a saint.

'Now do you understand why I acted as I did?'

'I do. You needn't apologize any further. I've already been told Mister Kakara can be difficult.'

'Not can be. *Is*. Almost all the time. Do you still wish to work for him?'

'I do.'

'Could I be nosy, and wonder why?'

'Perhaps because of the challenge,' Wolfe said.

'I've heard,' the woman said, carefully looking away from Joshua, 'that Kakara doesn't much care about what someone did before he arrives on Nepenthe. He feels he's his own law and can handle anything that happens on his world. He doesn't need to pay much attention to anyone else's laws . . . or to their outlaws.'

'Is that right?' Wolfe's voice was mildly interested.

The woman stared hard at him, and he returned her gaze, his expression bland, closed.

FOUR

Nepenthe had been built during the war, for the war, by its money, and when the war and the money ran out, it'd been abandoned as quickly as the nameless ten-mile-long chunk of igneous rock had swarmed with workers after the first Al'ar raid into the Federation.

It had been moved from its original orbit into a Lagrangian point off Garrapata and its rotation had been stilled. The planetoid was named ODS(M) (S)-386 and was ready to be fanged.

The sunward face of the moonlet was studded with solar energy cells, and the receptors were shielded. On the 'outward'-facing surface, where a jutting crag spoiled the illusion of a beef tenderloin abandoned on a grill, the rock had been cut away and a small domed outpost built.

The top of the crag was beveled flat, and the tiny world's single weapon installed there. It was a massive sun gun, hardly the most sophisticated of weapons but effective in defense, and was manned by hastily trained Garrapatian recruits.

Orbital Defense System (Manned) (Solar) Number 386.

Other planets in the Federation were given equivalent defense systems, while the Outlaw Worlds, officially called the Frontier Systems, were ignored, left open to not infrequent Al'ar assaults and even conquest.

With peace, no one wanted or needed ODS(M) (S)-386, but it was only abandoned for three years. Jalon Kakara needed a base for his merchant fleet, where the hastily converted transports wouldn't be troubled with registry, safety, or crewing regulations.

The barracks area was extended and became first docks, then shipyards. On the far side of the peak the sun gun had once topped, converters churned the rock into soil, added nutrients, and a park was sculpted. Then the entire planetoid was domed and given an atmosphere.

Where the sun gun had been, Kakara built his great palace. Energy was free, and so antigrav generators held the soaring, sweeping arcs of buildings, terraces, and decks above the ground's defiling touch, curving ramps connecting them, a dream of flight in stone and steel.

On one of those terraces Joshua Wolfe, obsequious in white coat, black trousers, and a disarming smile, polished the last glass until it gleamed, and set it with its brothers on a shelf.

He was on a verandah that opened on a swimming pool artfully made of rock so it looked like a sinuous forest pond. To his right was the lushness of Kakara's park, to the left the black-and-gray industrial boil of Nepenthe's heart.

Above and behind him, accessible by a seemingly unguarded ramp, were the multilevel rooms that made up Jalon Kakara and his wife's private apartments.

He had been on Nepenthe for almost a month and had yet to meet his master.

'Hey, friend. How's about some service?' The voice was, at the same time, tough and tentative.

The man it belonged to was medium size, overweight, and wore a lounging suit that had been custom-made for a bigger man, then hastily retailored.

'Good morning, Mister Oriz.'

The man eyed him with the cold look of a toad considering a fly's vitamin content. 'You know me, eh?'

'Yes, sir. The agency was kind enough to provide a description of all members of Mister Kakara's immediate staff.'

'First mistake, Taylor. You *are* Taylor, right? I ain't staff. I'm Mister Kakara's friend. That's all.' The cold eyes waited to be believed, looked away when they were satisfied, then returned to check.

Wolfe had been warned about Jack Oriz. Friend he might have been, as much as Kakara recognized the term. He also provided security for the magnate and, like many hangers-on, had a fine-honed sense of paranoia. One of the maids had said Oriz's first name had been different, but he'd changed it to wear Kakara's monogrammed hand-me-downs.

'My apologies, sir.'

'Too early to drink?'

'The sun's up, sir. And I'm on duty. What can I bring you?'

'You know how to do a Frost Giant?'

'Yes, sir.'

Wolfe took five bottles from a freeze cabinet, poured measured amounts into a double-walled glass, then unlocked another cabinet. He pulled on insulated gloves, took out a flask, opened it, and with tongs dropped a purple-streaked, hissing bit of nastiness into the mixture. What appeared to be flame shot up, then swirling mists rose around it.

He set it in front of Oriz with a flourish.

'Not bad,' the man said without the slightest note of approval. 'Mix yourself whatever you're having.' It wasn't a suggestion.

Wolfe refilled his coffee mug.

'Don't drink on the job, eh?'

'I don't drink at all, sir.'

'Another one of the reformed ones.'

'No, sir. Never started.'

'Then how'd you end up doing what you're doing?' Oriz asked.

'My mother owned five bars, so I grew up in the business.'

'What happened?'

'The war.'

Oriz grunted, lost interest. 'What do you think of working here?'

'So far, it's a good job, sir. I'm looking forward to meeting Mister Kakara.'

'Yeah, well, our business took a little longer than we thought. Jalon'll throw himself a welcome-home party tonight. You'll meet him then. It'll probably get wild.'

Wolfe shrugged. 'It's his world, and I'm drawing his silver. Why not?'

'Maybe you haven't seen real wild. You ever heard the joke about Jalon, the two whores, and the Chitet?'

He told it. The story was improbable, obscene, and made Kakara out as a sex-happy fool. Wolfe had heard it three times before on other worlds, each time with a different rich man as the center. The first version had involved the Earth-King Henry VIII and a pope.

When Oriz had finished, he laughed loudly, his eyes never leaving Joshua's face. Wolfe permitted himself a polite chuckle.

Oriz finished the last of his drink, stood.

'Another, sir?'

'More than one of those every couple hours and the party'll have to start without me. Besides, I got work to do.' He turned and waddled away. He veered slightly to the side once, almost slipping into the pool, corrected his course, and vanished down one of the ramps.

Wolfe looked thoughtfully after him, then knelt and began checking the underside of the bar's shelves. He found what he was looking for under the bottom one. It was a gray-green ovoid, a phrase-activated surveillance bug.

'Very cute,' he said below a whisper. 'Say the secret word or retell Oriz's little story, and win a thumping.

'I *am* looking forward to meeting you, Mister Kakara.'

It was late.

The series of rooms set aside for the party were packed. Joshua wondered where all the people had come from. Not even a yacht as big as the *Laurel* could have held them all. He'd seen a few of them in Kakara's absence, wandering around the sprawling mansion, planets without a system.

Now the sun had returned, and the magnate's well-paid friends swirled about him. The music that boomed around Wolfe as he made his way through the crowd, balancing a tray of champagne flutes, came from a quartet on a platform halfway up one wall. It was supposed to be Indian skitch, he guessed, its edges rounded by the distance from New Calcutta, the mediocrity of the musicians, and the tastes of the audience. Joshua thought wryly that the two or three dozen people present who might've been young enough to like the real stuff were more likely to bat their eyes and prefer the tastes – in everything – of their older and richer 'friends.'

He moved around a woman who was leaning against a replica of Michelangelo's *Victory* and staring contemptuously at a man sprawled on the floor at her feet. Someone had scrawled KAKARA RULES on the conqueror's knee.

Two women in old-fashioned tuxedos were dancing skillfully with each other.

An old man sat backward in a Chippendale chair, maneuvering a model of a *de Ruyter*-class monitor around as if he were ten years old.

A man Wolfe noted for his classically handsome features

was holding an intense conversation with the dancer in a Degas painting Joshua was fairly sure was real.

A troupe of ignored acrobats arced back and forth near the ceiling like playful swallows.

Joshua heard Kakara's voice before he saw him. It was loud, commanding, its edges blurred a little by alcohol.

'Damned straight she packed it in on you,' he said. 'You took her away from Potrero, di'n't you? Woman that's got her eye on the main chance, hell, she'll walk from you the minute she sees better. You were just the thing of the moment, just like Dardick or whatever his name is'll be the next on the list when she starts lookin' again.

'No wonder your da asked me to put you right. You got some kind of idea people do things for good reasons rather than because they just want to or because they've got any choice in the matter.'

Kakara wore black dress trousers with a black silk stripe up the side and a collarless silk shirt that had the Kakara house emblem, the jagged red lightning streak, in place of a neckcloth, no jacket. He was berating a slender man about half his age, who wore more conventional formal dress.

Standing around Kakara, nodding at appropriate intervals, were five other men and Oriz.

To one side was the small woman with dark hair whose picture Joshua had seen in Cormac's office. Her eyes were a little glazed, and she held a glass without appearing to notice it was empty.

Wolfe lowered the tray and stood unobtrusively to the side while Kakara continued:

'I'm sorry. But if you run across someone who's important to you – like Rita is to me – you make sure they don't get an opportunity to go in harm's way. It's the best for all concerned.'

He turned to the dark-haired woman and waited. After an interval, she nodded. He turned back, seemingly satisfied.

'Boy, you should count this a good lesson. Let's face it, that woman wasn't anything special. So she was pretty, so she did whatever she did to you in bed that set your little wick wiggling.

'You're rich, boy. You're going to learn there's a million more where she came from. Thing that's important, like I said, is to keep it from happening again. Not just with women, but with everybody.

'You find somebody you need – I mean, really need – you fasten 'em to you with whatever it takes. Money. Position. Power. Whatever. You make double-dogged sure they can't get a better deal elsewhere.

'Or, and this can be the most important thing, don't let 'em think they can do better. Make 'em afraid to start looking. Keep them tied to you, as long as you need them. That's the way to keep people loyal. And I'm pretty damned good at it.'

He spun suddenly and looked at Wolfe. 'Aren't I?'

'I assume so, sir,' Joshua said quietly.

'Assume? Don't you *know*?'

'I haven't been in your employ long enough to form an opinion. Sir.'

Kakara snorted. 'Opinions are like assholes. Everybody has one, and it's for sale. Right?'

Joshua kept the smile in place, said nothing.

'You're just like the others,' Kakara said. He reached out, took a flute from Wolfe's tray, drained it. He was about to turn, stopped, frowned, and his eyes held Joshua's.

They flickered away, and he shook his head, as if he'd just had a glass of icewater tossed in his face.

'No,' he said in a low voice. 'No, you're not.'

Joshua put a quizzical look on his face, nodded, and slipped off.

The dark-haired woman leaned back against the ten-foot-high chunk of driftwood that had been stained, lacquered, and declared art. She was looking out and down at the flaring lights along a shipway as construction robots crawled and welded. She didn't appear to be seeing them.

Joshua moved up beside her. Now his tray held an assortment of small liqueur glasses.

'Would you care for a drink, Captain Sidamo?'

The woman started, looked at him. Her face hardened. 'My name is Mrs Kakara,' she said. 'Are you making some sort of joke?'

'No, ma'am.'

'Are you one of Oriz's amateur spies? Or is my husband playing games again?'

'The bridge of the *PC-1186*,' Wolfe said. 'Cormac said you would remember that. You won't remember me, but I remember you. You were his logistics officer and I was one of his . . . clients every now and then. I don't think we ever were introduced.'

Once more Rita Kakara showed surprise. She looked about hastily. 'Careful. There are bugs everywhere.'

'Not here.'

'How do you know?'

'There was one behind that chunk of wood. I deactivated it an hour ago.' Wolfe didn't wait for a response. 'Now. Reach out, take one of the glasses. Taste it. You hate it. Give it back to me, and I am going to suggest another one, pointing at each.'

The woman hesitated, then obeyed.

'You're genuine,' she murmured. 'Did Cormac tell you what happened that afternoon on the patrol craft?'

'No. I didn't figure it was any of my business.'

'He always was a gentleman.' A smile touched her lips, and she was suddenly as young as Wolfe remembered her. 'Can you get me out?'

'I'm going to try.'

'When? How?'

'I don't know yet,' Wolfe said. 'But keep your track shoes handy . . . and this liqueur, Mrs Kakara, is Deneb Reducto. It's brandy that's had most of the water taken out and replaced with an herbal compound.'

Oriz was at his elbow. 'Jalon sent me over,' he said to Rita. 'He said to remind you it'll be a long day tomorrow.'

Rita moved her face into the semblance of a smile. 'How thoughtful of Jalon,' she said. 'I certainly wouldn't want a hangover. Thank you, Jack.

'I don't believe I'll try any of your wares, sir. That first taste should have warned me.'

Wolfe offered the tray to Oriz, who eyed him, then shook his head.

Wolfe bowed and moved toward a group of three men.

Joshua slid the rack of glasses into the washer, closed the door and touched the sensor. Steam boiled out, and he began loading another rack.

'Leave that,' a voice ordered. 'I need a drink.'

It was Jalon Kakara, appearing no drunker, no soberer than he had before.

'Yes, sir. What may I get you?'

There was a pale light from outside as the planetoid's program suggested dawn was close.

'In the back cabinet, there's a bottle. No label. I'll take about four fingers of it.'

Wolfe found a dark-brown bottle, poured a clear, colorless fluid, and passed it across. The big man warmed the glass in the palms of his hands, then sniffed deeply.

'Might I inquire as to what that is, sir?'

'On the world I come from, the government sets high duty on any alcohol. So we build our own. I keep some on hand.'

'Is it good?'

'Hell no! It's swill. I keep it around to remind me of . . . of certain things.'

Kakara drank, set the glass down with a clatter. 'So you don't think everyone's got a price, as does everything they believe, eh?'

'I didn't say that. Since I'm on your payroll I'd sound like several species of a fool if I did,' Wolfe replied.

'But you don't think that what people believe is on the block?'

'Sometimes,' Wolfe answered. 'Sometimes not. Sometimes it doesn't cost anything, either. People have a pretty good way of convincing themselves what they ought to believe at any given time without much encouragement.'

'Shit! Philosophy.'

Wolfe shook his head. 'Not at all, sir. Just talking about what I've seen.'

'The philosopher barman,' Kakara said. A corner of his mouth twisted.

He drained the glass, got up. 'Maybe I better keep you close. Find out more about what you think. That'd give you a chance to see whether I'm good at writing the music and then making anyone around me dance to it – and like it.'

'As you wish, sir.'

Kakara looked appraisingly at Wolfe, then slid off the bar stool and walked away.

Wolfe watched until he'd left the big room, then went back to stacking glasses in the wash rack.

His expression was thoughtful.

Joshua lay on a knoll in the center of the planetoid's park, on a towel. There were sandals, a pullover, knee-shorts beside him, and he had another towel over his hips. His eyes were closed.

He was not asleep. He floated out, away, toward the

invisible roof of the planetoid, where the artificial sun and clouds floated.

His fingers were splayed, thumb and forefinger touching, resting gently on his stomach.

I float . . . I see . . . the void around me . . . all elements are one . . . I feel the world about me . . . I reach, do not reach, for a way, for a place, where I may call, where the woman and I may flee from . . . the void . . . the emptiness . . . I bring nothing . . . I take nothing . . .

He *felt* someone's eyes on him, sat up slowly, yawning.

Rita Kakara left the path below the knoll and walked toward him. She wore a yellow sundress and was barefoot. Her feet made small springy indentations in the thick turf.

'Good afternoon, Mister "Taylor".' The quotes she put around Wolfe's name were barely noticeable.

'Mrs Kakara.'

'I suppose you've heard already.'

'No, ma'am. I've heard nothing. I haven't checked in today. I'm on the late shift.'

'Not anymore you're not. My husband's changed your assignment.'

'Oh?'

'He wants you to take charge of the bar on the *Laurel*. The bar and the commissary. Your contract will be adjusted accordingly.'

Wolfe rubbed his chin, thinking. 'Thank you,' he said. 'I gather it's a promotion.'

'It is. Even if it'll put you a bit closer to the fire.'

'I don't understand.'

'My husband doesn't handle travel well. Sometimes he becomes . . . upset easily. Too easily.' Rita looked about. 'Is it all right to talk?'

Wolfe was about to say yes, but the Lumina concealed in its pouch in his crotch warmed. He shook his head, slightly.

The dark-haired woman didn't catch the gesture, started to say more. Wolfe held out a hand, low, palm flat.

'Sorry,' she said. 'What I meant to say was that Jalon is a little sensitive about this. Some people might find it amusing that a man who made his riches as he did would have problems in space, and think he's afraid.

'That's not it at all.' Rita was talking a little too fast, Wolfe thought. But she wasn't doing a bad job of recovery.

'I think it's just that he likes his comforts, his own place, and sometimes isn't aware of it. The reason I wanted to mention it to you is to ask that you not judge him harshly if he snaps at you.

'Please don't take it personally.'

'Mrs Kakara, I do appreciate your taking the time, and I'll certainly do my best. I must say that so far the job has been such a pleasure that something as minor as that won't give me a problem at all.'

'I thought you'd understand.' She smiled and went back down the path.

Wolfe lay back down, then, after a moment, rolled onto his stomach. He remained motionless, and, after a space, his back moved slowly, regularly.

I look . . . my eyes are many . . . I see . . . I feel . . .

He *felt* a direction but made no move.

A few minutes later, he opened his eyes a slit.

To his right, on a hilltop nearer the mansion that overlooked the knoll, he saw a heavyset, medium-size man who moved like Jack Oriz walk away. Over his shoulder he carried a tripod, with what might have been a spyeye or directional mike mounted on it.

'Grayle, Grayle, *are you listening?*'

The response came through his bones, from the transponder against his breastbone:

'*I am.*'

'Instructions. I shall be leaving this burrow aboard a

ship. Follow. Do not allow yourself to be perceived. Stand by for immediate closure and boarding. Give this information to Taen. Clear.'

'*Understood.*'

Joshua took off the transponder and replaced it in the cutout copy of *The Barman's Guide to Fine Spirits*.

Joshua made a last check on the storage room, closed the door, and went to an intercom. 'Commissary to bridge. All items safely stowed.'

There was a double-click of acknowledgment.

Joshua went to one of the couches in the barroom, sat down, and leaned back.

Fifteen minutes later, a loudspeaker came on:

'All stations, all stations. Stand by for lift . . . five, four, three, two . . . we're gone.'

He *felt* beyond, outside, and *watched* as the *Laurel* came clear of the dock and moved toward the sky, and the illusion of a world vanished.

A great port opened, and the ship went out into blackness, then through the second lock, and was in the utter night/day of space.

Again the loudspeaker spoke:

'Time to jump, four seconds . . . three . . . two . . . one . . . now!'

The *Laurel* was somewhere else.

Wolfe heard an argument, then a blow. He looked up from the lemon he was peeling into a long curlicue and saw Rita Kakara stumble into the room, then down the corridor that led to the owner's suite. After a moment, Kakara followed, pausing only to glower at the two men at the bar.

'You didn't see anything,' Oriz advised.

'Of course not,' Wolfe agreed.

*

'Mister Trang, what's our destination?' Wolfe said.

'Offaly 18,' the ship's officer said. 'Not that it should matter to you. There'll be no leave granted, which is Mister Kakara's general policy, even his wife.

'Sorry, buster. You don't get the Grand Tour on his credits.'

'Since you like white wine, Mrs Kakara, here's something you might not be aware of.'

'Oh?' Rita pretended interest.

'It's a Chateau Felipe, from Rice XIX. Not that dry, very fruity, a bit of –'

The man beside her grabbed a handful of mixed nuts from the bowl on the bar, picked up his drink, and left.

'We're playing it by ear,' Wolfe said. 'I'm going to try to take you off as soon as we land. Do what I tell you, when I tell it to you. Wear shoes you can run in, clothes that won't stand out. *Don't* bring any baggage or a big handbag. No more jewelry than you usually wear.'

'The only thing I want out of this nightmare is me,' Rita said. 'And you don't have to worry that I'm going to behave like some flip-headed porcelain doll. I'll carry my own weight.'

Wolfe nodded once. 'Sorry. I *was* selling you . . . and Cormac . . . short.'

'**Open the mike to Taen.**' Wolfe spoke in Al'ar.

'**I am listening,**' the Al'ar said.

'*Here is what passes for a plan. It does not appear we shall be able to get the person we want away from the ship. Nor will I be permitted to leave. The best idea my brain provides is that we bring the* Grayle *in directly behind the* Laurel *as it's on final approach. Find out what dock it's going to be landed at, then put some covering fire down, while the woman and I –*'

'Don't even breathe heavy,' a voice behind him said.

Wolfe spun.

The door to his compartment was open. Standing in it were Oriz and two other men. Oriz held a blaster leveled on Joshua's chest.

Oriz stepped forward, ripped the bonemike off Wolfe's chest, and smashed it with a bootheel.

'It appears you aren't nearly as cute as you think you are, hey?'

Kakara hit Wolfe in the side of the head with the flat of a blaster, considered a moment, then hit him again.

Joshua's knees buckled, and he sagged back against the bulkhead. The right side of his face was a mask of blood.

He forced himself erect.

There were five others in the lavish suite: Kakara, Oriz, two bodyguards, and the ship's first officer, Trang.

'You aren't the first who's tried to pull something,' Kakara said. 'And I'm real sure you aren't going to be the last.

'What was the scheme? Who were you talking to?'

Wolfe didn't answer. Kakara started to hit him again, then turned to the officer.

'Trang, are you *sure* there's no other ships within range?'

'Yessir. We checked all frequencies, all wavelengths. Nothing.'

'Then who the hell was he talking to? Somebody on the ship?'

'Unlikely,' the sailor answered. 'That's a long-range transmitter he was using. Maybe, if it hadn't gotten smashed, I could've figured out something from whatever frequency it was set on. But . . .' He didn't finish.

The door slid open and Rita Kakara entered. She saw Wolfe's swollen face, masked her reaction.

'Rita, get out of here,' Kakara said. 'This isn't for you.'

'Why not? Whatever this man wanted to do . . . wouldn't

it have involved me? I want to watch whatever happens to him.'

'You think you do now,' Oriz said. 'But you won't in a little bit.'

'Shut up, Jack. Rita can stay if she wants,' Kakara said. 'But I don't want to hear you sniveling to show him any mercy. The son of a bitch – and his friends – wouldn't have shown us any.'

He hefted the gun and stepped toward Wolfe, then stopped. 'Jack. Let me borrow your penknife.'

Oriz took a small, ivory-bolstered knife from his pocket, opened it, and handed it to Kakara.

The shipline owner grinned, showing all his teeth. It wasn't a nice smile. 'Taylor, you ever see what a knife – a little bitty knife like this one – can do?

'I grew up hard, in the yards. The macs liked blades. Kept their women in hand. I saw what can be done . . . when you work slowly enough. Anyone'll tell . . . or do . . . anything.'

He licked his lips, set the pistol down on a table, and walked toward Joshua.

The Lumina warmed against Joshua's skin.

Wolfe's form wavered, vanished.

Trang shouted surprise.

The air blurred, and Wolfe was there, heel hand striking Kakara on the forehead. He stumbled back against the table, sending the pistol spinning to the deck.

Trang took three fast steps to the door; he was reaching for its control, when Wolfe knocked him down with a spin-kick and moved on, without finishing him.

A gun went off, and part of a bulkhead sizzled, charred.

Oriz had a hand inside his jacket, reaching for his gun. Joshua slammed into him, and he crashed into his two henchmen.

Joshua was turning, inside their guard. A backhand

rapped one of the men between the eyes; the man squealed and fell, both hands trying to put his face back together, gun dropping, forgotten.

The second man jumped back, let Oriz go down, and was in a fighting stance. Joshua snap-kicked, took him in the elbow. The man yelped, grabbed himself, took a knuckle-strike to the temple, and fell.

Oriz was scrabbling for his gun when Rita kicked him in the side. He grunted, rolled away.

Rita had his gun in both hands.

Kakara had come back to his feet. Rita was between Wolfe and her husband. Oriz pulled himself up.

'Rita! Give me the gun,' Kakara snapped.

'I'll get it. She won't shoot,' Oriz said.

The heavyset man had taken two steps when Rita shot him in the throat, blowing most of his spine into white fragments against the bulkhead. His head flopped once, and he fell forward.

The gun turned, and its bell-mouth held steady on Jalon Kakara.

He lifted two hands, trying to push death away.

'No.'

Wolfe's voice was soft.

Rita didn't move. She looked at Joshua, then back at Kakara. Her finger was firm on the firing stud.

Kakara made an unpleasant sound in his throat.

The dark-haired woman turned, tossed the weapon to Wolfe.

He caught it in midair. 'Now, let's go have a talk with the bridge about meeting some friends.'

Wolfe knelt in the open lock, holding the blast rifle that had been waiting in the *Grayle*'s lock on Kakara, the *Laurel*'s captain, and another officer. The side of his face was swollen, the blood only half dried.

'All right, Rita,' he said, his voice a little mushy. 'I have them. Go on into the ship.'

The woman put the safety on her blaster, started to obey, then walked over to Kakara.

The two stared at each other for a very long time.

Kakara was the first to look away.

Rita nodded, as if something had been settled between them, and went quickly into the *Grayle*.

'My ship's armed,' Wolfe said. 'Cut your losses, Kakara. Don't try to be cute.'

The big man stared at him.

'Whoever you are,' he said hoarsely. 'You better learn to sleep with one eye open. And don't make any long-range investments.'

'I never do,' Wolfe said. 'And I sleep with both eyes open. Always.' He slid one hand free, touched the lock sensor, and the door closed.

A clang came as the *Grayle* disconnected from the *Laurel*.

'Sir, shall we track them?'

Jalon Kakara didn't answer. His eyes were still fixed on the blank alloy portal of the airlock.

FIVE

'You have no crew?' Rita said.

'Don't much need one. The ship's automated.'

'So where was it hiding?'

'Dead astern of the *Laurel*. She doesn't have much of a sil-houette anyway, and nobody ever looks over his shoulder. Except in the romances to make sure the wolves are still there.'

Rita tried a smile, which graduated to a successful grin. Wolfe poured her another cup of coffee.

'Should I have shot him?' she asked.

'No.'

'Why not? The bastard gave me more than my share of bruises. Broken bones, twice. And if you were one of Cormac's people, you surely aren't a pacifist.'

'No,' Wolfe said, taking his cup to the washer. 'I'm hardly that. But death's a little final, sometimes.'

The planetoid of Malabar, and its attendant junkyard, was 'below' them.

The woman eyed the screen.

'Eleven . . . almost twelve years,' she mused. 'I hope I haven't built up something to be more than what it was.'

'Not from Cormac's lights. And if it is . . . you can always leave.'

'No,' Rita said flatly. 'Maybe I don't know what I should be wanting. I certainly didn't when I went for Jalon.

'I'll stay the course, if he'll have me. Because I know nobody ever, not *ever*, gets a third chance.'

'I . . . we owe you big,' Cormac said.

'You surely do.'

'Is there anything you need?'

Wolfe thought, smiled quietly. 'A time machine, maybe.'

Cormac looked at him. 'How far back would you go and change things?'

Wolfe started to answer, stopped. 'Maybe . . . all the way back to –' He broke off and said no more.

The port slid closed, and Wolfe went up the circular staircase to the control room. **'You may emerge from your burrow.'**

A panel slid open, and Taen came out.

'My apologies,' Wolfe said in Terran, then switched to Al'ar. **'I have no pride in having to hide you like this.'**

'It matters not,' the Al'ar said. 'I am relieved, in fact, because I do not have to injure my sensors with the sight of more humans. Now, have we adequately fulfilled the role of Noble Savior?'

'For the moment,' Wolfe said. 'And thanks for your appreciation for humanity.'

'This was received,' Taen said, pointing to a screen. 'I do not know how to decode it, but I suspect it is the response from the Federation Intelligence man.'

Wolfe went to the screen and studied the message for awhile.

'Cisco is depending one hell of a lot on my memory,' he muttered. 'It's an old hasty code we used during the war. I think. Let's see . . . OX4YM, RYED3 . . . I can't do it in my head anymore.'

He opened a drawer, took out a pad and pencil, began scrawling. Twice he got up to consult star charts on a screen.

'All right,' he said after some time. 'I think I have it. Most of it, anyway, and I can guess the rest. It *was* from Cisco, and it was setting up a meeting. We've got about two E-weeks to make it, with five days slop on either side.

'I think it's pretty safe. Cisco's going to set his ship down on an armpit called Yerkey's Planet. It's a single-planet system, with not much of anywhere to hide. If we can make a slow approach, ready to streak like a scalded cat if anything flickers . . . maybe. Just maybe.

'Ship. Take us out of this junkyard. Make two blind jumps when we have room, and put us somewhere in empty space, and I'll give you the ana/kata numbers at that time.'

'*Understood.*'

The *Grayle* lifted away from Malabar under medium drive.

Two minutes off, the emergency com frequency blared. 'Unknown ship, unknown ship. Cut drive, stand by to be inspected.'

'Ship! All weapons systems on standby.'

'*Understood.*'

Wolfe swung down a mike. 'This is the yacht *Otranto*, broadcasting on standard emergency frequency. Identify yourself, and give authority for your request.'

'*Otranto*, this is the *Ramee*. We made no request but demand you stand by for inspection. We are in pursuit of a dangerous Federation criminal.'

'Ship,' Wolfe said, 'give me any specs on the *Ramee*.'

'*No ship of that name found.*'

'Do you have any entry, anywhere, on the name *Ramee*?'

'*Otranto*, *Otranto*, this is the *Ramee*. Be advised we are armed, and will launch to disable unless you communicate instantly and cut your drive. Do not attempt to enter N-space. We will match orbit.'

'Ramee,' the ship said calmly. '*More commonly known as Petrus Ramus. An eminent logician. A native of ancient Earth, of the country then known as France. Most noted –*'

'Stop,' Wolfe said. 'With a name like that, a Chitet?'

Taen moved his grasping organs. 'From what you have told me, it would make sense that they would name their spacecraft after thinkers,' Taen said. 'Hardly a subtle maneuver, however.'

'Doubt if they care, this far from anything.' Wolfe keyed the mike. '*Ramee,* this is the *Otranto*. I must protest this piracy in the strongest terms. There is no one on board this craft but the captain and four crew members. We are delivering this craft to its new owners on Rialto.'

'This inspection will take only a few moments. Stand by. We will be sending a team across as soon as we are in conjunction with you.'

'So much for an honest face,' Wolfe said. 'Ship, do you have any ID on the *Ramee* from its dimensions?'

'*The ship resembles three classes of vessels. However, two of them are rare prototypes, so it is most likely the ship is a somewhat modified* Requesans-*class destroyer built by the Federation. I display its possible weaponry, performance.*'

Wolfe scanned the screen. 'Fast little bastard. Fine. Ship, give me a screen with the *Ramee* on it and its probable orbit in relation to us.'

Another screen lit. The Chitet craft, four times the size of the *Grayle*, was closing on the *Grayle* from directly 'ahead.'

'Cautious, ain't they? Ship, dump one missile out of the tubes. Do not activate drive, do not activate homing system, maintain on standby.'

'*Understood.*'

'At my command, you will go to full secondary drive. Put us as close to the *Ramee* as you can. As soon as you clear the other ship, activate the missile behind us and home it on the *Ramee.* Then take us back toward Malabar. I want an orbit that closely intersects the abandoned ships, emerges on the far side of the planet.'

'*Understood.*'

Breathe . . . breathe . . . reach . . .

Wolfe felt the Al'ar beside him stir.

Fire, burn . . .

'Ship, go!'

Drive-hum built around him. Wolfe had an instant to see the *Ramee* blur up onscreen, *felt* it pass, then, in a rear screen, saw the computer-created flare that represented his missile as its drive cut in and it shot toward the Chitet starship.

Ahead, the clutter of Malabar loomed.

'*The* Ramee *has launched three countermissiles. One miss . . . one bypass . . . third missile impacted. Our missile destroyed.*'

'I guess we couldn't hope to surprise them like we did the *Ashida,*' Wolfe complained. 'Ship, how long on the far side of Malabar will we be able to jump?'

'*At full secondary power, seventy-three minutes.*'

'What's the status on the *Ramee?*'

'*It has recovered and has set an intersecting orbit. My systems indicate it is preparing to launch an attack.*'

'I thought they wanted us alive.'

'If these Chitet are not experienced soldiers,' Taen said, 'perhaps they have great faith their weapons will do exactly as they wish and only cripple this ship and leave us to be captured.'

Wolfe managed a grin. 'Yeah. I believed that, too, once. But I'd just as soon not help them learn a missile's about as selective as a hand grenade in a nursery most times. Not when I'm about to be the dissatisfied consumer.'

'*Ramee* has launched. Three missiles. Probability of impact . . . fifty-three percent, plus or minus five percent.'

'I guess we made them lose their temper. Pisspoor for

folks who like to think they're cool, calm, and collected. Put us on an intersection orbit with the boneyard . . . correction, those abandoned ships.'

'*Understood.*'

'Give me a close-up screen.'

The ship obeyed. Wolfe looked at the blips.

'Ship, set a direct collision course for the biggest of the ships.'

'*Understood.*'

Once more the drive hummed.

'On command, I want you to change orbit radically, any direction, hold new course for three seconds, then return to previous course passing us close to Malabar.'

'*Understood.*'

The ships and their parent planetoid were scattered hundreds of miles apart, but on Wolfe's screen, and in his mind, that part of space was as crowded as any ocean harbor.

'Ship, what's the impact time on those missiles?'

'*Twenty-six seconds.*'

'When do we collide with the ship you're aiming at?

'*Twenty-nine seconds.*'

'At twenty seconds, obey my orders.'

'*Understood.*'

Wolfe's eyes followed the old-fashioned sweep pointer on the control panel. He could *feel* death close on him, black wolves with muscles of hydrogen ions.

Quite suddenly the ship's drive moaned, and the artificial gravity lost its focus. Wolfe felt 'down' move around him, swallowed hard, then everything was normal.

'*Missiles evaded.*'

One screen bloomed violet fire, blanked, and a second, shielded one repeated the view.

The forward half of one of Cormac's mothballed battleships vanished in a radioactive spray as all three of the Chitets' missiles struck.

'Well, Cormac did ask if I wanted one,' Wolfe said to himself. 'Duped their young asses, we did. Ship, will the *Ramee* be able to catch us?'

'*Estimate . . . possibly. But not within time frame you ordered until jump. However, they are maintaining pursuit. Not likely they will close distance as we pass through remainder of ships and the planetoid. Estimation of closest time they will be capable of launching attack: eighty-seven minutes.*'

'Well, thank Sheol for small favors.'

Wolfe realized he'd been standing, sagged down into his chair, massaged aching thigh muscles. He wiped a sleeve across his forehead, pulled it away wet. He turned to Taen.

'They *really* don't like us.'

'That is something I hope your Cisco can clarify.'

'He's got more than that to explain,' Wolfe said, a bit grimly.

Wolfe accepted the Lumina's flare, wrapped himself around it, let the flame become him, and reached out, beyond the spaceship's skin.

Void . . . nothing . . . I accept all . . .

He wasn't sure what he was looking for. Perhaps some sign of the Guardians they sought, perhaps a homing signal to the Great Lumina that might or might not exist.

He felt an attraction, turned in space.

His focus was abruptly broken, shattered, and he was back in the bare exercise room.

The Lumina was a dull, egg-shaped gray stone beside him.

All his mind could remember was the sudden angry buzzing, as if a boy had kicked over a hive of bees.

On Wolfe's arm were angry red welts, slowly disappearing.

The *Grayle* crept toward the dying red star and the bulk that had been named Yerkey's Planet.

Taen scanned the ship's screens. All were either blank or showed normal readings.

'The time allocated is almost over,' he said. 'Perhaps Cisco has already departed.'

'If so, then he'll try to set the meet up again,' Wolfe said. 'A good way to keep from springing a trap is to be very early or very late.

'Ship, how close are we to the planet?'

'*Three AUs, approximately. Do you wish ETA?*'

'Negative. I want a full orbit of the planet before we consider landing. Report any broadcasts on any frequency, any man-made objects observed.'

'*Understood.*'

The *Grayle* slid on, all unnecessary systems shut down, its sensors fingering emptiness.

'*I have one not-natural object located,*' the ship reported. '*It is a frigate, of the* Jomsviking *class. From its signature we have encountered this ship before.*'

'When a man who I called Cisco came aboard about a year ago?'

'*Affirmative.*'

'Can you tell what the frigate's combat status is?'

'*Not precisely. No weapons launch points are extruded. Slight discharge from drive tubes detectable, suggesting ship is ready to lift with minimal notice.*'

'Nothing ventured . . . all right. Take us in on a slow landing orbit. If that ship broadcasts anything, or if you pick up any other sign of artificial presence, drive at full power for space, and enter N-space, blind-jump, as soon as possible.'

'*Understood.*'

Yellow dust boiled around the *Grayle* as it landed, hung heavily in the thin atmosphere of the low-grav planet.

A man in a suit came out of the Federation frigate's lock, waddled slowly to a point about halfway between the two ships, and waited, listening to the whisper of his suit's air conditioner. After some time, a man in a suit, faceplate darkened, came out of the dust cloud. Wolfe walked to within ten feet of the man, stopped.

'Cisco.'

'You have the Al'ar?' the Federation Intelligence executive asked. 'Is he on your ship?'

'Seems to me that warrant you put out on me means I'm hardly honor-bound to answer.'

'All right,' Cisco said. 'I did that because I had to. I didn't have any choice.'

'People who take up your trade generally use that for an excuse.'

'This time it's the truth. The hell with it. I'm assuming you've got the Al'ar and have got some kind of operation going.' He held up a gauntleted hand. 'Let me come back to that.

'I wanted to tell you you were right. My superiors said those Chitet were renegades. I bought into that. But after what happened at Tworn Station . . . no more.'

'Very quick,' Wolfe said sarcastically. 'What gave you the hint? That there were three of their goddamned ships around? That their president or director or whatever he calls himself –'

'Matteos Athelstan. His title is Master Speaker.'

'Right. That he just happened to be at Tworn Station with about a trillion of what a woman called his religious caterpillars when the guns started going off?'

'Good, quick analysis, Cisco. No wonder the Federation took six goddamned months to figure out the war had started back then.'

'Knock it off, Wolfe. We're all in the dark on this one. You just happened to be the guy on point who set things off.'

Wolfe grunted, subsided.

'Fortunately, we were able to cover up what happened down there.'

'Why? Why does the Federation give a damn? Why'd you alibi them? Why don't you call up a division or so of the Navy and have them police these clowns up and put thumbscrews on this Athelstan until he sings?'

'Sure,' Cisco said. 'You've been out here in the Outlaw Worlds too long. The Federation doesn't work like that. Hell, no government does, not and be able to hold together for very long. And sure as hell your average citizen doesn't need to know that one of the most respected groups in civilization, known for quietness, efficiency, honesty, appears to have gone completely amok. We're trying to figure out the whole scope before we take action.'

'Meantime, you do nothing.'

Cisco made no response.

'All right. Let me take it now. Are you willing to admit there is a conspiracy? That it's a big one?'

Cisco nodded, then realized his motion couldn't be seen through the tiny faceplate and made an agreeing sound.

'You know the Chitet have a man inside Intelligence Directorate?'

'Yes. More than one. I think I can ID two, but there's at least two others,' Cisco said. 'But it's worse than that. I can't smoke them out because they've got cover farther up.'

'Inside the government?'

'Yes.'

'High up.'

'Yes. And in more than one branch.'

Wolfe muttered inaudibly. 'What are they after?'

'This is where it gets complicated,' Cisco said. 'Nobody knows. But I was able to set up a cutout operation and started some archivists digging into what we know about the Chitet, going all the way back.'

'Back what, four hundred or so years ago,' Wolfe asked, 'when they tried their little coup and got their paws slapped?'

He heard a surprised hiss from Cisco's microphone. 'There aren't a lot of people who know about that one.'

'I read history.'

'That's where we started,' Cisco went on. 'About two hundred years ago, not long after we made first contact with the Al'ar, the Chitet sent out an expedition to make contact with them.'

'Why?'

'The few records we've found don't say. And there's not much in the archives – somebody fine-toothed them and got almost everything to the shredder. Almost, but not quite.'

'What happened?'

'Something went wrong. They sent seven ships. None of them came back. No known survivors.'

'You're saying the Chitet took a hit like that and didn't scream to the government?'

'Exactly,' Cisco said. 'Obviously they were doing something they didn't want us to learn about. Ever.'

'What was their position during the war?' Wolfe asked. 'I was out of town and not reading the papers.'

'Unsurprisingly, they were fervent backers of the war effort and the government. Ran recruiting drives in their movement, raised money to buy ships, big on the various war bond drives, and so forth. Their then-Master Speaker, not Athelstan, hit the rubber-chicken circuit, always on the same theme: There can be but one imperial race in the galaxy, and it must be Man.'

'Well, something changed,' Wolfe said. 'In case you don't know it, they aren't after your Al'ar to slot him as the last survivor. At Tworn Station they were trying to take him alive.'

'That was my estimation,' Cisco said. 'Otherwise, they would've just dropped one nuke on the lid of that dome and let the ocean in to sort things out.'

'Maybe,' Wolfe said slowly, 'maybe they figure the Al'ar had something they could use. Something that'd let them pull another coup . . . one that'd succeed this time.

'You know they're buying every old warship they can get their hands on, preferably with the weapons systems intact.'

'Shit!' Cisco said. 'No. I didn't.'

'Now let's get personal. What are you – and FI, at least the part of it that isn't wearing dark suits and thinking logically – doing with me? Using me as your goddamned stalking horse?'

'I considered that,' Cisco said. 'But they're too close, and there's too many of them. I want to help you in whatever you're trying to do.' He gestured at the ship behind him. 'You can use me – and the *Styrbjorn* – if you want. But first I wanted to get some of the heat off you.

'I started a disinformation program a couple of months ago. You upped stakes and headed for the other side of the known universe, you've gone to ground inside the Federation, there's stories that your ship blew up, somebody killed you in a gunfight . . . as much as I can plant to confuse the issue.'

'Let me tell you something,' Wolfe said dryly. 'So far your little scheme isn't working. A Chitet ship jumped me when I was offplaneting . . . the last place I was at.' He ignored Cisco's start of surprise.

'And you best be careful on your own right,' he continued. 'Not that I give much of a shit, but if the Chitet inside FI figure out what you're doing, you could end up on the short end of a rope.'

'I'm careful,' Cisco said. 'I'm always careful. I'm using clean cutouts. Like our mutual friend who helped set up the meeting.'

'You still haven't answered the question,' Wolfe said. 'What do you want from me?'

'I want information,' Cisco said. His voice rose from his customary monotone. 'I'll ask the same questions I did before. What is the Al'ar looking for? Why was he wandering from homeworld to homeworld? Does he know what the Chitet could be after? Come on, Wolfe. I need help.'

Wolfe stood motionless for a space, then walked off, toward his ship.

'Wait! Goddammit, Wolfe, this can't be a one-way pipeline!'

Wolfe stopped, didn't turn. 'Right now,' he said slowly, his voice sounding muffled, 'I'll play the hand you dealt. I'll let you know when I need more cards . . . or have something to discard.'

He went on, and the form of his suit disappeared into the dust.

Ten minutes later, the ground shook under Cisco's feet. He turned on an outside mike and heard, dimly, the whine of a shipdrive.

The *Grayle* lifted through the dust and soared toward space.

Cisco watched the flare of its drive until it vanished, then walked back to the *Styrbjorn*.

SIX

The *Grayle* whispered through the darkness between stars. The only sound, beside the ship hum, was the dry voice of a man dead more than a thousand years:

> *'The trilling wire in the blood*
> *Sings below inveterate scars*
> *And reconciles forgotten wars.*
> *The dance along the artery*
> *The circulation of the lymph*
> *Are figured in the drift of stars . . .'*

Wolfe swung his feet off the bunk, touched the sensor, and the man's dusty voice stopped. He went toward the control room.

'I am sorry,' the ship said, and Wolfe imagined pique in the synthesized voice, *'but the task you require is beyond my capabilities, even if I were to shut down all non-life-support duties.'*

'Disregard. Resume normal functions,' Wolfe said. He tapped fingers on the control panel, thinking. 'You're sure you haven't got the vaguest idea where these Guardians might be located?'

'As I have said, that was why I was going from home-world to homeworld, seeking clues,' Taen said.

Wolfe frowned, then brightened. 'What we need is a computer. A *big* goddamned computer.'

'There is such a device on Sauros.'

'Which you can run?'

'Because I was working directly for the Command On High when I was hunting you, I was given a special, direct access code. I can use that to avoid the computer's safeguards and, from there, should be able to use the device, assuming standard coding, standard controlling,' the Al'ar said. 'We should have only one problem.'

'Yeah. You told me. It'll try to kill us without proper access.'

'I do not think the computer itself will attempt our deaths. When our Planners set up these devices, allowing for emergency use, I would assume they thought a user might not have full access information.

'Where the computer will try to kill us is on the way in, I suspect.'

'Big difference,' Wolfe said. He thought for a space. 'Maybe I know a better way. All this one will do is make me feel like a worthless asshole for a week.'

The bonemike against his chest vibrated.

'*No one told this man his brother had been killed by our forces?*'

'*He was told,*' Wolfe said shortly. '*He went mad. He retreated into a world where he had not been told.*'

'*And he is allowed to remain free, to live completely alone? No one in your society has rechanneled his mind to the truth? Or else, if that is not possible, ended his life as a gift?*'

'*We aren't as altruistic as the Al'ar,*' Wolfe said in Terran. '*Now shut the hell up, Taen. Something's wrong.*'

The tottering old house was dark, quiet, dead.

Wolfe moved across the street, stopped at the stainless-steel tube that was the mansion's pneumatic delivery system. When he'd last seen it, less than a year earlier, it'd been new. Now its sleekness was marred, gray. Someone had chalked an obscenity on it. Wolfe tried the access door. It had been jammed shut with a stick.

Wolfe went through the sagging gate and up the weed-grown path onto the sagging porch. He touched the com sensor once, then again, waited for almost half an hour.

Breathe . . . the earth reaches up . . . steady, unmoving . . .

He took two small, bent pieces of metal from his belt-pouch, held the knob steady, hissed surprise as the door came open.

A gun came into his hand as he moved to the side and waited. On the other side was nothing but silence. Silence and a familiar, too-sweet stink that rose above the customary smell of decay.

'The man's a rotten housekeeper,' he murmured. 'But still.'

He took a tiny light from his pouch, went quickly through the open door, flattened himself against the wall.

Nothing happened.

He moved his hand down the jam, found raggedness where a jimmy had pried, slid the door almost closed, snapped the light on, swept it around, turned it off.

'Mister Davout,' he said loudly. 'It's me. Joshua Wolfe.'

Silence.

Again, he turned the light on.

The hall was still stacked with years of high-piled coms. Davout had saved everything, from news, to entertainment, to devices in the sure and certain hope that one day his brother would return.

Wolfe moved the beam to illuminate one of the front rooms. Sealed boxes that had held music-fiches had been ripped open and cast aside.

He went down the hall toward the back stairs, keeping close to one wall. He walked in a strange fashion, crouched, centered, each leg sweeping toward the other in an inward arc, foot touching down toe-first, hesitating, then the full weight on the heel and the next leg moving forward.

The kitchen was still stacked with forgotten, unwashed dishes. But no odor came from them. Even the mold that had grown over them like a blanket had withered, died.

Wolfe took a deep breath, held it, then exhaled and started for the stairs.

Davout had cleverly used the newscoms kept for his brother's eventual reading as a booby trap, the papers baled, stacked precariously with barely visible wires here and there that, barely touched, would bring tons of paper cascading.

The stairs were a shambles of paper. A man's legs stuck out from under the bales. The smell came from him.

Wolfe grimaced, held the light between his teeth, lifted two of the bales away. Others threatened to tumble but didn't move.

The man killed by the trap had worn pants, not Davout's customary coveralls, and black boots, badly worn on the edges of the soles.

Wolfe touched the dry, withered skin.

'Dead two, maybe three months,' he said softly.

He lifted away more bales, pulled the man free, ready to jump to the side if more papers came down.

He turned the body over, shone his light on the face. He didn't recognize the man.

He went through the man's pockets, found lockpicks, plas cuffs, a folding stiletto, a few bills, an inhaler half full of a brown powder. He opened the vial, sniffed, wrinkled his nose, tossed the drug aside.

He stood, flashed his light up the stairway. Metal, not quite rusted, reflected the light. It was a long jimmy.

He stepped over the burglar's body and started up the stairs.

Davout lived in one long room on the top floor, windows

painted black against the light and the world. In the center of the room was the strange mélange of electronics that was Davout's computer, a bastard concoction of mostly military components the man had put together. There was a dim light from four screens, still scrolling endless numbers.

The little man lay on his back beside it, next to his overturned office chair.

Wolfe went to him and shined the light on his face.

Davout's skin was dry, withered. His lips were drawn back in a grin. His eye sockets were black, and something, rats perhaps, had nibbled away most of his ears.

His body showed no signs of violence.

His right hand was clasped over his chest, holding a piece of paper.

Wolfe gently lifted his hand and took the paper.

It was as brown, desiccated, as Davout's skin.

The Federation deeply regrets to inform you that no signs of your brother, Mister Stephen Davout, have been found in any of the worlds retaken thus far. We therefore have determined his status must be considered no longer MISSING but PRESUMED DEAD.

A representative of the government and a trained therapist will be calling on you to assist you in your hour of bereavement, and should you . . .

Wolfe put the years-old com back on Davout's chest, folded both his arms over it, and stood.

'I wondered if he always knew . . .' His voice trailed off.

He put the gun away, turned, went swiftly down the stairs and out of the house.

The shattered Al'ar battleship spun in the orbit it had found when the Federation warships left it in its death throes. The system's sun was very dim, very distant.

The killing blast had smashed the drive section of the crescent-shaped warcraft, and most of the crew had died in that moment.

The rest of the Al'ar had been left to their doom. There were blackened sears here and there on the odd reddish-violet metal skin, where destroyers had come close to the fangless monster and blasted away the lifeboat stations.

Wolfe floated out of the *Grayle*'s lock, set his helmet sight on the center of the battleship, touched a stud at his waist. White spray came from his suitjets, and he moved slowly across the half-mile distance toward the ship. He reversed as he approached the Al'ar ship and landed lightly, feet first, near the oval hatch.

Old memories came back, and he found the outer lock controls, pressed them. Nothing happened. Wolfe muttered a curse, took hold of the emergency toggle, and pulled.

Dead machinery came alive, and the hatchway yawned.

He saw the reflection of his face against the faceplate. It was white, drawn. He heard nothing but the rasp of his breathing.

Joshua floated inside.

After a long time, he came out. He pulled behind him an Al'ar deep-space suit and a second garment he had rolled up.

He knelt clumsily, and his lips moved soundlessly.

He pushed himself free of the ship, set his sight once more, triggered the suit drive, returned to the *Grayle*.

He did not look behind him.

'I do not understand why I will need a suit, especially not an on-planet outfit on my own world.'

'You will. Be silent. I do not wish to have speech with you at this time.'

'What is troubling your mind?'

'If you wish to have knowledge,' Wolfe said, 'it wasn't the happiest day of my life boarding that ship. There were a . . . lot of corpses. Some of them didn't die for a long time after the Federation ships finished with them.'

'But why should that bother you?' the Al'ar wondered. 'They are not your people. And dead is dead. Perhaps you are just upset at that Davout friend of yours.'

Wolfe gazed steadily at Taen.

The Al'ar met his gaze. Then Taen's head snapped back, as if he'd been struck.

He rose and left the compartment.

The *Grayle* plummeted toward the surface of Sauros, flared less than one hundred feet above the open ground, then settled toward the surface. It stopped about five feet above a flat, metalloid area that had once been used for the Al'ar polygonic 'dances.' The ship's lock opened.

Bulky packs were tossed out, and two space-suited figures followed them. The lock closed, and the *Grayle* lifted for space.

The two shouldered their packs and ran, stumbling awkwardly, toward a nearby building, careful to follow the winding path.

They disappeared inside.

The echoes of the shipdrive died in the streets of the city, a half-shattered wonderland of multicolored glass, stone, and metal, hues dulled by time and abandon.

No animal moved in the parks, no beings walked the streets.

Two hours later, another noise came, a rhythmic buzzing.

A small winged craft soared down a high corridor of stone, under an arching roadway, through the park, which the Al'ar had called a 'reaching-out' place. It orbited the park three times quickly, then another dozen times at its slowest speed, almost stalling.

Its operator reached a decision, and the robot banked and, at full speed, went back down the avenue, echoes of its passing dying as it went.

The two space-suited figures came out, returned to the path, and went through the park, into the city, the taller leading the way.

Neither spoke.

Sometimes the way was clear, sometimes rubble blocked their passage. Storefronts had collapsed, strange goods spilling across the road. But there had been no looting.

They walked for almost half an hour, then stopped in front of a half dome over a smooth ramp that led underground. They went into the cover of the dome and took off their suits.

'You appear to have taken the long way,' Wolfe said.

'Not at all,' Taen replied. 'We could have used the first burrow entrance. But then we would have had to use the civilian ways to reach this military entrance, and I do not know what shape they are in. I wonder that none of your people appears to have landed and collected the spoils of war.'

'Some might have,' Wolfe said. 'But not for long, and it would've been in the first days after the war. The Federation has all the homeworlds under watch now.'

'Ah. I did not know that. That is why the drone found me so swiftly when I first came to Sauros. I merely assumed my ship had been detected somewhere in space and followed.'

'No. They're scared shitless of whatever's still here. That's why we wore the suits, so their sensors wouldn't pick up any heat or other signs. We'll put them on again when we come back,' Wolfe said.

'If we come back this route,' the Al'ar added.

'You could also say if we come back at all.'

'I could. But I have confidence.'

The Al'ar opened his pack, took out what appeared to be a block of white plastic. He unfolded it until it became a thin square about eighteen inches on a side.

He touched a sensor, and the lines of a crudely drawn map appeared.

'The machine we seek, this computer, is one of three used by our Command On High. I learned of it only because the unit I headed that hunted you was assigned directly to them, and I filed my reports here.

'With luck, no one will have discovered it, and our task will be simple,' Taen said. 'I shall lead. Perhaps my presence will prevent any protective devices from activating.'

Wolfe nodded and shouldered his pack.

The two went down the ramp, disappeared from sight.

There was a neat hole in one corridor wall and, on the other side, a gaping, jagged opening.

'I do not like this,' Taen said. 'Someone who did not know the code came this way and triggered the weapon.'

Wolfe knelt, touched the deck, and *felt* around him. The Lumina in its hidden pouch warmed to his touch. He rose.

'Someone . . . maybe two, three people died when they set off this trap.'

'Terrans?'

Wolfe nodded.

'Yet there is no sign of a body. Still worse,' Taen said.

'Renegades don't worry about corpses,' Joshua agreed. 'These people would've been part of some organization.'

They went up a winding, curved corridor. The Al'ar abominated straight lines in length, so their buildings turned, swept, as did their roads and tunnels.

Wolfe had to stop three times to reorient himself as they went.

They went on another half mile. Twice Taen touched a blank section of wall, then told Wolfe it was safe to proceed.

The corridor ended abruptly. Taen stood in a certain place, took two steps at the side, and the wall lifted, revealing a high, rounded chamber. But no lights came on, and Wolfe smelled the old stink of seared flesh, ozone, *felt* fear and agony.

There were control panels ranked around the walls, but blaster bolts had torn and ripped them.

Taen made a soft noise of pain.

Once more Wolfe *felt* around him.

'Men were killed here,' he said softly. 'There aren't any bodies, so this must've been a Federation Intelligence group, not renegade looters. Probably one of our Analysis teams. Scientists, engineers, mostly. I guess they found this, tried to operate it.'

'And the machine killed them,' Taen said.

'Killing itself in the process.'

'No,' the Al'ar said. 'This is but an operating station. The computer itself is safe far away, far below us. But what upsets me is that I was wrong. I told you that the computer itself would have no safeguards. I was wrong. I wonder what else I am wrong about.

'**We must seek one of the secondary stations. I know the approximate location of one.**'

They stopped twice, ate rations from their packs that Wolfe hardly tasted, stopped a third time, slept briefly.

Wolfe woke with the memory of buzzing, felt the burns on his arm.

The man sprawled on his back, a look of mild surprise still visible. His build was slight, thin, and the face was that of a scientist, a thinker. His cheeks had begun to pull back into a rictus.

There was a hole where his chest had been and a pile of white dust above and below the hole where a strange decay was spreading.

'This was a looter,' Wolfe said. 'Somebody managed to land without alerting the Federation or else came down before the interdiction was put on.'

'What would he have sought?'

'Hardware. Programming. Raw knowledge, maybe. The word was your computers were faster, more intuitive than ours. I never knew anybody who'd operated both, so I can't say. He must've believed the story. He' – Wolfe looked around at the other six bodies – 'and his friends. They had enough brains to find this place . . .' He shrugged. 'Now what do we do?'

'I do not like this at all,' the Al'ar said.

'I'm not exactly overjoyed. What are our options? Find another world?'

'No. This is the only location I know for certain. We could spend the rest of our lives on other homeworlds' undergrounds, looking,' Taen said.

'And maybe running into another one of these nasty little traps,' Wolfe said. 'All right. We'll come up with another plan that doesn't require heavy thinking. Drop the computer idea.'

'We have one option. We could seek out the computer itself.'

'Which you said is under us. How far down did the Al'ar dig? I never knew of anything other than the upper civilian levels when I lived here, you know.'

'We dug . . . very deeply.'

'You said we could spend two forevers looking for a simple operating station. How will it be easier looking for Big Mama?'

'Easier in the looking because its location will be close to our Final Command Station. This is where we would have fought from, if you had landed on Sauros. Instead . . . we found another Way.'

'All right. And I would guess that there'll be even more traps for intruders.'

'Not just for Terrans,' Taen said. 'No Al'ar was permitted to go to these places without special permission, guides, and passes.' He paused. 'The machine will be as perfect a deathtrap as our finest soldiers could devise.'

SEVEN

The ramps curled down into darkness, broken now and again as still-sensing lamps flared, died as they passed.

Three levels below the military tunnel system, huge doors hung open. Inside was a great hangar with lines of in-atmosphere interceptors, sagging drunkenly, their skid-shocks slowly collapsing as fluid leaked away.

'We would have launched these when your ships entered Sauros' atmosphere,' Taen explained. 'Buildings above had been constructed with demolition charges so they would fall away at the proper time.'

'Clever,' Wolfe said neutrally. Both spoke in Al'ar. It seemed safer.

The next level was barracks for the pilots and maintenance crews, with long rows of resting racks stretching away into darkness. The padding on the racks had begun to unravel and trailed on the decks. Wolfe noted that nothing, not man, not rat, not cat, had made trails in the thick dust. He thought he could hear the faint whisper of a still-functioning air-circulation system.

Taen moved in front of Joshua as they went on. Wolfe found his hand hovering over his gun and grinned wryly, wondering what in this long-dead labyrinth would need shooting. Booby traps are impervious to a quick draw.

Taen held up a grasping organ, crouched, and pointed to the wall. Wolfe saw nothing, *felt* beyond.

Death . . . the snout of a blaster muzzle behind the metal-loid . . . trigger-sensor still alive . . .

They crawled under the sensor, got up, and went on.

The corridor they were in opened up, the walls hidden in the gloom, and another ramp went down, winding, turning. Joshua *felt* great space around him.

More and more of the automatic lights had failed, and so they took flashes from their packs, continued on.

Wolfe heard a whine of gears and went flat. The sound grew louder, and the ramp swiveled sideways, trying to dump them off. Joshua scrabbled toward the edge of the ramp as it turned, held it, and Taen's grasping organs had him by the leg.

He hung, gasping, over emptiness.

The Al'ar clawed his way up Wolfe's body, found a hold on the ramp, and they clung for long moments until the ramp settled back to level.

'I did not sense that coming,' Taen whispered.

'Nor I. I heard the sound of its machinery just before it began functioning.'

'But you sensed it before I. Perhaps you should lead. I must tell you that none of these devices was operative the times I was ordered to come this way.'

Wolfe hesitated, then obeyed. The Lumina was warm against his skin. The darkness around him was chill and smelled faintly of ozone.

The walls drew in once more, and they walked down a corridor that might have been on a spaceship.

At the end of the passage was a door. Wolfe was about to insert a finger into the opening sensor notch, then stopped. He knelt, peered into the slot, saw nothing.

He took the pack from his back, and pulled out a jimmy and a hammer. He motioned Taen out of the way, then tapped the dogs of the hinge free, caught the door as it tottered, and eased it to the deck.

Taen held up his grasping organs in a questioning gesture. Wolfe turned the door over and slid the tip of the jimmy into the sensor notch, turning his head away as he did.

A violet laser-blast flashed, burning a half-inch hole in the ceiling above them. Taen hissed, said nothing.

Their way was level once more. Taen came close, whispered, 'Now we are on the base level. What we seek should be close.'

Once more the walls were far-distant, invisible. Wolfe coughed, and sound echoed into the distance.

Taen took the lead again and went on, his head moving back and forth like a questing hound's.

Domes, some small, some huge, rose around them. Taen stopped at one.

'Here is the place we would have commanded the final battle from.'

Curious, Wolfe started to activate the door to the command center. Taen stopped him.

'Our business is not in there. Why should we risk encountering another trap?'

Wolfe held up his hands, agreeing, and abandoned curiosity.

He heard the purring of engines and then light crashed up around them, blinding them. The engine-sound grew louder, and something hovered toward them from the darkness.

Wolfe knew it from the war.

It was a four-barreled auto-cannon, triggers linked to motion detectors. Wolfe rolled as the cannon churned rounds, tearing up the metal deck where he'd been. The cannon swiveled, long-disused bearings squealing, spat a stream of solid bullets, and once more he rolled, coming up in a squat.

The Lumina burned against him as he frog-jumped sideways, and the cannon swept past him.

He froze, barely breathing. The cannon's pickups scanned the area he was in, found nothing, swept in increasingly greater arcs.

Wolfe inhaled sharply, about to dive for the gun's base, into its dead zone, and Taen rose from the darkness, blaster in both grasping organs, and blew the sensor off the cannon-mount.

The cannon blatted a burst into nowhere, ground into silence. It floated away, aimlessly, its guns looking here, there, nowhere.

Taen beckoned, and Wolfe followed him, around the great bulk of the command center.

An arched doorway rose from the deck. Taen tried the opening sensor. The door remained locked.

Wolfe took lockpicks from his beltpouch and slipped them into the slot. He *felt* as he moved them, trying to think as an Al'ar.

He felt a humming through the picks, jerked his hands out as the door slid smoothly open.

Inside were the banks of a great Al'ar strategy computer.

Taen slid his hand down a multicolored strip next to a rack, and around him screens lit. A larger screen, almost a yard on a side just in front of Taen remained blue-black, inactive.

'It lives!'

'It would have been a not life-enhancing experience if it had not, considering our passage,' Wolfe said.

'That is what you call sarcasm I would guess,' Taen said. 'I did not know it was possible to do that in Al'ar.'

The holograph rose in front of him, the computer's 'keyboard.' Dim green light formed vertical squares, and in each was a character or combination of characters in Al'ar.

'Let us hope that it will recognize me.'

Wolfe pulled up a resting rack and made himself as comfortable as possible.

Two hours later the dark screen in front of Taen blinked into life, swirled through a color wheel, shades unseen by Wolfe since he was last on an Al'ar world.

'Now we have a starting point,' Taen said.

'Start by asking about the Guardians.'

Taen's impossibly long fingers moved, screens showed figures, then a diagonal multicolored band appeared across the main screen. Taen's grasping organ shot out, and the screen blanked.

'That I do not like.'

'What occurred?' Wolfe asked.

'Be silent. Let me attempt the task again.'

Again his fingers moved against the 'keyboard,' and again the diagonal band flashed and Taen was cut out of the program.

'The machine has defenses and takes precautions. I thought I had a high-enough permission, what you call clearance, but any attempt to inquire in the area of Guardians produces a warning. If I persisted, I suspect the whole computer would shut down on me. Do you have a suggestion?'

'I think,' Wolfe said, 'we stay light-years away from that area. You realize that what just happened confirms the existence of the Guardians.'

Taen's hood flared slightly, then subsided. 'No, I had not yet . . . of course. Certainly it must. I wonder what has become of my intelligence? I am behaving entirely like a broodling.'

'Don't concern yourself,' Wolfe said. 'I never thought you were highly gifted in the arena of thinking.'

'Such is obvious,' Taen said. 'I chose to associate with Terrans.'

Wolfe looked at the Al'ar in considerable astonishment. 'Taen, did you just make a joke?' he asked in Terran.

'Perhaps I did. It was an error. **How shall we pursue the matter now?**'

'I wondered if there might not be some kind of block within the computer,' Wolfe said, 'so I brought some backup.' He dug in his pack and took out two microfiches, a viewer, and a notepad.

'This will take a few minutes,' he said, inserting the card into the viewer's slot. 'If we can't get 'em high, perhaps we can nail them down low.'

'What are these locations?'

'These are twelve battles fought during the war. I got them from the standard Federation history of the Al'ar war. We gave these battles their own names, which I assume could have different labels in Al'ar, so what you're looking at are just the ana/kata coordinates.'

'**Why were – are these battles special?**'

'Because these were fought in the middle of nowhere, for no discernible reason. All of them are deep inside the Al'ar sectors. Generally a Federation Fleet or Fleets would be traversing a certain area and be met with a sudden attack that ended only with the complete defeat of one or another force.'

'**What makes that extraordinary? There were many such fights.**'

'True. But these catfights appear to have been by accident, and especially ferocious, when our forces stumbled into yours. The Al'ar ships were already in place, as if they were holding a specific defensive position.'

'Perhaps,' Taen said, 'your security was inadequate. Perhaps our forces had advance knowledge of your Fleet movements and were able to prepare ambushes.'

'That was what the Federation Command worried about. I was consulted on two of the battles, which is why I remembered them. They'd assembled all data on the two events, but no one could find any congruence that might suggest a mole. They wanted to know if I could provide any interpretation of what happened. I failed. The explanation settled on was the imbecilic one of "aliens do alien things in an alien way."'

'Do not be angry at them. My own Command On High frequently used the same simplistic thinking,' Taen said.

Wolfe returned to Al'ar. 'I would like you to examine these locations on a small-scale starchart and tell me what the computer tells you about them.'

'I do not understand what you are seeking, but I shall obey. Rest yourself. This shall take some time, even with a device as sophisticated as this.'

'I have some interesting data,' Taen announced. 'First, I can confirm your hypothesis that these battles were anomalous, being fought far distant from any known Al'ar bases and not part of any known offensive plan. Look at these two. Nearly in the same location, yet fought seven years apart.

'What could have been so valuable about that sector of seemingly empty space that our forces would defend it so resolutely, as well as all the others?'

Wolfe's eyes gleamed. 'I can conjecture a better place to begin thinking,' he said. 'Take those two points and connect them. Project the line out.'

'I have done this.'

'Now take the other battles, and project a line from each of them to intersect with this line.'

'Shadow Warrior,' Taen said, and Wolfe thought he detected impossible emotion in his voice, 'the intersection point is at the fringes of our sectors, but well within the area of Al'ar control.'

'Worthy of consideration,' Wolfe said. 'Now, might you not wonder if our Fleets just happened to wander into these areas and were brought to battle because they were on the "approaches" to something very secret, something that perhaps even the forces assigned to defend them might not be informed of?'

'Such as the planet of the Guardians?' the Al'ar said. 'You do not have enough data to make such an inference.'

'Here might be an additional piece of data. Can you find out what units were involved in any of these battles?'

'Perhaps.' Taen's fingers blurred once more. Time passed.

'Unusual,' he said finally. 'I can find an order of battle for five of the earlier conflicts, but nothing on the later ones.'

'I find it significant,' Wolfe said, 'that all records of units can be blanked from the files of a strategy computer. This is generally done only when a formation is involved in something most secret. Such as defending the Guardians.

'Try to find out anything about any of those units, what we call the unit history, which is kept from day to day.'

'Our military also had the custom. I shall try.'

Wolfe watched as Taen again manipulated the machine. Quite suddenly a diagonal bar slashed across the main screen, and Taen blanked away from his search.

'The same cutout for security reasons as when we inquired about the Guardians?' Wolfe asked.

'Just so,' Taen said.

'Will you allow that as a second, possibly confirmatory bit of data?'

'I shall.'

'Might it not be interesting to return to our ship and make periodic jumps down that line, toward that point, to see what we might encounter?'

Taen turned from the 'keyboard.' His hood was fully flared. 'You might have found the path, Joshua Wolfe. I hope your thinking bears fruit.'

'Me, too. But let's look up something else, as long as we're up to our elbows in Al'ar secrets.'

'I cannot believe your Command On High placed such a low secrecy value on this file.'

'Why should they have?' Taen said. 'Now you are thinking like a Terran, not like an Al'ar.

'This information needed no higher a classification than to prevent the casual reader from seeing it. Otherwise, it offered what our leaders thought was a valuable insight into the dishonorable nature of the enemy, something any battle commander might find valuable.'

'I am sorry,' Wolfe said. 'I stand corrected. But this is in an older form of your language. I have trouble reading it. Would you give me its merits briefly?'

'I shall. This is the summary of what occurred when a group of Terrans who called themselves Chitet secretly visited our civilization, about two hundred Earth-years ago.

'They felt that they were predestined to rule the Universe and wished to form an alliance with the Al'ar to share this power with them.'

'Did the Al'ar know the Chitet had attempted a coup against the Federation about a hundred years before that?'

'They were informed of this by the leader of the expedition. They spent much time discussing the situation with the Chitet and were somewhat bewildered at just what secret powers my race was supposed to possess beyond the obvious, the known.

'These Chitet were equally vague about just what they sought, but said that their projections of future history showed, once the unexpected appearance of the Al'ar was integrated, that nothing in their projection would be altered. Their role as Rulers-to-Be was still a given.'

'What,' Wolfe said in Terran, 'was the response to that? Why didn't your leaders accept their offer? They could always have double-crossed them later. The Al'ar,' he said dryly, 'weren't exactly bound by human standards of fair play.'

'The offer was not accepted, according to this file, for two reasons. The first was that our leaders had not finally determined that war between our races was inevitable. Perhaps that was foolish of them. The second reason is that all traitors are always unreliable. A blade that slips once in the hand and cuts its wielder will most likely turn once more.'

'True. What happened then?'

'The head of the Chitet expedition evinced the Terran emotion called anger, and said if the Al'ar did not change their minds, when the Chitet returned to the Federation they would announce they had discovered secret battle plans for the obliteration of humanity. It is sad, but of course no such plans existed at that time.'

'Now that,' Wolfe said, 'was one of the dumbest-assed things I've ever heard of. Sit in the middle of the enemy and try blackmail. So that was why all seven of the ships were destroyed and their crews slotted. And these clowns call themselves the most logical folks who ever lived.' He snorted amusement.

'Of course,' the Al'ar said. 'I will make a side comment here. How can these Chitet be logical, if they, and I use your words, call themselves *most* logical?

'Logic is a condition, an absolute. Can a Terran be a little bit alive? A little bit dead?'

'You've never been to some of the bars I have on a Sunday night,' Wolfe said in Terran. He switched back to Al'ar. 'So all these years this must have been working at the Chitet. They valued the war, because they imagined that when it was won by the Terrans, they would be able to find this secret weapon, or whatever it was. And now they're trying once more. What in the – what can they be seeking?'

'Perhaps we should seek them out and ask them.'

'Perhaps so.' Wolfe looked thoughtful. 'But we've got a line to follow first.'

EIGHT

The *Grayle* banked into the street and hovered as her port slid open. Taen and Wolfe doubled from the shelter of the subway entrance to the ramp and went up it, and the ship climbed away.

'*I was observed entering atmosphere,*' the ship reported. '*A robot craft was launched to investigate, according to my sensors.*'

'Well, shame on you for getting sloppy. Will the bird, sorry, the craft come within observation range?'

'*Negative.*'

'Then don't worry about it. Ship, when clear of atmosphere, assume the electronic characteristics of a *Sorge*-type vessel. I remember that as being in your repertoire. Let's give the Federation patrollers some confusion if they pick us up.'

'*Understood. Request name.*'

'I guess it'd be subverting the purpose of a spyship to call yourself the *Philby*. Umm, you're now the *Harnack*. I don't think anyone will catch that.'

'*Understood.*'

'As soon as we're able, blindjump us away from Sauros. You will be given the coordinates.'

'*Understood.*'

Wolfe stretched hugely. 'Taen, I want a shower, about two pounds of near-raw animal tissue, a decent glass of fermented grape juice, and ten straight hours of sleep. And I'll kill anyone who gets between me and them.'

The ship answered: '*My sensors report a ship within range. It has not yet detected us but will within seconds. I shall not be able to evade detection.*'

'I made a promise,' Wolfe said. 'I'll keep it. Open all frequencies. Let's see who I'm going to murder.'

Five minutes later the call came: 'Unknown ship, unknown ship. Please cut your drive, and stand by for boarding and inspection.'

'Son of a bitch,' Wolfe swore. 'The singer's a little more polite, but I still don't like the song.'

'**The Chitet,**' Taen said.

'Yeah. I guess they're running their own interdiction out here, as well as the Federation Navy. How many goddamned ships do they have, anyway? Ship, what are the characteristics of the craft?'

'*I would identify the ship in question as being a light corvette, Federation-built,* Hamilton *class. It has superior armament, but its performance capabilities when new were inferior to mine.*'

'Finally,' Wolfe said. 'Something we can just run away from.'

'Perhaps,' Taen said, 'that may not be the best idea?'

Wolfe looked skeptically at the Al'ar. 'You will have to do some serious convincement to make me believe we should stand and fight a *Hamilton*-class corvette.'

'I think we can devise a strategy for that.'

'So what's the purpose, besides general piss-off at being chased around so much?'

'**In battle,**' Taen said carefully, '**sometimes a war leader can be distracted by the unexpected. Especially when it is aimed at himself and comes from nowhere.**'

'Hmm.' Wolfe considered.

'The corvette is broadcasting once more, with the same message,' the *Grayle* said. 'What should my reply be?'

'Stand by,' Wolfe said. 'All right. Let's start the ball rolling with your scheme. You can explain as we go.'

'Unknown ship, unknown ship, cut your drive immediately. We are armed, and will launch missiles unless you obey our command instantly. This is your last warning.'

'Now, this one I'm particularly proud of,' Wolfe said. 'Built her all by myself. Watch the third screen.'

He touched sensors, swung a mike down, touched other sensors. One screen showed the computer simulation of the approaching Chitet spacecraft.

The screen Wolfe had told Taen to watch cleared, and the image of a rather handsome woman appeared, wearing a Federation Naval uniform.

'This is the Federation Monitor ship *Harnack*,' Wolfe said, and the onscreen lips moved. 'Who is attempting to contact this unit?'

Static blared, then:

'This . . . this is the exploration ship *Occam*,' the voice said, now sounding unsure of itself. 'We are conducting an authorized control of the space around the planet Sauros. We request we be permitted to board and inspect your vessel.'

Wolfe touched sensors, and the woman onscreen frowned in anger.

'I say again, this is the Federation naval vessel *Harnack*. How dare you order a Federation ship to do anything?'

'Please stand by,' the voice bleated. 'I am summoning the captain.'

'*Occam*, eh? Another goddamned logician.' Wolfe grinned tightly, waited.

'This is Captain Millet of the *Occam*. My watch officer reports that you are a Federation naval vessel. Is that correct?'

'Affirm.'

'Would you please transmit your recognition signal?'

'**We do not have such data,**' Taen said.

'Neither do they. Spoofing people who want codes is easier than standing on your head in a zip-gee field. Ship, broadcast blue, green, blue-white colorbands.'

'Understood. Transmission complete.'

There was dead air for a time, then:

'*Harnack*, this is *Occam*. I do not understand your signal. That is not on the list of recognition signals we were provided.'

'*Occam*, this is Captain Dailey of the *Harnack*. I am thoroughly tired of this nonsense. By what right do you have to order any ship to stop anywhere at any time?'

'I have my orders from my superiors.' Now Millet's voice was as uncertain as his subordinate's. 'It is my understanding that such a matter has already been arranged between our governments.'

'This is *Harnack*.' The woman appeared completely outraged. 'Perhaps you are not aware of the function of a monitoring vessel. We operate directly under Federation High Command on matters of the most critical importance. I received no such information from my own superiors before undertaking my mission and doubt whether any such understanding exists.

'Now, sir, I have orders for you. You will cut your drive and stand by. I have already sent a com reporting this absurd incident. I propose to board you and examine your papers. Any attempts to resist will be met with the appropriate response. Do you understand, sir?'

A long silence, then:

'Message understood. We are obeying your instructions.' Then, plaintively: 'I am sure this matter will be settled to our mutual satisfaction.'

Again Wolfe smiled, a smile that was not at all humorous.

The watch officer waited nervously in the port. Beside him two other Chitet stood, hastily adjusting their best shipsuits.

He felt a hum of a shipdrive as the other ship closed with his, the clang as their ports met, sealed.

He stiffened to attention, determined to impress this martinet of a Federation captain before she could do his career any further damage.

The port opened, and utter horror burst out, impossibly thin and corpse-white, a nightmare that should no longer exist. The officer clawed for his pistol, fell dead with half his face blown away.

As the corpse fell, one of the other Chitet was killed where he stood; the second managed two steps and a gargling scream before he, too, died.

The *Occam*'s intercom chattered something as Wolfe cleared the lock. He wore a light Federation naval spacesuit, carried a pistol in one hand, a fighting knife in the other.

'That way,' he said, voice metallic through the suit's external speaker. 'To the bridge.'

A man looked around the port and ducked back as Wolfe fired, searing a hole in the bulkhead where he'd been. Joshua jumped to the passageway, sent three blaster bolts down it without looking, and ran in the direction he'd indicated.

There were five humans in quiet, plain-colored shipsuits on the bridge of the *Occam*. Four of them were still alive. The fifth lay sprawled across a nav table, blood from his slashed throat pooling on a starchart. The four had their hands in the air.

'Come on, Millet,' Wolfe shouted. 'Tell them, or I blow the atmosphere unit.'

The captain hesitated, then keyed a mike. 'All hands, all hands, this is the skipper. We have been attacked, and I have surrendered the ship. Do not offer any resistance. I repeat, do not offer any resistance.'

He looked at Wolfe, features invisible in the darkened faceplate. 'What do I do next?'

'All hands to Supply Hold Delta,' Wolfe said. 'Five minutes. If anybody shoots, we dump the air. Five minutes, we dump the air anyway.'

'But – what does the Federation – why – how can –' one of the other men on the bridge sputtered.

Wolfe sent a bolt shattering past his face in reply, and two screens on the control board fragmented. The man yelped and ducked.

'No questions, no goddamn answers! Let's go, let's go, let's go!' Wolfe shouted, herding them toward the compartment hatchway.

They moved, stumbling, not looking where they were going, eyes returning again and again to the impossible form of the Al'ar, standing silent, gun ready.

'So what did you do with the crew?' Cormac asked.

'We dumped them on . . . let's say a certain world where they'll be able to reach civilization in a week, maybe two. They had plenty of rations, two guns.'

'You're getting soft in your old age, Ghost Actual,' Cormac said. 'I can remember a time when –'

'That's what . . . someone else accused me of,' Wolfe interrupted. 'Guess that's the price of being lovable. Besides, they saw – or think they saw – some things I'd like people to learn about in a while. I'm trying to complicate some lives with this one.'

Cormac snickered, turned serious. 'Always wheels within wheels. Anyway, I can rig the ship the way you want it. I guess you'll want me to do it myself, right?'

'By preference. The only way three people can keep a secret is if two of them're dead.'

'All right,' Cormac said. 'You haven't gotten that lovable. Just as a guesstimate, I suppose you want me to rig you up a deepspace HAHO rig as well?'

'Just like the old days.'

'Except with different enemies.'

Wolfe shrugged. 'I never could tell the difference between folks who were trying to kill me. By the way. I need this stuff yesterday, and I mean yesterday.'

'Of course. Like always. You know, I could drag things out,' the shiprigger said. 'Make sure you're around for the wedding. I could use a best man.'

'You're getting married?'

'Yeah.' Cormac looked sheepish. 'I'm old-fashioned.'

'Not this time,' Wolfe said, real regret in his voice. 'I'm moving too fast to touch down.'

Cormac spread his hands. 'I tried.'

The *Grayle* and the *Occam*, slaved together, lifted away from Malabar, reached their first jump point, disappeared.

'*Countdown to fifth jump,*' the ship announced.

Wolfe put the book down on his chest and waited.

Time, space moved around him, and the *Grayle* came out of N-space. His eyes returned to the book, read two paragraphs, then he tossed the volume, *An Examination of the Relationship Among Ezra Pound, the Provençal Poets, and the Cygnus XII School of the Early 27th Century*, in the general direction of the overflowing bookcase. It thudded down, the magnet in its spine holding it in place.

'Now that,' he said softly, 'is easily the dullest goddamn book I've tried to read in ten years.' He went down the passage and rapped at the door to Taen's compartment.

'Come on, you alien monster. Let's see if you can break a few more of my bones.'

'So now we are in the heart of the Federation. Probably farther than any other Al'ar not on a diplomatic mission ever achieved,' Taen said.

'We are. And you'll be thrilled to note this section of

space is wildly different, far more colorful and exciting than any other we have transited.'

'Sarcasm **once more**.'

'When I was a boy,' Wolfe said, 'I couldn't wait until I made my first jump. Things were very glamorous in the romances, with ships hurtling past comets and planets and suns. I guess I thought it was like being on a bullet train at night, when you could look out and see the lights of the cities flash past. Then I found out that all you see is computer simulations unless you're too damned close, and there's nothing at all in N-space. More like the first time I rode the sea-train from Calais to New York, except there wasn't even the ocean to stare at.'

'**All hatchlings imagine things to be different than they are.**'

'Did I ever say that reminiscing with you is just about as much fun as watching rocks become sand?'

'This is the starship *Normandie* to unknown paired ships. Please respond.'

Wolfe, looking worried, swung the mike down. '*Normandie*, this is the tug *Foss Enterprise*. Go ahead.'

'This is the *Normandie*, First Officer Wu. Is that a *Hamilton*-class corvette you're pulling?'

'*Normandie*, this is the *Foss Enterprise*. That's affirmative. It's the mothballed *Hailsworth*.'

'I thought I recognized my screen projection, *Foss Enterprise*,' the woman's voice said. 'I was just curious. I commanded the *Hetty Green* during the war. I don't think I want to ask, but where're you taking her to?'

'You're right. You didn't want to know. She's headed for the knackers' yard.'

A sound very much like a sigh came from the speaker. 'Thanks, *Foss Enterprise*. What's the line . . . "but at my back/I always hear/Time's winged chariot," something or other?'

'That's "hurrying near," *Normandie*.'

'Yeah. That's it. This is the *Normandie*, out.'

Wolfe turned away the speaker. 'Nice to see there's at least one other sentimental slob out here.'

'I do not like this,' Taen replied. 'That was the fourth ship onscreen within the past few ship-hours. There are too many starships in this sector. There is too much chance of our being detected and challenged by either a Chitet ship or Federation Navy.'

'Now you're the one who's not thinking right,' Wolfe said. 'Here, inside the Federation, there's no reason for any naval vessel to challenge a ship proceeding on lawful business, and sure as hell no Chitet would dream of doing that. Hide in plain sight, and all that.'

'You are correct. I was thinking like an Al'ar, like an enemy.'

'This will be the last jump. Estimated distance from target world of Batan three ship-days' journey if all navaids correct,' the ship said.

The world twisted, changed, and the *Grayle* entered normal space.

Half filling the screen in front of them was the capital world of the Chitet.

By his conservative dress, the man onscreen might have been a preacher. He was not.

With further good news for our people, Master Speaker Athelstan announced a two percent reduction in the approved luxury tax. This, he said, was due to the excellent and mature response from us all when he announced last ten-month that we were consuming all too many nonessential goods and services. He promised that if this reasoned pattern continues, it might be possible . . .

Joshua turned away from the measured movements of the newscaster's face.

'Nice to hear that,' he said. 'It'd be a real pain if the bastard wasn't home to give us a nice, logical response to events.'

'It has been too long since I've done stupid things like this,' Joshua said.

He wore a bulky deepspace suit and stood next to a stack of metal rafts nearly as tall as he was, Cormac's High Altitude, High Opening rig. Short lengths of chain ran to rigid metal bars connected to the four corners of the bottom raft. The small hold of the *Grayle* was crowded.

'Twelve beat until the correct time,' Taen said. He sealed his own suit.

Joshua snapped his faceplate shut. 'Any time.'

'Atmosphere being removed.'

The slight ambient noise coming through the suit's insulation died.

The air rushing out into space tugged at the Al'ar, and he steadied himself against a stanchion.

The lock opened all the way, and Joshua stared out at the green-and-white bulk of Batan. They were only a few hundred miles above the planet, barely outside range of the Landing Authority.

Taen and Joshua slid the metal stack to the edge of the hold, and Joshua floated out into space.

The chains grew taut and pulled him gently away from the *Grayle*. The lock door closed.

He spoke into the bonemike. '*Execute orbital change as directed. You now are required to take commands from either this station or from the one who remains aboard.*'

'*Understood.*'

Joshua saw brief wisps from the ship's secondary drive, and slowly the two starships moved away from him.

'*Orient suit. On zero*,' the ship said, '*fire suit drive . . . five . . . four . . . three . . . two . . . fire.*'

Wolfe had turned as the *Grayle* instructed him and, on count, twisted the red handle on the canister attached to his stomach. Gas hissed for a time, then the cylinder was empty. He pulled two D-rings and let the container float away to find its own orbit as he began his descent into gravity.

He hung in a world of black and light, the small dots of stars moving around him while the great mass of Batan drew closer.

Wolfe ate twice, slept once while he closed on Batan. He woke, stretched within the confines of the suit, and sucked refreshment from the nipple beside the faceplate.

He blanked the faceplate and ran through the suit's entertainment suite, found nothing suitable and reopened the window on his womb.

He stared at the cold dead stars beyond, couldn't spot the *Grayle*, let the suit turn slowly until Batan was all that could be seen.

He watched the world turn, saw clouds spin, unwind, crawl over the planet's curve, and realized, dimly, that he was quite happy.

The programmed proximity detector brought him back from a dream he could not quite remember.

'*In-exosphere*,' the voice buzzed. '*Distance to ground, eight hundred miles.*'

Time passed. Again he ate, drank, voided into the suit's disposal compartments, dumped them, looked at his waste distastefully, then tucked into a vee and moved away from the debris.

'*External temperature rising*,' the suit sensor told him. '*Suggest deployment first generator within five minutes.*'

Wolfe thought he could feel atmosphere rush and turned on an outside microphone, heard noise as he hurtled down toward green and blue.

Four minutes later, he touched another sensor, and the first of the antigrav generators rafted above him released its catches, deployed to the length of its twenty-foot chain, and turned itself on slowly.

Wolfe felt gravity drag, and he was pulled upright by the chains linked to the shoulders of his suit.

He rode the generator for fifty miles while Batan stabilized under him, turning until it was still night below, then cut the generator away and free-fell until he saw the suit's metal turning a flecked heat-gray.

Three more times, as he fell deeper into the planet's atmosphere, he activated, then cut away the antigravity 'rafts' above.

He rode the last-but-one generator to ten miles above the surface, then cut loose from that.

Wolfe touched a key, and the tiny screens above his faceplate dropped down and showed him where he was in relation to his target. He decided he was a little long and to the east, but his position was acceptable. He retracted the screens and looked down.

It was about two hours before dawn in the city below, well within his desired arrival time.

He saw the mountain the city had been built against and deployed the last generator.

He grunted when it went on, feeling the jerk. 'Waited a little long,' he murmured, and dialed the power up until he hung motionless in the sky.

The dawn wind carried him behind the mountain, gave it to him for a shield. The wind eddied around the peak, back toward the city. Wolfe reduced power and bled off altitude.

Now he was in the first swell of daylight.

He looked below and saw the sun's rays touch a great palace's dark-gray stones. The spires were squared, tapering slightly to blunt tips, imagination constrained, dreams allowed but within limits.

The lake that was his target was just below. He thought the breeze was carrying him too close to the shore, chopped his power, and free-fell the last thirty feet to splash into the water.

He grimaced, muttered something about getting sloppy and out of practice, and let himself sink to the lake's bottom, some seventy feet down. He sunk to about midthigh in muck. The generator thudded against his helmet and slipped off into the mire beside him.

Wolfe unfastened the chains that held him to the generator, turned on the suit's integral antigrav generator until he nearly lifted clear of the mud, then began wading toward shore, following the compass direction illuminated above his faceplate.

It was slow, laborious going, but he was in no hurry.

After two hours, he turned on an exterior camera, swiveled it to look up, and saw the silver plate of the surface about fifteen feet above. He turned the antigrav off, settled down to wait.

Several times curious fish floated around, one an orange extravagance with long, white fins and an expression of incredible stupidity. Once the camera blipped alert, and he saw the oval of a boat move above him. At last the suit clock told him it was night again, and he turned the suit's antigrav on and went toward the land.

The boy and the girl sitting on the grass verge of the lake did not appear to be behaving in a calm, logical, Chitet manner.

She broke away from his embrace, slid the fastener of her soberly green tunic open, tossed it away.

The boy embraced her, and they lay back on the grass. A

few minutes later, she lifted her hips, wriggled out of her slacks. Her legs came up, curled around the back of his thighs as he moved over her.

Neither of them could have seen the metallic dome that broke the surface, rose, then submerged again.

Joshua surfaced once more around the curve of a small point, saw no one on the land, and waded ashore, a dark alloy gorilla in the night.

He went as quickly as he could into the trees, found one with a considerable overhang, ducked underneath the branches, and sat.

He unsealed his faceplate, drank in air that smelled like something other than sterility and Joshua Wolfe.

There were two moons overhead, one, slightly pinkish, racing past like an aircraft, the other, mottled orange, hanging motionless, half full, above and to one side of the residence of the Master Speaker.

There were many lights in the palace, and Wolfe supposed the Chitet leader was entertaining. He wondered briefly what their idea of entertainment would be, then decided that a rousing debate on whether Srinivasi Ramanujan would have been greater than Einstein if he'd lived was about the height of their decadence.

He unclipped the magclips of his pack, opened it, and took out a transceiver with an archaic key instead of a microphone.

The other device in the pack looked like a rather bulky small telescope, with a tripod. He extended and opened the legs, and set it in front of him. He peered through the eyepiece, focused it on the palace's central tower, locked the elevating wheels down.

Then he turned the transceiver on, swung the key out, and tapped K, K, K, K, waited.

The old dot/dash code came back from the *Grayle* in orbit off Batan: *R . . . R . . . R . . .*

When he heard the first letter, he turned a timer in his suit on.

He touched a stud on the scope, looked again through the eyepiece. Now the tower appeared to be lit by a strange, reddish glow.

Joshua moved back from the apparatus, careful not to disturb anything, and sent X . . . X . . . X . . . X . . .

The timer showed forty-seven seconds when he thought he saw something high above the palace, then heard the whine of the *Occam*'s secondary drive.

There might have been raving madness in the Landing Authority's control rooms and in Batan's aerial defense network. Wolfe heard, saw nothing except the ship plunging down, homing on the laser beam painting the tower.

It struck, and the palace exploded in a red-and-gray ruin, flames gouting high into the sky. Wolfe thought he saw the ruins of the *Occam* pinwheeling away to smash down in a courtyard but wasn't sure.

He sent Z . . . Z . . . Z . . . Z on the transceiver, then stowed it and the illuminator in the pack and set the melt-down timer to thirty seconds. He pushed his way out of the overhang and hurled the pack out into the lake. It sank rapidly. He barely saw the white flare as the detonator went off underwater.

'Federation pirates taking Chitet ships . . . an Al'ar on board . . . a suicide attack on Athelstan with one of his own craft,' he murmured. 'Yeah, Taen. I guess we have distracted them a little bit. Now we can go for the main chance.'

He looked again at the palace as explosions rocked the ground, almost knocking him down, then waddled away, waiting for the *Grayle* to home on his suit's signal.

NINE

DEATH STRIKES AT
CHITET MASTER

*Suicide Ship Smashes
Palace, Athelstan Safe*

Press for More

BATAN – Unknown attackers sent a starship crashing into the Residence of Chitet Master Speaker Matteos Athelstan.

Athelstan was slightly burned and concussed in the attack, but otherwise uninjured. At least 50 high-ranking Chitet officials and a greater number of his Residency staff were killed and more than four times that number injured when the starship slammed into the historic palace shortly after midnight, local time, this date.

A Residency spokesperson said that an important conference, the subject of which is secret, was being held, which accounted for the great number of government officials present at that late an hour.

The Residency, completed less than a year ago and first occupied by Speaker Athelstan, was regarded as a physical embodiment of the group, which now claims several billion adherents on over 100 worlds.

The Chitet's highest-ranking Authority Coordinator, Dina Kur, said no conceivable motive for the murderous attack is known, nor has any terrorist group claimed responsibility. The ownership of the starship and the type of ship are under investigation.

'Obviously,' Coordinator Kur said, 'the disturbed ones responsible for this outrage shall be brought to the bar, either by our own representatives of order or by others.

'The full force of our deductive processes and the weight of our entire culture will be brought to bear on solving this atrocity.'

'Outrage . . . atrocity . . . best get yourself a thesaurus, Dina, old son,' Wolfe murmured, then returned to the com.

'We call on all Federation officials and worlds to assist us in discovering the villains responsible for . . .'

'What in the name of several hells are you trying to pull off?' Cisco said. 'Are you and your goddamned Al'ar buddy on some kind of vendetta?'

'Now, Cisco,' Wolfe said mildly, 'use some of that Chitet logic that FI's so permeated with these days, and don't get your bowels in an uproar.'

'All right.' Cisco took a deep breath. 'What were – are you trying to accomplish trying to kill the head of the Chitet? I assume you know you missed him.'

'I wasn't trying to kill him,' Wolfe said. 'If I was, he'd be in his meat crate. Think, man.'

Cisco shook his head. 'I don't get it. Or you.'

'I'll just give you one thing you might get out of what happened. Look around. See who's frothing at the mouth in your organization. That might help you pick out a couple more moles. Looks like you've got more of them than a fruitcake's got fruit.'

Cisco smiled tightly. 'Thanks for helping me clean up my organization. I'm sure you're doing it strictly out of altruism.'

'That's me,' Wolfe agreed. 'Aren't you glad you looked me up last year when I was in a quiet sort of retirement?' His forced smile vanished. 'Goddammit Cisco, you built this monster. You're going to have to live with him, until it's over.'

'And when is that? What are you looking for? What are you after?'

Wolfe brought himself under control. 'I'll tell you when I figure it out. Right now, I'm still on the trail. The only reason I bothered to contact you was to tell you to keep your gunsels off my ass. I'm on to something, and it's very big.'

'With the Al'ar. How does he figure into it?'

'I won't answer that, either way. Maybe because I don't know.'

'So what am I supposed to do? Just sit here, listening to all the frigging whines from Earth Central, and nothing more?' Cisco demanded.

'No. I want you to keep watching the Chitet. If you hear of them getting close to me, let me know. You can use this same conduit. I'm monitoring it, through cutouts, about every E-week. But don't try to put a tracer on it.

'Cisco, you sent me down this rathole like a good little terrier, so you can goddamned well sit there with your net and see what comes out.'

'And not do anything, no matter what you decide to do? What comes next, Wolfe? Are you going to nuke Federation Control?'

The tight smile came back to Wolfe's face. 'Extreme times call for extreme measures, Cisco. I heard you say that, three or four times.'

'That was during the war!'

'Like you told me a year ago: Maybe mine's gone on longer than yours.'

Wolfe blanked the com without signing off. 'He's really going to hammer his arteries when those guys come out of the jungle with the rest of the story.'

'We are now,' Taen said, 'three jumps from entering what were Al'ar sectors. An interesting note, one that I think should be disquieting to us both: I experienced that strange buzzing sound once more when I was waiting for your signal to send the ship down against the Chitets. But it *felt* very faint, very distant.

'This last sleep period I felt it once more. It was much stronger. This suggests that whatever is causing this is either in the Al'ar sectors or is just beyond them.'

'I wonder why I didn't feel it when you did,' Wolfe said. 'And I wonder if we're the only two people in the galaxy who have.

'You're right. I don't like your information at all.'

NOTED MAGICIAN, MYSTIC, KILLED IN MYSTERIOUS FIRE

Press for More

BALTIMORE, EARTH – Leslie Richardson, 63, better known as 'The Great Deceiver,' was found dead in his houseboat moored not far from this city on the Patapsco River. He died, police said, of mysterious burns, possibly incurred by a freak

lightning strike on his boat, although the craft
showed no signs of fire damage.

Richardson acquired great fame as an illusionist
before and during the war, and was honored for
having devoted the War Years to touring and
entertaining Federation troops. He said he owed this
to the Federation because he had been working on
Glayfer XIX when the Al'ar landed and was briefly
a captive of the aliens. He was freed when a surprise
counterattack drove the Al'ar from the planet.

After the war, he announced, through his then-
manager, that 'the illusions I've worked for all these
years have lifted the veil,' and he retired from
performing to devote his life to contemplation and
writing about 'Other Worlds' he said he could catch
dim glimpses of through fasting and meditation.

The Great Deceiver was known for his charm and
self-deprecating humor as well as for his famed
tricks, one of which, the ability to seemingly
become invisible in the midst of a crowd, has never
been duplicated by anyone.

He is survived by . . .

*'Exiting N-space. One jump short of reaching point projected from
battles.'*

'Thanks,' Wolfe said.

Taen lifted grasping organs, set them back on his rack. **'I
find it what you would term amusing that you express
gratitude to your machine. It seems a thorough waste
of energy.'**

'You're right. And I'm polite to you, as well. Ship, do
you detect any sign of life?'

'Negative.'

'Do you detect any planets, asteroids, any habitable
place?'

'*Negative.*'

'Are there any signs of broadcast on any frequency?'

'*Negative.*'

'Make the final jump when you're able.'

'*Understood.*'

The world was cold, bleak, forbidding.

Wolfe looked again at the screen, then away from the gray and black wasteland. 'What's the environment like?'

'*Slight traces of oxygen. Not enough to support human life. Gravity half E-normal. Do you wish geological, atmospheric data?*'

'No.' He looked at other screens showing the far-distant sun and the other two planets in the system, both frost giants.

'Do you detect any transmissions, any broadcast sign of life?'

'*Negative.*'

'This makes no sense. There's a planet here, as close to Point Zed as possible, and it's deader than God.'

'**I suggest we make a circumnavigation,**' Taen said. '**The Guardians, if they are, or were ever, here, would hardly blazon their presence to the heavens.**'

'Ship . . . do as he says.'

'*Understood.*'

'**I am afraid you were correct. This world has never seen habitation,**' Taen said.

'Maybe . . .' Wolfe closed his eyes and let the Lumina carry him to the screen, through it to the desolation below. 'Ship,' he said. 'Turn through 180 degrees, then descend two hundred feet.'

'*Understood.*'

'What are you attempting?'

'Pure bluff. As if we just saw something.'

'*I have a launch*,' the ship announced unnecessarily as a rock outcropping spat fire at them. '*I am taking standard evasive –*'

'Cancel,' Wolfe snapped. 'Turn hard into the direction of the missile! Drop one hundred feet.'

'*Understood*,' the ship said, and the gravity twisted, contorted, '*but this is contrary to my programming.*'

'Full power now!'

'*Understood.*'

The missile, a gray-black tube with an adder's flattened head, flashed at them, past, and Wolfe thought he could see the alien lettering along its sides.

'Not prox-detonated,' he said, 'or –'

Steering jets flashed along the missile's flanks, and it rolled, then spun wildly, an aelopile, smashing into the ground just below the skimming *Grayle*.

'There's somebody home,' Wolfe said, hanging on to the control panel. 'Is there any way we can send flowers and gentle words?'

'I do not know of any.'

'Ship, get us the hell over the horizon. Full secondary.'

'*Understood.*'

'As soon as we're –'

'*I have a second launch.*'

'Damnation! Stand by to launch missile.'

'*Weapons station ready.*'

Wolfe hurried across the control deck and swung down a control station.

'Launch the missile,' he ordered. 'I have it under manual control.'

'*Understood.*'

'**Shadow Warrior, this is foolish,**' Taen said. '**You cannot think as fast as a ship-slayer.**'

'I'm not planning on thinking,' Joshua said. 'Now shut up.'

He *felt* the Lumina, forced away his own fear, tension.

Breathe . . . you are the void . . . you are the fire . . .

He was out, beyond the ship, riding just ahead of the blast wave of his missile, barely aware of his hands moving on the control panel as the missile came up and around toward the oncoming Al'ar rocket.

Touch the void, be part, be all, reach out, feel . . .

His awareness flashed out once more, floated above the crags as the long double-finned Al'ar ship-killer flashed toward him, then *felt* his own missile beside him.

Hands coming together, fingers outstretched . . .

Far away, in a safe, warm world, Wolfe's hands left the missile's control panel, splayed, moved together, and he heard Taen's hiss of alarm.

Touching . . .

Wolfe's missile veered into the path of the oncoming projectile, and flame balled over nothingness, then vanished, and a few, tiny metal fragments spun down toward the rocks below.

Wolfe stood over the missile controls. Taen was out of his rack, halfway across the compartment.

'Don't bother,' Wolfe said. 'It's dead. I killed it. Ship, get us the hell off this world. We've got some rethinking to do. I've had enough of this nonsense.'

'**How was that done?**' the Al'ar said. '**I knew you could project your awareness, but how could you affect what your rocket did without touching anything?**'

'I don't know. But I knew, as I took the controls of the rocket, that I could do it.'

The Al'ar stared at Wolfe. His hood flared suddenly.

'**Shadow Warrior,**' he said after a time, '**now I feel fear toward you. I no longer know what you are, what you are becoming.**'

TEN

Taen and Wolfe muscled the cylinder out of the lock, hastily set up its tripod legs, and ran for the nearby rocks as the *Grayle* lifted away into space. The cylinder slid three antennae out, and one swiveled up toward the sky.

The two space-suited beings stumbled on, moving as fast as the bulky suits and their heavy pack frames and slung blast rifles would let them. Wolfe kept glancing at the hillcrest. They'd made about a quarter of a mile when Wolfe saw the flicker of movement, knocked the Al'ar down, and flattened beside him.

A double-finned missile arced over the nearby hilltop and smashed into the cylinder. Smoke, fire flared up, and rock dust obscured the clearing.

Long moments later, it settled. There was a crater about thirty feet deep surrounded by splintered boulders.

Wolfe got to his feet, licking blood from his lip where the blast had smashed his head into the rim of his faceplate. He unclipped a lead from his suit and plugged it into an improvised connection on Taen's armor.

'I guess they told us.'

'**Your diversion was clever.**'

'We'll see if it fooled them into thinking we just dropped the sensor and scooted, or not. Then it's clever. But I sure hate to lose that snooper. Damned thing cost me too many credits to just throw away.'

'Would you rather have thrown away your life?'

'Nope. But I wish I wasn't such a stickler for authenticity and had thrown them the spare toilet instead.' Wolfe checked monitors. 'How thoughtful. It wasn't a nuke they dumped on us. Shall we press on and see what else the lion has protecting his den?'

'When you speak to other Terrans, do you also attempt to confuse them?'

'As often as possible.' Wolfe turned serious. 'Taen, do you have any sense of whether we're going after some robot deathtrap, or is there intelligence, such as maybe your Guardians, inside?'

'I do not know.'

'Second question. How many ways are they going to try to kill us? Anything besides the usual Al'ar methods?'

'I do not know that, either.'

'Elaborate.'

'Toward the close of the war, when we realized the Federation was slowly closing the trap, we experimented with many different types of weapons. I was not taken into the confidence of our leaders, so I do not know what devices may have been successful enough to be taken out of the laboratories and put in production.'

'You bring utter peace and confidence to my soul. Come on. We've got some hills to hike.'

CHITET MURDER CHARGES ROCK FEDERATION

Master Speaker Athelstan:
'Government Tried to Assassinate Me.'

Press for More

BATAN – Chitet Master Speaker Matteos Athelstan today accused the Federation of masterminding a

plot to murder him in last month's suicide-crash of
a starship into his palace.

The ship has now been identified as being the
Exploration Vessel *Occam*, an ex-Federation warship
disarmed and converted by the Chitet two years ago.
It was reported missing on a routine venture two
months before it dove into Speaker Athelstan's
Residency, and had been assumed lost with all
hands.

However, three days ago the surviving crew
arrived at a mining camp on the Outlaw World of
Triumphant, and claimed that they had been
hijacked by a Federation spyship of the *Sorge* class.

According to documents sent to this com, the
Occam's Master, Captain Millet, said they were
following their orders when a Federation vessel
identifying itself as the *Harnack* ordered it to cut its
drive. Captain Millet of course obeyed. The *Harnack*
then connected airlocks to the Chitet ship and,
when the lock was open, Federation sailors coldly
murdered four of Captain Millet's crewmen and
seized the ship.

They were imprisoned in a hold and then
released, with minimal supplies, on a dangerous
jungle world, no doubt, Master Speaker Athelstan
said, in the hopes they would be destroyed by the
savage beasts of that planet.

However, due to the inspired leadership of
Captain Millet and the other officers, the crew was
able to . . .

Wolfe slid to the knife-edge of the ridge, peered over, and
quickly ducked back.

The fortress sprawled across the hill beyond them,
although little could be seen aboveground. But the knolls

were a little too regular, the mounds winding between them too convenient.

He reconnected the com lead to Taen's suit. 'We're on it. How do we get inside?'

'**We fight our way in,**' the Al'ar said. '**I know of no way of communicating with whoever is inside, nor would they be likely to believe me, especially as I'm in the company of a Terran.**'

'In the old holopics,' Wolfe grumbled, 'I'd pretend to be your prisoner and then we'd jump 'em. Pity you come from a race that doesn't believe in silliness like that.'

'**Why should anyone bother taking an enemy alive, unless killing captives makes the others fight more fiercely, as Terrans do? Certainly we never concerned ourselves with our own prisoners.**'

'I know,' Wolfe said. 'But they vanished along with everybody else. Forget it. Why haven't they opened up on us? Surely they've got IR sensors.'

'**Perhaps, perhaps not. Perhaps they are waiting to see what our move will be, or perhaps they are waiting for us to move into the open.**'

Wolfe thought for a moment, then wriggled out of his pack. He took out a small tube, opened it, and took out a small, slim rocket. As the rocket came free, guidance fins snapped out of slots. He carefully pried at the tube and stripped five metal rods from it.

He clipped these into slots on the tube to form a launching rack.

'We've been where we are too long,' he said. 'Move over to behind that boulder there. And we won't need to be careful about anybody homing on our signals once the shooting starts.'

He unhooked the com cable and reeled it back into his suit. He ran awkwardly about thirty yards, set the rack down, slid the rocket into position, came back. Then he took what looked like binocs, except with an extra barrel in the center, from his pack and slithered back up to the ridge-crest.

Wolfe focused the viewer, put the crosshairs on one of the knolls, touched a stud on its side, then a second.

The small rocket shot into the air. Following the homing signal, it shattered against the knoll, a surprisingly large explosion for so small a device.

Instantly the knoll unmasked a multitube weapon, sending laser fire spattering in the direction the rocket had come from.

A moment later, a second pillbox exposed itself and put crossfire into the same area.

Joshua backslid into cover. 'Maybe they *don't* have infrared,' he said, putting his pack back on and crouching across to where Taen waited.

'Did you mark those two?'

'I did.'

'Now it gets interesting. Did you ever take part in an infantry assault?'

'Never. My fighting was in space or in-atmosphere.'

'That doesn't improve my mood.' Wolfe took off his pack, took out two round grenades, one anodized white, the other red, and an egg-shaped object almost as large as his head. He twisted a dial at the top. 'When I charge, you put one burst on that first pillbox, then concentrate on the second.'

'That sounds extraordinarily hazardous for you.'

Wolfe shrugged. 'It's about the only way to take out interlocking fire. But if anybody else starts shooting at me, discourage them. Try not to get killed.'

'That is not my desire at the moment.'

Wolfe thumbed the first grenade's activator, overarmed it into the open space in front of them, came to his feet, and ran forward. As he came into the open, he pitched the second grenade to his front, underhand, just as the first exploded and smoke boiled.

A moment later the second grenade blasted a flare of energy. Wolfe saw Taen's weapon fire past him, saw return fire from one of the turrets, then hurled the egg-shaped object high into the air.

It hit just short of the first pillbox, exploded, and the turret blew up, metal disguised as rock tearing with a screech audible above the crack of Taen's fire and the blind return blasts from the second pillbox.

He dove forward into smoke, feeling rounds smash into rock a foot away, pulled another grenade from its pouch, touched its stud and threw.

Again fire flashed and Wolfe, lungs searing, stumbled up, unslinging his blast rifle, and ran past the flare, sending rapid-fire bursts toward the second weapons bunker.

An explosion sent him tumbling, arm coming up to protect his faceplate. Another turret must have unmasked – a rocky column above him shattered and cascaded down.

Wolfe rolled twice, came up, and sent a burst at the weapons station, then *felt* death behind him and went flat.

A blade slashed as he rolled and saw a six-legged gray metalloid spider rearing over him.

The scythe on one arm lashed down and smashed his blast rifle as Wolfe yanked his pistol from its holster, fired twice.

The blasts took the spider in its leg segments, and the robot thrashed, toppled, as the Al'ar pillbox 'saw' movement and blew its carapace into fragments.

A moment later, Taen's weapon blasted the third pillbox into silence.

Coming from between the rocks were three more of the robots. Each was about eight feet tall, with a body like a round cigar and a small dome on top with a weapons tube jutting from it.

Wolfe knelt, held his pistol in a two-handed grip, and sent bolts smashing into the first. It shuddered, side-stepped, came on.

The one behind it reared as a ray from Taen's weapon took it head-on, and his second burst seared its belly open, revealing multicolored circuitry.

Wolfe sent a grenade spinning at the first, and the blast went off under it, seemingly harmlessly. But the robot froze in midstride, then sagged to the rocks.

The last spider was on Wolfe, cutting at him. Wolfe ducked, had its metalloid arm in his hands, trying to twist it. Inexorable force twisted, sent him down, and the scythe inched toward his faceplate.

Breathe . . . fire, burning all, blazing, wildfire, firestorm, beyond control . . .

He felt muscles tear, and the robot's arm bent, metal scraping. Wolfe rolled forward, came to his hands and knees under the nightmare, then stood, lifting against the greasy underside of the spider, pushing up, and the robot flipped onto its back, legs flailing.

Joshua saw his pistol, had it, and sent the rest of the magazine smashing into the robot as its legs flexed and died.

Taen was beside him. 'It is gone. And you are hurt.'

Suddenly Wolfe was aware of pain in his side, looked down, saw the black where a blast had burned his suit, and felt his suit's air hissing out.

He fumbled at his waist, but Taen's grasping organs were ahead of him, opening the patch and sealing the suit.

Wolfe swayed, and the Al'ar pulled him into the shelter of some boulders as another turret opened fire. The fire spattered harmlessly against boulders.

Breathe . . . breathe . . .

'Are you injured?'

Wolfe *felt* his body, shook his head, then realized Taen could not see the gesture.

'No. Not badly. Burned a little. Sorry. But I just lost my fondness for goddamned spiders.'

'Those devices surprised me,' Taen said. **'I had heard no stories of their development. I would guess they were completely experimental, since it was so easy to deactivate them.'**

'Easy for you to say,' Wolfe said. 'All right. We're inside their first line of defense. Let me see what I can discover.'

He sat, awkwardly.

Breathe . . . welcome the void . . . there is no pain . . . there is no fear . . . earth and water combine, restore your body . . . now reach beyond, find hei, *let* hei *surround you.*

Without realizing it his gauntleted hands touched, tried to link fingers.

He was above the planet's stony surface, looking down, looking at, looking through.

Here are weapons stations . . . here passageways . . . here there are . . .

Wolfe came back to his body's awareness, felt the flush of strength, energy, peace wash over him.

'Now we shall enter their fortress.' For some reason, it was natural to speak in Al'ar.

He took another, longer tube from his pack and got to his feet. Taen began to say something, fell silent.

They went between boulders, Wolfe dimly aware of something shooting, no awareness of where the blasts were striking. He went flat and crawled for almost fifty yards behind the cover of one of the mounded passageways.

Joshua came to an open space, hesitated, held up one hand for Taen to wait, went across the open space very fast.

Nothing happened. Wolfe beckoned, and Taen stumbled after him. He'd barely gained the shelter of a low cluster of rocks when a laser-blast shattered splinters behind him.

Taen looked at Wolfe and saw eyes staring, fixed on some strange invisible eternity through the faceplate.

Joshua's fingers moved automatically on the tube, and one end extruded until it was nearly four feet long. He opened a tiny compartment on the side of the tube, took what looked like a jeweler's eyepiece connected to an electrical lead, and positioned it in the center of his suit's faceplate.

He moved Taen out of the way, then stood, tube on one shoulder. It swept back and forth, then held steady on an open, completely unremarkable rocky patch.

Wolfe touched the firing stud and the rocket blasted out, flame spouting from the rear of the launch tube. The rocket exploded, smoke and flame gouting. Through the boil, they saw where the hidden hatch had been ripped open.

Wolfe tossed the launcher tube aside.

'Come,' he ordered, and Taen followed.

The hatch was only open about a foot, exposing a ramp, blackness. There wasn't room to squeeze through.

Wolfe took the hatch, hunched, and lifted. Metal shrieked, but the ramp did not move.

Taen was beside him, grasping organs beside human fingers. Wolfe felt resistance give, and the hatch shrieked open another foot.

Wolfe half pushed Taen through, followed him down.

Joshua *saw* clearly, led the way down twenty feet to where the ramp ended at a T-intersection, pulled Taen into it just as an automatic hatch slid across the rampway.

The silence came like a curtain of rain across Wolfe's mind.

He unsealed his faceplate, sucked clean, sterile air, *knowing* the fortress' atmosphere was still present.

'Welcome home, Taen,' he said.

Taen opened his suit, as well.

'No,' he said. 'I am not home. But I have reached a waystation on the journey.'

His voice echoed down the cold metal corridor.

They started down its curving length, moving carefully, weapons ready. They'd gone about seventy yards when, without warning, the deck fell away below them.

ELEVEN

Joshua rolled until he was falling facedown, then used his suit's steering jets to stabilize out of the beginnings of a spin. Craning his neck to the side, he saw Taen floating about three feet above him.

The Al'ar drew level with him and Wolfe realized their rate of descent was slowing. They'd dropped about five hundred feet and were falling at no more than a few feet per second when Joshua saw a deck looming below. He kick-snapped erect and bent his legs for the landing.

No impact came as the fortress' antigrav caught, held them. As they touched down, a metal roof crashed across, sealing off the tunnel they'd fallen down.

'Alice, and friend. Canned for the feast,' Joshua said. Taen did not respond, but scanned the walls and decks of the oval-shaped trap. Both still had weapons ready.

'I see nothing that suggests weakness that might be cut away,' Taen said.

'Nor I,' Joshua agreed. He tried to *feel* out, beyond. Through three-quarters of the arc, he could *feel* nothing but metal, rock. On the fourth, his *vision* went beyond, but only into emptiness. Then it met something and was hurled back.

Joshua shuddered, as if he'd been struck.

'What was that?' Taen asked.

'Somebody out there doesn't want to be watched,' Wolfe said.

'**Lay down the weapons,**' came a voice. It filled his mind and the tiny room.

Wolfe hesitated, noticed Taen had knelt, set his weapon down, did the same.

He *felt* someone, several beings, *watching* him, and squirmed, not comfortable.

The section of the wall slid open, and five Al'ar were in the opening. Two held long, slender weapons identical to Taen's. The other three wore dark ceremonial robes. The one in the center wore a Lumina stone on a metallic headband. He *knew* all of them to be Guardians.

'**Name yourselves.**'

'**Taen.**'

'**The One Who Fights From Shadows is the name I was given many years ago by another Guardian,**' Wolfe said. '**In Terran, Joshua Wolfe.**'

He felt his own Lumina warm as the Al'ar *reached* toward him.

Then the stone became cold as the Guardian turned to Taen. '**My senses did not tell me that another of us had remained behind.**'

Taen made no reply.

'**Why did you not make the Crossing with the others?**'

'**I do not know. Perhaps I was unworthy.**'

The Guardian began to speak, stopped, as if rethinking his words, then went on: '**You have spent time among these others, these groundlings. You have let your mind become corrupt. There was no "worth" to those who have gone, no "shame" to those who have remained here.**'

'**And how was I to sense this?**'

Wolfe blinked, thinking for an instant he'd detected impossible pain in Taen's words.

'If you did not go, then we must assume there is intent to your remaining. Perhaps it has to do with this one who accompanies you.

'Neither of you is the other's prisoner. You are working as a pair, as a conjoined unit? I find this a concept beyond visualization.'

'Nevertheless,' Taen said, 'it exists.'

The Guardian's attention shifted to Wolfe 'I am puzzled by the responses of this young one. Perhaps you might assist me in clarifying the murky pool.'

'I doubt that,' Wolfe said. 'I myself have little clarity of thought.'

'What do you seek?'

Joshua said nothing but slowly shook his head.

'Perhaps I can answer for both of us,' Taen said 'I began this search, looking for the Guardians, even though there was little but rumors. I sought to find why I was abandoned, and to be allowed either death or to join the others.

'This one, whom I had known when we were hatchlings, and whom I fought against in the time of war, joined me. What he hopes to gain, what he hoped to gain by studying our way in the time before war, I cannot tell you. But he was a strong pupil, both in the ways of fighting and in the ways of thinking. Since we have been together, he has become an adept, having talents even I was not aware could be gained. But I leap ahead.

'Before we could truly begin our search, we *felt* a threat, something unseen, unknown. Its onset is a buzzing, as of insects, but there is not true sound. I have felt an aura of blue when this happens; he has not. He has had some pain, some physical evidence, his outer layer showing bruises for a time accompanied by sharp pain, then the signs vanish.

'Both of *us felt* this had something to do with our quest, and feel this menace growing, and feel it especially strongly here in these parts of space that were once Al'ar.'

As Taen spoke, Wolfe felt an emanation from the first Guardian, then the others – something dark, strange, cold. Taen flinched as if he'd been struck and Joshua realized he, too, had felt what the Guardians had emitted.

'So,' Taen said, 'we were not becoming insane. This is real. What is it?'

The Guardian looked at his two fellows, then back at Taen and Wolfe. 'This shall be explained. But not at this moment. You. Terran. I cannot bid you welcome as an honored one. Our races fought too long and there was too much blood spilt for me to feel or say that. But you are now our guest. You will eat, sleep, learn here, and no one shall bring you harm or offer you shame. I am Jadera.'

The Guardian bowed slightly, and the Lumina on his headband flared, subsided.

Wolfe's vision blurred inexplicably, cleared when he blinked moisture from his eyes.

He realized there was a smile on his face.

Wolfe half remembered some of the foods they ate, but most were unfamiliar. They were the dishes of a state dinner, which no youth, even the son of an ambassador, would have been allowed. Some he liked, a few he had to force down, fingers crossed as his mind reminded him there was nothing in the Al'ar diet a Terran could not survive.

He wondered what the Al'ar foods tasted like to the aliens. To him, they were a flurry of flavors, mingling or sometimes overriding each other. Some were solid, but most were in heavy soups. A few came in covered, insulated containers, and were inhaled as a gas.

The room he ate in was huge, shadowed. Against the walls light-constructs flared, subsided. Beside each seat was a half dome on the table that delivered and removed each dish.

The Al'ar ate at small tables around him, conversing in low tones. Joshua wryly reminded himself the unemotional Al'ar were genetically incapable of performing a Prodigal Son routine and that he was the only one who was upset that Taen's arrival wasn't made more of.

At first he thought all of the aliens on the planet had been summoned, but then he realized many of them were present only in image.

He quietly asked Taen how this was done.

'A simple matter,' Taen said. 'Each sits in a booth with a background prepared to simulate this room. There is a communications device in front of him, and he has large screens around him. This way, we do not shrivel in loneliness, even though we are great distances apart at our duties.'

Wolfe turned to Jadera. 'If it is a permitted question, what are the duties of the Guardians on this planet?'

'You may ask, and I shall answer. There are many, ranging from maintaining this fortress to keeping watch for intruders to . . . the matter that brought you here, and that which I shall speak of at another time. Still others have rituals to attend to.'

'Rituals?' Wolfe asked. 'But we Terrans always believed – I do not know why – the Guardians were leaders of the flesh, not what we would term priests.'

Taen lifted a grasping organ, expressing surprise at what Joshua said.

'But how could that be?' Jadera responded before Taen could speak. 'How can a being lead in the body if he has not a vision, an ability to lead in the spirit?'

'Quite well,' Joshua said. 'Every time we Terrans have

had someone like that, we end up killing each other over which god is the better.'

'I have heard of this,' Jadera said. 'But it makes no sense. I have had it explained as what you Terrans call a god but understand it only as a concept in the mind, not reality. How could there be an argument, when there is but one truth?'

'How could there *not* be an argument,' Wolfe countered, 'when every believer in truth I have known or read of seems to think that truth belongs exclusively to him and his friends?'

'I guess we were foredoomed to war against each other,' Jadera said.

Wolfe's attention was drawn to a table not far from his, a strangely carved, octagonal piece of furniture. At it sat an Al'ar of great age. His corpselike pallor was mottled, marred.

When he saw Wolfe looking at him, his hood flared to its full size, his grasping organ touched a stud, and the Al'ar and where he sat vanished.

Jadera had noted what occurred. 'That was Cerigo. He is one who holds firmly to the old ways, and believes that we should have fought you the instant our races came in contact rather than waiting. He also lost his entire brood-cluster in the war, so he has little ability to stand the sight of Terrans.'

'And I lost those who bred me as well,' Wolfe said softly. 'Yet I still am sitting here. Perhaps his . . . truth is lacking in some areas.'

Jadera said nothing.

'Then we are what you call shamed,' Taen said in Terran, then returned to Al'ar. 'Please do not dwell on Cerigo and his behavior unless you must.'

Wolfe shrugged and turned back to his plate.

After a time, Jadera spoke again. 'When you were given your Al'ar name, did the Guardian who gave you that name tell you its history, or of the one he must have been thinking of when he bestowed it on you?'

'No,' Wolfe said, startled. 'I did not know of any such.'

'That is odd,' Jadera said. 'If he had not gone before, if he had not made the Crossing, I would inquire why not. When one of us is given his adult name, it is only after a long consultation, and the hatchling is given the opportunity to study the past and either accept or reject the name as being fitting.'

'Perhaps,' Taen said, 'it was because he was unsure of whether it was right to bestow a name on this one even though he was an honest Seeker of the Way. That Guardian, whose name I must not use, since he is gone, hesitated, and I was forced to remind him that the codex had been consulted and such a thing was not forbidden, even though it had not been done within memory. Perhaps he intended to give the history to this One Who Fights From Shadows at a later time. Perhaps the war prevented that from occurring.'

'But still,' Jadera said. 'The naming ceremony was not proper.'

He sat motionless for a moment. 'This must be rectified before any other matters can be dealt with, since one presses closely on the other.'

When the meal was finished, the Al'ar sat silently for a time, as was their custom.

Wolfe had done the same as a boy, among the Al'ar who taught him, and the old feeling of warmth, of belonging, came as he sat, still in voice and mind, among the Guardians.

Then, one by one, the projected visions of those elsewhere on the planet blinked out.

Jadera rose. 'I shall show you a burrow that we have modified as suitable for you.'

Another Al'ar led Taen away, and Joshua followed Jadera.

The chamber was octagonal, with a ceiling in various shades of purple that curved slightly downward at the corners. Where the resting rack would have been, soft, circular pillows in various colors had been piled inside a framework.

There was a table against one wall; a cup and a flask of some liquid sat on it.

'Is this satisfactory?' Jadera inquired. 'Does this not shame us? We have done the best we know, but we never envisioned a Terran as anything other than . . . as being our guest.'

Joshua noted with amusement that a covered vessel and a neat pile of soft clothes was set discreetly in one corner. 'More than sufficient.'

Jadera held out his grasping organs, turned, and left. Joshua yawned, undressed, and lay down on the pillows, wondering what they were normally used for.

His hand stretched out and found the empty holster his gun should have been in. A thought came that this was one of the few times in many years a weapon hadn't been ready at hand, yet he felt no anxiety.

Then he closed his eyes and sleep dropped like a curtain about his mind.

Wolfe was asleep, but not asleep. He dreamed, but what came and went in his mind were not dreams.

The universe his sac opened in was not the one he had known. It was already old, decaying toward rebirth.

He had a memory of those who'd chosen to breed him, and of those other adults who cared for his cluster as they swarmed, grew, fed, played.

Wolfe, dreaming, tried to feel happiness, contentment, anger, laughter, could not.

There was but satisfaction at being fed, at besting another or of helping another of the cluster against a third, then the lesser satisfaction of helping another better 'him'self.

He was Al'ar.

There were places set aside for hatchlings where no adult went. Some were mountainous, some covered with many breeds of ferns, from tiny ones that crumpled in his grasping organs to ones that towered above him and hid the sky. Other places had lakes and islands.

The hatchlings went into these places and formed groups or lived singly, doing as they had seen adults do, attempting those tasks adults did and they would do in their turn.

They fought, one against one, one against several, several against one.

Hatchlings died, but this was as it should be so the race would grow, would increase, would progress.

The one who had not yet been given a name killed more than most, and this was noted, both by his elders and other clusters.

There were five of them. When the third moon set, they met outside the cave their cluster was living in. They knew the direction to take, had walked most of it during daylight, thinking of other things so as not to alarm the hatchling who carried death with him.

That one without a name had built a burrow that was not a burrow but a challenge, foolishly, on the banks of a flowing waterway, with little cover and few places to flee other than into the water. But even the current would carry him toward the dens of beasts that would feed on Al'ar.

He had built a low fire from minerals he'd dug from the bank, under what the Wolfe-dreamer thought was a leafless tree carved of stone but was something that lived and grew.

The five stopped at the last bit of groundcover and looked long at the guttering fire and the motionless shadow of the one who seemed to have no fear.

They communicated in touches, grasping organs signaling who was to go forward, who was to come from the side, who was to wait until he was immobilized and then deal the killing stroke.

The one who had been chosen leader lifted his grasping organ, hood flaring, about to give the signal.

He came at them from behind, where he'd stalked them from when they left their cave.

The first died as a grasping organ darted into an eye socket, and 'blood' oozed, the second as a knee took 'her' in the back of the head, snapping the grouped tendons that was an Al'ar spine. The third swung with a club, missed as his target vanished, reappeared out of reach, and the club smashed into the fourth's chest. The last, the leader, had time to snap out a kick that sent the attacker stumbling.

The two from the cave came at him from either side.

The one Wolfe dreamed he was jumped straight up, turned and both his legs snapped out. He felt the kick land, felt body organs crush, felt death come.

The last turned to flee, but somehow the attacker was in front of him, slits of his eyes burning, fire demanding fuel, and the last one's spirit was that fuel and there were five young Al'ar sprawled dead, not far from a dying fire and a waterway.

It was not long after that the Choices were made. Some chose to breed, some chose to accept breeding. The tasks of the future were clear, and each picked the one he'd been called to as his lifework.

He had known forever what his own task would be.

Warrior.

Guardians further tested him, taught him.

Then they gave him a Lumina to hold, and a new name, honoring what he had done in the night, in the desolation.

He was the One Who Fights From Shadows.

There was no greater honor for an Al'ar than to be a warrior, except to be chosen as a Guardian.

He learned other skills while he refined those of the body. He learned the use of weapons, those that the Wolfe-dreamer could name as knife, gun, missile, others that had no name or image to him.

More important, he learned when not to fight but to flee or to dissemble and lie until the weight lay on his side.

He learned how to use vehicles that let him fly, both in various kinds of atmosphere as well as space.

He was taught how to help a ship transition from one part of the great Al'ar Empire to another.

Finally he was ready.

He was named a Keeper of Order, on the far edges of the Al'ar space. Here he would be in charge of the lives of the lesser beings the Al'ar ruled, beings of many planets and thoughts, but none of real worth.

Wolfe stirred, half woke, muttered in protest, then returned to the 'dream.'

The One Who Fights From Shadows knew the codex and ruled firmly, giving all as much life as he thought necessary, and bringing it to an end when the time for that came, as well.

Time passed.

Then the changes began.

Worlds fell out of contact with the parent culture.

Sometimes a handful of ships managed to flee to momentary safety, but as often as not the Al'ar inside them were dead or had twisted minds that could no longer make sense.

Other Al'ar Keepers of Order went into darkness, with no explanation for their death.

Something had come into their galaxy, something strange, something deadly, something unutterably alien.

Wolfe, in his dream, tried to feel *what that threat was, tried to* see *it, but his thrust was turned aside.*

The One Who Fights From Shadows was summoned to a great conference. All of the Al'ar homeworlds were linked together.

They were told the worst.

The Al'ar were doomed.

That which had entered their galaxy would be their destruction.

They could either stand and fight, or flee.

The Guardians had found a way to transition through space-time into another place, a place where they could not, would not be followed.

There was no debate, no reason for discussion. The path was clear.

To gain time, it would be necessary for some Al'ar, the best warriors, the strongest Keepers of Order, to counterattack, to hold back the evil until their people could escape.

The One Who Fought From Shadows knew he was one of the lucky ones and was lifted higher than others with the knowledge.

He was trained again, this time by Guardians, in ways to make his mind, his will harder than any metalloid, sharper than any blade or ray.

Special ships were built for the Keepers who would go out to that final battle, ships that dwarfed the biggest Al'ar battleships, but each crewed by only one being.

These ships had a single purpose, a single enemy.

The One Who Fights From Shadows was in the first

group. He leapt from change-point to change-point among the stars, each time knowing he was closer to the unseen enemy.

He came into 'real' space from his last vaulting point, and the enemy hung in space before him, a dark cloud blocking the stars it had already killed.

His grasping organs swept over weapons banks, and wave after wave of long-strikers shot forth.

He *felt* them strike home, *felt* the enemy's agony.

Far behind him, half across the galaxy, he knew the first of his people were preparing to flee to safety.

Then his foe regained strength and reached out, through space, through metal, for him, and took him, held him.

The One Who Fights From Shadows knew a moment, an eternity of red torment, fire, cried out, was no more.

Joshua Wolfe woke, shouting in pain, a dull buzzing in his mind. His arms, legs, and stomach were seared with red welts.

TWELVE

'How was that done?' Wolfe demanded.

'Fairly simply,' Jadera said. 'There are records of events. We know you possess a Lumina and have become skilled in its use. We used one of our own as a link and gave you the life of the honored one who previously bore your name.'

Joshua grimaced, caught a reflection of himself in a polished wall panel, looked away His eyes were deeply shadowed, his newly young countenance pallid from the night's 'dream.'

'So you – the Al'ar – were driven from your own universe into this one?'

'Exactly.'

'And now this . . . thing, whatever it is, is in our own space-time?'

'Not yet. But it threatens.'

'What is it? I could not determine.'

'We did not permit you to see. Now we shall. Follow me.'

'May I accompany you?' Taen asked.

'No,' Jadera said.

'Why is this not possible?' Wolfe asked. 'Is there danger? Taen is my partner. It would be good for him to have all knowledge that I do.'

'There could be some danger,' Jadera replied 'But it is not that. We try to avoid contact with . . . with what you are going to encounter. There is an Al'ar saying: "The scent of the falaas attracts the food-gatherer."'

'Or,' Joshua said, 'in Terran, "The bleating of the kid excites the tiger."'

'Just so.'

It took a moment for Wolfe to realize that Jadera had understood him. He started to comment, changed his mind, and followed the Guardian out the chamber door and to a slideway.

The room was an irregular polygon. The floor rose and fell in a series of small concave waves, and was flat only in the center. The ceiling was dimpled. The walls were crystalline with colors that were motionless when looked at directly, but shifted prismatically for peripheral vision.

'We shall need your Lumina for this.'

Wolfe turned his back, took the egg-shaped gem from its hiding place, a pouch between his legs slung on a thin band around his waist.

Jadera held out his hand, and reluctantly Joshua gave the Lumina to him.

Jadera walked across the humped floor easily, as if it were flat. Wolfe followed, moving carefully.

Jadera set the Lumina down in the center of the flat area, then took two other gems, each a bit larger than Wolfe's, from the pockets of his robes.

'Position yourself on the floor,' he ordered. 'You know how to liberate yourself from your body, do you not?'

'I do. But only for a moment.'

'Time is of no import now. It has ceased to exist. Once you have freed yourself physically, you will know how to do the rest.'

Wolfe sank to his knees, placing both hands, fingers

pointed inward, on his thighs. Jadera set the other two Lumina to form a line with Wolfe and his own gem.

'Now the machine is ready.

'Be advised, One Who Fights From Shadows, that what you are going to see is not real, although I use the word only as a label.'

'What is it then?'

Jadera considered his words. 'This enemy was not native to our original galaxy, or so it is believed, but comes from yet another time and space. It has more than a fourth-dimensional presence, unlike you and I.

'Therefore, what you will see, all your experiences, will be what your mind and your Terran culture suggests.

'To understand this more completely, imagine that you are a being in only two dimensions, such as in one of your hanging pictures. Now imagine that somehow you are lifted from that picture and inserted into what we call the "real world." Forgive my use of this obvious fiction.

'You would be only able to perceive cross-sections of this other, three-dimensional world, so an object, your Lumina, perhaps, would appear as a series of varying-sized ovals, smaller at first, then larger, then smaller as it moved past your perception.

'Similarly, you, who consider yourself a three-dimensional being, perceive the Al'ar in a manner that we are not.'

Joshua blinked, began to ask something.

'No. Concentrate on the matter at hand,' Jadera said. 'Experience all, but remember it is all ultimately false and will give you no more than a hint of what is out there.'

He returned to the door and touched the wall in several places. 'You may begin to *see* whenever you wish.'

He left the room, and the door slid closed behind him.

Breathe . . . breathe . . .

Joshua lifted his hands, fingers splayed, thumb and forefinger touching, in front of his face.

Zai . . . Accept all . . . welcome the universe . . .

Reflexively his fingers came together into knife-edge, interlocked.

The void reaches out . . . accept ku . . . all is one . . .

He appeared to be in a huge cavern, the walls dank, dripping. It was illuminated by unknown phosphorescence.

The stone under his feet was worn to a wide, smooth path by the passage of numberless beings.

He heard that insect-buzzing once more. It came from ahead of him.

He went down the path, and the buzzing grew louder.

There was a wall visible through the dimness and, in its center, an enormous door.

It was like no door he'd ever seen. It was a dark stone, broken with obsidianlike streaks. It and its frame were carved with symbols and letters Wolfe thought might be an archaic form of Al'ar script. It seemed to open on either side, and above and below.

The buzzing grew louder.

Wolfe reached out, touched the door, felt heat.

The stone shimmered, became opaque, and he was in emptiness. There was a distant galaxy, its stars swirling as if he were seeing it over millions of years.

He was somehow closer, so stars were all around him. There was a scattering of red giants, more white dwarfs, still more dark, burned-out black dwarf stars. In the far distance, he saw the white heat from a pair of supernova.

As he watched, the light flashed, died. Where the supernova had been were neutron stars, falling into collapsars.

This universe was contracting, blue-shifting, dying toward its phoenix rebirth.

The being called Wolfe now saw something strange.

The space between the stars was not dark, was not night, but was filled with millions of minuscule red dots. He could see them pulsing, but they had no light of their own.

He shuddered, feeling fear, feeling death in their swirling life.

He willed himself to move closer, to study them.

Pain washed over him, flaring as if he'd been cast into a great, invisible fire.

Before he could scream, before he could move, he was on the far side of the portal, crouched in a fighting stance in the strangely floored room.

The three Luminas blazed in front of him, not with the usual multicolored lights, but solid red, the same red as he'd seen in that distant galaxy.

Then their light died, and they were nothing more than unimpressive, gray oval stones.

Breathe . . . breathe . . .

Jadera came into the room.

'You have seen.' It was not a question.

Wolfe rose, bowed to the three stones. It seemed correct. 'I did. That is the universe from which you came?'

'Yes. I assume you also saw some sort of a door, a gateway?'

'I did.'

'That represents the rift in space, in time, that we created to leave that universe for this. Because it cannot be sealed we Guardians were created, to stand watch against our ancient enemy. You saw it?'

'I saw something between the stars, in space, that appeared red to me. It had filled the distance between the nearest ones completely but was patchier farther out, toward the ends of the galaxy.'

'That was it.'

'What is it?'

'Once more, I must remind you, there are no correct words for it. Not in my language, not in yours.'

'It reminds me, for some unknown reason,' Wolfe said slowly, 'of what we call a virus.'

'I know the term. Except this virus can take anything, take all for a host, from small, living beings to planets to the space between them. Perhaps it even infects the very fabric of space. Once these things have been touched by our enemy, they become different. If they lived once, they live no longer, at least not in the form we call life. Inanimate objects become part of the creature, the being, as if their particles have been altered to match its own.

'Call it a virus, if that pleases you. It is a single entity; it is many. It bears a resemblance to your microorganism in two other ways – it is all-consuming and it is always growing, increasing.'

'I saw but one galaxy. What of the others in that universe?'

'I assume they are "infected" by this time, since within the last time periods we have been aware that the enemy is looking about for new territory to grow into.'

'This universe?'

'Yes.'

'So it followed you.'

'It has not yet followed us. But it appears aware of our flight, as if we somehow left a trail.'

'Thanks,' Wolfe said, changing language. 'So humanity's next. And we can't run like you Al'ar did.'

'What would your people have done if they had our powers and were threatened by this being? Would Terrans have done differently?'

'No,' Wolfe admitted. 'But what you said doesn't make me feel any fonder of you at the moment.'

Jadera remained silent, and Wolfe thought he sensed indifference.

'Can this enemy be fought?' Joshua asked

'It could have been once.'

'You speak in the past. Please explain.'

'I shall show you. Come.'

Taen was waiting in the hall outside. Wolfe quickly explained what had happened.

'I was told what you would see by another Guardian,' the Al'ar said. 'I will say I have no regrets at not looking at the enemy who destroyed my people's home and sent us into exile in this terrible universe you inhabit.'

Wolfe eyed him, made no comment.

Jadera led them into a circular room. A featureless gray column five feet high and a foot in diameter rose to one side. Jadera walked behind it and touched places on the column.

There was darkness and then a huge Lumina appeared. It was about the size of Wolfe's head.

'This is an image of the Overlord Stone,' Jadera said, 'the greatest of all Lumina. It is said that all the other stones hived from this one, although how that could be possible is not known.

'This stone, like its smaller sisters, is actually little more than a lens, and gives the properly trained adept something on which to focus his powers – even his wishes, if he is of a high enough level – and causes certain events to occur that seem impossible.

'The Lumina were native to our original universe. They were used by many generations of Al'ar as tools to help build our powers to fight, to move in hostile environments and times. They are weapons, learning tools, many things, depending on who *looks* into them, with what desires.

'When the enemy appeared, our forefathers were just beginning to use this great Lumina to explore other possible universes. We thought it might even be possible to enter those of the past and future, although no one had yet accomplished that.

'Then, as I said, the enemy came, and all of our efforts were concentrated on defeating that horror.

'As you dreamed in our records, one was the original One Who Fights From Shadows. He and his fellows died an honorable death giving us valuable time to flee.

'Once we had reached this universe, we tried to close the rift, but were unsuccessful.

'We positioned one of our starships close to the rift and created Guardians to watch for any signs that our enemy might sense us and follow. While a handful of us kept watch, the rest of the Al'ar expanded into this new galaxy and began settling new worlds.

'After some time, we encountered humans.

'We studied your techniques for moving planetoids, improved them, and, about one hundred years ago, positioned this world you are on to replace the Guardians' ship and armed it to be nearly impregnable, although you proved that there is no fortress that cannot be assaulted with success.

'The rest is as you know it.

'Eventually we realized that only one race could exist in this universe, and the other would be doomed to extinction.'

'And so you started the war,' Wolfe said. 'I'll accept you believed you had to wipe us out. But what made you think we were as eager to shed blood as you?'

'That was first prophesied by some of our more conservative elders, beings like Cerigo. We studied the matter further, and realized that those who predicted the worst were right, after we found what you beings did to your more primitive ancestors.'

'You mean such as the North American First Men, those we call Amerinds? There are still many of them, and they occupy high posts and are respected in the Federation.'

'But are they as they were, before better-armed humans came on them and forced them to live a certain way? And is the way they live now the way they would have grown, would have built their own culture if they'd been undiscovered?'

'No one can say,' Wolfe said in Terran. 'Probably not. They would have found their own way, made their own civilization.'

'And *they* are human, of your own breed. Do you really believe Terrans, once they won the war, would have accepted and lived in peace with complete aliens like us?'

Wolfe remained silent for a long time. He finally shook his head slowly.

'When we knew of the inevitable destruction to come,' Jadera went on, 'once more we used the Overlord Stone, the Mother Lumina, to seek another world and then to go to it.'

The Lumina hanging in the air shrank and was surrounded by a lattice of shimmering crystal that looked like pure, many-colored light, a spindle with rounded ends. Stars came into being around it, and Wolfe realized he was looking at a small artificial world, built solely to house the Lumina.

'We put the Lumina in this small satellite, exactly in the geodesic center of the Al'ar worlds, and the necessary focus was applied so our people could free themselves.'

Taen shuddered.

Jadera appeared not to notice. 'Then the only ones left were the Guardians . . . and this one.'

'So why was I not permitted to make the Crossing?' Taen demanded.

'I do not know. There are always incongruities. If you wish, now we could use our powers and attempt to help you go with the others.'

Taen's grasping organs raised, lowered, and his hood flared, subsided.

'Once, not long ago,' he said 'there could have been nothing else to desire.

'But that was then. Not now. There is another task I must be prepared to undertake.'

The two Al'ar looked at each other, then Jadera turned back to Wolfe. 'We Guardians were to remain for a time, to make sure you Terrans could not deduce where we went, nor follow us. Then we were to make the Crossing ourselves, taking the Lumina with us.

'But then we *felt* the enemy reaching for us, *looking* for that still-existing rift into this universe.

'It is strange that not long ago we discovered a way we might have closed that rift to seal the enemy off and let him die as his universe dies . . . or let him be consumed when it is reborn. But it would have taken all the Guardians' power, plus calling on other forces, and once again using the great lens of the Mother Lumina.

'Which we cannot do.'

'Why not?' Wolfe asked.

'The Overlord Stone is gone. Now we are trapped in this time, and will go in death with everything else when our enemy arrives, which will be soon.'

'What happened to it?'

'Your Federation has it.'

Wolfe jerked back. 'No,' he said. 'That is false, and I do not know how your perception was arrived at.'

'That is the only explanation,' Jadera insisted.

'It cannot be,' Wolfe argued. 'First, I was brought into this matter by a high-level Federation Intelligence official. He was – as far as I know still is – using false Lumina stones to try to find out what is going on. All he knew was that one single Al'ar might have survived, and commissioned me to find him, then later to kill him. At no time did he even mention a Mother Lumina.'

'High-ranking officers do not always tell their subordinates more than what they must know. I think in Terran it is termed not letting one hand know what the other does.'

'I am very aware of that,' Wolfe said. 'But this man, this one called Cisco, gave me all his raw data. There was no mention of the Overlord Stone anywhere in it. If the Federation had it, wouldn't they have given me different orders? And if they did have the Overlord Stone, it seems they would have insisted I take Taen alive, not kill him.'

Jadera thought. 'There appears to be merit in your reasoning,' he said grudgingly.

'Now I shall provide a puzzler,' Wolfe went on. 'The Federation doesn't know about the Mother Lumina, but the ones who call themselves Chitet do. They even know to call it the Overlord Stone.'

'Who are these Chitet?'

Wolfe explained the group, their onetime attempted rebellion against the Federation, and his and Taen's murderous encounters with them.

'This,' Jadera said, 'is truly a puzzlement, as you said.

While I consider it, I think it is time I show you why I said what I did about the Federation having stolen the Overlord Stone.

'Now it is time to show you some deaths.'

THIRTEEN

Federation Hides Deadly Secret:

DEATH STALKS DREAMERS

*Do the Al'ar Somehow Murder
from Beyond the Grave?*

By the Federation Insider's Special Investigation Team

A strange, supernatural death has struck at least a dozen of the Federation's most noted psychics and mystics, a special investigation by your Federation Insider has discovered.

According to secret police reports that were provided to your Insider's newshounds by concerned higher-ups within the government, these vision-favored men and women all died in the same manner: burning to death in awful agony. Yet none of them had time to scream or cry for help, since in several cases loved ones or others were nearby and heard nothing.

In one horrifying case Lola Fountaine, who has frequently made predictions for your Federation Insider over the years, was in the company of her business advisor and best friend when she suddenly clawed at her throat, and her body, the terrified friend told police, showed a terrible rash, then turned red, as if burning, then the flesh charred and boiled, lifting away from the bone. 'Yet,' she went on, 'there were no flames, and I felt no heat.

'It was almost like Lola was struck by some strange disease, some virus, that killed her by fire before she had time to call for help,' the friend went on.

Lola was not the only one.

The first to die, Federation officials believe, was the late Leslie Richardson of Earth, once known as 'The Great Deceiver,' whose body was found on his houseboat two months ago.

With at least a dozen dead, the Federation Insider queried officialdom as to why this horror is being kept secret. None of those we questioned had any response other than 'No comment.'

There are only two similarities to the deaths: All of the victims were known for their extraordinary powers; and all of them specialized in psychic investigations of the monstrous Al'ar.

Other known victims, and the circumstances of their death, are . . .

FOURTEEN

The crystal spindle's fire gleamed no more. It hung, dead, in emptiness, far from the nearest star. There were two other ships nearby. Joshua recognized them as Federation long-range scoutcraft, probably *Foley* class, built within the last five years.

'So the Federation did find the Lumina,' he said. 'Why was Cisco lying to me?'

'As I said previously, my explanation is that the one hand knows not what the other does,' Jadera said.

'You said there were deaths here,' Taen said, 'so something beyond the discovery of the Lumina occurred here.'

'It did,' Jadera agreed. He went to another screen, touched its surface.

The image showed the Lumina carrier ship, then moved past it, into emptiness. Then there was something visible, something too small to show up on the screen.

It was the body of a human. He wore no spacesuit, and most of his head had been shot away.

'Here is the first death. None of us can tell what might have happened. One Who Fights From Shadows, bring your Terran eyes to this, so we may learn and decide what must be done next.'

'Suit up,' Joshua said in Terran. 'We'll go visiting.'

*

The entry lock of the Al'ar ship bulged outward, and three beings moved through its viscosity into space.

'Are you hearing this band?'

'I am,' Wolfe said. 'You correctly set my suit's communicator.'

White mist came from the driver on Wolfe's suit, what appeared to be green light from the belts of the two Al'ar, and they moved toward the Lumina's carrier-ship.

Wolfe looked back at the Al'ar craft. Like his *Grayle*, its bulk belied the size of the crew – only ten Al'ar had been needed to man the craft before it lifted away from the Guardians' world.

The ship was named *Serex*, which translated as Swift-Strider. It was a light cruiser and looked as starkly alien as it was, with a sickle-shaped 'wing' that housed the drive, fuel and weapons pods, and twin ovals that hung inside the c-curve at the front for the crew.

The cold past ran down his spine, and he remembered the war, seeing other Al'ar cruisers snap out of N-space toward him.

The Lumina's carrier-ship loomed close, and he reversed, braked briefly, and touched down on the skin of the craft. It was ridged, and he used the ridges as handholds to follow the two Al'ar to the entry lock.

Jadera touched the circle in two places and it bulged expectantly. They pushed their way through.

Wolfe looked at his suit's indicators and saw there was zero atmosphere.

The ship's interior was a single circular room, the walls lined with screens, controls. Coming down from the ceiling and up from the floor were two pylons about a foot in diameter.

The three-foot space between them was empty.

'Here is where the Lumina would have been?' Wolfe asked.

'Just so. The suspending forcefield has been shut down.'

Wolfe went back to the lock and examined its edges closely.

'There are signs of damage,' he said. 'Someone forced the entryway and entered who did not know the pattern of this entrance.'

'A Terran.'

Wolfe nodded, then realized the gesture couldn't be seen. 'Almost certainly,' he said. 'Would there have been any devices protecting the Lumina?'

'None. The stone's potency is lessened by anything that blocks any sensory approach.'

'So this person would have entered and seen the Lumina hanging in midair. How would it have appeared? Blank, dull, like mine, when I am not using it?'

'No,' Jadera said. 'The Overlord Stone is always reflecting a measure of the energy going into the smaller stones.'

'So somebody – maybe a couple, three somebodies – boards this ship, and here's the biggest jewel they've ever seen. Real hard to figure what comes next,' Wolfe mused aloud, without keying his mike. He looked around the chamber again. No thoughts, no impressions came.

'Let's go look at the other exhibits,' he said.

The first Federation ship's outer lock yawned. Wolfe maneuvered into the small portal, saw the inner lock door was also open.

He ran his fingers along the edges of the lock, then looked at black smudges on his glove's fingertips. He unclipped a light from his belt and pulled himself into the ship's interior, the two aliens behind him.

There were ten dead men inside, grouped around the

unfolded chart table. Their bodies had exploded when the lock was blown open, then, as the years passed, withered into dry mummies. Their blood and body fluids were dried red, brown, gray spatters on the bulkheads and overhead.

Wolfe glanced at the bodies, then went past them to the scout's main control panel. There was a gaping hole to one side. Wolfe touched it, again saw black on his fingertips.

He examined the controls, found the EMERGENCY OVER-RIDE switch.

'Try to pull that outer door closed and turn the locking wheel as far as it will go,' he asked.

Taen obeyed. 'It appears to have sealed.'

Joshua closed the override switch, saw indicators flicker feebly to life.

'There's still air in the bottles. Stand by.' Again, he examined the control board, touched sensors.

Overhead lights glowed into faint yellow life.

An indicator on his suit's panel moved sluggishly. Joshua opened his faceplate.

'We have atmosphere,' he said. 'Unseal your suits.'

The thin air smelled dead, dusty.

The two Al'ar slid their faceplates up.

'Why did you do this? We have no need of their atmosphere,' Taen asked.

'Because it's hard as hell to do a shakedown with gauntlets. Shut up. I want to pay attention to what I'm doing.'

Wolfe took his gloves off and, beginning with the first man, trying not to look at his twisted grimace, he systematically went through the pockets and pouches of the torn shipsuit. He did the same for the other nine men.

'Not a bit of ID,' he said, sounding unsurprised. 'Now for the ship's log.'

He sat at the pilot's chair, again fingered controls.

Nothing happened.

He looked to one side, saw a small slot where something the size of a ship's log cartridge would have been. The slot was empty.

He found the ship's safe. The door had been blasted open, and papers were scattered on the deck. He knelt, went through them.

'No ship's roster, no orders, no nothing.'

He went to one corpse, touched the crumpled skull, closed his eyes.

He *felt* back into dim time, *felt* surprise, horror, agony.

'Do you know what happened?' Jadera asked. **'We were unable to determine who was the murderer, since all of the Terrans died by violence.'**

'Pretty sure. Let's take a look at the other ship. I'll predict we'll find one more body.'

'We do not need to investigate that ship unless you need to,' Jadera said. **'It is just as you said. How did you know?'**

Joshua didn't respond but pulled his gauntlets on and turned their wrists until they clicked sealed.

The second scoutship showed no sign of damage, and Wolfe opened the lock and entered. There was still air in the ship. As the inner lock cycled open he wrinkled his nose, smelling what he'd expected, an echo of the familiar sweet stench of an unburied corpse.

This man had died more quickly than the others. A blaster bolt had cut him almost in two. Over the years the body had decayed slowly, the ship's conditioner system fighting against corruption: skin pulled tight against bone, ripped, tore. Fingernails, hair grew as flesh vanished. The corpse leered at Wolfe.

Wolfe went to the controls, touched sensors, and the panel came alive. He scanned it.

'Plenty of fuel . . . air . . . we'll take this one back with us.'

He spun around in the chair. The two Al'ar stood on either side of the corpse, their eyeslits fixed on him.

'**First,**' he said, '**is we get rid of** *that*.'

Joshua found a thick plas tarp, rolled the remains into it, and the three lifted the tarp to the lock and cycled it out into space.

He found his lips moving in almost-forgotten phrases as the body orbited away aimlessly.

'Now, Joshua Wolfe,' Jadera said in Terran. 'Tell us what happened.'

'It's pretty obvious,' Wolfe said. 'These scouts have four-man crews for most missions. Two men and one kills the other, three and it's two against one, five is cost-ineffective.

'They send them out in three-ship elements.'

'**Ah. There is one ship and one man missing.**'

'This is what I think happened,' Joshua went on. 'Possibly these scouts came on the Lumina craft by accident, although I find that almost impossible to believe. They've got good sensors, but space is pretty big the last time I checked.

'Maybe the Lumina ship radiated some kind of signal that could be received by someone, and they were just being curious as to the source of this signal. Or maybe they were following up on something Naval Intelligence picked up on one of the Al'ar homeworlds.

'I don't know. It doesn't matter.

'I do know that at least one member of the crew was Chitet – maybe the man that's missing, although that's not likely.

'They found the Lumina carrier ship, boarded it, saw the Lumina. The biggest goddamned jewel any man could believe. Somebody got greedy. I'd guess . . .'

Wolfe stopped, thought for a time.

'Jadera,' he asked slowly, 'if someone, someone who had never been trained, concentrated on the Lumina, what would he *see*? Anything at all?'

'That is almost an impossible question to answer,' the Al'ar Guardian said. 'But I can hazard a thought. If someone saw the Lumina as what you said, a jewel of inestimable value, and he gazed into it, the Lumina would most likely reflect what he brought to it.'

'Dreams of glory,' Wolfe said.

'This is so. I would imagine he would suddenly find his mind filled with all manner of possibilities.'

'So we have,' Wolfe went on, 'our dreamer, whom the Lumina has just taken to the roof of the temple. So he arranges a conference on some pretext aboard one ship. One man – or woman – is left on each of the other two. Standard policy.

'Our villain arranges to be the last to arrive, waits until he knows everybody's unsuited, then blows the lock safety and the inner door open.

'He goes to this ship, kills the man here, and then, or maybe later, shoots the man on the third ship and pitches him out the lock.

'At leisure, he tries to make sure he – or she – is going to be able to disappear, and destroys all the crew IDs and the ship's log so, he hopes, nobody can know which of the twelve did it.

'Then he vacates for parts unknown, and fame and fortune, in the third ship with the Lumina.'

'Why did he not use the ship's weapons to destroy the other two, and leave a completely clean trail?'

'I don't know,' Wolfe said. 'But I can make a pretty close guess.

'Murder doesn't come as easy as people think it does. Especially the first time out. It scrambles the brain a trifle. I remember serving a bounty once on a woman who murdered her family for the death benefits and then forged their names on bank records after it was already known they were dead.

'Our friend managed to commit eleven murders successfully. Now he's suddenly up to his bellybutton in gore. These were people who were his shipmates, maybe even his friends until a few hours ago.

'All he wants is out and away.'

'I do not understand all of your words,' Jadera said. 'But it appears you are making sense.'

'I do,' Taen said. 'He is.'

'So our man flees with the Lumina. What would he do with it? Sell it?' Wolfe asked.

'He might think of doing that,' Jadera said. 'But it would certainly take a measure of time to do. Particularly if any of the details were known in the Federation. But more likely he would, especially if he spent some time considering the stone, thinking into it, and understanding what it was *telling* him, realize it could be used to get him far greater riches than just selling it could ever bring.'

'What could it give an unskilled man, one untrained in using a Lumina?' Joshua asked.

'It could give him certain insights, feelings that he could follow. What someone intended, what someone was really planning, really thinking. It is likely that a man who would think of killing, who did kill, would be encouraged by the Lumina to go in evil ways. It, of course, is unconstricted by human or Al'ar customs or laws.'

'So he's gone to ground somewhere and is busy trying to become the Great Nefarious Something-Or-Other. I can think of a couple of ways to go looking for him,' Wolfe went on. 'But first we've got to worry about the Chitet.

'I said before that I thought there was a Chitet mole –
sorry for the slang, an agent – among the men and women
on these ships. Some time between the discovery of the
Lumina aboard the ship and the killings, he or she managed
to dump a report off into N-space.

'The Chitet got that report. That's what put them in
motion, looking for anything resembling a Lumina or anything like an Al'ar, since they were specifically interested in
the Mother Lumina.

'Now, if they believe this is the root of all Al'ar
power . . . no wonder they've been getting a little testy
lately.

'Next the Federation hears about all this activity, and it's
wandering around trying to figure out what the hell is
going on. That's why they came to me.'

'Yes,' Jadera said. 'That makes uncommonly logical
progression. So what we must do is find out more
about this scout team so we are able to track the murderer and recover our Lumina. You said you knew of
some ways.'

'I do. That's why we'll need this ship. It'll give me a
starting point – inside the Federation. I'll start by –'

A warning shrilled in his speaker.

It came from the *Serex*.

'*Jadera . . . our sensors report transmissions coming from the
ship you are aboard, being broadcast into N-space.*'

'Son of a bitch,' Joshua swore. 'Somebody boobytrapped
this goddamned thing.'

Taen and Jadera looked about, as if they would be able to
see the source of the transmission.

Breathe . . . feel . . . reach out . . .

The Lumina was warm against Joshua's skin.

He *saw* the vibrations their hurried questions made in
the air, *felt* the waves the transmission from the Al'ar ship,
and something else.

He pushed past the Al'ar and pulled the inner lock door open. He reached under the sill of the outer lock door and pulled out a black, soft cylinder about a foot long that had been worm-curled out of sight.

'Kill it!' he ordered, and threw it on the deck.

Taen's sidearm came out, and he touched the firing stud.

The air shattered with the blast as the bolt struck the transmitter, and the metal deck seared.

There was silence.

'Back to your ship, Jadera, Taen,' Wolfe ordered. 'Somebody already found these ships and set a little alarm between the time you Al'ar came here and now. Maybe they were hoping the murderer'd come back to the scent. I'll bet the bug was set by the Chitet.

'That transmitter's shouting for backup, and I'll bet it's not far away. The Chitet have everything riding on this card.'

'What will you do?' Jadera asked.

'They'll want to track whoever was here. They can't know about the Guardians. You two return to the planet. I'll hang on here and give them something to chase.'

'You are being foolish,' Jadera said. 'We can fight them with the *Serex*.'

'They'll be coming in something big, too big for you. Goddammit, they're buying battleships! Let them chase me around for a while. If I could run rings around your watchdogs in the war, I know I can play the fox with these sobersides.'

Jadera hesitated, then closed his faceplate.

'Come on, Taen,' Wolfe said. 'I'll get back as quickly as I can.'

'No,' the Al'ar said. 'My life, my death, my doom are with you. I shall remain.'

Wolfe started to snarl something, then stopped.

After a moment, a smile came, went.

'You have my gratitude. And it's nice to have another damned fool around. Now get unsuited and strap in as best you can. I'll try to figure out master pilot tactics in what time we've got left. Life's going to get very interesting.'

Ten minutes after the *Serex* vanished into N-space, something shimmered on one of the scoutship's screens.

Joshua didn't need to key the Jane's-ID sensor.

It was the sleek, mottled darkness of a monstrous battlecruiser, only light-seconds distant.

FIFTEEN

'Those goddamned Chitet have too much money – or know too many of the right people,' Wolfe swore.

'You know that ship?'

'Know of it. Class of three. Laid down during the war, never finished. It was designed to beat up most of your ships and outrun anything it couldn't kill.

'Let's see what kind of legs it's got after we give 'em something to think about.'

Wolfe touched sensors and felt the scoutship lurch as two missiles fired, jumped briefly into N-space, emerged and exploded.

Two miniature suns – solar flares – blossomed.

'Now if they're blinded, they won't know just where we're going. I hope . . .'

Wolfe cut in the scout's stardrive and sent it into hyper-space.

The familiar sensations came, were gone, and the ship was in another part of the galaxy.

Joshua keyed another jump location, and as he did space blurred and the Chitet warship appeared.

'Son of a bitch! He had time to get a tracer on us! I didn't know beancounters made good E-warfare types.'

Again he touched the jump sensor, and again the scout went in, out of N-space.

Wolfe swung to another panel, opened the com net, set it to scan.

'Let's see if anybody out there's talking. Maybe we can find somebody to hide behind.'

There was nothing but the snarling static of the stars around them, then: 'Unknown ship, Unknown ship, this is the Chitet Police Vessel *Udayana*. Please respond.'

'The hell with you, sweetheart,' Wolfe snarled.

'Unknown vessel, this is the *Udayana*. Be advised the pickup in your ship detected Al'ar speech. Stand by for a patch transmission.'

'What is this?'

'I guess their bug was better than I thought,' Wolfe said. 'And now they're getting cute.'

A new voice came over the com. 'This is Chitet Authority Coordinator Dina Kur. I have been told there is an Al'ar aboard the vessel I am addressing. You are best advised to surrender immediately. We intend no harm, but rather a mutual sharing of knowledge.'

'Yes,' Taen agreed. '**I share my knowledge of everything with them, and they share their knowledge of pain-causing with me.**'

Wolfe looked at the Al'ar in some astonishment. 'I think you just made a joke.'

'**Impossible. You are deluded from the strain.**'

'That's twice.'

'You have the word of the Chitet government,' the com went on. 'Here is a recorded message, intended for you, made by our Master Speaker.'

Another voice came: 'This is Master Speaker Matteos Athelstan, addressing either Joshua Wolfe or a member of the Al'ar race. You have now been contacted by a high-ranking representative of our government and told that we wish to obtain certain data. We will guarantee both of you shelter from your Federation pursuers and sanctuary against any charges by the Federation.

'The Chitet are an old and honorable culture, and we

wish to welcome you. Please do as the conveyor of this message instructs you.'

After a pause, Kur's calm tenor came back. 'That was our Master Speaker. You have five minutes to prepare to obey the commands of the vessel that is tracking you. This is the last option to avoid possible violence. Please use logic, and realize there is no benefit to be gained by further resistance.'

'**Jump, One Who Fights From Shadows. There is no benefit to be gained from these people.**'

Wolfe obeyed.

The next time they came out of N-space they saw the *Udayana* – and three other, smaller ships in a fingers formation.

Wolfe launched a missile, and two of the Chitet ships sent out countermissiles.

As he readied the controls for another jump, the *Udayana* launched. Wolfe slammed the jump button as the missile broke out of N-space and detonated.

The edge of the shockwave caught them just as they entered hyperspace, and the scoutship rocked and tumbled in reality as well as their hyperspace-altered perceptions.

'The hounds are a little close,' Wolfe said. 'I'm not as good a fox as I used to be.'

'**What direction are you moving us in?**'

'Toward the Federation. We're well into it now. I hoped that they'd break off if company was around, but I'm not very lucky today.' Wolfe took a deep breath. 'There's another option.'

'**Which is?**'

'I can call for help to the Federation. To Cisco.'

'**That would be not sane.**'

'Of course not. But the Chitet are going to kill us for sure. Maybe with FI we can have time to lie to them for a while.'

Taen thought. 'Or, maybe, if they materialize in time, we can use the confusion to slip between the two forces.'

'Even better.'

Wolfe jumped twice in rapid succession.

Now they hung in space near an occupied system – their com scanner blipped through transmission groups on several channels.

Joshua scribbled code groups from memory, then set controls on the com to the special frequency Cisco had given him and opened his mike.

'X20FM . . . DL3WW . . . DO098 . . . PLM2X . . .'

He finished the groups and punched in another jump.

'Let's get close to their sun and tart around there. Give us some time to stall.'

When they came out of hyperspace, a planet was just 'above' them, about the size of Wolfe's thumbnail.

'I didn't know I could shave it this near a planet,' he muttered. 'Taen, can you drive this thing?'

'I have been watching you,' the Al'ar said. **'And I was cross-trained on older Federation vessels. I can try, as long as the Chitet do not make an attack.'**

'I don't have them on any screen,' Wolfe said. 'Maybe we lost them. But I won't bet on it. Keep about this distance offworld, so we can jump.'

He went to the chart table, opened it, and pulled out a catalog. 'If I knew what I was looking for . . .'

Ten minutes later the com beeped at them.

'I could do with a little luck right now,' Wolfe said, and touched the RECEIVE sensor.

The screen lit, and it was Cisco's face, disheveled, sleepy.

'Broadcasting en clair, Wolfe. We have a monitor on your frequency and he got me up. All code groups came through except one. Understood your problem.

'Suggest immediate rendezvous. Will be there on same item I was aboard last meeting to provide security. Standing by.'

'Just that goddamned frigate you were pooting around in before? Come *on*, Cisco.' Wolfe keyed the SEND sensor.

'Cisco, this is Wolfe. We're being chased by a battle-cruiser. I say again, a frigging battlecruiser, with three smaller friends. Same wonderful people as before if that part of the message got garbled. You better get ahold of the nearest Federation base and get some serious backup. Stand by for rendezvous point.'

He returned to the catalog, thumbed pages. 'Oh-ho. Maybe this.'

He took a microfiche from a cabinet. Its label read: OFF-WORLD WEAPONS STATIONS — TAURUS SECTOR — COORDINATES, DESCRIPTIONS. CLASSIFICATION: MOST SECRET.

'I think I have the Chitet ships onscreen now,' Taen said.

Wolfe paid no attention as he slipped the microfiche into a viewer and scanned.

'Now this might do us up fine,' he murmured, and went to a screen. 'Just reachable. All right. Here's what we're going to do. I've got us a place to duck into until Cisco and his friends show up.'

'**What is it?**'

'You'll see.'

Wolfe went to the com and sent hastily coded coordinates through it, then replaced Taen at the controls.

'Now we go to ground. Or if they've scrapped our den out, we get killed.'

Once more the scoutship shimmered into hyperspace.

SIXTEEN

The abandoned orbital fortress was a double-sided tetrahedron, Command-and-Control capsules set above and below the five weapons/living positions. The circular stations were connected by tubeways. It sat just beyond the three Federation worlds it had been built to defend, in the same orbital plane.

Wolfe and Taen stood in the scoutship's lock, waiting as the ship closed on the station. Both of them had booster packs for their suit drives.

The *Udayana* had not yet come out of hyperspace when the scout's autopilot spun the ship, and the secondary drive hissed, killing the ship's velocity.

'Four . . . three . . . two . . . let's go.'

The Al'ar and human pushed away from their ship as it spun on its gyros once again and, at full drive, shot away toward the closest Federation planet.

Wolfe killed his remaining relative velocity, then aimed himself at the station. Taen was a dozen yards behind.

They were a few hundred yards from the station when the ranging radar on Wolfe's suit *bonged* and a pointer appeared on his faceplate.

The Chitet ship had just come out of hyperdrive and was closing on them. Seconds later, space distorted in three other places and the *Udayana*'s smaller escorts flashed into being.

Taen and Joshua braked, landed on the fort's outer skin, and crouched toward the nearest lock.

It was sealed.

Wolfe muttered, unclipped a blaster. He touched his helmet to Taen's. 'I'll cut our way in when – if – they go right on by like they're supposed to.'

The *Udayana* closed on the fortress. Wolfe found himself holding his breath.

He saw the white glare of braking jets.

'Son of a bitch,' he muttered. 'They *always* chase the wrong thing in the romances.'

He pointed the blaster at the seal, fired briefly, wedged the lock door open, and the two slid inside.

'Did they set any wards when they closed this station down?' Taen asked.

'Damfino,' Wolfe said. 'If they did, we'll surely run into them, the way our luck's been running. I just hope they didn't see the gun go off.'

He shone a light briefly on the lock's interior, aimed carefully and blew the inner dog away, then flattened against the lock wall.

Air howled past, subsided, and Wolfe felt the clang as still-functioning damage portals closed inside the fortress. He forced the inner lock door open, and the two went into the station.

There was an emergency repair box on the bulkhead near the lock door, and Wolfe closed the inner lock door and slid a patch over the hand-size hole he'd blown in it.

He went to the damage portal, found the entryway, and opened it.

Taen followed him, touched his helmet to Wolfe's. 'What now?'

'Now we get out of the tin cans. I'd rather take a chance on breathing space than not be able to fight.'

Silently the two unsuited.

'I assume they will be boarding us,' Taen said. 'All we have to do is make their lives as miserable and short as possible until the Federation appears.'

'*If* the Federation appears,' Wolfe corrected. 'And if they bring something bigger than Cisco's spit-kit.'

'**I am looking forward to this**,' Taen said. '**It goes against my nature to always be running, as I have since my people left this space.**'

Wolfe didn't answer, but knelt and put his hands flat on the deck.

He *felt* pain, fear, death.

He stood, looked at the Al'ar, and half smiled.

'There are worse walls to have your back against. Now let's see how badly they defanged this beauty.'

The *Udayana*'s cargo bay was filled with men and women. They stood quietly in ranks, waiting for the commands to begin their well-planned attack.

A speaker crackled: 'Seal suits.'

Faceplates clicked.

'We will use the station's docking bay to debark. Make your last checks on your weaponry.'

There was no need to respond.

'I have been informed,' the voice said through a hundred suit speakers, 'that Authority Coordinator Kur has decided to personally take charge of the prisoners when they are taken.

'This is a chance to win high status and recognition. Our enemy will use any strategy, any deception to take us, to make us allow our emotions to rule and then destroy us.

'Think well, think carefully. Fight hard, fight with the intelligence you have been trained to use.'

None of the Chitet cheered as the speaker clicked off. They would have been shocked at the suggestion.

'**Do you suppose the Federation will arrive before they kill us?**'

'I don't even know if they're on the way,' Wolfe said honestly.

'If so, and we are not able to slip away in the chaos their arrival will bring, have you considered what we will tell them?'

'Have you decided to allow them to capture you?' Wolfe asked, a bit surprised.

'I am not sure. But for the sake of our discussion, let us suppose I shall.'

'Sure as hell we can't tell them about the Guardians, nor their planet.'

'No. I specifically referred to what lies beyond, in our old space-time. What you are calling a virus.'

'Do you think any of them would find truth in those words?' Wolfe said, switching to Al'ar.

'It *is* a remarkable concept,' the Al'ar said. 'Does the one you call Cisco have the mental reach for that?'

'Again, I do not know.'

'But we must try.'

'Why? Why do you give a diddly damn if the virus comes through into our space? Wouldn't that be an ultimate victory for the Al'ar?' Wolfe said.

Taen looked down, ran a grasping organ through the dust that covered the sensors of the control panel in front of him, then spoke in Terran.

'No. Life is life, whether Al'ar or human. That other – that virus – is something else. And we have all agreed I am corrupted.'

The deck jolted beneath them, and the slam of explosions came.

'As you said before, now it begins,' Wolfe said.

'And, most likely, ends.'

The Chitet moved into the station slowly, methodically. A squad would secure an area, take up firing positions, and a second squad would move through them to the next location.

They moved almost like professionals.

Almost.

Joshua's fingers rippled across the controls.

'You perform as if you are familiar with these weapons systems,' Taen commented.

'Not really. I was aboard a couple of these stations during the war for a few days.'

'Your movements are deceptive, then.'

Three screens lit simultaneously. Joshua studied them, frowning. 'Damn. They made sure this lion's toothless. No missiles, no guns, no nothin'. I guess we'll just have to take four cards and pretend there's a kicker.'

He turned to another, very dim screen.

'Come closer . . . closer . . .' he said softly, hand poised over a contact.

A hatch slid back on the skin of the fortress, and a triple-barreled missile launcher appeared.

An alarm squawked at a weapons station aboard the *Udayana*.

'Sir,' a rating said.

'I have it,' the officer in charge of the position said. 'Chaingun . . . target . . . fire!'

As the sailor pressed the controls, the officer snapped, 'Cancel that! There's nothing in those tubes!'

It was too late.

Four hundred collapsed-uranium shells roared out the multiple muzzles of the close-range weapon and tore into the station, smashing the deactivated launcher . . .

. . . and the platoon of Chitet who were just entering that weapons compartment.

*

Sirens bellowed, echoed through the deserted tubeways of the fortress.

'Now let us measure our foes,' Joshua said in Al'ar.

Taen extended a grasping organ. Wolfe touched it, then slipped out the hatch.

The reserve platoons waiting in the bay shifted, murmured as the alarms threatened chaos around them.

'Silence in the ranks,' an officer snapped, and the women and men were motionless.

A slender man wearing a black shipsuit appeared on a catwalk above them, lifting a heavy blaster.

He opened fire as the officer began to shout an order, and the bolts cut through the ranked Chitet.

The screams drowned out the sirens.

Return fire shattered the catwalk's railing, but Wolfe was gone.

The squad moved slowly down the corridor. Two men flattened on each side of the door, while a third booted it open, peered inside. Their officer stood to one side.

'Nothing, sir.'

'Next,' the woman said calmly.

They moved to the next doorway. One man kicked at the door, and it swung inside.

He peered in, and the officer saw him convulse, drop.

He rolled as he fell, and the woman had a moment to gape at his slashed-open throat as blood fountained.

Taen came out of the compartment, slender weapon spitting flame.

'Sir,' the officer said into his mike, 'we have twenty-seven casualties . . . eleven dead. More suspected – there are units no longer in touch.'

'Continue the mission,' came from the *Udayana*.

'Yes, sir.'

The voices were still calm, controlled.

There were three of them. They prided themselves, as much as a Chitet permitted himself pride, on being better soldiers than the others. After all, they had been Federation Marines before realizing the truth, deserting, and joining the ranks of those who lived logically.

They worked together smoothly, clearing passageways, reporting back to their officer on their progress.

Secretly they held him in contempt for not having the courage to stay with them, but none of them said anything.

They came to a place where several tubeways joined. They saw nothing.

They chose a new passageway, started down it.

Breathe : . . fingers touching . . . power focusing . . . accept Zai . . . become one . . . become all . . .

One of them thought he heard something, looked to one side.

A blur, and then there was a man in a black shipsuit beside them. He took one step forward, leapt, and one leg shot out.

It took the first man at the angle of his jaw, and his neck snapped cleanly.

Joshua landed on his hands, rolled to one side just as the second man fired, blast searing the metal deck. Wolfe curled into a front-roll, and his legs lashed into the second man's groin.

The third's aim was blocked. She moved to one side, as Wolfe back-snapped to his feet, ducked under her swinging gun and struck twice, the first blow crushing her solar plexus, the second her throat.

The second man was trying to scream, backing away, gun forgotten.

Wolfe double-stepped forward, lunged, arm snapping

forward, hips and shoulders turning. His palm smashed into the man's face, driving his septal cartilage into his brain.

Joshua watched the final body crumple slowly.

Fingers touching . . . welcome Zai *. . . let the void take you . . .*

The air shimmered, and there was no one in the corridor except the three corpses.

Each member of the medical team towed an antigrav stretcher behind him. They had four armed men for security, yet still moved slowly, checking every passageway.

They spun, hearing a clang, saw a duct cover from the overhead air system rolling to a halt.

One medic laughed nervously, and they turned back, and then someone shrieked.

Standing in front of them was an impossibly thin, grotesquely white being.

One Chitet lifted his gun, was shot down.

Taen pulled a grenade from his weapons belt, thumbed its detonator, and rolled it into the center of the team.

He ducked around a corner as a bolt shattered the wall next to him, heard the crash as the grenade detonated.

The Al'ar stepped back into the corridor, surveyed the dead, the bleeding, then lifted his weapon and, aiming carefully, finished the job.

'Sir,' the officer reported. 'We're still taking casualties. We don't know how many of them there are. There's one man in a black coverall . . .'

'That will be the renegade Wolfe,' his superior said.

'. . . and no one knows how many Al'ar. They're all around us, sir!' His voice cracked.

The other's tones remained controlled, calm. 'Very well. When one Al'ar – and Wolfe – have been captured, you have permission to kill the remainder.'

'But — yes, sir.' The young officer breathed deeply, reminded himself of the necessity for calm, stood. There were seventeen men and woman crouched around him, sheltering behind weapons mounts. Two hours ago, there had been thirty.

Fire . . . burn . . . take . . . all is yours . . .

'Sir,' one of them said. 'Look.'

The officer noticed that a hose, hydraulic, he thought, had come loose from a mount. Suddenly the hose stiffened, began flailing, and a dark, acrid fluid sprayed out.

Two Chitet jumped for the hose, had it, then it slipped through their fingers, continued thrashing, the solution vaporizing as it showered them.

The officer saw a small round object coming toward him.

It seemed to move very slowly. He had all the time in the world to dive away from the grenade, shouting a warning. The grenade hit, bounced, exploded, and the fumes ignited. The ball of flame grew, devoured the Chitet, and they screamed, danced a moment in agony, died.

Joshua came out of the doorway fast, kicked the closest man in the side of the knee, went around him for the second.

He hit him with a hammerstrike to the temple, knew he was dead, and forgot him.

The third man's rifle was coming down from port arms. Its front sight blade caught Joshua's shipsuit, ripped it and tore his flesh.

The gun went off beside his waist, and the muzzleblast seared across his stomach.

Wolfe had the gun by the barrel, jerked, front-kicked into the man's stomach, tossed the weapon away. The man buckled, clutching himself. Joshua doubled his fists, struck down at the base of the man's neck, let the body fall away.

The first man was flat on the deck, gagging, cuddling his knee like it was a child, trying to end the pain.

Joshua high-stepped above him, drove his heel down into the man's throat, spun away.

Breathe . . . breathe . . .

His hands came together.

Feel the earth . . . invoke chi *. . .*

Burn-agony seared, was recognized, denied, went away.

Wolfe ran down the corridor toward sudden shots.

Taen shot down the last of the five as Wolfe came in at the far end of the long room. '**They have bravery.**'

'They do. For which the hell with them. Come on. I can *feel* them above, in front of us. We've got to pull back toward one of the command caps.'

Taen slid another tube into the slot of his weapon and followed Joshua down the tubeway.

Let the wind take us . . .

The alarm gonged needlessly. The watch officer had seen what was on screen.

Three Federation battleships had come out of N-space and were, a nearby prox-detector told him, less than fifteen minutes from intercept. A gnat-swarm of other ships snapped into being around them.

The officer slapped a button and sirens howled. The *Udayana*'s watch frequency blared:

'All ships in vicinity of the Magdalene 84 Orbital Fortress. I say again, all ships in the vicinity of the Magdalene 84 Fortress. This is the Federation Battleship *Andrea Doria*.

'You are ordered to cease all unlawful activity immediately and immediately surrender to this task force.

'Resistance will be useless. Any attempt to open fire on any Federation ship will be met with the full force of our missiles.

'I say again. Surrender immediately. Our ships will match orbits with yours and board. Do not resist!'

The *Udayana*'s commander was beside the watch officer. 'Three battleships . . . a dozen destroyers . . . Mister, cut us loose from the station!'

'Sir?'

'I said seal the ship! Get us away from this station and jump into N-space! Move, mister!'

The watch officer began to say something, caught himself. He issued hasty orders.

The sentries in the boarding bay of the fortress had barely time to duck out of the way as the Chitet battlecruiser's lock irised shut. Seconds later, the station's outer lock closed.

They gaped and then felt the vibration as the *Udayana* broke away from the fortress into space.

One of them stammered a question, but no one had an answer.

Then their suit speakers crackled:

'Fellow Chitet. This is the captain of the *Udayana*. We have been ambushed by superior forces of the Federation. To avoid exposure and damage to our cause, it is necessary for those of you on special assignment to give up your lives for the cause.

'Under no circumstances can you allow yourselves to be captured, or to provide anything that might be damaging to the greater cause.

'You served well. Now serve on. Your sacrifice shall not be forgotten.'

'Our rescuers appear to have arrived,' Taen said.

'Yeah,' Wolfe said. He saw the sniper who'd been shooting

at them from behind a massive generator, and sent a bolt smashing into the man's chest. 'Now let's try to stay alive long enough to be rescued.

'I hate anticlimaxes.'

One of the Chitet ships bulleted toward the Federation units, vanished in a expanding ball of gases before it could launch a missile.

The *Udayana* and its two surviving escorts drove away from the fortress at full drive, then vanished into N-space.

The Federation admiral on the bridge of the *Andrea Doria* cursed and looked at the man in civilian clothes beside him. 'We should have hit them without warning. Now we've got nobody to hang.'

The Federation Intelligence executive shrugged. 'They're not important. We can take them later. What's on that fortress is.'

The admiral picked up the microphone, and the ancient words echoed down the corridors of the great ship:

'Land the landing force.'

Federation soldiers spilled from the airlocks into the bays of the station.

Here, there, scattered knots of Chitet fought back. Only a handful of them disobeyed orders and tried to surrender.

The others died, as ordered.

'Do you know, One Who Fights From Shadows, I have a possible solution to our problem with the Federation.'

Wolfe looked at Taen. The Al'ar's eyeslits were focused on him.

Suddenly Taen's head lifted, he looked beyond, then dove forward atop Joshua.

The bolt from the Chitet blaster took Taen in the back, tearing away his grasping organ and shoulder.

Wolfe heard a shout of joy as he rolled out from under the Al'ar.

Across the chamber he saw a Chitet, blaster snout aiming.

There was no thought.

There was no focus, no *Zai*.

Wolfe took Taen's death from his mind and cast it at the Chitet.

The man screamed in impossible agony, fell dead.

Wolfe did not know if he had been the only Chitet left in the compartment, nor did he care.

He knelt beside the Al'ar.

Taen's eyeslits were closed.

Joshua felt something leave, something that had been the last of a time when there was youth, no blood, no death.

His mind was still, empty.

Time passed. It may have been long, it may have been a few moments.

He *felt* a presence.

He looked up.

There were three men in the compartment. Two were Federation soldiers. They held blast rifles leveled.

The other was Cisco.

He held a wide-barreled pistol in his hand, pointed down at the deck.

Joshua got to his feet, walked forward.

Cisco lifted the gas gun, fired.

The capsule hit Wolfe in the chest, exploded.

Joshua stumbled.

He *felt* the savage insect clamor in another galaxy, building in triumph.

Then there was nothing.

BOOK THREE

THE DARKNESS OF GOD

For

Guy Glenn

Tom McManus

and

Ken & Candy Leggett

without them, the perspective
might've gotten a
little different

ONE

A Federation battlefleet whispered through subspace. In a compartment aboard its flagship, the *Andrea Doria*, two men stared down at Joshua Wolfe's body. One was a fleet admiral, the other a Federation Intelligence executive.

A third man wore coveralls and combat harness. He sat in a chair, a blaster held casually in his lap.

'How many safeguards does he have?' Admiral Hastings asked.

'Every damned one we could build into his mind, sir,' the second man, Cisco, answered. 'He was one of our best before he turned renegade.'

'You think you'll be able to get what you want without killing him?'

'We have to,' Cisco said grimly. 'FI doesn't have anything else.'

The first man pursed his lips. 'Well, you built him, you ran him, so you'd *better* be able to peel him like an onion.'

'Yes, sir. I've already got our best psychs on standby.'

The admiral left the compartment without responding. Cisco took something from his pocket and examined it. It was a gray, featureless stone with a few bits of color in it. 'Stay dead like that,' he said softly. He put it away, then swung to the guard.

'How much longer are you on shift?'

'Two hours and some.'

'Stay careful,' Cisco warned. 'We don't really know what we have here, so don't get casual.'

The guard stared at Cisco. 'Yes, *sir*,' he said, putting heavy emphasis on the last word. Cisco nodded, then went out. The hatch slid closed.

'Yes, *sir*,' the man said again. 'Yes, sir, Master Cisco, large-charge spymaster sir.'

He glanced at Wolfe.

'Guess I oughta kick you in the shins a time or two, eh, since shit always flows downhill, huh?'

The man tightened the black band around his biceps, then pulled the small lanyard. The bell from the ancient ocean-ship *Lutine* clanged three times through the high-ceilinged, wooden-paneled chamber.

By the third peal, the room was silent.

The man cleared his throat.

'The Federation exploration ship *Trinquier*, overdue on planetfall for three weeks, is now considered lost.

'All Lloyd's carriers involved with this matter are advised to contact their policies' beneficiaries.'

Another continuum . . . red spray across the stars, connecting them, holding them, blood-syrup of death, nothing living but a single invader . . .

Joshua Wolfe, between death and life, felt the touch of the alien and pulled back in horror.

The drug Cisco'd shot him with still washed through his system; nothingness clung.

Cisco has the Lumina. I am naked.

Defeat.

No. You had strength before. Find it now. The Lumina gave you nothing but kimu.

Joshua struggled, fell back, floated away once more.

Time passed.

Once more a bit of life came, angry, yammering.

Rouse yourself. Now. There will be no time when we reach Earth. You must strike first.

No. Easier to drift, to drown.

Images came, went, like old-fashioned photographs looked at casually, then cast into a fire, twisting, warping as they vanished:

The corpselike face of an Al'ar, grasping organs blurring through a series of strikes. Then the alien stopped, waited for the young Joshua Wolfe to echo his movements. The Al'ar was named Taen.

. . .

*The hissing, invisible **kill-barrier** in the prison camp, not far from his parents' graves.*

. . .

The Al'ar, about to open the scoutship hatch, whirled, but not in time, grasping organs coming up, but late, too late as the death-strike went home. The dirty, ragged boy pulled the corpse away and clambered into the ship, went to the controls.

He sat behind them, stared at their utter alienness, felt fear shake his spine. He forced himself to breathe, as he'd been taught, then remembered all he'd learned, all he'd been told, from any prisoner who'd been inside an Al'ar ship.

Tentatively, he touched a sensor. The hatch behind him slid closed.

He touched two more, and the panel came alive; he felt the shuddering of power behind him.

A cold, hard smile came to Joshua Wolfe's lips.

. . .

Joshua wore the uniform of a Federation major. Behind him were ranks of soldiers in dress uniform. A general held an open velvet case with a medal inside. His words were 'highest traditions of the service,' 'without regard for his own safety,' and 'refused to recognize the severity of his wounds, but insisted on returning to his weapon,' and so forth.

They had little meaning to Wolfe. All he heard was death and killing.

. . .

Joshua, wearing fighting harness with blaster ready, cat-paced through the empty streets of Sauros' capital. But there was no one to kill. The Al'ar had gone, utterly vanished.

. . .

The face of the man who called himself Cisco, saying there was yet one more Al'ar, and Joshua was to hunt him down.

. . .

The last Al'ar, blurring out of concealment, striking at Joshua. Taen.

. . .

The shadows of the Al'ar Guardians, telling him why they'd fled their home-space for Man's universe, showing him the invader Joshua's man-mind could only see as a ravening virus, devouring world after world, system after system, jumping across and filling the spaces between them.

. . .

The emptiness in the Al'ar ship where the great Lumina stone had hung before it was stolen by a shadow drenched in blood.

. . .

Taen, as the Chitet bolt took him in the back, slumping in death.

. . .

Death . . . that welcomed.

It would be very easy to let the animal-mechanism shut down. Nothing was ahead but pain under the not-gentle hands and tools of the FI interrogators.

Death.

Defeat.

The red crawl of the 'virus' would continue through another galaxy and on and on.

Wolfe stirred.

Can you reach out? Can you find anything? The Al'ar Guardians?

Nothing.

Something came, or rather returned to him. An echo, far worlds distant.

The ur-Lumina he sought?

Nothing once more.

Again. Feel for anger, feel for fear, feel for those who hate you, who want you.

Another flicker, far distant, a man who hated with a white-hot heat, remembering the woman Joshua had freed and returned to her lover, now her husband.

No. Not him. Not Jalon Kakara.

A red-orange sear of flame, stone pinwheeling up as the Occam smashed down from its orbit into a dark gray palace, the frantic yammer of a world whose leader had almost died.

The Chitet.

He felt them.

Looking for Wolfe, looking for the Great Lumina, cult-mind sweeping, hunting.

Then the drug took him back down into its embrace.

'This is utterly absurd,' Cisco said in a near-snarl.

Hastings looked at him coldly. 'Orders are orders, and these certainly are from an unimpeachable authority.'

'Sir,' Cisco began, 'this makes no sense. We have Wolfe secured. I can't think of anything anybody's got that could ruffle the *Andrea Doria*'s hair. So why the hell are we ordered to divert and transfer him? We're only, what, half a dozen jumps from Earth now? Utterly no sense whatsoever,' he said, ignoring the mindcrawl suggesting a reason.

'Consider an explanation, mister,' Hastings said. 'We're well within the bounds of the Federation. I hardly think even your Chitet would try to grab him here. We beat them, remember? We drove them away. They aren't anything to worry about, at least not for us. Once you have your spy debriefed, it'll be a simple matter for the police to take care of matters.

'You're being paranoid, Cisco. I'd rather suspect ComFedNav wants to keep my battle group close to the Outlaw Worlds, rather than have us waste the time and energy to go all the way back to Earth, dump off one man, and then jump back out here.

'The pickup group specified in the order seems more than large enough to keep a countergrab from happening.'

'Admiral Hastings,' Cisco said, 'you saw what the Chitet had around that fortress. That was a goddamned battleship!'

'An old battlecruiser, actually,' Hastings corrected. 'I think you're being a bit hysterical, Cisco. Don't forget the orders are not just for Wolfe, but for you and your entire team to transfer as well. But I'll give you this. When we rendezvous with the other ships, if there's any irregularity, I'll refuse to turn him – or you – over to them. And I'll reauthenticate the original orders with ComFedNav right now. Does that satisfy you?'

Hastings glowered at the FI executive.

'No,' Cisco said. 'But that's the best I'll get, isn't it?'

Four ships waited – one frigate, one armed transport, and two sloops – as the Federation battlefleet emerged from the nowhere of N-space.

'This is the Federation Naval Force Sure Strike,' came the com from the *Andrea Doria*. 'Challenge Quex Silver Six-Way.'

'*Andrea Doria*, this is the FNS *Planov*. Reply Cincinnatus Yang.'

'That's the correct response, sir,' the watch officer reported to the *Andrea Doria*'s captain. 'And I checked the Jane's fiche.

That's the *Planov* onscreen. Current Nav-Registry still carries her and her escorts as being in commission.'

'Tell them we're beginning the transfer,' the ship's captain said. She turned to Admiral Hastings. 'Sir?'

'I see nothing wrong,' the admiral said. 'Cisco?'

The agent's eyes flickered. 'There's nothing apparent, sir,' he conceded.

'Do your people have the – package ready?'

'Yes, sir.'

'You may begin the transfer, then,' Hastings told the ship's captain.

'Ready?'

'Ready, sir,' the senior FI tech reported to Cisco.

'Get him on board.'

The tech triggered the antigrav unit, and the bubble stretcher holding Joshua Wolfe lifted off the deck. Two men steered it through the hatch of the *Andrea Doria*'s shuttle; the other seven men in the FI detachment followed.

Cisco gestured at Admiral Hastings, something like a salute.

'See you on Earth,' Hastings said in response, without returning the salute.

Cisco nodded and boarded the boat after his men.

Hastings waited until the shuttle lock slid shut, then he grimaced in distaste to his aide. 'The air's better when the spooks are gone,' he said.

The young blond woman grinned at him. 'Guess it's nice Earth's a decent-sized planet, sir.'

Hastings guffawed and clapped his aide on the back. 'Let's get up to the bridge and make sure they're well on their way.'

The *Andrea Doria*'s shuttle nosed up to the *Planov*'s stern, and a cargo lock yawned between its twin drive tubes. A mag-probe touched the shuttle's nose and drew it inside the transport.

'We have your ship,' the com crackled. 'Unloading.'

Ten minutes passed.

Hastings looked sideways at the *Andrea Doria*'s captain. 'Very slow, even if they are unloading flatlanders. Your boat crew needs drill.'

'They'll get it, sir,' the officer said, anger touching her voice. 'My apologies.'

'This is the *Planov*,' the com said. 'Loading complete. Stand by.'

The armed transport's lock opened, and the shuttle slid out, tumbling. There was no sign of its drive activating.

Abruptly the *Planov* and her three escorts vanished into N-space.

'Courteous bastards,' the aide murmured, but Hastings' attention was on the monitor and the slowly revolving shuttle.

'Something's wrong,' he snapped. 'Captain! Send a boarding party to the shuttle!'

'Yes, sir.'

'Have them armed!'

The captain's face flashed surprise for a bare instant. 'Sir!'

Ten suited men floated around the *Andrea Doria*'s shuttle. Two hung near the craft's nose, two near the drive tube. The other four clustered around the airlock. All had heavy blasters clipped to their suits.

'No external damage to ship,' the team's leader, Sergeant Sullivan, reported. 'No sign of lock damage.'

'Cleared to enter.'

Two men braced on either side of the lock, weapons ready, while the leader touched the lock door sensor.

The outer lock door slid open.

The leader, with one other man, went inside. 'Cycling inner lock,' he reported.

Static snarled, then:

'Son of a bitch!'

'Report!'

'Sorry. This is Sergeant Sullivan. Everyone on board's dead! Unconscious, anyway!'

'What about the prisoner? The man in the stretcher?'

'No stretcher, sir. Wait a minute. One of the women is sitting up, sir. I've got my outside pickup on.'

Very faintly the men on the bridge of the *Andrea Doria* heard:

'What happened?'

'Gas . . . They were waiting for us . . . gassed us . . . didn't give us a . . .'

Then silence. Sullivan's voice came:

'She's passed out, sir.'

'Well?' said the woman with alabaster features fine enough for a museum.

'Pretty standard, Coordinator Kur,' the medical tech said. 'They first hit him with Knok-Down, maybe a more concentrated blast than normal. Then they kept him under, almost to the point of needing a life-support system. Suppressing conscious thought, pain, and so forth.'

'Any damage?'

'I assume you mean mental. Probably none.'

'How long to bring him out of it?'

'Three, perhaps four hours.'

'Summon me when he's fully conscious.'

Wolfe opened his eyes slowly. The compartment around him swam, then steadied. He was in a comfortable bed. The air smelled of disinfectant. He felt ship-hum in his bones.

Sitting in a chair beside him was a woman wearing conservative, dark clothes, almost a uniform. She was perhaps five years older than Wolfe, and he found her beautiful, in a chill, forbidding way. *Like a statue*, he thought.

Behind her stood two men, also wearing dark clothes. Their hair was close-cropped, and they might have been brothers. They each held blasters aimed at Wolfe's chest.

'Welcome, Joshua Wolfe,' the woman said. 'I am Authority Coordinator Dina Kur. You are now in the hands of the Chitet.'

TWO

Wolfe eyed the two men with guns.

'Honest, I *really* appreciate the rescue,' he said. 'So you won't have to shoot me more than once or twice to make sure I'm beholden.'

'There is no point in facile cleverness,' Kur said. 'Let me put it to you clearly. We are aware you seek the stone called the Overlord Stone or Great Lumina, as do we.

'We consider you our most dangerous enemy, since you have circumvented our plans on several occasions, including the destruction of an entire Chitet mission and its ship on the planet of Trinité; then you severely damaged a patrol cruiser of ours in your escape. We are also aware of your hijacking of the patrol vessel *Occam*, and using that ship in an attempt to murder our Master Speaker, Matteos Athelstan. Under normal circumstances, you would be immediately put to death for crimes against the Chitet and, ultimately, the future of humanity. But these are not normal times or circumstances.

'You also, in the company of an Al'ar, purportedly the last Al'ar alive, investigated a certain area where the Great Lumina had been, and where we had set alarms. I was aboard the *Udayana*, and followed you to the abandoned planetary fortress where you held off our forces until the Federation could arrive. Our cause gained many martyrs that day. What happened to the Al'ar who was with you?'

'He is . . . gone beyond. Dead,' Wolfe said.

'So we assumed, and that made your continued existence, as long as you do not further jeopardize the Chitet, essential, at least for the moment,' Kur said. 'He was killed, and you were taken by the Federation. We were informed by reliable sources you were being returned to Earth as a captive, so evidently those you thought to be your friends have changed their positions. Or you have.

'Regardless, you are going to assist us in our quest, Joshua Wolfe.'

Her voice had remained utterly, inhumanly cold. 'Our Master Speaker is aboard this vessel to ensure that all goes well, and that we will be successful in recovering the Great Stone the Al'ar called the Overlord Stone.'

'I am going to help,' Joshua agreed.

'Don't play me for a fool, Joshua Wolfe,' Kur replied. 'I'm not going to listen to nonsense about a sudden realization of the truth of our beliefs. We are not on the road to Damascus, nor are there many visions in N-space.'

'Oh, but I am going to cooperate,' Wolfe insisted. 'For I already know how to find the Chitet – sorry, the former Chitet – who murdered eleven men and women and stole the Great Lumina. But I'll need your resources to recover it.'

Kur stared at him, without blinking. 'This decision is well beyond me,' she said. 'I must consult with Master Speaker Athelstan.'

Wolfe 'freshed, ate, and slept, feeling the last of the drugs wash out of his system. He asked if he could work out, and his request was denied, without explanation.

His guards were changed every hour, and never varied their routine. They sat, eyes fixed on Joshua, never answering anything he said, nor volunteering anything of their own.

Two ship-days later, Authority Coordinator Kur returned. With her were three Chitet. Two were men, average looking, calm-expressioned. One wore a close-cropped beard. The third was a small woman who, in another setting, might have been considered quite pretty.

'Master Speaker Athelstan wishes to speak with you,' Kur announced. 'Now, listen closely, Joshua Wolfe.

'Your life is important to you, I assume. It is also important to us, at least until we have fully exploited you and whatever knowledge you possess.

'You will continue to be watched by gun-guards such as those who have been with you since your capture. It is known that you're a master at most forms of combat, armed or otherwise.

'We have also heard stories which appear preposterous about your other abilities, which I assume you acquired from the Al'ar at one time or another.

'We can take no chances, Joshua Wolfe, even if it means sacrificing whatever leads you might provide toward the Overlord Stone.

'These three are an additional safeguard. They are Guide Kristin,' Kur indicated the woman, 'and Lucian and Max.' Lucian was the bearded one. 'They are among our most highly trained security specialists, and have formerly been assigned to the private bodyguard of Master Speaker Athelstan, so you should respect and be wary of their skills.

'You do not need to know their family names. Kristin speaks for the team. They have orders to kill you if ordered, and if anything, I repeat anything, appears wrong, to destroy you instantly, without waiting for a command from Master Speaker Athelstan or myself. Remove your tunic, please.'

Joshua obeyed. Kur stepped out of the room again, and returned with a small flat black case.

'Put your hands in front of you,' she ordered. 'Guards,

each of you stand to one side, so you have a clear field of fire. If Joshua Wolfe attempts anything, kill him.'

The guards obeyed. Kur took a flesh-colored pouch with thin straps from the case. 'Turn around,' she ordered. She touched the object to the base of Joshua's spine. It felt cold for an instant but quickly warmed. She ran the straps around his waist, touched them together, and they joined seamlessly.

'Replace your clothing,' Kur said. 'That object, as you can probably surmise, is explosive. It is phototropic, and will gradually take on the coloration of your skin, though you should exercise care about disrobing in public, because the camouflage is not perfect.

'The charge is shaped, so someone standing next to you when the device is detonated would be unharmed, and only momentarily deafened.

'You, on the other hand, would have your spinal cord shattered. If you attempt to remove the charge, a signal will be sent to the operator, and he or she will instantly detonate it.'

Joshua sat down, leaned back. It felt as if he had padding against his spine, no more.

'The woman or man controlling the detonator to that device is watching a monitor at all times, a monitor carrying your image,' Kur said. 'You do not need to know how far away the operator is, nor even where he or she is, nor where the monitor is. If you are moving, one of these three will have a tiny camera concealed about his or her person. If you are in one place, the camera will be hidden there. It might also be more than one camera, so there's no point in finding and destroying one single pickup.

'If the operator sees anything amiss on the monitor, or if you vanish from its screen . . .'

'Quite clever,' Wolfe said. 'I see you three are now my closest and best friends.'

'That is an excellent way to think,' Kur said. 'Now, Master Speaker Athelstan awaits.'

'You were once in possession of a Lumina,' Athelstan said, stating a fact, not a question. He appeared in his fifties and could have been a successful merchant banker. Wolfe had seen him once before, on a vid interview. He'd ascribed the glitter in the man's eyes to camera flare. There was no such excuse now.

There were three others in the compartment, which was soberly but richly paneled: Kur, Max, and a Chitet in his early thirties who was Athelstan's aide.

'I was,' Wolfe said. 'The Lumina was originally purchased by one quote Judge end-quote Malcolm Penruddock of Mandodari III, stolen from him by a spec thief named Innokenty Khodyan. I recovered the gem on a warrant, and Khodyan got dead in the process.

'I interviewed Penruddock about his interest in the Lumina —'

'At the behest of Federation Intelligence,' Athelstan said.

'It was . . . and also for my own interests. But your Chitet killed Penruddock and his wife before I found out very much. Almost killed me.'

'He did not deserve the Lumina,' Athelstan said. 'He'd been quietly approached to sell it, but refused. That left us no other course.'

'Must be nice to be sure of who deserves what and when. And that's not quite how it went,' Wolfe said calmly. 'Credit me with a bit of intelligence. You first commissioned Innokenty Khodyan to steal the Lumina from Penruddock, using a fence named Edet Sutro as a cutout. You killed him on Trinité. For a group of people who think themselves philosophers, you sure trail a lot of bodies.'

'Nowhere does it say philosophy cannot resort to direct action to accomplish its goals,' Athelstan said. 'And our goals are great, encompassing not only the salvation of humanity, but enabling it to reach the next level of evolution as well.'

'There was a Chinese once,' Wolfe said, 'who said, "Those who would take over the Earth and shape it to their own ends never, I notice, succeed."'

'Lao-tzu lived long before the Chitet,' Athelstan said. 'And there were those of his time who came very close. Buddha. Confucius. The group of Jews who created Jesus. Mohamet . . . But there's no point in this sparring. I assume the Federation has the Lumina.'

'They do.'

'Does that cripple you? What powers did the stone give? We have one, but none of our savants have been able to do more than the most minor trickeries with the object.'

Wolfe's eyes flickered. *So they have one now.* 'I can still find the Mother Lumina for you,' Wolfe evaded.

'How? We have searched hard for it, for almost seven years without result.'

'Obviously you were looking in the wrong places,' Joshua said. 'And you didn't have a ferret with sharp enough teeth.'

'I agree. The facts dictate the truth.' Athelstan's head bobbed slightly, as if he'd just recited a prime canon of his faith. 'Tell us how to look, and we shall.'

'Not quite that easy,' Wolfe said. 'If I just tell you, my continued existence, as your knob-rattler Kur has pointed out, would become a little redundant. So even if I knew, exactly, I wouldn't tell you.'

'You were our captive once,' Athelstan said. 'And the head of the interrogation team reported you had suicide devices installed in your mind against forcible questioning and against any psychotropic drugs we have access to. I assume she was correct.'

'I'd be a fool not to say yes,' Joshua said.

'How do we seek the Overlord Stone?' Athelstan said. 'My security coordinator will obey your orders.'

'I await instructions,' Kur said, showing no resentment.

'First, here's what I know,' Joshua said. 'The Al'ar placed the Overlord Stone in a ship, actually a satellite. It was set in space in a certain place of importance to the Al'ar. Sometime after the war, three Federation scoutships found it. I assume this discovery was not an accident.'

Kur looked uncomfortable. Athelstan nodded for her to speak.

'Some Federation investigations on Al'ar homeworlds suggested the existence of the ur-Lumina,' she said reluctantly. 'The Federation issued orders for a naval patrol to visit the area of interest. We learned of this patrol shortly before it transshipped, and were able to insert one of our agents aboard one of the ships. The agent was equipped with an N-space blurt-transmitter, and was able to report the discovery to us. We had ships standing by capable of capturing the scoutships, and dispatched them immediately. But when they arrived, they found –'

'Eleven corpses, two ships, and no Lumina,' Wolfe said. 'Your boy changed his mind while he was sitting around twiddling his thumbs, and decided to render unto Caesar instead of the Chitet. And he wanted to be Caesar.'

'So we assumed,' Kur said. 'We went in search of the individual.'

'Who is she?'

'How did you know it's a woman?' Kur demanded.

'Because of the care you've taken not to mention her sex,' Wolfe said.

Kur eyed him, then went on. 'Her name is Token Aubyn. She was a lieutenant in the regular Federation Navy. All E's on her quarterly reports. An officer with a great career in front of her. She'd been secretly raised as a member of our culture, and chosen to infiltrate the Federation military.'

'Home system?'

'Vidaury III, although she spent time on VI as well before she enlisted.'

'I assume you've toothcombed that system without results or leads?'

Kur nodded.

'Token Aubyn,' Wolfe mused. 'Pretty name for somebody that cold-blooded. You have a full dossier on her?'

'We do.'

'I want it. All of it,' Wolfe said. 'No dandy little crossouts for Chitet snitches and sources.'

'But –'

'Be silent, Coordinator Kur. We must give Wolfe every possible aid,' Athelstan said.

'After all,' Joshua said, 'it's not as if you plan on letting me escape with anything I learn here, now is it?'

Athelstan didn't answer, but his cold eyes held Wolfe's.

Joshua went through the fiche on Token Aubyn quickly, letting his senses, his training, reach for what might be in the data. Then he read, viewed everything very slowly, twice.

Security Coordinator Kur and his alternating guardians waited stolidly.

There weren't many holos or vids. Kur told Joshua that Aubyn reportedly hadn't liked having herself recorded.

The best holo Joshua could find was a head-and-shoulders cameo of Aubyn in full-dress Federation uniform.

'That was her graduation picture from the Academy of Flight on Mars, taken at her parents' insistence,' Kur said.

'Where are they now?'

'Dead. In an accident two years ago.'

'Convenient.'

Wolfe examined the portrait. Aubyn wasn't pretty, but striking. Dark hair, worn very short. She was the gamin type, with hooded eyes just turned away from the lens.

Other documents said she was slender, a bit over average height.

'What about her love life?'

'Nothing known.'

'Come on, Kur. Everybody plays pinch-and-tickle sometimes.'

'Not necessarily,' the woman protested. 'Especially in Aubyn's case. Her parents were deep-cover types, so she grew up in a house full of secrets, on two planets. Then, when we gave her our long-range plans for her, she would have been a fool to endanger everything by listening to her glands.'

'How romantic you Chitet are.'

Wolfe ran the fiche forward.

'Now here's something interesting,' he mused. 'The final competition for the Academy of Flight broke down to her and one other person. He died just before the final oral examinations. In another accident.'

'We checked into that thoroughly,' Kur said. 'It *was* an accident. Aubyn was half a planet away when this boy died.'

'I say again: convenient.'

He returned to the fiche.

'You either did a good job of programming Aubyn, or else she already had her calling. No zigs, no changes of major. Chosen field of study at the Academy . . . sociology. And her thesis was on "The Dynamism of a One-Party State."'

'I fail to see any significance in that,' Kur said. 'When we have convinced the people of the Federation of the benefit of our ways, of course there won't be any necessity for dissenters.'

'Thus spake Savanarola,' Wolfe murmured. 'Did you ever consider that Aubyn was doing research for her own idea of a one-party state? One with Token Aubyn as dictat?'

'Oh,' Kur said. 'That's insane – and of course we didn't

allow ourselves to consider any options that didn't make sense. Our error.'

'Do you have data on the eleven men and women she murdered who were in her minifleet?' Wolfe asked.

'We do.'

'Then let's start looking for a hole for me to go down,' Wolfe said.

'I don't follow.'

'Isn't it logical that Token Aubyn, once she decided to steal the Lumina and desert both the Federation and your – social circle to boot, had brains enough to know better than to go home, especially with something that would give her the powers it would?'

'Of course. We've spent a great deal of time trying to find her throughout the Federation and even the Outlaw Worlds. Do you think you can provide a lead?'

'I do.'

'Since you're experienced with the Lumina,' Athelstan put in, 'what powers will she have?'

'I'm not sure,' Wolfe lied. 'But that's for later, anyway.'

'So she went somewhere. If we're lucky, maybe she didn't just pick someplace out of an interstellar gazetteer. Maybe she got an idea from her shipmates. There isn't much to do on those little spitkits but talk, and since Aubyn was a newbie, everybody would've been eager to tell her all the war stories everyone else had heard until their eyes turned green. Maybe somebody talked about his or her homeworld, and maybe that sounded like just the place for a woman with big ambition, no scruples, and God in her pocket. Maybe somebody talking about that place was what gave Aubyn the idea in the first place.'

Wolfe lay in near-total darkness. He'd been moved into a larger chamber, but it was as sterile as the one he'd been revived in.

Across the room Guide Kristin sat in a low chair. A reading light pooled around her head and shoulders, and she appeared intent on her reading matter, *A Consideration of Logic As It Should Be Applied in Daily Circumstances*, written by one Matteos Athelstan.

Wolfe, momentarily exhausted, turned his mind away from his search and considered her. Her blond hair was sensibly close-cropped. He'd seen the thrust of her breasts under her sensible garment, but had no idea about what the rest of her body looked like, other than it was slender.

He found her face somewhat attractive, a curving vee. It reminded him a bit of an Earth-Siamese cat. *At least*, he thought, *she doesn't have the screeching voice of a Siamese.* He smiled.

The woman looked up, saw Joshua's eyes on her, and quickly looked down at her book.

Interesting, he thought. He blanked her, let himself reach out, *feel* through the ship.

A faint direction came to him, as if he were shouting in a wilderness and heard a tiny echo from a hidden grotto. He let 'himself' float in that direction.

There the Lumina is. Of course Athelstan would keep it close. In his office safe. Not original. But secure, at least. For the moment. But perhaps . . .

Now I shall try something.

Reach toward it . . . touch it without touching . . . fumbling . . .

Joshua Wolfe was outside the ship, hanging, floating in N-space.

Find ku, find the Void again. Let the Lumina take you beyond. Warmth, feeling warmth back toward the Federation. Out there . . .

He jerked back, feeling the chill hatred of the invader, the 'virus.'

No, not there. Not yet.

Look elsewhere. Let the small find the large. Confusion. There are others. But they're small. Feel . . .

Ah! There!

'Why did you pick Rogan's World?' Kur said.

'Because,' Wolfe said, 'I'm guessing she heard about Rogan's World from Dietrich, who grew up there. Nice that he happened to be the motor mate on the scout she commanded as well. Looking at his service record — three court-martials, two nonjudicial punishments — I'd guess he was an excellent representative of the planet.'

'You've been there?'

'Nope. Always wanted to, though.'

'Why?'

'Because of the delicate aroma of corruption,' Wolfe said. 'And money.'

Kur eyed him skeptically.

Wolfe sat up in bed, yawning, as if he'd just awakened. Kristin was instantly alert. Wolfe took the robe from the chair beside the bed, pulled it on as he stood.

'Ship air dehydrates me,' he said, walking toward the fresher. 'Can I get you some water?'

'No,' the Chitet said.

Wolfe went into the fresher, took a metal glass from its clip, filled it, and drank. He grimaced at the cold, completely flat taste, then clipped the glass back in its holder.

'I'm grateful,' he said when he came out, 'you don't insist on watching me *everywhere*.'

'Even an animal in a zoo is allowed a private area,' Kristin said. 'And there is nothing in that fresher that can be used as a weapon.'

Joshua went back to the bed, sat down.

'I'm curious,' he said. 'Why do you insist on taking the midnight to eight watch?'

'Because I am in charge of my team,' Kristin said. 'Security training dictates an escape attempt is most likely going to be made in the early hours of the morning.'

'I'm not planning to escape.'

'Good,' Kristin said. 'Then you shall continue to live.'

'Another question,' Wolfe persisted. 'Does your camera, or pickup, or whatever it is, transmit sound to whoever's sitting on my personal doomsday switch?'

Kristin looked at him, slowly shook her head from side to side.

'Just curious,' Wolfe said, pulling the robe off and lying down again.

No. I am not trying to escape. Not yet.

'I understand most of these requests, and agree with them,' Master Speaker Athelstan said. 'They certainly fit what I would romantically expect a master rogue and gambler to have. But we may not be able to acquire the exact model of ship you've specified, since the operation must be mounted immediately.'

'A yacht's a yacht,' Wolfe said. 'Something big, impressive, ultra nouveau, that's all we want. Oh yeah, something I forgot – Pick some kind of uniform for the crew to wear. With gold braid.'

Athelstan considered, decided Wolfe wasn't making a joke, nodded. 'One question,' he said, 'and this is to satisfy personal curiosity. You specify the ship's library must contain an edition of the complete works of this Earth-poet Eliot. Why?'

'Eliot does more than Hume can,' Wolfe said, 'to justify God's ways to Man.'

'I still don't understand. But then,' Athelstan said, 'I've never been much of a one for poetry. Utterly illogical.'

'It's interesting you should say that,' Joshua said. 'Most poets think they're more logical than the rest of us.'

Athelstan smiled tightly. 'Amusing conceit. Do you agree with them?'

Wolfe shrugged. 'Depends on how bad my hangover is.'

Athelstan frowned.

'By the way,' Joshua said. 'We'll need some kind of linkup with an expensive comp-catalog. I'll take care of outfitting the rest of the crew myself. You might be too – logical.'

'That one,' Wolfe decided. 'And that one, and – not that one. Too virginal. Not that one either. Makes you look too available. For too low a price.'

He touched sensors, and the next set of catalog holographs swam into life. He kept his eyes away from Guide Kristin, whose face was red with embarrassment.

'You find this quite amusing, don't you,' Kur said, her voice showing a trace of anger.

'Lady,' Wolfe said in exasperation, 'you're the one who says I've got to go looking for Token Aubyn with gunguards *and* these three mad bombers. So I'm going to be standing out a little. That's fine, because that's the quickest way to get Aubyn to notice us. But don't tell me how to dress the set, goddammit. I could've used Lucian or Max for my main companion, but I don't think I can fake being a manlover for long. And I'll be suiting them up as soon as I finish with Kristin anyway. You want all of us to mouse in like good brown Chitet? Won't that make Aubyn wonder why her fellow bow-and-scrapers happen to be on Rogan's World? Wouldn't she maybe send a couple dozen goons to check matters out?'

'If she's even there,' Kur said skeptically. 'I find it hard to accept that one man can put a pin on the map after hundreds of our best minds have analyzed the situation over the years. And I find your continual insults of our culture rather distasteful.'

'Funny. I find your continual attempts to kill me the same,' Wolfe said. 'You're bitching about wearing an expensive gown, and I've got a bomb up my ass. Now shut up and let me keep on with my frills and bows. One other thing. What about the ship?'

'You'll have it in time,' Kur said. 'It offplaneted Batan this E-day.'

'Good,' Wolfe said. He looked at Kristin and decided to take pity. 'You pick the next two outfits.'

'No,' the woman said. 'I have no experience being a – a . . .'

'Popsy is one of the old words,' Wolfe said helpfully. 'But give in to your worst impulses, woman, and go crazy. Even Chitet have been known to smile and dance in the moonlight. I know. I saw a couple of them.'

He thought for an instant her face flickered, but decided he'd been wrong.

THREE

Dear Scholar Frazier:

I'm sending this brief note via a completely trustworthy graduate student of mine, with instructions to hand-deliver it to you, and no one else, for I fear to trust it to conventional means, even if it were coded.

I would strongly recommend against your continuing to seek funding for the expedition to the Al'ar homeworld of Sauros we spoke of at the last seminar. I know this must surprise you, because of my initial enthusiasm, and I'm fully aware of your need to reestablish your credentials, particularly in the field you first became well known in.

However, very unofficial word has reached me that all contact with the team from Halcyon III's Universidad de Descubrimiento has been lost. As you know, they were investigating A887-3, another of the Al'ar homeworlds, and were partially funded by the Federation.

These are unsettled times, so this might not be as worrisome as I find it, but there are two rumors I've heard involving the expedition that need passing along, and two very definite facts:

The first rumor is that the Halcyon III team 'cast some extraordinarily strange messages prior to their disappearance, messages that make it appear as if they'd gone mad. The messages supposedly mention a 'red death,' a 'walking between the stars,' among other hysteria.

The second rumor is that two other expeditions, also projected toward one or another of the worlds formerly held by the Al'ar, have been cancelled. Supposedly these two expeditions would have gone into the 'center' of the Al'ar fringe worlds – the same sector that A887-3 is in.

I'd discount these stories, except for my two facts:

The first and most disturbing is that the heirs and beneficiaries of the scientists on the Universidad expedition have had their death benefits paid in full, even though no official notice of death has been made. This suggests to me that someone at a very high level knows what happened, but no one is willing to admit to it.

The second fact is that I've been advised by my department head to ignore any stories about Halcyon III, and to pass along to her the name of anyone spreading such tales, for transmission to what she called the 'proper authorities.'

I protested, of course, reminding her of our long tradition of free speech, but she scowled at me and asked if I remembered the necessary restrictions on speech back during the war. I said I certainly did, and considered most of them imbecilic. She told me that if I wished my annual review to go as smoothly as it should, I'd take heed of her warning and stop being silly.

I don't know what to make of all this, Juan. But I certainly think you should be warned.

Something seems to be going wrong out there in the former Al'ar worlds, and I'd suggest you stay well clear until there's further data.

Best,

'Liz

Scholar Eliz Shulbert
L'Ecole de Science
Janzoon IX

FOUR

Wolfe's chill eyes swept the hotel lobby. 'This'll do,' he said.

The manager fawned slightly. 'You mentioned you have quite precise requirements?'

'I do. We'll take the penthouse suite in the tower for myself and my personal assistant, and the entire floor below it for my staff and the crew of my yacht. I'll also need the next floor to be vacant. I despise noise when I'm trying to sleep.'

The manager realized his eyes were bulging and corrected the situation. 'But – there're already guests on some of . . .'

'Inform them that their charges to date are on my bill, and you'll assist in finding them acceptable rooms elsewhere in the hotel – or else help them relocate to another, equally prestigious hotel.' A large bill changed hands. 'If they insist on staying . . .' Wolfe shrugged.

The manager managed to look as if he were bowing without moving. 'I'm sure with such generosity – I'm sure there'll be no problem.'

'Good. Also, I'll need one of your private dining rooms on constant standby, a conference room, and three of my men added to your staff to ensure proper security.'

'As you wish, Mister Taylor.' The manager spun. 'Front!'

A platoon of bellboys scurried forward and began sorting the mountain of luggage, including the fourteen matched bags in pink reptile hide.

Kristin stepped close to Wolfe. She no longer wore the drab simplicity of a Chitet. Her blond hair, starting to grow out, had a slightly iridescent streak curving along the hairline above her left ear. She was wearing tight red silk shantung pants, sandals, and a bare-midriff blouse in white.

'I feel like everyone is watching us,' she murmured.

'Not us,' Wolfe corrected. 'Mostly you.'

A bit of a smile appeared.

Lucian and Max were also dressed for their roles, one wearing a black-white checked silk shirt, the other a green-patterned shirt, with the currently popular white false-leather tight jackets. They wore dark trousers, short boots. Neither man bothered to conceal the bulge of a holster on his right hip.

Wolfe was all in black, a silk turtleneck, finely woven wool pants, and a black jacket.

'You'll see,' he told the manager, 'that my ship-crew is taken care of when they finish porting arrangements?'

'But of course.'

This time the bow was real.

Kristin wandered through the huge, multilevel suite in a completely un-Chitet-like manner. Everything was stained wood, old paintings, and antiques, and the aroma of money hung close. Wolfe followed, saying little. Part of him was remembering another woman, named Lil, in another hotel on another world; the rest of him was concentrating on – something else.

'You know,' she said, 'I almost think you're trying to seduce – I mean, convert me away from what I believe in. There is no rationale for this luxury . . . but it certainly feels nice.'

Wolfe didn't answer. He had his eyes closed, facing one of the enormous windows that looked out over the smoky industrial city of Prendergast, Rogan's World's capital, toward the hills that ringed the port.

'Is something the matter?' she asked.

Wolfe's eyes opened.

'No. I was just trying to see if anybody's watching or listening.'

'Lucian, Max, and I all checked for bugs,' she said. 'We're *all* very well trained.'

'In another life,' Joshua said, 'I wore both belt and suspenders.'

'What are suspenders?'

'Something to keep the chicken from crossing the road. Never mind. We're clean as far as I can tell.'

Kristin turned away and appeared intent on the view.

'Master Speaker Athelstan told us that everything depends on finding this person,' she said carefully. 'I took that to mean our charade must be as perfect as possible.'

Wolfe waited.

'So if I'm supposed to be your – your popsy, then, or whatever you call it, well, then, we should . . .' She broke off, furiously coloring.

'You blush too easily,' Wolfe said gently, not letting himself smile. 'But don't worry about it. You sleep anywhere you want to. If anybody happens to insert a spybeam without me noticing, well, we had a fight and you're miffed. All right?'

Kristin nodded, still not looking at Joshua.

'Which brings up a question,' Wolfe said. 'How come the twenty-four-hour-a-day watch isn't being kept? Did somebody decide I'm telling the truth and I'm not going to cut and run from you?'

'I can't answer that,' Kristin said. 'But there have been additional measures taken that aren't quite so obvious. And don't think they're trusting you any more than before.'

'They, eh? Not us.'

'What?'

'Never mind. So we're down, we made a big splash, yacht and all, and we're in place as fools with money.'

'Rogan's World,' mused Joshua. He lifted a snifter to his lips, sipped. 'Where honesty's a word in the dictionary between *hogwash* and *horseshit*. And everything's for sale and they have everything you want.' He considered the snifter. 'I never thought I'd find Hubert Dayton again. I've got one bottle hidden . . . somewhere, against the Day of Reckoning.'

Kristin wore a thin blue robe, with a satin and lace gown under it in the same color. The remains of a lavish room service meal littered the linen tablecloth on the mahogany table.

'To success,' Wolfe toasted.

Kristin lifted her waterglass in return.

'That's a sinful practice,' he said.

'Why? I've never liked alcohol,' Kristin said. 'It distorts your judgment and makes it easier for you to do stupid things.'

'Precisely why I'm quite fond of it.' He spun his chair and looked out over Prendergast. 'I wonder why all commercial ports get so crooked so easy,' he said.

'Maybe because when everything's got a price tag on it, you start believing everything does have a price tag on it.'

'Not bad,' Joshua said.

'Thank you. And when everything's just passing by,' Kristin went on, 'maybe it's easy to think you can do whatever you want, and pass on with the current, or else whatever you did'll be washed away in the morning.'

Joshua nodded. 'I'll buy into that one, tentatively, my little epigrammatist.

'So, here we have a spaceport – shipyard – heavy manufacturing – and by the way, Rogan's World produced half a dozen Federation politicians whose reputations, shall we say, spread a stain far beyond their reach. And at least as many artists in various mediums. Wonder if corruption is a spore-bed for creators?

'Interesting, change, though. According to the 'pedia I scanned, nothing and nobody interesting's come out of Rogan's World for quite a while. Since just after the war, to be precise.'

'What does that mean?' Kristin asked.

'Probably nothing. But it could be somebody doesn't want Rogan's World to draw any attention at all.'

Kristin looked frightened. 'Could the Overlord Stone give somebody *that* kind of power?'

Wolfe nodded.

'So how do we find Token – that woman.'

'Good,' Wolfe approved. 'The less we use her name, the safer it is. For I don't truly know what the Great Lumina could give, especially to someone who's been using it for as long as she has.'

'How do we find her?' Kristin asked.

'We don't. We let her find us.' Wolfe smiled. 'Apropos of absolutely nothing, I like your perfume.'

'Oh. Oh. I thought the name in the catalog sounded – interesting. Thank you.' Kristin looked somewhat confused.

'How long have you been bell captain?' Joshua asked.

'Oh, seven, eight years,' the woman said. Her name tag read HAGERSMARK. Long enough to be able to help our guests in whatever ways they want.' She pocketed the bill Wolfe handed her.

'Supposing that I – or one of my crew – wanted company?'

'Easiest thing in the world,' Hagersmark said, looking bored. 'Any variation you want.'

'What about – inducements that don't happen to be legal?'

'I don't know that word.'

'Things to smoke, inject, whatever.'

'Like you said, whatever.'

'Just curious,' Wolfe said. 'But what I'm really interested in is action. This hotel seems a little – quiet.'

'The management likes to keep it that way,' Hagersmark said. 'They figure guests can find their own joyspots. Or bring 'em back here. As long as you pay, you can do whatever you want. But you want action. I assume . . .' She rolled fingers as if manipulating a set of dice.

'You assume,' Wolfe said.

'How big?'

He handed her a bill.

'That suggest anything?'

The woman eyed it, reacted.

'You *do* mean action,' she said. 'Best bet's a private game. But you'll need to meet some people to set that sorta thing up. Be around in the right places. Best bet's either Nakamura's or the Oasis. The Oasis generally attracts a little looser crowd.'

'Thank you,' Wolfe said.

Hagersmark started toward the door, then stopped. 'So that's your game, eh? Everybody in the hotel was wondering.'

'I'm just someone who mostly lives the quiet life,' Wolfe said. 'But every year or so I like to vary things.'

'Of course, sir,' she said piously. 'Have a nice, quiet time.'

A day later, Wolfe was waiting for Kristin to finish dressing when the discreet tap came at the door.

Max was sitting across from him, watching.

He *felt* out, uncurled from the chair he was in. 'Kristin. Stay out of sight.'

'What's wrong?'

'We've got visitors. And the desk was supposed to buzz us before anyone came up.'

The knock came once more.

'I'm ready,' she said. 'Shall I call for backup?'

'Not yet. Max, you get out of here, too. But be ready for life to get interesting. Don't do anything unless I start screaming.'

The Chitet hesitated, then hurried into one of the bedrooms and half closed the door.

Wolfe went to the door and opened it. Two men stood outside. Both were young, wore full evening dress, and had cold eyes above careful smiles.

'Mister Taylor?'

Wolfe nodded.

'We're sorry to intrude, but perhaps a moment of your time might be beneficial to us both.'

'So Hagersmark didn't stay bought,' he murmured and beckoned them in.

'A drink?' he offered.

'No, thank you. We don't want to take up any more of your time than necessary. My name's Henders, this is Mister Naismith.'

'I'm at your service,' Joshua said courteously.

'My associate and myself understand that you're a man who's interested in the sporting life.'

'At times.'

'Perhaps you weren't aware that the two clubs that you might find most congenial – I refer to the Oasis and Mister Nakamura's establishment – are, in fact, private.'

'No. The person who told me about them didn't mention that.'

'That's why we thought we might pay a visit, and arrange for you to become a member of both casinos.'

'How convenient,' Wolfe said. 'I assume "membership" also carries other benefits?'

The younger of the two men scowled, but Henders kept his smile.

'In fact, it does. There are other establishments in Prendergast and across Rogan's World that welcome members. But the real advantage for a man such as yourself is the availability of exchange currency at any hour of the night or day. Also, since there's an unfortunately high crime rate on Rogan's World, in the event of your having significant winnings, our organization can arrange an escort to wherever you wish, or even for a bank to open at any hour for a deposit.'

'And, of course, should I decline membership, it's not unlikely that I might get mugged, should I happen to be a winner,' Wolfe said wryly.

'Such things have happened.'

'I further assume that the cost of such a membership is high.'

'We predicate the cost on a member's evident assets,' Henders said, looking pointedly about the suite. 'In your case, especially considering the rather impressive display you've made since you've been here, it might indeed be expensive. But well worth the cost, I can assure you.'

'And the levy is . . . ?'

'That would depend on how long you plan on staying,' the man said. 'Generally, we like to have our members current on a weekly basis. However, for longer stays, or for permanent residents, other, more equitable arrangements can be made.'

Wolfe strolled to the bar, poured a small pool of Armagnac into a snifter.

'I must say, I admire Rogan's World,' he said. 'Generally, the first gunsel who tries a shakedown is a featherweight.'

'What the hell are you talking about?' snarled Naismith. 'This is a perfectly legit offer.'

'Of course it is. I'm merely making light conversation.

My response, in most cases, to such a hit is quite rapid. I find the second level of goonery, after they've recovered from finding their junior in an alley, is markedly superior.'

'I know you have your own security element, Mister Taylor,' Henders said. 'But I don't think you're aware of the organization you may be challenging.'

'Oh, but I think I am,' Wolfe said. 'That's why I was complimentary about Rogan's World. I've noted you gentlemen aren't the usual bluff-and-bluster back-alley types with alligator mouths and jaybird asses, but actually have links to significant people. I don't object to payoffs,' he went on. 'It's an accepted part of my operating cost. But I'll be triple-damned if I'll play the fool and slip any punk who taps my shoulder and breaks bad the dropsy.'

'I see,' Henders said. Naismith couldn't decide whether to get angry or just stay puzzled. 'You certainly have analyzed the situation quickly and, I must say, correctly. I think, Mister Taylor, you might become a valued addition to a certain group here. You appear to have a great deal of wisdom.'

'Not wisdom,' Wolfe said. 'Common sense. How much?'

'We would consider – ten thousand credits appropriate. At least for a starter. If circumstances indicate otherwise, that amount can be lowered.'

'Or raised, if I'm sufficiently lucky.'

Henders inclined his head

Wolfe went into another room. The two gangsters looked at each other. The younger man licked his lips nervously.

Wolfe came back in with a leather envelope, thick with bills.

'Here,' he said. 'The credits are clean, good, and out of sequence, and it's a pleasure to be part of your – organization.

'Now, if you'll excuse me, we have plans to dine tonight. Perhaps at Mister Nakamura's.'

The two men left.

Max came out of the bedroom. A gun was in his hand.

'Why'd you pay them? I completely fail to understand your reasoning in allowing us to be victimized.'

'Which is why you're a Chitet and I'm a gambler,' Wolfe said. 'Kristin! I'm starving to death!'

'I see why you're the ranker of the trio,' Wolfe said. 'I don't think Max had a clue.'

'He's a good man,' Kristin said defensively. 'Maybe I realized the nature of the situation a little faster than he did because I've been around you more.'

'Probably,' Wolfe said. 'Crookedness can be contagious.'

Kristin smiled. She wore a clinging gown, muted silver with deep burgundy flowers on it, low-cut, Empire-waisted, and utterly diaphanous. Under it was – perhaps – a sheer bodystocking.

Wolfe wore a white short-waisted formal jacket, matching pants, black silk shirt, and a white throat scarf.

He shifted position and moved the bomb at the base of his spine to a more comfortable position. 'I once told somebody that I heard Time's winged chariot at my back, but I never thought it'd end up as a literal expression,' he murmured.

Kristin quirked an eyebrow.

'Just a private thought,' Joshua said.

Kristin cut a bite, chewed. 'This is wonderful. What is it?'

'On a Chitet menu, it'd no doubt appear as muscle tissue from a juvenile steer, wrapped in a shell of dough, with cow secretions, plus various fungi.'

'Pish,' Kristin said. 'That won't affect my appetite. We

do that kind of word game as play when we're growing up.'

'Play? What you're tucking away is boeuf Wellington. Named after a general who was pretty good at waiting for his enemy to make the first mistake.'

'Of course we play – I played – when I was a child. What do you think Chitet do? Just march up and down in formation and drone prime numbers at one another? We're people, like any other,' Kristin said, a bit of heat in her voice. 'We just happen to have a better way of thinking, of living than anybody else.'

Wolfe started to say something but thought better of it. 'Okay. I was wrong. You're creatures of the sun, the light, and the dancing waves. Now eat your vegetables or I won't read you any more Charles Peirce before bed-time.'

'I know who he was,' Kristin said.

'See my point?'

Kristin looked puzzled. 'No. I don't.'

'Never mind.'

Joshua heard music coming from another part of Nakamura's as they strolled out of the restaurant.

'Care to dance before we go to work?'

'No,' Kristin said. 'I never learned how. My creche didn't see the point of doing anything when music played, anyway. It's enough to simply appreciate it intel-lectually.'

'Take that, Dionysus,' Wolfe said.

'Precisely,' Kristin said. 'The Apollonian side must con-trol events, or everything is chaos.'

'Sometimes chaos can be fun.'

'And who is whose prisoner?' Kristin retorted.

'Point and match to Guide Kristin,' Wolfe said.

They continued into the casino.

Joshua considered the half-full room as a formally clad man glided to him.

'Mister Taylor? Welcome to Nakamura's. Might I inquire as to your pleasure?'

'Nothing right now,' Wolfe said. 'But I do have a question. Is Mister Nakamura present?'

'Mister Nakamura passed on over a year ago,' the pit boss said. 'The club is currently held by a consortium of businessmen.'

'I see,' Wolfe said. 'Perhaps another time I might be interested in your tables. But not at the moment. Come on, Kristin. The Oasis calls.'

'This,' Wolfe said, 'might become my home away from home.'

'Why?' Kristin asked. 'It looks just like Nakamura's. Why this one instead of the other?'

'Because this one looks a bit – closer to the bone, shall we say? Observe the bar, and the half-dozen young women who gave both of us the scan when we walked through. Expensive companions for the evening – or the hour. Or consider the gamblers.'

'I don't see anything unusual.'

'See how many have friends standing behind them. Friends who just happen to have bulges in their hip pockets or under their arms. Friends with blank faces and eyes that never stop moving.'

'Oh. You mean you wanted a crooked place to gamble?'

'Sssh, my love. Don't disparage the jam pot. And we might be able to find an honest game here. Or turn it into one.'

'Now I don't understand what you're thinking any more than Max does,' Kristin said.

'You don't have to.' Wolfe took a wad of credits from his pocket. 'Here. Go spend these. Come back when you need more.'

'I really don't understand gambling games,' she protested, 'although of course I've studied probability theory.'

'Good. Think popsy. Lose in a spectacular manner.'

Wolfe noted a heavy, short man strolling through the gaming room, his eyes comfortably assessing the night. His expensive clothes wrapped him like a toad in a turban. Three blank-faced men flanked him, a fourth walked unobtrusively in front.

'That is —?' Wolfe asked the croupier, indicating with his chin.

'Mister Igraine. The owner.'

'Ah. Is he a plunger?'

'I assume you mean does he play? Frequently. And well,' the croupier said. 'If you'd be interested in one of his private games, it might be arranged.'

Wolfe looked back at the dice layout, then saw Kristin hurrying toward him.

'Look!' Kristin said excitedly. She was holding up a thick sheaf of bills.

Wolfe spun a chip to the croupier and picked up his dwindled stake. 'I'll go sit and sulk for a while,' he said. 'Try to remember where my luck went. And I'll think about what you said about Mister Igraine.'

He led Kristin to a quiet corner. 'Obviously you're doing better than I am,' he noted.

'These people don't know anything about the odds,' she said. 'I've never gambled before, but it seems pretty simple. I know you told me to lose, but am I supposed to look like a complete fool?'

Wolfe laughed.

'Once a Chitet . . . Very good, Kristin. You'll start a new legend as the bimbo who never loses.'

'So do I gamble some more?'

Wolfe considered. 'I don't think so. I've set the scene,

and dropped maybe fifteen thousand. That ought to be enough. Tomorrow night we'll reap what I hope we sowed.'

A chill wind blew across the city, clouds swirling past overhead, but the penthouse's balcony had three braziers, with what looked like real wood burning in them.

Kristin looked across the city's lights at the hills in the distance.

'Maybe she's over there . . .'

'Maybe.'

She moved closer to him. 'It's late,' she said.

'It is,' he agreed. 'But gamblers and raiders work best by moonlight.'

'Among others,' Kristin said, her voice low.

Wolfe looked surprised.

'Yes,' he said, almost in a whisper, 'among others.'

He stepped closer, until his hip touched her buttocks, waited for her to step away. Kristin didn't move. He slid his arms around her waist, nuzzled her hair.

Joshua felt her breathing come more quickly.

He slowly turned her to him. Kristin lifted her cat face, eyes closed, lips parted.

He kissed her, felt her tongue come to meet his. He slid the straps of her dress off her shoulders, and her bare breasts were firm against him.

The kiss went on, and her lips moved under his, tongue darting.

He picked her up in his arms, carried her through the suite's living room into a bedroom, started to lay her on the bed.

'No,' she said. 'My shoes . . .'

'Don't worry about it. We have maids.'

She lay back, naked to the waist, legs curled, her eyes half-open, watching as he undressed.

He touched the light sensor, and the room was dark except for a stream of light from the doorway.

Joshua went to the bed and knelt over Kristin, one arm around her, the other sliding her dress up, cupping her buttocks, kneading them. She was not wearing a bodystocking, but had shaved her body smooth.

She moaned, lifted her leg across the back of his thighs.

'Yes,' she whispered. 'Oh yes, my Dionysus.'

Kristin stifled a scream, writhed against him, then collapsed, her legs sagging back to the bed. Joshua stayed on his knees, lifted her legs about his waist, caressed her breasts slowly.

'I'm back,' she said after a time.

Joshua moved inside her, and she gasped.

'Not yet,' she whispered. 'Give me a moment.'

'One and only one.'

'Maybe,' she said, 'there is *some* merit to chaos.'

'In its place,' he agreed. 'Logic doesn't belong in the bedroom.'

'I should be able to argue with you,' she said. 'But I don't think my brain is working right now.'

Joshua lifted her buttocks, pulled her close against him. 'Never interfere with success,' he said.

'No . . . I mean yes,' she managed as he began moving slowly inside her. She rolled her head from side to side, wrapped her legs more tightly about him. 'Oh yes. Send me away again.'

Joshua came out of the bedroom, robe wrapped around him. Lucian was scanning some papers.

'I'll have instructions for you in an hour,' Wolfe said. 'Then nothing. We won't go back out until tonight.'

Lucian looked at Joshua with disapproval, said nothing, picked up a com and touched buttons.

It was an hour after dawn.

Joshua picked up the tray room service had just brought and took it back into the bedroom.

Kristin was at the window, naked, leaning on the railing.

Joshua put the tray down, dropped his robe, walked up behind her, and kissed her back.

'Do you think anybody down there can see us?' she asked.

'Probably,' he said cheerily. 'And they're getting ready to record every single lascivious move.'

Kristin giggled.

'That's a nice sound,' he said.

Kristin didn't reply for a while, then:

'This doesn't change things.'

'Sure it does,' Wolfe said. 'It means you don't have to sleep on the couch unless you want to. And you already said you had permission from Athelstan to be flouncing around like you are.'

'You know what I meant.'

'I know what you meant,' he agreed, hands sliding around her body, cupping her breasts, pulling her against him.

'Joshua, I don't think I can do it anymore. I'm sore.'

'Umm-hmm.'

'You're not stopping.'

'Ummm-umm.'

'Oh. Oh. Oh GOD!'

'It's time for work, people,' Wolfe said. 'Here's the order. Kristin, Max, I want you with me. Pick the best two of the gun-guards as backup. Get them into formals. Ten, no, fifteen more in the heavy lifter we've rented. If Kristin or I call for backup, bring the gunnies in ready for shooting. Lucian, I want you standing by our flit, pretending you're the chauffeur. We may need to leave in a hurry and we want our back guarded.'

'Negative, Wolfe,' the bearded man said. 'My orders are to stay with you.'

'For the love of – does it do any good for me to swear on – on *Critique of Pure Reason* that I don't have any intention of double-crossing you? And there's already two of the team on me like white on rice?'

'Negative,' Lucian said firmly. 'You may have subverted one of us,' and he gave a pointed look at Kristin, 'but some of us know where our duty lies.'

'That's enough,' the woman snapped. 'I still command, and I still speak for this gathering. You, Lucian. In the other room. Now!'

The Chitet looked sullen, but he obeyed. Kristin followed, slamming the door hard behind her, and Wolfe heard loud voices.

Passing from grandeur to grandeur to final illusion, Wolfe thought hopefully. He and Max avoided looking at each other.

Kristin and Lucian came back out and sat down.

'As long as we're all getting along so well,' Wolfe said. 'What's the possibility of my being permitted one lousy little gun? There's no –' He broke off. Both Kristin and Lucian were shaking their heads.

'Oh well,' he said. 'I'm glad to get you two to agree on something. So I'm going in naked, then. But if anybody even twitches, I want somebody to put a bolt through him. We still aren't even in sight of the target.'

'You've done quite well for yourself this evening,' Igraine said. His voice was as smooth and oily as his hair.

'Compared to last night,' Wolfe agreed. 'You would think I'd have learned to stay away from dice by now.'

'So roulette is your game,' Igraine said. 'Mine, too.'

Wolfe had carefully noted the attention the casino's owner paid the wheel in his inspection tour the night before.

'I like it,' Wolfe said. 'Especially when it's straight, with only a single zero.'

'I have no need to be greedy,' Igraine said.

'*Faites vos jeux, m'sieurs,*' the *tourneur* intoned. There were eight others around the wheel.

Wolfe put on the cloth a stack of chips from the considerable pile he'd already won.

'*Manque,*' he said.

Igraine reached out, tapped the enameled letters of *passe*. The *tourneur* nodded, and other bets were made.

'*Rien ne va plus,*' he announced, spun the crosshandles with his fingers, and flipped the ivory ball against the wheel's rotation.

The wheel slowed, and the ball bounced, bounced again, stopped in a compartment.

'*Quatre,*' the *tourneur* said.

'Congratulations,' Igraine said. 'Again?'

Wolfe nodded.

It was either very late or very early.

But no one appeared sleepy.

There were about forty people around the table now, and the only sound was the *tourneur*'s voice, the whisper of the spinning wheel, the clatter of the ivory ball, and the low murrnur after the clatter stopped.

The wheel had only two bettors, Igraine and Wolfe. Chips were stacked high beside Wolfe, and credits piled next to his untouched drink. Igraine had nothing in front of him.

Lucian stood across from Wolfe, Max was next to him, and Kristin on Joshua's other side.

Igraine's shirt was sweat-soaked, and his hair hung in disarray over his forehead.

The *tourneur* had closed the table twice, and guards had brought first chips, later credits.

'*Rouge*,' he announced.

'*Non*,' Wolfe said, stepping back, and the *tourneur* spun once again.

The ball dropped into the zero compartment.

'You have a sixth sense about things,' Igraine complained.

'It felt like about time for zero to hit,' Joshua said. He pushed chips forward.

'*Rouge*.'

'*Noir*,' Igraine said.

He glanced at the *tourneur*, nodded imperceptibly.

Wolfe *felt* out, *felt* the man's foot shift to the right, *reached* out. The *tourneur*'s body twitched a little, again. The man looked worried.

'*M'sieur?*' Wolfe inquired.

The *tourneur* licked his lips, spun the wheel.

'*Deux. Rouge.*'

Wolfe collected his winnings.

'All right,' Igraine said. 'That's enough.'

'For you,' Wolfe said. 'But I'm still playing.'

'By yourself, then.'

'You can't afford the game?'

Igraine started to say something then clamped his mouth shut.

'You still have something to bet,' Wolfe said. He looked around at the club. 'One roll. All of this,' he indicated the money in front of him, 'against the club. You play black, I'll stay with red.'

Someone behind Wolfe said something, and a woman gasped. He didn't turn.

Kristin's hand slid closer to the gun in her tiny break-away purse.

Igraine gnawed at his lip, suddenly smiled.

'Very well. Spin the wheel!'

The *tourneur*'s foot moved, tapped the hidden switch

under the carpet. The wheel spun, the ball bounced wildly about.

Red/black/red/black flicker, slowing, the ball rattling from compartment to compartment, rolling, dropping into a red compartment . . .

Wolfe *reached* out, *felt* white smoothness, *pushed* . . .

The ivory ball clicked to rest.

'*Vingt-quatre*,' the *tourneur* said. '*Rouge*.'

'Did you do that?' Kristin demanded.

'I'm not sure,' Wolfe lied. 'I sure wanted that ball to jump a little bit.'

'Without a Lumina.'

'I was probably just lucky.'

'Joshua,' Kristin said. 'I'm not a fool. I know probabilities, and there's no way you could have won that many times with so few losses.'

'Sure there is,' Wolfe said. 'Igraine had to win that many times to get the club, didn't he?'

'Not proven and an example of illogical thinking,' Kristin said. 'So now we own a gambling club. That'll be the trap for Aubyn?'

'No,' Wolfe said. 'It's just the beginning.'

Kristin yawned. 'Tell me about it in the – oh my. It is morning.'

'Gamblers, raiders, and lovers keep late hours, remember?'

'Not this raider. I'm beat.'

'Are you sure?' Joshua asked, running a tongue in and out of her navel.

'I am. Go to sleep. You've got too much nervous energy.'

Wolfe woke suddenly. His sheets were sweat-soaked. He blinked around, then remembered where he was.

It was past midday, and the suite was silent. Kristin lay next to him, breathing steadily, regularly.

Red . . . creeping from star to star, fingers, tentacles reaching toward him . . .

Wolfe shuddered.

Can it sense me?

Impossible.

He lay back, tried to blank his mind, but *felt* the invader, pulsing like a bloody tumor, out there in the blackness.

Quite suddenly something else came.

It was almost as foreign, almost as alien.

But it comforted.

Light-years away, beyond the Federation, he *felt* them.

The Guardians, truly the last of the Al'ar, hidden in the depths of the nameless world they'd tunneled deep into. Waiting. Waiting for Wolfe, waiting for him to return with the Lumina.

Waiting for the 'virus.'

Waiting for death. Hoping it would be welcome.

He was awakened a second time by soft warmth around him, moving, caressing.

Joshua looked down, and Kristin lifted her head.

'I didn't want you to think I don't like doing it with you,' she said.

'Never crossed my mind,' Joshua said.

'Good,' she said, sitting up, bestriding him, her hands guiding, then she gasped as she sank down, enveloped him. 'Oh good.'

'Preposterous,' the well-dressed man said.

'Not at all,' Wolfe said calmly. He walked to the end of the conference table, looking at each of the ten men in the room, trying to feel their response. 'I've owned the Oasis for two weeks now and have managed to almost double my receipts. I think it would be logical for you gentlemen to allow me to take a minority position in Nakamura's. Both clubs attract much the same clientele, and it's senseless to compete.

'You'd not only see improved profits, but you wouldn't have any of the problems of running a casino – which none of you, I've observed, had any experience doing prior to Mister Nakamura's death.'

'Why should we let you muscle in?' a fat, mean-faced man said. 'We've done very damned well for ourselves in the past year.'

'We have indeed,' the first man said. 'We've learned the peculiarities of the trade, and are familiar with who to – deal with, and who to ignore.'

'Matter of fact,' the fat man said, 'whyn't you let us buy you out? Seems more logical.'

He laughed.

'That's very amusing,' Wolfe said. 'And I do admire a logical man.'

His smile was thin.

Wolfe's fingers crept up the doorframe, found the sensor. Violet light flashed. His hand continued feeling the doorway. He found another alarm, neutralized it.

He was one of two dark spots against the dark stone of the alley. Both he and Kristin wore close-fitting black jumpsuits and balaclavas.

Wolfe's hand dipped into a pouch, then moved swiftly around the door's lock. There was a sharp click.

He picked up a long, thin prybar, slid it into the crack, and lifted, straining. There was a loud clatter from inside; Kristin flinched involuntarily.

'Now, if they don't have a sound pickup . . .'

Wolfe cautiously opened the door, staying well away from the opening. No auto-blaster ravened, no alarm tore the night. Wolfe lifted away the wooden balk he'd jimmied out of its slots.

'Now, milady, if you'll hand me the first of those interesting packets we prepared earlier . . .'

FIRE RAVAGES NITE SPOT

Popular Club Destroyed
In Mysterious Inferno

<u>Press for More</u>

PRENDERGAST – A series of predawn blasts rocked the capital, totally destroying Nakamura's Nightclub. According to fire and police officials, arson is suspected, since none of the casino's elaborate fire and security alarms went off. The damage is vast, and the well-known club, long a favorite of Prendergast's monied socialites, must be considered totally destroyed, said a spokesman for the consortium that has operated the club since . . .

'What comes afterward?' Kristin asked. She was curled in Wolfe's arms.

'You mean tomorrow? They'll try to make sure I'm a good example of what not to grow up to be.'

'I know that,' Kristin said. 'I've already instructed the guards like you told me to. And I think you're insane. I mean after we get the – after we get what we came for.'

'If we get it,' Wolfe corrected.

What?

You Chitet try to kill me?

I try to get out from under, with the ur-Lumina?

Kristin lay in silence, waiting.

'There is no after,' Wolfe said, his voice unintentionally harsh.

*

They took Wolfe just as he was going toward his lifter, just outside the hotel. Three men came out of the shrubbery, guns leveled, and Naismith slid from a parked lifter holding a big-barreled riotgun steady.

'Anyone moves, everyone dies,' Henders said calmly as he came up the driveway.

The doorman saw the artillery and became a red-clad statue.

One of Henders' men moved behind Max and the other two security men with Wolfe, expertly searched them, and took their guns.

'You ought to get yourself some new punks from the repple-depple,' Naismith cracked. 'If you come back.'

'Shut up, Naismith,' Henders said. 'Mister Taylor, if you'd come with us, please? Someone wants to talk to you quite badly.'

They have him, the signal went up to the orbiting *Planov*.

'Very well,' Master Speaker Athelstan said. 'Continue monitoring.' He turned to a man sitting at a control board. 'I am not completely assured the subject hasn't made an ally of these gang members. Be prepared for instant activation of the device.'

'Yes, Master Speaker,' the man said, and rechecked the trigger for the bomb on Wolfe's back.

They rough-frisked Wolfe before pushing him into the sleek gray lifter that appeared as the thugs hustled him away from the hotel.

Confusion . . . confidence . . . certainty . . .

'He's clean,' the searcher reported.

'A man with the overconfidence of his congeries,' Henders said.

Wolfe looked mildly impressed. 'Not bad,' he said. 'But how about "A gun limits the possibilities"?'

'I'd agree,' Henders said, 'but only for the sap on the far end of the barrel.'

Wolfe shrugged.

They put him in the middle of the backseat, with Naismith and another thug on either side of him, guns almost touching his sides. Henders got in beside the pilot, turned in his seat, and kept his pistol pointed at Joshua's head.

'The head of my organization isn't pleased with you,' he said. 'You'd better have some explanations.'

Wolfe yawned. 'I generally do,' he said.

He closed his eyes and appeared to go to sleep.

Henders looked worried, then held the gun ready.

The warehouse was gray, anonymous, on a dingy street close to the spaceport. Henders pressed a button, and a door slid open. The lifter floated in and grounded, and the canopy lifted.

They muscled Wolfe out and took him along a bare concrete corridor, then down steps to a door. A guard stood outside with a heavy blaster.

Without a word, he opened the door, and Henders, Naismith, and the third gunman pushed Joshua inside.

The room was almost big enough to have an echo; dark-paneled wood walls hung with jarringly modern anima-art. There was a door to one side that was closed.

Naismith and the gunman stood to either side of Joshua, guns aimed.

At the far end of the room was an old-fashioned kidney-shaped desk. Leaning against it was a strangely misshapen man. From the waist down, he was tiny, almost small enough to be a jockey. Above that, he had the barrel chest and muscled arms of a stevedore. He wore his thinning hair long, tied into two queues that dangled behind his ears.

He had a strong, determined face, but with the pouty, small mouth of a decadent.

'You can call me Aurus,' he said. 'That's as good as anything else. It means gold, and gold's what I am.'

His voice matched his shoulders: deep, full of authority. Aurus went on, without waiting for Wolfe to respond.

'Taylor, we get a lot of damned fools here on Rogan's World, of a damned big variety. But you're something new.'

'Always nice to widen a man's experience,' Joshua said.

'Don't crack wise,' Aurus advised. 'I don't give a rat's ass if you go below with or without your teeth, and it's hard to talk through a mouth full of blood. A fool,' he repeated. 'Of a unique sort.

'You downplanet with enough pizzazz for a circus, obviously trying to catch somebody's eye. Fine. I'm good-hearted, there's always room for somebody else in my organization, so I send a couple of my best operators out to meet you. No problem. Everything goes well; Henders comes back and tells me here's someone we can do business with.

'Three days later, you clip poor goddamned Igraine out of his joint. I really want to know, before you die, how you counter-rigged his wheel. I'd ask the croupier, but Igraine fed him to the eels last night.

'So you're a fast mover, I now think. Then you go and jump the cits that front Nakamura's place and tell them you're the new mensch on the dock. Did you ever consider they were working for me? Did you ever think maybe you should've talked to me before you started pushing your muscle around?

'Not you. Throw a bomb, get the heat worked up, and think you just pulled some sort of brilliant move. Dickhead. Let me be the first to advise you, Mister Taylor. Your flashing around is going to do nothing but cost me money, and get you dead.'

Aurus' face was getting redder. He went behind his desk,

lifted the stopper from an elaborately worked decanter, and poured a drink into an equally fancy snifter. Henders walked from behind Wolfe to the side of the desk, holding his gun steady.

'Contrary to what you just said, I *did* think about talking to you,' Wolfe said, before Aurus could lift his glass. 'But I didn't think it was worth my while.'

'You didn't . . .' Aurus shook his head in disbelief. 'No. You didn't think. All you did was –'

Wolfe's hand flashed out, palm up, fingers curled. He had Naismith's gunhand at the wrist, twisted once, and bone shattered with a sharp crack. Wolfe, now with Naismith's gun, spun away as the gunman on the other side pulled his trigger.

But Wolfe wasn't there, and the blast seared into Naismith's side, ripping through his stomach wall. Naismith screamed in utter agony and fell sideways as his guts spilled, a stinking pile of pink, gray, red.

Joshua shot the gunman in the head, and blood spattered high to the ceiling.

The man who'd called himself Aurus was scrabbling in a compartment behind the desk for a gun.

Henders fired and missed, and Joshua crouched, aimed, fired.

The blaster seared Henders' arm away, and his gun cartwheeled across the desk.

Joshua shifted his aim and fired. His first bolt took Aurus in the shoulder, smashing him back against the wall. He flopped against it, mouth opening to shout, to scream, and Joshua blew his chest apart.

The door came open, and Joshua shot through the gap without aiming. He heard a shout of pain.

He ran, crouching, for the desk, and went prone behind it, pistol aimed at the doorway. He heard shouts, running feet. The door crashed open, but nobody came in.

He saw the barrel of a heavy blaster and took aim. A head flashed into sight, was gone before he could fire.

'Shit,' the shout came. 'They got th' boss.'

Another voice: 'C'mon, Augie. We're gone!'

There were more shouts, running feet, and the sound of lifter drives whining to life. It was quiet then except for Naismith's moans and the whir of the anima-art's motors.

Joshua went to Naismith and shot him in the head. Then he went to the door and looked out. The body of the guard was sprawled just beyond it. Wolfe went up the steps and found the warehouse deserted, its door yawning.

'Thieves *do* fall out,' he said to himself.

He went back down into Aurus' office.

Henders was barely conscious, clutching the cauterized remains of his arm.

Wolfe kicked him sharply, and the man screamed, bit if off.

'I'm not getting soft,' Joshua said. 'But maybe somebody'll be interested in hearing the details from a survivor.'

He reached into a jacket pocket, took a card from a case.

The card read only:

John Taylor

INVESTMENTS

He wrote the com number of his hotel, and

Perhaps we should talk

He dropped the card on Henders' chest, took the magazine from the blaster, tossed the gun into a corner of the room, and left.

Henders tried to sit up, collapsed.

After a time, he started moaning.

'You're blood-crazy,' Master Speaker Athelstan said firmly.

Joshua looked around the compartment, meeting hostile stares from Kristin, her duo, and Security Coordinator Kur.

'I do not believe this,' he said. 'Not one of you understands the fine art of making a good impression, do you?'

'Perhaps,' Kur said, 'we don't have your obviously wide experience in criminal matters.'

'Obviously not,' Wolfe agreed.

'It does not matter whether we understand or approve,' Master Speaker Athelstan said. 'A course of action has been determined by you. There is no other choice than to follow it. Joshua Wolfe, what comes next?'

Joshua held out his hands.

'Business as usual.'

'You had no gun hidden,' Kristin asked.

'No.'

'Yet you killed five men who *did* have guns.'

'Four. Henders should be alive, if a medico showed up in time.'

She stared at him.

'Perhaps,' she said finally, 'we have not been careful enough with you.'

Eight nights later, a message was waiting when Wolfe returned from the Oasis near dawn.

The screen was blank except for six numbers.

Joshua went out of the hotel, found a public com, dialed the numbers.

A synthed voice said, 'Yes?'

'This is John Taylor. I was given this number.'

There was a hum for almost thirty seconds, then:

'At 1730 hours today, leave your hotel and walk east along Fourteenth Boulevard. You will be met. Come alone and unarmed.'

The line went dead.

FIVE

Joshua spotted them as he left the hotel: two men behind, a man and a woman far ahead, across the boulevard. There'd be other pairs down the side streets. It was a classic box pattern, hard to elude, more likely intended to show Wolfe the opposition's resources than anything else.

All were pros, and none showed the slightest interest in Wolfe.

He was grateful he'd convinced Kristin not to put a shadow backup, and to play it straight, at least at first.

'If they're trying to kill me,' he reasoned, 'at least that'll bring 'em further into the open. I'm pretty sure I can duck another attempt by thuggery, if they're no better than the late idiot who called himself Aurus.'

But he still felt clammy fingers at his back as he walked. He made three blocks before a long, sleek lifter pulled out of a side street. Its window hissed down.

'Mister Taylor?' The driver was young, freckled, friendly looking.

'Yes.'

'I'm your transport.'

Wolfe got into the luxuriously appointed vehicle. The driver waited for a slight hole in traffic, then sped across the boulevard. He took a left, two rights.

'I didn't bring any backup,' Wolfe said.

'Of course,' the young man said. 'I'm just careful.' Two smaller lifters, with four men in each, came from side streets, fell in behind Joshua's vehicle.

'Yours?'

'Mine,' the driver acknowledged.

'You are careful.'

'Sorry, sir, but I'll have to check you before we go inside,' the driver said, trying to sound truly apologetic.

Damn them for untrusting bastards and not taking that damned bomb off. Wolfe caught himself grinning. *How dare these Chitet think I'd ever do anything nefarious or possibly dare to haul ass without giving them the chance to blow me up. I'm shocked. Shocked, do you hear me?*

He got out of the lifter, pretending to be impressed by the looming, colonnaded gray stone building they'd landed in front of, and the forested grounds around it, while he was *reaching* out, *feeling* . . .

The driver took a sweep from the door pocket and moved it across Wolfe, who turned, raising his hands, a bored expression on his face, as the sweep moved up his spine.

The driver's expression blanked, just as the detector's needle pegged and a buzzer sounded. He looked perplexed, then shook his head and paid no notice to the alarm triggered by the bomb. He continued on, moving the sweep under Wolfe's armpits, around his waist.

'You're clear,' he said. 'So let me take you inside to Advisor Walsh.'

'Won't be necessary,' a jocular voice came from the mansion's steps. 'The mountain has come to Yahweh, or however it goes.'

The man appeared as cheery as his voice and his driver. He was small, balding, with twin ruffs of white hair above his ears, and a smile accenting the lines of happy aging on his face. But his eyes were obsidian, and the two men flanking him looked equally dangerous.

'Mister Taylor, you've wreaked some havoc on my organization,' he went on. 'I'm Edmund Walsh, and I think we should have a talk.'

'I suppose you expect me to begin with some sort of moral lecture on how I'm so outraged by this new generation of villains like yourself, who lack all respect for tradition, the amenities, and so forth,' Walsh said. 'I had Sathanas' own time finding Hubert Dayton,' he said. 'Finally had to buy a bottle from your hotel. I believe this is how you like it, however.'

He handed Wolfe a half-full snifter and a glass of ice water.

'It is, sir,' Wolfe said. 'And no, I wasn't necessarily expecting a lecture about the good old days. Wasn't expecting or not expecting anything, to be precise.'

'Good,' the old man approved. 'What they call no-mind, eh?'

He noted Wolfe's flicker.

'Oh yes, Taylor. I'm hardly an oaf. When I heard the report of the damage you did to Aurus and his goons, I suspected there was a bit more to you than just being quick with a gun. Some say a man properly trained could even control objects. Such as roulette balls?'

Wolfe smiled politely, sipped Armagnac, and made no response.

'Anyway, back to where I started. You'll have to bear with me, Taylor. I'm getting old and have a tendency to ramble. You'll likely find that weakness in yourself, as you age.' The black eyes glittered. 'That's assuming you plan on getting older.'

'It's on my agenda.'

'Good. At any rate, one reason I won't talk to you about

how gunnies like me were such noblemen in our youth, when the world was young and every day promised a new fool to hijack, is I got the same lecture from some other old bastard back then. I read me a little history, and found what he'd said to be complete codswallop. Goons is goons, as they say. And I suppose we all end up romanticizing the past.'

Walsh dropped ice cubes into a glass, poured from a pitcher. 'I'd dearly love to be saltin' it back with you,' he said, letting a bit of false sentiment into his voice, 'but the stomach won't stand for it. Most of it's synth lining, but still I've got to live the clean life. At least they don't have me on pablum yet.'

Walsh walked out of the bar-cubby down a long, high-ceilinged hall, into a drawing room with bookcases and tables holding ship and machine models. On the walls were testimonials to Walsh's virtues. He motioned Wolfe into a large leather chair, sank into one across from him. 'Admire my digs?' he asked.

'Imposing,' Wolfe allowed.

'Glad you didn't say you liked this pile of rubble,' Walsh said. 'Damned cold and hard to heat. You know why I choose to live here instead of somewhere comfortable?'

'Because you want to impress the gunsels?'

'That,' Walsh admitted. 'But there's something else. When I was a boy, my mother used to come here. At the time the place was the home of a shipbuilder. A hard, hard man named Torcelli, who'd cut his way to the top and wasn't about to let anybody get up beside him. My mother was one of his mistresses. She brought me here twice. Torcelli saw me, and got uncomfortable about something. I've wondered if I'm his bastard, but I doubt it. Mother wasn't exactly the choosiest with her attentions, and his seed would've been weak by then.

'But the place took my mind, and I never let it leave me. I guess that gave me some sort of visible goal, eh? Get on top my own way, then buy this relic and restore it to prove I'm at least as good as Torcelli was. Better, since I've been here longer.'

Walsh drank water. 'Not that this matters,' he said. 'But when you retire, or anyway step back from the day-to-day battles, you find yourself thinking back. Wondering what made you do this, do that, and what you gained or lost from it.' Walsh looked out a window. 'See, over there, by the lake? My elk. There's six of them. Had them brought in from Earth. Ungainly bastards they are, and they're hell on my roses. I guess I'll have a roast one of these years, eh?' He put his glass down, leveled his eyes on Wolfe. 'Even though he didn't bother to clear it with me, I can't say I disagreed with Aurus' wanting to kill you. You *did* put a dent in his immediate plans.'

'A man who can't hang on to what he has doesn't deserve it,' Wolfe said.

'I'll agree with those sentiments. Ruthlessness is an imperative in my organization – and, I truly believe, in any other thriving organism. However, some feel that you've gone a bit far, a bit fast.'

'I didn't see much of anything in my way,' Wolfe said.

'At the level you began at, that probably is true. Even Aurus had begun to slacken off lately. However, that doesn't mean you can make that assumption about anyone and everyone.'

'Such as you.'

'Such as me. I may be old, but I'm still a far bigger shark than you, sonny. Don't ever forget that an old tough is merely a tough that's gotten old.'

'I try not to underestimate my opponents,' Wolfe said. 'Or to judge everyone as an opponent without reason.'

Walsh waited a moment, then nodded. 'You aren't stupid,' he said. 'Take a look at the walls, and tell me what you see.'

Wolfe obeyed, walking slowly through the drawing room, examining a holo here, an old-fashioned photograph or framed tab story there. He lingered at one, which showed Walsh, not many years younger than he was now, at the podium at a banquet. Smiling faces, men, women, looked up at him, hands caught in the moment of applause. Wolfe noted the unknown symbol on the podium, moved on.

Walsh waited patiently until Wolfe returned to his seat, drinking Armagnac. 'Well?'

'Like you said, I'm not stupid,' Wolfe said. 'I got two impressions from all those plaudits. First, and least important, is that you've had a helluva long run here on Rogan's World, and it doesn't look like there's many who don't owe you.'

Walsh nodded once.

'But that wasn't, I think, what you wanted me to get,' Wolfe continued. 'I'd guess it was a suggestion that all things come to him who waits, and seeing pictures of Edmund Walsh over the years might make me think about developing patience. Or else.'

'No,' Walsh said, nodding, 'you aren't stupid.'

Wolfe waited for something else, but Walsh seemed content to remain silent. He drained his snifter. 'So what do you want me to do?' he asked.

'Just what you're doing,' Walsh said. 'Gambling is one of the areas I've never been happy with. A little too unorganized for my tastes. I need a good man in place. You've got two clubs now – and you can have whatever of Aurus' goodies you fancy. But no more fancy grabs, eh? Nothing that makes headlines. You'll get more, in good time. And it won't be a long time, either. But don't get greedy for a while. Stick around, and you, too, can end up with people throwing banquets for you as an elder philanthropist with a colorful past. Even giving you government titles that don't pay shit, but get you a lot of respect. Get antsy now, though, and . . .'

Walsh didn't finish.

Wolfe stood. 'Thank you for the wisdom, Advisor Walsh.'

His voice was nearly devoid of irony.

'I don't like it at all,' Wolfe repeated. 'That was Aubyn in the picture, sitting beside Walsh. So we're close. But if Aubyn – or Walsh – had been interested in making any kind of a deal, he would've said something, instead of playing "tomorrow's another day." He knows good and well gangsters don't listen to promises. So the only reason I could figure for the meeting is Aubyn wanted to take a look at me. She got it, and now she's trying to figure out her next move. Think about it, Athelstan! She's thinking about tactics, and we're picking our noses and looking at pictures on a wall! That means she's ahead of us.'

Onscreen, both Athelstan and Kur started to speak, stopped. Kur inclined her head in deference.

'Thank you,' Athelstan said. 'First, I'll voice my obvious suspicion – that you're trying some subterfuge to derail our plan.'

'Why should I?'

'Perhaps,' Athelstan said, 'because you've sensed the ur-Lumina, feel that you can seize it on your own at a later time, and realize once we have possession it's absolutely lost to you.'

'Utterly illogical,' Wolfe said. 'You've no reason to think that except your own suspicions. Or paranoia.'

Athelstan's lips pursed, then he recovered. 'Admitted. I withhold the canard for the moment.'

'Another possibility,' Kur put in. 'You're frightened.'

'Hell yes I'm frightened,' Wolfe said. 'This Aubyn has had the biggest goddamned brass lantern as a toy for five years, rubbed it all she wanted, and has a whole goddamned battalion of genies lined up for all I know. She's clever, she's mad, and she's a sociopath. I'm ground zero for her while you sit up there in your spaceship thinking lofty thoughts.'

'Be careful,' Kur warned.

'Why? You'll kill me? What do you think Aubyn wants? To get in my pants?' Wolfe turned to the other three in the room – Kristin, Max, and Lucian. 'What do you think? Are we just running scared?'

Max made no reply.

'Insufficient data for me to make a judgment,' Lucian said.

'Negative,' Kristin said. 'Wolfe's analyses have been correct thus far.'

'Joshua Wolfe,' Kur put in, 'calm down. You've run agents, you know how easy it is for one to panic when he's one step short of his target. Haven't you ever had to order anybody to hold fast?'

'I have,' Wolfe said grimly. 'Three times, no more. I lost my ferret twice, barely made the hit the third time. Then I started paying attention to the man on the ground.'

'This is not a democracy,' Athelstan said firmly. 'There is generally but one logical way, and since I've been chosen to speak for the Chitet, I have decided we should stay the course. We are getting close to our target. To withdraw now would be to abandon all our accomplishments.'

Wolfe stared at the screen. 'I've won a lot of money from people like you,' he said quietly. 'People who think what they've thrown in the pot gives them some kind of rights on the showdown.'

'You're not assessing the situation with proper logic,' Athelstan said. 'Continue the mission.'

Walsh waited while the woman with hooded eyes paced back and forth, thinking.

'No,' she decided. 'there's nothing more to be gained by waiting and observing. Proceed as we discussed.'

'I don't feel like making love tonight,' Kristin announced.

'Nor I,' Joshua agreed, leaning across her and turning off the light. 'I wish that your fearless leaders had heard the old Earth-Chinese proverb that of the thirty-four possible responses to a problem, running away is best.'

'Master Speaker Athelstan knows what is right.'

'Yeah,' Joshua agreed. 'For Master Speaker Athelstan. Never mind. Go to sleep. It's liable to get noisy pretty quick.'

Joshua lay back, trying to quiet the jangle. After a time, he felt Kristin relax into sleep. Then he took tension, fear, anger from his toes, moved it upward, pushing it as a broom sweeps water, up his body, through his arms, through his chest and into his brain. He found a color for these things, deep blue, coiled the tensions, the fears into a ball, forced it out of his body, and made it float precisely three inches above his head, between his eyes. He ordered his mind to obey him, that all would be doomed if that blue ball sank into his body once more.

Joshua was almost asleep when he *felt* something. Far out, across the city – although when he reached for it, nothing was there.

Then it returned, brooding, dark.

Wolfe slid out of bed, dressed in dark shirt, pants, and a pair of zip boots. He returned to the bed, and lay on his back.

Waiting.

The door to the bedroom crashed open, and Wolfe was crouched in a defense stance as Kristin half shrieked and sat up.

Lucian was in the doorway, gun in his hand, eyes wide. 'They killed him!' he cried. 'They've killed him!'

Suddenly he burst into racking sobs, and the gun fell onto the carpet.

Wolfe heard the blare of the vid in the room outside and ran into the living room.

Onscreen was dark space, lit by the flaring ruin of a starship. For an instant Wolfe was thrown back years, to other screens and other ship-deaths.

Then the smooth commentator's voice registered:

'. . . still unknown registry and origin, although sources within Planetary Guard advise the ship had been in a geosynchronous orbit over Prendergast for at least two months.

'I repeat the flash: An unknown starship, orbiting just off Rogan's World exploded minutes ago. Initial reports suggest the ship was attacked by unknown assailants. We have no word as to the ship's name or registry, nor any information about passengers or crew.

'We have a news crew en route, and another on its way to Planetary Guard headquarters. These images are coming to you courtesy of the Guard, from one of the navsats offworld.

'Please stand by for further details.'

The screen blanked, but Max continued staring at it.

'Master Speaker Athelstan,' he said in a whisper. 'The bitch got him. She killed him.' He exploded onto his feet, shouting. 'Goddammit, she killed him! She killed Kur . . . all of them!'

Kristin, naked, was in the bedroom door. Her face was blank in shock and horror.

'Come on,' Wolfe shouted. 'She hit first! We're next!' He ran back into the bedroom, scooping up Lucian's gun on the way. Lucian was crouched on the floor, head in his hands, sobbing, repeating over and over: 'It's ended . . . The dream is gone . . . It's ended . . .'

'Come on, man! Or die with your frigging dream!'

Lucian didn't move.

Wolfe hurried into the gun-guards' quarters and found them as shattered as Lucian. He found the team's cashbox, smashed it open, and shoved wads of credits into his pockets.

'What are you doing?' Max demanded. His gun was wavering, but still aimed at Wolfe.

'We're getting out of here,' Wolfe said. 'Or else we'll be as dead as Athelstan.'

'No,' Max decided. 'No, we can't leave. No, we can't –'

Wolfe was on him, gun crossblocked out of the way as it went off, blasting a three-inch-wide hole in a painting of a shepherd and his flock and the wall behind it. Joshua struck Max once on the forehead with the heel of his hand and let him fall.

One of the gun-guards had his pistol half drawn, and Wolfe kicked him back against the wall. He had Lucian's gun in his hand, and the other guards froze.

'Get your things and get out,' he ordered. 'Move! We'll try for our ship at the yard!' He didn't wait for a reply, but darted into the main room.

Kristin had found a pair of blue pants and a red pullover; she sat on the floor of the bedroom, sorting through boots very methodically and slowly.

Wolfe yanked her to her feet. 'Out! Now!'

Kristin started to protest, nodded dumbly.

'Come on, Lucian!'

'Lost . . . All lost . . .'

Wolfe could spare no more time. He grabbed Kristin's hand and pulled her out of the suite toward the private lift.

The glass-fronted lift's door slid closed, and Wolfe punched 2.

'Where's your gun?'

Kristin's hand felt her waistband, then she shook her head.

'Good,' Wolfe said sarcastically. 'One gun against – Jesus God!'

Two tactical strike ships with the insignia of the Planetary Guard broke through the cloud cover and dropped down toward the hotel. They banked, then hovered about one hundred feet above the hotel's roof. Flame spat from one, then the second. Wolfe slammed the lift's emergency buttons. It obediently stopped, and the door slid open.

Wolfe pitched Kristin out onto thick pile carpet as the missiles smashed into the hotel, and exploded.

The tower rocked under the impact, and alarms howled.

Kristin was crying, whimpering. Wolfe lifted her face, slapped her hard, twice. 'Come on, soldier! Or die right here!'

Kristin shook her head violently, then her eyes came back to normal. 'Where . . . What . . .'

'Find the emergency exit. There's got to be one somewhere.'

There was, at the end of the long corridor. Doors were opening, and bewildered men and women were stumbling out. Wolfe pushed through them, found the stairs, clattered down their long, cement-gray steps, hearing siren screams clamoring everywhere.

A man with a gun stood at the door leading into the lobby. Wolfe shot him without asking questions, took his gun, and they went on down, into the underground parking structure.

There was no one in the attendant's booth, and Wolfe went to a wooden cabinet, yanked it open, and found a rack with ignition keys dangling from it.

'Good. Organized,' he muttered. He scanned the gravlifters parked nearby. 'A-27 – here it is.' He pulled a set of keys from a numbered hook, pulled Kristin toward a nearly new sleek luxury lifter. He pointed the ignition sensor at the vehicle, and the door slid up.

'Inside,' he ordered, and Kristin managed to fumble her way into a seat.

Wolfe slid in, pushed the sensor into the ignition slot, let the drive whine to life. He lifted the craft and steered it up the ramps, toward the exit.

A bright red heavy gravlifter was just grounding, blocking the exit, red and blue lights flashing. Firemen wearing exposure suits piled out, heavy-laden.

Wolfe slid the drive-pot to full thrust, brought the stick up, and sent the lifter careening across the wide sidewalk onto the boulevard. A fireman saw him and barely dove out of the way.

There were other firecraft grounding on the boulevard, and he saw someone waving. Someone aimed a gun, fired, and the bolt went somewhere Wolfe couldn't see.

At full power, he sent the lifter down the street, made one turn, another, then banked the craft up into the darkness and smoke as the hotel gouted fire like a torch.

SIX

Wolfe held his breath and sliced through the bomb strap. Nothing happened. He pulled it away, feeling it tear at his skin like a bandage long in place. He let the bomb thump to the lifter's floor.

Kristin watched dully, making no attempt to stop him.

He started to say something, rethought his words. 'You'll get over it,' he said gently. 'Everybody's Christ gets killed sooner or later.'

'You don't understand,' Kristin said. 'It wasn't just Athelstan – it was a whole dynasty that woman murdered. Kur – Athelstan's aides – his best logicians – Aubyn may have destroyed us.'

Again Wolfe held back his words.

'That's as may be,' he said. 'A little martyrdom never hurt a good cause. But later is for mourning. Right now, we've got to think about our own young asses.'

'It doesn't matter,' Kristin said. 'You can go your own way – go wherever you want. I'll try to get off Rogan's World somehow. Perhaps – when – if we recover, we'll mount another operation against Aubyn for the ur-Lumina.'

'You want to get slapped again? Knock off the defeatism. You ain't dead till you're dead, as the eminent grammarian said. I dragged you out of that hotel; I can drag you a few feet further. Besides, I might need somebody at my back.'

'How do you know I won't kill you?' Kristin asked. 'I guess that's what Athelstan and Kur would have wanted me to do.'

'Lady, a piece of advice: stop second-guessing corpses.' Wolfe's voice sharpened. 'Now pull it together, dammit!'

The image of that universe-encompassing 'red virus' filled his mind.

'I can't – won't – say why,' he went on. 'But there's no time for you to wander back to Batan and debate, oh so goddamned logically, whether you're coming back for the Mother Stone and what color your little pink dresses ought to be.'

Kristin took several deep breaths. 'All right. What do we do? Take your thirty-fourth easiest option and run?'

'No. Aubyn'll be expecting that. We do what any good – if maybe suicidal – gravel-cruncher's supposed to.'

'A little obfuscation here,' Wolfe said, as he grounded the lifter in an alley behind a business loudly proclaiming itself to be HJALMAR'S LIFTERS – ONLY THE BEST IN PREVIOUSLY OWNED ANTIGRAVITY DEVICES. He opened the lifter's engine lid, located the tool compartment, and muttered under his breath when all he found was a bent screwdriver and a crescent wrench whose jaws barely met. 'How are you at deactivating proximity detectors?'

'I never learned how,' Kristin said.

'And what *are* they teaching the young these days?' Joshua said. 'Tsk.'

He unscrewed the registration plates of his lifter and changed them for one of Hjalmar's finest. 'In case somebody happens to be alert,' he said, 'I'd rather not get stopped.'

He considered the night. The whole planet seemed focused on the still-roaring inferno seven miles distant.

'Now watch and learn something,' he told Kristin. 'Normally any lifter's proximity detectors are up front. Here, just below the driving lights on the traffic side. Pop the little panel, like so. All that you have to do then is yank this wire – here – and the same one on the backup unit. The drive won't pick up any closing signal. Handy thing to know, if you plan on, say, ramming a baby carriage or something scummy like that.'

He realized he was babbling a little, from fear of what was to come as much as relief at having the bomb gone.

'And now we go marching through Georgia,' he said.

Wolfe shot the two guards outside Walsh's mansion and steered the gravsled through the gates. There were lights on in the mansion's east wing.

'Out!'

Kristin obediently tumbled onto the grass. An alarm clanged from the gates, but Wolfe paid no mind.

He turned the lifter toward the west wing, set the height designator at five feet above the ground, and slid the drive-pot to full power.

As the lifter accelerated toward the mansion, Wolfe jumped out and went flat.

Someone heard the turbine whine, ran out of the main entrance, saw the speeding lifter, and shot at it twice. Going about sixty miles an hour, the lifter smashed into the stone building, flipped, and crashed through the great bay windows. A moment later it exploded. All the lights in the mansion died.

'That's our calling card,' Wolfe said. 'Let's go introduce ourselves.'

There were shouts, screams, and another alarm went off. Wolfe ignored them and trotted across the dark lawn and up the steps.

A man – perhaps the shooter – was gaping at the flames

starting to flicker in the far wing. Wolfe shot him neatly in the neck.

'Where . . . ?' Kristin started.

'Shut up.' Wolfe reached out, *felt*, and went through the door into the house.

'Breathe gently,' Wolfe advised.

Edmund Walsh, half-dressed, obeyed. His face was white, silhouetted in the glow from a pocket flash on the bureau in front of him.

'Move away from the dresser,' Wolfe ordered.

Walsh did, moving very slowly, hands lifting to shoulder height as if they belonged to a marionette.

Wolfe pocketed the gun beside the light. Walsh started to protest. Wolfe reached out and stroked the old man along the neck with three fingers. Walsh dropped bonelessly. Joshua shouldered him. 'One little memory trot, and we can be on our way.' He turned off the flash and dropped it into a pocket.

Joshua went unhurriedly across the drawing room to the wall lined with testimonials, holographs, and photos behind the glare of the flash. He pulled one holo free and tossed it to Kristin. 'Don't lose this. We'll need it.'

Emergency power went on, flickered, went out.

Wolfe listened to the shouting from the other wing and heard the screams of firelifters approaching. 'Out the back,' he decided. 'Look for something to steal.'

The windowless delivery vehicle sat behind the mansion's kitchen. The ignition key was in place, the lifter's driver probably having reasoned that no one but a desperate fool would dare steal from Edmund Walsh.

Joshua slid Walsh into the back, started the drive, lifted the craft silently, and sent the lifter across the grounds, away from the flames and excitement. He found an unguarded rear gate and floated down the long avenue toward the city.

'What we need,' Wolfe said, 'is something nice, quiet, and dark. Like – like this.'

The sign read FLORIET REGIONAL PARK, and the entrance was blocked by two barrels. Wolfe shut off the lifter's lights, grounded the craft, rolled a barrel out of the way, moved the lifter through, and replaced the barrel.

He lifted the 'sled without turning the lights back on and went slowly along a curving, narrow drive. He passed slides, swings, and climbs, then grounded the lifter in the playground's center.

Wolfe propped Walsh against a wooden clown with peeling paint. He started slapping Walsh on the cheeks with two extended fingers, not hard, not gently. 'Stop faking,' he said. 'The nerve block wore off a couple of minutes ago.'

Walsh's eyes came open. 'You're better'n I thought, Taylor. I didn't think you'd live through our little demonstration – let alone come back this fast.'

'I am better. A lot better. But I don't have time for compliments. I need some information.'

'Fresh out.'

'I don't think so,' Wolfe said. 'I'm in a hurry, so it's going to hurt. Show him the picture.'

Kristin handed him the holo of Edmund Walsh being feted at a banquet, standing behind a podium with an unusual symbol on it.

'What's the emblem mean?'

Walsh compressed his lips.

Wolfe set the gun on the sand and took Walsh's left hand. Walsh tried to pull away but wasn't able to. Wolfe slid two fingers down to Walsh's little finger, twisted.

Walsh yelped.

'Ring finger.' Joshua broke that one as well.

'Middle . . .'

'Stop!' It was Kristin.

Wolfe turned, stared at her. She shuddered, turned away.

'Middle finger . . .'

'I'll tell you!'

The bone snapped with a crack, and Walsh stifled a scream.

'I *said* I'd tell you!'

'Talk.'

'It's the logo of the Fiscus-MacRae Fund.'

'What's that?'

'A big – really big – research firm,' Walsh said, biting his lip against the pain. 'They do political research, sociological studies – that kind of thing.'

'Yeah,' Joshua said. 'That kind of thing. Nice cover – you can do anything you want to with something that vague. Nobody's going to ask who's coming, who's going, or why, whether they're gangster or pol. And research justifies a ton of electronics, doesn't it? Enough for a whole world's command center. Not stupid at all.'

He pointed to a woman sitting at the podium table, a mildly striking woman with short, dark hair. Her face was in silhouette, and it was hard to say what she was looking at. 'Who's she?'

He *felt* Walsh stiffen.

'I don't know.'

'You'll run out of bone joints before I run out of patience,' Wolfe said.

'Oh, I'm talking, I'm talking. I was just trying to remember –'

Wolfe broke his index finger.

'I'm telling you the truth!'

'You're more afraid of her than you are of me?'

Walsh stared into Wolfe's eyes. His head moved up, down, a bare inch.

'We'll have to rectify that,' Joshua said. 'Kristin, you might want to go back to the lifter. This is going to get messy.'

'No,' she said. 'I'll stay.'

'Then stay quiet. Listen closely, Edmund. I'm going to hit you once, just above the cheekbone. Your eye is going to come out of its socket. I'm going to pull it out by the ganglion then pull until the ganglion snaps. After that – who knows? We'll concentrate on your face, first, because that'll be pretty damned gory, and second, because it doesn't do any lasting damage. But I'll leave you your tongue, hearing, and one eye. You want fear – we'll deal on that level. If you still aren't talking, I'll get something sharp from the lifter, and we'll start down from your navel. Look at me! Do you think I'm bluffing?' Wolfe turned the flash on his own face and waited.

'No,' Walsh muttered after a moment. 'You're not bluffing. You'll do it. But she'll do worse.'

'I agree,' Wolfe said. 'She's had more practice than I have. But there's a difference. I'm now. She's later.'

'How much of a start will you give me?' Walsh said.

'When you talk, I leave.'

Walsh slumped back against the statue. 'I don't have any choice. She's the deputy director of Fiscus-MacRae. She uses the name of Alicia Comer. I don't know much about her,' he said. 'She's not from Rogan's World. I heard she's a helluva fund-raiser, which is why Fiscus-MacRae uses her. She was one of the founding partners, come to think.'

'Walsh, you're still lying. But that doesn't matter. Where does Comer live?'

Walsh hesitated, then told him.

'Where's the fund located at?'

That, too, came out.

'All right,' Wolfe said. He rose.

'You're a bastard, Taylor,' Walsh managed.

'I know,' Wolfe said. The gun slid into his hand, and Wolfe touched the trigger. Kristin half screamed as the bolt sliced through the old man's head and blood sprayed across the clown.

'You told him you wouldn't . . .' Kristin managed.

'Yeah,' Wolfe said, his voice flat. 'I lied. I do things like that.'

Low-power lasers made lines in the near-dawn darkness in an irregular figure, sealing off an area around the spacecraft. Ten bodies still littered the tarmac. Seven were variously dressed; three wore the livery chosen for Wolfe's pilots. Morgue 'sleds to one side of the ship-park waited for the scattering of police to finish their work. Three noisy 'cast teams waited, held back by an angry cop. No one paid much attention to the rangy man wearing a coverall that said SPACEPORT GROUND HANDLER as he walked up to the cop.

'Are your officers out of the ship?' he asked.

'Uh – yes. I think so.'

'Good. Mister McCartle wants the ship moved down-row, into one of the hangars.'

'Nobody said anything to me about that.'

'He told me you'd know,' Wolfe said. 'Said the police wanted it out of the way to keep off souvenir hounds and like.'

The policeman hesitated, looked into Wolfe's eyes, then smiled. 'Oh. Yeah. That makes sense. Which hangar?'

Wolfe looked pointedly at one of the reporters, who'd edged closer. The cop leaned closer, listening.

'Eight-Six-Alpha,' Wolfe said. 'All the way down to the end, in A row.'

'You need any help?'

'Not unless there's still bodies inside.'

'Nope. Taylor's crew must've come out shooting, not that that did them much good. Regular Kilkenny cats here. Doesn't seem to be any damage to the ship, but maybe you want to not do any VTOing.'

Wolfe half saluted and went through the line of light, through the ship's hatch. The lock closed behind him.

Joshua slid into the pilot's seat, unlocked and activated the controls. Eyes closed, he touched sensors. 'I do not like the feel of this beast,' he muttered, touching the secondary drive sensor.

The drive hissed into life.

Wolfe picked up a com button, stuck it to his larynx. 'Rogan Prime Control, this is the *Eryx*.'

'*Eryx*, this is Prime. Be advised your ship has been seized by proper authorities. I can't allow you to lift without authorization.'

'Prime, this is the *Eryx*. Police Captain McCartle in command. I've been ordered to relocate this ship to the police field for a complete analysis. Plus we don't want the ship sitting around for gawkers. This whole mess is too loud anyway.'

'Hell,' the voice swore. 'I'm always the last to get the word.' There was silence, as Wolfe *felt* out for the woman. 'All right. How do you want to lift it?'

'Don't put me in the regular pattern, Prime. I'll be holding 1,000 feet, course 284 magnetic, on visual.'

'That was 1,000 feet, course 284, *Eryx*. You're cleared to take off.'

'Thanks, Prime. *Eryx* out.'

The yacht settled down on an almost-deserted open stretch of road, where a gravlifter waited. It grounded, skidded, lazily turned on an axis, and settled, blocking the road. The gravlifter's canopy lifted and Kristin ran toward the ship. The lock opened, and she went up the gangway and through the open lock door into the control room.

Wolfe nodded as she sat down in the copilot's seat, and took the *Eryx* off again.

'That wasn't the best landing I've seen,' Kristin said.

'Not my fault,' Joshua said. 'I'm the original hot-dog danny normally. This pig you found in a boneyard and decided would make a good yacht's got more slop than a hophead's legs.'

'We had to move quickly.'

'So you did,' Joshua grunted. 'Let's hope it'll hold together long enough to get us offworld and somewhere.'

'What's your plan?'

'It's changed,' Wolfe said. 'I was hoping to find the Lumina and go straight after it.'

'What about Aubyn?'

'I don't give a damn about her,' Wolfe said. 'No Lumina, no power. Nor do I give a shit about how Rogan's World is run anyway. But she's with the Lumina now, so it's going to be a two-for-the-price-of-one goat rope.'

'How do you know where she is?'

'I *know*.'

'Can you take her?' Kristin said.

'That's what we're going to find out. Grab the controls, and keep it level. I'm going to be busy for the next few seconds.'

Reaching out .

Feeling . . .

Wolfe jumped in his seat, feeling the death-sweep rush toward him.

Shit. The bitch is waiting for me. I wonder if she's got enough power – if she's used the Lumina enough – to kill me with just her mind.

Unknown.

Breathe . . . breathe . . .

All right. We'll have to go and have ourselves a look.

'I've got the con,' he said, and sent the *Eryx* swooping down toward open farmland below. There were no buildings, vehicles, or workers in sight, and he landed the ship behind a long, high mow of drying grass.

He slid to a com, touched sensors. 'Central Library,' he requested.

The screen blanked, lit with a rather unimaginative panel of books.

Wolfe touched keys; F,I,S,C,U,S,-,M,A,C,R,A,E#F,U,N,D

FILE FOUND

V,I,S,U,A,L,#H,E,A,D,Q,U,A,R,T,E,R,S

SEARCHING . . .

The screen showed a sprawling series of ultramodern buildings, centering around a glass pyramid that might've been a cathedral.

'Son of a bitch,' Wolfe swore. 'Old Edgar Allan's got a *lot* to answer for.'

'What does that mean?'

'Nothing.' Wolfe thought. 'Since we don't happen to have a battalion or two of marines in our back pockets, I guess I'll just wander in and see what's going on.'

'Joshua?'

'What?'

'Why doesn't Aubyn have troops surrounding the building, if she controls Rogan's World? I surely would if I were her.'

A bit of a smile came to Wolfe's mouth. He leaned over and kissed her on the cheek. 'And I'm very glad you're not. Why no soldiery? I don't know. Maybe Aubyn thinks the most important thing is for nobody to know who's the puppet master here. Hell, for all I know, she's aware of her enormous crimes and doesn't think she morally deserves the army.'

He didn't voice his real thought: that Token Aubyn didn't think she needed any backup.

'That doesn't make any sense,' Kristin complained.

'Since when does *anybody* make any sense? All right. I'm betting I'll find Aubyn – and that other thing – in the main building. I'm bringing this hog down on the other side of that rise. That should give you cover against direct fire.'

He picked up a bonemike from the control board, fitted it around his neck. 'If you don't hear anything – or you hear a lot of male screaming in my general tone of voice, get away from the ship, back into the city, and go to ground. Here. Take the credits we took from the hotel. That'll get you a good running start in case Aubyn's the vindictive sort. And good luck.'

'Aren't you the one who's going to need the luck?'

'I am. Wish I still believed in it.'

Not far from Fiscus-MacRae's central building were two monolithic abstract sculptures, set by themselves in the rolling lawn.

Inside one, two men crouched behind a semiportable blaster, peering through a vision slit just above ground level. One lifted a microphone. 'This is Two-Seven. One man, approaching from the east. I think he came from that ship that grounded about fifteen minutes ago. Shall we drop him?'

Inside the building a balding man with the muscles of a weightlifter spoke into his com. 'This is Kilkhampton. Stand by.' He looked at the woman once known as Token Aubyn.

Her eyes were closed. They opened. 'No,' she ordered. 'We'll let him get closer. Is he armed?'

The bald man looked at another screen. 'I see some sort of ferrous material mass at his waist. Probably a pistol.'

'Let him come. He's outgunned.'

The bald man eyed Aubyn, then opened his com.

Joshua Wolfe walked slowly, steadily, toward the building. His hands were at his sides, well away from the holstered sidearm. His breathing was slow, deep. In through the nose, out through the mouth, sixteen breaths a minute.

He stopped, held his hands out level, and his breathing slowed, four deep inhalations per minute. He *felt* out, beyond.

Inside the building, he *felt* the Great Lumina, a deep hum beyond hearing, a glow beyond vision. It swirled in his mind like a maelstrom, pulling him forward, pulling him toward death. He tried to take its power, failed. Another was blocking him, someone closer, more familiar with the Lumina's power.

Aubyn.

He *felt* her waiting for him, an ant lion deep in her pit, a spider waiting for the web twitch.

She was *reaching* for him, for his mind.

He refused contact. Forced himself away.

He noted the men hidden in the statue/gun emplacement, and other armed men equally well camouflaged around the seemingly deserted institution. There were other guards inside the building. They, too, were recognized.

He *reached* beyond them, beyond Rogan's World, into space. He felt the shrieking of the 'red virus' in space as it clawed toward Man's worlds.

He *reached* beyond that, beyond Man, toward a nameless world deep in the void.

He *felt* the touch of the last of the Al'ar, the Guardians, waiting for him, waiting for the Lumina.

He took strength, brought it back.

Again he *reached*, this time into memory.

The one he'd thought was the last of the Al'ar; Taen, lifted his head, and a Chitet bolt took him. Taen fell, dying, dead, across Joshua.

Wolfe remembered that moment, brought it forward. His breathing changed once more, quickening, almost panting, but far too regular, coming from his diaphragm.

Joshua felt the roar of life, of death, blood pouring through his veins. As he had once before, he took Taen's death and cast it forth, like a net. He let it sweep out, around, over the towering glass building.

'What the hell's he doing, just standing there –'

Kilkhampton gagged suddenly, as if struck in the throat, grabbed for his chest, half rose, and toppled across the control board.

Aubyn was on her feet. She grabbed for his com.

'Any station – all stations – report immediately!'

There was no response.

Aubyn started to key the sensor again, tossed it away. She left the room and walked quickly but calmly for the lift.

Wolfe entered the huge circular room and looked around. There were two mezzanine balconies above, then the diffused crystalline light from the faceted-glass roof. To one side was a large reception desk of exotic woods, with an elaborate com. No one was behind the desk.

There was a body sprawled near one wall, a gun lying not far away.

The marble floor formed a swirl of black and white, leading the eye to the lift at the far end. The air smelled as if lightning had struck nearby not long ago. Wolfe's breathing was slow, regular, deep.

A woman waited in the center of the room. She was about ten years younger than he was, not pretty, but striking. She wore a hand-tailored deep blue business suit. Her dark hair was cut close and looked a little like a cap.

She appeared unarmed.

Joshua drew his pistol with two fingers and spun it clattering across the marble to the side. Aubyn jumped in surprise, then recovered. Her eyes, hooded, sought Wolfe's.

'I am Token Aubyn,' she said. Her voice was low, musical.

'You do not need my name,' Joshua said.

'You are not a Chitet,' she said.

'No.'

'But you were helping them.'

'For my own purposes.'

'Which are?'

Wolfe looked up at the glass ceiling. 'Congratulations,' he said. 'One crystal makes another invisible. Nice way to hide something in plain sight.'

'I am trying to *reach* you,' Aubyn said calmly, not responding to what Wolfe had said. 'What I call mind-seizing. But you're different from others – from other minds I've chosen to use for my purposes. Your thoughts are different. Alien. I almost feel like I did when I first saw the crystal, and thought into it and knew I had to have it for my own.'

Again, Wolfe made no reply.

'The crystal,' Aubyn said, 'what I've heard is called a Lumina, is mine. I found it. I killed for it. And I'll kill again. This is my world, and soon I'll be ready to reach out for more.

'You – or those Chitet fools I once believed knew something – cannot, must not stop me.'

Wolfe *felt* discordance, as if someone had rubbed a finger along a wet glass, a glass with a hidden flaw in it, and the growing tone that could not be heard *felt* wrong, *was* wrong.

'I am not a fool,' Aubyn went on. 'I know the Lumina, and what it can give. So even though you're strong, stronger than I thought at first, I must deal with the situation immediately. You must die now.'

There was nothing to see, but Wolfe *felt* energy sear, *saw* it as a flashing ball. He took it, welcomed it, and it was gone.

Aubyn looked startled.

Joshua felt force, coming down, crushing force, coming from all directions. He fought, tried to stand, but it was too strong. He slipped sideways and fell heavily, half-curled, one hand resting on his ankle.

Aubyn walked toward him.

Wolfe lay motionless.

Aubyn's footfalls were very loud on the marble.

Wolfe's right hand flickered to his boot top, and a tiny, six-pointed, razor bit of steel flashed.

Aubyn jerked as the shiriken scarred her face and blood spurted.

Joshua *felt* the Lumina then.

Zai . . . I welcome this . . . I accept this . . . ku *. . . reach . . . reaching . . .*

The room was filled with a great luminescence, hard, cold, all the colors that could be imagined, and he took its power, sending, receiving as it rebounded, building.

He dimly heard shattering glass, then the grating, rending of alloy beams as they cracked, smashed.

There was something floating in the middle of the room, a great gem of many facets, each facet flashing.

The Lumina.

Wolfe came to his feet.

All the universe held was Token Aubyn's eyes, boring into his. Aubyn's eyes, and somewhere beyond, the Lumina.

Joshua *reached*, welcomed the Lumina's energy, welcomed the thin Al'ar force from far beyond in interstellar space, shaped the power, focused it, and the room flared with intolerable light.

Wolfe shouted – fear? rage? – as Aubyn's body exploded into a sheet of flame for a bare instant. Then it was gone, and her unscathed body collapsed to the floor. Not far from her body was a gray, indistinct stone, about the size of Wolfe's head.

The Lumina.

Wolfe stumbled toward her and made sure she was dead. He spoke into the bonemike. 'Bring the ship in. We've got a cargo to load.'

He let himself sink back to the floor, felt the chill of marble against his cheek, and welcomed nothingness for a time.

SEVEN

'For a renegade,' the comfortable-looking man named Fordyce said, 'your Joshua Wolfe has been doing very, very well by Federation Intelligence. Are you sure you aren't running a *very* deep private operation here?'

Cisco shook his head. 'No, sir. I've been with FI too long not to remember my pension whenever I start getting too creative.'

'Of course,' Fordyce drawled blandly. 'Certainly I never thought of such subterfuge, but was content to soldier my way up through the ranks, knowing my innate ability would be recognized in the fullness of time.' He roared with laughter.

The title on the entry door to his secured suite read OPERATIONS DIRECTOR.

'You must admit,' Fordyce went on, 'he has done us a world of good. Athelstan dead along with almost all of his advisors and security people, which puts a big crimp in the Chitet's ambitions for a few dozen years. Admirable, simply admirable. If he were still on the payroll, we'd have to promote and gong him a couple of times. And I won't even consider the seven rather senior officials in FI who decided, after the debacle on Rogan's World, to either take early retirement or transfer to less, shall we say, active sections of the government. Rather a good job of smoking the moles out, I'd say.'

'Yes, sir,' Cisco said. 'So what do you wish done about Wolfe?'

'I'd say nothing. Let him sneak back to his Outlaw Worlds and mind his own business.'

'We can't do that, sir.'

'Why not?'

'We've picked up some very strange data,' Cisco said. 'You're aware of those Al'ar objects called Lumina?'

'I am.' Fordyce's tone became flat, disapproving. 'Manna for oo-ee-oo-ee idiots and mystics.'

'The Al'ar didn't think so,' Cisco persisted.

'That doesn't mean they have any relevance to us,' Fordyce said. He waited for Cisco to withdraw the point, but the gray man just sat, lips drawn into thin lines. Fordyce sighed. 'Very well. What new data about these Lumina further complicates the issue of Joshua Wolfe?'

'We've been getting reports of some sort of a super Lumina the Al'ar had at the end of the war. I don't know if it was a secret weapon that didn't quite work out, or what, for it was never deployed as far as I can tell,' Cisco said. 'Supposedly this is what the Chitet were after, and why they hijacked Wolfe when I had him comfortably zombied and on the way back here for debriefing.'

'Of *course* this Great Lumina would give anyone who touched it superpowers,' Fordyce said cynically. 'Such things always seem to have a reputation like that.'

'That's the story,' Cisco said reluctantly. 'Supposedly this woman who bossed Rogan's World, who was called Alicia Comer, but who was in fact a deserter from the Federation Navy named Token Aubyn, had possession of this Lumina, and used it to carve her way upward.' Cisco told Fordyce as much of Aubyn's history as he'd been able to get from Naval and FI records.

'Interesting,' Fordyce said, lacing his fingers on his desk. 'I still view the whole matter skeptically. Now let me return your question to you: What do you want to do about Wolfe, assuming that he has possession of this ruddy great chunk of colored glass? Put out an all-Federation hue and cry? That'll certainly attract attention, particularly with the rather strange happenings these days.'

'No, sir. But I'd like to let word slip out at a high level that FI's very interested in talking to him. Alive only. Anyone who can provide his services to us will be appropriately, if quietly, rewarded.'

'That seems a viable alternative,' Fordyce said. 'I assume you can do it through the usual conduits – old boys and such?'

'I can.' Cisco started to rise. Fordyce held out a hand.

'A few minutes ago, I referred to the current level of excitement. Have you been following events?'

'Not really, sir. Since I got out of the hospital from the gassing, I've been concentrating on Wolfe.'

'Things have been a little unusual of late. Quite some time ago, we lost one of our spyships. The *Trinquier*, which was operating under civilian cover as an exploration vessel, vanished. Then an investigative team – straightforward scientific chaps – on one of the Al'ar homeworlds disappeared, after making some very aberrant screams for help. We had to make some threats in the scholarly community to keep that silent. Finally, we sent out a task force – six ships, including the *Styrbjorn* – seven weeks ago, to investigate along the *Trinquier*'s projected mission plan. The entire task force has fallen out of communication. We're presuming all six ships are lost, with no explanation whatever.'

Cisco sat down heavily. 'The *Styrbjorn*? I used that ship a few times. Sharp crew. Good captain. There's no way they could be surprised – or get into an accident.'

'Unusual, isn't it?' Fordyce said. 'I'm starting to get a very strange feeling. We may be in for *extremely* interesting times.'

EIGHT

'So it's just like the old-fashioned romances. Logic – common sense – probability are discarded, and one man defeats an entire kingdom,' Kristin said. 'You have the Lumina, and we Chitet have nothing.' She sighed, got up from the control chair, and went to Wolfe. 'I suppose you'd better hold true to the romance and kiss the princess you've won.'

'That I can do.'

After a while, she pulled back. 'Although I'm not much of a princess.'

'You're more of one than I'm a prince,' Joshua said.

'So you have me to do with what you will. What do you will?'

'Let us see,' Joshua said, twirling nonexistent mustachios. 'First I shall remove all your clothes except your space boots. Then slather you with freshly made tartar sauce. I'll wake the six furry creatures I have back in cold storage . . .'

Kristin laughed. 'I never realized you had a sense of humor before.'

'I generally don't, when somebody's got a gun on me.'

'No, seriously, what . . .'

The ship jolted, went in and out of N-space. Wolfe's stomach crawled. Kristin slid out of his lap as he came out of the chair. 'Not good,' he said. 'Ships aren't supposed to do that without giving hints. Let's go see the worst.' He started for the engine spaces.

Four hours later, they knew the worst.

'Less than sixty drive-hours and this drive'll make a good ship anchor,' Wolfe said. 'Damn these bargain-basement yachts.'

He called up a gazetteer onscreen and opened a voice sensor.

'Nearest inhabited planet,' he said.

The screen blinked twice, then an entry scrolled:

Ak-Mechat VII. Class 23. Currently exploited for minerals. Est. pop. 7,000. No controlled field. No cities. Three populated sites, little better than mining camps, are located as shown . . .

Figures scrolled.

'Two jumps,' Wolfe said. 'Not good. Then a goodish chug on secondary. And it's a bit chilly. I'm not considering hollering for help.'

'Is there any other choice?' Kristin asked.

'Surely. Press on regardless for real civilization and hope my mechanical diagnostic abilities are pessimistic.'

'Could they be?'

'No.'

'I just realized I always wanted to visit this Am-Kechat.'

'Gesundheit. But it's Ak-Mechat.'

Kristin quietly slid open the hatch to the small freight compartment. The space was empty, except for the Great Lumina. It hung in midair, fluorescing colors. She heard, over the increasingly shrill hum of the ship's drive, deep, slow breathing, coming from nowhere. She heard the clank of metal; she saw a thin piece of alloy steel lift, stand on end, then bend in an invisible vise. The steel clanged to the deck and Joshua appeared. He was naked, drenched in sweat. For an instant Kristin didn't register. 'You did that,' she said.

Wolfe took several more breaths before he nodded. 'I still don't quite have full control. I wanted the metal to bend, and then fall slowly to the deck.'

'When you do — what then?'

Wolfe shook his head. 'I can't tell you. And I doubt if you'd believe me, anyway.'

'I just read, in one of your books, about a queen who believed as many as six impossible things before breakfast. Try me.'

'All right. I want to use the Lumina to close a door, or maybe seal a door. Something that I think's here, with us in this spacetime, has to be either destroyed or put on the other side. And then the door must be sealed.'

'I have no idea what you're talking about.'

Joshua picked up a towel from the deck, wiped his forehead. 'Neither do I, most times. Forget about it. I'm for a shower, anyway.'

'Need your back scrubbed?'

'Always.'

Kristin rolled her head back and screamed as Wolfe drove within her, holding her knees crooked in his elbows, forearms pulling her against him.

She came back to herself, was aware of hot water needling her face, her breasts. Wolfe set her down. She managed a smile. 'I was somewhere else,' she said.

'So was I,' Joshua said. He kissed her, eased her feet to the deck.

'What are you going to do about me?' she asked.

'Not sure,' Wolfe said, picking up the soap from the deck. 'I guess I'll turn you around and scrub your back. Like this.'

'Mmmh. No. Stop for a minute. I meant – you aren't going to let me come with you.'

Wolfe's hand stopped for a time, then continued, rubbing in a small circle. 'Lady,' he said slowly, 'I don't think you want to come with me.'

'Why not? I'm not going back to the Chitet.'

'My turn to ask why not,' Wolfe said.

'I'm not sure yet,' Kristin said. 'But – something died. Changed, anyway, when Master Speaker Athelstan got killed.' She was silent for some time. 'No,' she said softly. 'I'm lying. Things changed some time before that. After – after we started making love.'

'Sex shouldn't change what you believe,' Joshua said. 'Or the way you live.'

'No,' she said softly. 'No, it shouldn't.'

Again there was a long silence. Joshua leaned close, whispered in her ear.

She giggled, bent forward a little, hands on her upper thighs. 'Like this?'

She gasped.

'Like that,' Joshua managed.

They came out of N-space on the fringes of the Ak-Mechat system. Wolfe went back to the drive chamber, ran a diagnostic program, and returned to the bridge. 'That drive is about as defunct as it's possible to get without going bang or maybe even thud,' he announced. 'I can't chance an in-system jump. So it's a long, hard drive for planetfall. Get out a good book.'

Kristin slept, her breathing a gentle bubbling.

Joshua lay beside her, *feeling* out. He *felt* the red, the burn, the soundless buzzing insect roar of the life-form that had destroyed the Al'ar's universe and was reaching into his own. He pulled back from the searing pain as it built.

He *felt* the red presence, the 'virus' far closer now than before.

Wolfe took the ship in slowly, making two transpolar orbits of Ak-Mechat VII as he killed speed and altitude. 'They weren't being funny about the field being unmanned,' he said. 'All I'm getting from down there is a navbeeper. Guess if anybody's got any incoming cargo they make private arrangements. We'll land next time around.'

But the *Eryx* didn't make it. Minutes short of the field, holding at about three hundred miles per hour, fire spurted out the drive tubes and the secondary drive went silent. Wolfe looked at Kristin, who was double-strapped into a control chair. 'This one might be tough. I'm gonna try to porpoise it in.'

He brought the ship down, down, until it hurtled barely twenty-five feet above rocky outcroppings. 'Last time around I thought I saw moors around about here,' he muttered. 'Come on, Heathcliff.'

He felt the controls getting sloppy, vague in his hands. They were fifteen feet above gray rocky death.

'Gimp one for the winner,' he prayed, flaring external foils, and the *Eryx* climbed briefly, shuddered, near stalling. He pushed the nose down, and the rocks were gone. Wolfe saw the many-shaded browns of water and land.

He yanked the main stick hard back. The *Eryx* tried to climb again, reached vertical, then stalled, toppled, and fell, pancaking onto the dark moor of Ak-Mechat VII.

Wolfe forced the fuzzing blur from his brain and pushed his eyelids up. The control room was a murky skew of wiring, screens, and instruments that'd popped from their housings. Kristin sagged in her chair, a bit of blood seeping from her nostrils.

The antigrav was gone, and the deck was at a twenty-five-degree angle. Wolfe unsnapped his safety belts and got up. His body was battered, bruised.

He staggered to Kristin and unfastened her. He started feeling for damage; her eyes came open. She coughed, then sat up quickly and vomited.

'I'm all right,' she said, wiping her mouth with the back of her sleeve. 'That was a hard one.'

'I think we'd best see about leaving,' Joshua said, as the ship rolled back until the deck was almost level. 'I don't think we're on any kind of firmness.'

He made his way to the lock, where there were three packs made from cut-apart crew coveralls. Two held supplies, the third the Lumina.

Wolfe manually cycled the inner lock, went through the chamber, peered through the tiny bull's-eye, then opened the outer lock door.

The *Eryx* was half-buried in mire that was pulling the ship deeper second by second.

'Come on, lady. All ashore that's going ashore,' he shouted, grabbing the packs and muscling them to the lock. He chose a patch of muck that looked a bit more solid than the rest, and tossed one pack onto it. It didn't sink.

'Now you,' he said, and half threw Kristin after the pack. She landed half on the solid place, nearly slipped into the mud, but recovered.

Wolfe threw the other pack and the Lumina to her, poised, and jumped. He looked around. Close mountains rose gray against gray overcast, lighter gray clouds that looked like rain. Behind him were the foothills they'd almost crashed in. All around was the moor, stretching empty and brown, with dark waters ribboning through the land.

Beside them the *Eryx* rolled once more, and this time its open lock went under. Air gouted in bubbles, and the *Eryx* sank deeper and vanished. A single muddy bubble broke with a *glop*.

'At least we're not leaving footprints,' Wolfe said. He put the tied-together trouser legs of the pack holding the Lumina over his neck and tied the other, more unwieldy pack behind. He waved toward the mountains.

'Let's go find some civilization. I need a drink.'

They moved quickly, in spite of bruises and the swampy land. Joshua *felt* ahead, and went surefootedly from solid hummock to matted tuft, slowly heading toward the mountains where the gazetteer had said the mines were. He hoped they'd find the field first, and that it wouldn't be completely unmanned.

They'd made several miles when thunder growled, and they looked for shelter. A hilltop rose ahead, and they made for it. There were two large boulders with a patch of soft mosslike growth between, sloping down to a stretch of black, open water. Wolfe took Kristin's pack, unzipped it, and took out a rolled section of plas. He secured the plas to the boulders with paracord, then spread insul blankets under the shelter.

'A garden of unearthly delights, madam.'

Kristin looked about them. 'Actually, this *is* beautiful,' she said. 'Look at the way the moor goes on forever and ever, and the little flowers in the moss here.' She eyed the pool of water nearby. 'Would there be monsters in that?'

'Damfino,' Joshua said. 'Whyn't you go play bait? I'll try to rescue you before the horrid beasties get more than a nibble or two.'

She kicked moss at him, stripped off her coveralls and boots, and cautiously waded into the water. She kept her gun in one hand for a while, then set it close at hand on the bank and started splashing water about. 'Come on, you filthy disbeliever. Clean your vile hide,' she called.

Wolfe obeyed, taking soap down. They washed, shivering as it grew colder, and the storm grew closer.

'Look,' Kristin pointed into the water. A foot-long brown creature drifted past her foot. 'A fish?'

'Maybe.'

'Could we eat it?'

'Maybe. Come on, Lady Crusoe. Later for the local fauna. We brought dinner.'

They'd finished the self-heating ship rations before the storm broke, and rain came down in soft, drifting waves around the shelter, beading on the plas, then pouring down it. Joshua leaned out and let rain drizzle on his tongue, feeling like a boy. Bitter, but drinkable, he thought, and ducked back into the shelter.

Kristin, aided by a small flash propped on a rock, was arranging the blankets. She slid into the improvised bed. 'Are you planning to sit up all night?'

Joshua joined her, lying back against the moss. Kristin turned the flash off and put her head on his shoulder. After a while, she sighed. 'This is nice. It's like this is the only world there is.'

'Maybe it'd be nice if it were.'

'Why couldn't it be? We could eat fish, and – and maybe the moss is edible. We could live on love for our desserts. These shipsuits won't ever wear out. And maybe you'd look good in a long beard, my little hermit of Ak-Mechat.'

Wolfe laughed, realizing the sound was almost a stranger.

Kristin ran her fingers over his lips. 'I do *like* this,' she said again. 'All alone on what feels like an island.'

'Thus proving John Donne a liar,' Wolfe said, yawning.

'I know who he was, you overeducated name-dropper,' Kristin said. 'I had to analyze the illogic of some Christian thinkers when I was in creche, and he was one of them.'

'Damned odd training the Chitet have for their war-riors,' Wolfe said.

'But I didn't think John Donne was always wrong. We all *are* part of the main, aren't we?'

'Hasn't been my experience,' Wolfe said, voice chilling, remembering a teenage boy in an alien prison camp, alone, staring down at rough graves.

'Or have you just chosen not to be a player?' Kristin asked. 'I read the fiche Chitet Intelligence had, Joshua. It was pretty scanty, but it said you were a prisoner of the Al'ar when you were a boy, and then you escaped and were a soldier until the Al'ar vanished. Perhaps if I'd gone through something like that, I wouldn't feel connected to the main very securely either.'

'Sometimes,' Joshua said, 'it's the least painful way.'

'Which is why you've gone through so much for the Lumina. Just for your own benefit. Of course.'

Wolfe was quiet for a very long time.

'You Chitet sharpen your razors way too damned much,' he said. 'Goodnight.'

The field was as advertised – nothing more than a square mile of hardpack, with reflectors at the perimeter. There was no sign of life. Two stripped wrecks lay drunkenly nearby, not far from a long shed, with the navbeacon in a square cupola atop it.

The shed was unlocked, and had a sign, stamped in dura-lumin:

Welcome to Ak-Mechat Vll.
Feel free to use any of the mokes inside. There are
three destination settings: Graveyard, Lucky Cuss,
and Grand Central. If you break one of them, fix it
or leave some credits so we can. It could be a long
hike for the next sourdough.

'I was hoping,' Wolfe said, 'there might be at least a watch-man with a com we could rent to call offworld. Let alone something like a freelancer with a ship for hire. Ah, for the rough freedom of a pioneer world.' He scanned the sign again. 'Naturally, according to the gazetteer, Graveyard's the biggest mining town. Wonder who the cheery bastard was that named it?'

'Why didn't they build the field near the mines?' Kristin asked. 'Or relocate it, once they found whatever they're digging out.'

'A lot of people like to see visitors coming from a long way off,' Joshua said. 'Or maybe none of them could agree about where the new field ought to go. The less I try to figure out why people do things, if I don't have to, the better I sleep at night.'

'Joshua, do we have enough credits to get someone to pick us up?'

'Probably,' Wolfe said. 'But we're not looking for simple transport. At least not for long. Eventually, I need a ship of my own. I'm pretty sure they don't run passenger lines where I'm headed. But there's all kinds of ways to pay for things. Mount up, and let's see if we can make Graveyard before dusk.'

The moke was as simple as engineering could make it: a nearly rectangular craft with a bench seat behind an open windscreen, a small cargo department, controls for start-ing/stopping the drive, a joystick, an altitude control, and the three buttons for the programmed destinations, with a small satellite-positioning screen that gave nav instruc-tions.

Wolfe and Kristin loaded aboard the least-battered moke, lifted it out of the shed, and followed the screen's directions. The moke beeped if they tried to make any devi-ation from the preset course.

It grew colder the closer they got to the mountains, and clouds lowered. A wind spat flurries of snow into the cockpit. They were moving uphill, following a track that had been leveled some time ago by earth-moving machinery, curving between trees, storm-twisted evergreens with hand-size leaves.

'We're not going to make it before nightfall,' Wolfe said. 'Let's start looking for the least dismal place to camp.'

A creek crashed over rocks not far from the trail, near a downed tree and a cluster of rocks that would serve for a windbreak. They grounded the moke and lifted out their packs. Wolfe used the plas to form another tent with the downed tree as a back, and Kristin spread the blankets. He found dead branches for a fire, piled them high, and sparked them into smoky life with his blaster on low.

'What do you want to eat?' he asked. 'Stew, featuring the ever-popular mystery meat, or seven-bean cassoulet?'

'Let's go with the stew,' Kristin said. 'The tent's too small to chance the cassoulet.'

Wolfe set out two mealpaks, then opened the improvised pack that held the Lumina. 'I'd like to try something,' he said, 'and I need a lab rat.'

'Charming way to put it,' Kristin said, sitting crosslegged on the blanket. 'And I can't say I care for doing anything with *that*.'

'Why not? It's just a tool that was built by some weird-looking folks.'

'There's too much blood – too much strangeness about it,' Kristin said. 'But go ahead. What are you going to try to do?'

'I won't tell you – I don't want to suggest anything. But whatever you feel like doing – try not to do it.'

Joshua knelt, set the Lumina in front of him, and breathed deeply, slowly, for several minutes. Then his breathing came quickly, and his hands came out, palms up.

The gray, nondescript stone flamed to life.

Wolfe's fingers curled, and the heels of his hands touched. Kristin started to get up, then sank back. She moved once more, returning to her cross-legged position as Wolfe's breath exploded out.

'No,' he said. 'It didn't work.'

'You wanted me to get up, and go out to the lifter, right?'

'I did.'

'Why didn't the Lumina make me do it? You've used it to kill people. Why did it fail on something simple?'

'I don't know.' Wolfe thought about it. 'Maybe because you're close to me – maybe because you're strong-willed. Or maybe I didn't have a gut-drive to make you do something.'

'So you're not an Al'ar,' Kristin said.

'No.'

The thought flashed:

Not yet. Wolfe thought – hoped – he felt relief. 'All right,' he said. 'Once more. Think of something. Anything.'

Kristin closed her eyes and was silent. Wolfe began breathing rhythmically once more.

His breath pattern stopped.

'A black tube,' he said. 'With something white, reflecting at the top. Some sort of industrial tool?'

'I'd give that one a close, but lousy on the interpretation. I was thinking about that formal you bought for me, back on Rogan's World, that I never had a chance to wear. With pearls.'

Wolfe looked at her for a long time. 'When – if – we get a chance, I'll get you some more pearls. And take you somewhere you can wear them.'

The dusk shattered in a scream, and Wolfe and Kristin rolled out of the shelter, guns ready.

A creature slashed madly at the ground, three yards on the other side of the moke. It was about twelve feet long, moved on four legs, and was almost Wolfe's height at the shoulder. It had long, dark brown hair, with two arms ending in scoop-shaped claws. It had no neck, and its skull was set close into its shoulders, with red, glaring eyes and dark incisors lining a circular mouth.

Kristin was kneeling, aiming, pistol butt cradled in her left palm, elbow on her knee as the monster screamed again, stumbled toward them, reared, claws stretching.

'Wait,' Wolfe said, his voice calm.

Reach . . . *nothing is here . . . calm . . . peace . . . not prey . . . not enemy . . . soft wind . . . not harm . . .*

The beast roared again, but this time not as loudly.

Calm . . . not prey . . . not enemy . . . wind . . . full belly . . . not-thirst . . . not-hunger . . .

The creature stood still for an instant, then turned, and, unhurriedly, shambled away.

Kristin let out her breath, lowered her gun. 'Now why did *that* work?'

'Let's add another guess,' Wolfe said. 'Fear is an excellent motivator.'

'Let's see if you're still at peak drive,' Kristin said. 'Read my mind now.'

Wolfe began to breathe, then a smile came. 'I got the signal perfectly.' He came toward her, lifted her in his arms, and carried her back into the tent. 'It didn't hurt that you were playing with the slider on your shipsuit,' he said.

'I'm still transmitting,' Kristin said throatily. 'Do you know how I want to love you?'

Her hands reached for his suit fastener and pulled it down; her head came forward and she took him in her mouth.

Early the next morning, they reached Graveyard.

NINE

EMERGENCY BULLETIN

LANCET, EDINBURGH, SCOTLAND, EARTH

A new, **highly infectious**, almost **invariably fatal** disease has been reported on several worlds at the fringes of the Federation and appears to be spreading rapidly with no discovered means of transmission.

SYMPTOMS AND SIGNS

The incubation period is unknown. The onset is very rapid, beginning with **intense pain** and a **high fever**, spiking as high as 106–109 degrees Fahrenheit. The pulse is rapid and thready and hypotension occurs. Almost immediate **inflammation** of the entire skin occurs, accompanied by **delirium**, **confusion**, and **incoordination**. The secondary stage of the disease produces what appear similar to **deep burns**, with destruction of the epidermis and dermis over the entire body. Unusually, the common loss of feeling accompanying deep burns never occurs, and **pain** continues to grow to an intolerable pitch. Patient

will enter advanced shock almost immediately,
while disease continues to destroy tissue. Death
generally follows within one to two hours after the
first symptoms are noted.

DIAGNOSIS

No recoveries known from full onset of disease. The
few survivors evinced only beginning signs of the
disease which then disappeared without any
treatment. Current fatality estimates: Over 99%.

ETIOLOGY

Unknown.

EPIDEMIOLOGY

Unknown.

TRANSMISSION

Unknown. Disease seems to strike at random. Two
reports, which cannot be taken as believable,
suggest those who had contact with the Al'ar or
who have 'psychic abilities' (phrase not admitted as
meaningful) are most at risk.

TREATMENT

None reported as effective. Patient should be treated
for extreme shock and given standard third-degree
burn treatments. Beyond that, treatment is
symptomatic.

WARNING WARNING WARNING WARNING

This disease is highly contagious, with no known
cure, and few reported recoveries. Patients should be
isolated, as should medical teams involved with

their treatment. Any information suggesting effective diagnosis or treatment should be immediately communicated with this station. To prevent possible panic, this information should be regarded as **highly secret** and should not be given to the general public or media.

TEN

The canyon was a deep vee-notch, with bluffs towering overhead. There were half a dozen mine entrances cut into the walls, high rectangles. Around each were scattered outbuildings.

There was a mine not far distant from the track, and as the moke slid past, a long line of ore cars slid out, controlled by a miner in a tiny overhead gravsled.

Kristin waved, but the man had no response until he realized what he was looking at. Then he waved back frantically, almost tipping over the 'sled.

'It appears,' Joshua said, 'that Graveyard's male-female ratio's about normal for the outback. What a place to settle down, Kristin. Total adulation until somebody gets drunk or jealous and grabs for a gun.'

They rounded a corner, and Graveyard spread below them. There was one central street, with a dozen dirt ruts radiating off it. Buildings, mostly prefab, dotted the canyon's floor and walls; rocky outcroppings covered with dirty snow lay between them. Above the town were large, two-story buildings.

'Superintendents' quarters,' Joshua said. 'Looks like things have gotten prosperous enough to have absentee owners.'

'How do you know?'

'If they were palaces, the owners'd be here. Hired help never gets mansions.'

'You've been on worlds like this.'

'I've been on worlds like this,' Wolfe agreed.

There was a hand-lettered sign:

GRAVEYARD
POP. 400

Someone had crossed out the population, and scrawled

500 and still booming!!

A man sat against the sign. One hand was propped up with a stake, and there was an ace of spades pinned to his open palm.

There was a fist-sized hole in his chest.

Joshua lifted an eyebrow but didn't say anything. He drove the moke down the central street at quarter speed, eyeing the buildings. Some appeared to be residences, others had signs: HARDWARE, EXPLOSIVES, COMPUTERS, GROCERIES, DRY GOODS, ASSAYERS, GALACTIC COMMUNICATIONS. There were other, larger signs: THE BIG STRIKE, HAMMAH'S HANGOUT, THE DEW DROP INN. Others were operated by those with less imagination or a more direct approach: GIRLS. ALK. GAMBLING.

They passed a small building with a very neat sign on it:

First Church of Christ, Lutheran
Pastor Tony Stoutenburg
'First Find Peace in Your Heart,
Then Give It to Others.'

'Now there,' Joshua said, 'is the loneliest man in Graveyard.' Kristin smiled briefly.

There was one ornate building on the street. It had started life as several modular shelters stacked and butted end-to-end, then workers had laboriously planed the twisted wood of Ak-Mechat into siding and fastened it into place. Others had cast and painted dragon heads from plas, and fastened them to the upper cornices.

There was a neat sign:

THE SARATOGA
Proprietor: Richard Canfield

On its porch, seemingly oblivious to the cold, was a tall, slender man with immaculate shoulder-length blond hair. He wore brown, formal-looking clothes, tucked into knee-high boots. Gems glittered at his cuffs, fingers, and one earlobe.

Wolfe raised a hand.

The man eyed Wolfe, nodded in return, and went back into the Saratoga.

'You know him?'

'I know who he is. And what he is. I was rendering professional courtesy.'

'Canfield? And a gambler?'

'Sharp, lady. Very sharp.'

Wolfe hesitated, then swung the controls of the moke around and grounded the machine in front of the Saratoga. 'This'll likely be the center of things,' he said. 'Maybe a little bit safer than renting a hovel on some backstreet. You go register, and I'll find out where to get rid of this beast.'

'Which brings up a question,' Kristin said. 'What name do I register under?'

'Our own, of course,' Wolfe said. 'Honest folk like us have nothing to hide.'

*

The room was fairly large, with a big bed, furniture that'd been antiqued with a blowtorch, and fake wood paneling. There were photographs on the walls, not holos, of ancient Earth scenes.

'You won't believe what this room costs,' Kristin said.

'Sure I would,' Joshua said. 'When you're the only game in town you set your own prices. Plus it's warm, dry, and better than a cribhouse. Just what a horny miner who's got more credits than sense wants when he gets paid. Or, since there's still some freelancers working the hills, when he thinks he's found something out there in the rocks.'

Kristin looked skeptical, bounced on the bed. 'At least it doesn't squeak,' she agreed.

'Fine. I don't believe in advertising,' Joshua said.

'Now what?'

'Now we start whining for help.'

'An open com line to where?' the small man with the large beak asked.

'I'll make the connection,' Wolfe said.

'I can't allow that.'

Wolfe dropped another bill on the counter. Then a second.

'All right,' the man said. 'Go in that booth there. I'll cut the controls through to you.'

'No,' Wolfe said. 'I want you to take a walk with my friend here. Show her some of the sights of Graveyard.'

'That's against corporate regulations!'

'I know you wouldn't dream of eavesdropping, but I'm a *very* private man,' Wolfe said. Three more bills fluttered down. The man put out a finger, touched them.

'For how long?'

'Not long,' Wolfe said. 'I'll go looking for you when I'm finished.'

*

'You've been out of touch for a while,' the distorted voice said from half a galaxy distant.

'Been busy.'

'So I gather,' the voice said. 'Don't know if I should be talking to you.'

'Oh?'

There was nothing but star-hum for a bit.

'All right,' the voice said reluctantly. 'I didn't get where I am by picking sides. FI would like to talk to you, real bad. And I don't mean with you as a free agent.'

'That's a known.'

'Did you know they've put the word out that anybody who grabs you and delivers you to Cisco or one of his bottom-feeders will get absolution? Alive only, which I suppose is a blessing.'

'I didn't. Am I hot publicly?'

'Not yet. But sooner or later some bravo'll open his mouth to the law.'

'Of course. You thinking about collecting?'

There was a blurt of static.

'Come on, Wolfe. I've seen what happens when some-body decides to pin your hide to the wall. I'm not an operator anymore, either. I just sit here and put people in touch with people they'd like to do business with.'

'Good,' Wolfe said. 'I don't like dealing with ambitious folks.'

'What do you need?' the voice asked. 'And what's in it for me?'

'I need a ship. Clean, fast, armed if possible.'

'How much you willing to pay?'

'Once I've got the ship – whatever the price tag is.'

'Once you've got the ship – come *on*, Wolfe. Once I've won the Federation lottery I can afford to buy a ticket. Ships are expensive.'

'They didn't used to be.'

'You didn't use to be Federation Intelligence's poster boy, either.'

'All right,' Wolfe said grudgingly. 'I'll hunt elsewhere.'

'No,' the voice said. 'I didn't say I couldn't get you one. But since it doesn't sound like you're sitting on barrels of credits right now, we'll have to find another way of payment.'

'That's what I told somebody not too long ago,' Wolfe said. 'So what's the tag?'

'Now we're doing business,' the voice said. 'Let me consider a couple offers I've got lying around.'

The voice went away. After a while it came back.

'There's this official on a certain world who seems to think he's a minor deity. Some people I know would like him to discover the joys of disembodiment and see what he's like in a new incarnation.'

Wolfe took a deep breath. 'I don't have much choice.'

'Good. This one won't be . . . Wait a second. Cancel the above, my friend. I've got something a whole lot better. And it won't mess with any morals you have left. The bodies shouldn't start bouncing until you're well out of town.'

'What is it?'

'Very simple. I've got a package – or rather some people I know have a package. They want it delivered to some people on another world.'

'What's the catch? Seems there's always enough hotrods around for courier runs,' Wolfe said.

'The package itself is hot – in both old-fashioned senses of the word. And the ship-driver I'm going to use I have – some small questions about. He may or may not have done me wrong a couple of years ago, so I want somebody I can trust with him.' The voice paused. 'Oh yeah. The people it's going to are also warmish.'

'Break it down, man.'

'Fine. I've got twenty-five pounds of fissionable material somebody on World A wants taken back to his, her, or their Old Sentimental Home, so a group of people who call themselves Fighters for Victory can build a little bitty bomb.'

Star-hum.

'You interested?'

'I'll do it.'

'Good man. I assume you'll have some specifications about being picked up, wherever you are, since you never were a trusting soul.'

'I will.'

'Nice to be partners again, Joshua.'

Wolfe let the little man have his office back. He seemed grateful, scurrying about like a chipmunk making sure his grain hadn't been discovered. Joshua looked for Kristin, found her down the street, talking to a medium-size cheerful man with a neatly trimmed beard.

'Joshua, this is Pastor – it is Pastor, right? – Stoutenburg. Joshua Wolfe.'

'Honored,' Wolfe said. 'Not sure I've met many ministers in my life.'

'We seem to be a declining breed,' Stoutenburg admitted. 'Christianity's a little old-fashioned and slow these days. But at least I'm not as extinct as priests.'

Wolfe inclined his head and didn't open the argument.

'Pastor Stoutenburg – Tony – has been giving me the history of Graveyard.'

'Such as it is,' Stoutenburg said. 'It can be summed up pretty briefly: Find minerals, dig minerals, use credits to look for new sins.'

'Has anybody had any success?' Joshua asked. 'With the sins, I mean.'

'Not that I'm aware of,' the preacher said. 'But they seem fairly content recycling the old ones.'

'Are you making any headway?'

Stoutenburg shrugged. 'I'm not looking for rice Christians, but I think I'm getting a few more folks at my services every week.' He grinned. 'Since we're on an Earth seven-day week, twenty-two-hour day here, I refuse to believe the reason is I'm the only place where you can come down on a Sunday morning without having to pay for quiet.'

'What's the town like?' Kristin asked.

'Really? Seven hundred to a thousand people, everyone dependent on the mines. There are, so far, half a dozen major veins of stellite. Most everyone except for me spends good weather wandering the hills looking for more, and the possibilities of success are good. It appears most people think riches are either here or right around the corner, so why not spend it like they already have it. I won't grant Graveyard the honor of calling it Satan's favorite resort – we're not big enough or decadent enough for that yet – but there's a sufficiency of people building its reputation.' Stoutenburg nodded with his chin. 'Here's one of our finest boosters.'

Wolfe turned and saw Canfield strolling toward them. Ten feet behind him were a very large man with a shaven head and an angry expression and a medium-size man clad in all gray. Both openly wore holstered pistols. Wolfe noted with interest the guns were heavy current-issue Federation military blasters.

'Morning, Father,' Canfield said. 'Who're your friends?'

Joshua introduced himself and Kristin.

'I don't suppose,' Stoutenburg said, 'that it makes any difference to remind you I'm not a priest, Canfield. Father doesn't apply.'

'Sorry . . . Father. It's easy to forget.' Canfield eyed Wolfe. 'So you're a guest at my establishment – and talking to the representative of the other half. Trying to copper your bets, Mister Wolfe?'

'No,' Joshua said. 'It was figured out a long time ago which way I'm intended.'

'Which is?'

Joshua smiled blandly. Canfield looked puzzled, then smiled in return.

'Are you planning on settling here in Graveyard?' he asked.

'We're just passing through.'

'Ah,' Canfield said. 'Well, may your stay be a successful one.' He inclined his head to Kristin, then moved on.

'I wonder if he'll ever figure out that we're all just passing through,' Stoutenburg said gently.

'Probably not,' Joshua said. 'His kind take their markers far too seriously.'

They were just finishing dinner when the shouting started in the nearby gaming rooms: 'Cheat . . . Bastard double-counter . . . Goddamned rayfield scummek . . .' Kristin swiveled; Joshua managed to watch out of the corner of his eye, still appearing disinterested.

Three men dragged a fourth out the casino entrance. One wore the green eyeshade of a croupier; the other two were the gray man and the shaven-headed behemoth who'd accompanied Canfield. The fourth wore the high plas boots of a miner and a clean, patched shirt and pants.

The miner broke free at the door and swung at the croupier. The man in gray struck him down from behind with an edged hand, and the big man kicked him hard six times. Now he had a broad smile on his face.

'Joshua! Do something,' Kristin hissed.

'No. Wrong time to play Samaritan.'

The big man stopped, walked around the miner, aimed carefully, and sent his boot crashing into the side of the man's head. The impact sounded mushy, as if bone had already been broken.

The other two picked up the motionless miner, pushed the outer door open, and threw him out into the street.

The big man swaggered back through the dining room, looking at each table, each diner. No one held his gaze for more than a moment. He stopped at Joshua and Kristin's table, and glowered at them. Joshua felt Kristin's hand slide to her waist, where her gun was hidden. Wolfe stared back at the big man, his face calm.

The man blinked, jerked his gaze away, and went back into the casino, the other two behind him.

'Poor planning,' Wolfe said as he picked up the dessert menu.

'Why? What?'

'A good gambling hell always has a back door,' he said.

Kristin said her appetite was ruined, so Wolfe called for the check and signed it. They started out.

'Wait,' Wolfe said. 'Let's look in the other room.'

Kristin started to object, then closed her mouth, followed him.

There were dice tables, a line of gambling machines, several green-topped tables where men with false smiles and quick hands waited. Canfield leaned against the bar in the back. He saw Wolfe and came to him.

'I'm surprised you haven't come in looking for action before,' he said.

'I'm afraid you misjudge me,' Joshua said. 'I'm not a gambling man.'

Canfield looked surprised, then recovered. 'Perhaps your lady?'

'She tried it once, but got bored with always winning,' Wolfe said.

Canfield smiled coldly, nodded, and returned to the bar.

'I'm afraid I misspoke,' Wolfe murmured. 'Playing at his tables would hardly be considered gambling.'

'I'm a little angry with you,' Kristin said.

'I know,' Joshua said. 'But we've got enough problems without taking on somebody else's. Besides, the Canfields are self-eliminating.'

Kristin climbed into bed, shut off her lamp, and rolled over with her back to Joshua.

Joshua was already dressed when Kristin woke.

'Joshua,' she said softly. 'I was wrong last night. We *do* have enough troubles of our own. Don't be mad at me.'

Wolfe came over, sat down on the bed. 'Funny, *I* was just going to apologize for last night. And I'm never mad at you.' He kissed her. 'I've just got some people I want to talk to. I've decided we need something to keep our minds busy until the ship gets here. So I'll meet you for lunch.'

He kissed her again, and she pulled the covers away. 'Now, don't do that,' he said. 'Or I'll never get out of here.'

'Would that be a bad thing?' she asked, her voice silky.

'As I said before, I refuse to get involved in theological disputes.'

Wolfe buzzed their room and asked Kristin if she wanted to meet him in the dining room.

As she crossed the lobby, Canfield approached her. 'Mrs. Wolfe . . .'

'The name is just Kristin,' she said.

'Kristin, then. I wanted to make sure I – or anyone else at the Saratoga – haven't done anything to upset either of you.'

'What makes you think we're angry?' Kristin asked, realizing with amusement she was echoing Wolfe's words.

'Well, I thought I recognized your friend as being one

who's of the sporting sort. I was wondering why he refused my invitation to join us at the tables, and wanted to make sure nothing was amiss.'

'Nothing's wrong, Mister Canfield. Perhaps Mister Wolfe just isn't sure you can cover the size of his bets.'

Canfield flushed, stammered. Kristin bowed and went on into the dining room.

Joshua rose, kissed her as he held a chair out. 'I saw you chatting with Canfield.'

'I was. He wanted to know if we were miffed at him '

'Miffed? No, we're not miffed,' Joshua said. 'He's upset because we didn't stumble into his thimbleriggery?'

'I assume that means a fixed game?'

'It does.'

'Well, then . . .'

Joshua laughed when Kristin told him what she'd said to Canfield. 'That must have tweaked him a little. By the way, some of the people I talked to said Canfield's not only got the Saratoga, but runs the games in three other places. Your friend Tony was right – he's hell-bent, pun possibly intended, on running this town. He also seems to have an interest in a couple of the bordellos, and owns a lot of the open property around Graveyard. And he buys any high-grade stellite that happens to come his way. For about thirty-five percent of the market value. The assay office pays sixty percent. But Canfield doesn't ask where you got it.'

'What's stellite?' Kristin asked.

'Interesting metal,' Wolfe said. 'Kind of pretty. Light purple in its natural state. High heat application can change the color to a dozen or more different shades. Corrosion-, wear-, stress-, and heat-resistant, very light-weight, so it's used for internal stardrive controls and other delicate, high-stress applications. Or machined, worked, and polished, it can be jewelry. Ultra-expensive. As I said, you've led a sheltered life, m'dear. If you'd seen the holos of the rich and insipid, you surely would've seen examples of it dangling hither and yon.'

'I've never been interested in yons,' Kristin said. 'Especially on the rich. So Canfield is the boss of this town?'

'Not quite yet,' Wolfe said. 'He'll need to own a mine or two before he can rename Graveyard. But he's working on it. Now, let's eat, for I've got to meet a man after lunch.'

'I want to come with you.'

'Sorry. I love you enormously. But this one's way too dirty for you. In the literal sense.

'What's the matter?'

Kristin was staring at him. 'You never used the word "love" before.'

Joshua met her eyes, then looked down at the menu. 'That's right,' he said after a while. 'I haven't, have I.'

Wolfe left the main street, hiking up a rutted sidetrack toward one of the mines. He appeared not to notice a medium-size man in gray following him from a distance.

There was no fence, no guard around the mine. He sauntered toward the yawning high-roofed horizontal main shaft. A man wearing a white safety helmet spotted him. 'Hey!'

Wolfe walked to him.

'What's your business?'

'Looking for a man named Nectan.'

'He's down th' hole. I'm Redruth, th' super. You ain't workin' for me, you ain't here. And you sure ain't goin' down. Too damned dangerous.'

'What happens when the owner comes to visit?'

'Huh?'

'Doesn't he have friends? Don't they get to see what's making him rich?'

'That's different!'

Wolfe extended a bill. 'Think of me as a friend.'

Redruth considered it, shook his head. 'Naw. Too damned dangerous.'

Another bill joined the first, then a third.

'You get killed, it's your ass.'

'I get killed, shove me up a drift, drop the ceiling, and swear you never saw me,' Joshua said.

Redruth grinned. 'Get a helmet an' ear protection from the toolman over in that shed. There'll be a lift goin' down in twenty minutes or so.'

Joshua nodded his thanks.

The man in gray watched from a distance.

The lift floated close to the high ceiling. The driver leaned back.

'You ever been in a workin' mine afore?'

'Not stellite. And not this big.'

''Kay. Thisun's a good 'un,' the driver said. 'No wood on th' planet t' speak of, so they pitpropped with metal, so it's safer'n your house.' A chain of ore cars rumbled past below, a man in a sled controlling it from above, and the two sleds slid past, almost bumping.

'Now's th' fun part,' the man shouted, and Wolfe's stomach moaned as the sled suddenly fell, straight down an absolutely vertical shaft.

'We bet on who c'n go down th' fastest,' the miner bellowed at Wolfe, apparently paying no attention to his controls.

'Let's lose this one,' Joshua shouted back.

'What?'

'Never mind!'

The miner pushed a stick forward, and the lift slammed to a stop. Joshua's guts didn't.

Breathe . . . breathe . . .

'That was interesting,' he shouted as a new noise grew around them.

'Yer all right, Mister. Most tourists puke f'r half an hour, I pull that on 'em.'

'I used to run a roller coaster in another life,' Wolfe said.

'What?'

'Never mind.'

The sled floated down another passageway as deep as the one far above them. Machines growled and groaned around them, seemingly without human control. Joshua spotted a few men here and there, keyboardlike control panels hung around their necks. Then the lift driver grounded the sled near a passage that led sharply upward.

'G'wan up th' slope to the face,' the miner shouted. 'Nectan's up there, likely. I'll wait here. Don't want t' get too close. I'm what they call claustrophobic.'

A long conveyor belt almost filled the shaft, and chunks of rock bounced along it toward the main passage. The air was hot and smelled of machine oil and ozone. In spite of the earmuffs, the grinding scream tore at Wolfe's hearing. At the end of the belt was a square machine with a metal-framed clear operator's cage on the side. The screeching stopped for an instant, the machine moved forward an inch or two on wide tracks, and the worm began tearing at the rock again. Wolfe climbed onto the machine's body, carefully made his way to the back of the cage, waited until the grinding stopped, then crashed his fist against the back of the cab.

A dirty face turned, eyes gaped in surprise, and the machine's howl lowered. The operator opened the door, motioned Wolfe inside.

There was a tiny seat beside the operator's station, and Wolfe sat. The man closed the door, and there was almost complete silence.

He grinned at Wolfe's expression. 'Like night 'n' day, don't it be? An' there's real air t' suck on.'

Wolfe nodded.

'So who th' hells're thou?'

'Joshua Wolfe.'

'I assume thou has business.'

'I do, Mister Nectan. I want to talk about the time you let a man named Canfield bankroll your prospecting.'

Nectan shook his head.

'Nay, nay. I learned m' lesson well. No need t' repeat it.'

'Left arm,' Joshua said. 'Broken in two places. Lost most of your teeth on one side. Four broken ribs.'

'An' still don't sleep right of a night,' Nectan said. 'So thou can be well outta here, an tell Canfield I said I'd naught speak, an' I'm a man of m' word.'

Wolfe looked at him, and Nectan started to get angry. He glared at Wolfe, then the anger faded from his face.

Wolfe was breathing slowly, regularly.

'Who're you – I mean, who're you with?'

'I'm with me,' Wolfe said. 'I collect all sorts of interesting facts. Sometimes I put them to use.'

'M' da always said I was born a fool an' I'd likely die one, t' boot,' Nectan grumbled. 'All right. You ask. I'll answer. An' th' only reason I'm doin' it is 'cause I hope one day Canfield reaches for something that's way beyond him.'

The man in gray watched Joshua Wolfe walk away from the mine, back toward Graveyard, and went after him.

The road wound down, through huge boulders, high piles of spoil. The wind was cold this high above the canyon floor, and the man pulled his coat tighter about his shoulders as he hurried downward. He came around a bend, saw the empty track in front of him, and swore. Wolfe must've started running.

He broke into a trot, then heard a metallic *snick* behind

him. The man skidded to a stop, almost falling. He lifted his arms away from his body very slowly.

'Good,' Joshua approved. 'Thought you'd recognize a safety going off.'

He walked forward, fished the man's pistol from its holster. 'Nice choice of iron,' he said. 'Anderson Variport. Just like the Federation big boys carry. Now let's step over here where it's peaceful, and have a chat.'

'How did you spend your day?' Joshua asked jovially.

'I went for a walk after you left,' Kristin said. 'And I ran into Tony — Pastor Stoutenburg.'

'Uh-oh,' Joshua said. 'You've got to watch those men of the cloth. First you're praying together, then — then they come up with strange ideas like marriage. Be careful.'

'I'm careful, you loon,' Kristin said. 'He was going out looking for funds —'

'Begging.'

'All right, begging. I asked if I could go with him. He said he'd rather I didn't, that he was going into the bars, and I might be misunderstood. I said I could handle things, and he said I could go.'

'How did you do?'

Kristin flushed. 'All right.'

'What's all right?'

She looked away, cheeks red. 'Seven hundred and ninety-seven credits, and two IOUs.'

'Good heavens.'

'Plus six proposals of marriage, seven miners who wanted something else, and a woman in one of the girlhouses who wondered if I was looking for a job.'

'Twice good heavens. What a productive morning. It looks like you've found a real home here in Graveyard.'

'Tony said he would've thought he was lucky if he'd made fifty credits,' Kristin said.

'There's nothing like good works,' Joshua said.

Kristin noticed Joshua was wearing a gun. Not the small pistol she knew he had tucked out of sight in his belt, but a large, heavy military blaster worn on an equally military-looking weapons belt. 'What's that for? Are we expecting trouble?'

'I *always* expect trouble. I decided I needed to be a little more open in my habits. And somebody I met this afternoon decided to give this to me.'

'Where did you go?'

'To chat with a miner. Fascinating line of work. I may take it up as soon as hell gets a nice ice-frosting.'

'About Canfield?'

'About Canfield. And then I had another little talk with one of his men – that charmer in gray who helped Canfield's main bully the other night, who used the name Saratov. The bald goon's chosen name in these parts, by the way, is Brakbone. Delightful folks around here, I must say.'

'Joshua, what are you doing? Why are you doing this?'

'I got bored,' Wolfe said. 'And Mister Canfield irritates me.'

'How did you get the man in gray to talk to you?'

'I exerted charm and lovability.'

'What's he going to tell Canfield?'

'I seriously doubt,' Wolfe said, 'if he'll be communicating anything of import within our lifetimes. Now, is there anything on the wine list that's dated in years instead of days of the week?'

Kristin woke to the soft thump of Wolfe's bare feet hitting the floor, then saw him silhouetted against the open window, naked, with his pistol ready. Her own reflexes cut in, and she was crouched beside the bed, pistol ready.

'I heard shots,' Wolfe said. 'Two of them.' He cautiously

peered through the window. 'Lights, about a block down,' he said. 'Other people heard them as well.'

The bedside lamp flickered on, and Wolfe started dressing.

'What're you doing?'

'Involving myself in other people's business.'

'Why?'

'To redeem myself in your eyes and esteem.'

Before she could decide whether to laugh or worry, Wolfe had his boots and coat on, and was at the door. He buckled his gun belt on.

'Join me if you want. I think this is going to be interesting. The pot may have boiled before I put it on the fire.'

Ten minutes later Kristin was dressed and in the street. So was half the population of Graveyard. They were crowded around a small semicircular hut just off the central street. The door stood open, and, as she approached, two men dragged out a third, whose head was lolling.

Kristin heard him muttering: 'Di'n't do it . . . di'n't do nothin' . . . jus' wan'ed sleep . . . had a li'l too much t' drink . . . mad at Raff, wan'd t' sleep it off . . . woke up an' he was dead . . .'

Somebody shouted, 'Lock him up in the assayer's vault.'

Someone else bellowed, 'Why waste th' time? He blew off Raff . . . do th' same with him! Right here, right now!'

There were yells of agreement, but the two men bulled through the crowd without yielding.

Canfield stood near the door to the hut.

'Come on, boys,' he shouted. 'Settle down! Killing Steadman won't bring del Valle back, now will it? Come on, now. Drinks are on me! Let's give old Raff a proper sendoff!'

The crowd clamored approval, streamed toward the Saratoga.

Kristin saw Wolfe walk up to Canfield and ask him something. Canfield frowned, snapped a retort. Wolfe stood there, waiting. Canfield grimaced, then nodded his head. Wolfe went into the hut.

Canfield hurried after the crowd, but Kristin followed Wolfe.

There was a body sprawled on the floor to the right of the entrance. A man with a medical hardcase was bent over the corpse, and there were three kibitzers. He stood. 'One shot. Took del Valle just below the sternum. Death would have been almost instantaneous.' He clucked. 'Amazing Steadman could shoot that straight, as inebriated as he appears.'

'A minute of your time, Doctor?'

The man surveyed Joshua.

'And who're you?'

'Someone who's curious.'

'Go on to the bar with the others. I'd as soon not go through the gore more'n half a dozen times. And I need a drink.'

'As a favor, Doctor.'

The man looked angry, then, as Wolfe held his eyes, his face softened. 'You're new,' he said. 'Anything to do with any kind of law?'

'Not for a while,' Wolfe said.

'That's a pity. We could use some around here. All right. Hell, I probably need to rehearse what I'll tell those drunk yahoos anyway. The dead man's Raff del Valle. Exploratory geologist and miner. Highly respected. Which means he found two mines, made a mint, and let everybody help him drink it away. Didn't bother him – he said he liked looking for it as much as finding it. Maybe more, because he was sober then, and he had a temper when he set to drinking.

'The guy who shot him's Lef Steadman. He picked Raff up out of the gutter, moved him into his hooch here, bankrolled him for his last *Wanderjahr* looking for traces, and was his partner. Fifty-fifty split, I heard, expenses off the top. Del Valle came back three days ago happier'n a pig in shit, which meant he'd found something.

'Or thought he had. Anyway, he started drinking, and he and Steadman had a series of arguments. They didn't get loud, so nobody knew what they were about. Probably one of 'em wanted to change the split, assuming del Valle got lucky for a third time. Anyway, things finally broke down to a shouting match at the Big Strike, and Steadman stomped out, swearing he was going to hammer Raff the next time he saw him.

'Pretty obvious what happened. Del Valle must've not thought Steadman was serious and come back here with a skinful. Came in the door, and saw Steadman laying for him. He had time to get a shot off – which drilled a hole over by that window – then Steadman put him in his meat locker. Simple enough. Now all we've got to do is figure what to do about Steadman.'

'What're the choices?' Wolfe asked.

'Either he gets lynched, which is the odds-on favorite, 'cause Raff was a popular lush, as I said. Or else somebody takes pity and busts Steadman out and he makes tracks for Lucky Cuss or Grand Central, and tries to get offplanet before somebody with a grudge happens to run into him.'

The man shrugged.

'I'd go seventy-thirty. Against.'

Wolfe's lips quirked. 'I'll take a hundred of that.'

The man looked surprised. 'Why?'

'Let's say – I like the long shots.'

The doctor smiled. 'Why not? Give me a chance to even up what I owe Canfield. Jung – Nyere – you heard him. You're . . .'

'Wolfe. Joshua Wolfe. You can find me at the Saratoga.'

The other two men nodded understanding.

'Good,' the doctor said. 'Now, if you two'll give me a hand with the body, I'll lock up here.'

'If it's no bother,' Wolfe said, 'I'll take care of that for you, and turn the key over to Canfield.'

'You playing detective?' The doctor didn't wait for a response. 'Surely. Why not. Give Steadman a chance. A man ought to go down with all his colors flying. Come on, boys. Let's get the stiff on ice. I'm real thirsty.'

Kristin waited until the three had left, half dragging the corpse. 'So you don't think it happened that way?'

'Don't think. Know.'

'How? Through the Lumina?'

'No. Pure common sense. Look around.'

Kristin calmed herself and tried to breathe the way she remembered Wolfe doing, tried to blank her mind and turn it into a receptor.

The building was about ten by forty feet. The main room took up most of that. To the rear on the right was a closed door Kristin assumed hid the fresher, and on the left a divider that marked off the cooking area.

There was one door, and three windows, one larger one on the side where del Valle's body had lain, two smaller ones on the other side. There wasn't much furniture – two chests, one open wardrobe crudely made from shipping crates, two beds, two improvised desks. There were two boxes holding books and fiches by each bed, and a larger box with a lid at the foot of each bed.

Kristin looked at the titles. One held *Elements of Geology*, *Mineral Analysis*, *Field Guide to Ak-Mechat*, other geological titles and, incongruously, Burton's multivolume *A Thousand Nights and One Night*. The other bookcase contained books with titles such as *Million-Credit Thinking*, *Turn Yourself into a Money Machine*, and *Self-Improvement Through Riches*.

'Just from their reading matter,' she said, 'he's guilty as blazes.'

Wolfe chuckled from where he was quickly rummaging through del Valle's box of papers. 'Did you find anything that looks official? Like maybe a land claim?'

'No. Do you want me to go through this box? It'll probably have his papers.'

Wolfe crossed to it, quickly sifted through the few papers and fiches that defined Steadman's life. 'Nothing here, either,' he said. 'And we're running short of time, I think. I can smell a lynch mob in the building. Look at this.' He held out a pistol. 'This is Steadman's gun. It was lying on the floor. I picked it up in the confusion.'

'Pretty standard,' Kristin said. 'A 12-mill-bell Remington-Colt.'

'Take a sniff of the barrel.'

Kristin obeyed. 'Nothing.'

'Like it maybe hasn't been fired for a while? Can't tell by the magazine, which is only half-charged. Now look at the setting.'

'It's on wide aperture.'

'Try to reset it.'

Kristin pushed at the inset lever below the blaster's bell mouth. She grimaced. 'Stuck. Evidently Steadman didn't trust his ability at snap-shooting – and didn't clean his gun very often.'

'Interesting observation,' Wolfe said. 'The way the story goes is del Valle came into the hut. He saw Steadman sitting behind his desk – there. Steadman had his pistol aimed, but he was drunk. Del Valle had time to draw, and shoot. He put a nice neat – notice, he *was* a marksman – hole over here by this window. Before he could correct his aim, Steadman dropped him. Then Steadman passed out until the crowd got here. Nice neat murder for profit, blown because the idiot had to get drunk before he had courage enough to kill Raff del Valle, and got himself too drunk.'

'So they say,' Kristin said.

'Uh-huh. And there's something else interesting about this window we really don't have time for. Come on. We've got to wake up the land office clerk.'

Fortunately the clerk slept in a small apartment above his office. Wolfe bullied him into full consciousness, asked two questions and got sleepy, grumbled answers, and told the man to go back to sleep.

'Now, let's see what's going on at the Saratoga.'

A slattern was draped over a bench outside the hotel muttering, 'Hangin's too good . . . hangin's too good . . .'

'I see the elite have already assessed the situation,' Wolfe said. 'Keep your gun ready.'

They went inside.

The dining room and bar were full, and the harried barkeeps were simply giving bottles to anyone who asked. Two women who took their hair color and personality from a bottle were behind the beer taps, and the room was a shout of judgment.

A miner stood on top of the bar, shouting, 'Dunno why we're all jus' talkin' . . . We know who done it, an' likely why, t' screw poor Raff outta his new claim . . . why wait?'

There was a roar of approval.

'We ain't got no courts anyhow,' he finished in a surprisingly reasonable tone.

Canfield's bodyguard, Brakbone, leaped onto the bar. 'He's right! Let's get this thing over with right now!'

'No!' someone cried out behind Joshua. 'He's wrong!'

Wolfe – and the crowd – turned, and saw Stoutenburg at the entrance.

'Oh shit,' somebody said in the silence. 'Now we gotta get preached at.'

There was laughter.

Stoutenburg ignored the comment, pushed his way through to the bar. 'I know a lot of you – most of you – think I'm no more than some sort of nag. But the book I believe in says "Judge not, lest you be judged." Think about it for a minute, and don't pay any heed to whether Somebody greater than you said it that you maybe haven't learned to believe in it yet. Think about what would happen if you made a mistake – had too much to drink or smoke or 'ject, and you did something terrible. Would you want somebody deciding what to do with your life right then, in the heat of passion? Especially if they'd been drinking, smoking, or whatever? Shouldn't a man's life be considered in calmness, sobriety?'

'Naw,' somebody shouted. 'Di'n't somebody say you get a jury of your peers? Ol' Lef, he got messed up an' kilt Raff, so we got messed up an' now we're gonna kill him. Ain't that justice?'

The mob, enjoying itself, roared with laughter.

Stoutenburg flushed, held his anger back.

'Come on, Tony,' Canfield said, coming out from behind the bar. 'Father. We respect you for being honest, but nobody believes that old-fashioned stuff.'

'Don't they?' Stoutenburg shouted.

Canfield pretended to survey the crowd.

'Doesn't look like it from here. Looks to me like everyone's pretty happy with the decision that's been reached. Except for maybe Steadman.'

He waited until the laughter died.

'What do you want, Father? A trial?' His voice turned mocking. 'The preacher wants a trial.

'That sounds very good,' Canfield went on. 'But just for openers, who'll defend Steadman? We've all got to live with each other come tomorrow morning.'

'I don't,' Wolfe said.

Silence grew, except for a drunk giggling in a corner. Wolfe walked to the bar, the sound of his bootheels very loud. 'I don't,' he said once more. 'Let's have a trial. I'll defend Steadman.'

'And who the blazes are you?' somebody shouted.

'Get the hell outta here,' Brakbone snarled. 'Goddamned outsiders got no right to be talkin' anyway.'

'Who made you an insider?' Wolfe asked. 'Canfield imported you two months ago, and all of a sudden you're an original settler?'

Brakbone stepped back, suddenly unsure.

'All right,' Canfield said loudly. 'Let's have a trial. That'll make everything acceptable, won't it? I'll be the prosecutor. Joshua Wolfe here'll try to fake us out. But we know what the verdict'll be, don't we?'

There were shouts of agreement.

'Somebody fetch Steadman,' someone yelled. 'Man oughta get a fair hearing to his face before we kill him.'

Lef Steadman was trembling like he had a fever, partially fear, partially the wake-up pill that he'd been fed that sobered him but also produced a hangover like the unoiled hinges of hell.

'Why're you doin' this?' he whispered to Wolfe.

'I'm a good citizen and your new best friend,' Joshua said. 'Now keep your damned mouth shut, no matter what, or I'll rip your windpipe out.'

Canfield paced back and forth, clearly enjoying the situation. Kristin stood next to Stoutenburg. Wolfe noted with approval she had one hand inside her jacket, on her gun butt.

'We don't need to worry about oathing,' Canfield said. 'We can tell who's lying and who's not. Prosecution goes first. Get Doctor Nonhoff up here.'

The doctor wasn't much soberer than the rest of the

crowd by then, but he made his way through what he'd found, and what he thought had happened.

'Your witness,' Canfield said.

'No questions.'

'All right,' Canfield said. 'I guess the only other testimony we need is from Lef Steadman.'

Steadman stood up, and somebody threw a bottle at him. It missed and smashed against the back of the bar.

'Hold it down,' Canfield shouted. 'Anything else like that and I'll close the bar!'

Steadman told his story. Yes, he was Raff del Valle's partner. Maybe former, after tbe argument last night. Yes, he'd put up the credits for him to go out on an exploratory survey looking for a new stellite vein on a fifty-fifty split if del Valle found something. He'd even let him live with him when he came back into Graveyard from the mountains.

Del Valle had come back boasting that he'd found something big, bigger than either of his other two strikes. Steadman had suggested they register the claim right away, but del Valle had said there was no hurry. He'd filled out the form papers, and they would take them to the land agent in the morning.

In the meantime, he was thirsty. So they started from bar to bar. Steadman kept arguing with the older man, begging him to get the registration filed, that he might get drunk and blab the location, and somebody would steal their claim.

'I was drinkin', but not as heavy as Raff, an' he lost his temper, like he does – did – when he's sweet as a peach. He finally said he was goin' for me, an' I best clear out. I got out of whatever place we was drinkin' at, an' thought I'd best go back to th' hooch, an' get some sleep. I made it, an' remember losin' my guts outside. Thought I'd best sit up, try'n sober up some, so I wouldn't go an' puke in my blankets. I must'a passed out like that.'

He stopped. There was silence.

'Then shoutin' sorta brought me to,' he said, 'an' there were all those people around, an' Raff was dead on the floor.'

'Very nice,' Canfield said. 'I don't think diminished capability is much of a defense. If we even believe it. I think he was pretending to be as drunk as he was, setting up an alibi. Your witness, Wolfe.'

'One question,' Wolfe said. He took the Remington-Colt from his belt. 'Is this yours?'

'I dunno,' Steadman said. 'Lemme have a look at it.'

Wolfe gave it to Steadman, and a gun jumped into Brakbone's hand. Steadman yelped in panic.

'Don't worry,' Joshua said. 'It's defanged. Nice piece, by the way.'

Brakbone growled, reholstered his pistol.

'Yeah. It's mine,' Steadman said. 'Had it around for a couple of years, only started carrying it a month or so ago. Sorry I had to look at it, but I ain't much of a pistoleer.' He handed the weapon back to Joshua.

'No further questions,' Wolfe said.

Steadman lifted his head, and there was black fear in his eyes.

'What kinda defense are you? You gonna let them just kill me?'

'Go sit down,' Wolfe said. 'And remember what I told you.' Deliberately, he let his hand brush his gun butt. Steadman flinched and stumbled back to his chair.

'I think we've got enough,' Wolfe said, and voices in the crowd echoed him: 'Yeah. Kill the bastard!' 'Shoot 'im!'

'Not quite yet,' Wolfe said calmly. 'Let's consider a couple of things. Start with the sequence of events. According to Doctor Nonhoff, Steadman was sitting at his desk when del Valle came in. He was drunker than a lord, so he would've had to have the pistol in his hand, waiting to assassinate his partner. But somehow he didn't shoot first. Del Valle hauled iron and, at about seven feet, put his bolt three feet away from Steadman, and punched a hole in the wall next to the window. Maybe he was drunker than Steadman by then. But that's still pretty crappy shooting.

'At that point Steadman came to enough to shoot del Valle quite accurately in midchest. A nice neat hole, according to Doctor Nonhoff. Anyone want to see Steadman's pistol? Here,' Wolfe said, handing it to a burly miner. 'You've been hollering for a lynching loud enough. Take a look at the gun.'

The miner fumbled it in his hands. 'It's a gun.'

'Brilliant, sir,' Wolfe said. 'Notice it's set on wide aperture. To make the hole Doctor Nonhoff said it did, it should've been set on narrow. If Steadman had shot del Valle the way it's set now, it would've made a big wide messy crater, right? So reset it for me.'

The man pushed the small lever, then pushed harder, his teeth set. 'There! Damn thing felt like it was rusted solid!'

'Indeed,' Wolfe said. 'Does anyone but me think it's interesting that when I picked the gun up in Steadman's shack, it was on wide aperture? And remember he just said he wasn't much of what he called a pistoleer, so as a gunfighter he would've wanted a wide shotgun blast to have any hope of hitting anything. So what must've happened was he reset the aperture, shot del Valle, then reset it before he passed out.'

There were mutters. Somebody said, 'That's not enough.'

'Another little thing,' Wolfe said. 'Pity that Remington-Colt's not a powder-burner, so this isn't that indicative either. But the pistol doesn't smell like it's been fired anytime since the Al'ar War to me.'

'Like the man told you,' Canfield said. 'That *isn't* enough. If Brown here could've moved it once, someone could've moved it earlier.'

'Yeah,' Brakbone said. 'Like him.' He pointed to Joshua. 'You're the on'y one said it was set on wide.'

The crowd agreed, but not as loudly as before.

'Sure I could've changed it,' Wolfe said. 'But let's assume for the moment I didn't. Let's try another explanation for what happened. Del Valle made an ass of himself when he was drunk. Steadman got out of there, threw up, staggered into his hut, and passed out sitting at the desk. His gun ended up on the floor. Who knows how it got there. Maybe it got in his way and he yanked it out of his belt and dumped it on the floor; maybe it fell out when he was being dragged out after the shooting. He's passed out, so we can forget about him for the moment.

'Then del Valle shows up. He's drunk, too. But he's not so drunk he doesn't see somebody laying for him, somebody with a gun pointing through the side window. Somebody with a heavy Federation pistol that holds a nice, hot beam. Maybe something like this Anderson Vari-port.' Wolfe slid the weapon he'd taken from Saratov out of its holster, then replaced it. 'Nice piece. I've only seen one other like it since I've been in Graveyard. Del Valle draws, snaps a shot, misses. The man in the window doesn't.'

'Bullcrap!' That came from one of the bartenders.

'If someone wants to go take a look at the shack from the outside,' Wolfe went on, 'he'll find there's jimmy marks on the window, enough to snap the lockbar and get the window open, so the iso-glass wouldn't mess up the shot. And there's a nice scrape on the left-hand side of the window, where someone might've braced a blaster to make sure he didn't need but one shot. That would've made the shooter right-handed.'

Wolfe looked at Brakbone. 'You're right-handed, aren't you? And you carry an Anderson.'

'What the hell are you talking about?'

'Just making an observation.' Wolfe paused. 'This lawyering is thirsty stuff. Somebody pass me a beer.'

There were a few laughs. One of the blowsy women drew a mug and leaned it across the bar. Wolfe drank heartily.

'Thanks,' he said. 'Here's something else. The paperwork. Steadman said del Valle wrote up the claim form. I just checked with the land office clerk, and del Valle hasn't filed anything in two years.'

Canfield's expression flickered for an instant.

'I went through both their gear,' Wolfe said. 'I didn't find any claim.'

'Steadman must be lying,' Canfield said.

'Possibly. Murderers do things like that. Now here's something else. I've noticed a lot of people around here have a hobby of going out on the land every chance they get, and trying to see if they can strike it rich like del Valle did.'

'Sure,' a woman said. 'On'y way you'll stop bein' a comp'ny fool or a wage slave.'

'No question,' Wolfe agreed. 'And today I talked to a man who had another kind of hobby that was even more interesting. Seems he and his partner used to help anybody interested in prospecting. In the old days it used to be called grubstaking. These two loaned prospectors the credits, and all they wanted back was ten percent interest per week, plus five percent of the principal. If you didn't, or couldn't, pay, it could get somewhat painful, I was told.'

Wolfe deliberately stopped, looked around the crowd. 'I see some people out there who're looking away from me,' he said. 'I guess you know what I'm talking about.'

'I assume you're going to make some kind of point out of all this,' Canfield said.

'I think so. I talked to another man who found something, or anyway he thought he did. It looked to him like a very promising claim. His two "partners" decided they wanted the mine to be in their names. He argued with them. He went to the hospital, and the claim was filed in their names. But that mine didn't pan out, because the two went back to their old ways. One of the grubstakers was named Saratov.'

He heard a low growl from the crowd, like a tiger awakening.

'That's one of my employees,' Canfield said. 'And I haven't seen him since this afternoon.'

'Maybe he's busy,' Wolfe said. 'Since this isn't a court of law,' he went on, 'I've got a suggestion. Saratov's partner, like most of you know, is Mister Brakbone here. What say, before we go and do something rash like kill Lef Steadman, we send somebody to inspect Brakbone's quarters, looking for interesting pieces of paper? I think a man's life might be worth that, don't you?'

'The hell you will!' Brakbone shouted, and dove at Wolfe.

Wolfe heard Canfield shout, 'You stupid shithead!' as Brakbone was on him, reaching for a stranglehold. Wolfe's hands went up under his and took both arms by the muscles, pinching sharply. The two tottered back and forth, struggling. Brakbone shouted something, harsh alk fumes stale in Wolfe's face.

Joshua suddenly bent both knees, stepped forward, pushed up on Brakbone's left arm, and turned, pulling and ducking under the man's left as he stumbled forward, off-balance. Wolfe turned sideways and snapped a knife-hand strike into Brakbone's lower ribs. The man grunted in pain, flailing for balance as Joshua pivoted around him and struck for his groin. The strike missed. Brakbone kicked, catching Joshua in the chest, and Joshua stumbled back. Brakbone came in, and Joshua snap-kicked for Brakbone's head. Brakbone's hands blocked; Joshua crouched, let the momentum of his kick spin him, and whipped his leg as he fell, sending Brakbone tumbling.

Brakbone's pistol dropped out of its holster. As he fumbled for it, somebody kicked the gun into the crowd, and Brakbone came to his feet.

The two men circled. Joshua aimed a knife strike toward Brakbone's throat, Brakbone ducked aside, whirled and swept a kick into Joshua's gut. Wolfe doubled over, pulling for air, let himself fall sideways, away from Brakbone's follow-through, and rolled back to his feet.

Brakbone had a fixed, tight smile on his face. People were shouting, Wolfe paid no mind. Circling . . .

Brakbone sent two punches at Joshua's head. He ducked them, threw a sword-hand hooking punch at Brakbone's temple. It missed the death-spot but smashed into his cheekbone.

Brakbone yelled in pain, tried another kick. Joshua ducked it, struck, missed.

Breathe . . . breathe . . . all the time is yours . . . let the wave take you . . .

Brakbone attacked again, and Joshua stepped sideways, toward the big man, his forearm snapping up in a block. Brakbone's arm was flung away, and Wolfe smashed his knuckles into Brakbone's chest, kept moving into him, striking, striking, and Brakbone fell hard on his back.

Brakbone rolled away from Wolfe's foot stamp, back-snapped to his feet, and struck. Wolfe blocked one strike, then another, came in hard to smash Brakbone's lower side with his palm.

Ribs snapped, and Brakbone howled. He stood, swaying.

No sorrow, no joy, as I take what is not mine to take . . .

Wolfe's right hand came up, curled, and he struck down, barely a touch, near Brakbone's collarbone. Brakbone's hands reflexively grasped his throat, then fell away as his eyes rolled up and he fell bonelessly forward.

Wolfe stepped aside, let the corpse crash to the floor.

There was complete silence.

Suddenly Canfield had a gun in his hand.

'This is utter goddamned nonsense,' he snarled. 'Next you'll be accusing *me* . . .'

Breathe . . . breathe . . .

'Put the gun down, Mister Canfield.' It was Stoutenburg.

'No. I'm leaving – let all of this bullshit settle down. When you've come to your senses, then – then we'll see what happens next.'

'That's a good idea,' Stoutenburg said, taking a step forward. 'But I don't think you should leave. I do think we deserve some explanations. Now, or in the morning.'

'Not a chance, preacher. Don't make me shoot you.'

'You're not a depraved man, Mister Canfield. You won't shoot an unarmed man.'

Canfield was panting as if he'd run a hard mile.

Stoutenburg took another step.

Kristin's gun was out, aiming. But the minister blocked her aim.

'Just give me the gun,' Stoutenburg said. 'There's been more than enough killing.'

He was only two feet from Canfield, reaching out.

Wolfe saw, as if his eyes were inches away, Canfield's finger touch the trigger stud, exert pressure . . .

All is still, all is solid, all is stone, there can be no motion, all is ice . . .

Canfield's finger whitened, but the gun didn't fire. Tony Stoutenburg took the gun by the receiver, twisted gently, and had it in his hand.

'I think that's all,' he said mildly.

'Now what?' Wolfe said, stretched in a steaming bath, feeling his bruises, letting the water outside, the blood within, wash the pain away.

'Now what about what?' Kristin said. She was still dressed, sitting on the bed.

'Since you stuck around after I left, did anybody have any ideas about what to do about Canfield? Or will the lynching bee reconvene tomorrow night, after the hangovers subside? I assume nobody's going to let him out of the assayer's vault anytime soon and let him make a run for it.'

'Tony said he'd get some of Graveyard's reputable citizens together, and set up some sort of council. I guess they'll have a court or something.'

'So law, order, morality, and straight poker games come to Graveyard.' Wolfe yawned. 'And all the players take the fun to Lucky Cuss or Grand Central. Hardly seems worthwhile.'

'You sound like you're sorry you got involved.'

'Not sorry at all. Canfield was a reek in the nostrils of the Lord. But why the hell does one yutz mean that we've got to have parking regulations and dress codes all of a sudden?'

'What do you want? Anarchy?'

Wolfe started to say something, stopped. When he spoke again, the levity was gone from his voice.

'I don't know. Sometimes I wish I did.'

The little man who acted like a chipmunk woke Wolfe early the next morning and gave him a slip of paper with a message. It was a simple code Wolfe remembered from the war.

IN-SYSTEM. ETA YOURS THREE E-DAYS. BE READY. There was no name on the slip.

'You could stay on,' Stoutenburg said. 'Kristin hasn't told me anything about either of you, but I have the idea neither of you has any kind of a home.'

'That's true enough, Tony,' Wolfe said. 'But there's something I've got to take care of. It's maybe a little bit bigger, maybe a little more important than Graveyard.'

Stoutenburg inclined his head. 'If you say so. You know, at one time, I dreamed of having a big parish. Maybe being a bishop, even. But things happened to me, like I think they've happened to you two. And now I think what I see around me is more than enough.'

'Very nice,' Wolfe said, without irony. 'I wish I had your clarity of sight.'

'Joshua,' Kristin said, as they were loading the moke, 'I've got something to tell you.'

Wolfe turned, leaned back against the moke's body. 'You're not going with me.'

'How did you know?'

He shrugged. 'I knew.'

'They need law around here,' Kristin said. 'You won't – can't do it. I told Tony I would.'

Wolfe nodded. 'He's a good man,' he said obliquely. 'And you'll make a good cop.'

'You know,' she said, 'when Tony took the gun away from Canfield . . . That proved something to me. You don't have to use violence. There's always another way.'

Wolfe glanced at her, thought of saying something, changed his mind. 'Nice if you're right,' he said, voice neutral.

'And didn't you once tell me that there isn't any after?'

'I did.'

'Did you mean for us when you said it?'

'Yes,' Wolfe said honestly. 'For everything.'

'I still don't understand.'

'Again . . . I can't tell you.'

'You see?' Kristin's eyes were pleading, hopeless.

Wolfe stared down into them and took a deep breath. He

took Kristin in his arms, kissed her, chastely. 'Thanks, angel,' he said. 'Like I said, Tony's a very good man.'

A ship lay in the center of the empty port. It was sleek, angled, dull black. Two gunports were open, chaingun barrels in battery.

One tracked Joshua's 'sled as it floated across the field. He drove the moke to the shed and put it inside. He came out, carrying the two packs Kristin had bought for him.

The port slid open, and a bearded, big man came out. He held a gun pointed down at the ground, carefully not aiming at Joshua. 'You're Wolfe,' he said. 'I recognize you from the holos back during the war. I'm Merrett Chesney.'

'I've heard of you.'

'You're a little late.'

'Some unexpected business came up.'

'We better bust ass. The client's in a hurry.'

'So am I,' Wolfe said. He started for the port, stopped, and stared off at the gray mountains in the distance for a long time.

Then he boarded the ship, and the lock slid closed behind him.

ELEVEN

TO: All Concerned Federation Administrators
& Executives, Grade 54 and Above

FROM: Department of Information

1. Due to certain out-of-the-ordinary events, it has
become necessary to impose immediate screening on all interstellar transmissions, particularly
those intended for or emanating from any media
source.
2. Screening must be made on ALL transmissions
involvlng references to rumors of a 'red death,' a
'burning death,' or 'interstellar disease.'
3. Also to be screened is any mention of
Federation ships disappearing mysteriously or
encountering any unusual phenomena.
4. Media heads on your respective worlds or areas
of responsibility should be notified of these con-
ditions immediately.
5. It is also suggested that this is in no way a
restriction of either the Federation-guaranteed
freedom of speech or freedom of communication, but rather it is an attempt to help

concerned parties avoid either causing panic or
making errors of judgment that might prove
hard to correct at a later date.

> Joseph Breen
> Minister of Procedures
> Department of Information
> Federation Headquarters
> Earth

TWELVE

'You travel light,' Chesney said. 'A virtue in these times.'

'It didn't start out that way,' Joshua said, then forced his mind away from Ak-Mechat VII.

'When does it ever?' Chesney laughed harshly. He checked the control panel, nodded satisfaction, and swiveled in his chair. 'I think the closest I ever came to actually meeting you was off some beastly Al'ar planet. A1122-3 it was. Horrid tropical world. I was beating up the oppos to give one of your teams cover on an insert.'

Wolfe thought back.

'You were trying a prisoner recovery,' Chesney said.

Wolfe remembered.

'It got a little ugly,' Chesney went on. 'I had seven old *Albemarle*-class spitkits, and we were zooming and shooting and dancing all over the heavens and then two Al'ar frigates came out of nowhere. We lost three, and were very damned grateful that was the worst it got.'

'It wasn't any prettier on the ground,' Wolfe said.

'I never heard what happened, actually,' Chesney went on. 'Never had the proper clearance. No one around to be rescued, then?'

'No,' Wolfe said slowly. 'No, there were almost seventy civilians down there.' He remembered the stumbling, nearly brain-dead men and women who'd been through Al'ar interrogation.

Chesney waited for more details, eyes gleaming a little. After a while, he realized that was all Wolfe proposed to say. 'Ah well, ah well,' he said. 'A long time ago, wasn't it? But back then we were most alive, at our finest. Pity those days aren't still around, isn't it?'

'I don't think so,' Wolfe said. 'We're still paying, and I don't think the debt'll be settled by the time I die.'

Chesney shrugged. 'War debts, deficits – those are for governments to worry about, not warriors like you and me.'

'I wasn't talking about the money,' Joshua said shortly.

Chesney looked at him cautiously. 'Well, that's as may be.' He paused, then changed the subject: 'I s'pose one thing we should settle is the pecking order, then. It's my ship, so I'm in command normally. However, I'm hardly a fool. When we insert and extract your areas of expertise, I'm demoted to first mate. Agreed?'

'That sounds reasonable.'

'Good,' Chesney said. 'Very good indeed. I happen to have a small bottle of a good, perhaps excellent if my shipper is telling the truth, Earth-Bordeaux. Shall we seal our partnership?'

Chesney was as experienced as Joshua in long, dull N-space passages, and so the two stayed out of each other's way as much as possible. The ship was small, a converted eight-crew long-range scout of the *Chambers*-class, which Chesney had named the *Resolute*. The engine spaces had been roboticized, as Wolfe had done with his own ship, the *Grayle*. The crew spaces were still anodized in the soft pastels the Federation thought lessened tension, and Wolfe supposed Chesney preferred them that way; they must remind him of his service days.

Something nagged at Wolfe, something about Chesney. But it didn't surface, and so he let his back brain worry at it. He spent the long hours working with the Lumina in his carefully locked compartment, reading from the ship's extensive library, or sleeping. He took over the cooking, since Chesney's idea of a good meal was to reconstitute a steak, fry it gray, and cover it with freeze-dried mushrooms and whatever soup came to hand.

Chesney had hidden a bug inside the wardrobe catch, which Wolfe found and deactivated within an hour after jumping from Ak-Mechat VII. Neither man brought it up.

Wolfe discovered Chesney had more than one good, perhaps excellent, bottle of wine aboard. He nipped constantly, on the sly, an experienced secret toper. Joshua wondered if he was as sly about his alcoholism when alone. Since they were far from action, and a *Chambers*-class ship in transit could be piloted by a drug-hazed gibbon, Wolfe said nothing.

Four ship-days out, Chesney told Wolfe the destination and the clients. They were to pick up the bomb materials on Bulnes IV, then make a short jump to deliver it to the rebels on Osirio, barely twelve light-years distant. 'Seems straightforward enough,' he said. 'Don't suppose, Joshua, you'd be willing to dig through the library, see what the piddling match is all about, though? Not that it matters, but it might be interesting. Even valuable, if the slok comes down.'

Wolfe obeyed, also curious, and reported some success.

'I suppose it's some government-take-all planet with a colony, dissidents dissidenting from the official policy, helping rebels and that, then?' Chesney said. He'd been quick to inform Wolfe that not only did he despise politics, but he utterly hated any government that did more than maintain a military and police force.

'Not exactly. The whole situation's interestingly backward. Better listen closely,' Joshua said, 'because I don't think I'll get it right more than once. Osirio, where we're to deliver the package, was the mother planet. Evidently their best and brightest went out to Bulnes, where we're supposed to make the pickup, and colonized the system. Osirio was brain-drained and is currently in a state of what the 'pedia called decadent autocracy. Aristocratic thugs who run things badly, much like Earth's czars, so there's an active little rebellion bubbling. Assassinations, no-go districts, the stray conventional bombing here and there. The rebels, as far as I could tell, don't have any particular program other than blasting the rascals out. The real dynamism is on Bulnes IV, but the government of Bulnes owes its legitimacy to the mother planet.'

'Good Lord,' Chesney said.

'Yeah. They're afraid if Osirio falls, they'll tumble right after it.'

'Who's right?'

Wolfe shrugged. 'The people out of power aren't killing as many people as those in power. Yet. Maybe they'd do better, or maybe they'd start their own pogroms if they won.'

'Thank heaven it's not for us to say,' Chesney said. 'But with a mess like that, it's certainly tempting to make the easy profit.'

'I don't follow,' Wolfe said.

'The way that wonderful voice we contract our services through set the deal, we get 250K when we pick up the plutonium, or whatever it is, 750 on delivery.'

'I know.'

'We could do a little personal renegotiation, arrange to get the 750 from the rebels first, then write off the 250 and go about our merry way, then, couldn't we?' Chesney saw the expression on Wolfe's face. 'No, I s'pose not. Probably be too messy to arrange, not to mention dangerous while we loop around their silly world, bickering. We'll play the cards as they lay, I suppose.'

*

Chesney was fond of talking about the war, particularly about the atrocities of the Al'ar. Wolfe listened and made little comment. Chesney seemed less interested in conversation than in his own monologue.

One time, after third-meal, Chesney asked Joshua, 'What made the bastards so cruel? Why'd they kill so many women, children, and civilians who weren't even Federation officials?'

'That wasn't cruel to them,' Wolfe said. 'Women breed warriors, children – what they called **hatchlings**,' he said in Al'ar, '– grow up to be warriors. As somebody back on Earth once said, "kill 'em all. Nits grow up to be lice, don't they?" The Al'ar think – thought anyone who does things the hard way is a complete fool.'

Chesney looked away for an instant, as if some very private thought had surfaced, then back at Joshua. 'You were their prisoner, when you were a child, or so the fiches had it, which was why the Federation made you into a supercommando,' he said. 'So you dealt with them face-to-face.'

'Sometimes.'

Chesney shuddered. 'That would've been horrifying. Like walking into a spider's web. But at least you got to see them when you killed them. That must've been a pleasure.'

Joshua said nothing.

'Thank heavens,' Chesney said, 'they're dead, or at any rate gone from this spacetime. We don't need any more nightmares like them, right?'

Wolfe thought of the 'virus' that had driven the Al'ar from their own universe and was now invading Man's. Again he kept silent.

They came out of N-space on the fringes of the Bulnes system and wormed their way toward the fourth planet. There were three planetary fortresses orbiting the planet and patrol ships crisscrossing the world.

'Piffle,' Chesney said. 'Their security chatters like a band of langurs, never keeping silent to see what's going on around it. This should be as easy as stealing coins from a dead man's eyes. Their search patterns are lattices like your grandmother's pie.'

'I don't think my grandmother made pies,' Wolfe said. 'I remember her being quite busy representing her district.'

'All right, then your first popsy's see-everything blouse.'

'I wasn't that lucky,' Wolfe said amiably. 'My first love was the daughter of the Federation's secretary of state. She wore tunics that fastened at the neck, hung loosely, and never gave me anything to dream about, plus the baggy knee-trousers that were the style then.'

'Ah, but once you got the tunic off,' Chesney said, deliberately lascivious, 'then you beheld a garden of delights?'

'Nope,' Joshua answered. 'I never even kissed her, and I'm not sure she knew I did more than exist. In any event, it was more pouting than passion on my part.'

'Ah,' Chesney said. 'Unlucky you. As for me, my first was the tutor my father brought in to teach my brothers some language or other. A definite tart. But when my father caught us doing the naughty, that was the last we saw of her. I've often wondered . . .' Chesney shook his head.

'What happened to your great first love?' he went on, changing the subject, making conversation while his fingers touched sensors and the *Resolute* closed on Bulnes IV.

'She went away to school and married the graduating valedictorian when she was a freshman. Perhaps a successful marriage was what she intended for a career. They both were killed in the Al'ar raid on Mars.' Joshua remembered the girl's easy smile, seldom directed at him.

'Just as well – that she married someone else, I mean,' Chesney said. 'A warrior doesn't need any more anchors than his own mind can provide.'

'Yeah,' Wolfe said sarcastically. 'That's us. Footloose, carefree rebels, leaving a trail of broken hearts as we wander the stars.'

Wolfe came out of his compartment yawning. Chesney was at the control panel, on the com. He saw Wolfe, said, 'Received . . . clear . . .' into the mike, and broke contact.

'You've got contact with our customers?' Wolfe asked.

'Right. First an hour or two ago, then they put out another signal just now,' Chesney said quickly. 'Damned amateur worrywarts. Babbling like they've never heard of intercepts or locators. Had to cut them off, as you heard.'

'The only way conspirators get experience is the hard way,' Joshua said, easing into the copilot's seat. 'Unfortunately, most get dead in the learning.'

'And isn't that the truth,' Chesney said heartily. 'They even had a password for us. "Freedom or death." How terribly jejune. We're about sixteen hours from planetfall, by the way. How about some coffee?'

'Sure,' Wolfe said, getting up. 'Have it ready in a minute.'

'Keep one hand for yourself,' Chesney warned. 'I might be jinking us around a trifle. There might be a det-bubble or two I've missed.'

'Interesting place to schedule a pickup for,' Wolfe said. 'Right in the middle of university grounds. Very clever, unless they're professorial, in which case it's suicidal.'

'Which way would you bet?'

'Six to five. Against. On anything.'

'That's safe,' Chesney said. 'Now, if you'll excuse me, I'm about to be somewhat busy.'

Chesney brought the *Resolute* screaming in from space, just at dawn. 'Hopefully they'll think we're a meteorite for a moment or two, and by then we'll be below their radar horizon and invisible long enough to grab the geetus,' he said. 'Buckle up.'

He flared the ship barely a thousand feet up. Wolfe heard antigrav generators groan and saw red warnings flash on the control panel.

'Shut up,' Chesney grunted to the blinking lights. 'Stop sniveling, you bitch.' His fingers danced across sensors, and Wolfe remembered a pianist he'd seen.

Chesney was very good, he decided, as the ship spun and dodged without, as far as Joshua could see, any warnings of detection.

'Always well,' Chesney grunted, 'to be careful. Touchdown, six minutes . . .'

There was a city below. He extruded spoilers, killed the drive. 'Don't want to go *too* slow,' he said. 'Or some traffic cop'll throw a rock and knock us down. One minute sixteen. Here we are.'

He put reverse thrust on as the *Resolute* shot over long rows of housing into open country, then towers and great buildings loomed ahead, gold and red brick in the dawn's light.

'And here we be,' he said, braking sharply. The *Resolute* bucked and fell a few feet, and Chesney moved the slide-pots of the antigrav system up, and the ship stabilized. 'Just on time.'

The *Resolute* settled toward a huge cement pad, marked with regular lines. Beyond was a large stadium. The *Resolute* touched down with never a jar. 'I'll keep it just grounded, so we don't punch a nice easy-to-spot ship-sized crater in their parking lot,' Chesney said. 'Perhaps you'll see to the niceties, then? Do take a gun. Freedom-lovers can prove most unreliable.'

Wolfe picked up his heavy blaster, went to the lock, opened the inner and outer doors, and looked out. On one side was the stadium, on the other a low building, on a third a large grove.

He extruded the gangway as a small gravsled came from behind the building and shot toward the *Resolute*. There were two women and a man aboard, and, in the back, a large case.

The lifter grounded ten feet from the *Resolute*, slewed sideways, its skids striking sparks from the tarmac.

'Freedom,' one of the women shouted as she jumped out.

'Or death,' Wolfe replied dryly, wondering if enough starships grounded on Bulnes' campuses for a password to be needed.

'I'm Margot,' the woman said.

'And I don't have a name, and hope that isn't your real one, either,' Wolfe said. 'Never give away what you don't have to.'

The woman appeared angry, then perplexed.

The other two lifted the case out and staggered toward the *Resolute*. Margot glanced at Joshua as if expecting him to help. Wolfe didn't move, but kept the gun ready. She gave him a dark look and helped the other two.

'All right,' she said when the case was in the lock. 'You'd best lift, before the Inspectorate makes a sweep over us.'

'You're forgetting something,' Joshua reminded her.

Her eyes flickered. 'Oh. Yes. Sorry,' she said. 'Sorry I forgot, but my mind was on security.'

Joshua decided she was a rotten liar. The other woman brought a packet from the gravsled. Wolfe opened one end.

'It's all there,' Margot said. 'Don't you trust us?'

Wolfe made no reply, shuffling notes. 'Good,' he said at last. 'Now get away from the ship. We're going straight up and out.'

The three ran to the gravsled, and the driver lifted it away.

'Go!' Wolfe shouted to Chesney and hit the close sensor on the lock.

It slid shut as the *Resolute* went vertical. Wolfe grabbed for a handhold and fell against the lock door as the secondary came on, then gravity shifted as the ship's own system went on.

He looked out the tiny bull's-eye port at the shrinking parking area, the suddenly tiny gravsled, and, from the copse of trees, two gravlighters lifting out of concealment. 'Hit it hard,' Wolfe called. 'Our customers just got stopped!'

Wolfe let the radiation counter clatter for a moment, shut it off, and set it down beside the case. 'Whatever's in there is hot,' he said. 'I have no intention of opening it, even in space wearing a suit. I'll take their word it's what the rebels want.'

'Good,' Chesney said. 'What about the money?'

'It's real, as far as I know,' Joshua said. 'But I'm hardly an expert on Bulnes' coins of the realm. Here, give me a hand.'

He and Chesney lifted the case down the passageway, lashed it down in the small cargo hold, and returned to the control room.

'I need a drink,' Chesney said. 'You?'

'Maybe later.'

Wolfe waited until Chesney had the cork out of the bottle, about to pour.

'How much did the Inspectorate pay you to rat them out?'

The bottle jerked and wine spilled across the table. 'What *are* you talking about?'

'Come on, Merrett,' Wolfe said. 'When I came out of my room, before we went in-atmosphere, you were talking to somebody. You heard me, jumped like a goosed doe, then came up with a cockamamie explanation that the rebels were the chatty sort. How much?'

Chesney eyed Wolfe. Joshua took a small pistol out of his shirt, laid it down on the table, put his hand on top of it.

'Half a mill,' Chesney said reluctantly.

'Where's it to be delivered? I assume you're not planning to go back to Bulnes and collect?'

'I have a number-call account. They're transferring funds now.'

'Good,' Wolfe said. 'You can com your banker right now, and transfer 250K to an account number I'm going to give you. Remember, the split's equal, right?'

Chesney blinked, then a smile creased his face. 'You don't care about them any more than I do.'

'Why should I?' Joshua said. 'I'm no more political than you.'

Chesney picked up his glass, drained it, refilled it. 'You know,' he said, 'I might have found myself a real partner.'

'Maybe,' Joshua said. 'But don't think that game works twice. Not on me, not on the people we're making the delivery to.'

'Of course not,' Chesney said. 'For openers, their security – the Inspectorate I heard you call it – wouldn't have any reason to pay me if they had both sets of baddies and the geetus as well, now would they? This way, they've already made the transfer, and now they're waiting for me to tip them the wink once I reach Osirio to get the rest. They'll be waiting a *very* long time. Partner.'

THIRTEEN

NOT FOR PUBLIC RELEASE

Do Not Distribute Below Executive Level

The management of Hykord Transport GmbH has determined we will no longer accept cargoes either directly or for transshipment from companies who are part of our Galactic Efficiency Group for the following sectors:

Alkeim, Garfed, Montros, Porphyry, Q11, Rosemont, Saphir, TangoZed, Ullar, Y267, and Yttr.

In addition, no cargo intended for any of the so-called Outlaw Worlds will be accepted.

Finally, we no longer accept shipments to any scientific or military presence in the worlds formerly part of the Al'ar sectors.

This decision has been reluctantly reached not because of various distressing rumors, which are utterly absurd to anyone who takes a moment to consider their probability, but due to the hugely increased insurance premiums leveled.

Management hopes that this situation will change shortly, and Hykord Transport GmbH will be able to return to its proud motto: 'You Crate It, We Carry It. Anywhere, Anytime.'

FOURTEEN

'It looks tropical down there,' Chesney said gloomily.

'The gazetteer agrees with you,' Wolfe said. 'I quote: "Most of the planet is tropical to subtropical, with extensive rain forests which have been heavily exploited by the Osirians. These forests are the home of many interesting fauna, including the primeval and exceedingly dangerous tarafny, click here for holo, many species of snakes, including the aggressive, dangerous-to-man . . ."' Wolfe let his voice trail off.

'*This* is the motherworld,' Chesney said in amazement. 'They're not decadent – you have to have accomplished something for it to get rotten. And why am I always going to places where the bugs are not only bigger than I am, but carnivorous?'

'You must've been lucky in another life,' Wolfe said.

'Ah well,' Chesney sighed. 'Here we go. In-atmosphere. Ring up our clients if you would, and see if they've got the soup on.'

Wolfe touched sensors, opened a mike. 'Freedom,' he said.

There was a crackle of static. He tried again.

'Or death' came back.

'Inbound per your instructions,' Wolfe said. 'ETA . . .' he glanced at Chesney.

'Fifty-eight minutes,' the pilot said.

'In five-eight. Will monitor this freq. Do not broadcast except for emergencies,' Wolfe said.

There was the acknowledging click of a mike button.

'Well,' Wolfe said. 'Perhaps a professional. Or at least someone who's read a book or two.'

'Here's the plan,' Chesney said, and his fingers touched points on the map on a secondary screen. 'I'm bringing it in over this ocean, hopefully without being noticed. I'll low-fly to shore, then ground it here, which is the grid location they gave us, on what looks like a beach, next to this river here. If anything goes wrong, we withdraw gracefully, leaving big black streaks. Remember, my finances have been a little close lately, so the missile tubes are for show only. The only armament the *Resolute* has are the chainguns, so we shouldn't play the bravo. Comments?'

'Other than it looks easy, which scares me, none.'

'Buckle up.'

Osirio swallowed their screens as they closed, and Joshua dimly heard atmosphere-roar. The screen went to gray for an instant, then came back with a real-time visual: thick cloud cover below, blanking everything. Chesney switched to infrared.

'Nothing much down there,' he said. Wolfe examined the blotches along the shoreline, saw nothing change, flipped the scanner through various spectrums.

'I've got a little wiggle about where we're headed,' Joshua said. 'Signals within the ninety-one-point-five megahertz range.'

'Diagnosis?' Chesney's voice was tense.

'Don't know.'

'Must be a village. I'd guess they'd have some kind of com to civilization. Just like amateurs to pick a place they can sit and drink beer in while they wait.'

'Maybe.'

'Wolfe,' Chesney said worriedly. 'I've got a –'

Alarms roared as the com blared: 'Ambush! The Inspectorate's holding the town! Break off! Go for –'

'Strong radar signal,' Joshua said. 'We are being tracked.' His voice was cold, emotionless, very clear.

'Understood,' Chesney said. His voice could have been a duplicate of Wolfe's.

Another alarm shrilled.

'We are targeted,' Joshua said.

'Your call.'

'Maintain flight pattern . . . Stand by for evasive action . . .'

A third alarm gonged.

'I have a SAM launch,' Wolfe said. The alarm rang twice more. 'I have two more launches.' He could have been talking about the weather.

'Give me music. We're blown,' Chesney ordered.

Joshua touched two sensors, skipped two, tapped three others.

'ECM broadcasting.'

'Results?'

Joshua waited.

'Results, dammit!'

'Negative on one and three – I have a lock on two – two is wavering – he's lost contact with us . . . Two self-detonated.'

'Your call.'

'Stand by – wait – wait – roll right, dive 300 feet, jink left,' Joshua ordered. 'On my command . . . four . . . three . . . two . . . NOW!'

Chesney's fingers swept the control board, and the *Resolute* dove sideways, corrected, banked left.

'One toppled . . .' The slam of an explosion rolled the ship.

'That was three,' Wolfe said. 'A bit close. Stand by . . . I have another launch – max evasive action – jink left – left – right – climb five-zero . . .'

Breathe . . . breathe . . .

'Two more launches,' he said.

'They're trying to pin us against that ridge.' Chesney's voice cracked.

'Continue evasive maneuvering.' Wolfe's voice was quite calm.

Breathe . . . breathe . . .

'Christ,' Chesney moaned. 'What I'd give for one lousy little air-to-air –'

'Missile closing – jink right!'

Another explosion rocked the *Resolute*.

'Missile one – miss.'

Joshua *felt* death, *felt* the second missile, remembered a time he'd used his mind to warp a countermissile into a target, remembered the fear, *felt* death once more, and hurled a rocket, a ghost that never was, at the image onscreen.

He *felt* the power of the Lumina in the compartment behind him, *felt* it glow into life, *felt* its colors whorl around the empty room. He *felt* the missile in his hands, closed them like talons, and the missile image was gone.

'Missile two self-detonated,' he said, and again *reached* for the third. He *felt* nothing, there was nothing, there was no power within, nothing reached out. 'Dive,' he ordered, and the *Resolute* dove toward the sea not 200 feet below.

Then there was nothing onscreen.

'Missile three missed,' he reported. 'Evidently lost its target.' He touched a sensor, saw an exhaust flare. 'I have it headed toward space.'

'And we're going after it,' Chesney said. 'This is too much like dangerous.'

'Negative,' Joshua said.

'I said –'

'Remember the deal, Mister,' Wolfe snapped, and his tone had the long-disused sharpness of command.

Chesney caught his breath. 'Sorry. Your call.'

'Over the village full-tilt and straight for those mountains,' Wolfe said. 'Right over the SAM site.'

'Understood.'

A screen showed a cluster of buildings rushing at them, with gray-green lifters and three mobile launchers, two low-altitude chainguns that started yammering as they passed overhead. Then they were over the village and there was nothing but jungle onscreen and the rising mountain ahead.

'Take her over the ridge crest then the nap of the earth until I say. Then we'll look for a hiding place to put her down on, and figure out what to do next.'

'Understood,' Chesney said, then the habits of the past took hold, and he automatically added, 'Sir.'

The *Resolute* sat in dimness, sixty feet underwater. The lock slid open, and a man in a spacesuit floated out. There was a long, sealed roll tied to his shoulders. He unspooled a wire from a reel at his belt, opened a small door beside the lock, and plugged the reel in.

'Am I communicating?' Wolfe said.

'Very clear,' Chesney answered. 'I still think you're over-cautious in wanting a wire for a com. They can't be monitoring *every* freq.'

'Nobody had a SAM site in that village, either.'

'Strong point.'

'Stand by,' Wolfe said, and pushed away from the lock. The river's sluggish current took him away from the ship. He activated the suit's antigrav unit and came to the surface.

Fernlike trees reared high on either side of the river,

with smaller growth below them and some brush on the ground. Water churned as the antigrav unit sent him toward a climbable bank. Half a dozen loglike objects lay along it. One of the logs slithered off into the water as Wolfe approached.

'There are some *really* big snakes in these parts,' he reported.

'Man-eaters?' Chesney asked.

'I'm not going to give them my arm as an experimental hors d'oeuvre.' Wolfe clicked on an outside mike, and jungle sounds poured in. One of the snakelike creatures opened a long, toothed slit of a mouth, and the booming roar deafened him until the mike automatically cut the volume.

'That was your friend the snake,' Wolfe reported. 'He's wondering whether he wants to fang me . . . He just decided it wasn't worth the bother and went swimming.'

Wolfe waded ashore, unsnapped the roll, and took out a small cylinder. He moved to one of the trees, activated his antigrav to maximum power until he weighed no more than ten pounds, and climbed hand-over-hand up the trunk to about a hundred feet above the ground. Clinging to the trunk, he used his gun butt to tap a spike into it and hung the box from the spike.

'I hope,' he said, 'this jerry-rigged bastard works.'

'No reason it shouldn't,' Chesney said. 'If it locates from a suit in space, it should work fine by itself with all this thick, smudgy atmosphere to go wading in.'

'I would've thought, after all those years playing sojer boy, you would've learned the basic rule that when it's something you need, it's guaranteed to break.'

'I'm a romantic,' Chesney said. 'Speaking of which, I assume the air's perfumed and smells of exotic spices.'

'Hang on a minute,' Wolfe said. He cut power a little, let himself drop down the tree from limb to limb until he thudded into soft, decaying leaves at the base. 'Now I'll satisfy your curiosity,' he said, unsealing his face plate.

'Well?'

'Not exactly attar of roses,' Wolfe said. 'Try old armpit, shit, and stale beer.'

'Typical jungle.'

'Typical jungle,' Wolfe repeated. 'One down, one to go.'

He went back into the river and drove toward another tree, a few hundred yards downstream.

'Freedom,' Wolfe said patiently into the two microphones in front of him. He heard nothing but dead air.

'Ah, the romantic life of a soldier of fortune,' Chesney murmured.

Wolfe waited fifteen minutes then tried again: 'Freedom.'

'It appears the Inspectorate scooped our clients up,' Chesney said. 'We've been doing this for three hours now. Do you know anybody else who might need a do-it-yourself bomb?'

The speaker suddenly crackled. 'Or death.'

'They're on freq one,' Chesney reported. 'And their password's not only stupid, but it's now got a long gray beard.'

'I receive you,' Wolfe said.

'Name yourself,' the speaker said.

'Your supplier,' Wolfe said.

'Give name of person providing materials.'

'Almost enough for me to get a location,' Chesney said. 'And what they want's still crappy security. The Inspectorate could've pulled that woman's toenails out by now.'

'Margot,' Wolfe said.

'Good,' the voice said. 'Are you still onworld?'

'Perhaps,' Wolfe said.

'Are you still willing to make delivery?'

'Affirmative.'

'If you're onplanet and close to where the meet was blown today, give us your location and we'll come to you.'

'I have him,' Chesney said. 'Lousy triangulation, but he's broadcasting from –' he looked at the onscreen map, and where two red lines intersected,'– about one ridgeline over, if this map is correct. They could get here in what, two hours?'

'You've obviously never hiked the bush,' Wolfe said, and keyed the mike. 'Negative on your suggestion. Somebody's leaking on your side, in case you hadn't noticed. We'll come to you.'

There was a long silence, then the voice came back. Even on the tinny FM band, it reeked suspicion. 'We don't know *who* betrayed us. Dislike idea of giving present location. You could be Inspectorate on our frequency.'

'True,' Wolfe said. 'But I already know where you are. If missiles don't start incoming in the next few seconds, suggest your paranoia unjustified.'

Again, a long silence. 'Very well. We have no choice, do we? We'll await your arrival. ETA?'

'Sometime day after tomorrow. Probably in the morning,' Wolfe said. 'Out.' He shut off the com.

'Whyn't you get behind the controls and ready for a fast getaway,' he suggested. 'Just in case we're the ones who got located and we weren't chatting with noble freedom fighters.'

Chesney obeyed. 'So we're going to go for a walk,' he said 'And you're right, I've done very little forest-crawling. Do we go in nice, air-conditioned spacesuits so we don't have to get close to the local fauna?'

'Nope,' Wolfe said. 'Too bulky, too slow, too easy a target.'

'I'd rather be an armored target than a naked one,' Chesney complained. 'And how'll we navigate? I understand a satellite positioning system can be a double-edged sword.'

'It can,' Wolfe agreed. 'I've booby-trapped a few myself. We'll print out the map, and I'm going to invent a brand new device you might've never seen. It's called a compass.'

'Christ,' Chesney groaned. 'The things I do for greed.'

The ship surfaced at dawn and slid to the bank; the lock opened. Wolfe and Chesney got out. They carried Wolfe's two packs and pistol belts. Wolfe had a blast rifle slung over his shoulder. In the lock was the bulky case with the radioactive materials, a suit antigrav generator strapped underneath it. Joshua activated the generator, turned it to high, and picked up the case by a cargo strap as if it weighed no more than a pound or so.

'I wish I had a better arsenal,' Chesney complained as he stepped onto the bank. 'Why is it, every time I take an assignment, I think I've got everything I could conceivably use, and the only things I don't have are what I really need?'

Wolfe shrugged. Chesney took a small box from his pocket and pressed sensors. The *Resolute*'s lock closed, and it slipped underwater. 'I always feel naked outside the ship,' he said.

'Good,' Wolfe said. 'Naked men stay scared. Scared men stay alive. Let's hoof.'

An hour later, they passed through the ruins of a village. The wooden huts had been burnt, and there were blast holes in some of the roofs. Three trees had rotting, sagging ropes looped around them, and a few bones scattered nearby.

Wolfe *felt* screams, agony, prolonged death.

'How long ago did this happen?' Chesney asked.

'Maybe a year, maybe a little longer.'

'Who did it?'

'Maybe rebels, maybe soldiers. As a guess,' Wolfe said,

'I'd go for the government. The farmers would've come back if it'd just been "revolutionary justice."'

'Nice people,' Chesney said.

'Would it have been any more civilized,' Wolfe said, voice harsh, 'if they'd razed the village from the air? Or is it worse because somebody had to look in somebody's eyes as he killed him? Or her?'

Chesney didn't answer. They went on.

Wolfe counted paces, consulted the map, and stopped regularly to pour water from his wine-bottle canteen into its plas cap and float the tiny needle he'd magnetized atop it before going on.

They stopped when the glow that was the barely visible sun was approximately overhead. Chesney let the case down to the ground, and wheezed. 'Gad. Weight-schmeight. It's the mass somebody ought to figure out how to eliminate.'

'Einstein did,' Wolfe said. 'And our customers are going to use his cookbook.'

'I meant – never mind what I meant.' Chesney opened his pack, took out two ration paks, and tossed one to Wolfe. He lifted out a small bottle of wine, looked at it longingly, but put it back. He touched the heater tab, waited a few moments, opened the pak, and grimaced.

'I've *got* to learn to not buy things just because they're a bargain. What is this glop, anyway?'

Wolfe had his own pak open. 'Interesting,' he said. 'I'd guess some centuries ago it was intended for soldiers that might've been Earth-Japan émigrés. This would be bean paste, this pickled cucumber, this, well, some sort of mussel, shellfish, which you put on the rice. The small plas pak's soy sauce.'

'What's this green stuff ?' Chesney said, sampling.

'Wait! That's . . .'

'Hot – hot . . .' Chesney managed in a strangled tone, and unsealed the wine bottle that now served as a canteen and gulped down water.

'Some sort of ground-up root,' Wolfe continued. 'Wasabi, I think I remember hearing it called.'

'Sadistic bastards!' Chesney moaned.

'Doesn't – this – damned hill ever end?' Chesney panted.

'It'll be downhill tomorrow. And think how easy it'll be on the way back.'

'I can't – I keep thinking about the other side of this goddamned ridge that we'll have to climb before then.'

'It's easier if you don't try to talk,' Wolfe advised.

'I'm a pilot, which means anything but a ground-pounder,' Chesney said, ignoring the advice. 'Why I ever –'

Underbrush rustled; horror rushed them. Wolfe saw pincered legs, claws, a glaring multifaceted eye as he pinwheeled sideways, blast rifle flying away. The beast clawed at him, missed, spun on its own tracks.

Chesney had his gun out and snapped a shot. The bolt blew off two of the creature's legs, and it shrilled agony and rage.

It reared, segmented body towering over Wolfe.

He *felt* for its brain, found nothing but raw savagery as his pistol came up, fired twice, and dove away as the creature screeched once more, and came down. He put another bolt, then a third into its side as it writhed, then, forcing himself to stay calm, aimed and blew its single eye into spattering gore.

The nightmare flailed and thrashed about.

'Get around it,' Wolfe shouted, and Chesney, moving very fast for a man of his size, pushed through the brush to the uphill side.

'Come on,' Wolfe ordered, and the two men went uphill at a run.

The creature's death agonies – if that was what they were – continued as they pushed on.

'Gods – no. That thing doesn't deserve a god,' Chesney said. 'What was it? That taradny or tarafny you were reading about? We should've looked at the holo.'

'Hell if I know,' Wolfe said. 'But I surely don't want to run into its big brother if it isn't.'

Chesney nodded.

'I – notice,' Wolfe managed, 'you're not panting any more.'

'Too – scared.'

'Can we build a fire?' Chesney asked. 'I assume you know how to rub two wet sticks together, and all that woodsy lore.'

It was dusk, and they'd just finished another ration pak. They'd crested the ridge an hour earlier, and Wolfe had found a campsite on the far side, where a spring began the long run down into the valley below.

'No,' Wolfe said.

'But what about that tarantula's brother?'

'I'd rather worry about him than somebody from that village who might be airborne with a snooper and an air-to-ground. Bugs are maybe – heatseekers are for sure,' Wolfe said.

'Oh well,' Chesney said. He took the rather fancy coat that was the only rainproof he had out of his pack, and rolled himself up in it. 'Mrs Chesney's favorite son wasn't meant to sleep rough,' he complained. 'I'll be tossing and turning till dawn.'

Wolfe found a rock, zipped into his waterproof coat, and put the rifle across his knees. Moments later, Chesney's breathing grew into a whiffling snore, his beard ruffling like a sail. Wolfe grinned wryly.

Breathe . . . breathe . . .

He *felt* the Lumina, back in the *Resolute*, *felt* it flame. He *reached* out, around them, *felt* nothing, no one. He let his senses flow, like lava, over the next crest, down the long slope to the sea, toward the village where the SAMs had been, far distant.

He *felt* people, *felt* warmth, warmth of their homes, their fires. He tasted hard cold metal, like blood, and knew the Inspectorate and its missiles were waiting. He *felt* its outposts, *felt* men worried about the morrow, worried about the patrols that would range into the mountains, looking for enemies.

Joshua brought himself back and listened to Chesney's measured snore. He *felt* the night around him, *felt* no menace.

He *felt* another presence, *felt* fright somewhere below, somewhere in the valley they'd traverse in the day. His hand drew a line toward it in the dirt. He tried to *feel* how many there were, what they looked like, what they thought – he failed.

He opened his eyes and looked at the line he'd drawn. It followed the same azimuth he was trying to hold to, toward where the two lines from the radio-locator on the map came together.

Suddenly exhausted, he sagged back against the rock. Rain pattered on his head, and he pulled the hood of his coat up. The rain grew harder. *Sleep now*, he told his body. *Feel nothing.*

Joshua came fully awake, hearing a voice. The rain had stopped. He didn't move, but his finger slid the safety off the rifle. Then he realized the speaker was Chesney. He was speaking clearly, in a low voice, but in a strange, affected accent: 'My dear chap . . . I have utterly *no* idea what you're talking about. No, I can't say I see any resemblance to me and this horrid boy, so stop waving that holograph in front of me. Absurd to so accuse a Federation officer!'

Wolfe was about to shake him awake, but *felt* no danger, no threat in the surrounding blackness. Chesney sighed, rolled over, snored twice, then spoke again: 'Certainly not! I've been too busy, what with the peacetime closures around this base, to even breathe. I certainly didn't know she'd taken a – a lover. I'm completely shattered. Good heavens, man, can't you recognize the obvious? It must've been some back-alley goon that tried to rob them, and things went terribly awry. I must say I object to this entire line of questioning, and wish to notify my commanding officer I seem to be in need of legal assistance.'

Once more a long silence, then: 'Certainly not guilty, Admiral.'

Now his voice went low, became a conspiratorial mutter: 'Yes. Yes, of course. It'd be an utter disgrace for an innocent man like myself to be a convicted – disgraceful for the service, as well. You have no idea how I appreciate this. Yes, yes. And I thought you didn't believe me, when I told you what must've happened to her and that man . . . Of course I'll make sure I never come back here, or have anything to do with the Navy. Why should I? These fools have tried and convicted me.'

Then, in a gloating voice: 'Trevor? You were wrong. Quite wrong.'

Chesney laughed chillingly, then his breathing choked, and Wolfe knew he was awake. Joshua took in a slow breath, let it rasp against the roof of his mouth, and exhaled noisily.

'Wolfe?'

Joshua snorted, coughed. 'What?'

'I – just wanted to know if you were awake,' Chesney whispered. 'Sometimes my – my snoring bothers people.'

'Not me,' Wolfe said, in a carefully sleep-filled voice. 'I can sleep through the crack of doom.'

'Good,' Chesney said. 'Goodnight again.'

Wolfe knew he wasn't sleeping, but listening.

Finally Wolfe's mind, drunken monkey that it was, gave him what he'd been looking for on Merrett Chesney. There'd been three separate tabloid sensations. First a war hero, a special operations veteran of many close-fought engagements, was accused of murdering his wife and her lover.

Then a second scandal broke. The hero had been keeping a terrible secret. His real name wasn't Chesney, but . . . Wolfe's mind sought for the name but couldn't bring it up. A rich youth, parents near the top of their planet's social set. The boy had been unhappy, but seemed to settle down once he was placed in a military school. During one summer leave, there'd been an explosion at the family's mansion, an explosion that was at first blamed on a faulty power grid. Further investigation had found the blast came from a land mine stolen from a military depot that'd somehow been set off in the kouse.

Wolfe tried to remember how many had been killed. He couldn't, but he was sure the family had been obliterated, except for the son, who'd been out with a girl that night. But he had refused to name her, refused to soil her reputation. There'd been a trial, but the jury couldn't quite convict him of murder in the first degree, and it settled on a secondary charge. The boy would have served five E-years or so before he was released and disappeared.

That had been the end of that until that highly decorated Federation Navy commander, Merrett Chesney, had been accused of murder. Investigation revealed he'd fraudulently enlisted at the beginning of the war. He'd been a model sailor, quickly commissioned and volunteered for special operations, although there'd been whispers he wasn't averse to enriching himself if it didn't interfere with his duties.

Chesney had married well during the war and, as soon as

the Al'ar vanished, set to work spending his wife's inheritance. When the money began to run out, both developed wandering eyes. Then the wife and one of her lovers had been murdered – beaten to death, as Wolfe remembered.

The third sensation was after Chesney was convicted. Before the penalty phase of the trial was completed, he'd escaped, with the connivance of at least one fellow officer. That officer's body had been found next to a hangar where a patrol ship had been kept, a ship that was now missing.

No one had much time to look for Chesney: The postwar interregnum was swirling chaos. Everyone assumed he'd fled to the Outlaw Worlds and hopefully met a deserved fate.

Nice choice of partners, Wolfe, Joshua thought wryly. *Maybe I should have stayed on Ak-Mechat VII.*

'Do not move,' the voice said.

Joshua stopped in midstep, let his boot ease to the ground.

The woman came out of the brush. Her clothes were worn but clean, her face dirt-streaked, although that might've been an attempt at camouflage. She held an old sporting rifle ready, and Joshua noted it was very clean.

He'd sensed someone ahead for about five minutes, just after they'd struck the path they were following. 'Freedom,' he said.

'Or death,' the woman answered, but the gun stayed leveled.

'We have what you've bought,' Chesney said, moving a hand toward the case he was lugging, freezing when the gun barrel was focused on the middle of his chest.

'Put down the rifle, and unfasten your gun belts,' the woman ordered.

They obeyed. A man came from the other side of the path and picked up their weapons.

'Are they carrying any communications gear?'

The man patted them down hastily, eyes meeting Wolfe's nervously, then looking away. 'Nothing,' he said. 'But in that case . . .'

'Don't open it,' the woman and Chesney said in near unison. Wolfe grinned, and a smile almost made it to the woman's lips.

The man shrank back as if it were a tarafny.

'You,' the woman said, indicating Wolfe with her gun barrel. 'Carry it. You go first.'

Joshua picked up the case, slung the strap over his shoulder, and started off.

Ten minutes later, the woman pushed aside brush, and they went up a narrow, skillfully camouflaged side track. The ground had been planted with a tough grass that didn't show bootprints.

They came to a creek about five feet wide and crossed it on the flattened chunk of alloy that served as a bridge. There was a sentry on the other side, young, alert. He looked at Wolfe and Chesney with an expression somewhere between hostility and awe.

They entered the camp. There was a rocky cliff, with a protruding rock shelf that covered the entrance to a low cave that went back for almost fifty feet. There were at least twenty men and women in the camp. A man came out of the cave. 'You can call me Andros.'

Joshua's lips quirked. 'I'm tempted to introduce myself as Homme. But I'm John Taylor. This is – Archibald Tuesday.' Chesney frowned for a minute, then recovered.

'Good,' Andros said. 'No one needs real names until the war is over.'

'Sometimes not even then,' Wolfe said.

'True. But we do not plan on taking our planet in the direction of Messieurs Dzhugashvili and Ulyanov.'

Chesney was puzzled, not understanding what Wolfe

and Andros were talking about. The woman had a faint smile on her face.

'I assume that is what we are paying so dearly for?' Andros indicated the case.

'It is.'

'Very, very good. Now the tide will be on the turning.'

It was just after dark. The rebels had prepared a meal while Chesney and Wolfe washed at the creek. For guerrillas, Chesney said, they ate like gourmets. Fish wrapped and baked in an aromatic leaf, three kinds of unknown vegetables, a meat that tasted like pork dipped in a fiery sauce, then fruit. They drank a cool herbal tea. Their plates and utensils were military-issue plas.

Joshua and Chesney sat just outside the cave mouth with Andros and the woman who'd been introduced as Esperansa. Their guns and packs had been returned and now lay beside them. The other rebels were farther back in the cave, talking quietly over the remains of their meal. There were around forty now, about half of the band, Andros said. The others were out on patrols or staked out on ambushes on the other side of the ridge. 'By rights,' Andros said, 'we should have had a roaring fire and a feast. But infrared detectors have taken the romance out of being a guerrilla.'

'Never mind,' Wolfe said. 'Neither of us believe in parties when we're working.' He looked around the cave.

'Something I'm curious about. You're not planning on assembling the – device here, are you?'

Esperansa laughed aloud. 'No, Mister Taylor. Not here. But I shall not tell you where I'll work.'

'Don't want to know,' Joshua said amiably. 'The only thing I'd like to know is the recipe for that pig we just ate.'

'Pig?' Andros looked puzzled. 'Oh. You mean the baked tarafny?'

Chesney sat suddenly upright, eyes wide.

'We think it's quite fair. The tarafny tries to eat us,' Andros said, pretending not to notice Chesney's dismay, 'so we eat it first.'

'Never mind about the recipe,' Joshua said. 'I don't think, assuming the tarafny is the same charmer we encountered on the trail, it'd be very practical to keep a cageful aboard a starship. Now, perhaps we should talk business?'

Andros poured himself another glass of tea. 'Certainly.' He turned. 'El-Vah,' he called. 'Would you bring me that brown envelope that's in my bedroll?'

A young man came out of the cave carrying the fat envelope. He was armed with a pistol. He gave Wolfe and Chesney a cold look and sat down a few feet to the side.

'Let me ask something first,' Andros said. 'You two are quite a team. When the Inspectorate sprung their trap, we were just outside the village. We saw your ship and knew you were doomed. But you escaped their missiles and came back through their midst, showing your contempt for the swine. I've never seen or heard of such piloting, such skill. Our cause would be greatly helped if we had an attack craft such as yours, with you two piloting it. We could strike real terror in the pigs we've sworn to destroy.'

'How much?' Chesney asked flatly. 'I come expensive, especially since there'd be only one of me, which makes it easier for them to pick a target. And my friend here isn't cheap, either. I won't tell you who he really is, but he was a high-ranking commando officer during the Al'ar War, and has great skills fighting on the land as well as in the air.'

'Ah?' Andros considered Wolfe. 'We could certainly use a master tactician, someone to train our recruits, perhaps lead us in raids until our own officers gain greater experience.'

'Is anyone planning on asking me if I'm interested?' Wolfe asked.

'I don't know if you would be,' Andros said. 'For I must

tell you what we're paying for that package you brought from Bulnes practically bankrupts our treasury here on Osirio. You would have to wait for payment until our coffers are replenished from Bulnes, or from some of our out-system supporters. Not that we would be ungenerous. We would pay what we could now, and give ten times that once the Inspectorate has fallen.'

'I've got other commitments,' Joshua said. 'Sorry.'

'I don't have anything in the fire right now,' Chesney said. 'But one thing a freelancer can't do is fight on the if-come. People have a tendency to forget about what they owe once they've won. Wasn't it Machiavelli who suggested a lord who actually paid his mercenaries any other way than by the sword was a damned fool?'

'I understand,' Andros said. 'And I am sorry we could not afford your further services. So here are the credits we were able to raise.' He held out the envelope.

'*Able* to raise?' Chesney said, disbelief becoming anger.

Andros shook his head. 'It would have been so much simpler if you'd been interested in joining us,' he said, reaching behind him. 'As it is, I'm truly sorry . . .'

Joshua's small hideout gun snapped from his sleeve and he shot Andros in the face. The man rolled on his side, his half-drawn pistol falling into the dirt.

El-Vah drew his pistol. Wolfe shot him in the chest. The boy made a surprised sound in his throat and tumbled backward.

Wolfe heard shouts from the cave as Esperansa brought up her rifle, fumbling with the safety. Two blasters crashed simultaneously and she fell forward onto her face.

Blast rifle up, Wolfe sent a burst into the cave. He tossed Chesney his gun belt, stuffed the brown envelope into his shirt, and shouldered his pack.

'To the trail,' he snapped. 'Back the way we came. Stay just ahead of me.'

Chesney nodded, buckling his gun belt on, hefting his pack. 'What about the case?'

'Leave it. They almost paid for it.'

Somebody shot at them, and the bolt smashed into the ground nearby. Wolfe sent another burst at random and started running, pistol belt slung over his shoulder.

The sentry in the middle of the path looked bewildered. 'What is happening? What –'

Chesney shot him in the head. He spasmed, throwing his rifle high overhead, fell back into the creek. They went over the bridge, and Wolfe kicked the length of alloy down into the water on top of the sentry's body.

He caught up to Chesney. 'We walk like hell for a count of one hundred,' he ordered. 'Then you keep walking for another hundred count, and go off into the brush and wait for me.'

'What're you going to do?'

'Double back, ambush them, then join you. For pity's sake, don't shoot somebody coming up the path whistling. It'll be me.'

'Right.'

'Especially since I still have the envelope with the money.'

'Let's go,' Chesney said. 'I can hear them coming.'

They went on. It was just light enough to dimly follow the path. Wolfe counted carefully, calmly: ninety-eight . . . ninety-nine . . . one hundred.

He ducked to the side, and Chesney kept moving.

Wolfe *felt* out, *felt* them coming. But he didn't need the Lumina. He saw figures in the dimness, pelting up the trail. He stepped out and fired a long burst.

There were screams, wild shots. Another burst followed the first, then Wolfe went uphill once more. *Damn, but I wish I had some grenades*, he thought with the part of his mind that wasn't counting.

At fifty, he stopped, frowning. He thought for a brief moment, then turned off the path.

Chesney lay prone, pistol pointing back down the path, ready to fire. He shrieked involuntarily as a hand came down on his shoulder, and Wolfe crouched beside him.

'God, god, gods,' he almost sobbed. 'Don't *do* that, man. My heart's not up to that. Why didn't you –'

'Wasn't sure there might not be a mistake,' Wolfe said.

'I heard you shooting them up,' Chesney said, voice nervous. 'Did you get them all?'

'Nope. I'm not that efficient a killer.'

'So what's next? Are we going to have to keep running?'

'We are – but I've got a way to slow them down, or anyway give them somebody else to worry about.' He dug into his pack. 'I brought these along in case we needed a diversion,' he explained, holding up two spacesuit emergency flares. He took the end cap from one, inverted it, and put it on the other end.

'Wolfe, everybody on the goddamned planet'll see that!'

'Hope so,' Joshua said, and slammed his hand against the cap. White fire hissed upward nearly a thousand feet, and blossomed into a series of red-green-red-green flashes.

Joshua sent another one after the first. Chesney was still utterly bewildered.

'Now we turn left,' Wolfe said. 'We'll move parallel with the ridge crest until dawn. Then we'll turn uphill again, and cross into our own valley. Up and at 'em, soldier.'

Minutes after they started moving, they heard the whine of gravlighters and saw lights in the sky.

'Down, and hope the Inspectorate's shitty with people-sniffers,' Joshua ordered.

Explosions boomed, and the ground shuddered around them.

'Good,' Joshua said. 'Bomb that old jungle. Always do it the easy way.'

There were high screams from the sky, and a pair of scoutships dove down. Fire blossomed from their bellies, and rockets slammed into the mountain.

'They'll keep that up all night, if I know my amateurs,' Wolfe said, 'then land troops on top of the mountain and sweep down. When – if the Inspectorate discovers the cave, they'll have something to keep them busy, and they won't be looking for us.'

Just before dawn they heard gunfire and explosions. 'They found them,' Chesney said.

'Maybe,' Wolfe said. 'Or maybe they're shooting up each other or a really offensive tree.'

'I hope they get the bastards.'

'Why? They did something stupid,' Wolfe said, 'and it seems to me they've already paid for it.'

'I don't like people who try to kill me.'

'An understandable emotion. I frequently share it.'

Chesney was staggering by the time the sun came up. Joshua found an impenetrable thicket, and they pushed their way into it. Chesney went immediately to sleep, not offering to stand guard.

Wolfe let his senses float out but *felt* nothing. He calmed himself, breathing steadily, and let his body relax while his mind watched.

Around midday, Chesney grunted and woke up. He saw Wolfe sitting cross-legged, counting money. 'How much do we have?' he asked.

'A little less than half a million,' Joshua said. 'Again, it appears real.' He shook his head. 'They should've bargained instead of going for the guns. Two-thirds isn't bad soldier's pay.'

Chesney nodded agreement. 'You're right,' he said. 'Lord knows I've taken less and not cried all night. But why the hell can't people stay honest?'

Wolfe looked at him without replying.

Chesney had the grace to turn away.

They moved slowly, quietly, following the mountain crest, until almost midnight, then they holed up until just before dawn. Aircraft constantly passed overhead, scoutships, lighters, gravsleds. But none slowed, so Wolfe paid no mind.

They crossed the few open spaces at a trot, listening carefully first. 'We're making a big circle,' Wolfe explained. 'We'll have one more night in the open, then make the *Resolute* not long after first light.'

'Oh Lord, a consummation devoutly to be made,' Chesney misquoted fervently. 'I never knew I could smell so bad. I'm going to *live* in the fresher until further notice. Is that what it's like being a soldier?'

'Nope,' Wolfe said. 'It's when you don't know you stink and don't care either that you start soldiering.'

That night, when Chesney slept, Wolfe slid over beside him. He picked up Chesney's pistol and pushed its bell mouth firmly down into the ground they lay on. He wiped the dirt from the outside of the barrel, and set it back down near the pilot's hand.

Chesney touched controls on the tiny box and waited.

Brown water roiled, and the *Resolute* surfaced. Its secondary drive hummed, pushing it close to the bank. Its lock door opened, and the gangway slid out. Wolfe started down the bank.

'Joshua.'

Wolfe stopped.

'Turn around, Wolfe. I don't like being a back-shooter unless I have to.'

Joshua obeyed.

Chesney had his pistol aimed in both hands at Wolfe's chest. 'I really don't think three-quarters of a mill is enough for two people,' he said, and his voice gloated as it had when he told Trevor he was wrong. 'And I don't think I'll be sharing it with our mutual friend, either.'

'You don't want to do that, Merrett,' Joshua said.

'Oh, but I have to,' Chesney said, and his voice had a tone like the ring of cracked crystal. 'I know you weren't sleeping. I know I was talking in my sleep. No one must know about me. No one.'

'I said, don't do it,' Wolfe said calmly.

The dirt-clogged barrel of Chesney's gun was aimed steadily at Wolfe. 'But I'm going to,' Chesney said.

Wolfe turned, started up the *Resolute*'s gangway.

Merrett Chesney laughed again, convulsively jerking the trigger.

'Chesney's dead,' Wolfe said into the blank screen.

'How?'

'He didn't believe people tell the truth sometimes,' Joshua said.

'What does that mean?'

The transrnitter hissed for a while.

'All right,' the voice conceded. 'He was a strange one at best. I suppose you knew about him?'

'I learned.'

'He was so afraid of anyone finding out, and I think everyone knew. Oh well. So what next?'

'No changes,' Wolfe said. 'I've got nearly three-quarters of a million credits. I take my cut, drop the rest off with you.'

'What's the split?'

'I'm going to take my fifty percent of what we agreed on, plus half of his fifty percent for general aggravation,' Joshua said. 'You get the rest.'

'Pretty damned generous,' the voice said.

'Why not? I've got a ship now, so I can afford to keep up the old ties.'

'Good. Nice doing business with you,' the voice said. 'Stand by to record.'

Wolfe scanned the control panel of the *Resolute,* found the recorder, and switched it on.

The voice reeled a set of coordinates, then: 'Got them?'

'I do.'

'Good.' There was a moment of silence. 'Wolfe . . . I'm sorry about what happened – but you understand how business works.'

Wolfe lifted an eyebrow.

'Clear,' the voice said, and the contact was broken.

The coordinates were for open space, far between systems, near the fringes of the Federation. During the war a great battle had been fought here, and the shattered hulks of starships, Federation and Al'ar, still spun in aimless orbits.

A medium-size, ultramodern starship hung in space at exactly the specified points.

Wolfe opened his com. 'Unknown ship, this is the *Resolute.*'

'Go ahead, *Resolute*. You have the credits?' It was an unfamiliar voice. Wolfe shrugged. He hardly expected his contact to meet him personally.

'I have.'

'Come on across, then.'

Wolfe breathed, *felt* across the distance. There was nothing. No warmth, but no threat. He tucked his hideout gun into his waistband, put on a spacesuit, buckled on a heavy blaster, went into the lock, and cycled himself into space.

It was dark, except for the far-distant glimmer of forgotten suns. Wolfe turned on a suit spotlight, jetted across the short distance to the other ship, and touched down next to its lock.

The outer door was open. Wolfe went into it, closed the lock door, and let the lock cycle.

The door opened into luxury. Stepping out of the lock, Wolfe saw three men with guns. They wore strange helmets that fit snugly from the base of the neck over the top of the head and down over the forehead. Reflecting goggles hid their eyes.

They held blast rifles leveled.

Joshua slowly lifted his hands, grimly cursing his carelessness.

A man came out of a compartment. He also wore a helmet, but instead of a suit he wore a uniformlike tunic with a jagged crimson streak on the chest.

'If you move, you're dead,' said a voice in Joshua's speaker.

The man took Wolfe's gun, gingerly unfastened his helmet, and lifted it away. His hand came back very quickly with an air-hypo against Wolfe's neck, and he pressed the stud. Wolfe jerked aside, but not in time.

'There.' The voice came from another room. 'That's got you.'

A door slid open. Out came Jalon Kakara. He walked over to Wolfe. His eyes were alive with rage, hate. 'I warned you,' he said, and smashed his fist into Wolfe's face.

'I warned you,' he said again.

FIFTEEN

SECRET

By the authority of Federation Millitary Regulation 267-65-909, the following INACTIVE RESERVE UNITS are REACTIVATED and will participate in Federation maneuvers as soon as they are at full TO&E strength:

783rd Military Police Battalion
43rd Starport Security Detachment
12th Public Information (Active) Detachment
7th Long Range Patrolling Unit (less 17th Troop)
96th Logistical Command
21st Scoutship Flight
78th Scoutship Flight
111th Scoutship Flight
831st Heavy Transport Wing
96th Field Headquarters Support Company
4077th Field Medical Unit
3411th Field Medical Unit
9880th Field Medical Unit

All members of these units are to report IMMEDIATELY, and are permitted to use any civilian transportation necessary, and are authorized the highest priority in reaching their units. Members of these units should advise their dependents they will be on extended active service and, at this time, there is no capability for dependents to travel with them, nor will their new posts allow dependent housing. This activation is a purely routine test of the Federation's ability to mobilize. There is no cause whatsoever for alarm or false rumor.

FOR THE COMMANDER:

Tara Phelps
Vice Admiral
Federation J-1

SIXTEEN

'I told you,' Kakara went on, 'to sleep with one eye open –
but you didn't. You just went on about your merry way, as
if you could steal my wife and there'd never be any paybacks to worry about.'

Wolfe tried to speak, couldn't.

Kakara grinned. 'Can't talk, can you? Just so you know,
you've been hit with about two hundred cc's of HypnoDec.
Your automatic body controls function, but that's about it.
Go ahead. Try to walk.'

Wolfe's sluggish mind tried to work, tried to reach out,
tried to *feel* the great Lumina a few hundred yards away in
the *Resolute*.

He was empty, drained, half-stunned.

'You see,' Kakara gloated. 'You see? Now here's the way
things are going to work. You've gotten a preliminary
dosage. So right now you're suggestible. I'm programming
you now, just like a frigging computer.' He turned to his
aide. 'Hit him with the rest of the dose.'

The man obeyed.

'Good,' Kakara said. 'Now I can tell you to kill yourself,
if I wanted to. But I don't. We need you, Wolfe. Go to
sleep! Sleep!'

Wolfe's eyelids drooped, he sagged, fell forward.

'Catch him,' Kakara ordered, and two of the suited men
had Wolfe's suit by the utility belt.

'Good,' Kakara said. 'Very, very good. Move him into the lab, strip him, and body-search him. Check his body cavities, make sure the son of a bitch doesn't have any surprises. If there are any, it'll be your asses.'

'What about his ship?' one of the suited men asked.

'Destroy it,' Kakara ordered.

Somewhere, deep in some distant ocean, Wolfe's mind stirred, felt red panic, horror. Somehow he pulled himself up, pushed toward the surface miles away.

Somehow he *reached* out . . .

Or perhaps the Lumina *reached* for him.

'Never mind,' Kakara said. 'I changed my mind. Don't waste the energy. Let the ship rust with the others.'

Joshua heard words, repeated over and over.

'Wake up, wake up, come on, man, wake up. Dammit, something's wrong!'

Wolfe floated toward the sea's surface.

'Nothing is wrong,' a calm, sterile voice said. 'We possibly gave him too much HypnoDec, and he's taking some time to come back to awareness.

'Do not fret, Kakara. All worry does is shorten your life.'

Wolfe heard an inarticulate snarl of rage, was just below the surface.

'Yeah,' Kakara said. 'Yeah, he's back with us. I saw his eyes flicker. Can you hear me?'

'I can hear you,' Wolfe said.

'Can you understand me?'

'I can understand you.'

'Is he telling the truth?'

'He is,' the calm voice said. 'Perhaps he's not fully able to analyze what you say, but your speech, your orders are absorbed, and will be retained in his memory.'

'Good,' Kakara said. 'I want to give him something that'll eat at him. Listen to me, Wolfe. I know who you are,

I know everything about you. Joshua Wolfe, prisoner of the Al'ar, commando hotshot during the war, worked for Federation Intelligence, fell on hard times like most soldiers when there's no public tit to suck on, ended up in the Outlaw Worlds as no more'n a bounty hunter. Freelanced for FI, got on their wrong side, is currently hotter'n hell, though there aren't any wanted posters up yet.

'How about that shit?

'When you stole Rita – I don't know why, but you're going to tell me – I told you not to make any long-range investments, didn't I? Jalon Kakara gets what he wants. *Always*. So I started looking for you. I started by back-tracking. There's some dead people around, thanks to you. I started with that bitch at the employment agency who sent you to me. She didn't know shit – that resume you mickeyed up fooled her good. But she's dead. I don't like people who play games with me.

'But then I had a dead end. I figured I'd been had by a pro, and there aren't many slick ones. So I had my security people – I've got real good ones, you know – start looking in the sewers people like you live in. One name kept coming up. Joshua Wolfe. But the holo I got didn't match the one on your employment record, so I set it aside.

'But your damned name kept appearing again and again. And most of your compatriots could be accounted for: dead, working, or with good alibis. And this Joshua Wolfe liked working as either a gambler or a barkeep when he was undercover.

'So I took a chance. I play poker like that, too. Get a feeling about things – and I'm damned seldom wrong. And I remembered the number of crooks who've had their faces rebuilt when the heat was on. I went looking for you. Looked hard. Posted a big reward. Real big.

'Nothing for a while, and I was starting to think I was wrong, when I got a call from somebody you know. He said you were doing a job for him, but he'd be willing to hand you over for a price I was willing to pay, if you got out alive. He even left a message for you. "Like I said, it's only business," he told me to tell you. Nice friends you got, Wolfe. I would've cleaned up his loose end, but he's a very cagey player and hard to locate. Sooner or later, though, I'll get a lead, and wrap him up, too. Doesn't all that make whatever brain's not doped up squirm, Wolfe? Make you finally realize who you went up against?

'Now I'll tell you what I want you for, but I bet if your mind was working you would've figured it out by now. You're going to tell me where Rita is, and, since I assume you didn't take her for yourself, who the bastard is who's got her.'

Wolfe's breathing came fast, and his fingers clawed.

'No, you fool!' the sterile voice came. 'You just alerted one of his compulsion modes. Continue and he's not unlikely to have a brain hemorrhage or even suicide!'

'All right, all right,' Kakara's voice went. 'Forget what I just said about Rita.'

Wolfe's breathing eased.

'This is like walking through a minefield,' Kakara complained. 'All right, Brandt, what do I do now? And don't ever call me a fool again. I only give people but one warning.'

'My apologies,' the voice said, undisturbed. 'Tell him to come fully awake.'

'Wolfe, wake up. See, hear, feel,' Kakara said.

Wolfe surfaced. He felt the table he was lying on, and the restraining straps. He opened his eyes.

Standing next to Kakara was a slender, balding rather friendly-looking man in his early sixties, wearing old-fashioned glasses. He was dressed a bit formally, in an expensive lapel-less jacket and pants and tip-collared shirt.

'Joshua Wolfe,' the man said, 'I am Doctor Carl Brandt. Have you ever heard of me?'

'No,' Wolfe said.

'That is good,' Brandt said. 'For I've always despised the limelight.' He surveyed Wolfe with a smile. 'You must forgive my pride, but I consider you my creation. For quite some time I worked for Federation Intelligence. I am the one who devised the various mindblocks and suicide programs that you've been conditioned with so you wouldn't have to worry about torture, drugs, or pro-longed interrogation. Very seldom have I had the chance to examine one of my field operatives, particularly one who's been through as much stress as you. While you were unconscious, I ran a battery of mechanical tests, and I am certainly impressed with your mental stability, at least as far as physiological means could determine. I would dearly like to have some time with you, and perform a complete analysis, but Kakara said that's impossible. Since I'm now working for him, I'll just have to watch from the sidelines, I'm afraid.'

'You see, Wolfe?' Kakara said. 'You can't even escape by dying. Somebody warned me all of you hotshot spooks were loaded for bear, and if anybody fooled around with your mind, tried to interrogate you or use heavy drugs, you'd kill yourself. Shut your brain off permanently, cause a heart seizure – they said there could be a dozen ways you'd been modified to suicide. So I went looking for a good head-splitter, and got lucky. I've found the harder you work, the luckier you get. I ended up with the guy who put you – or anyway the people like you – together.

'Another precaution I took. I kept hearing stories about how you could do things other people couldn't, and I remembered how you managed to hypnotize me, and some other people so we thought you were invisible. Or maybe you even *can* make yourself invisible. The reality doesn't matter much. A couple of people my men talked to said it was because you spent so much time with the Al'ar. They said you were about half Al'ar yourself. Jesus, no wonder I get the skincrawls around you. You're a goddamned monster like they were. That gave me some problems. Then Doctor Brandt told me about something you probably never heard of.'

'The Federation was well aware of the Al'ar's mental abilities,' Brandt said. 'They mounted a crash program to find a way to keep the Al'ar from exerting their powers against men. They tested several versions in combat, but none seemed to work, except for those helmets you saw Mister Kakara's men wearing. They were tried out in a raid just before the Grand Offensive, and appeared to make men invisible to the Al'ar, or at any rate the postaction report said the Al'ar were confused at their appearance. There wasn't time to put the helmets into production before the Grand Offensive, and then, when the Al'ar vanished, there wasn't any need for them. I had read the preliminary reports, and was able to find a handful of the experimental models. It would appear the reports were correct, wouldn't it? You certainly weren't about to do anything to prevent your capture.'

'You see?' Kakara said. '|We've got you fore and aft, as they used to say. All right, Doctor. Enough talk. How do we get this bastard to do what we want?'

'Quite simple,' Brandt said. 'You cannot ask him to reveal his secrets. But you can order him to take us to wherever your wife is. And you can order him to make sure she expects friends, not enemies. Ask simple, direct questions, and you'll receive a direct answer. Don't ask for any interpretations or extrapolations. Even with the drug, he has enough free will to avoid answering those. Or else his avoidance mechanisms will be activated.'

A slow, dirty smile spread across Kakara's broad, battered face. 'All right, then. Take me to Rita.'

The sea was a tempest above. Wolfe sank deeper, deeper.

'Set your nav coordinates for the deep space settlement known as Malabar, in the Outlaw Worlds,' he told Kakara.

Kakara poured himself another drink, lifted it in a toast to the rigid figure of Joshua Wolfe. They were alone in the ship's luxurious captain's suite. 'Let me tell you what's going to happen,' he said, 'once I get Rita. First, I'll kill you, because I don't want any chance of a slipup, and I'm still not sure what you are, a man or an Al'ar. But you won't die easy.

'I thought I'd kill this man, whoever he is, next. But then I considered . . . I think I'll have some fun with Rita first. Show that bastard what I used to like to do to her. But this time, I'll let it go further than I did. Then I'll kill him. Slower than you died.

'As for Rita . . . I thought for a while I'd kill her last,' Kakara said, breathing heavily. 'But there's worse things than death. After I finish with her, maybe let some of my men have their fun too, I'll leave her alive. Maybe I'll drop her on a world I can think of, with some supplies. Put a bird with a camera on her, and watch what happens. There's – things, I've never been sure what they are, might be interested in her . . . I'd like that.'

Kakara wiped his mouth with the back of his hand. 'Yeah,' he repeated. 'I'd like that.' He sat for a time, just staring at Wolfe. There was a tap at the door. 'Come in.'

A man wearing Kakara's jagged crimson flare on a uniform tunic came in, with a sheaf of printout. 'I have some preliminary data on Malabar, sir.'

'Give me a verbal,' Kakara ordered. 'Wolfe, this is Pak, one of my analysts. He's helped make Kakara Transport what it is. I use him for the cute details that I'd just as soon nobody know I need. Like what shipping line president likes to hire cute young men for traveling companions, or who grafted who during the war. I set him to work finding out about Malabar. Go ahead, Pak.'

'Malabar's the name for the biggest planetoid,' the man said. 'It's not much more than a moonlet in an asteroid belt, system bap-bap-bap, coordinates thus-and-so, one-time Special Operations Naval Base during the war. After the war it was turned into a parking place for parts of the mothballed fleet.'

'Huh! We ever arrange to get a ship from there, back when we were getting started?'

'No, sir. It's pretty well on the fringes of nowhere. It's got a reputation for being a smuggler's base, an illegal ship-yard, a transshipment point, and so forth. Not much shows on the surface – most everything's underground. No esti-mates on current population. Somehow it's been converted to private property, even though the mothballed ships are evidently still there.'

'Any government?'

'None I could find. The official caretaker for the scrapheap is someone named Cormac. An ex-Spec Ops pilot, highly decorated, frequently reprimanded. That's the only name he uses now, but his full name is Cormac Pearse. Discharged with the rank of commander.'

'Rita was a pilot during the war,' Kakara said. 'I got the idea she was involved with that stupid commando shit, too. Wolfe, is he the one?'

Joshua said nothing.

'Shitfire,' Kakara said in exasperation. 'Do you know this man Cormac?'

'Yes.'

'Did he know Rita Sidamo?'

'Yes.'

'Well, well. So Malabar's where we're going, and it's a real den of thieves, eh? Pak, is that something for us to worry about?'

'Negative, sir,' the brown-skinned man with the calm face said. 'I've never known criminals, or anyone on the wrong side of the law, to stick up for anyone other than themselves . . . or possibly for an immediate gain.'

'And there surely isn't an advantage going up against Jalon Kakara. Still . . . Send in Captain Ives. I think we'll visit Malabar with a little muscle.'

Five ships broke out of N-space. One was Kakara's liner, two were converted troop transports, two more were scout-ships. All wore the jagged crimson insignia.

About three E-diameters distant floated dead starships, warships, liners, freighters, and yachts, orbiting close to the largest planetoid in a scattered asteroid belt.

In the liner's main salon and in the two troopship holds, armed men stared at tall screens, listening to Jalon Kakara:

'. . . the bastards have been very happy here on Malabar, taking a ship of mine here, a cargo there, for five or six years. It's taken us that long to track them down, but finally we've found their little den of thieves. The Federation does-n't seem interested in intervening, although I've requested support half a dozen times or more.

'Most of you know Jalon Kakara, and know he doesn't stand interference, and if pressed he has a way of taking care of things in the most effective way possible, if maybe not the way bleeding hearts would prefer.

'That's you, men. Some of you have worked for me in the past on ticklish little jobs like this, and you know how you're taken care of. You've already seen the insurance poli-cies, no questions asked if anything happens to you, seen the weapons you're issued, and know how promptly you're paid if the mission is successful. This whole operation will be on the same level. All I want is no more Malabar. Not ever. When we pull out, we'll set blasting charges so no other jackals will be able to use this den. And as far as what happens to the men – and women – who're down there . . . They've cast themselves beyond the law, haven't they? Now the law – *my* law – has winkled 'em out. We'll deal with them the best, most permanent way we know, won't we?'

There were hungry roars of approval.

Jalon Kakara motioned, and the pickup went dead. 'That's as much as they need to know.' He walked across the bridge of the liner to another com, where Wolfe sat. Joshua wore a tiny receiver in one ear, and Brandt, standing to one side, out of pickup range, wore a bonemike. Kakara picked up another mike, positioned it on his breastbone.

'Go ahead,' Kakara said. 'Make the call.'

Wolfe sat motionless.

'*Mister* Kakara,' Brandt said in reproof.

'Sorry,' Kakara grudged, then said, precisely, 'Wolfe, contact Malabar without arousing alarm.'

Far down, Joshua fought for control of his mind, his lips. They moved silently, then spoke aloud: 'Malabar Control, Malabar Control. This is the –'

'*Corsair*.' Brandt's whisper was loud in Joshua's ear.

'This is the *Corsair*. Request approach and docking instructions.'

Wolfe waited, not patiently, not impatiently. Finally: '*Corsair*, this is Malabar' came from the com. 'We're a private port, and don't grant approach or landing permission without reason.'

Wolfe sat motionless, as if the information had no meaning.

Kakara pursed his lips angrily. 'Go ahead,' he whispered. 'Contact your friend Cormac. Tell him it's all right. Tell him who you are. Just like the last time you talked to him.'

Just like the last time . . .

'Malabar, this is *Corsair*. Request you contact Cormac. Tell him I shackle Wilbur Frederick Milton unshackle. Sender Ghost.'

'*Corsair*, wait.'

Time passed, then: 'Ghost,' a different voice said, 'this is Cormac. Golf Alpha.'

'This is Ghost India,' Wolfe said.

A few seconds passed, then: 'Welcome back to Malabar, Joshua. I assume everything's well with you.'

Wolfe made no reply.

'Joshua,' Cormac said, 'are you all right?'

'He's got a virus,' Brandt whispered. Kakara nodded, keyed his mike.

'You have a virus.'

'I'm all right,' Wolfe said. 'I have a virus.'

'Well, come on down, and tell me where you acquired that fine fleet I see. Evidently times've been good.'

Wolfe made no response.

'You're doing fine,' Kakara prodded.

'I'm doing fine,' Wolfe echoed.

'Guess it doesn't hurt to be warmish with the Fed, eh? Good. Tell your ship captains to switch to channel 643, and I'll have Control give them individual docking instructions. As for you, you rogue, I've still got the De Montel you didn't finish last time.'

'Good,' Kakara said. 'Why don't you and Rita meet me?'

'Good,' Wolfe said. 'Why don't you – you and Rita meet me?'

'That's what we planned,' Cormac's voice said. 'See you in a few, Ghost India.'

'Ghost India. Out.'

'Now,' Kakara gloated, 'now it'll all come paid.'

He turned to the bridge.

'Captain Ives. Take the deck. Have two men with rifles meet me in the forward lock.'

'Yes, sir.'

'I'll disembark first with Brandt and Wolfe. Stay linked with me, and I'll give the word for the main attack. We've got a chance to nip 'em in the bud now, and if their leaders are down our job'll be even easier.'

'Yes, sir.'

'Let's go, Wolfe. This is what they call the hour of reckoning.'

Kakara was suited up, except for his helmet. He took an expensive live-mask from its pouch, pulled it over his head, and tugged at its earlobe on-sensor. The mask took a moment to warm up and mold to his features. Kakara now was a balding, bearded, benevolent-looking man who might've been a banker. 'Like I said, I think of everything,' he said, and pulled his helmet on, sealed it, and closed the faceplate.

'Cycle the lock,' he ordered. 'Entering Malabar. Go first, Wolfe.'

Joshua obeyed, walking carefully, one alloy-suited foot in front of the other.

His mind clawed, spat like a caged catamount, *reaching* out, swirling as the deep ocean currents swept him helplessly around.

Then he *felt* another wave, far distant, growing from nothingness, from another ocean, one that held everything, held the 'red virus,' held the Al'ar Guardians.

He remembered long years ago, on a gray shore, being very small, and watching someone he loved dive into a cresting wave, and he felt fear for that person. Then the person's hand waved, and he was swimming safely on the far side of the wave as it curled, broke, smashed into shore. Another wave loomed, and feet kicked, and the man – it was a man, his father – swam forward, was swept up by the wave, lying in it, cradled like Joshua's mother cradled him, one hand jutting out, the other along his side, and the wave held him, and he was using the wave, letting its power carry him toward . . .

'Come on, Wolfe,' Kakara ordered. 'On through.'

The outer lock of the liner closed, then the outer lock of Malabar.

Joshua felt the whirr of machinery, then heard it dimly as air filled the lock and the inner door slid open.

The five men went into a bare room.

'Where's your friend?'

Wolfe made no response.

Kakara hesitated. 'We'll unsuit,' he ordered, and twisted his helmet off. 'Take off your suit.'

Wolfe slowly obeyed. As he stepped out of the lower half of the suit, a speaker crackled. 'Joshua, this is Cormac. A slideway was stuck, so we're running a little behind. Be there in a moment.'

Kakara smiled thinly. 'I like a man who's in a hurry to get what he's due,' he almost-whispered, then started as a wall panel slid away, revealing a long, dimly lit hall. 'What do we do, Wolfe?'

'Go down there,' Joshua said. 'He will meet us.'

Kakara motioned them forward, his other hand near his holstered gun.

They started down the corridor, first Wolfe; then Brandt, beside and a little behind him; then Kakara and the two gunmen.

The great, friendly wave was roaring, coming closer, but still far, far away . . .

A panel slid open about thirty yards distant, and Rita Sidamo and Cormac stepped out. Rita wore a close-fitting tunic, Cormac his familiar khaki pants, faded shirt, and old sleeveless sweater. Neither appeared armed.

Wolfe fought to cry out, to strike, but he could do nothing.

'It's nice seeing you again, Rita,' Kakara said, stripping off the mask and drawing his pistol.

'It is you,' Rita said, her voice cold with loathing, but

utterly unsurprised. 'I thought you might have changed, might've been able to let go of things, but –'

'Neither of you move,' Kakara said. He keyed his bone-mike: 'Ives, send in the men.'

Cormac leaned back against the passage wall. He shook his head sadly. 'Kakara,' he said, 'you're just about a thorough utter damned fool and someone should have put you out of your misery years ago.'

'The only one who'll be doing any killing is me,' Kakara said. 'Both of you, get your hands up. Now! Connors, Amtel, take them!'

The two men drew their guns, walked forward.

The wave was closer, much closer, its hissing promise of danger loud, very loud . . .

Rita started laughing.

'Jesus God, but Cormac's right. You're so damned *dumb*.' The two holo images vanished as a door panel slid away, and the real Cormac shot Amtel and Connors. The panel closed as Kakara snapped a shot, and the bolt crashed harmlessly into the nearby wall.

The wave broke . . .

Now everyone was underwater, and Kakara's shout of alarm was blurred. Wolfe was in no hurry, had all the time in the universe. The drug still flowed in him, but there were antibodies, leukocytes surrounding each molecule of HypnoDec, isolating it, eliminating it . . .

Wolfe was turning, hands, feet in the reflexive attack stance . . .

Kakara spun, almost falling, pistol coming up . . . Brandt's mouth was open. He was shouting.

Wolfe sidekicked him forward as Kakara fired. The bolt smashed away Brandt's lower jaw and upper cheekbone. He shrieked, clawed at himself, fell.

Kakara's gun bucked with the recoil. He pulled it back on target, and Joshua was crouched, spinning, then up, and his foot caught the blaster, sent it whirling ten feet away to clatter against the deck of the passageway.

Joshua *felt* out, *felt* behind the passageway wall, *felt* Cormac and Rita. Cormac had his gun in one hand, his other on a panel-opening sensor. Joshua *felt* inside the sensor, *felt* its tiny parts. One of them bent, and the lock was jammed. He turned to Kakara. Now there was all the time in the world.

Kakara's eyes were wide in fear.

'You told me once you were good with a knife,' Joshua said softly. 'There's a blade in your pocket. Get it.'

Kakara's eyes never left Joshua's face. His hand swooped into a pocket, came out with a long folding knife. It snapped open with a click.

'No Al'ar secrets,' Joshua mocked. 'No games. Come to me, Jalon Kakara. You're mine.'

Now Joshua was riding the wave, part of it, its power his, spray and foam, and he saw his father laughing from the shore, a woman beside him, his mother; young, alive . . .

Kakara came in cautiously, left hand extended at chest level, right about a foot below, behind the left, holding the knife like a fencer holds his foil, moving sideways, circling, moving toward Wolfe's weak side.

He slashed, and Joshua wasn't there, ducking under the slice, then coming up. Wolfe's right hand blurred, and the back of his fingernails whipped across Kakara's forehead, just a touch but drawing red lines, and then blood poured.

Kakara lunged from a crouch, forefoot sliding out. His knifepoint touched Wolfe's breastbone, then glanced away.

Joshua spun inside him, drove his elbow back into Kakara's shoulder, had his forearm in his left hand, yanked him down toward his knee as it snapped up, and Kakara's ribs smashed. Kakara screamed, fell. Joshua sprang away, waited for him to recover.

The man came halfway to his feet, charged, knife hand slashing, back, forth. Wolfe jumped to one side, struck down with a claw hand, and Kakara's ear ripped, tore, dangled down on his cheek.

A very faint smile came to Wolfe's lips, stayed there.

Kakara lunged once more, and Wolfe's left hand shot out palm first, smashing into Kakara's face below the eyebrow. Kakara's eyeball split as if it had been smashed with a hammer, and clear fluid poured down his face.

Kakara backed away, half-blind, bloody as a bull after the picadors, knife weaving a steel blockade against Wolfe.

'Enough,' Wolfe said. 'Let's finish it.'

Joshua snapped a block with his right hand, kicked into Kakara's armpit, turned inside Kakara's guard, and struck the knife from his hand almost delicately.

Kakara balled his hands into fists, but it was too late.

Joshua shouted and struck Kakara full force in the solar plexus with a right spear-hand. He didn't have time to scream as Wolfe recovered and drove his palm into Kakara's forehead.

The big man's skull smashed like a thin-skinned melon as Joshua reached with his right, tapped four fingers sharply against Kakara's heart, denied it permission to beat, and let the corpse slump to the deck.

The wave was nothing but foam, and there was sand gritting under Joshua's knees, and he rolled sideways, came to his feet in the shallows, laughing, tasting the ocean's salt.

Wolfe stood in an empty corridor, the taste of salt strong in his mouth, four bodies at his feet. There was a smashing sound, and a door panel ripped off its slide, and Cormac and Rita came out, guns ready. When they saw the bodies, both relaxed.

'For a man with a virus infection, you seem to have done all right,' Cormac said.

'The bastard ambushed me,' Wolfe explained. 'Had me under a hypnotic.'

'You did fine, Ghost,' Cormac said. 'But why the hell didn't he screen you, make sure what you were going to say meant . . .'

'He told me soldiers weren't worth anything once they were off the public tit,' Wolfe said. 'A man who thinks like that isn't going to care about one phonetic letter instead of another.'

'I figured something was wrong when Control told me the shackle code you gave him. You never were the kind of slob who uses the same one twice, so that was enough to put my boys in motion. But thanks for the second warning, Ghost India instead of Actual,' Cormac said.

'He was always like that,' Rita said. 'Bull your way through, and everything'll fall into place.' She looked at the body. 'Didn't work this time, did it, Jalon?'

'I assume you can lumber to our quarters under your own power and let the rest of that hypnotic wear off,' Cormac said. 'Rita'll escort you. I'll go make sure Kakara's goons are policed up.'

'They shouldn't be much of a bother,' Joshua said. 'One of Kakara's toadies said thieves never fight together. I think their morale is being shaken right about now.'

'So he thought he was coming into a nest of thieves, eh?' Cormac laughed humorlessly. 'Didn't anybody suspect I anticipate visitors and have a welcome committee on standby? Kakara was a long way from being the first to want to pluck this ripe, dangling fruit called Malabar. Who was it who said a man must be moral to live beyond the law?'

'I forget,' Joshua said. 'Jesse James, maybe. Or Tamerlane.'

Cormac went back through the panel into the hidden passage and was gone.

Rita was still staring down at Kakara's body. 'You probably hurt him a lot worse than I would've,' she said. 'But you should've let me kill him.'

'You weren't around,' Joshua said blandly, thinking of the jammed lock.

'I didn't mean now,' the woman said. 'I mean back when you pulled me away from him. Back aboard the *Laurel*.'

Joshua grimaced. 'Yeah,' he said. 'I guess I should have.'

The five men, all experienced at reconning hostile artificial worlds, entered the big, empty chamber cautiously, keeping low, guns moving, pointing like searching eyes.

Small gunports opened behind, above them.

'Now?' a scarred man asked.

'Now,' said a woman who, but for her hard, knowing eyes, could've been his daughter, and gunfire spattered.

A trapdoor opened as one of Kakara's officers stepped on it, the antigrav generator at the bottom of the shaft activated at full reverse thrust, and he fell screaming. The dozen men behind him shrank back and huddled against the walls.

A voice spoke: 'The rest of the passage's on hinges too, boys. Better throw away the guns.'

The men looked at each other, then threw their blasters down the hall.

'That was sensible,' the voice said. 'Just stay where you are. There'll be somebody along to collect you in a while. Maybe if you're good we'll feed you a beer.'

The room was circular, opulent, with scarlet drapes hanging from a high ceiling. There were tables with half-eaten meals, half-empty glasses. It was deserted.

The seven men entered. One picked up a glass and was about to sample its contents.

'Don't,' his leader hissed. 'Poison!'

The man dropped it. It smashed on the marble floor.

Then the room was full of laughter, rich, amused, female.

One man tried the door they'd entered through and found it locked. The other doors were locked as well.

'What do we do now?' one whispered.

Echoing laughter was his only reply.

The two scoutships hung in space just off Malabar, 'above' the docked liner and troopships.

Two missiles floated from the back side of the planetoid, and fire hissed from their tails as they went to full drive. Alarms shrilled on the scoutships, and one managed a countermissile launch. The second was too slow, and vanished in a ball of greasy flame and quickly vanishing smoke. A third, fourth, and fifth missile arced around the planetoid's surface, overloading the first scoutship's sensors.

It too exploded soundlessly.

'This is Malabar Control,' came through the speakers on the bridge of Kakara's liner. 'We have taken or killed all of your men. Jalon Kakara is dead. Surrender, or we shall launch missiles against your ships. Reply immediately on this frequency.'

The voice was Cormac's.

On the bridge, Captain Ives looked at Pak, who avoided his gaze.

'You have thirty seconds,' Cormac's voice said.

Ives picked up a com.

'We'll sort through them,' Cormac said cheerily, 'then arrange for one of our ships to dump them somewhere not too far from civilization, on its next run with the goodies . . . Not that I'm sure what's still civilization. Things have been getting decidedly strange.'

'I know,' Wolfe agreed. He picked up the snifter, swirled it, sipped, and set it back down. 'I better not have any more of this before dinner,' he said. 'I've been leading a clean life lately, and I'm sort of out of training.'

'Just as well,' Cormac said, draining his beer. 'I'm starving. Rita, where are we going to eat?'

'Fifth Level,' she said. 'They're doing a victory banquet. I already accepted.'

'You want company, Joshua? I can think of a couple of lovelies who wouldn't mind meeting the Hee-ro of Malabar.'

Kristin's face came to Wolfe, was pushed away.

'Like I said, I'm living a clean life lately.' He stood.

'Joshua,' Cormac said, 'you said you knew that things were weird out. Did you have anything to do with that?'

'In a way.'

'Are you away from it now?'

Joshua slowly shook his head. 'Now I'm about to dive straight into the middle of things. Let's go. If this is likely to be my last meal, it might as well be Trimalchian.'

SEVENTEEN

FEDERATION URGES CALM

Martial Law Temporary Measure to Quell Rioting

<u>Press for More</u>

NEW DJAKARTA, EARTH – Federation spokesperson Lisbet Ragnardotter announced today that the martial law recently proclaimed on many Federation worlds should be considered strictly a 'temporary measure.'

She cited the recent rioting on Starhome and Ganymede as justification for the extreme measures, and said the emergency proclamations will be withdrawn as soon as what she termed the 'currently unsettled situation' is stabilized.

'Those Federation worlds we have been forced to temporarily withdraw from will be strongly supported, and as soon as the current military buildup reaches proper strength, they will be reinforced.'

She stressed there is no cause for alarm by any Federation citizen, and said that the current flood of rumors are 'palpably false to any logical man or woman, and should be ignored. Those spreading these wild tales should be reprimanded for attempting to destabilize the situation and, if they persist, reported to the proper authorities.'

No questions were allowed at the conference, and no information was available about the reported loss of Federation units somewhere near the Outlaw Worlds.

EIGHTEEN

Michele Strozzi looked out at the workmen swarming over the scaffolding that marked where the new Residence was rising. *His* Residence, he thought with quiet satisfaction. He waited until the whispering died, then turned. Twenty-seven men and women looked back at the slender, quietly dressed man.

'Very well,' he said. 'Is it agreed that, in the present state of emergency, I speak for the Order, and shall continue to do so until peace has returned and a proper consensus may be found?'

There were nods, quiet yeses.

'Good. I could practice false modesty and thank you for the honor, but I truly believe I am the best suited to represent the Chitet at this time and possibly in the future. Hopefully you will continue to agree with me. I have been made Master Speaker because I have argued we must take immediate action, rather than continuing to moil about in the shock and distress caused by the death of Master Speaker Athelstan and most of our hierarchy.'

'I think most of us here agree on that,' a man with a neat goatee said. 'But what, exactly, should this action be? There's been the conflict.'

'I do have a plan, one which I think will be the best for the Order. However, indulge me for a few moments, and consider history. A bit more than three hundred years ago, we attempted to bring order to Man's worlds and replace the Federation, or, at any rate, install our brightest minds at its head. Obviously we were premature, and Man had not yet developed his fullest logic, for we were defeated, and our leadership either imprisoned or sent into exile. We bided our time, knowing that the battle had only begun.

'A hundred years later, on consideration of the Al'ar phenomenon, our then-Master Speaker realized we had erred in assuming we could continue at leisure to develop our culture, our society, and allow Man to recognize our superiority when it became obvious.

'Further analysis was done, the process and records of which seem to be lost, and our Master Speaker determined, for the ultimate good of Man, that we must seek an alliance with the Al'ar, since it was clear to him they possessed talents superior to Man's. With such an alliance, we might learn these talents and continue assisting Man in his progression toward rationality. We were rejected by the Al'ar, and our envoys destroyed.

'We returned to our normal passive ways, and time passed. Perhaps this was an error in our logic, and we should have pressed matters. I believe it was, but my synthesis isn't complete. Eventually, as we had predicted, war broke out between the Al'ar and Man. We firmly backed the human cause, having come to the realization that if there could be no cooperation between Al'ar and Chitet, they must be unutterably destroyed. The manner of their destruction is still unknown, but they vanished from our known universe, just before the final attack was to be made. Whether this was some sort of mass suicide or an interdimensional shift is unknown. Certainly since the Al'ar seemed completely alien to this spacetime, the second theory seems the most probable to me.

'In the midst of the celebration over the war's end, our

new Master Speaker, Matteos Athelstan, made a remarkable jump in logic, using techniques and sources that are still being sought. He decided that the Al'ar had not only fled the threat of destruction by Man, but that they also recognized a greater threat in the offing, one which they would be unable to defeat and hence refused to confront. He did not know what it was, or even what form it might take, but determined, as you all know well, to recover any and all Al'ar artifacts that seemed pertinent to their weaponry and thinking and turn their benefits to our Order. This included the Lumina stones and, when the existence of the ur-Lumina, the Overlord Stone, was discovered, that became the prime area of concern.

'At this point our matrix of events intersected Joshua Wolfe, who we quickly realized was our most dangerous enemy, the one who's brought greater destruction to the Order than anyone in its history. Master Speaker Athelstan captured this man, if he is indeed just a man, and attempted to use him in our quest for the Overlord Stone.'

'Just a man, you said?' a very old man asked.

'Wolfe spent time among the Al'ar,' Strozzi said. 'He was supposedly their captive at the beginning of the war, although I privately wonder if that is a fact or a cover-up Wolfe or his sometime superiors in Federation Intelligence promulgated.

'I personally believe that Master Speaker Athelstan erred slightly in his thinking about Joshua Wolfe, accepting that he was truly a renegade, rather than an agent in deep cover working for Federation Intelligence. Certainly it's absurd to think one man could wreak the havoc he has managed.' Strozzi glanced reflexively at the ruins of the Residence.

'At any rate, Master Speaker Athelstan met his death attempting to use Wolfe to find the Overlord Stone. As you all know, Master Speaker Athelstan was very careful about security. Perhaps he was too careful, since we still have no idea exactly what happened on Rogan's World. All records of the event appear to have been destroyed with Master Speaker Athelstan's ship. However, we have sent skilled operatives to Rogan's World, and they have analyzed the situation. We have some tentative appreciations:

'1. Joshua Wolfe was not killed in the debacle, but survived the destruction of Master Speaker Athelstan. Whether he was a causative factor is unknown.

'2. He managed to secure the Overlord Stone from the traitor and murderess who had possession of it, and he fled, possibly with the connivance of those Chitet who had been ordered to guard him closely. That last is a mere theory, though. But it is absolutely known that he has possession of the Lumina and that he killed Token Aubyn and destroyed her political machine that controlled Rogan's World.

'Where Wolfe went from Rogan's World is unknown. What he intends to do with the Overlord Stone is unknown. What Joshua Wolfe has to do with this present emergency in the former Al'ar Worlds, the so-called Outlaw Worlds, and the settled systems close to them within the Federation is also unknown.

'My belief is that Wolfe is indeed connected with the strange events that have come upon us, strange events foreseen by Master Speaker Athelstan. It is my belief that *all* of the events I've discussed, this possible alien entity that is wreaking so much havoc, the Overlord Stone, the Al'ar, and Joshua Wolfe are inextricably linked. It is also my belief that we are being invaded, that there is a new alien race no one knows anything whatsoever about, and they are infinitely more hostile than the Al'ar. We must act immediately to save Mankind.'

'I would like to see an analysis of your thinking, Brother,' a woman said.

'I cannot provide it at the moment,' Strozzi said frankly. 'There are some quantum leaps I'm not yet able to justify mathematically. But I know I am right, just as Master Speaker Athelstan knew he was right, and events bore him out.'

'Accepting for the moment your thesis,' the woman continued, 'have you a course of action?'

'I do,' Strozzi said. 'The place where the ur-Lumina was found is, I believe, a locus. The ship where the Overlord Stone was found had been deliberately placed where it was by the Al'ar, and they did nothing by accident or without considerable deliberation. I also note that the earliest reports of the current phenomena came from sectors close to that point.

'I propose we send two or three of our finest reconnaissance craft, manned by the most skilled and experienced crews, to that sector, and, just within range of communication, our most powerful battlefleet, ready for the most immediate response to any eventuality. To prevent any errors, I shall accompany that fleet.'

'What do you expect to happen?'

'I don't know,' Strozzi said.

'Isn't there considerable risk to the recon ships?' someone else wondered. 'And, conceivably, to yourself? We do not wish to sacrifice another Master Speaker.'

'There is,' Strozzi said quietly, 'considerable risk to all Mankind right now. We must not delay. I feel the Overlord Stone will once again return to where it was found, and it will be returned by Joshua Wolfe. And when it does, we shall, we *must*, be ready to strike.'

NINETEEN

'Well?' Rita asked. Cormac was at the ship's controls; she leaned back in the navigator's seat.

'Phew,' Wolfe said. 'I thought I knew how messed up things have been lately. Not even close, was I?' He handed back the three fiches of recent newswires. 'The world hasn't become a better place in my absence.'

'And you're going back into it? You sure?' Cormac asked.

'I don't have any choice,' Wolfe said flatly.

'You could always give up the Saint George complex and get into a deep hole with us,' Rita suggested, 'at least until things shake out a little and you can see through the mud a bit more clearly.'

Joshua smiled politely.

'It was worth a try,' she said. 'We'll be breaking out of N-space in – four ship-hours.'

Joshua turned end for end and touched down on the *Resolute*'s hull. He keyed the lock door sensor's pattern. It slid open, and he pulled himself inside the lock, looked back.

Cormac's ship, a former Federation deep-space scout, hung about half a mile distant. Its signal lights blinked.

G-O-O-D L-U-C-K S-E-E Y-O-U N-E-X-T T-I-M-E T-H-R-U.

'Not in this life,' Joshua said, waving a hand in farewell before he entered the *Resolute*.

Wolfe smelled tangerines, heard the long wail of a saxophone; a memory came, went, too brief to do more than make him smile, and the *Resolute* came out of N-space.

The ship hung in the darkness between stars. Joshua checked all screens. 'Nothing but nothing out there,' he said to himself. 'Now to see what we shall see.'

The Lumina sat in a padded case in the center of the control room. He picked it up, carried it to an empty storeroom, and put it in the middle of the floor.

Joshua stripped and took a hachiji-dachi stance facing the Lumina, legs spread, body straight, relaxed, hands curled into fists. He took slow breaths in, breathing from his diaphragm, held them, exhaled. Breathe five . . . hold seven . . . exhale seven . . .

Wolfe bowed deeply to the Lumina, sat cross-legged on the deck without using his hands.

Breathe . . .

His mind reached for the Al'ar stone.

The Lumina flared, colors flashing across the walls as if it were a spinning multicolored mirror-ball, but the head-size stone stayed motionless.

Then very slowly it rose into the air and hovered at Wolfe's eye level.

Joshua's breathing came faster, and the colors swirled around him.

Then he was in the control room, and his presence moved from sensor to sensor. Screens blanked, showed new displays. The navigation computer whined for an instant, then stopped, and its screen lit.

SET FOR JUMP

A sensor was depressed, with no finger, no hand visible. The *Resolute* vanished into N-space.

Joshua 'returned' to the storeroom, but did not 'enter' his body. He moved outward, beyond the hull of the ship, into the confusion of hyperspace.

But there was no confusion now. He was in a constantly changing cage, a lattice that moved, enlarged, shrank, dipped around him. Beyond it were the objects of conventional space as they moved in their orbits, so many clockwork mice.

He heard sounds, the hiss of suns, the crackle of radiation, the hum of quasars.

Wolfe saw his ship as a loose assemblage of various atoms, then, more deeply, as a spaghetti-heap of vibrating 'strings.' He let it go far past him, then he was in front of it as it flashed past.

Wolfe laughed. He felt like taking the *Resolute* in his hands, remembering the toy ship he'd had as a child; he wondered what had happened to it, but stopped himself.

He shifted until he was floating above the *Resolute*, keeping it company as it went from one point to another to a third, following the irrational logic of its computers. To Wolfe, it made perfect sense. Perhaps he could jump 'ahead,' await the *Resolute* when it left N-space – but he hesitated.

In that instant, he returned to the storeroom, and the Lumina settled to the deck. It was now a small gray boulder, with only a few flecks of color. Joshua stood without using his hands and went out of the storeroom. There was no sweat on his forehead; his face showed no sign of strain.

'If I can do that again,' he said, 'I might be getting somewhere.'

The dead voice whispered dry words into the darkness.

Wolfe turned the audio off, stared out into the silence between the stars.

*

The *Resolute* flew low over the planet that was dead without ever having been born, empty, desolate.

He *felt* the missiles tracking him, the metallic death one grasping-arm sensor-touch away, *felt* the strangeness, the terror under the world's dry, silent stone.

'This is the One Who Fights From Shadows,' he broadcast in Al'ar yet again.

There was a faint crackle on a speaker.

'You are received,' a voice answered. 'Welcome back. We feared you had gone beyond, had met the real death when you ordered us to flee and you remained behind to fight those you said were the Chitet.'

'I live,' Wolfe said, and fatigue showed in his voice. 'But Taen met his doom at their hands.'

'That we knew,' the voice said, and Wolfe recognized it as that of Jadera, the Al'ar who was the head of the tiny handful of aliens who'd chosen not to make the Crossing with the rest of their race, but remained behind as Guardians to hold off the 'virus' that had driven them from their own universe into Man's. 'We felt him pass, feared you had gone with him, for we are not able to sense your life as we could an Al'ar's.'

'He died well,' Joshua said, 'as the warrior he was.'

'Of course,' Jadera said. 'There could be no other possibility ... Or for us. The time is very close now. Our mutual enemy has gained a foothold in this galaxy, and is ready to transfer its center, its nucleus, here. We were preparing for an attack, knowing that we could not succeed without the Great Lumina, which I sense you have.'

'I do.'

'And do you know how to use it?'

'I am learning.'

'Enter your home, then, One Who Fights From Shadows, and we shall ready ourselves for the last battle.'

A radar screen flickered, showing movement on the ground below. Wolfe zoomed a forward screen to its highest magnification and saw a rocky hillside yawning open – the entry port to an underground Al'ar hangar.

Once before, Joshua had eaten Al'ar foods in this shadowy great cavern, with light-sculptures flaming on the walls. But then it had been as much of a banquet as the Al'ar were capable of, welcoming Taen. But if they weren't capable of much celebration, Joshua thought, their mourning was equally nonexistent. Half a dozen times the half dome on the table in front of him opened, and he took the plate it held and ate. Jadera sat across from him equally absorbed in his meal.

Finally replete, Joshua made no move to accept the next plate offered. Jadera did the same. They sat in silence for a time, as was the Al'ar custom.

'I have a question,' Joshua said. 'When an Al'ar dies, like Taen did, does his – spirit, I suppose it should be called, make the Crossing?'

'A good question,' Jadera answered. 'I do not know. That was the hope of some of our more romantic brothers.'

'Utterly impossible,' an Al'ar at a nearby table said. 'No one who died in our previous galaxy appeared in this one. Dead is dead.'

Joshua half smiled. He recognized the alien, Cerigo, who had lost his broodmate and offspring during the war and carried his hatred for Man close, like a favorite garment.

'I thank you for honoring me with your presence, Cerigo. Last time, you refused to eat with me.'

'I would do the same this time,' Cerigo said. 'But we shall fight together soon, and only a worm allows enmity to one who will share the blooding.'

'Thank you.'

Cerigo made a noise Wolfe took to be an acknowledgment.

'Cerigo reminds me of an admiral I served under,' Wolfe said. 'He always spoke in an animal-growl, too. But very few of us could fight as hard as he did.'

'Cerigo was a great ship leader once,' Jadera said. 'An admiral, in charge of what you call a *battleship*. He was one of our best commanders.'

'Not good enough,' Cerigo said. 'For I did not kill enough Men for it to matter.'

'Cerigo has been selected to be in command of our attack,' Jadera said.

'Good,' Wolfe said. 'A man who hates well generally fights well, as long as he does not allow his animal side to rule.'

'There is no worry of that,' Jadera said. 'Cerigo is far too experienced a warrior to succumb to any . . . what you call *emotion*,' he finished, then changed the subject. 'None of us have seen the Overlord Stone for a great time,' he said. 'Some of us have never witnessed it at all. Would that be possible?'

'You hardly need ask permission of me,' Joshua said, 'for it is your property.'

'No longer,' Jadera said. 'We discussed the matter while you were gone, and agreed that if you succeeded in returning alive with it, you would probably be the most capable to use it against the invader.'

'You assume much of my capabilities,' Wolfe said.

Jadera made no response.

Wolfe opened the case that sat at his feet and lifted the Lumina out.

Around him other Guardians stirred, and lifted their grasping organs.

Wolfe *felt* their power, took it into him, let the Lumina

lift from the floor, float in the room's center, its kaleido-scope colors flaming.

He looked around, at the corpse-white long faces, their attention fixed on the Lumina.

'Will this tool, this weapon, suffice?' he asked.

Jadera turned to him. 'We do not know. But we have other devices prepared which might help. Come.'

Wolfe couldn't see the far walls or the roof of the hangar. But it seemed small, barely large enough to house the monstrous battleship that loomed over their heads.

Its fuselage was a flattened cylinder, reminding Joshua of a shark. It had two thick 'wings,' one curving forward, the other aft. At the tip of each wing were weapons stations, and other podlike stations were studded irregularly along the ship's body. It was commanded from another pod, located just under the shark's chin, where a remora might hang. Its stern bristled with ungainly antennae for the ship's sensing and ECM capabilities.

The ship was a mile long, perhaps longer, greater from wingtip to wingtip.

'I never – thank the Powers Beyond Myself –' Joshua said, 'saw or even heard of anything like this during the war.'

'It was still in final testing when the war ended,' Cerigo said. 'Our Command On High was trying to determine where its deployment would be most effective. It was intended to be able to deal with an entire Federation battlefleet by itself, needing escorts only for its antimissile screen.'

'Taking this ship out against the invader is very noble,' Wolfe said carefully, making sure he would give no offense.

'But one single ship cannot ever succeed in a mission, and all aboard it will be doomed, without coming close to accomplishing their task.'

He remembered history, remembered a doomed great ocean-ship called the *Yamato*.

'We realize that,' Cerigo said. 'However, the final reports from those who stayed behind in our home universe suggested that fusion weapons appeared to set this – this entity, whatever it is, back. These we could deploy successfully. We also have a sunray, such as you used against us from your planetary fortresses. The ship is also armed with countermissiles, in the unlikely event it encounters any Federation ships before it reaches the target zone. Perhaps not enough, but there was no other option, besides curling in our burrows waiting to be spaded out and skinned. The Al'ar were never burrowing worms.'

'All this is meaningless noise,' Jadera said, 'since you have recovered the Mother Lumina. Now we are capable of fighting on an equal plane, or so I believe.'

'I feel,' Wolfe said, 'like an aborigine who s just been given a machine gun without an instruction manual and told to take care of those bastards who're wiping him out.'

'Not a bad comparison,' Jadera said, also in Terran, then reverted to Al'ar. 'Do you actually think we know anything ourselves?'

The Lumina floated in the middle of the room. Joshua sat cross-legged underneath it. Al'ar, either in the flesh or in projection, were clustered around him. Occasionally one or another would wink out as other duties called.

'Our strategy,' Jadera said, 'will be to fight from the great ship, which we have named the *Crossing*. We have other ships – three for each Al'ar – which have been roboticized, so in fact we have a fleet of more

than 160 craft, including the *Nyarlot*. Each is capable
of launching missiles into the invader when we close.
We suggest that you attempt to strike the invader with
the Lumina's force. Perhaps you may hurt it, more
likely you might be able to force it back, through the
rift into the universe it came from, once the Al'ar
home.'

Joshua sat thinking.

'Do you have a better plan?' Jadera asked.

'I do not,' he said.

'We should begin our strike from where the Lumina
was positioned, in its satellite,' Jadera said. 'Perhaps,
even though the Al'ar are gone, such positioning may
increase its power.'

'Very well,' Joshua said in Terran, and rose. 'Let us go to
war.'

TWENTY

'You may or may not be pleased, Admiral Hastings,' Cisco said, 'that I specifically requested the *Andrea Doria* and its battlefleet for this mission.'

'I'll be honest,' the officer said. 'I'm not. I'm not sure, with everything else going wrong around us, this is the most important mission my ships and men should be used for. We've pulled back from who knows how many worlds in the past few months. Others have evidently fallen into chaos, anarchy. Entire sectors aren't reporting. We've lost at least sixteen fleets . . .'

'Eighteen,' Cisco corrected. 'That's confirmed. More likely twenty-three.'

'To what? To something nobody can even see?'

'That's also been corrected,' Cisco said. 'Although the information won't make you feel any better.'

'What the *hell* are we fighting?'

Cisco motioned him to a corner of the bridge, away from the other officers. 'You don't have the proper clearance,' he said. 'No one else aboard the *Andrea Doria* does either, but I was advised by my superior I should inform you of the Federation's current explanation for these events, so you'll understand the importance of your orders. It appears our universe has been invaded by some sort of single-cell — although "cell" is not the right word — being, an entity that's capable of making interstellar flights, jumping from star to star.'

'That's impossible!'

'It certainly is,' Cisco agreed. 'And I'll give you an even less possible truth: This being, this alien, appears to be able to alter the very nature of matter, to make it disassemble itself, then reassemble in the form of the alien's structure.'

Hastings looked at Cisco. 'That violates every single principle I have ever learned,' he said. 'This alien is capable of altering string, of altering its vibrations, its resonance, into – into what?'

'Into its own form of matter,' Cisco said. 'Into itself. Not matter, not antimatter.'

'So everything will become part of it eventually? Stars, planets, space, people?'

'If that theory's correct,' Cisco said, 'yes. Maybe not people, though. I assume you've heard the stories of the "burning disease"?'

'I have, and they're as utterly unbelievable as what you just told me. Preposterous!'

Cisco didn't reply.

Hastings' shoulders slumped. 'I'm not a fool, Cisco. Obviously there's *something* out there, something utterly unknown that's slowly destroying everything. So how do we fight it?'

'No one knows yet,' Cisco said. 'The Federation has anyone and everyone working on every possible solution.'

'With obviously nothing but theory so far?'

'As far as I know,' Cisco said. 'Needless to say, none of this is to be discussed with anyone until I personally advise you differently.'

'I wouldn't anyway,' Hastings said. 'I don't need to be in command of sailors who think me mad.' He took a deep breath. 'But how is destroying this Chitet fleet going to solve matters?'

'First, the Federation hardly needs traitors among its own,' Cisco said. 'Second, the Chitet have attempted to league themselves with other aliens in the past. The Al'ar. Now we've gotten word that they've assembled their warships and moved them into the Al'ar Worlds.'

'Why?'

'We don't know,' Cisco said. 'But we know where they are. We have a highly placed source within the cult, someone who recently recognized his patriotism.' Cisco's lips twisted into a smile. 'Or else no longer wanted to back a loser.'

'I have the coordinates but little else,' Hastings said. 'What are your orders, once we emerge from N-space, assuming the Chitet are there?'

'We can expect around a hundred ships,' Cisco said. 'All Al'ar War vintage, but well reconditioned. None bigger than the battlecruiser you drove away when we recovered Joshua Wolfe from them. They're to be given one chance to surrender, and if they do not accept, they're to be destroyed in detail. The Chitet must *never* be allowed to work against Man again.'

Hastings nodded, managed a smile. 'At least it'll be good to have a nice, simple battle to fight,' he said, 'instead of nothing but confusion.'

TWENTY-ONE

'Are we ready to lift?' Joshua asked.

'*All systems go*,' the *Grayle* reported.

'Did you miss me?'

There was a silence. Joshua was about to withdraw his question, then: '*By "miss," analysis indicates that I am supposed to provide an emotional response, that is, your absence created a negative condition in me. Further consideration suggests you are intending what is listed in my files as a "jest" or "joke." However, I do admit a preference for being used, for being active, rather than being in a state of nonbeing, such as I have been since landing on this planet.*'

'Well dip me in a bucket,' Joshua said in some amazement. 'Cormac ought to change his name to Viktor. Okay, Monster. Take it on out of here.'

'*Understood.*'

The *Grayle* came clear of the hangar floor, and the door opened. The ship moved slowly out over the wasteland, then climbed for open space.

'**Lifting clear,**' Joshua reported. '**Time until entering N-space, approximately twelve ship-minutes.**'

'**You are heard,**' Cerigo's voice came over a speaker. '**We will lift in approximately five of your minutes, enter N-space approximately fifteen of your minutes afterward. We will therefore emerge at the desired** point in exactly eight of those minutes after you. Is that correct?'

'Correct. This is the *Grayle*, clear.'

The contact alarm gonged as Federation ships came out of N-space. Michele Strozzi heard someone swear, ignored it. 'We were betrayed,' he said calmly to his admiral, Ignatieff.

'Yes, sir. Should we attempt to withdraw?'

'No,' Strozzi decided. 'They'll pursue us, and we do not need to have an enemy at our back. Eventually we'll have to confront the Federation, to make them realize we're right in what we're doing. How many of them are there?'

Ignatieff asked an electronics officer and relayed the answer: 'About 160, sir.'

'They outnumber us,' Strozzi said. 'But the Federation's ships are mostly manned with recruits, and ours with veterans. They've been subject to peacetime economics; we've kept our men fully trained. Admiral Ignatieff, destroy this Federation fleet. Perhaps this is our beginning, even though it was not in my projection of coming events.'

'Yes, sir'

The Federation ships came out of N-space in battle order, a huge crescent, sweeping toward the Chitet fleet.

'As I promised you, Admiral,' Cisco said. 'The Chitet. Do you wish the honors?'

Hastings took the mike his aide held out. 'This is the Federation battleship *Andrea Doria*,' he said. 'I order all vessels not under Federation command to immediately signal blue-white-blue as a signal of surrender. You have five minutes to comply, or you will be attacked.'

'Captain,' a weapons officer reported, 'one of the ships has launched missiles. I've activated countermeasures.'

'There's your answer,' Cisco said.

'Very well,' Hastings said, switching to another frequency. 'All ships. This is the *Andrea Doria*. Authentication Witnal. Attack!'

Missiles spat from the Chitet ships at the oncoming Federation fleet, and countermissiles flashed back. Explosions dotted space and quickly vanished. Other, greater blasts came as the Federation took hits, and ships pinwheeled out of formation or drove 'down' or 'up' in senseless directions.

The Chitet launched a second wave of missiles as they closed on the Federation.

Too many Federation weapons crews were inexperienced, but there were still veterans of the Al'ar War among them.

Aboard one Federation ship a warrant officer in his sixties pushed a lieutenant out of his way and crouched over a launch station, cursing as his prosthetic leg creaked.

'Target acquired,' he said, his voice level. 'Launching – One launched – Two launched . . . Now, goddammit, Lieutenant, watch how I'm trying to spoof 'em. The first one goes for the incoming missile . . . closing . . . Got the son of a bitch! The second goes right on through the debris, uses the crap to mask itself against their countermeasures – don't go to autopilot but keep the controls and you ride it right on into the . . .'

The Federation missile smashed into the bow of the *Udayana*, into its electronics bays, and explosions tore at the battlecruiser, ripping the bridge decking three floors above like an ancient tin can.

Michele Strozzi was sent spinning into a control panel, blood spattering the screens beside him. He sprawled motionless for an instant, then stumbled to his feet. He saw Admiral Ignatieff's head lying next to him, looked for his body, saw nothing.

An aide was beside him, arm around his shoulders. 'Sir, lie down,' she shouted.

He looked at her, opened his mouth to say something reassuring, inspiring. Blood poured out, drenching her tunic, and his eyes went dull and he went down limply.

The aide knelt, keening in loss, and another missile smashed directly into the bridge. The *Udayana* exploded in a long sheet of flame.

The Federation forces swept forward, the ships on the ends of the formation following orders, trying to bend the vast C around the Chitet to encircle the fleet. But the center of their pattern was already broken, and the battle center was a swirling catfight.

'All Federation ships,' someone – no one ever admitted to the command – ordered, 'break formation and choose your own targets. I say again, go for their throats!'

The *Grayle* left N-space for Armageddon. Wolfe gaped at the madness, keyed his com.

'*Nyarlot, Nyarlot,* this is the One Who Fights From Shadows. There's some kind of battle going on here.'

'Who is fighting?'

Wolfe took a moment to examine his screens, calm himself. 'It appears to be a Federation fleet . . . I don't know who they're against – maybe Chitet? Maybe civil war?'

'**What should we do, One Who Fights From Shadows?**'

'I don't know,' Wolfe said.

'Whose enemy are they?' Cerigo said. 'Should we stand aside? Will they leave us alone, let us fight our own battle, fight the battle for them as well? Can we explain in time, and would they believe us? Would they join us? We stand by for your will.'

Joshua took a deep breath, gave an order.

On the bridge of the *Andrea Doria*, the ship's executive officer glanced at a master screen and screamed in utter horror, seeing something out of a nightmare vanished long years before.

The Al'ar ships came from nowhere, sweeping forward in a *grasping hand* formation, a phalanx of corpse-white death.

It seemed to some watchers they came slowly, instead of at their light-second-devouring real speed.

At their head was a monstrous winged shark, scimitar-shaped, beyond any memory of the Al'ar terrors. It was flanked by the robot ships, flying in fours, two abreast, two slightly behind the first pair, as the Al'ar held their grasping organs in combat stance.

Shipskins bulged, split, and birthed slender missiles that trembled once and homed in on their targets. Some Federation or Chitet ships had time for countermissile launches, but too many didn't see the doom from nowhere.

The Al'ar formation lifted 'above' the spinning pandemonium, swept past, reversed course, and came back in a second attack.

A Chitet frigate spat four missiles at the *Nyarlot*; five countermissiles launched and closed on the missiles. There were three explosions, then a fourth, larger one on one of the *Nyarlot*'s fighting pods.

Guardians died, and the ships they controlled veered away from the fight, uncontrolled.

Wolfe *felt* their deaths and flinched. He saw the out-of-control ships and reached for them, as he'd once taken and crushed a missile. The ships were his. Wolfe didn't notice that the ships broke formation and regrouped – not as the two-two they'd attacked in, but as five fingers, four ships almost parallel, the fifth guarding the rear, human fingers reaching for human throats.

He sent them into the madness, controlling them as they fired their missiles. Federation and Chitet ships were there, past, gone. He came back, dimly aware of the *Nyarlot* somewhere behind, volleying its own killers toward the human ships.

A ship he knew, a ship he'd been aboard, was close to 'him,' but he veered his fighting formation away, away from the *Andrea Doria*.

Wolfe's face had a tight, skull-like grin.

'Whiskey element, engage Chitet vessels at 320-12,' Hastings ordered. 'Hotel, please respond to this station. I say again, Hotel, respond if you are still capable. Quebec, regather your elements.' He was as calm as if he were on a peacetime exercise, or moving models on a map.

Cisco stood beside him, trying to stay out of the way, trying to make sense of the madness that englobed them.

Then there was something else on the bridge. It was an Al'ar, an Al'ar nearly fifteen feet high.

Someone shrieked, and a blaster smashed through the Al'ar and blew a hole in the deck above the apparition. The Al'ar stepped forward, and its grasping organ reached. Cisco shrank back, but the organ came on, came on.

His hand fumbled in a pocket, came out with a gray stone, the Lumina he'd taken from Joshua Wolfe, and brandished it like a talisman. The Al'ar brushed it aside and it smashed to the deck and shattered.

The alien changed, and for an instant Cisco saw Joshua Wolfe reaching for him. Then the grasping organ touched Cisco's chest, and he screamed, flung back as if smashed by a blaster bolt.

The Al'ar vanished.

Hastings had time enough to manage, 'What in Mithra's holy name was . . .' Then three missiles hit the *Andrea Doria*, and it broke in half. The rear half exploded, the forward section spun away from the battle, into an orbit without end, vanishing into emptiness.

Then there were fewer ships and fewer still as Chitet ships broke and ran for hyperspace, and Federation ships went after them, or fled on their own. There were no more than a dozen of Man's ships left in that outer darkness.

'**End contact,**' Cerigo commanded, and Wolfe obeyed, pulling his 'fingers' back, away. He sat on the bridge of the *Grayle*, panting as if he'd fought a tournament.

'**The way is clear,**' Cerigo said.

'Yes,' Joshua agreed. '**Slave all ships to mine. Now we must approach our real enemy.**'

The *Grayle* emerged in the depths of what had been the Al'ar Worlds. Joshua *felt* redness, death, change, all around him, and his body burned, as if too close to an all-surrounding fire. The stars were dim, the planets indistinct, their shapes blurred, red around them, consuming them, changing them into itself.

The *Nyarlot* and the robot-ships were there.

Joshua *heard* hisses of rage from the Guardians aboard the *Nyarlot* as they sensed their ancient enemy.

No commands were given, none were necessary, and the ships spat heavy missiles at the entity, at what should have been empty space, but Wolfe saw it as red-speckled, pulsing like a diseased organ.

Nuclear fires blossomed, died.

Joshua's burning pain ebbed, returned more strongly, ebbed once more.

He *saw*, aboard the *Nyarlot*, a fighting pod, as Al'ar flesh smoked, curled, and blackened, and Guardians fell, dying, dead.

A small sun was born in nothingness as the Al'ar sunray activated, and fire ravened at the alien.

Joshua felt it shrink, writhe.

The sunray burnt itself out, and the alien gathered its force, its power.

Suddenly the *Nyarlot*'s drive went to full power, and it drove away from the *Grayle*.

'**Die well, One Who Fights From Shadows,**' came Cerigo's last broadcast. '**Die as we die. Die as an Al'ar.**'

The *Nyarlot*'s engines, fuel, and missiles exploded as one. Flame seared at Wolfe's eyes, and his screens blanked for a moment. He *felt* the Guardians, the last of the Al'ar, leave this spacetime.

'**May you be on the Crossing,**' he said without realizing it. The pain was gone momentarily, and he *felt* the invader recoil. He took the deaths of the Guardians and threw them at the 'virus' as he'd once hurled Taen's death at his murderer to slay him.

The Lumina floating behind him was a flare of solid white, starlike, flaming hot.

Now he saw the invader not as the 'red virus,' but, in flashes, as the Al'ar might have, great writhing fanged crawlers, worms, the monstrous worms that had forced the ground creatures who became the Al'ar from their burrows to the surface and then to the stars.

The worms became the serpent of Midgard, gnawing at Yggdrasil for an instant. But Wolfe's 'eyes' went beyond, saw the bits that composed the 'virus,' reached below the molecular, the atomic levels, and *felt* the resonance of its ultimate bits.

He allowed the resonance for an instant, absorbed it, then forbade it.

The alien strings/not-strings hummed down into silence, and there was a vortex of nothingness, absolute nothing, not matter, not energy, not antimatter, at the core of the invader, spreading, eating, a not-cancer.

Far away, Joshua *felt* the rift in space, then was standing in the huge cavern, hearing the dripping of liquid from its walls, and the monstrous stone door, carved with strange symbols, was in front of him.

The door to the universe the invader had come from yawned open. Behind him, coming toward him, he *felt* the invader, trying to flee, trying to return to its own place, the universe it had created that became itself.

Wolfe stretched out a hand, and the door boomed shut, and the sound of the booming echoed through creation. He reached up, pulled rock from the ceiling, and it cascaded down with a rumble, burying the passage to the door that his mind had created from a different reality, sealing the rift between universes.

The 'virus,' the invader, was around him, and he *felt* it, had it cupped in his hands. He considered it coldly, then denied it permission to exist.

A soundless scream came, like the tearing of dimensions, and the invader was gone.

Joshua Wolfe hung in space. He was enormous, he was subatomic. He *felt* the rhythm around him, normal, strange, warm, cold, dark, light.

Stars were above, below, next to him. He studied them for a long time. Some he knew, others were strange. Far in the distance was a familiar yellow star. He approached it, saw its nine worlds. He leaned over one, blue, green, and white, and knew it for his birthplace.

Wolfe stretched out a hand to touch Earth.

His nose tickled.

Joshua Wolfe was on the bridge of the *Grayle*. Behind him, the Lumina rotated, sending its comfortable, familiar colors around the control room. Wolfe thought of a ceiling, of an artist. His nose still tickled.

He scratched it.

Then he burst into laughter, great, booming waves of total amusement.

TWENTY-TWO

The *Grayle* orbited a system that had lived and died long before Man, a system without a name, only a number. Its planets had been devoured when the sun went nova, and now there was nothing but the dying star and a tiny starship.

Wolfe relaxed in a chair, gazing at the screen in front of him. He poured the last of the bottle of Hubert Dayton he'd husbanded in the ship's safe for years, savored its burn, tasted the grapes of Gascony, remembered a winding road, a girl's laughter, the acrid smell of woodsmoke as the pruned vines burned, a cold wind coming down from the massif, a storm minutes behind, and the welcome flicker of the fire in the tiny cottage ahead.

'A long time ago,' he said, lifting the snifter in a toast. 'Quite a run,' he said. 'They gave me quite a run indeed.'

A line from the long-dead poet came:

'In my end is my beginning.'

He said the words aloud in Terran, then again in Al'ar. Something that might have been a smile came and went on his lips. He drained the snifter.

Wolfe stood. He gave a series of coordinates.

'*Understood,*' the *Grayle* said. '*Awaiting your command.*'

The flames of the red giant reached for him, welcoming.

'Go.' The ship's drive hummed to life.

He crossed his arms across his chest, brought them slowly out, palm up, as his breathing slowed. The Great Lumina roared life, incandescent as never before. The bits of matter that had been Joshua Wolfe stilled, were motionless.

Joshua Wolfe's corpse slid to the deck. The slight smile still remained on his lips.

The *Grayle*, at full drive, plunged into the heart of the dying sun.

BACKBLAST

INTRODUCTION
TO 'BACKBLAST'

'Backblast' was written as a hoot – Warren Lapine asked if I was interested in doing a story inspired by art, just as in the old days of SF magazines. I said I'd try.

'Backblast' is the result.

When putting together this omnibus, all of us (Lapine, Betancourt, myself) tried to fit the story into the trilogy as seamlessly as possible.

It didn't work out.

So, for those keeping a chronology, 'Backblast' occurs after the end of the Al'ar-Human war, but before the events of the Shadow Warrior books.

BACKBLAST

Lorn Ware checked the bubble, slightly moved the leveling screw, stepped back from the double tripod and bar her recording apparati clung to. She unclipped the remote viewer/shutter release from her belt harness, looked into it. Right screen, foreground was a roseatted circle of stone she named a monument, though why the Al'ar should've put one up in the middle of nowhere was a puzzlement.

Just like, she thought, *everything, or almost everything about the Al'ar is a mind-shatter.*

On the left of her mini-screen was a huge Al'ar transmission tower, the closest of the long line that marched across this sere world from the abandoned, half-finished underground base to the middle of nothing, where the line simply stopped.

It would be a great holograph.

Artistic as all hell, she thought. *Just like Herr Uber-Digger-Schwanz Frazier ordered. Perfect for the cover of the semi-annual report, sure to peel more funds for the Univee out of the government.*

Until a real analyst happens to take a look at things.

She put that aside. *Dad always said Man can't serve two masters,* she thought wryly. *But what about Woman?*

She shivered as a chill, dead wind whispered past, then checked her timesend, and jolted. *How'd it get so late? You're piddling about with a bare minute-forty before the run . . .*

Ware concentrated on her viewer, listened for the barely audible near-subsonic tone of building power, hovering over the release switch, not trusting the automatic shutter.

Picturesque as anybody could want when the violet are fireballs toward me, jumping from tower to tower and past . . .

She caught a flicker from the corner of her eye, started to turn.

The blast of raw energy tore her body apart before she had time to scream.

Scholar Juan Frazier ran a hand over his nearly-bald skull as if anticipating new growth. The small twittering man with the hooded eyes reminded Joshua Wolfe of some species of bird, perhaps a woodpecker; or possibly the reptilian *hultsma* of Vega VI.

'Isn't it a bit irregular to send an investigator all the way from the Federation to inquire about an accident that's already been fully reported?' Frazier asked carefully. 'Not to mention expensive?'

'Probably,' Joshua agreed blandly. 'But I'm a local boy, free-lancing in the Outlaw Worlds, so it wasn't that many jumps for me. As for irregular, I heard rumors there's been insurance problems on other university-funded projects.'

'You don't have any idea, though, why the Univee . . . damnit, I hate that word . . . isn't satisfied with the information I provided,' Frazier persisted.

'Not really,' Wolfe said. 'But I'd guess it might be because your project's funded through the government. You know how *they* like to ask questions.'

'Ah,' Frazier said. 'Ah, of course. Of course that's it.' He visibly relaxed, but his eyes stayed fixed on Joshua.

His long office was cluttered with terminals, reports, a few models of Al'ar apparatus and, incongruously, an architect's holograph of an elaborate lakeside home.

There was a port behind him, looking out at the jumble

of temporary buildings around the low mounded entrances to the Al'ar base, and, not far distant, Wolfe's grounded spaceship, the *Grayle*.

'As I understand it,' Wolfe said, 'your team is currently trying to put the Al'ar power grid back on line, correct?'

'Not just on line, but also trying to determine what that power was intended for. Another base? An exotic weapons system? Perhaps a launch-base? And all of this is but part and parcel of our complete investigation of all Al'ar remnants on Five.' Frazier touched a sensor, and a wallscreen lit.

Planet A-6343-5, the fifth planet of the arbitrarily numbered star system, given the A-prefix as a former Al'ar world, hung in space. The perspective closed on the planet.

'Here is the base we're at,' and a dot lit on the map. 'Transmission towers run out to . . . here.' A line sketched onscreen.

The screen changed, and showed a single tower.

'This is the end of the line,' Frazier said. ' Or so we call it.

'Our first questions are,' and Wolfe heard in his mind the tapping as earnest students began numbering their lecture notes, 'what was going to be built here. Or, conceivably, what could be underground here, although none of our resonations have yet discovered anything. Why was this end-point so far from the base? Why are there only a scattering of buildings along the route?'

'I've scanned your reports,' Wolfe said. 'Since the base appears unfinished, maybe the Al'ar were just starting to develop this world.'

'No,' Frazier said. 'That's not good enough. At least, I don't think that's the answer. Do you know anything about the Al'ar power source?'

'Just a little,' Wolfe lied. He remembered very well the deep hum of the huge tower near the Federation embassy that was his boyhood home; and after that the tower beyond the internment camp his parents had died in.

'No one quite understands why the Al'ar chose to build these towers so, perhaps monolithic, might be the word,' Frazier went on, deep into his subject. 'Especially since their cities are so ethereal. But then, I suppose no one will ever understand the Al'ar, now they've vanished.'

Wolfe's face remained immobile.

A laser pointer touched the tower onscreen. 'This upper arm carries the main transmission, which is more or less fixed in position at a right angle to the direction of power transmission.

'On a developed Al'ar world, power would be transferred to the second arm, then diffused downward to receptors below, most generally atop whatever building they powered.

'Actually the power would be routed to these cylinders, call them holding tanks if you will, below the second arm, then transferred up. Here, just below the lower arm, you'll note these small columns. We think those were used to fine-tune the power transmission downward.

'At any rate, those columns, about your height, are where our problems have been occurring, and the reason our project's stalled for the moment.' The small man's mouth twisted, and, surprisingly, emotion came into his voice. '*Damn* me but I'm sorry someone had to die! Especially that much against the odds! With all that desert to incinerate . . .'

'There were four previous backblasts,' Wolfe said. 'And the fifth killed Lorn Ware.'

Frazier nodded jerkily.

'What was she doing out there?'

'That's what makes it worse,' Frazier said. 'What she was doing wasn't really necessary. She wanted to get some holos of the test. Lorn said they'd make a spectacular exhibit at the University . . . Univee as they all call it now, and I suppose I'd better adjust to it. She thought it might help when our budget was up for renewal, since it appears we're sort of stalled in place, and the government wants to see results for its investment.' He shrugged small shoulders. 'Who was I to argue? I'm not exactly a specialist in raising money.

'Maybe if I *were* . . .' his voice trailed off.

Wolfe waited politely, but the man didn't continue. After awhile, Joshua said, 'So she just happened to pick a place where the flashpoint happened.'

'Scholar Northover wondered if maybe that monument out there . . . there's some kind of Al'ar stonework, which we call a monument . . . might've drawn the blast,' Frazier said. 'Like lightning is drawn to a high point. He's the electro-magnetic specialist with the team, so perhaps there's merit to his theory, and the monument was badly shattered.'

'Was there anything of a similar nature to draw the other four blasts?' Wolfe asked.

'No. Or, at any rate, nothing that we can determine.'

'I'd like to take a look at the accident site,' Wolfe said. 'If there's a gravsled I could borrow? I don't think I can get lost.'

'I'll com the garage, and have one waiting. If you plan on eating with us, the next meal is at 1800 hours.'

'Thanks. Speaking of which . . .' Wolf took an elaborate timepiece off his wrist, opened its back. 'I'm still on Zulu shiptime.'

'1430. The planet-day is 29.5 hours,' Frazier said. 'It'll seem like forever. But why don't you borrow one of these? They make life a little simpler.'

He opened a desk drawer and took out a slender black device with a synthetic hook/eye strap, gave it to Joshua. 'Let's see . . . that's unit 56,' he said, and turned to a small domed case. He touched sensors on it. 'And it's . . . 1143 now . . .'

'That's a time-send,' Frazier explained. 'Everyone on the team carries one. It's nothing but a receiver, linked to a common sender. Set the sender when you land on any world for any length day, and all the units show exactly the same time, so there's never any trouble about synching watches, let alone making sure everyone has a timepiece that's capable of that wide an adjustment.'

'Convenient.'

'Especially when you have such a small team,' Frazier went on, 'and you're trying to keep some sort of order. It's handy when anything potentially hazardous is being investigated.'

'How many people are on the expedition?'

'Twenty-three,' Frazier said. 'Sorry. Twenty-two, now.'

'And you're on first-name terms with them? Like you evidently were with Ware?'

'I . . . we like to think of ourselves as friends,' Frazier said. 'Mostly, then, yes. Although there are some who prefer formality.'

'Of course,' Wolfe said. He eyed a rather ornate ring on the middle finger of Frazier's hand, was about to ask something when the door slid open, and a woman came in. She was a bit older than Wolfe's 35 years, athletically built, large-breasted, mildly pretty. Her hair was long, pulled back and then wrapped around her neck for convenience, and she wore an untailored set of ship coveralls.

'Scholar,' the woman said, 'we've got some preliminary pickups from the mole on the 14th level, if you're interested.'

'I am,' Frazier said. 'Maybe we've found something worth sending someone down to investigate.' He rose. 'Oh. Pardon me. Joshua Wolfe, this is Scholar Mikela Tregeagle. She's the expedition comptroller, adjutant, wheel-greaser, executive officer . . . the one who never makes a mistake.'

'Hardly,' Tregeagle said, and her polite smile made her suddenly lovely. 'I've merely been with Scholar Frazier for eight years now, so I should know by now what's supposed to come next.'

'I'm pleased to meet you, Mister Wolfe, although the circumstances aren't the best.' Tregeagle grimaced. 'Lorn Ware was one of our best. I don't think anyone was a harder worker.'

'Except maybe you, Mikela,' Frazier said.

The smile she gave him for payment was very warm. Frazier seemed not to notice.

'If you'll excuse us, Mister Wolfe,' he said. 'The garage is near the bubble's main entrance.'

'I saw it when I landed,' Joshua said. 'I'll try to not be any trouble while I'm here. I'm sure the questions the Univee . . . pardon, the university, has can be cleared up in a day or two and I'll be on my way.'

Wolfe left the expedition base, walked the quarter kilometer to his ship. The air was thin, slightly acrid.

As he approached, the airlock opened, and a gangway slid down. He entered the ship.

'Greetings,' he said.

— *Greetings*, — the *Grayle* answered.

'This situation may become interesting,' Wolfe said. He issued careful instructions. 'Now to worry about me,' Wolfe said. 'Starting with the fact I'm chatting with a goddamned box.' He went to a bulkhead near the airlock, touched a stud. The wall slid open, revealing racked pistols, rifles, grenades, machine weapons, even a semi-portable blaster. He considered carefully, took a tiny dart-like knife of black obsidian sheathed on a worked silver chain from a rack, put it on so the knife hung down the back of his neck; stuck a narrow tube-blaster in his halfboot, went back to the port.

'Wish me luck,' he said, and went back into the dry desert wind.

A burly man waited beside a small lifter. He wore stained, worn coveralls and the lines on his hands had ground-in grease in them.

'You're the snooper,' he greeted Wolfe.

'More a paper-shuffler than anything else,' Joshua said, holding out his hand. 'Joshua Wolfe. You're Dov Cherney.'

The man ignored Wolfe's hand.

'I am. Why's the university so interested in Lorn?'

'I'll put it brutally,' Wolfe said. 'Insurance companies don't like to pay out near as much as they like to take it in.'

'A lot of people die,' Cherney said.

'They do,' Wolfe agreed. 'So what's your especial interest in Ware?'

'I don't think that's any of your business.'

'I think it became my business after what you just said.' He stared hard at Cherney, and the man's eyes dropped.

'Lorn was a friend of mine.'

'Scholar Frazier said everybody on the team is friends.'

Cherney snorted.

'I didn't believe it either,' Wolfe said. 'Unless there were twenty-three angels here.'

'Not hardly.'

'How special a friend was Ware to you?' Wolfe said, keeping his voice neutral.

'She was . . .' Cherney suddenly hiccuped, and turned away, blinking.

Wolfe waited until the big man turned back.

'Sorry,' Cherney said. 'I'm not used to things like this.'

'Stay that way,' Wolfe advised. 'It's harder in the short run, but better.' He didn't explain. 'Go on.'

'I thought a lot of her,' Cherney said. 'She was easy to talk to.'

'Just talk?'

Cherney flushed. 'Yes, dammit!'

'Her choice or yours?'

'Hers,' the man grudged. 'I wanted . . . wanted what I never got.'

'How much did that bother you?'

Cherney started to get angry again, caught himself. 'Quite a lot,' he said. 'I'm being honest. I lost my wife and son in a stupid accident two years ago. Saw the Univee was hiring for offworld, so I thought that'd get me out of things. Didn't think I'd get the job, but I guess scholars always need somebody who knows which end of a wrench fits your hand.

'Lorn used to come down here and talk. Suppose she wanted somebody to talk to who wouldn't rank on her. Which I didn't. But I guess I thought more of what was going on than she did.'

'Rank on her?'

'Lorn and Tranh Van are . . . were . . . still working on their degrees, so they were the dot and carry types for the expedition,' Cherney went on. 'I guess Lorn didn't realize what a pain in the ass scientists can be, not wanting to do anything outside their specialty, especially if it involves physical work.

'Lorn never had time for her own specialty.'

'Photography?'

'Hell no. That was something Frazier decided she'd be good at. She's taking her degree in alien psychology, but Toni Acosta . . . that's Scholar Acosta to anybody lower-ranking than God or Frazier . . . keeps anything in that area, Al'ar or people, welded solid.

'So it was go here, do this, clean that, and Lorn was getting sick of it.'

'Did it show?'

'Damned right it did. She was worried Tregeagle was

going to ship her back on the next resupply. The exec'd had more than a couple of what she called guidance sessions with Lorn.'

'What was Lorn Ware like?'

Cherney considered. 'I thought she was the prettiest, nicest thing I'd ever met,' he said softly, and again had to find control. 'But I'll be honest, Wolfe.

'There were those who don't . . . didn't agree. They thought she was a little too one-way. She *was* very determined to make it big, and didn't have much use for anyone who wouldn't . . . or couldn't . . . help her.'

'Like you?' Wolfe's tone was equally soft.

Cherney jerked as if struck, growled, and a fist balled.

Joshua's right leg moved back half a foot, and his hands curled slightly. He was suddenly in a barely noticeable crouch.

But Cherney's hands opened, and his shoulders slumped instead. 'Yeah,' he said tonelessly. 'I guess like me. I just wish she hadn't tried so hard. Maybe . . .'

He was silent for a moment, then looked up at Joshua.

'But maybe not. There's your lift, Mister. Sign the trip-ticket and logbook before you take it out.'

Wolfe sat on the plinth of the shattered Al'ar monument, staring up at the transmission tower the backblast had reportedly come from.

He looked at a small holo in his hand. A young woman sat in a sidewalk café in some city. It was summertime wherever the holo had been taken, because the woman wore stylishly baggy shorts and a twin vee-top over small breasts. Lorn Ware.

Yes, pretty, Wolfe thought. Perhaps 25 E-years. Hair cut efficiently short, like most of the other scientists. Expression half-smiling, as if she'd been complimented before the shutter opened. Wolfe couldn't read anything else from her face.

He rested his head on one hand, closed his eyes, let his Al'ar-trained senses reach out.

The wind tasted bitter, like the past, too well remembered. Very faintly, it brought a mind-scent of a time long ago, when he had been a student of Al'ar ways, when he'd earned the Al'ar name, One Who Fights From Shadows.

Then war had come, and he'd been first their prisoner, then one of their most deadly foes, striking from nowhere, deep inside their systems.

At the war's height, the Al'ar had vanished, leaving their home planets in perfect order, and Man's galaxy a shatter of planets and ships, a galaxy that only now, eight years later, the Federation was beginning to put back together.

Outside the Federation were the lawless Outlaw Worlds, and beyond them the empty Al'ar systems.

A-6343-5 was between the Al'ar and the Outlaw worlds.

Joshua *felt* back into the past, *felt* for the Al'ar, almost saw their corpse-white forms as they built the towers. His most terrible enemies and his best . . .

His eyes blurred for an instant, and he wiped a sleeve across them, ignored the knife-force of the past.

Emptiness came, then he *felt*, very faintly, Man's arrival. The presence grew stronger, and he sensed Ware's presence. For an instant there was something else, then a flash of agony and the long swirl down into death.

He forced his mind back, *feeling* for that something else.

Wolfe stood, looked again at the transmission tower, then walked slowly to the broken monument.

He ran a hand across the blast-shattered stone, then looked out at the empty desert.

'Cute,' he murmured. 'Very damned cute indeed.'

He smiled, but his smile was not pleasant.

Wolfe had been inside one of the Al'ar hidden bases twice, once when the Al'ar still held it. Even now, eight years later, his skin still crept, his arms wanted to be cradling a heavy blaster, and his senses reached for some warning before an Al'ar came from nowhere to kill him.

He felt sweat on his temples, unobtrusively wiped it away.

No one noticed – they were watching the woman 75 feet above move from handhold to alloy handhold toward the control deck about ten feet distant from her. The climber was Scholar Tregeagle, and Wolfe began to believe what Frazier had said about her vast competencies.

The chamber was enormous, more than a kilometer long, and as high, filled with glittering machinery, silent now, but looking like they needed no more than a signal to growl into life.

They were nearly two miles underground, and had descended on an antigrav generator crudely welded into an Al'ar descent tube that no one had been able to activate.

There were half a dozen scientists in the chamber beside the zebra-painted 'mole' that floated two feet above the deck. The robot bobbed slightly in a stray air current, and Wolfe thought it was eager to be released to hunt deeper into the cavern after more Al'ar secrets.

'What do you think that is up there, Raoul?' Scholar Frazier asked, and Wolfe wondered why he didn't use the man's title.

"I'm not sure,' a bearded man said. 'I hope it's adjustment controls for the grid. Maybe I can figure out from there what's causing these frigging backblasts.'

Scholar Frazier moved closer to Joshua. 'That's Scholar Northover, our electronics man.'

Wolfe nodded, wondered why Northover wasn't up there with Tregeagle instead of trying to figure out the Al'ar machinery from a distance.

Tregeagle reached for a stanchion, pulled herself onto

the deck. There was a spattering of applause, and the woman bowed elaborately.

Joshua ate without talking, feeling eyes touch him, flinch away when he raised his head. He'd been introduced around by Scholar Frazier's deputy, Tregeagle, before the meal. A few scientists had tried cautious, nervous questions about what was new or interesting in the Federation, quickly dropped when they learned Joshua was based in the Outlaw Worlds, sectors they evidently thought were made up of murderers, barbarians and the déclassé.

Not far wrong, Wolfe thought. *Which is why I like them.*

He finished his meal, took the plate to the cleaning station at the end of the messhall. There were no scraps left from the processed protein slab the hand-scribbled menu had called 'Meaty Surprise,' nor from the vegblok that'd accompanied it.

Wolfe scrubbed the plate with waterless detergent, held it under the rinser for a second, then placed it in the nearby rack.

He leaned back against the wall and waited patiently until most of the scientists were looking at him.

'I just wanted to offer my apologies,' he said, not sounding apologetic at all, 'but it'll be necessary for me to interview each of you singly about the unfortunate accident.' He put a deliberately artificial smile on his face, wiped it away.

'Saying that I feel like some sort of policeman,' he said, and his eyes swept the narrow messhall. He didn't see the response he'd hoped for. It had been a cheap shot in the dark at best.

'Perhaps, Scholar Tregeagle, I could use your office.' Again, it wasn't a request. The woman nodded.

'The quicker begun, the quicker ended,' he said. 'Scholar Acosta, if you'd be willing to go first?'

The small woman pursed her lips, then got up.

'Very well,' and bustled out of the room, leaving Joshua to trail in her wake.

If Frazier reminded Wolfe of a woodpecker, Toni Acosta was a shrike, a butcher-bird. Within a few moments, she'd shredded Scholar Frazier ('nice enough, but years beyond being able to head an expedition'); her compatriots ('largely idiots who bussed every posterior in sight for their post-ings,' and the dig itself ('poorly organized from the outset, oriented toward gadgeteering and gimmickry instead of analyzing and understanding the Al'ar psychology, which should be the real beginning and purpose of any investiga-tion.'); and left the blood-dripping remains impaled on branches for later savories.

Joshua noted his mind was running to Earth-bird analo-gies, and wondered if he was homesick. He shuddered involuntarily, which answered his question, and turned back to business.

'Your opinions are interesting, Scholar Acosta,' he said. 'What about your colleague?'

'You mean student Ware? Hardly my colleague.'

'What was your opinion of her?'

'Utterly incompetent, like almost everyone studying psychology these days.'

'Strong condemnation.'

'Piddle,' Acosta snapped. 'Hardly nasty enough for these numbwits with addled psyches, trotting around trying to bring everyone down to their level, hoping that'll enable them to understand their own sewer-pipe thinking.'

'You're generalizing.'

Acosta looked at Wolfe sharply. 'Perhaps,' she said slowly, 'I should be more careful with my words. But what an interesting choice of words. Clerk-interviewers don't generally think in those terms nor use words like general-izing. Are you what you seem?'

'As the cliché goes,' Wolfe said, 'what you see is what you get.'

'But perhaps not everyone sees you the same.'

Wolfe nodded his head a bare inch.

'My specific objection to student Ware,' Acosta said, 'was she was more interested in self-advancement than learning. By that I mean she was the sort who'd come up with a flashy explanation for a series of events to attract the greatest attention, rather than spending any amount of time *thinking* about the events she'd observed before theorizing.

'I would expect, if she'd lived, she would have become a sudden wonder in the Federation, publishing some book that would neatly explain why men don't get along with women, or why women should do without men, or something of that sort.'

'Was she any good at photography?'

'Who knows? She was such a snoop, always looking after other people's business, that I thought Mikela . . . that's Scholar Tregeagle . . . assigned her those duties to keep her busy. You know, I caught her going through my files once, although she said she was just looking for a paper I'd written on Al'ar life-patterns. But after I told her to get out of my office I found she was prying into my personal fiches, which I keep well-guarded, I might add.

'I always wondered who else's secrets she tried to pry into. If she'd died some other way, say a mysterious fall down in the caves, well, I don't know what I might be thinking.

'I suppose there's a bit of validity to the notion a psychologist isn't much better than a nosy-one at best, but she took things to an extreme.'

Something Acosta had said earlier struck Wolfe.

'A couple of minutes ago you used two unusual examples of what Ware might write about in the future, why men don't get along with women, or why they should do without men. Were those deliberately chosen?'

'No,' Acosta said quickly. 'They merely jumped to mind. But after all, do *men* get along with women? What's your feeling on the matter?'

Wolfe didn't answer, but kept his gaze on the psychologist. Her eyes met his, darted away.

'Yes, I lied about Lorn Ware,' Mikela Tregeagle said, sounding undisturbed. 'I certainly would have sent her home on the next resupply ship, and the evaluation I'd send to her department head at Univee would not have been good.

'I lied because she is dead, and her father . . . he's a widower, by the way . . . should be allowed to mourn his daughter without any qualifications. *De mortuis nil*, and all that.'

'What were her problems?'

'Mister Wolfe, I don't see why you're so interested in Lorn Ware's character or lack of same. I should think you'd restrict your inquiry into the accident that killed her, and, speaking personally, I wish you'd put in a request for more safety equipment for our team, to prevent further occurrences of this nature.

'We should be able to conduct all testing, all exploration of this base without human involvement, but we only have that single mole.

'Heaven knows what sort of boobytraps the Al'ar could have set down there, that're still armed and waiting.'

'That's a valid concern,' Wolfe said. He'd almost died a dozen times coming too close to alien leave-behind death devices. 'But, to be honest, I was asked to provide full details about this person. I'm not sure, but I think my company is considering involving itself more closely in these expeditions from the outset.

'I suspect they feel accidents are as much made as just happen.'

'What, the old evil saw that people determine their own fate?' Tregeagle said. 'Leave it to an insurance company to drag that one up.'

Wolfe shrugged. 'I'm not even their full-time employee, Scholar Tregeagle. Just a day laborer.'

'Scholar . . . poo,' Tregeagle said, and her brilliant smile came. 'Some of us . . . like Scholar Acosta . . . love titles more than we perhaps should. I don't care. Call me Mikela.'

'Certainly,' Wolfe said. 'Would you mind being a bit more specific about Ware's failings?'

'If you don't attribute them to me, I shall. First she was extraordinarily ambitious, to the point I felt she'd do whatever was necessary to advance her career.'

'You're not the first to tell me that.'

'I'm hardly surprised you already knew that,' Tregeagle said. 'It was patently obvious to almost everyone.'

'I'd guess Dov Cherney wouldn't be part of that almost everyone.'

'No,' Tregeagle said. 'No, he wouldn't. What she did, or perhaps tried to do to him, is an example of my second criticism of Lorn. She wanted everyone to like . . . perhaps love her.

'She was willing to go to any extreme to make that happen.'

'Cherney told me she just used him as a confessional. He wanted more, but didn't get it, he said.'

'Well, if Dov told you that, I'll choose to believe him. Why not? The truth wouldn't matter anyway.' Tregeagle sighed. 'Poor Dov. He surely deserved . . . deserves . . . better. Personally, I'll put what Lorn did to him as another reason to dislike her.'

'It takes two to make a relationship,' Wolfe suggested. 'If she didn't want to play, that doesn't make her a villain.'

Mikela's eyes took his, held them for an instant. Then her smile came again. 'Of course not,' she murmured.

'Were there any complaints about Ware prying into other people's business?'

Tregeagle looked startled.

'No,' she said emphatically. 'Why? Has anyone . . .'

'Just a standard question,' Wolfe reassured her smoothly.

Expedition custom, Wolfe learned, was to stay up as late as you could, for Five's night was almost endless.

He waited in the cleaned-out store-room he'd been given for a sleeping chamber until his timesend read 2700 hours, then slipped out into the dimly-lit corridor. The base was silent except for the hum of humidifiers, heaters, and the bedroom corridors were closed.

Wolfe carried a towel and soap container as a support for a possible thin alibi that he was looking for the refresher and couldn't find it.

He stopped at one door, hearing the groans of someone deep in a nightmare, noted the nameplate – Northover, the electronics specialist – for a possible inquiry into the nature of dreams, went on.

Ware's room was locked. Joshua took a flat finger-sized bit of plas from a pocket, held it to the keyhole, fingered a sensor. The pick vibrated in his hand, and the lock opened.

He went in, slid the door closed, touched the light sensor.

The room was a near-duplicate of his – folding bed, desk, book/fiche case, keyboard and screen, and a partial 'fresher in an alcove. The room had been stripped bare, and Ware's possessions were in a case and a metal-bound trunk on the bed. Both were sealed with straps.

Joshua selected the trunk, and took a small case from his pocket. He took a pair of tiny snips from it, cut through the metal as if it were paper.

The trunk held what he wanted – fiches, a few battered books, and Ware's papers. He riffled through them like the professional thief he'd been trained as, set some aside for immediate attention, others for later investigation.

Two hours later, he had something interesting. It was an expensive leather book, inscribed, in masculine handwriting:

To Lorn
I wish I could be there with you, but I can't, so
write about everything so you won't forget to tell
me everything. Love you

                                              Da

The diary's paper was rich-feeling, hand-laid. Wolfe leafed through it, scanning entries. The first dozen or so pages were filled with careful handwriting, obediently listing everything that happened to Lorn Ware on her arrival on Five. Then the entries grew less and less, made days apart.

Joshua half-smiled. She was no better at a journal than he was. He turned a few pages, and stopped. Pages had been roughly torn from the book, more than a dozen of them.

He held the book up to the light sideways, saw the dent of writing on the unripped pages.

Amateur night, he thought. *Destroying the whole book would've been a lot –*

The door smashed open and Dov Cherney was on him, swinging a torque bar nearly a meter long.

Wolfe rolled sideways, and the bar crashed into Ware's trunk. Joshua snap-kicked to his feet as Cherney whipped the bar sideways at his waist.

Joshua's hand blurred, and he had the burly man's wrist in one hand, and the bar spun out of Cherney's grip. Wolfe's hand twisted, and the sound of the bone snapping was loud in the small room.

Cherney screamed and Joshua stepped into him, back-handed a knuckle-strike to the man's forehead and smashed back against the wall.

Joshua recovered as Cherney collapsed half-on, half-off the bed.

Moments later, there were people in the doorway. One was Frazier. Just behind him was Scholar Acosta.

'Put him somewhere safe,' Wolfe ordered. 'And have everyone assembled in the messhall in an hour.

'It's time for a chat.'

The signal had come two weeks earlier. Wolfe had finished a moderately nasty piece of business on Vavasour IX involving a man who'd run away from his wife with his company's assets and his teenaged stepdaughter.

The *Grayle* hummed through N-space, and Wolfe drowsed over a battered book. He was considering his penthouse on Carlton VI, the dry shudder of the martini he seldom allowed himself when he was operational, the raw beef seasoned with olive oil, capers and cheese, and what sort of Armagnac he'd finish the meal with.

He next thought about the company he might choose on that night, but set that aside. Carlton VI was still too far away for indulgences like that.

The com buzzed.

Wolfe set the book aside, went out of the master cabin, up steps to the bridge.

He studied the symbols on the screen, touched sensors. After a time the screen cleared, then read:

CALL TO BE RETURNED IN ONE E-HOUR.
STAND BY.

Joshua went to the galley. He dropped a brownish chunk from one freezer into a stone bowl, took bread and cheese from a stasis-locker, carved off two pieces, put one in the bowl, buttered the other, grated cheese on top of it, and clipped the bowl into a slot in the oven. He set the oven, pressed a sensor.

By the time he'd cut two wedges of cheese, the smell of the French onion soup filled the galley.

He returned to the master cabin for his book, went back to the galley. When the soup was ready he ate slowly, intent on his reading.

He cleaned his dishes, returned to the bridge and sat in front of the screen for the few minutes remaining. He showed no sign of impatience, his face quite expressionless.

The com burped static, and RECEIVING scrolled across it.

'Wolfe,' a neutral voice came.

'Yes,' Joshua said. 'No picture?'

'No picture.'

'I'd appreciate some authentication, then.'

'Golightly Seven Quill Quill.'

Wolfe's eyebrows lifted slightly.

'Didn't know that was still current.'

'It isn't,' the voice said. 'We keep it active for a few old-timers we call on every now and then.'

'I'm listening.'

'An agent just got dead on an archeological dig. We don't know if it was an accident or not.'

'Where?'

'One of the Al'ar pioneer worlds. A-6343-5.'

'Name?'

'Lorn Ware. She was going to Havelmar University. She'd already done some contract work before she went to school. Nothing serious, just the standard take a vacation among the stars and deliver a package sort of thing. She did all right, so we kept her on the possible list.

'She initiated contact this time, and said she was having

trouble paying tuition and did we have anything.

'This dig on Five had just come up, and we like to keep track of anything that goes on around any of the Al'ar worlds, so we suggested she might want to apply for the job. Since it's Federation funded, it was simple to make sure she got it.'

'Does anybody on the expedition know she's Intelligence?'

'Negative. Not even the director or the Univee itself.'

'You sure?'

'Dammit, Wolfe, don't you think we know how to run a clean op?'

'No,' Wolfe said. 'I don't.'

There was silence for a moment, then harsh laughter.

'Allah's teeth, but Cisco warned me you were a rough cob.'

'How is he?'

'Fine. Said to say he still thinks you're a shit.'

'Compliments flow when the elite meet,' Wolfe said. 'What're you willing to pay for me to investigate?'

'Don't suppose I can call on your patriotism,' the voice said.

Wolfe remained silent.

'I understand you've still got some kind of reserve commission,' the voice tried next. 'We could always recall you.'

'You could always *try*.'

'For the first time, I'm starting to agree with something Cisco thinks,' the voice said. 'All right. Federation Intelligence agrees to pay you whatever your standard per diem is, plus all expenses, plus thirty thousand credits when you turn in your report.'

'That's a little steep for something you think might be an accident.'

'Wolfe,' the voice said, 'we treat anything that's even *vaguely* connected to the Al'ar like it's radioactive.

'You know that.'

*

Twenty faces looked at Wolfe in various stages of bewilderment, sleepiness and vague anger.

'Where's Scholar Acosta?' Wolfe asked.

'Probably thinks this is beneath her,' Raoul Northover said. Someone chuckled.

'I'll get her,' Mikela Tregeagle said, and left the room.

'I said before I wasn't happy feeling like some sort of a policeman,' Wolfe began. 'I didn't and don't. But for all purposes, from now on you might as well consider me a Federation official, properly constituted, and –'

A scream from outside interrupted him.

Wolfe was the first into the corridor. The tube blaster was in his hand.

Tregeagle stood in the doorway to Acosta's office, shaking, sobbing.

Joshua pulled her out of the way, looked in.

The shrike had impaled her last victim.

Scholar Toni Acosta was sprawled next to her desk, chair overturned beside her. Her face was purple, twisted, and Joshua smelt shit.

A triple-stranded wire was twisted deep into her neck.

'That saved me some elaboration about my exact credentials,' Wolfe said flatly an hour later. 'But you can assume they're legitimate.'

Acosta's body had been moved to a cold-locker, next to the store-room Cherney had been barricaded in, and the team reassembled in the messhall.

'Scholar Acosta was murdered, of course,' Wolfe went on. 'As was Lorn Ware.

'From here on,' he said, 'things are going to get very bumpy indeed.'

'Sorry, Wolfe,' Northover said, not sounding sorry at all. 'But there's no way the Ware kid could have been murdered.

'Not unless you either think the Al'ar leave ghosts

behind or that somebody's figured out how to aim those goddamned backblasts.'

'I'm not thinking either one,' Wolfe said. 'I know how Ware was killed, and you aren't close.'

'I should suppose that's a relief,' Northover said, 'since I've been the man at the start switch on all the grid tests.'

'Which means you're alibied.'

'So is everyone else,' Northover said. 'I hate to shatter your cleverness, Wolfe. But the test that killed Ware happened at 1700, exactly.'

'So the report said.'

'We're a tiny team,' Northover went on. 'When anything important happens . . . and there's nothing more important than trying to make that power grid work . . . everyone has a job. A job where he's either in full view of somebody else, or else he's monitoring instruments and recording the results.

'That means every single one of us!

'So if Lorn Ware was murdered . . . who did it?

'And I'm not going to believe anything you come up with about two or more people working together, either.'

The wind was stronger when Wolfe grounded the gravlift beside the monument, keening sadly, and sending an occasional whisper of sand across the stone.

Northover and Wolfe got out of the lifter, and Wolfe took him to the monument.

'You see that stake with the red handkerchief on it?' Wolfe said. 'That's where Ware had her equipment set up.'

'I saw it before,' Northover said. 'And I went over the site carefully.'

'Not carefully enough,' Wolfe said. 'Or you would've noticed something. Take a good look at the monument. The blast tore hell out of it, right?'

'Obviously,' Northover said. 'I do have eyes.'

'Use them, then! Look at the edges of the stone, where the blast hit. See the angle? That angle goes straight out into the desert, away from the transmission tower!'

The wind was suddenly very loud to the bearded scientist.

'Christ with a spanker,' he said finally. 'It sure as hell is. So the blast came . . .'

'From out there. Don't bother running a backplot,' Wolfe said. 'I already did. There's a nice big rocky outcropping, perfect for landing a gravlifter on, and for hiding footprints.'

Northover swiveled, looked back, beyond the stake.

'Sure,' Wolfe said. 'If you dug up sand from the impact area and analyzed it – assuming you've got the right instruments – I'll bet you'll find that "backblast" was nowhere near the wavelength the Al'ar used for their power-casts.'

Northover was looking back and forth.

'Okay,' he said finally. 'I'll buy into it. But how was it done? Some kind of robot device?'

'From where?' Wolfe asked bleakly. 'One of you brought it with him . . . or her? I'm supposed to believe that one of you is some kind of ex-saboteur or something and capable of rigging something like that from a handful of wire and bellybutton lint?

'Sorry. I've read the background files on everybody here. Nobody qualifies.

'Even if I believed that, there'd be another problem. Assume there was some kind of blaster with a timer that somebody managed to pre-aim, knowing *precisely* where she was going to set up her recorders.

'She walks into position, the timer goes off, and she gets spattered. That's known as having God in your lap, and I'm an atheist.'

Wolfe suddenly noticed Northover was a little white.

'My apologies,' he said. 'I forget some of us are still civilized.'

'Never mind,' the scientist said. 'Go on.'

'Then, after Ware's dead, our murderer comes back here, unobserved, secures her gear and scoots before anybody arrives. The body was supposedly found about 1830 or so. That whole plot sounds like some kind of romance, and I'm not romantic any more,' Wolfe said.

'You're right,' Northover said thinking for awhile. 'We were all together, talking about the test afterward, and then somebody . . . I think it was Cherney . . . said Ware was missing, and we went looking for her. Not enough time.

'But dammit, Wolfe, we are all accounted for at 1700!

'Every single bleeding one of us!'

'Son of a bitch, squared,' Joshua muttered. 'Cubed.' It was a day and a half later, very late at night, and Northover was still right.

Wolfe had made up twenty little cards with each team member's name and where they were supposed to have been at 1700 hours, when the test was made and Ware died, and had them laid out on his tiny desk. For 15 minutes before and after the blast, everyone was well accounted for.

All right. Consider all options. Was Ware in fact killed just at 1700? Of course, because she had to be at her recorders when the test was made. She wouldn't necessarily have been there a few minutes before or afterward. The killer had to have her at a precise spot at a precise time. That suggests some kind of robot, doesn't it, Wolfe? But then somebody would've had to pick the fiendish thingie up afterward, and there wasn't time for that, so that's out.

But why was she killed at precisely 1700?

At 1700, Wolfe realized, *everybody including the killer, would be ostentatiously accounted for. The precision was for the alibi, not the murder.*

Which gives me absolute zip-null!

He glowered at the cards, and there was a gentle tap at the door. He swept the cards into a drawer.

'It's not locked,' he said.

The door opened, and Mikela Tregeagle came in. She wore a white blouse, with two buttons at the throat undone, and close-fitting fawn pants. She was barefoot.

'I guess you and I are the only ones still up,' she said, closing the door behind her. 'I tried to sleep, but my mind keeps working, keeps remembering, and I thought maybe I'd mix myself some milk. It's a pity that Juan keeps a dry camp, or I'd be looking for a drink.

'Then I saw your light on under the door, and thought I'd intrude.'

'You're not intruding.' Wolfe stood, and slid his chair toward her. 'Here. Take a pew.'

'I'll sit over here,' she said, and sat on the bed.

'I'd offer you something,' Wolfe said, 'if I had anything.'

'I'm all right,' Mikela said. She looked away from him, at the wall. 'So what happens next, Joshua? Aren't you going to run out of questions soon?'

'Possibly.'

'Then what?'

'The Federation ship we sent for'll have specialists aboard. They'll take over.'

'And what'll you do then?'

Wolfe didn't answer.

'Go back into the night like the mysterious being you are?'

'I'm not mysterious.'

'Oh, but I want you to be,' she said, lying back on the bed. 'Everyone thinks field work is glamorous. If they really knew. You spend a year or so sucking up to anyone with money who's a scientist hopeful for funding, which is never enough to do it right.

'Then you go out with the same people, the same faces

you've been on eight, ten worlds with. Sometimes they're friends, sometimes maybe they were even lovers, maybe now they're enemies.

'You've heard all their jokes, all their stories, and they know all yours as well.

'About the only real pleasure is finding something new, and what the hell are we finding here? Another goddamned Al'ar base, and the only mystery is there's nothing at the far end, so far, although I know we'll find something sooner or later.

'Otherwise this is no different than what, seven or eight identical bases?

'We'll be out here for another year, maybe two, then go back to the Univee and spend another two years making everything neat and tidy and publishable so all our enemies can have something to throw rocks at.

'Then I start trying to raise money again for wherever Juan wants to go next, and the cycle begins all over again.'

'In the wrong light, anybody's job looks crappy,' Wolfe said, feeling like a sententious ass.

'Maybe . . . but I'm still glad you materialized, regardless of the circumstances. It gets tiresome when everybody knows everything about everyone.'

'Everything except the most important thing,' Wolfe said. 'Who killed Lorn Ware and Toni Acosta.'

'Oh, that'll come out, sooner or later,' she said. 'Which means it's maybe not the most important thing at all.'

'What do you think is the most important thing?'

Tregeagle's fingers moved to her blouse, unfastened another button. She looked up at Joshua, and her eyes were bright, glittering. 'For me,' she said huskily, 'right now, it's what it's like to kiss you.'

'There actually might be an answer to that,' Joshua said. He crossed to her, knelt beside the bed. Her mouth opened under his, and he cradled her head in one hand.

Her tongue slid into his mouth, her lips moved under his.

Joshua unbuttoned her blouse, pulled its tails out of her pants. Her breasts were firm, erect.

Her hand moved down, unfastened the snaps of her pants, pulled them open. She wore no underclothing.

'Yes,' she breathed when the kiss ended. 'I do want to know more about my stranger.'

'So you still don't have any idea who the murderer could be,' she said, much later, in the near darkness. They were still joined.

'Lots of ideas,' Wolfe said. 'None worth thinking about, let alone mentioning.'

'I tried to play detective this afternoon,' Mikela said. 'What about the idea that Dov Cherney killed Lorn, and then somebody else killed Acosta?'

'Two killers among 20 people? Aren't we supposed to be shaving with Occam's Razor?'

'Oh well,' Tregeagle sighed. 'I guess I'll stick to being a dig-and-delver. Speaking of which,' and she wriggled against him, 'I do like your delver.'

'Thanks,' Joshua said, and kissed her. 'Delving with you isn't a bad way to spend an evening.'

'Morning. It's very late,' she said.

'Yes.'

'Aren't you sleepy?'

'Not very. But shouldn't you be thinking about going back to your room? I'd rather keep our business our business.'

'In a while,' Mikela said. 'As for anyone knowing, you don't know how things work on an expedition. Everybody probably knows everything, like I said. But when it comes to sex, everybody pretends not to know.

'But you're right. It might complicate things. And

there's at least one somebody I'd just as soon not have know.

'Although what he'd do about it . . .'

She stopped. Wolfe waited, but she didn't continue. He caressed one breast, tweaked her nipple until it was firm, and her breathing quickened. She lifted one leg across his thighs, moaned as he moved slowly, steadily in her.

'Dov,' Wolfe said calmly, 'I know you didn't kill Scholar Acosta. But what about Lorn Ware?'

Cherney stared at him through the swollen purple ruin of his face. His forearm was shrouded in a plascast. 'You wouldn't believe me if I said no, so yeah, I killed her. Killed both of them with my Al'ar deathtouch,' he snarled.

'Thank you. Go back to your goddamned meditations,' and Wolfe slammed the storeroom door a bit harder than he'd planned.

'I get the idea you're groping at straws,' Northover said. He sat in the middle of the gravlifter's front seat, eyes fixed straight ahead.

'I am,' Wolfe admitted. 'Do you have any other ideas?'

Northover shook his head. Wolfe steered the gravlifter toward the transmission tower, climbed until the craft was level with the second level.

'This was the first one that backblasted, right?'

'That's correct. But I don't know what you hope to find. I examined this tower closely from every angle, with as long a lens as I have. Whatever's causing these problems has got to be in the main generating apparatus, not on the tower.'

Wolfe looked curiously at Northover.

'You checked this tower out from a distance? Why didn't you do what we're going to do and land on it?'

'I don't think the arm would support something as heavy as a lifter,' Northover said, not looking at Joshua.

'Come on, man. This is antigrav, remember? You could have a pilot hover the damned thing while you clambered around.'

'I . . . couldn't. I can't.'

'Why not? You don't weigh more than 45, 50 kilos.'

Northover took a deep breath, looked away from Wolfe. 'I'm acrophobic,' he said.

'Oh,' Wolfe said. 'That's why you had Tregeagle shinnying up that wall in the cave instead of going yourself.'

'She . . . and Juan . . . Scholar Frazier . . . are the only ones who know. I told her when I first interviewed for the team, last expedition. She said it didn't matter, she couldn't see any reason an electronics analyst had to be a mountain climber.

'Then, when this project was presented, she remembered what she said, thought it was pretty funny, and said she'd do the climbing for me as recompense. Matter of fact, she did go out on the arms of this tower after the first back-blast, but didn't find anything.'

'I see.'

'She's quite a woman. I've sometimes wished that I'd met her ten years ago.'

'Why ten years?'

'That would've been before she met Juan, and fell in love with him.'

'Oh?'

'They're lovers,' Northover said. 'At least they were, some years back.'

'Why don't they partner in the open?'

'He's married.'

'But obviously not faithful,' Wolfe pressed.

'I don't know the reason. Maybe he's religious, or figures he's got some kind of duty to his wife, who I've never met. I'm pretty sure . . . hell, I flat know she still loves him. So why she does like she does . . . I don't know.

'But I've got enough trouble understanding my own life, so I don't have time for anybody else's.'

'Why does she do what she does?' Wolfe asked.

'Never mind,' Northover said. 'I shouldn't have said what I did.

'Look, Wolfe. I've been trying to force myself, but I'm not going to be able to get out onto that arm, like you want.'

'Don't worry about it,' Joshua said. 'You just sit where you are, and I'll tell you if I find anything. You tell me what it means.'

'All right,' Northover said. 'But if I get a panic attack . . .'

'We'll drop down and ground the lifter immediately.'

'All right. I'll try.'

Wolfe brought the lifter close to the tower. The huge lower arm hung over him.

A light blinked on the lifter's instrument panel.

'Signal,' Northover said. He picked up a mike, keyed it.

'Northover and Wolfe. Who's 'casting?'

The light went suddenly dead. Northover looked at Wolfe puzzledly, then shook his head. 'Twenty damned people on this world, and we still get wrong numbers. Man and technology, the perfect union.' Northover forced a laugh, clipped the mike back on its rack.

Joshua took climbing line from the back seat, tied it securely to the gravlifter's crashbar and gingerly stepped out onto the arm. He looked about for an anchoring point.

'Will I hurt anything if I tie the lifter to one of these puppies?' He pointed to the row of round seven-foot-tall columns Frazier had theorized were used to fine-tune the power transmission to the receptors below.

'Nope,' Northover said. 'They're as solid as everything else Al'ar. Probably you could lift the tower by them.'

Wolfe threw a double half-hitch around the column,

anchoring the gravlifter, then made his way gingerly across the arm.

'This'll be interesting,' he said. 'Not knowing whether what I'm looking at is . . . what ho.'

'What is what ho?'

'Evidently you're wrong about these columns, and Scholar Tregeagle missed something,' Joshua said. 'They're a bit more fragile than you thought. Here's one that's worn through, right down at the base.' He moved across the slippery alloy almost to the end of the arm, avoided looking at the long drop to the sands below, and knelt next to the column, examined the fault.

'Not worn through,' Wolfe said. 'Cut. Or maybe the weld or whatever joined it to the deck plating didn't hold. Correction. It had some help. There's hammer-strikes on the far side. On both sides, rather.

'Try this one, Northover. The column was cut, I don't know how recently, but I'll bet not long ago. Maybe by a blaster on narrow aperture? Then somebody hammered it out a ways, then back.'

'I've seen holos of other towers on other planets,' Northover said. 'And gone over them a millimeter at a time. I've never heard of anything like this. The Al'ar didn't practice shade-tree engineering.'

'No,' Wolfe said. 'But maybe somebody human does, who wanted to create a backblast.'

'Why would anyone want to do that?'

'Let's go look at another tower,' Wolfe said. 'Then I'll try an answer.'

He started toward the gravlifter, stopped as he heard, almost felt, a deep hum.

'Somebody's running the grid,' Northover shouted. 'Come on! We've got to get out of range!' He fumbled at the anchoring line. 'Goddammit,' he swore. 'It won't come!' He jerked at the rope, further tightening the knots, then, in utter panic, jumped behind the controls of the gravlighter.

The hum was growing louder, and Wolfe felt his hair stand on end. The metal was more slippery than before, and Joshua felt like he was on ice. He forced his way, almost falling, toward the tower the gravlifter was anchored to, just as Northover slammed thrust to the lifter's drive.

It jerked forward, the half-hitches held, and the gravlifter flipped, hurling Northover out.

He fell, screaming, but Joshua had no time for his death. The grid's power-hum was louder, and Wolfe felt pain grow, pain like his nerves were being stripped from his body.

He rolled over the side, dropped ten feet to the lower arm, found his feet. But that was no refuge. He remembered Frazier's explanation that the power would come up the angled arm from the 'tanks' on the main tower.

He ran, nearly falling, to where it C-curved, slid down the curve, then leapt straight out, onto the top of the 'tank.' He almost fell, regained his balance, saw, hidden in the depths of the tower, notches that were some sort of service ladder.

He half-fell, half-jumped and had his hand in one notch, dangled as just above him, a series of violet fireballs slammed across the sky, dancing from tower to tower and the gravlifter exploded like a bomb.

The fireballs vanished.

Joshua swung, found another hand-hold, then his feet were in a notch. Quite suddenly his body spasmed. He held on until the reaction passed, then began the long, precarious climb down.

He'd walked almost two kilometers toward the base when the first gravlifter found him.

'Four dead now,' Scholar Frazier moaned. 'Gods, everybody wants to be famous, but not for something like this! And who'll be next?

'We're huddled in our rooms waiting for the next murder, scared witless it'll be us.'

'There won't be any more murders,' Joshua said firmly. 'Now sit down, and put yourself together. I've got some questions.

'First. That holograph of the house on the wall? Where's it located?'

'What? What the blazes does that have to do with anything?'

'Shut up and answer my goddamned question,' Wolfe snapped. 'Some bastard tried to kill me three hours ago, and did kill Northover. I'm the one who ought to be sitting there jelly-fishing, not you!'

Frazier gasped a handful of breaths like they were the last ones promised. He looked at the architect's rendition of the lakeside mansion.

'This is absurd . . . but it's not anywhere. I'll never be able to afford something like that. My wife and I had it made as, well, a dream-scheme. She said maybe it'd be a good luck charm, or encourage me to make some great discovery and win the Nobel or the Federation Prix d'Découverte or something that's got a big fat wad of credits attached, and we'd find a lake and build our house.

'I kept telling her I'm not much more than a science-drudge, hardly a Schliemann or Vauxton, and I'll never be in the history books. But she keeps saying next time, next time I'll find something big.' He smiled wistfully. 'She's got more faith in me than I do.'

'Evidently,' Wolfe said. 'Considering your affair with Mikela Tregeagle.'

Frazier jolted. 'How did you find out . . . who told you?'

Wolfe didn't bother answering.

Frazier's face was red. 'That was something I suppose shouldn't have happened.'

'Happened?'

'Yes. It was three expeditions ago, and we'd been out a long time. Too long. I was getting discouraged, and Mikela has always been there for me. She was the one who raises the money, finds compatible team members, keeps everything smooth . . . really they ought to make her the expedition head.

'But she never wanted that, she told me.' Frazier caught Wolfe's expression. 'Sorry. I veered. Three expeditions ago, things happened between us. The affair lasted until the project's end.'

'Why did it end? Tregeagle looks at you like it's still going on.'

'It's enough for you to know it's ended, isn't it?'

'No,' Wolfe said, voice flat. 'Talk.'

Frazier swung around in his chair until he was facing out the port, back to Joshua. 'I'm not worthy of her.'

'Why not?'

'I'm . . . I'm impotent,' he said, voice muffled. 'I caught some kind of virus and . . . I'm completely incapable. No erection, no orgasm, not anything.'

'So?' Wolfe was unimpressed. 'Love isn't defined by just sex. Or perhaps love wasn't the reason you let the affair happen.'

'Who knows why it started,' Frazier snapped, turning back. 'But I surely loved her . . . love her now. Can't you understand, Wolfe? I'm not a man any more. And now you're shaming me further.'

'I've got a lot more sympathy for four corpses than for your lousy little ego,' Wolfe growled.

'You're right,' Frazier mumbled. 'You're right. But you can sit there all day and tell me I'm a neurotic, but that doesn't change how I feel.

'That's the only reason I can't let myself object when Mikela does . . . does what she does.'

'You mean sleep with other expedition members?'

Frazier nodded. His face held a pleading look. 'I don't know. I really don't know for sure about that. I couldn't let myself think about that. Good God, Wolfe. How far down do you have to drag me?'

'Last question,' Joshua said. 'That ring you wear. The diamond's real, isn't it? As are the four, no five *falera*-stones. Where'd you get it?'

'It was a present,' Frazier said.

'Who gave it to you?'

Frazier told him.

Joshua reached far under the desk, touched cold metal. He pulled, and the magnetic clip let go. Wolfe examined the small, rounded-edge square.

'And you thought you were a friggin' professional,' he muttered in complete disgust.

The storeroom door slammed open, and Dov Cherney jerked up from his half-doze. Wolfe was across the small room, and picked him up by the throat.

'I've had enough bullshit,' he said, his eyes hard, glittering. 'Now, first I have a question. Then you and I are going to take a little walk and sit down with some nice friendly people.'

'Get bent.'

Wolfe whiplashed his knuckles twice across Cherney's face.

'I said, I have a question. You're going to answer it, or I'm going to smash that cast and break your goddamned arm so it'll never heal.

'Then I'll start on the other one.

'Don't even think you've got any legal rights now. I'm so far outside the law I could make you the fifth corpse and walk away without anyone saying one single word.

'Believe me, brother. You're going to talk to me.

'Now, here's the question. Lorn Ware wasn't sleeping with you. So who *was* she screwing?'

Joshua grounded the gravlifter just beyond the last transmission tower and shut off the drive. He clambered out, and walked away from the vehicle into the desert.

He let the silence build around him, entered it.

Again, the past whispered, again he *felt* the Al'ar presence.

Then it vanished, and there was nothing but the dry wind.

'Shit,' he said to himself, almost in a whisper. 'I should've known . . .'

He didn't finish the sentence, but got back in the gravsled, touched sensors. The drive purred alive, and he brought the lifter off the ground, spun it, and sent it fast along the line of towers, leaving a swirling line of sand behind him.

'*This Joshua Wolfe,*' PA speakers and belt coms blared. '*All team members will assemble immediately in the messhall. That is an order from Scholar Frazier. I say again, assemble immediately.*'

A worried Frazier stopped Wolfe outside the messhall.

'I went to get it, like you told me. But it's gone. Somebody took it.'

Wolfe grunted. 'Wonderful. Absolutely wonderful.'

*

Joshua looked at the twenty scientists. Some looked scared, some worried, some curious. Dov Cherney glowered, Mikela Tregeagle sent a quick smile.

He stood behind a small cardtable. On it was a plas pitcher full of water, a glass, a recorder and something hidden behind the pitcher.

'We'll start at the beginning,' he said. He held up the recorder.

'This is an official hearing, called by a properly constituted Federation law enforcement official under emergency circumstances.

'That official is myself, Colonel Joshua Wolfe, Federation Armed Forces.'

There were a few gasps.

'I was originally sent here by Federation Intelligence to investigate the death of one of their operatives, Lorn Ware.'

He sipped water.

'The reason for her presence doesn't need to be hidden. FI monitors all investigations into the Al'ar, for reasons I'm not privy to, but could theorize on. But that's of no matter.

'Ware was what we call a contract agent. She'd done some small jobs for FI, and wanted to keep on the payroll.

'Maybe she wanted prestige. Almost all of you have remarked on her ambition. Maybe she needed the money.

'Or perhaps she liked playing spy. She was, as some of you've told me, quite curious about things that weren't normally her concern.

'I don't know if she was constitutionally like that, or if she suspected something after the expedition reached A-6343-5.'

'What the hell was there to suspect?' Frazier snapped.

'I'll get to that in a moment. Ware was, as I've said, ambitious. I don't know, and don't particularly care what her sexual preferences were.

'Dov Cherney was attracted to her, and was rejected.

'Mikela Tregeagle was not.'

'Joshua!' Tregeagle was on her feet, her expression puzzled, hurt, the look of a proud mother watching a favorite child forget his recital lines. 'That's not true!'

'Sit down, Mikela,' Joshua's voice was gentle. She stared at him, then obeyed.

'Yes, it is true,' Wolfe went on. 'I don't know what set Ware off. Maybe pillow talk. Or maybe I've got it all wrong, and Ware smelled something in the beginning, and

Tregeagle decided to find out how much she knew, and seduced her.

'Like she did me.

'As a sidenote, I'll add Tregeagle also put a recorder in her own office after I stupidly decided to use it for my interviews. Mikela isn't a woman who leaves things to chance, it appears.

'In any event, Ware started looking for evidence. Evidence of large-scale embezzlement. Embezzlement that I'd suppose goes back for some years. That's a fairly serious criminal offense, and when the University will learn about it, there'll be civil trials I imagine.

'But this was a government expedition, funded by the Federation. And embezzling public funds is right up there with murder.

'Particularly when the whole investigation of these towers is specious. There's nothing out there under or near that last tower. I *know*, even though the way I acquired that knowledge isn't legally or scientifically admissible.

'I'll bet Mikela knew you were working a dry hole. Maybe some others did, too, but didn't say anything for fear the grant would be cut. Or maybe not. That's another paper trail for the lawyers.'

People turned, craned at Tregeagle. Mikela's eyes held on Joshua's face.

'How much was taken, and under what guises, I don't know,' Wolfe continued. 'There's many, from misreporting your salaries as greater than they are and pocketing the difference to fraudulent invoices from nonexistent contractors to whatever.

'Of course, the longer the project continued, the greater the opportunity.

'There are only two possible suspects. One is Scholar Juan Frazier: He probably didn't take very long for Ware to dismiss, with his poor little dream of someday having enough money to build a house by the side of a lake.

'That left Scholar Mikela Tregeagle, who somehow had the money to buy Frazier an incredibly expensive ring. Maybe that's what caught Ware's eye. I don't know.

'Tregeagle had access to *all* funds, not just the safe with petty cash, but everything. I'd suspect she's been stealing from the Univee for quite a few years, and this particular dig isn't her first adventure in larceny.

'Tregeagle was the one who raised the money from the beginning, and set up the budget for each expedition, unaudited by anyone, least of all by her former lover, Frazier.

'Their affair, at least physically, stopped some time ago for reasons that don't matter. But the two stayed together.

'Perhaps Mikela still loves Frazier. Or perhaps she sees an easily-duped fool. Or perhaps she believes she loves him, and hides the hate even from herself. I'm hardly a psychologist, but that could explain her affairs. I wonder how many of you Mikela "just happened" to encounter at a convenient place and time.'

Wolfe saw eyes flicker in his audience, heard someone sigh.

'Ware began gathering evidence, snooping in any file, any computer, any fiche, she could access. And Tregeagle caught her out. How much information Ware found, I don't know, nor do I know if Ware was able to conceal her evidence somewhere or if it was destroyed after her death.

'When Mikela Tregeagle discovered the prying, Lorn Ware had to die.

'Now, if Scholar Tregeagle were a common thug, an ordinary villain, she would have simply waited until she and Ware were alone somewhere, maybe underground in the Al'ar base next to a nice long fall, as Acosta suggested, and there would have been a terrible accident.

'But that was too easy, wasn't it, Mikela?'

The woman didn't answer, sat quite still with her hands

folded in her lap, looking unblinkingly at Wolfe.

'She had to get cute. She came up with an elaborate scheme. First to cleverly sabotage the transmission towers to produce backblasts. I don't know how she learned that could be done, but I assume the prosecutor will find some paper she found.

'Since Scholar Northover was an acrophobe, and Tregeagle knew, that probably gave her the last piece to the plan.

'She visited the first tower, made certain cuts to the directional columns, and that produced a backblast to her complete satisfaction. Later she went back and hammered the columns back into place, so her sabotage was nearly unnoticeable. What were the odds of anyone actually landing on top the arms and examining them closely in any event?

'Three more incidents, and everyone was convinced the power grid was very chancy, and anything could happen. She'd prepared the stage most carefully for her "accident."

'She'd already arranged for Lorn Ware to become the team photographer-recorder, and so, on this fifth trial, she no doubt had Frazier tell Ware to record the event, of course specifying that odd monument be in the picture for artistic reasons. Frazier doesn't remember things that way, but perhaps Federation interrogators will help his memory.

'Tregeagle waited not far from the monument until Ware arrived and set up her equipment, then shot her, most likely with one of the heavy demolition blasters. I'd guess Tregeagle wasn't sure of her aim at that range, and wanted to make sure.'

'Impossible,' Frazier said. 'If you're arguing she used the test-blast as a cover . . .'

'I am,' Wolfe said.

'Then your whole theory falls apart. We were all together

at 1700 hours, when Scholar Northover triggered the pulse.'

'Agreed,' Wolfe said. 'But the murder happened a bit before then.'

He pulled the straps of the timesend on his wrist free. The ripping sound was very loud.

'Nice gimmick,' he said, turning the device in his hands. 'Gives everyone a common signal. Or maybe not, if somebody has access to the transmitter in Frazier's office, and manually transmits a signal to one timesend, and the person on the other end sets up her equipment and moves carefully into the target zone exactly when she was ordered to.

'Right in line with a nice rock to stand on so there's no footprints, but a pity that monument's in the line of fire. Particularly when Tregeagle's shot cuts a nice hole in the monument that gives a clear line to the real line of fire.

'But Mikela's in a hurry, and doesn't notice. She gets her gravlift airborne, hauls back to base, and is where she's supposed to be well before the real 1700 rolls around.

'Cute,' Wolfe said tiredly. 'A little too cute.'

He took the hidden object from behind the pitcher. It was his tube blaster. Holding it pointed down at the deck, he started toward Mikela.

Tregeagle jumped up, yanking the team's missing handweapon, an archaic blaster, from a leg pocket of her coverall.

'Oh no,' she said. 'Oh no. This is all a lie. And I don't listen to lies. I didn't listen to them from Lorn, I won't listen to them from you.

'Drop the gun, Joshua.'

Wolfe's fingers opened, and the tube blaster clattered to the deck.

'Are you going to kill us all, Mikela?' Joshua said softly. 'That's your only other option.' He took a slow step toward her, then another.

His muscles were fluid, taut. His mind whispered: *wind, wind, unseen, unheard, behind you, beside you* . . .

A chair clattered. Dov Cherney was walking toward her, face frozen, lips moving silently, reaching for her with his one good hand. Mikela swung the gun on him, then she faltered, her eyes gaping.

Joshua Wolfe blurred, vanished.

She spun back, finger punching the firing stud. The gun bucked and blew a fist-sized hole in the back wall.

A blurred figure became Wolfe, diving forward and Mikela fired again, blast just over Wolfe's shoulders, and then she spun away, mountaineer's grace. Cherney had her for a moment, clumsily pulling her against his chest with his free arm.

She drove an elbow back, and doubled him as the blaster went flying. Tregeagle ran for the door. Frazier was up, hands bird-clawing at Tregeagle, trying to stop her. She shoulder-blocked him, and Frazier tumbled back over his chair.

Joshua scooped up his tiny blaster as Mikela slammed through the door. He went after her.

She was at the end of the corridor, at the outside door. She yanked it open, and he shot at her legs, drilled a thumb-sized hole in the doorway, and she was outside.

He ran to the door, booted it open. Tregeagle was running for one of the entrances to the Al'ar caverns.

'Stop!' Wolfe shouted. 'There's nothing there!'

She veered, seeing the *Grayle* in the distance, gangplank extended, lock closed.

Wolfe knelt, braced, fired again, trying to wound her, but the close-range weapon sent its bolt a meter wide.

He ran after her, sucking harsh alien air, sand crunching under his feet.

But she was faster, clattering up the gangplank, smashing her fist again and again against the lock controls.

Over her head, unnoticed, one of the *Grayle*'s weapons bays slid open, and the gleaming barrels of one of the ship's chainguns peered out.

It traversed downward. The wounded-dragon millisecond roar echoed across the desert as the ship followed Wolfe's orders and fifty three-quarter-inch collapsed uranium rounds shredded Mikela Tregeagle's body.

Joshua Wolfe stood over the mound that was as much a monument as Mikela Tregeagle would probably have.

The members of the expedition stood knotted together, as if huddling against a winter gale. No one spoke. Then, one by one, they walked back, into the expedition's buildings.

No one had met his eyes, and no one spoke to him.

Wolfe waited until they were gone, then turned back to the grave.

From memory, he quoted an ancient poem. The dry wind and the silence swallowed his words.

STEN

Chris Bunch and Allan Cole

THE FIRST BOOK IN AN ACTION-PACKED
SF ADVENTURE SERIES.

Vulcan is a factory planet, centuries old, Company
run, ugly as sin, and unfeeling as death. Vulcan
breeds just two types of native – complacent or
tough. Sten is tough.

When his family are killed in a mysterious accident,
Sten rebels, harassing the Company from the metal
world's endless mazelike warrens.

He could end up just another burnt-out Delinquent.

But people like Sten never give up.

DRAGONMASTER: BOOK ONE
STORM OF WINGS

Chris Bunch

**THE ACTION-PACKED NOVEL FROM ONE
OF THE GREATEST WRITERS OF FANTASY
ADVENTURE.**

The land between the volcanic kingdoms of Deraine,
Sagene and Roche is ruled by the sword and by the
outlaw. But the schemes of men and nations hold
scant interest for Hal Kailas. For him the only true
power in the world is that of the dragons . . .

As a child he loved to climb the high cliffs around
his village and watch the dragons nesting there –
huge, savage beasts with wings that blackened the
sun. His only dream was to grow wings – or learn to
ride a dragon.

But when the uneasy peace of the kingdoms is
shattered by war, Hal's dream becomes reality. For
this is a conflict such as the world has never seen.
For the first time, the fearsome wild dragons have
become living weapons, ridden by men of cold
daring and ruthless ambition.

And the greatest of them is Hal Kailas,
Dragonmaster.